High Praise for *Holder of Lightning*:

"Farrell's formidably long and richly detailed fantasy debut launches a new series that's sure to delight fans of Celtic fiction. Much intrigue involving a multitude of mostly well-drawn characters and little bloodshed make for a relatively leisurely plot by the standards of this subgenre. Powerful scenes of magic-wielding and the vividly depicted Celtic society, though, should hook persistent readers, who will be glad for the glossary of character and place names, a guide to the Daoine calender, a list of the holders of the Lámh Shábhála and more at the end of this challenging book."
—*Publishers Weekly*

"Besides great, fast-paced fun, full of politicking and betrayal, Farrell's tale is a tragic love story with a surprisingly satisfying ending."
—*Booklist*

"Portraying a young woman's journey to self-acceptance and self-mastery, Farrell's first novel, a series opener, will particularly appeal to fans of Celtic–based fantasy."
—*Library Journal*

"Farrell weaves Celtic lore with elements of epic fantasy to create a rich and imaginative world in this first book in a new fantasy series, *Cloudmages*. Despite the occasional derivative notes in the plot—readers will be reminded of that granddaddy of fantasy, *The Lord of the Rings*—the book still has the power to capture the reader with its entertaining blend of Celtic magic, heroic and romantic characters, and dynamic plot. This series opener is recommended for libraries with strong fantasy collections and is sure to be popular with teen fantasy devotees, who will eagerly await the next book. —*VOYA*

"An absorbing tale fu_____ined despite being only the_____ *cus*

The Cloudmages

HOLDER OF LIGHTNING

MAGE OF CLOUDS

Holder of Lightning

The Cloudmages #1

S. L. Farrell

DAW BOOKS, INC.

DONALD A. WOLLHEIM, FOUNDER

375 Hudson Street, New York, NY 10014

ELIZABETH R. WOLLHEIM
SHEILA E. GILBERT
PUBLISHERS

http://www.dawbooks.com

First Paperback Printing, January 2004
1   2   3   4   5   6   7   8   9   10

*This one's for Devon
who made me write a "real" fantasy*

And for Denise, who is part of all that I do.

ACKNOWLEDGMENTS

My appreciation to Padraic Lavin, Treasa Lavin, Daragh O'-Reilly and Johnny Towey, who comprise the musical group OSNA, whose self-titled CD *Osna* (Celtic Note, CNCD 1002) I purchased while in Ireland. Whenever I wanted some special inspiration or needed to fall into the mood of the novel, I put their CD in the player. I've been unable to find any other recordings by this group in the U.S., but this is one fine effort. Thank you for the sonic inspiration! You can find Celtic Note at http://www.celticnote.ie on the internet.

And while I'm mentioning the music which was always playing in the background, I should also give a nod to Capercaillie and Cherish The Ladies, groups that also found quite a lot of time on the CD player during the course of the writing.

THE CELTIC WAY OF LIFE by the Curriculum Development Unit (The O'Brien Press Ltd., 1998) is a small but interesting book giving an overview of daily life among the Celtic people of Ireland, and it served as a quick source of inspiration for some of the aspects of life in the fictional Talamh an Ghlas.

For a more detailed and in-depth look, THE COURSE OF IRISH HISTORY by Professors T.W. Moody and F.X. Martin (Roberts Reinhart Publishers, 1995) proved invaluable. The book is essential reading for anyone interested in a detailed and well-researched overview of the history of Ireland.

My apologies in advance to speakers of Irish Gaelic.

Through the book, I have borrowed several terms from Irish and though I've made my best attempt, any mistakes in usage are my own and are due to my limited understanding of the language.

Many thanks to Sheila Gilbert for seeing the story and loving it, and for making me part of the "family" at DAW.

If you're connected to the internet, my web page can be accessed from www.farrellworlds.com—you're always welcome to browse through.

CONTENTS

Part One: The Sky's Stone

Part Two: Filledah

Part Three: The Mad Holder

Part Four: The Shadow Rí

Part Five: Reunion

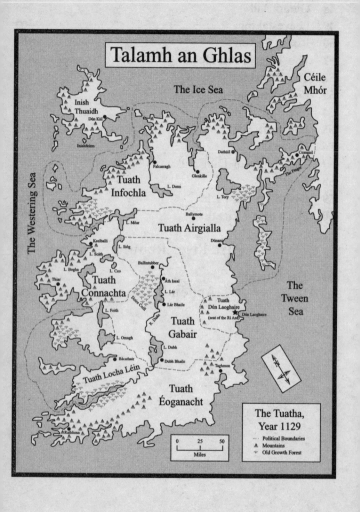

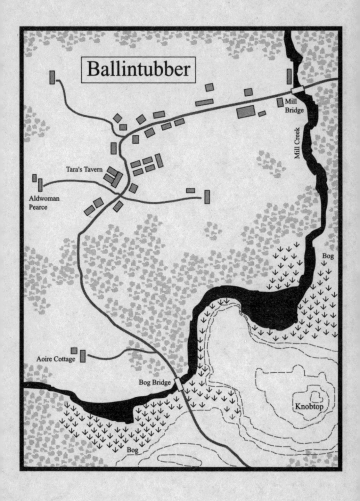

Ballintubber

Mill Bridge

Mill Creek

Tara's Tavern

Aldwoman
Pearce

Bog

Aoire Cottage

Bog Bridge

Knobtop

Bog

PART ONE

THE SKY'S STONE

1

A Fire in the Sky

THE stone was a gift of the glowing sky.

Jenna wasn't certain exactly when the first shifting curtain of green and gold shimmered into existence among the stars, for her attention wasn't on the vista above her. She shouldn't have been out this late in the first place— she should have been bringing the sheep into their pen even as the last light of the sun touched the hills. But Old Stubborn, their ancient and cantankerous ram, had insisted on getting himself stuck on a rocky ledge on Knobtop's high pasture, and Jenna had spent far too long pushing and prodding him down while trying to avoid being butted by his curled horns. As she shoved the ram's wooly bottom back down toward the winter scrub grass where the rest of the flock was grazing, her dog Kesh barking and growling to keep Old Stubborn moving, Jenna noticed that the silver light of the stars and crescent moon had shifted, that the landscape around her had been brushed by gold.

She looked up, and saw the sky alight with cold fire.

Jenna gaped, her mouth half open and her breath steaming, staring in wonder at the glowing dance: great sheets and folds of light swaying gracefully above like her mother's dress when she danced with Halden at the Corn Feast last month. The lights throbbed in a strange silence, filling the sky high above her and seeming to wrap around Knobtop. Jenna thought there should have been sound: wailing pipes, or a crackling bonfire roar. There was power there;

17

she could feel it, filling the air around her as if a thunderstorm were about to break.

And it *did* break. The light above flared suddenly, a goldshattered flash that dazzled her eyes, snatching away her breath and sending her staggering backward with her hands before her face. Her heel caught a rock. She went down hard, the air going out of her in a rush and a cry, her arms flailing out on either side in a vain attempt to break her fall. The rocky, half-frozen ground slammed against her. For a moment, she closed her eyes in pain and surprise. When she opened them again, the sky above her was dark once more, dusted with stars. The strange lights were gone, and Kesh was whining alongside her, prodding her with his black-and-white muzzle. "I'm all right, boy," she told him. "At least I think so."

Jenna sat up cautiously, grimacing. Kesh bounded away, reassured. One of the rocks had bruised her left hip through her woolen coat and skirts, and her neck was stiff. She'd be limping back down to Ballintubber, and Mam would be scolding her not only for getting the sheep back so late, but also for getting her clothes so dirty. "It's *your* fault, you stupid hard-head," she told Old Stubborn, whose black eyes were gazing at her placidly from a few strides away.

She pushed angrily at the rock that had bruised her. It rolled an arm's length downhill. In the black earth alongside where it had lain, something shone. Jenna scraped at the dirt with a curious forefinger, then sat back, stunned.

Even in the moonlight she could see a gleam: as pure a green as the summer grass in the fields below Knobtop; as bright as if the glowing sky had been captured in a stone. Jenna pulled the pebble free. It was no larger than two joints of her finger, rounded and smooth. She rubbed it between fingers and thumb, scrubbing away the dirt and holding it up to the moonlight. With the touch, for just that second, another vision overlaid the landscape: she saw a man with long red hair, stooped over and peering at the ground, as if searching for something he'd lost. The man halted and looked toward her—he was no one she recognized, and yet . . . She felt as if she *should* know him.

But even as she stared and the man seemed to be about to speak, the vision faded as did the glow from the pebble. Maybe, she thought, none of it had ever been there at all; the vision and the brilliance had simply been the afterimage of the lights in the sky and her fall. Now, in her hand, the stone seemed almost ordinary, dull and small, with no glow or spark at all, though it was difficult to tell under the dim moon. Jenna shrugged, thinking that she would look more closely at the rock later, in the morning. She put the pebble in the pocket of her coat and whistled to Kesh.

"Let's get 'em home, boy," she said. Kesh yipped once and circled the flock, nipping at their heels to get them moving. The sheep protested, kicking at Kesh and *baaing* in irritation, then started to move, following Old Stubborn down Knobtop toward the scent of peat and home.

By the time they came down the slope and crossed the ridge between the bogs and saw the thatched roofs of Ballintubber, Jenna had forgotten about the stone entirely, though the dancing, glowing draperies of light remained bright in her mind.

The expected scolding didn't come. Her mam, Maeve, rushed out from the cottage when she heard the dull clunking of the tin bells around Old Stubborn's neck. Kesh went running to her, barking and racing a great circle around all of them.

"Jenna!" Maeve said, her voice full of relief. She brushed black hair away from her forehead. "Thanks the gods! I was worried, you were so late getting back. Did you see the lights?"

Jenna nodded, her eyes wide with the remembrance. "Aye, I did. Great and beautiful, and so bright. What were they, Mam?"

Maeve didn't answer right away. Instead, she threw her shawl over her shoulders and shivered. "Get the sheep in, then clean yourself up while I feed Kesh, and we'll go up to Tara's. Everyone's there, I'm sure. Go on, now!"

A while later, with the flock settled, her clothing changed and the worst of the mud brushed away from her coat and from her hands, and Kesh (and herself) fed, they walked down the lane to the High Road, then north a bit to Tara's, the dirt cold enough to crunch under their boots, the moon frosted silver above. The tavern's windows were beckoning rectangles of yellow, and the air inside was warm with the fire and the heat of bodies. On any given night, Tara's was busy, with Tara herself, gray-haired and large, behind the bar and pulling the taps for stout and ale. Often enough, Coelin would be there, playing his fiddle or giotár and singing, and maybe another musician or two would join him and later someone would start dancing, or everyone would sing along and the sound would echo down the single lane of the village and out into the night air.

Jenna liked to listen to Coelin, who was three years older. Coelin had apprenticed under Songmaster Curragh, dead of a bloody cough during the bad winter three years ago. Jenna thought Coelin handsome, with his shock of unruly brown hair, his easy smile that touched every muscle in his face, and those large hands that spidered easily over his instrument (and which, aye, she sometimes imagined running over her body). She thought Coelin liked her, as well. His green eyes often found her when he was singing, and he would smile. "You're too young for him," Mam had said one night when she noticed Jenna smiling back. "The boy's twenty. Look at the young women around him, girl, smiling and preening and laughing. Half of them have already lifted their skirts for him, I'll wager, and one day soon one of them will miss her bleeding and pop up big and there'll be a wedding. You'd be a piece of blackberry pie to him, Jenna, sweet and luscious, devoured in one sitting and as quickly forgotten. Look if you want, and dream, but that's all you should do."

Tonight, Coelin wasn't playing, though Jenna thought that half of Ballintubber must be pressed inside the tavern. Coelin sat in his usual corner, his instruments still in their cases. Aldwoman Pearce stood up alongside the huge fireplace across from the bar, a mug of brown stout close at hand, and everyone staring at her furrowed, apple-shaped face. ". . . in the Before, the sky would be alive with mage-lights, four nights out of the seven," she was saying in her trembling voice that always reminded Jenna of the sound of a rasp against wood. When Jenna and Maeve walked in, she stopped, watching them as they sidled along the back of the crowd. Cataract-whitened eyes glittered under over-hanging, gray-hedged brows, and she took a long sip of the stout's brown foam. Aldwoman Pearce was Ald—the Eldest—in Ballintubber, over nine double-hands of years old. "I've buried everyone born before me and many after," she often said. "And I'll bury more before I go. I'm too old and mean and tough for the black haunts to eat my soul." Aldwoman Pearce knew all the tales, and if she changed them from time to time as suited the occasion, no one dared to contradict her.

Aldwoman Pearce set the glass down on the mantel again with a sharp *clack* that made half the people jump up, startled. The noise also narrowed Tara's eyes where she stood behind the bar—mugs were expensive and chipped ones were already too common. Aldwoman Pearce didn't notice Tara's unspoken admonition; her gaze was still on Maeve and Jenna.

"In the Before, when the bones of the land were still alive, mage-lights often filled the sky," Aldwoman Pearce declared, looking back at the others. "They were brighter and more colorful than those we saw tonight, and the cloudmages would call down the power in them and use it to war against each other. In the Before, magic lived in the sky, and when the sky became dark again, as it has stayed ever since for hands upon hands of generations, the cloudmages all died and their arts were lost."

"We've all heard that story a thousand times before," someone called out. The voice sounded like Thomas the Miller, who lived at the north end of the village, but Jenna, craning her head to see over the crowd, couldn't be sure. "Then what was that we saw tonight? I saw my shadow, near as sharp as in the sun. I could have read a book by it."

"Aye, that you could, if you owned a book and if you could read at all," One Hand Bailey called out, and everyone laughed. Jenna's mam had a book, a fine old thing with thick pages of yellow paper and gray-black printing that looked more perfect than any hand could have written. Thomas claimed he could read and Jenna's mam had shown him their book once, but he claimed it must have been written in some other language, because he couldn't read it all. Sometimes Thomas read stories from the book bound in green leather that Erin the Healer owned, but Jenna wasn't alone in wondering whether Thomas simply made up the things he supposedly read.

"Tonight we saw the signs of the Filleadh," Aldwoman Pearce declared. "The first whisper that the bones of the land have stirred and will walk again, that what was Before will be Now. A hint, perhaps—" She stopped and glanced at Jenna's mam again; a few of the others craning their necks to look back as well. "—that things that were hidden will be found again."

Some of the people muttered and nodded, but Thomas guffawed. "That's nonsense, Aldwoman. The Before is Before, and the bones of the land are dead forever."

"The things I know aren't written in any of your books, Thomas Miller," the Ald sneered, tearing her hard gaze away from Maeve. "I know because my great-mam and great-da told me, and their parents told them, and so on back to the Before. I know because I hold history in my gray head, and because I listened. I know because my old bones *feel* it, and if you had a lick of sense in your head, you'd know it, too."

Thomas snorted, but said nothing. Aldwoman Pearce looked around the room, turning slowly, and again she fixed on Maeve. "What do *you* say, Maeve Aoire?"

Jenna felt more than saw her mam shrug. "I'm sure I don't know," she answered.

The Ald sniffed. "This is a portent, I tell you," she said ominously. "And if they saw the lights all the way in Dún Laoghaire, the Riocha will be like a nest of hornets hit with a stick, and will be buzzing all around the whole of Talamh an Ghlas. The Rí Gabair will be sending his emissaries here soon, because we all saw that the lights were close and within his lands." With that, Aldwoman Pearce drained her stout in one long swallow and called for more, and everyone began talking at once.

By the time Tara's clock-candle had burned down another stripe, Jenna was certain that no one in the tavern really knew what the lights had been at all, though it certainly made for a profitable evening for Tara—talking is thirsty work, as the old saying goes, and everyone wanted to give their impression of what they'd seen. Jenna slipped outside to escape the heat and the increasingly wild speculation, though Maeve was listening intently. Jenna shook her head as the closing door softened the din of a dozen conversations. She leaned against the drystone wall of the tavern, looking up at the crescent moon and the stars, gleaming and twinkling as if their stately transit of the sky had never been disturbed.

She smelled the odor of the pipe a moment before she heard the voice and saw the glowing red circle at the corner of the tavern. "They'll be going for another stripe, at least."

"Aye," Jenna answered, "and they'll all be complaining of it in the morning."

Laughter followed that remark, and Coelin stepped out from the side of the tavern, his form outlined in the glow from the tavern's window. He took a puff on the pipe, exhaling a cloud of fragrant smoke. "You saw it, too?"

She nodded. "I was up on Knobtop, still, when the lights came. With our sheep."

"Then you saw it well, since it looked as if the lights were flaring all around old Knobtop. So what do you think it was?"

"I think it was a gift from the Mother to allow Tara to sell more ale," Jenna answered, and Coelin laughed again, with a full and rich amusement as musical as his singing voice. "Whatever it was, I also think that there's nothing I can do about it."

"That," he said, "is the only intelligent answer I've heard tonight." He tapped the pipe out against the heel of his boot, and sparks fell and expired on the ground. Coelin blew through the stem and tapped it again, then stuffed the pipe in the pocket of his coat. "They'll be calling for me to play soon, wanting to hear all the old songs tonight, not the new ones."

"I like the old songs," Jenna said. "It's like hearing the voices of my ancestors. I close my eyes and imagine I'm one of them: Maghera, maybe, or even that sad spirit on

Sliabh Colláin, always calling for her lover killed by the cloudmage."

"You have a fine imagination, then," Coelin laughed.

"Your voice has a magic, that's all," Jenna said, then felt herself blushing. She could imagine her mam listening, and telling her: *You sound just like one of them.* . . . Jenna was grateful for the dark. She looked away, to where Knobtop loomed above the trees, a blackness in the sky where no stars shone.

"Ah, 'tis you who has the magic, Jenna," Coelin said. "When you're there listening, I find myself always looking at you."

Jenna felt her cheeks cool, and she stopped the laugh that wanted to escape. "Is that the kind of sweet lie you tell all of them, so they'll come sneaking out to you afterward, Coelin Singer? It won't work with me."

His eyes glittered in the light from the window, and the smile remained. " 'Tis the truth, even if you won't believe it. And you can tell your mam that the rumors about me are greatly exaggerated. I've not slept with all the young women hereabouts."

"But with some?"

He might have shrugged, but the grin widened. "Rumors are like songs," he said. He took a step toward her. "There always has to be a bit of truth in them, or they won't have any power."

"You should make up a song about tonight. About the lights."

"I might do that," he answered. "About the lights, and a beautiful young woman they illuminated—"

The door to the tavern opened, throwing light over Jenna and Coelin and silhouetting the figure of Ellia, one of Tara's daughters and Coelin's current favorite. "Coelin! Put out that pipe of yours and . . ." A sudden frost chilled Ellia's voice. "Oh," she said. "I didn't expect to see *you* out here, Jenna. Coelin, Mam says to get your arse inside; they want music." The door shut again, more vehemently than necessary.

"Ellia sounds . . ." Jenna hesitated, tilting her head at Coelin. "Upset," she finished.

"It's been a busy night, that's all," Coelin answered.

"I'm sure."

"I'd better get in."

"Ellia would like that, I'm certain."

The door opened again. This time Jenna's mam stood there. Coelin shrugged at Jenna. "I should go tune up," he said.

"Aye, you should."

Coelin smiled at her, winked, and walked past her to the door. " 'Evenin', Widow Aoire," he said as Jenna's mam stepped aside.

"Coelin." She let the door shut behind him, and crossed her arms.

"We were talking, Mam," Jenna said. "That's all."

Maeve sniffed. Frown lines creased her forehead. "From what I saw, your eyes were saying different things than your mouth."

"And neither my eyes nor my mouth made any promises, Mam."

Inside the tavern, a rosined bow scraped against strings. Maeve shook her head, revealing the silvery gray that touched her temples. "I don't trust the young man. You know that. He'd be no good for you, Jenna—wouldn't know a ewe from a ram, a bull from a milch cow, or potato from turnip. Songmaster Curragh got him from the Taisteal; the boy himself doesn't know who his parents are or where he came from. All he knows is his singing, and he'll get tired of Ballintubber soon enough and want to find a bigger place with more people to listen to him and brighter coins to toss in his hat. He'd leave you, or you'd be tagging along keeping the pretty young things away from him, all the while with children tugging at your skirts."

"So you've already got me married and your grandchildren born. What are their names, so I'll know?" Jenna smiled at her mam, hands on her hips. Slowly, the frown lines smoothed out, and Maeve smiled back, her brown-gold eyes an echo of Jenna's own.

"You want to go in and listen, darling?"

"I'll go in if you're going, Mam. Otherwise, I'll go home with you. I've had enough excitement for a night. Coelin's voice might be too much for me."

Maeve laughed. "Come on. We'll listen for a while, then go home." She opened the door as Coelin's baritone lifted in the first notes of a song. "Besides," Maeve whispered as Jenna slipped past her, "it'll be fun to watch Ellia's face when she sees Coelin looking at you."

2

A Visitor

IN the morning, it was easy to believe that nothing magical had happened at all. There were the morning chores: settling the sheep in the back pasture, cleaning out the barn, feeding the chicks and gathering the eggs, going over to Matron Kelly's to trade a half dozen eggs for a jug of milk from her cows, doing the same with Thomas the Miller for a sack of flour for bread. By the time Jenna finished, with the sun now peering over the summit of Knobtop, it seemed that life had lurched back into its familiar ruts, never to be dislodged again. In the daylight, it was difficult to imagine curtains of light flowing through the sky.

Jenna could smell Maeve frying bacon over the cook fire inside their cottage, and her stomach rumbled. Kesh was barking at her feet. She opened the door, ducking her head under the low, roughly carved lintel, and into the warm air scented with the smell of burning peat. The cottage was divided into two rooms—the larger space crowded with a single table and chairs and the kitchen area, and a small bedroom in the rear where Jenna and her mam slept. Maeve had helped Jenna's father—Niall—build the wattle and daub house, but that was before Jenna had been born. She often wondered what he looked like, her da. Maeve had told her that Niall's hair was red, not coal black like Jenna's and Maeve's, and his eyes were as blue as the deep waters of Lough Lár, and that his smile could light up a dark night. She knew little about him, only that he wasn't from Ballintubber, but Inish Thuaidh, the fog-wrapped and

cold island to the north and west. Jenna tried to imagine
that face, and sometimes it looked like one person and
sometimes another, and sometimes even an older Coelin.
She wished she could see the memories that her mam saw,
when she rocked in the chair and talked about him, her
eyes closed and smiling. Jenna had no memory of Niall at
all. "He was killed, my love," Maeve had told her years
ago when Jenna had asked, curious as to why she didn't
have a da when others did, "slain by bandits on his way to
Bácathair. He was going there to see if he could gain a
berth on one of the fishing ships, and maybe move you and
me there. He always loved the sea, your da."

When Jenna grew older, she heard the other rumors as
well, from the older children. "Your da was fey and
strange, and he just left you and your mam," Chamis Redface told her once, after he pushed her into a thicket of
bramble. "That's what *my* da says: your da was a crazy
Inishlander, and everyone's glad he's gone. You go to Bácathair, and you'll find him, sitting in the tavern and drinking, probably married to someone else and talking
nonsense." Jenna had flown at Chamis in a rage, bloodying
his nose before he threw her off and Matron Kelly came
by to pull them apart. When Maeve asked Jenna why she'd
been fighting with Chamis, she just sniffed. "He tells lies,"
she said, and would say nothing else.

But she wondered about what Chamis had said. There
were times when she imagined herself going to Bácathair
and looking for him, and in those fantasies, sometimes, she
found him. But when she did, invariably, she woke up before she could talk with him.

The man you thought you saw, after you fell . . . He *had
red hair, and his eyes, they might have been blue* . . . Jenna
tried to shake the thought away, but she couldn't. She saw
his face again and found herself smiling.

"I'm glad to see you're so pleased with yourself," her
mam said as she came into the tiny house. "Here's your
breakfast. Give me the milk and the flour, and sit yourself
down." Maeve slid the wooden plate in front of Jenna,
along with one of the four worn and bent forks they owned:
eggs sizzling brown with bacon grease, a slab of brown

bread with a pat of butter, a mug of tea and milk. "This afternoon I have to give Rafea two of the hens for the bolt of cloth she gave me last week."

"Give her the brown one and the white neck," Jenna said. "They're both fat enough, and neither one lays well." Jenna slid her fork under a piece of bacon. "Mam, I think I'll take the flock back up to Knobtop this afternoon."

Maeve's back was to her as she cut a slice of bread for herself. "Up to Knobtop?" she asked. Her voice sounded strained. "After last night?"

"It's a nice day, the grass was good up there yesterday, and this time I'll be sure I'm back earlier. Besides, Mam, in all the old stories, the mage-lights only come at night, never during the day."

Her mam hadn't moved. The knife was still in her hand, the bread half cut. "I thought you might help me with the hens." When Jenna didn't answer, she heard Maeve sigh. "All right. I suppose I shouldn't be surprised. Aldwoman Pearce'll be talking about it, though."

"Why should Aldwoman Pearce care if I go to Knobtop? Because I was there last night?"

"Aye," Maeve said. She set the knife down and turned, brushing at the front of her skirt. "Because of that, and . . ." She stopped. "Ah, it doesn't matter. Go on with you. Take Kesh, and keep Old Stubborn out of trouble this time. I'll expect you back before sundown. Do you understand?"

"I understand, Mam." Jenna hastily finished her breakfast, gave Kesh the plate on the floor while she put her coat and gloves back on, and took the half loaf of brown bread her mother gave her, stuffing it into a pocket of the coat. "Come on, Kesh. Let's get the sheep . . ." With a kiss for her mam, she was gone.

By the time they reached the green-brown flanks of Knobtop, the sun had warmed Jenna and her coat was open. The sky was deep blue overhead and dotted with clouds, sailing in a stately fleet across the zenith. The sheep moved along with Kesh circling and nipping at their heels, their black-faced heads lowering to nibble at the heather. As they rose higher, Jenna could look back north and west and see the thatched roofs of Ballintubber in its clearing beyond the trees lining the path of the Mill Creek, and looking eastward, glimpse the bright thread of the River Duán winding its way through the rolling landscape toward Lough Lár. By noon, they were in the field where Jenna had seen the lights.

She didn't know what she had expected to see, but she found herself disappointed. There was no sign that anything unusual had happened here at all. Kesh herded the sheep into the largest grassy slope, and the flock set themselves to grazing—they paid no more attention to the area than they did to the pastures down in the valley.

Jenna found a large, mossy boulder and sat down to rest from the climb. "Kesh! Keep them here, and don't let Old Stubborn get away this time." She pulled her mam's brown bread from her pocket; as she did so, the pebble she'd picked up the previous night fell out onto the ground. She leaned down to pick it up.

The touch of it on her fingers was so cold that she dropped the stone in surprise, then picked it up carefully, as if she were holding a chunk of ice. In the sunlight, there was the echo of the emerald brilliance the rock had seemed to possess when she'd first found it. She'd never seen a rock this color before: a lush, saturated green, crenellated with veins of pure, searing white that made her pupils contract when the sun dazzled from them. The stone looked as if it had been polished and buffed with jeweler's rouge.

And so cold . . . Jenna closed her right hand around the stone, thinking it would warm as she held it, but the cold grew so intense that it felt as if she'd taken hold of a burning ember. As it had last night, another vision settled over her eyes like a mist, as if she were seeing two worlds at once. The red-haired man was there again, still stooped over as he paced the slope of Knobtop, and again he turned to look at her. "I lost it . . ." he said, and then he faded. Other, stronger voices came to her: a dozen of them, two dozen, more; all of them shouting at her at once, the din clamoring in her ears though she could make out none of the words in the chaos.

Jenna cried out (Kesh barking in alarm at her voice) and

tried to release the stone, but her fingers wouldn't open. They remained stubbornly clamped around the pebble, and the icy burning was climbing quickly from her hand to her wrist, onto her forearm, past the elbow . . . "No!" This time the words were a scream, as Jenna scrabbled frantically at her fisted hand, trying to pry the fingers open with her other hand as the cold filled her chest, pounding like a foaming, crashing sea wave up toward her head, crashing down into her abdomen. The voices screamed. The cold fire filled her, and Jenna screamed again in panic. She could feel a surging power pressing against her, each fiber of her body taut and humming with wild energy. She lifted her hand, concentrating her will, imagining her fingers opening around the stone. Her fingers trembled as if she had a palsy, then sprang open. Coruscating light, brighter than the sun, flared outward, arcing in a jagged lightning bolt that struck ground a dozen strides away.

The stone fell from her hand. A peal of thunder dinned in her ears and echoed from the hills around Knobtop. Breathless, Jenna sank to her knees in the grass.

Whimpering, Kesh came up and licked her face while she tried to catch her breath, as the world settled into normalcy around her. Old Stubborn *baaed* nearby. Jenna blinked hard. Everything was normal, except . . .

Where the lightning bolt had struck, there was a black-ened hole in the turf, an arm deep and a stride across. The dirt there steamed in the air.

Jenna's intake of breath shuddered in amazement. "By the Mother, Kesh, did I . . . ?"

The stone lay a hand's breadth from her knee. Cradled in winter-browned heather, it seemed pretty and harmless. She reached out with a trembling forefinger and prodded it once. The surface seemed like any other stone, and she felt nothing. She touched it again, longer this time: it was still chilled, but not horribly so. She picked it up, careful not to close her hand around it again. "What do you think, Kesh?"

The dog whimpered again, and barked once at her.

Gingerly, she placed the stone back in her pocket.

*　　*　　*

"Is everything all right?" Maeve asked as Jenna brought the flock back to Ballintubber. "Thomas said he saw a bright flash up on Knobtop, and we all heard thunder even though the sky was clear." The worry made her mam's face look old and drawn. "Jenna, I was worried. After last night . . ."

All the way down from the high pasture, Jenna had debated with herself over what she'd tell her mam. She'd thought at first that she'd tell her everything, how she'd found the stone after the lights, how it had seemed to glow, how the cold fury had consumed her until released. She wanted to describe the man she'd seen in the misty vision, and ask her: *Could it be Da?* But looking at Maeve now, seeing the anxiety and concern that filled her eyes, Jenna found that the carefully rehearsed words dissolved inside her. The fright she'd felt had faded and she seemed unhurt by the experience—why bother Mam with that now? Besides, she wasn't sure she *could* explain it: Mam might think she was making up tales, or wonder if Jenna had gone insane like Matron Kelly's son Sean, whose brain had been burned up by a high fever when he was a baby. Sean talked as poorly as a three-year-old and babbled constantly to creatures only he could see. No, better to say nothing.

Jenna plunged her hand into her coat pocket, letting her fingertips roam over the pebble there. The stone felt perfectly normal now, like any other stone, not even a hint of the coldness. Jenna smiled at her mam.

"I'm fine," she said. "A flash? Thunder? I really didn't notice anything." Jenna wasn't used to lying to her mam—at least no more than any adolescent might be—and she was surprised at how easily the words came, at how casual and natural they sounded. "I didn't see *anything,* Mam. I thought I might, after last night, but everything was just . . ." She shrugged, and brought her hand out of her pocket. ". . . normal."

Maeve's head was cocked slightly to one side, and her eyes were narrowed. But she nodded. "Then get the sheep in, and come inside. I have some stirabout ready to eat."

She continued to regard Jenna for a long breath, then turned and entered the cottage.

That was all Jenna heard on the subject. She took the stone out of her pocket that night after her Mam was asleep, hiding it in a chink in the wall next to her side of the bed and covering it with mud. It was dangerous, she told herself, and shouldn't be handled. But every morning, when she woke up, she looked at the spot, brushing her fingers over the dried mud. She found the touch comforting.

That night, she dreamed of the red-haired man, so real that it seemed she could touch him. "Who are you?" she asked him, but instead of answering her, he shook his head and wandered off toward Knobtop. She followed, calling to him, but she was caught in the slow motion of a dream and could never catch up. When she woke, she found that she couldn't remember his features at all; they were simply a blur, unreal.

She looked at the mud-covered spot where the stone lay, and that, too, seemed unreal. She could almost believe there was nothing there. Nothing there at all.

Over the next few days, the excitement in Ballintubber about the lights over Knobtop gradually died, even though the stories about that night grew with each telling, until someone listening might have thought that entire armies of magical creatures had been seen swirling in the air above the mount, wailing and crying. A good quarter of the village of Ballintubber had been up on Knobtop that night, too, if the tales that were told in Tara's were to be believed. But though the tales grew more elaborate, the night sky over Knobtop remained dark for the next three nights, and life returned to normal.

Until the fourth day.

The day was gloomy and overcast, with the lowering clouds dropping a persistent cold rain that permeated through clothing and settled into sinew and bone. The world was swathed in gray and fog, with Knobtop lost in the haze. Ballintubber's single cobbled lane was a morass

of puddles and mud with occasional islands of wet stone.
The smoke of turf fires rose from the chimneys of Ballintubber, gray smoke fading into gray skies, and the rain
pattered from the edges of thatch into brown pools.

Rain couldn't alter the pace of life in Ballintubber, nor
in fact anywhere in Talamh an Ghlas. It rained three or
four days out of seven, after all, the year around. Rain in
its infinite variety kept the land lush and green: startlingly
bright and refreshing drizzles in the midst of sunshine;
foggy rains where the clouds seemed to sink into the very
earth and the air was simply wet; soaking, hard spring
downpours that awakened the seeds in the ground; summer
rains as warm and soft as bathwater; rare winter storms of
snow and sleet to blanket the world in white and vanish in
the next day's sun; howling and shrieking hurricanes from
off the sea that lashed and whipped the land. Rain was
simply a fact of life. If it rained, you got wet; if the sun
was out or it was cloudy, you didn't—that was all. The
chores still needed to be done, the work still went on. A
little rain couldn't bring the activity in Ballintubber to a
halt.

But the appearance of the rider did.

Through the open doors of the small barn behind Tara's
Tavern, Jenna saw Eliath, Tara's son and youngest at
twelve years of age, currying down the steaming body of a
huge brown stallion. Jenna was pushing a barrow of new-
cut turf toward home; she detoured to see the horse, which
looked far too large and healthy to be one of the local work
animals. "Hey, Eli," she said, setting down the barrow just
inside the door where it was out of the rain.

Eli glanced up from his work. The horse turned his great
neck to glance at Jenna and nickered. She went over and
rubbed his long muzzle. Eli grinned. "Hey, Jenna. That's
some animal, isn't it?"

"It certainly is," she said. "Who does it belong to?"

"A man from the east, that's all I know. He rode in a
while ago, stopped at the tavern, and asked Mam to send
me to get the Ald. I think he's Riocha; at least he's dressed
like a tiarna—fine leather boots and gloves, a jacket of
velvet and silk, and under that a léine shirt as white as new

snow, and a clóca over it all that's as thick as your finger and embroidered all around the edges with gold—the colors of the clóca are green and brown, so he's of Tuath Gabair." Eli plucked at his own bedraggled woolen coat and unbleached muslin shirt. He plunged a hand into a pocket and pulled out a large coin. "Gave me this, too, for getting Aldwoman Pearce and taking care of the horse."

"Where is he now?"

"Inside. Lots of other people there now, too. You can go in if you want."

Jenna glanced at the tavern, where yellow light shone through the streaks of gray rain. "I might. Can I leave the barrow here?"

"Sure."

There were at least a dozen people in the dim, smoky interior of the tavern, unusual in midafternoon. The stranger sat at a table near the rear, talking with Aldwoman Pearce. Jenna caught sight of a narrow face with a long nose, brown eyes dark enough to be nearly black, and a well-trimmed beard, a slight body clad in rich clothing, a delicate hand wrapped around a mug of stout. His hair was long and oiled, and the line of a scar interrupted the beard halfway to the left ear. Jenna could hear his voice as he spoke with Aldwoman Pearce, and it was as smooth and polished as his clothing, bright with the accent of the upper class and permeated with a faint haughtiness. The others in the tavern were pretending not to watch the stranger's table, which made it all the more obvious that they were.

Coelin was there, also, sitting at the bar with a mug of tea and a plate of scones in front of him, talking with Ellia. Tara was in the rear of the tavern, hanging the pot over the cook fire. Jenna went over and stood next to Coelin, ignoring the barbed glance from Ellia, behind the bar.

"Who is he?" Jenna asked.

Coelin shrugged. "Riocha. A tiarna from Lár Bhaile, if he's to be believed. The Tiarna Padraic Mac Ard, he says."

"What's he talking to Aldwoman Pearce about?"

Coelin shrugged, but Ellia leaned forward. "Mam says he asked about the lights—didn't Aldwoman Pearce foretell that the other night? Says he saw them in Lár Bhaile from across the lough. When Mam told him how they were flickering around Knobtop, he asked to speak to the Ald.''

"Maybe he'll want to speak with you, Jenna," Coelin said. "You were up there that night."

Jenna shivered, remembering, and shook her head vigorously. She thought of those dark eyes on her, of those thin lips asking questions. She thought of the stone in its hole in the wall of her cottage. "No. I didn't see anything that you didn't see here. Let him talk to the Ald. Or some of the others here who say they saw all sorts of things with the lights."

Coelin snorted through his nose at that. "They saw things with the ale and whiskey they drank that night and their own imaginations. I doubt Tiarna Mac Ard will be much interested in that."

"Why's he interested at all?" Jenna asked, glancing over at him again. "They were lights, that's all, and gone now." Mac Ard's eyes glittered in the lamplight, never at rest. For a moment, their gazes met. The contact was almost a physical shock, making Jenna take a step back. She looked away hurriedly. "I should go," she said to Coelin and Ellia.

"Ah, 'tis a shame," Ellia said, though her voice was devoid of any sorrow at all.

"Come back tonight, Jenna," Coelin said. "I made up a song about the lights, like you suggested."

Despite her desire to be away from Mac Ard and the tavern, Jenna could not keep the smile from her lips, though the pleased look on Ellia's face dissolved. "Did you now?"

Coelin tilted his head and smiled back at her. "I did. And I won't sing it unless you're there to hear the verses first. So will you come?"

"We'll see," Jenna said. Mac Ard was still looking at her, and Aldwoman Pearce turned in her chair to glance back also. "I really need to go now."

As Jenna rushed out, she heard Ellia talking to Coelin— "Keep your eyes in your head and the rest of you in your pants, Coelin Singer. She's still just a gawky lamb, and not a very pretty one at that . . ."—then the door closed behind her. The cold rain struck her face, and she pulled the cowl of her coat over her head as she ran through the puddles to the barn and retrieved her barrow of peat.

She hurried back to the cottage through the rain and the fog.

3

A Song at the Inn

JENNA had just lit the candles on the shelves to either side of the fireplace. The sun was down or lowering—the rain persisted, and the sky slipped from the color of wet smoke to slate to coal as the interior of their house slowly darkened. Maeve was peeling potatoes; Jenna was carding wool. They both heard the sound of slowly moving hooves through the drumming of rain, and Kesh lifted his head from the floor and growled. Leather creaked, and there were footsteps on the flags outside the door. Someone knocked at the door and Kesh barked. Maeve looked at Jenna.

"Mam, I forgot to tell you. There's a tiarna who was at Tara's . . ." Maeve set down her paring knife and went to the door, brushing at her apron. She opened the door. Mac Ard stood there, a darkness against the wet night.

"I'm looking for Maeve Aoire and her daughter," Mac Ard said. His voice was deep and gruff. "I was told this was their home."

"Aye, 'tis," Maeve answered, and Jenna heard a strange, awed tone in her mam's voice. "I'm Maeve Aoire, sir. Come in out of the wet, won't you?" Maeve stood aside as the man ducked his head and entered. Kesh growled once, then slunk away toward the fire. "Jenna, put your coat on and take the tiarna's horse out to the barn. At least it'll be dry there. Go on with you, now."

By the time Jenna got back, Mac Ard was sitting at the table with a plate of boiled potatoes, mutton, and bread, and a mug of tea in front of him. Kesh sat at his feet, waiting for dropped crumbs. His boots and clóca were drying near the fire. Maeve sat across from him, but she wasn't eating. Her face was pale, as if she might be frightened, and her hands were fisted on the table, fingers curled into palms. She glanced up as Jenna came through the door, shaking water from her hood and sleeves. "It's not raining as hard as it was," she said, wanting to break the silence. "I think it'll stop soon."

Her mam simply nodded, as if she'd only half heard. Mac Ard had turned in his chair, the legs scraping across the floorboards. "Sit down, Jenna," he said. "I'd like to talk with you."

Jenna glanced at her mam, who gave her a slight nod. Jenna didn't sit, but went over to Maeve, standing behind her, and resting her hands on her Mam's shoulders even as Maeve reached up to pat Jenna's hand reassuringly. One corner of Mac Ard's mouth lifted slightly under the beard, as if he found the sight amusing.

"I didn't expect to hear the surname Aoire, so many miles from the north," he commented. He stabbed a potato with a fork, brought it to his mouth, and chewed. "It's an uncommon name hereabouts, to be certain. Inishlander in origin."

"My husband was from the north," Maeve answered. "From Inish Thuaidh."

"Husband?"

"He's dead almost seventeen years, Tiarna Mac Ard. Killed by bandits on the road."

Mac Ard nodded. He blinked, and the dark eyes seemed softer than they had a moment before. "I'm sorry for your loss," he said, and Jenna thought she heard genuine sympathy in his voice. "For a woman as well-spoken and comely as yourself, he must have been an exceptional person for you to never have remarried. This is his daughter?"

Maeve touched Jenna's hands. "Aye. She was still a babe in arms when Niall was murdered."

Another nod. "Niall Aoire. Interesting. Niall's not an Inish name, though. In fact, my great-uncle was named Niall, though he was a Mac Ard." The tiarna sipped at the tea, leaning back in his chair. He seemed to be waiting, then took a long breath before continuing. "Four nights ago, I was standing on the tower of the Rí's Keep in Lár Bhaile, when I saw colors flickering on the black waters of the lough. I looked up, and I could see the glow in the sky as well, to the north and west beyond the hills. They were nothing I'd ever seen before, but I'd heard them described, in all the old folktales. Mage-lights."

He drummed the table with his fingers. "A dozen or more generations ago, I'm told, my own ancestors were among the last of the cloudmages as the mage-lights in the sky weakened. Then the lights vanished entirely, and with them the power to perform spells. If you listen to the old tales, with the lights also went other magics as well: that of mythical creatures and of hidden, ancient places. Now half the people think of those tales as myth and legend, no more than stories. At times, I've thought that, too. But looking at the lights, I felt . . ." He tapped his chest, leaning forward, his voice dropping to a hoarse whisper. "I felt them calling me, here. I went running down from the tower, and dragged the town's Ald back up so that I could show him. 'By the Mother-Creator, those are mage-lights, Tiarna,' he said. 'They can't be anything else. After so long . . .' I thought the poor old man might cry, he was so moved by the sight of them. So I asked the Rí's leave to come here, because they called me, because I wanted to see where they'd chosen to return." His eyes found Jenna, and again she felt the shock of that contact, as if his gaze could actually bruise her. "I'm told that you were up there that night, on Knobtop."

She wanted to shout denial, but couldn't, not with her mam there. "Aye," she started to say, but the admission was more squeak than word. She cleared her throat. "I was there."

"And what did you see?"

"Lights, Tiarna Mac Ard. Beautiful lights, rippling and swaying." She could not stop the awe the memory placed in her voice.

"And nothing more?"

"They flashed at the end, brighter than anything I'd ever

seen. Then they were . . ." Her shoulder lifted. "Gone," she finished. "I told Kesh to bring the sheep along, and we came back here."

Mac Ard ruffled Kesh's head and fed him a piece of the mutton. "Strange," he said. "And nothing else happened? Nothing else . . . unusual?" His eyes held her. Jenna found herself thinking of the stone hidden in the wall in their bedroom, not six strides away from Mac Ard, and of the cold lightning that flared from it and the red-haired man. She could feel her cheeks getting hot, and her mouth opened as if she wanted to speak, but she forced herself to remain silent as Mac Ard continued to stare. She thought that he could see through her, could sense the lie of omission that lay in her gut, burning, all the worse because now she was lying to a Riocha, one of the nobility of the land. Mac Ard's nostrils flared on his thin nose and he almost seemed to nod. Then he blinked and looked away, and the terror in her heart receded.

"How odd," Mac Ard said, "that the mage-lights would choose to reappear here."

"I'm sure neither of us know why, Tiarna," Maeve told him.

He pursed his lips. He glanced back once at Jenna before turning his attention to her mam. "I'm sure you don't. Tell me this, Widow Aoire, did you know your husband's family well?"

Maeve shook her head. "I was born and raised here. The truth, Tiarna, is that I know very little about them, and never at all met any of them. The farthest I've ever been from Ballintubber is Bácathair, a few months after my husband's death. I went there to see if the gardai could help me find out more about how he died, and who the murderers were."

"And did the gardai help you?"

Jenna saw Maeve's head move softly from side to side. "No. They had nothing more to tell me than I already knew, nor did they care much about the death of 'some Inishlander.'"

Mac Ard nodded slowly, contemplatively. "I've taken enough of your time and hospitality," he said. "Let me repay you. I understand that there's a young man with an excellent voice who sings at the inn where I'm staying tonight. Come back there with me; be my guests for the evening, both of you. We can talk more there, about whatever you'd like."

Jenna had to stop herself from grinning, both from relief that the tiarna's interrogation seemed to be over, and at the suggestion to go to Tara's. Coelin had promised her a song, and she hadn't wanted to ask, with the awful weather. But if the tiarna insisted . . .

"Oh, no, Tiarna," Maeve started to say automatically, then glanced back at Jenna. He smiled at her and nodded, as if they shared a secret.

"Your daughter wants you to accept," Mac Ard said. "And I would be honored."

"I don't—" Maeve began. Jenna tightened her arms around her mother's shoulders, and felt her sigh. "I suppose we'd also be honored," she said.

The rain had subsided to a bare, cold drizzle. Mac Ard brought his stallion out from the barn. "You want to ride him?" he asked Jenna. She nodded, mutely. He picked her up, hands around her waist, and placed her sideways astride the saddle, handing her the reins. He patted the muscular neck, glossy and as rich a brown as new-turned earth. "Behave yourself, Conhal," he told the horse, who snorted and shook his head, bridle jingling. "That's a special young woman you hold."

For a moment, Jenna wondered at that, but then Mac Ard clucked once at Conhal, and the horse started walking, startling Jenna. They moved up the lane to Tara's, Mac Ard and Maeve walking alongside. The tiarna seemed to be paying most of his attention to Maeve, Jenna noticed. His head inclined toward her, and they talked in soft voices that Jenna couldn't quite overhear, and he smiled and, once, he touched Maeve's arm. Her mam smiled in return and laughed, but Jenna noticed that Maeve also moved slightly away from the tiarna after the touch.

Jenna frowned. Her mam had never paid much attention to the other men in Ballintubber, though enough of them had certainly indicated their interest. She'd always rebuffed them—some gently, some not, but all of them firmly. But this dark man, this Mac Ard . . . He seemed to like Maeve, and he was Riocha, after all. Maeve had always told her how Niall, her da, was strong and protective and loving, and she could imagine that this Mac Ard might be the same way. . . .

The conversation inside Tara's stopped dead when Tiarna Mac Ard pushed open the door of the tavern so that Maeve and Jenna could enter, then, as quickly, the chatter resumed again as everyone pretended not to notice that the tiarna had brought company with him. Tara came out from behind the bar, and shooed away old man Buckles from one of the tables. "What will you have, Tiarna Mac Ard?" she asked with an eyebrows-raised glance at Maeve. Mac Ard tilted his head toward Jenna's mam.

"What do you recommend?" he asked.

"Tara's brown ale is excellent," Maeve said. She was smiling at Mac Ard, and if she remained a careful step away from him, she also kept her gaze on him.

"The brown ale, then," Mac Ard said. Tara nodded her head and bustled off. Maeve sat across the table from Mac Ard; Jenna went over to where Coelin was tuning his giotár. Ellia was there also, her arm around Coelin. He glanced up, smiling, as Jenna approached; Ellia just stared.

"So the tiarna found you, eh?" he said. "He came up right after you left and asked where you lived." Coelin glanced over at the table, where Mac Ard's dark head inclined toward Maeve. Coelin lifted an eyebrow at Jenna. "Seems he likes what he found." Ellia grinned at that, and Jenna frowned.

"I don't find that funny, Coelin Singer," she said. She lifted her chin and turned to walk away.

Coelin strummed a minor chord. "Jenna," he said to her back. "I'm sorry. I didn't mean to offend you." She looked over her shoulder at him, and he continued. "So what did he ask you? 'She's the one who was up there,' he said to me. 'I know this. I can *feel* it.' That's what he told me, before he even knew who you were."

"What did the tiarna mean by that?" Jenna asked.

Coelin shrugged. "I'm sure I wouldn't know. What did he say to you? What did he ask?"

"He only asked whether I saw the lights, that's all. I told him that I had, and described them for him."

"We *all* saw them," Ellia said. "That's nothing special. I could describe the lights for him just as easily, if that's all he wants to know." She tightened her arm around Coelin. Jenna looked at her, at Coelin. She tried to find a hint in his bright, grass-green eyes that he wanted her to stay, that her presence was special to him. Maybe if he'd spoken then, maybe if he'd moved away from Ellia, if he'd given her any small sign. . . .

But he didn't. He sat there, looking as handsome and charming as ever, with his long hair and his dancing eyes and his agile, long-fingered hands. Content. He smiled, but he smiled at Ellia, too. *And he'd let either of us lift our skirts for him, too, with that same smile, that same contentment.* The thought struck her with the force of truth, the way Aldwoman Pearce's proclamations sometimes did when she scattered the prophecy bones from the bag she'd made from the skin of a bog body. There was the same sense of finality that Jenna heard in the rattling of the ivory twigs. *You're no more to him than any other comely young thing. His interest in you is mostly for the reflection he sees of himself in your eyes. He flirts with you because it is what he does. It means no more than that.*

"I'll be going back to my table," she said.

"Stay," he said. "I'll be singing in a minute."

"And I'll hear you just as fine from there," Jenna answered. "Besides, you have Ellia to listen to you."

A trace of irritation deepened the fine lines around his eyes for a breath, then they smoothed again. His fingers flicked over the strings of his giotár discordantly. Ellia pulled him back toward her, and he laughed, turning his head away from Jenna.

She went back to the table. Mac Ard was leaning toward Maeve, his arms on the table, his hands curled around a mug of the ale, and her mam was talking. ". . . Niall would go walking on Knobtop or the hills just to the east, or follow the Duán down to Lough Lár, or go wandering in the forests between here and Keelballi. But he always came back, was never away for more than a week, maybe two at the most. There was a wanderlust in him. Some people never seem satisfied where they are, and he was one. I never worried about it, or thought he was traipsing off with some lass. Once or twice a year, I'd find him filling a sack with bread and a few potatoes, and I'd know he would be going. Jenna—" Maeve glanced up as Jenna approached, and she smiled softly, "—she has some of that restlessness in her blood. Always wanting to go farther, see more. I don't know what Niall was searching for, nor whether he ever found it. I doubt it, for he was wandering up to the end."

Mac Ard took a sip of the ale. "Did you ever ask him?"

Maeve nodded. "That I did. Once. He told me . . ." She looked away, as if she could see Jenna's da through the haze of pipe and peat smoke in the tavern. Jenna wondered what face she was seeing. "He told me that he came here because a voice had told him that his life's dream might be here." Meave's eyes shimmered in the candlelight, and she blinked hard. "He said it must have been my voice he heard."

Coelin's giotár sounded, a clear, high chord that cut through the low murmur of conversation in the bar. He'd moved over near the fire, Ellia sitting close to him and a mug of stout within reach. "What would you hear first?" he called out to the patrons.

On any other night, half a dozen voices might have answered Coelin, but tonight there was silence. No one actually glanced back to Tiarna Mac Ard, but everyone waited to see if he would speak first.

Mac Ard had turned in his chair to watch Coelin, and Jenna could see something akin to disgust, or maybe it was simply irritation, flicker across his face. Then he called out to Coelin. "I'm told your teacher was a Songmaster. He must have given you the 'Song of Máel Armagh.' "

"Aye, he did, Tiarna," Coelin answered. "But it's a long tale and sad, and I've not sung it since Songmaster Curragh was alive."

"All the more reason to sing it now, before you lose it."

There was some laughter at that. Coelin gave a shrug and a sigh. "Give me a moment, then, to bring it back to mind . . ." Coelin closed his eyes. His fingers moved soundlessly over the strings for a few moments; his mouth moved with unheard words. Then he opened his eyes and exhaled loudly. "Here we go then," he said, and began to sing.

Coelin's strong baritone filled the room, sweet and melodious, a voice as smooth and rich as new-churned butter. Coelin had a true gift, Jenna knew—the gods had lent him their own tongue. Songmaster Curragh had heard the gift, unpolished and raw, in the scared boy he'd purchased from the Taisteal; now, honed and sharpened, the young man's talent was apparent to all. Mac Ard, after hearing the first few notes, sat back in his chair with an audible cough of surprise and admiration, shaking his head and stroking his beard. "No wonder the boy has half the lasses here in his thrall," Jenna heard him whisper to Maeve. "His throat must be lined with gold. Too bad he's all too well aware of it."

Coelin sang, his voice taking them into a misty past where fierce Máel Armagh, king of Tuath Infochla four hundred years before, drove his ships of war from Falcarragh to Inish Thuaidh, where the mage-lights had first shone in the Eldest Time and where they glowed brightest. The verses of the ancient lay told how the cloudmages of the island called up the wild storms of the Ice Sea, threatening to smash the invading fleet on the island's high cliffs; Máel Armagh screaming defiance and finally landing safely; the sun gleaming from the armor and weapons of Máel Armagh's army as they swarmed ashore; the Battle of Dún Kiil, where Máel Armagh won his first and only victory; Sage Roshia's prophecy that the king would die "not from Inish hands" if he pursued the fleeing Inishlanders to seal his victory. Yet Máel Armagh ordered the pursuit into the mountain fastnesses of the island and there met his fate, his armies scattered and trapped, the Inishlanders surrounding him on all sides and the mage-lights flickering in the dark sky above. The last verses were filled with the folly, the courage, and the sorrow of the Battle of Sliabh

Míchinniúint: the Inish cloudmages raining fire down on the huddled troops; the futile, suicidal charge by Máel Armagh in an attempt to win through the pass to the Lowlands; the death of the doomed king at the hands of his own men, who presented Máel Armagh's body to Severii O'Coulghan, the Inishlander's chief cloudmage, to buy their safe passage back to their ships. And the final verse, as Máel Armagh's ship *Cinniúint*, now his funeral pyre, sailed away from the island to the south never to be seen again, the flames of the pyre painting the bottom of the gray clouds with angry red.

The clock-candle on Tara's bar had burned down a stripe before Coelin finished the song, and Mac Ard's hands started the applause afterward as Coelin eased his parched throat with long swallows of stout. "Excellent," Mac Ard said. "I've not heard better. You should come to Lár Bhaile, and sing for us there. I'll wager that in another year, you would be at the court in Dún Laoghaire, singing to the Rí Ard himself."

Coelin's face flushed visibly as he grinned, and Jenna saw Ellia's eyes first widen, then narrow, as if she were already seeing Coelin leaving Ballintubber. "I'll do that, Tiarna. Maybe I'll follow you back."

"Do that," Mac Ard answered, "and I'll make sure you have a roof over your head, and you'll pay for your keep with songs."

The patrons laughed and applauded (all but Ellia, Jenna noticed), and someone called out for another song, and Coelin started a reel: "The Cow Who Married the Pig," everyone clapping along and laughing at the nonsensical lyrics. Mac Ard inclined his head to Maeve, nodding once in Jenna's direction. "Those were her ancestors the boy sang of," he said. "And your husband's. A fierce and proud people, the Inishlanders. They never bowed to any king but their own, and they still don't." He sat back, then leaned forward again. "They also knew the mage-lights. Knew how to draw them down, knew how to store their power. Even then, in the last days of the Before, in the final flickering of the power and the cloud-mages. They say it's in their blood. They say that if the mage-lights come again, when it's time for the Filleadh, the mage-lights will first appear to someone of Inish Thuaidh."

Jenna saw Maeve glance toward her. She wondered if her mam had felt the same shiver that had just crept down her spine. "And are you thinking that my daughter and I had anything to do with this, Tiarna Mac Ard?" Maeve asked him.

Mac Ard shrugged. "I don't even know for certain that what we saw were mage-lights. They may have just been some accident of the sky, the moon reflecting from ice in the clouds, perhaps. But . . ." He paused, listening to Coelin's singing before turning back to Maeve and Jenna. "I told you that when I saw them, I wanted to come here. And I . . . I have a touch of the Inish blood in me."

4

The Fire Returns

JENNA left before the clock-candle reached the next stripe: as Coelin sang a reel, then a love song; as Mac Ard related to Maeve the long story of his great-great-mam from Inish Thuaidh (who, Jenna learned, fell in love with a tiarna from Dathúil in Tuath Airgialla, who would become Mac Ard's great-great-da. There was more, but Jenna became lost in the blizzard of names.) Maeve seemed strangely interested in the intricacies of the Mac Ard genealogy and asked several questions, but Jenna was bored. "I'm going back home, Mam," she said. "You stay if you like. I'll check on Kesh and the sheep."

Her mam looked concerned for a moment, then she glanced at Ellia, who was leaning as close to Coelin as she could without actually touching him. She smiled gently at Jenna. "Go on, then," she told Jenna. "I'll be along soon."

It was no longer raining at all, and the clouds had mostly cleared away, though the ground was still wet and muddy. Her boots were caked and heavy by the time she reached the cottage. Kesh came barking up to her as she approached. Jenna took off her boots, picked up a few cuttings of peat from the bucket inside the door, and coaxed the banked fire back into life until the chill left the room. Kesh padded after her as she went from the main room to their tiny bedroom and sat on the edge of the straw-filled mattress. She stared at the mud-daubed hole where the stone lay hidden. *"They say it's in their blood,"* Tiarna Mac Ard had said. *"When I saw them, I wanted to go there. . ."*

Jenna dropped to her knees in front of the hole. She picked at the dried mud with her fingernails until she could see the stone. Carefully, she pried it loose and held it in her open palm. So oddly plain, it was, yet . . .

It was cold again. As cold as the night she'd held it in her hand on Knobtop. Jenna gasped, thrust the stone into the pocket of her skirt, and left the bedroom.

She sat in front of the peat fire for a few minutes, her arms around herself. Kesh lay at her feet, looking up at her quizzically from time to time, as if he sensed that Jenna's thoughts were in turmoil. She wondered whether she should go back to Tara's and show the stone to Mac Ard, tell him everything that had happened on Knobtop. It would feel good to tell the truth—she knew that; she could feel the lie boiling inside, festering and begging for the lance of her words. Mam certainly seemed to trust the tiarna, and Jenna liked the way he spoke to her mam, and the way he treated the two of them. She could trust him, she felt. And yet . . .

He might be angry to find that she'd lied. So might her mam. Jenna swore—an oath she'd once heard Thomas the Miller utter when he'd dropped a sack of flour on his foot.

The ram, in the outbuilding, bleated a call of alarm. A few of the ewes also gave voice as Kesh's ears went up and he ran barking to the door. Jenna followed, pulling the muddy boots back over her feet, guessing that a wolf or a pack of the wild pigs was prowling nearby, or that Old Stubborn had simply got himself stuck somewhere again. "What's the matter with—" she began as she walked toward the pens.

She stopped, looking toward Knobtop.

Something sparked in the air above the peak: a flicker, a whisper of light. Then it was gone. But she'd seen true. She could still see the ghost of the light on the back of her eyes.

"Kesh, come on," she said.

She started toward Knobtop, her boots sloshing through the muck.

By the time she started walking up the mountain's steep flanks, the sky flickered again with flowing streams and billows of colors, tossing multiple shadows behind her over the heather and rocks. Kesh barked at the mage-lights, lifting his snout up to the sky. They were brightening now, fuller and even more dazzling than they'd been the last time. By now, Jenna knew, someone in Ballintubber would have seen them. They'd be tumbling out of Tara's, all of them, gawking. And Tiarna Mac Ard . . .

She imagined him, running to the stable behind Tara's, leaping on his brown steed and riding hard toward Knobtop . . .

She frowned. Now that the lights had appeared again, she didn't want to share them with him. They were hers. They had given her the stone; they had shown her the red-haired man.

The stone . . . She could feel its smooth weight now, cold and pulsing in the woolen pocket. She pulled the stone out: the pebble glowed, shimmering with an echo of the sky above, the colors tinting her fingers as she held it. The mage-lights seemed to bend in the atmosphere directly above her, swirling like water, as if they sensed her presence below. Jenna lifted her hand, and the mage-lights coalesced, forming a funnel of sparkling hues above that danced and wriggled, lengthening and elongating. Jenna started to pull her hand away, but the funnel of mage-light had wrapped itself around her hand now, like a thread attached to the maelstrom in the sky above her. As she moved her hand, it stretched and swayed, a ball of glowing light attached to her wrist. She could feel the mage-lights, not hot but very, very cold, the chill creeping from wrist to elbow, to shoulder. Jenna tried to pull away, desperately this time, but they held her like another hand, gripping her shoulders, the cold seeping into her chest and covering her head.

She swam in light. She closed her eyes, screaming in the bright silence, and she could still see the colors, melding and shifting.

Ethereal voices called to her.

A flash.

A deafening peal of thunder.

Blackness.

Kesh was licking her face.

Jenna rolled her head away, and the movement sent pain coursing through her neck and temples. Kesh whined as she shoved him away. "Get off," she told him. "I'm fine." She sat up, grimacing. "I hope so, anyway."

She was still on Knobtop, but the sky above was simply the sky, starlit between shreds of clouds slowly moving from the west. She looked down; she was holding the stone, and it throbbed like the blood in her head, pulsing cold but no longer shining. She was suddenly afraid of the pebble, and she started to throw it away, drawing her hand back.

Stopping.

The mage-lights came to you. *They came to* you, *and the stone . . .*

She brought her hand back down to her lap.

Kesh whined again, coming up to rub against her, then his head lifted, the ears going straight, his tail lifting and a low growl coming from his throat. "What is it?" Jenna asked, then she heard it herself: the sound of shod hooves striking rock within the copse of elm and oak trees down the slope of Knobtop. Jenna stood. Whoever it was, she didn't want to be seen here. She put the stone in her pocket and lifted the hem of her skirts. "Come, Kesh," she whispered, and ran. There was a small stand of trees fifty strides away, and she made for the darkness there. She stopped once she was under their shade, looking back through the tree trunks to the field. She saw the horse and rider emerge from under the trees: Tiarna Mac Ard, astride Conhal. The tiarna made his way slowly up the hillside, looking at the ground, glancing up at the sky. Kesh started to run out to them, and Jenna held the dog back. "Hush," she whispered. Mac Ard wouldn't be finding the mage-lights tonight, and she didn't want him to find her, either, or to have to explain why she was here. "Come," she said to Kesh, and slipped deeper into the shelter of the woods, making her way down the slope toward home.

*   *   *

Her mam looked up from the fire as Jenna opened the door. "Your boots are muddy," she said.

"I know," Jenna said. Sitting on the stool at the door, she took them off.

"I was worried when you weren't here."

"I went walking with Kesh."

"On Knobtop." The way Maeve said it, Jenna understood it was not a question. She nodded.

"Aye, Mam. On Knobtop."

Maeve nodded, worry crinkling her forehead and the corners of her eyes. "That's where he said you'd be." She didn't need to mention who "he" was; they both knew. "You look cold and pale," Maeve continued. "There's tea in the kettle over the fire. Why don't you pour yourself a mug?"

Wondering at her mam's strange calmness, Jenna poured herself tea sweetened with honey. Maeve said nothing more, though Jenna could feel her mam's gaze on her back. By the time she'd finished, Kesh barked and they heard the sound of Mac Ard's horse approaching. The tiarna knocked, then opened the door, standing there in his clóca of green and brown. Maeve nodded to the man, as if answering an unspoken question, and he turned to Jenna. He seemed too big and too dark in the cottage, and she could not decipher the expression on his face. He stroked his beard with one hand.

"You saw them," he said. "You were there." When she didn't answer, he glanced again at Maeve. "I saw your boot prints, and the dog's. I know you were there." His voice was gentle—not an accusation, just a sympathetic statement of fact.

"Aye, Tiarna," Jenna answered quietly.

"You saw the lights?"

A nod. Jenna hung her head, not daring to look at his face.

Mac Ard let out a long sigh. "By the Mother-Creator, Jenna, I'm not going to *eat* you. I just want to *know*. I want to help if I can. Did you see the lights first, or did you go there and call them?"

Jenna shook her head, slowly at first then more vigorously. "I didn't call them," she said hurriedly. "I was here, and I heard Old Stubborn making a commotion and went outside to check and . . . I thought I saw something. So I went. Then, after I was there, they came." She stopped. Mac Ard let the silence linger, and Jenna forced herself to stay quiet, though she could see him waiting for her to elaborate. "Did *you* see them, Tiarna?" she asked finally.

"From the tavern, aye, and as I was riding toward the hill. They went out by the time I reached the road and started up Knobtop. I saw the flash and heard the thunder when the lights vanished." He held his right arm straight out, and ran his left hand over it. "I could feel my hair standing on end: here, and on the back of my neck. I rode up to where the flash seemed to have come from. That's where I saw the marks of your boots." He let his hand drop. His clóca rustled. His voice was as soft and warm as the blanket on her bed. "Tell me the truth, Jenna. I swear I mean you and your mam no harm. I swear it."

He waited, looking at Jenna, and she could feel her hand trembling around the wooden mug. She set it down on the table, staring down at the steaming brew without really seeing it. She was trembling, her hands shaking as they rested on the rough oaken tabletop.

"I was there," she said to the mug. "The lights, they were so . . . bright and the colors were so deep, all around me . . ." She lifted her head, looking from Mac Ard to her mam, shimmering in the salt water that suddenly filled her eyes. "I don't understand why this is happening," she said, sniffing and trying to keep back the tears. "I don't know why it keeps happening to me. I don't want it, didn't ask for it. I don't know *anything*." The stone burned cold against her thigh through the woolen fabric. "I . . ." She started to tell them the rest, how the mage-lights had glowed in the stone, how the power had arced from it, how the pebble had seemed to draw the mage-lights tonight, all of it. But she saw the eagerness in Mac Ard's face, the way he leaned forward intently as she spoke of the lights, and she stopped herself. *You don't know him, not really. The stone was* your *gift, not his.* The voice in her head almost seemed to be someone else's. "There isn't anything else to tell you, Tiarna," she said, sniffing. "I'm sorry."

Disappointment etched itself in the set of his mouth, and she realized that the man was genuinely puzzled. He shook his head. "Then we wait, and we watch," he said. He turned to Maeve. "I'll stay at Tara's for another day, at least, and we'll see. The mage-lights may come again tomorrow night. If they do, if they call Jenna, I'll go up there with her. If that's acceptable to you, Widow Aoire."

Maeve lifted her chin. "She's my daughter. I'll be with her, too, Tiarna Mac Ard."

He might have smiled. Maeve might have smiled back.

Mac Ard brushed at his clóca, adjusting the silver brooch at the right shoulder. "Good night to you both, then," he said. He gave a swift bow to Maeve, and left.

5

Attack on the Village

THE night sky stayed dark the next night. Tiarna Mac Ard remained at Tara's, coming to Jenna's house that evening and escorting the two of them back to the tavern, where they listened to Coelin with an eye on the window that showed Knobtop above the trees.

But it remained simply night outside. Nothing more.

The next day broke with a heavy mist rolling in from the west, a gray wall that hid sun and sky and laid a sheen of moisture over the village. The mist beaded on the wool of the sheep as Jenna and Kesh herded them to the field behind the cottage. Kesh was acting strangely; he kept lifting his head and barking at something unseen, but finally they got the last straggler through. Jenna walked the field perimeter once, checking the stone fence her father had built, then calling Kesh—still barking at nothing—and closing the gate.

She smelled it then in the air, over the distinctive tang of smoldering peat from their own fire and those in the village: the odor of woodsmoke and burning thatch. Jenna frowned, surveying the landscape. There was a smear of darker gray beyond the trees lining the field, and under it, a tinge of glowing red. "Mam!" she called. "I think there's a fire in the village."

Maeve came from the cottage, wrapping a shawl over her head. "Look," Jenna said, pointing. Her mam squinted into the damp air, into the gray, dim distance.

"Come on," she said. "They may need help . . ."

They didn't get as far as the High Road. They heard the sound of a galloping horse racing toward them down the rutted dirt lane, and Tiarna Mac Ard came hurtling around the bend, his hair blowing and his clóca billowing behind him. He pulled Conhal to a mud-tossing halt in front of them, dismounting in a sudden leap.

"Tiarna Mac Ard—" Maeve began, but then the man cut off her words with a slash of his arm.

"No time," he said. "We need to get you and your daughter out of here. Into the bogs, maybe, or over—" He stopped, whirling around at the sound of pounding hooves, as Kesh ran barking and snarling toward the quartet of onrushing horses.

White fog blew from the nostrils of the steeds and the mouths of the riders.

"Kesh, no!" Jenna shouted at the dog. Kesh stopped, looked back at Jenna.

They could have gone around him. There was easily room.

They ran the dog down. Jenna screamed as she saw the hooves of the lead horse strike Kesh. He yelped and rolled and tried to escape, but the horse's muscular rear legs struck his side and Kesh went down under the three behind, lost in the blur of motion and clods of flying dirt. *"Kesh!"* Jenna screamed again, starting to run toward the bloody, still form in the dirt, but Maeve's arms went around her as Mac Ard stepped between them and the horsemen. *"Kesh!"*

The lead rider pulled his party to a stop before Mac Ard. The man threw his clóca back, and Jenna, sobbing for Kesh, saw a sword on his belt. "Where's your blue and gold, Fiacra De Derga?" Mac Ard called to the rider. "Or are those of Connachta too cowardly to show their colors when they go plundering in Gabair?"

The rider smiled. His hair was flaming red—a deeper red than that of the man in Jenna's vision—and his eyes were cold blue. "Padraic Mac Ard, what a surprise. I haven't seen you since our cousin's wedding feast a year ago last summer." Pale eyes swept over Maeve and Jenna. Jenna wanted to leap at the man, but Maeve's arms held her tightly, and Jenna clutched at her skirts in frustration and anger. In the folds caught in her left fist, she felt a small, cold hardness beneath the wool. "And what interesting company you keep. Is this the Aoire family the village Ald told me about before she died, the Inishlander's wife and daughter?"

"These people are formally under Rí Mallaghan of Tuath Gabair's protection. That's all you need to know."

De Derga smiled. He lifted himself in his saddle with a creak of leather and looked about ostentatiously. "And where *is* Rí Mallaghan? I don't seem to see him at the moment, or any royal decree in your hand." His gaze came back to Mac Ard. "I only see you, Padraic. If I'd known that, I'd have left my companions with the rest of my men." The three men behind De Derga laughed as he *tsked*. "One lone tiarna is all Rí Gabair sends when mage-lights fill the sky? I find that incredibly foolish. When word came to Rí Connachta that people on our eastern borders had seen mage-lights, he sent out over two dozen to follow them. And last night . . . well, you saw them better than us, didn't you, up on that hilltop?"

Jenna let her hand slip into the pocket of her skirt. The stone pulsed against her fingertips, as frigid as glacial ice.

"You would always rather talk a man to death than use your sword, Fiacra."

De Derga spread his hands. "It's my gift. Now, step aside, as I'll be taking the women back to Thiar."

Mac Ard unsheathed his sword, the iron ringing. Jenna heard her mam's intake of breath. "Be careful, Tiarna," she said, one hand extended to Mac Ard, the other still around Jenna's shoulders. Jenna slipped from her mam's grasp, a step away; she took her hand from her pocket, her hand fisted. De Derga laughed.

" 'Be careful,' " he repeated, mocking Maeve's tone. He shook his head at Mac Ard. "Your taste was always common, Padraic."

"Get off your horse, Fiacra, so I can separate your babbling head from your shoulders."

De Derga sat easily as his mount stamped a foot and

shook its head at the smell of the weapon. "No. I think
not."

"You have no honor, De Derga. And I'm shamed that
you'd let your men see that."

(Throbbing against her skin . . . Searing cold rising up
her arm, filling her . . .)

"My men have seen me fight often enough, cousin, and
they know that I could take you as easily as this woman
you're shielding. They also know that I won't be goaded
into doing something foolish when the battle's already
won." De Derga waved a hand, and Jenna noticed that the
trio behind had drawn bows. "So, Padraic, the choice is
yours: sheathe that weapon and return to Lár Bhaile, or
we'll simply cut you down where you stand."

This time it was Mac Ard who laughed. "Let's not lie to
each other, Fiacra. You can't let me go back and tell my
Rí that you were here in his land."

A muscle twitched in De Derga's mouth. "No," he said.
"I suppose I can't." He waved a hand to his men as Mac
Ard let out a scream of rage and charged toward De Derga,
his sword swinging in a great arc. Bowstrings sang death.

"No!" Jenna screamed, and the fury seemed to burst
through her skin, ripping and tearing through her soul,
spilling from her open mouth.

She lifted her hand.

In one blinding instant, arrows flared and went to ash in
mid-flight. The horses screamed and reared, and four jagged bolts of pure white erupted from Jenna's hand, the
lightnings snapping and crackling as they impaled the riders, striking them from their saddles and arcing as they
slammed the bodies to the ground. The discharge from the
stone was blinding, overloading Jenna's eyes even as she
saw the riders fall; the sound deafened her, a sinister crackling like the snapping of dry bones. Someone screamed in
agony and terror, and Jenna screamed in sympathy, her
voice lost in the chaos, her mind awhirl with the cold power
until, swirling, it bore her down into oblivion and silence.

6

Bog And Forest

SHE awoke with a start and a cry, and Maeve's hand brushed her forehead soothingly. "Hush, darling," she said, but her eyes were full of worry.

"Where are we?" Jenna asked. She sat up—they were sitting in the midst of bracken, and Tiarna Mac Ard was crouched a few feet away, his back to them. Jenna could smell the earthy, wet musk of bog, and water trickled brightly somewhere nearby. Two saddle packs were on the ground near them, and a bow with arrows fletched like those of the men who had attacked them. The memory came back to her then, awful and fierce: Kesh lying dead on the ground, the men from Connachta threatening them, the cold, terrible lightning from the stone. "The riders . . ." she breathed with a sob. "The man you called De Derga, your cousin . . ."

"Dead." Mac Ard said the word gruffly, his voice low. "All dead. And by now their companions know it as well, and are hunting us." He glanced back at Jenna, and his expression was guarded. "They'll also know that it wasn't a sword that cut them down."

"I . . ." Jenna gulped. Her stomach lurched and she bent over, vomiting acid bile on the ground. She could feel her mam stroking her back as the spasms shook her, as her stomach heaved. When the sickness had passed, Jenna wiped her mouth with the sleeve of her coat. "I'm sorry," she said. "They're—" She couldn't say the word. Mac Ard nodded, watching her as she leaned into the

60

comforting arms of Maeve, as if she were a little child again.

"Jenna, the first time someone fell to my sword, I did the same thing you just did," he said. "I've seen men hacked to death during a battle, or crushed under their horses. Eventually, it bothers you less." He leaned over, as if he were going to stroke her hair as Maeve did, but pulled his hand back. He pursed his lips under the dark beard. "I'd be more worried about you if it didn't bother you. But I have to tell you that what you did . . . I've never seen the like."

The stone, cold in her hand . . . Jenna felt in her skin pocket, then glanced frantically around her on the damp ground.

"Would you be looking for this?" The stone glistened between Mac Ard's forefinger and thumb. He turned it carefully in front of them. "Not much to look at it, is it? Something you might miss entirely, if it was just lying there."

"That's *mine*," Jenna said loudly. "I found it."

"Jenna—" Maeve began, but Mac Ard snorted as if amused.

"A *cloch na thintrí*, it's called," he said. "A lightning stone. And you had it all along. When I asked you about the mage-lights, you must have forgotten to tell me about the cloch you found." He could have sounded angry. He didn't; he seemed more disappointed.

Jenna looked at the ground rather than at him.

"Your da would have known the term," Mac Ard continued. "I'll wager he brought the stone here himself, or knew that this one lay there on Knobtop, waiting for the mage-lights to return. And, aye, Jenna, now it's yours." He stretched out his hand, and dropped it in Jenna's palm. It was warm, an ordinary stone. "Keep it," he said. "It gave itself to you, not to me."

Jenna put it back in her skirt, feeling Mac Ard's eyes on her. "How . . . ?" she started to say, but Mac Ard lifted a finger to his lips. "Later, you'll know all you want to know, and more."

Jenna stared at the tiarna, trying to see past his dark

gaze. He seemed calm enough, and not angry with her. After a few breaths, she looked away. "Mam, where are we?" she asked once more.

"In the bog on the other side of the bridge," Maeve said. "Tiarna Mac Ard carried you here when you collapsed, after—" Her mam stopped.

"Mam, what's happened? Why did those men come here?"

It was Mac Ard who answered. "They came for the same reason I came—because they saw the mage-lights. I didn't think Rí Connachta would be so foolhardy as to send his people here. I was the one who told Rí Mallaghan of Gabair that we didn't need to concern ourselves with the other Tuatha." He scoffed angrily. "I was a damned fool, and damned lucky to be alive. Tara's son Eliath came running into the tavern this morning, said that the Ald's cottage was afire and that there were a dozen men on horseback there. I left the tavern then, and rode for your home. De Darga saw me as I brought Conhal out of the stable, and followed. The rest you know."

"Where's Conhal?"

"With three of us, we couldn't outrun the others with one horse, so I turned him loose. Hopefully he'll find his own way home. As for the others, they're scouring the countryside now, looking for us. We've seen them twice while we were here; once a pair of riders, then four more who crossed the bridge and went up on Knobtop. Look . . ." He stopped, pulling brush aside so that Jenna could see the bog. They were on one of the grassy, overgrown hummocks that dotted the marsh. She could see the peat-stained open water of the Mill Creek a little bit away, and beyond the creek was the rise of the northern bank and the low hills that concealed their house. Beyond the hills, she could see a column of black smoke smeared across the sky. She knew what it was even as her mam spoke.

"They burned the cottage," Maeve said. Her voice was strangely calm. "Everything we had . . ."

"The Rí Gabair will give you all and more, once we get to Lár Bhaile. I promise you that."

Maeve's eyes flashed, and Jenna heard the mingled anger

and sorrow in her voice. "Will the Rí give me back the scarf that Niall gave me the night he first came to me? Will he give me the cups and plates that Niall made with his own hands, or the pot with blue glaze I fired for him? Will I see the first linen shirt I made for Jenna, when she was just a babe? The Rí can give me money and build a new cottage, but he can't give me a tithe of what's been destroyed."

"I know that," Mac Ard replied softly. "I wish it were different, Maeve—may I call you that?" Jenna's mam nodded. "Good. And please call me Padraic. I wish I could undo my words to Rí Mallaghan and that I had come here with my own squad of gardai, as he wished. Maybe then none of this would have happened. But I can't unsay the words, and I can't ease your loss. All I can do now is try to keep us alive."

"How?" Maeve asked. She looked at Jenna. "You don't want her to—"

"No," Mac Ard said quickly. "She doesn't need more blood on her hands, nor do I think she knows how to control the stone or whether she could repeat what she did. I certainly don't know the answer to that. The Connachtans will expect us to make for Lár Bhaile, so they'll be watching the High Road and the River Duán. They can't stay here long, however—they know word will eventually reach the Rí's ears about this raid and he'll send soldiers after them."

"So what do we do?"

"We find a place to hide for a few days."

Maeve shook her head, hugging Jenna. "Where? I don't know of such a place. They would find us here, eventually."

"I agree," Mac Ard answered. "So we'll go into Doire Coill."

Jenna cried out at that and Maeve shook her head. "Have you gone mad, Tiarna Mac Ard? You take us from one death to another."

"I take us from sure death to a hope for life," he answered. "They'll be searching the bogs soon enough, Maeve. We can't stay here. We need to go, and we need to go now while we can."

Maeve was still shaking her head, but Jenna felt her

mam's arms relax around her and knew that she'd made a decision, staring at the smoke rising from the ruin of their lives. Everything they'd known was gone; their only ally was Mac Ard. Jenna leaned toward Maeve. "We have to trust him, Mam," she whispered. "We have to."

She could see the lines at the corners of her mam's eyes relax as she made the decision. "All right," she said finally. "We'll follow you. Padraic."

Jenna knew that most of the tales were simply that—stories to frighten the children. The residents of Ballintubber had a thousand tales and legends and stories about the half-wild land that surrounded them. The Rí Mallaghan might proclaim himself king over Tuath Gabair, but in truth, his rule only extended to the small towns, the villages, and the occasional squares of farmed land: tamed patches of a landscape that had seen vast, misty centuries when legends walked alive.

Legends *still* walked, if the stories were to be believed, in those hidden places where humankind came infrequently, or not at all. Doire Coill was one of those places, a lingering remnant of a greater oak forest that had once stretched from Lough Lár to the Westering Sea, and north and south for leagues, a wall of trees shading meandering bogs and hidden valleys, where giant elk and ferocious knifefangs had roamed. Most of the forest was gone now, eroded by axes, time, and changing climate. Yet portions of it yet existed, here and there through the peninsula of Talamh an Ghlas. Doire Coill was not the largest of these or the most well known, but it loomed large in the stories Jenna had heard. One Hand Bailey, in his cups at Tara's, had often spoken of the time he'd lost his hand.

"Oh, I'd heard the tales, aye," Jenna could remember his drunken voice saying, low and slurred with alcohol. "Rubbish, I thinks, because I was young an' stupid. So I takes me old horse and cart down the High Road past Knobtop, thinking that Doire Coill weren't likely to miss one of those nasty old black oaks, and wouldn't that make a great pile of lumber for the selling. That's what I thought, and every day of my life since I've regretted it. Me an'

Daragh O'Rheallagh started a'sawing at the closest trunk to the road with a two-man blade, and at first it went fine, though I thought I heard the trees rustling angrily at the sight of the metal, and a cold wind came out from underneath the trees like the forest was breathin', a foul breath of dead and molderin' leaves. Didn't see any animals, which was strange: not a squirrel, not a bird, not a deer; like they'd all gone, knowing what we were doing and afraid of it. We kept at our sawin', wantin' to get out of there as quick as we could—the noise dead in the stillness, the tree sittin' there hating us, the sawdust piling at our feet. Then, all a' sudden, it fell, before it had any right to do so, like it *chose* to fall. Crushed poor Daragh under it before he could move, and the saw blade snapped with an awful noise an' whipped out, an' it sliced me hand right off me arm. I thought I'd die there meself, but I managed to tie a scrap a' cloth around me arm quick to stop the bleedin'. Wasn't no such luck for Daragh; he was already dead, his head smashed and his brains dashed out on the ground. I came back here quick as I could, and six men and the new Widow O'Rheallagh went back to get Daragh's body out from under the tree. When they got there, it was gone. Not a trace of 'im was left. I swear it—ask Widow O'Rheallagh herself, or Tom Mullin over there, who went with 'em. Doire Coill's an evil place, I say. I already gave it me hand, and that's all a' me it's to get. I won't go in there again, and them that do are nothin' but fools."

Bailey's words resonated in Jenna's head as they left the hummock in the bog and started heading south, moving parallel to the rough line of the High Road and taking care to stay hidden from possible watchers on the rising flanks of Knobtop. It was getting near dark, with all of them tired and soggy nearly to the waist, when Jenna noticed that the ground underneath their feet was firmer, and that the trees around them were twisted, thick-trunked oaks hung with parasitic mistletoe, huddled together in a dark mass.

They were within the indistinct edges of Doire Coill, west and south of Ballintubber. Somewhere to their left, the High Road to Lár Bhaile (and beyond to Dún Laoghaire) passed within a stone's throw of the forest's leaves before

turning sharply east to meet and cross River Duán at the
village of Áth Iseal, a good full day's journey from Ballintubber on horseback. Between Áth Iseal and Ballintubber,
there were few human habitations—and in the empty space
between no one gave allegiance to Rí Gabair or any king.

"How long do we need to stay here?" Maeve asked.
Jenna looked at the deep green shadows under the trees.
She let the pack she carried fall to the ground. Contrary
to what One Hand Bailey had said, she saw life enough:
black squirrels bounding through the tangled limbs above
them, starlings and finches flitting from branch to branch.
The trees here were ancient: they had seen the first movement of humankind through this land, and Jenna sensed
that they remembered and were not pleased. Mac Ard's
boots crunched on a thick carpet of old leaves and acorn
caps.

"Two days, maybe a few more," he said. "The Connachtans can't stay longer without risking open war, and I don't
think they want that. Two days, and we can chance the
High Road again."

"Two days," Jenna repeated. "Here in Doire Coill."

"It's a forest, that's all," Mac Ard told her. "Don't worry
yourself over silly tales. I've been out here before, at the
edge of the Doire, and slept under its branches. I had
strange dreams that night, but that's all."

"We'll need a fire," Maeve said. "So we don't freeze
during the night."

"There's a tinderbox in one of the packs. A fire will be
safe enough after the sun goes down and they can't see the
smoke, I suppose," Mac Ard said. "We're far enough off
the High Road. If we go a bit farther in, the trees will
shield the light . . ." Maeve looked at Jenna as Mac Ard
started to rummage in the packs.

"He knows what he's doing, Mam. And if he hadn't
come to help us, we might be dead."

Maeve nodded. She went to Mac Ard and began helping
him. An hour later, they were huddled in a tiny clearing
with a small fire of dead wood that they'd gathered. The
warmth of the fire was welcome, but to Jenna, the flickering
light only seemed to intensify the darkness around them,

encasing them in a globe of bright air while blackness pressed in around them. They'd eaten a loaf of hard bread and a few slivers of cheese from the pack, with water that still tasted of the bog from a nearby stream. Maeve and Mac Ard sat close to each other, closer than Jenna had ever seen her mam sit to another man. She was pleased at that, huddled in her cloak across the fire. She watched them through the flame, talking softly together, with a brief smile once touching her mam's lips. Jenna smiled herself at that. Maeve had rebuffed the advances of every man in Ballintubber, from what Jenna had heard and seen, but this Mac Ard was different. Jenna wondered, for a moment, how her own da might have reacted to what happened, and that brought back to her the events of the day, and she wanted to cry, wanted to weep for Kesh and the soldiers she'd killed and the lives that she'd left destroyed behind her, but there were no tears inside her.

She was dry, cold, and simply exhausted.

Wings fluttered somewhere above and behind her, startling Jenna. The rustling came again, loud and closer, and a huge black crow swooped low across the fire and lifted to land in a branch near Mac Ard. It cawed once, a grotesque, hoarse cough of a sound. Its bright eyes regarded them, the glossy head turning in quick, abrupt moves. "Nasty thing," Maeve said, glaring at the bird. "They're thieves, those birds, and scavengers. Look at it staring at us, like it's waiting for us to die."

Mac Ard picked up the bow and nocked an arrow. "It won't stare long," he said. He drew the bowstring back, the braided leather creaking under the strain.

"Hold!"

The voice came from the darkness, and a form stepped from the night shadows into the light of the fire: a man, old and hunched over, attired in ragged leather and fur and supporting himself with a gnarled oaken staff. The crow *cawed* again, flapped its wings, and flew to the man, perching itself on his left shoulder. "Who are you?" Mac Ard asked, the bow still drawn and the arrow now pointed at the chest of the stranger.

"No one worth killing," the man answered. His words

were understandable, but thick with an odd accent. He seemed to be staring somewhere slightly to the side and above Mac Ard, and in the gleam of the firelight, Jenna saw the man's eyes: unbroken, milky white pupils.

"He's blind, Tiarna," she said.

The man laughed at that, and at the same time the crow lifted its head and cackled with him, the two sounds eerily similar. "This body's blind, aye," he said, "but I can see." The man lifted his right hand and stroked the crow's belly. "Dúnmharú here is my eyes. What he sees, I see. And what I see now is two village folk and a tiarna, who know so little they would light fires under these trees."

"This is not your land," Mac Ard answered. "This forest is within Tuath Gabair, and belongs to the Rí. And you've still not given us your name."

The old man's amusement was loud, echoed by the crow. "My name? Call me Seancoim," he answered. "And Rí Gabair can claim whatever he likes: his cities and villages, his bogs and fields. But the old places like this forest belongs to themselves, and even Rí Gabair knows that." He grinned at them, gap-toothed, and gestured. "Now, follow me. I'll take you where you'll be safe."

"We're safe enough here," Mac Ard said.

"Are you?" Seancoim asked. "Do you think your young woman's sky-magic can protect you here?" He glanced up with his dead eyes. A strong wind stirred the tops of the trees, and Jenna could hear their limbs groaning and stirring. At the edges of the firelight, branches writhed and stretched like wooden, grasping arms, and the sound of the wind through the trees was like a sobbing voice, mournful. The hair raised on Jenna's forearms and the light of the fire shuddered, making the shadows move all around them. "Mam?" Jenna called out.

"*Stop!*" Mac Ard commanded Seancoim, and he brought his bow back to full draw. The crow stirred, wings fluttering, and at the same moment the arrow snapped in half like a twig even as Mac Ard released the bowstring. The crow settled again on Seancoim's shoulder; the wind in the trees died to a breeze, the leaves rustling. "Put out your fire and follow me," Seancoim repeated. "The tiarna can keep his sword in his hand, if it makes him feel better. But it won't do him any good here, and the trees hate the smell of iron."

With that, the old man turned, shuffling slowly into the darkness, his staff tapping the ground before him.

7

Seancoim's Cavern

JENNA wrinkled her nose at the smell: musty earth, and a strange, spicy odor that could only be Seancoim himself. A draft wafted from the entrance of the cavern, the mouth of which was a narrow slit in a rocky, bare rise another stripe's walk deeper into the forest. Yellow light beckoned beyond, outlining the stone arch, and she smelled burning peat as the wind changed.

"It's warm inside," Seancoim said, gesturing to them as he ducked into the passage. Dúnmharú cawed and leaped from his shoulder, disappearing into the cave. "And light. There's food as well, enough for all. Come." He vanished inside, and Jenna saw her mam glance at Mac Ard. "We've followed him this far," she said.

"I'll go first," Mac Ard answered. He drew his sword and, turning sideways, followed the old man. Maeve waited a moment, then went into the opening with Jenna close behind.

Beyond the narrow passage, the cavern widened significantly, the roof rising to follow the slope of the hill, the sides opening up quickly left and right. The passage led slightly downward a dozen strides, and Jenna found herself in a large room. A central fireplace ringed with stones sent smoke curling upward toward the roof, lost in darkness above. The low flames from the peat sent wan light to the stone walls, and Jenna could dimly see another passageway leading deeper into the hill. Along the wall were several querns, small stone mills used for grinding corn and other

grains. Hung everywhere around the cavern were racks
with drying herbs and various plants laid over the wooden
rods. Some of them Jenna recognized: parsley, thyme,
lemon grass, mint; others were entirely unfamiliar. The
smell of the herbs was almost overpowering, a barrage of
odors.

Dúnmharú had roosted on a rocky shelf nearby. Beyond
the drying racks and querns, there was almost no furniture
in the room. If it was a home, it was a bare one. Jenna
could see a straw pallet laid out near the fire, a bucket of
water, and a long wooden box that Seancoim eased himself
down on. He leaned his staff against the box, but it fell to
the stones and the sound echoed harshly.

"It's not pretty," he said. He leaned down and placed
the staff within reach. "But it's dry, and warm enough, and
not susceptible to enemies burning it down." He glanced
at Maeve as he said that, and Jenna heard her mam's intake
of breath. Mac Ard scowled, walking around the perimeter
of the cavern, his sword sheathed now but his hand on
the hilt.

"This is where you live?" Jenna asked, and Seancoim
laughed.

"Here, and other places," he answered. "I have a dozen
homes in the forest, and a dozen more I've forgotten about
over the decades."

Jenna nodded. "You live alone?"

Seancoim shook his head. "No. There are others like me
here, a few, and I see them from time to time. And there
are more of my people, though not many, in the old forests
that are left, or in the high mountains, or the deepest bogs.
We were the first ones to find Talamh an Ghlas."

"You're Bunús Muintir," Jenna said. The word was like
breathing a legend. The oldest poems and songs spoke of
the Bunús Muintir, of the battles that had raged between
the Bunús and Jenna's people, the Daoine. In the poems, the
Bunús were always evil and horrific, fierce and cruel war-
riors who had allied with spirits, wights, and demonic
creatures.

"Aye, I am the blood of Bunús Muintir, and I know your
Daoine songs." Seancoim said. "I've heard them, and like

all history, they're half true. We were here when your ancestors came into this place, and we fought them and sometimes even bred with them, but Daoine blood and Daoine
swords proved stronger, until finally those of the pure lineage sought the hidden places. There were no final battles,
no decisive victory or defeat, despite what the songs tell
you. True endings come slowly. Sometimes they come not
at all, or just fade into the new tales." Groaning, Seancoim
stood again. "There's bread there, on the ledge near Dúnmharú, baked two days ago now, I'm afraid. There's still
some of the last blackberries of the season, and smoked
meat. That's all I have to offer and it's not fancy, but it
will fill your bellies. Go on and help yourselves."

The bread was hard, the berries mushy with age and the
meat tough, but Jenna thought it strangely delicious after
the day's exertions. She finished her portion quickly, then
broke off a hunk of bread and went outside. The clouds
had parted, and a crescent moon turned the clouds to silver
white. She was above the trees, looking down on their
swaying crowns. She could see Knobtop, rising up against
the stars to the north, farther away than she'd ever seen
it before.

The wind lifted her hair and brushed the forest with an
invisible hand. She thought she could hear voices, singing
not far away: a low, susurrant chant that rose and fell, the
long notes holding words that lingered just on the edge of
understanding. Jenna leaned into the night, listening,
caught in the chant, wanting to get closer and hear what
they were singing . . .

. . . aye, to get closer . . .

. . . to hear them, to touch their gnarled trunks . . .

. . . to be with them . . .

Beating wings boomed in her ears: Dúnmharú touched
her shoulder with his clawed feet and flew off again, startling her. Jenna blinked, realizing that she stood under the
gloom of the trees at the bottom of the slope, a hundred
strides or more from the cavern, and she had no idea how
she'd come to be there. She whirled around, suddenly
frightened at the realization that she hadn't even realized
that she was walking away. The last few minutes, now that

she tried to recall them, were hazy and indistinct in her mind.

Small with distance, Seancoim beckoned at the cavern entrance, and Jenna ran back up the hill toward him, as if a hell hound were at her heels.

"So you *do* hear them," he called to her, as the crow swept around her again before settling back on the old man's shoulder. "Some don't, or think it's only the wind moving the trees. But they sing, the oldest trees, the ones that were planted by the Seed-Daughter after the Mother-Creator breathed life into the bones of the land. They remember, and they still call to the old gods. It's dangerous for those who hear: the enchantment in their old voices can hypnotize, and you'll find yourself lost in the deepest, most dangerous parts of the wood. Most who go to listen don't return."

Jenna looked over the forest, listening to the eerie, breathy sound. "Should we leave?" she asked.

The old man shrugged. "The unwary should be careful, or those whose will isn't strong enough. That last, at least, doesn't describe you, now that I've told you the danger."

"You don't know me."

"Oh, I know you well enough," he chuckled.

Jenna shook her head. The wind shifted and the tree-song came to them louder than before, the chant rising in pitch. "What is it they're singing? It sounds so sad and lonely."

Seancoim leaned heavily on his staff, as if he were peering into the dark. "Who knows? I certainly don't. They speak a language older than any of ours, and their concerns aren't those of humans." He turned, and his blind eyes stared at her. "There are other magics than the sky-magic you can capture in a cloch na thintrí," he told her. He extended his hand toward Jenna. "Let me hold it," he said to her.

Jenna took a step back, clutching at the stone hidden in her skirt. "I know you have the stone," Seancoim said. "I saw the lights over the hill there, through Dúnmharú's eyes." Seancoim pointed at Knobtop. "I could feel the power crackling in the sky, as it has not in many lifetimes, and I feel it now close to me. You can't hide a cloch na thintrí from me, or from any of the Bunús Muintir. I can feel the stone. All I ask is to hold it, not to keep it. I promise that."

Jenna hesitated, then brought the stone out and laid it on Seancoim's lined palm. He closed his fingers around it with a sigh. He clasped it to his breast, holding it there for several long breaths, then holding out his hand again, his fingers unfolding. "Take it," he said. "Such a small stone . . ."

"I'm sure it's not powerful, like the ones the cloudmages in the songs had," Jenna said, and Seancoim laughed.

"Is that how you imagined them, with stones the size of their fists hung on chains around their necks, the way the songs and tales tell it?" The crow cackled with him. "Is that the source of your knowledge?"

Jenna nodded. "You must know how to use the cloch," she said. "You have magic, too: using the crow for your eyes, the way you broke the tiarna's arrow or how you knew I had the stone . . ."

"I gave you the answer just a moment ago, but evidently I need to repeat it: there are other magics than that of the sky." He stared upward, as if looking at a scene only his blind eyes could glimpse. "Once my people knew them all: the slow, unyielding power of earth; the shimmering, soft gifts of water. Some of them we know still. Others aren't for us humans at all, but belong to others, like the oldest of the oaks here in Doire Coill, or other creatures who are sleeping for the moment." His chin tilted down once more, and he seemed to laugh at himself. "But you asked if I know how to use your cloch na thintrí, didn't you? The answer to that is 'No.' Each stone teaches its owner in its own way; yours has already begun to teach you."

"You talk as if the stone were alive."

"Do you know that it's not?" Seancoim answered. He smiled, a darkness where teeth once had been, the few teeth left him leaning like yellow gravestones in his gums. The wind died, and the tree-song faded to a hush, a whisper, then was gone. "There, they've finished. We should go inside—it's late, and there are things walking out here that you don't want to meet. Your tiarna will want to leave with the morning, and you need sleep after this day."

Jenna could feel exhaustion rise within her with Sean-coim's words. She yawned and nodded, following the man through the cavern's entrance. Seancoim continued on into the darkness past the fire, but Jenna stopped. Her mam and Mac Ard were asleep, next to each other even though on different pallets. Her mam's hand had trailed out from underneath her blanket, and it rested near Mac Ard's hand, as if she were reaching for him. She could sense Seancoim's attention on her as she stared, her breath caught in her throat. She wanted to smile, happy that her mam wasn't ignoring Mac Ard as she had the others, and yet afraid at the same time, wondering what it might mean for her.

"She is a woman and he a man, and both of them hand-some and strong," Seancoim whispered, his voice echoing hoarsely from the stones. "I can tell that your mam is at-tracted to the tiarna, even if she resists the feeling. That's natural enough. It's been a long time for her, hasn't it, to feel that way about a man?"

Jenna swallowed hard. "Aye," she said. "A long time. I just wonder . . . Does he feel the same? After all, he's Riocha, and we're . . . nothing."

Seancoim took a step forward. Bending close, he seemed to peer at the sleeping Mac Ard with his blind eyes before rising with a groan. "I think he does, as much as he can. He's a hidden man, this tiarna, but there's room in him for love, and if he's Riocha, he's perhaps less prejudiced than many with his lineage. But—" he stopped.

"But?"

Seancoim shrugged. "He's also a man with his own ambitions."

"How can you know all that? You can't see . . . I mean, is that magic, too?"

"Perhaps." Seancoim grinned at her. "Isn't it what you want to hear?"

"I want my mam to be happy. That's all."

"What about yourself?" he asked.

Jenna could feel heat rising from her neck to her throat, her cheeks burning. Her mam stirred on the pallet, turning, her hand sliding away from Mac Ard. Jenna let go of the breath she was holding. Twin tears tracked down her face.

"Too much has changed for you today," Seancoim said. Somehow, he was standing next to her again. "Too much changed in the space of one sun." His hand went around her shoulder. She started to pull back, then allowed herself to sink against him, the tears spilling out. His chest smelled of herbs and leather and sweat. She clung to Seancoim, weeping; still holding her, he went to the box next to his pallet. "Wait a moment," he said, and lifted the lid. A sweet, spice-filled aroma filled the air with the movement. Inside were several small leather bags, and Seancoim shuffled through them, muttering, before snatching one up with a cry and handing it to Jenna.

"Here," he said. "One day, you will need this."

"What is it?" Jenna asked, sniffing.

"Brew it as a tea, and drink it, and you will forget what is most painful to you," Seancoim told her. "There are some things that no one should remember, be it in song or tale or memory. When that time comes for you, you'll know."

Jenna glanced again at her mam and Mac Ard. "I don't think I want to remember today," she said, and the tears started again. Seancoim let the lid of the box close, sat on it, then drew her to him again. They sat, and Jenna stayed with him, crying for Kesh and her home, for her innocence and for her mam, letting Seancoim rock her until sleep finally came.

In the morning, Jenna found herself curled up on a pile of straw and old cloth close to the fire, which had dwindled to glowing coals. Seancoim's small leather bag was still clutched in her hand. No one else was in the cavern, and pale light filtered in through the entrance. Jenna got up, put the bag in her skirt with the stone, wrapped her coat around her, and padded outside.

Below her, the forest was wrapped in white mist and fog, the sun a hazy brightness just at the horizon. Seancoim was nowhere to be seen, but Mac Ard and Maeve were standing a few feet down the slope, talking with their heads close together. She started to go back inside, not wanting to interrupt them, but the rock under her foot tilted and fell back with a stony *clunk.* Maeve turned. "Jenna! Good morning, darling."

" 'Morning, Mam. Where's Seancoim?"

"We're not certain," Maeve answered. "He was gone when we woke. He refilled the water bucket, though, and left some fresh berries on the shelf."

We're not certain . . . Jenna nodded and found herself smiling a bit, hearing the plural. Mac Ard was smiling at her as well, teeth flashing behind the black beard, the smile slightly crooked on his face. She wanted to know what he was thinking, wanted to know that her mam would be safe with him, wanted to know that they could, perhaps, be a family.

But she knew there could be no answer to those questions. Her bladder ached in her belly. Jenna shrugged, turned, and left them. Later, having relieved herself behind a convenient screen of boulders, she came back to find that Seancoim had returned with Dúnmharú on his shoulder.

". . . riders on the High Road," he was saying to Mac Ard and Maeve. "They were tiarna—had to be, with those great war steeds, the heavy swords at their sides, and that fine clothing—but they weren't showing colors on their clóca."

"Which way were they riding?" Mac Ard asked.

"That way," Seancoim answered, pointing south, away from where Knobtop would have been, had they been able to see it through the fog.

Mac Ard nodded, the lines of his face deepening and a scowl touching his lips. Jenna saw his right hand tighten around the hilt of his sword. "The Connachtans are looking for us well away from Ballintubber, then, and the High Road's not safe. I'd hoped . . ." His voice trailed off.

"There are other ways," Seancoim said.

"Other ways?"

Seancoim shrugged. The crow flapped its wings to keep its balance. "The forest you call Doire Coill goes away east and south from here, until it meets the tip of Lough Lár. A loop of the High Road passes close by again, as well, and it's not far from there to Áth Iseal and the ford of the Duán—a few miles. No more. I can lead you there in a day and a half."

"You would do that for us?" Maeve asked.

"I would do it for *her,*" Seancoim answered. He pointed to Jenna, his blank white eyes looking in her direction.

"Why me?" Jenna asked.

Seancoim gave Jenna his broken smile. "Because the Bunús Muintir have our songs and tales also."

"What is that supposed to mean?" Mac Ard said.

"It means what it means," Seancoim answered. The smile vanished as he looked at Mac Ard. "That's all."

"I'm suspicious of those who hide their intentions in riddles," Mac Ard retorted. "I'm especially suspicious when that person's a Bunús Muintir."

Seancoim snorted. "If I wanted you dead, Tiarna Mac Ard, you would already *be* dead."

Mac Ard scowled. "Are you threatening us?"

"It's no threat at all. Only the truth. All I had to do was leave you where you were in the forest—that would have been enough on a night when the trees were singing. If I wanted to be more certain, I could have led you into the truly dark places farther in, or I could have poisoned the food I gave you, or murdered you while you slept, or led your enemies here to find you. I could have had the trees call you, or sent for the old spirits who haunt this place, or sent the beasts that dwell here, or used the little magic I have of my own. There were a dozen ways and more for you to die, Tiarna. I could have avenged a few of the Bunús deaths at the hands of you Daoine, if that was my intent. Yet it seems to me that you're still breathing, because I hear you spouting paranoid nonsense. This is *my* home in which you walk, and it doesn't care if you are Riocha or not, Daoine or Bunús Muintir. Those things aren't important. They aren't even important out there, where they often seem to be. You have no idea what you risk here. You also have no idea of the greater events in which you've been caught."

"Then tell me," Mac Ard said. "Enlighten us." Jenna found that she disliked the mocking tone in the man's voice. For the first time, she started to wonder, seeing the way he treated Seancoim. She remembered what Seancoim had said last night: *"He's also a man with his own ambitions."*

Seancoim shook his head. "You're not ready to hear that tale yet. You're not ready to understand or believe it. You're not even capable of seeing who is your real enemy."

The crow cawed and fluttered away to a nearby branch. Seancoim glared at Mac Ard with his dead eyes, his staff clenched tightly in his hand as he pulled his bowed back more erect. Mac Ard glowered back, and Jenna thought for a moment that he would draw his sword or shout a challenge. But the anger in the Mac Ard's eyes slowly faded, and at last he bowed to Seancoim: a swift, passing inclination of his head. "I apologize," he said. "I shouldn't offend someone who offered aid when we were in need."

Seancoim tilted his head toward Mac Ard. "You're still in need," he said. There was no acknowledgment of Mac Ard's apology in his voice, but the corners of his mouth turned up.

The irritation flashed again in the tiarna's eyes, and Jenna stepped close to Seancoim, putting her hand on his arm. "Aye, we *are* still in need," she said, looking pleadingly at her mam. "We understand that."

"Aye," Maeve echoed. "We do."

Seancoim seemed somewhat mollified. His posture relaxed, and Dúnmharú returned to his roost on the old man's right shoulder. He sniffed again. "And I will help you," he said. "I will do what I can."

"These men who are looking for us," Mac Ard said. "If they realize we're in Doire Coill, or if they suspect that we're here, they will come after us. This isn't simply a walk in the woods."

Seancoim coughed, Dúnmharú cackled with open beak. "The forest takes care of itself," he said to Mac Ard. "A few men? They're no threat to Doire Coill, not even if they all carry axes and fire."

Mac Ard looked dubious at that statement, but Jenna remembered the singing of the trees. Seancoim glanced up at the sky, as if he could see the fog-shrouded sun. "If you don't wish to follow me through the forest, you could stay here in my cave. I have business to the east, but I can come back here and lead you to the High Road in a few days."

Jenna watched her mam glance at Mac Ard and shake her head slightly. "We'll go with you," Mac Ard said. "The sooner we reach the Rí's city, the sooner we'll be safe."

"Sometimes there is no such thing as safety, wherever you go," Seancoim answered. "But we'll leave as soon as you're ready."

8

The Cairn of Riata

EVEN by day, the forest was dim. They moved through valleys of fog-shrouded trees, pacing alongside fast-moving brooks whose foam made the dark water seem almost black by contrast. They caught rare glimpses of sky, blue now that the high mist had burned off, and every so often walked through columns of gold-green light, their boots crushing a thousand tiny images of the sun on the forest floor.

Jenna had often walked through the woods near Ballintubber, but they felt different: lighter, airier, with the trees spaced farther apart and well-worn paths meandering among them. They were old, too, those woods, but Jenna had never felt that the forest itself watched her, judging her and deciding whether it would allow her to stay.

She felt a Presence here. Here, there were musty vapors rising from the ground, and red-crowned, sinister mushrooms peering from between piles of decaying leaves decades old, screens of mistletoe and bramble that tugged at her with thorny fingers, vine-wrapped hollows between close-set oaks in which night nestled eternal. There were trails that Seancoim followed: thin, narrow paths that might have been made by deer or other animals, twisting through the underbrush and vanishing suddenly. Doire Coill was a maze where they found themselves walking the bottom of a hollow with sides too steep to climb, all white fog ahead and behind, so that they moved between walls of brown and green until Seancoim turned into a hidden break that

Jenna knew she would have missed, a narrow pass through to another fold of land bending in a slightly different direction, all of them leading to some unseen destination. And if she had found herself suddenly alone and lost, it would do no good to cry for help. The forest swallowed sound, muffling it, making words indistinct and small. Jenna was certain that she would call only whatever fey creatures Doire Coill held within its confines.

By the time the sun had reached its height and started to decline, Jenna knew that if Seancoim were to vanish into the fog around them, they would never find their way back. She said nothing, but the scowl that lurked on Mac Ard's face and the frown twisting Maeve's lips told her that the other two realized it as well.

As evening approached, the hillsides spread out slightly to either side of them before curving back in to each other, so that they walked in the center of a bowl several hundred strides across, the trees all around them with open sky directly above. In the center of the bowl, gray with the persistent fog, a dolmen loomed, a pair of massive, carved standing stones two people high with another block laid over the top, large enough that several people could walk between them abreast as if through a door. Arrayed around the central stones in a circle were six cairns covered with earth and grass, the narrow entrances of the passage graves arranged so that each looked out onto the central stones. Seancoim continued to walk between the graves toward the dolmen as Dúnmharú flew away to land on the capstone, but the others stopped at the entrance to the valley of tombs. Jenna stared at the dolmen, at the notches carved in them that were Bunús Muintir writing, wondering what was inscribed there.

"Who is buried in this place?" Mac Ard asked. "These must be the graves of kings and heroes, yet I've never heard anyone speak of this valley."

"You're not supposed to know it," Seancoim answered, "though a few Daoines have been here and seen the graves. We've kept it hidden, in our own ways, because the last chieftains of the Bunús Muintir rest here." He nodded in the direction of one of the mounds. "Maybe you would know this one. In there is Ruaidhri, who fought the Daoine at Lough Dubh and was wounded, and died weeks later."

"Died from the wounds from Crenél Dahgnon's sword," Mac Ard said. To Jenna, the name seemed to draw echoes from the hills around them, like clouds running before a storm, and she thought she heard the angry whispers from the mouths of the passage graves, or perhaps it was only the wind blowing across the entrances.

Seancoim shook his head, while Dúnmharú flapped his black wings angrily. "That's not a name one should speak here, but aye, that's the Daoine Rí whose blows shattered Ruaidhri's shield and killed him, and Lough Dubh would be the last time any of the Bunús Muintir chieftains would put an army on the field." Seancoim pointed to the largest grave, aligned directly with the dolmen at the far end of the valley. "There is Riata. Do you know of him?"

Jenna shook her head, as did Maeve, but Mac Ard took in a breath that caused Seancoim to laugh. "Ah," he said, "so you *have* listened to some of our old tales. Riata—he was the last, and perhaps the most powerful, of the Bunús cloudmages. The mage-lights vanished for us a scant three generations before you Daoine came. If they hadn't, if we had our mages wielding the clochs na thintrí when the Daoine came, then perhaps all that would be left of *your* people would be a few haunted barrows. Or perhaps if we hadn't become so dependent on that magic, we would not have been so easily displaced when you came." He lifted his hands and let them fall again like wounded birds. "Only the gods can see down those paths."

"Do we have to stay here?" Jenna asked. "It's getting late." The entire valley was in deep shadow now, and Jenna felt cold, though the sky above was still bright.

"It's late," Seancoim agreed, "and it's not safe to travel here at night. We'll stay there." Seancoim pointed to the ridge beyond the valley.

Mac Ard grimaced. "That's a long climb, and close to this place."

"They say restless ghosts walk here, and Ruaidhri is among them," Seancoim answered. He cocked his head at Mac Ard. "If I were Daoine, I might be afraid of that."

"I'm not afraid of a spirit," Mac Ard said, scowling. "Fine, old man. We'll stay here."

"Aye, we will," Seancoim told him, "unless you want to go back on your own." He turned away, calling Dúnmharú back to him, then walking on through the dolmen. After a moment, Jenna and the others followed, though Jenna walked carefully around the dolmen rather than going under its capstone, and didn't look into the cold archways of the barrow graves at all.

Jenna had thought that it would be impossible to sleep that night, unprotected under the oaks and so near the Bunúis tombs. Exhaustion proved stronger than fear, and she was asleep not long after she lay down near their tiny fire, only to be awakened sometime later by a persistent throbbing near her leg and in her head. She opened her eyes, disoriented. The fire had died to embers. Her mam and Mac Ard were asleep, sleeping close to each other and not far from her; Seancoim and Dúnmharú were nowhere to be seen. Jenna blinked, closing her eyes against the throbbing and touching her leg—as she did so, her hand closed on the stone under the cloth. It was pulsing in time with the pain in her temples. As she lay there, she thought she heard her name called: a soft, breathy whisper wending its way between the trunks of the trees. *"Jenna . . ."* it came, then again: *"Jenna . . ."*

Jenna sat up in her blankets.

There was light shifting through the leaves: a rippling, dancing, familiar shining high in the sky and very near. She thought of calling to her mam, then stopped, knowing Mac Ard would awaken with Maeve. Part of her didn't want Mac Ard to see the lights, didn't want his interference. Jenna rose to her feet and followed the elusive glimmering.

A few minutes later, she stood at the rim of the valley of Bunús tombs, looking out down the steep, treeless slope to the circles of graves and the dolmen at its center. She could see them very clearly, for directly above the valley the mage-lights were shimmering. Their golden light washed over the mounds of earth and rock in waves, as if she were watching the surface of a restless, wind-touched lake. The valley was alive with the light.

"Jenna . . ." She heard the call again, more distinctly this time, still airy but now laden with deeper undertones: a man's voice. It came from below.

"No," she whispered back to it, afraid, clutching her hands together tightly. The stone pulsed against her hip, cold fire.

"Jenna, come to me . . ."

"No," she said again, but a branch from the nearest tree touched her on the back as if blown by a sudden wind, pushing her a step forward. She stopped, planting her feet.

"Jenna . . ."

The lights flared above, sparks bursting like a log thrown on a bonfire, and a tree limb crashed to the ground just behind her. Jenna jumped at the sound, and her foot slid from under her. She took another step, trying to recover her balance, only now the ground was tilted sharply down, and she half ran, half fell down the long, grassy slope to the valley floor, landing on her knees and hands an arm's length from the rear of one of the barrows.

"Come to me . . ."

The mage-lights splashed bright light on the dolmen, sending black shadows from the standing stones twisting wildly over the mounds. Jenna could feel the stone throbbing madly in response, and she took it in her hand. The pebble glowed with interior illumination, bright enough that she could see the radiance between her fingers as she held the stone in her fist. Having the stone in her hand seemed to lend her courage, and she walked slowly between the graves toward the dolmen, though she could feel every muscle in her body twitching with a readiness to flee.

As she stepped into the open circle around the dolmen, she saw the apparition.

It stood before the barrow of Riata: a man's shape, long-haired and stocky, clad in a flowing clóca of a strange design which left one shoulder bare. The form shifted, wavering, as if it were formed of clear crystal and it was only the reflection of the mage-lights on its polished surface that rendered it visible. But it moved, for one hand lifted as Jenna recoiled a step, her back pressed up against the carved surface of the standing stone. There were eyes watching her in the spectral face. It spoke, and its voice was the one that had called to her. The words sounded in her head, as if the voice was inside her.

"You hold the cloch na thintrí," it said, and there was a wistful yearning in its voice. Its face lifted and looked up at the mage-lights, and she could see the glow playing over the transparent features. "They have returned," it said, its voice mournful and pleased all at once. "I wondered if I would see them again. So beautiful, so cold and powerful, so tempting . . ." The face regarded Jenna again. "You are not of my people," it said. "You are too fair, too tall."

"My people are called the Daoine," Jenna answered. "And how is it you know our language?"

"The dead do not use words. We lack mouth and tongue and lungs to move the air. I speak with you mind to mind, taking from you the form of the words I use. But I feel the strangeness of your language. Daoine . . ." It said the word slowly, rolling the syllables. "I knew no Daoines when I was alive . . . There were other tribes, we knew, in other lands, but here there were only the Bunús Muintir. My people."

"You're Riata?" Jenna asked. She was intrigued now. The ghost, if that's what it was, had made no threatening moves toward her, and she leaned forward, trying to see it more clearly. The ghosts and spirits of the tales she'd heard in Ballintubber were always bloody, decaying corpses or white vapors, and they cursed and terrified the living. This, though . . . the play of light over its shifting, elusive form was almost beautiful, and its voice held no threat.

"I was called that once," the specter said, sounding pleased and sad at the same time. "So that name is still known? I'm not forgotten in the time of the Daoine?"

"No, not forgotten," Jenna answered, thinking that it might be best to mollify the spirit. *After all, Tiarna Mac Ard had known of him.*

"Ahh . . ." it sighed. A hand stretched out toward Jenna,

and she forced herself to stand still. She could feel the chill of its touch, like ice on her forehead and cheek, then the hand cupped hers and Jenna let her fingers relax. In her palm, the stone shot light back to the glowing sky. "So young you are, to be holding a cloch na thintrí, especially this one. But I was young, as well, the first time I held it . . ."

"*This* one?" Jenna asked. "How . . . ?"

"Follow me," it said. Its hand beckoned, and from fingertips to elbow the arm seemed to reflect the intricate curls and flourishes of the lights above, as if the patterns had been carved into the limb. The phantom glided backward into Riata's tomb, its cold touch fading.

"I can't," Jenna responded, holding back from the yawning mouth of the barrow. She glanced up at the lights playing over the valley, at the stone in her hand.

"You must," Riata replied. "The mage-lights will wait for you." Then the presence was gone, and nothing stood in front of the passage. "Come . . ." whispered the voice faintly, from nowhere and everywhere.

Jenna took a step toward the barrow, then another. She put her hand on the stone lintels of the opening: they were carved with swirls and eddies not unlike the display in the sky above and on Riata's arm, along with lozenges and circles and other carved symbols. She traced them with her fingers, then walked into the passage itself. Darkness surrounded her immediately and Jenna almost fled back outside, but as her eyes slowly adjusted, she could see in the illumination of the mage-lights and the answering glow from the cloch na thintrí that the walls were drystone, covered with plaster that was now broken and shattered, the stones piled to just above the height of her head and capped with flat rocks. The passage into the burial chamber was short but claustrophobic. The walls leaned in, so that while two people could have knelt side by side at the bottom, only one standing person could walk down the corridor at a time. Once, the walls must have been decorated— there were flecks of colored pigment clinging to the plaster and her touch caused more of the ancient paintings to crumble and fall away. Here and there were larger patches where she could see traces of what, centuries ago, must have been a mural. Jenna was glad to finally reach the relative spaciousness of the burial chamber. She glanced back: through the passage, she could see the dolmen awash in the brilliant fireworks of the mage-lights.

The burial chamber itself had been constructed with five huge stones, forming the sides and roof. The air was musty and stale, and the room dim, touched only by the reflections of the lights, the cloch na thintrí's illumination. At the center of the room was a large, chiseled block of granite, and set there was a pottery urn, glazed with the same swirls and curved lines carved on the lintel stones. Around the urn were beads and pieces of jewelry, torcs of gold and braided silver that glistened in the moving radiance. Clothing had once lain here as well; she could see moldering scraps of brightly-dyed cloth. These had been funeral gifts, obviously, and the urn undoubtedly held the ashes and bones of Riata. But his specter had vanished.

"Hello?" she called.

Air moved, her hair lifting, and she felt a touch on her shoulder. Jenna cried out, frightened, and the sound rang in the chamber, reverberating. She dropped the cloch na thintrí, and as she started to reach for it, the pebble rose from the floor, picked up by a hand that was barely visible in the stone's glow.

"Aye," Riata's voice said in her head, full of satisfaction, the tones dark and low. " 'Tis true. This was once mine." Pale light stroked the lines of his spectral face, sparking in the deep hollows where the eyes should have been. His voice seemed more ominous, touched with hostility. "Or more truthfully, I once belonged to it. Until it was stolen from me and found its way to another."

"I didn't steal it," Jenna protested, shrinking back against the wall as the shadowy form of Riata seemed to loom larger in front of her. "I found it on the hill near my home, the first time the mage-lights came. I didn't know it was yours; I never even knew of you. Besides, it's only a little stone. It can't be very powerful."

Cold laughter rippled the dead air of the tomb, and the stench of death wafted over Jenna, making her wrinkle her nose and turn her face away. "I don't accuse *you* of stealing it," Riata's voice boomed. "This cloch na thintrí has owned many in its time and will own many more. Dávali had it before me, and Óengus before him, and so on, back into the eldest times. And it may be little, but of all the clochs na thintrí, it is the most powerful."

"It can't be," Jenna protested. "Tiarna Mac Ard . . . he would have said . . ." *Or he didn't know,* she suddenly realized. She wondered if he would have handed it back to her, if he had.

"Then this tiarna knows nothing. This cloch even has a name it calls itself: Lámh Shábhála, the Safekeeping. The cloch was placed here when I died, on the offering stone you see in front of you. And it was taken over a thousand long years ago—I felt its loss even in death, though I didn't have strength then to rise. For hands upon hands upon hands of years I slumbered. Once, centuries ago, the lights came again to wake me and I could feel that Lámh Sháb-hála was alive with the mage-lights once more. I called out to Lámh Shábhála and its holder, but no one answered or they were too far away to hear me. With the mage-light's strength, I was able to rise and walk here among the tombs when the mage-lights filled the sky, but few came to this place, and though they were Bunús Muintir, they appeared to be poor and savage, and seemed frightened of me. None of them knew the magic of the sky. I realized then that my people had declined and no longer ruled this land. But someone held Lámh Shábhála, or the lights could not have returned. For unending years I called, every night the lights shone. Then, as they have before, the mage-lights died again, and I slept once more." The shape that was Riata drew itself close to her. "Until now," he said. "When the mage-lights have awakened again."

"Then take the stone," Jenna said. "It's yours. Keep it. I don't want it."

Riata laughed again at that. "Lámh Shábhála isn't mine, nor yours. Lámh Shábhála is its own. I knew it wanted me to pass it on as it had been passed to me. I could feel its desire even though the mage-lights had stopped coming a dozen years before I became sick with my last illness, but

I held onto it. There were no more cloudmages left, only people with dead stones around their necks and empty skies above. I believed my cloch to be as dead as theirs; in fact, I prayed that it was so. I should have known it wasn't. Lámh Shábhála is First and Last." The voice was nearly a hiss. "And a curse to its Holder, as I know too well, especially the one who is to be First."

The stone hung in the air in front of Jenna, held in invisible fingers. "Take Lámh Shábhála," Riata said. "I pass it to you, Jenna of the Daoine, as I should have passed it long ago. You are the new First Holder."

Jenna shook her head, now more afraid of the stone than of the ghost. Yet her hand reached out, unbidden, and took the cloch from the air. She fisted her hand around the cold smoothness as Riata's laughter echoed in her head.

"Aye, you see? You shake your head, but the desire is there, whether you admit it or not. It's already claimed you."

Jenna was near to crying. She could feel the tears starting in her eyes, the fear hammering at her heart. The cloch burned like fiery ice in her hand. "You called it a curse to its holder. What do you mean?"

"The power of the land is eternal, as is the power of the water. Their magics and spells, for those who know how to tap and use them, are slower and less energetic than that of the air, but more stable. They are always there, caught in the bones of the land itself, or in the depths of the water. The power within the sky ebbs and flows: slowly, over generations and generations of mortal lives. It has done so since before my people walked from Thall Mór-roinn to this land and found Lámh Shábhála here. No one knows how often the slow, centuries-long cycle has repeated itself. There were no people here when we Bunús Muintir came to Talamh an Ghlas, but there were the standing stones and graves of other tribes who had once lived here, and we Holders could hear the voices in the stone, one tribe after another, back and back into a past none of us can see. The mage-lights vanished for the Bunús Muintir four times, the last time while I was still alive. The sky-power returned once for you Daoine, then vanished again. Now the mage-lights want to return again."

Jenna glanced down the passage of the tomb. Multicolored light still touched the dolmen, brightening the valley. "The mage-lights have *already* returned," Jenna said, but Riata's denial boomed before she could finish.

"No!" he seemed to shout. "This is but the slightest hint of them, the first stirrings of Lámh Shábhála, the gathering of enough power within the stone to open the gates so that *all* the clochs na thintrí may awaken and the mage-lights appear everywhere. For now, the lights follow Lámh Shábhála—and that is the danger. Those who know the true lore of the mage-lights also know that fact. They know that where the lights appear, Lámh Shábhála is also there. And they will follow, because they want to hold Lámh Shábhála themselves."

Jenna continued to shake her head, half understanding, half not wanting to understand. "But why hold the stone if it's a curse?"

A bitter laugh. "The one who holds Lámh Shábhála gains power for their pain. Some believe that's more than a fair barter—those who have never held the cloch itself. It's the First who suffers the most, not those who come after, and you are the First, the one who will open the way. So watch, Jenna of the Daoine. Watch for those who follow the mage-lights, for they aren't likely to be your friends."

Jenna thought of the riders from Connachta, and she also thought of Mac Ard. But before she could say more, Riata's shape stirred. "The mage-lights beckon," he said. "They call the stone. Do you feel it?"

She did. The cloch was throbbing in her hand. "Go to them," Riata said. His shape was fading, as was his voice, now no more than a whisper. "Go . . ." he said again, and the apparition was gone. She could feel its absence, could sense that the air of the tomb was now dead and empty. She called to him—"Riata!"—and only her own voice answered, mocking. The mage-lights sent waves of pure red and aching blue-white shimmering down the passage, and Jenna felt the stone's need, like a hunger deep within her-

self. She walked down the passage and out into cold fresh
air again. The mage-lights wove their bright net above her,
a spider's web of color that stretched and bent down
toward her, swirling. She raised her hand, opening her fingers, and the light shot down, surrounding her, enveloping
her in its flowing folds. The whirlwind grabbed her hand in
its frigid gasp, and she screamed with the pain of it: as the
brilliance rose, a sun caught in her fingers, consuming her.

Hues of brilliance pulled at her. Knives of color cut into
her flesh. She tried to pull away and could not, and she
screamed again in terror and agony.

A flash blinded her. Thunder filled her ears.

Jenna screamed a final time, as the cold fire seemed to
penetrate to her very core, her entire body quivering with
torment, every nerve alive and quivering.

Then she was released, and she fell into blessed darkness.

9

Through the Forest

"JENNA?"

The smell was familiar—a warm breath laden with spice. Jenna opened her eyes to see Seancoim crouching alongside her. The dolmen towered gray above her, rising toward a sky touched with the salmon hues of early morning, and Dúnmharú peered down at her from a perch on the capstone. Jenna blinked, then sat up abruptly, turning to look at the tomb behind her. "Riata," she said, her voice a mere hoarse croak. Her throat felt as if it had been scraped raw, and her right arm ached as if someone had tried to tear it loose from its socket. She could feel the cloch na thintrí: cold, still clutched in her fist, and she slipped it back into the pocket of her skirt, grimacing with the effort. Something was wrong with her right hand—it felt wooden and clumsy, and the pain in her arm seemed to emanate from there.

"You saw him?" Seancoim asked, and Jenna nodded. Seancoim didn't seem surprised. "He walks here at times, restless. I've glimpsed him once or twice, or I think I might have."

"He . . ." Jenna tried to clear her throat, but the effort only made it hurt worse. She wanted to take her hand out from where it was hidden in the woolen skirt, but she was afraid. ". . . called me. Spoke to me."

Seancoim's blind eyes narrowed, but he said nothing. He opened the leather bag at his side and rummaged inside, pulling out a smaller leather container capped with horn.

"Here. Drink this." Jenna reached out. Stopped. The skin of her right hand was mottled, the flesh a swirling pattern of pale gray and white, and the intricate tendrils of whit-ened flesh ached and burned. Her fingers were stiff, every joint on fire, and the damaged skin throbbed with every beat of her heart. She must have cried out, for Dúnmharú flew down from the capstone to Seancoim's shoulder. The Bunús Muintir took her hand, examining it, pushing back the sleeve of her blouse. The injured area extended just past her wrist.

"Your skin is dead where it's gray. I've seen it before, in people who were caught in a blizzard and exposed to bitter cold," Seancoim said. Jenna felt tears start in her eyes, and Seancoim touched her cheek. "It will heal in time," he said. "If you don't injure it further."

"Jenna!" The call came from the ridge above them. Maeve and Mac Ard stood there, her mam waving an arm and scrambling down the slope into the valley, Mac Ard following more carefully after her. Maeve came running up to them, glancing harshly at Seancoim. "Jenna, are you all right? We woke up and saw the lights, and you were gone—" She noticed Jenna's hand then, and her own hand went to her mouth. "Oh, Jenna . . ."

Jenna turned the hand slowly in front of her face, a con-tortion of pain moving across her features as she flexed her fingers slowly. The swirling pattern on her hand echoed the carved lines of the dolmen. Her mam took her wrist gently. "What happened, darling?" she asked, but Jenna saw Mac Ard approaching, and she only shook her head. *He had the cloch in his hand, and he gave it back to me . . .* Mac Ard came up behind Maeve, putting his hands on her shoulders as she examined Jenna's injury. Jenna saw Mac Ard's gaze move from her hand to the carvings on the dolmen, then back again. For a moment, their eyes locked gazes, and she tried to keep her emotions from showing on her face. *Watch for those who follow the mage-lights,* Riata had said. She wondered how much Mac Ard knew or guessed, and if he had, did he regret not keeping the stone when he had it.

"I'm fine, Mam," she said to Maeve. "The pain's easing

already." It was a lie, but Jenna forced a small smile to her face, pulling her hand gently away from her mam.

"I'll make a poultice that will take away the sting and speed the healing," Seancoim said. "There are andúilleaf flowers still in bloom in the thicket near the camp." His staff tapping the ground ahead of him, he shuffled away between the barrows.

"Jenna," Mac Ard said. "We saw the lights. Did the stone . . . ?"

"*I* hold the stone," she answered, far more sharply than she intended. Belatedly, she added: "Tiarna."

His eyes flashed, narrowing, and his hands dropped from Maeve's shoulders. "Jenna!" her mam said. "After all the tiarna's risked for us . . ."

"I know, but we've risked our own lives as well," Jenna told her, watching Mac Ard's face more than her mam's. "We lost our home, and poor Kesh is dead. We're not Riocha, with fine clothes and buildings and the Rí waiting for us to return. We know farming and planting and raising sheep; we're not used to fighting or intrigue or even traveling. He's going back to what he knows. We're going forward into a situation we don't understand at all. We're caught up in something, and . . ." She stopped, closing her mouth. . . . *and I think he knows more about it than he's telling us.* Emotions warred inside her. *That doesn't mean he's evil. Your mam's right; he* has *risked himself for you.*

And the question: *Do I tell him? Do I tell him what Riata said about the stone?*

No, she decided. *I don't. Not right now.*

"Jenna . . ." Maeve breathed, then glanced back at Mac Ard. "She's hurting, Padraic. It's the pain talking."

"I know, Maeve," he answered. His voice soothed, though Jenna thought she saw irritation in the folds around his eyes and mouth. Then his face cleared entirely, and he stepped forward, opening his arms as if he were about to sweep Jenna up and carry her.

"Thank you," she told him. "I . . . I could use your help."

She cradled her arm to her waist, feeling in her head the cold, cold pulsing of the stone. She let Mac Ard support her as they walked back to their campsite.

*   *   *

"Take this."

Seancoim handed Jenna a wooden cup. A vile-looking, thick whitish liquid steamed inside, with bits of pale stems floating in the mixture. He gestured at the wrapping around her right hand and arm. "The brew is made from andúil-leaf, like the poultice I gave you," he said to her unspoken question. "It'll take away what's left of the pain."

Maeve and Mac Ard were packing away what little they had, and the embers of the fire had been covered with moist dirt. Jenna took the cup from Seancoim and sipped the concoction. It was bitter and lukewarm, and she made a face. "Drink it and don't complain," Seancoim growled. "We've a good walk ahead of us yet today, and you don't need to be thinking about your hand."

Jenna took a breath and lifted the cup to her mouth, trying to ignore the sharp smell of the andúilleaf and gulping it down quickly so she couldn't taste it. She wasn't entirely successful. *"Uch!"* she said, wiping her mouth and handing the cup back to Seancoim. "It's awful."

"Good. That will make it less likely that you'll want it again." He handed her a small bag. "Here," he said. "This is the rest of the andúilleaf I gathered. I'll tell you how to make the brew before I leave you. When you get to the tiarna's city, find a good apothecary and show him this; if the herbalist has any knowledge at all, he'll know what it is, so you can get more if you must."

"I won't *want* more, I promise," Jenna said.

Seancoim only nodded uncertainly at that. "Can you feel the draught working?"

Jenna nodded: its fire had settled in her stomach, and was reaching outward. Her hand felt almost normal under the wrappings, and she could flex her fingers easily.

Seancoim patted her on the shoulder, then stuffed the cup back in his pack. "It's time to go," he announced loudly.

They started off again through the forest. Even though the day was clear and sunny, Doire Coill remained dim and shadowed, and the walk was, if anything, more difficult than their passage the day before, as Seancoim led them up one

ridge and down another. The land was flattening, though,
each ridge a little less high and steep than the one before,
until by noon they were walking through a rolling plain,
with the trees set close together and the floor of the forest
choked with underbrush. Seancoim led them in a wandering
pattern through the wild growth, and they had to go single
file behind him, with thorns snatching at their clothes on
every side and branches threatening to bump unwary heads.
Though Seancoim moved this way and that, never keeping
to a straight path—impossible anyway in the dense forest—
Jenna felt certain that they were bending north again, as
well as east, so that their path the last two days described
a small arc looping deeper into Doire Coill than one would
have expected. She wasn't certain how she knew this, but
in her head she could feel the valley of the tombs where
Riata slept, and it was now behind and to their left. Once,
when they came across a fire-cleared glade, Jenna moved
next to Seancoim, talking softly to him so her mam and
Mac Ard could not overhear.

"I wonder," she said to him, "if we couldn't have cut in
a straighter path across the forest and missed the valley
last night."

Seancoim didn't look at her. His blind eyes stared
straight ahead. "Sometimes the best path isn't the straight-
est one."

"Did you know . . ." She stopped, feeling a tingling in
her hand under the bandage. ". . . what would happen?"

"In truth, no," he answered. "But I suspected that something would. I've been hearing the call of Riata for several
months, whispering through the wood. The last time I
passed by the valley of the tombs, with a bright moon
above, I saw him walking restlessly outside near the dolmen, looking up at the night sky. When you came, I realized that it might be that the Last Holder needed to meet
the new First, so I made certain our path went by the
tombs."

"You know about this cloch, then," she said. "He called
it Lámh Shábhála. Can you tell me—what will it do to me?
What does it mean to be the First?"

Seancoim shrugged under his furs. "I know the magic of

the earth, not the sky, and they're very different. Jenna, it's been four centuries since the mage-lights last came, and you Daoine had Lámh Shábhála then. For the Bunús Muintir . . . well, the last time we possessed the cloch you hold was not long after you Daoine came here, an entire *age* ago and all the tales have been so twisted and distorted in the tellings and retellings that much of the lore can't be trusted, or is so wrapped with untruths that it's difficult to separate the two. Each time, the cloudmages must learn anew. I can tell you very little that I know with a certainty is true."

"I'm scared, Seancoim," Jenna said, her voice husky and broken.

He stopped. He took her injured hand in his gnarled, wrinkled fingers. "Then you're wiser than anyone else who is searching for Lámh Shábhála," he said.

The land flattened out into a plain, and Jenna noticed that the trees were no longer so closely huddled together. The oaks were now less numerous than maples, elms, and tall firs, and the ground less boggy than the wide valley where Ballintubber sat. The woods grew lighter, with the sky visible between the treetops, and Jenna became aware of the bright singing of birds in the trees above them, a sound that she realized had been missing in Doire Coill. Ahead, they could see where the trees ended at the verge of a large grassy field, which ran slightly downhill to a wide, brown strip of bare earth bordered on either side by a stone fence.

"There is the High Road coming up from Thiar in the west and Bácathair to the south," Seancoim said. He pointed to the left. "That way, the road runs north to cross the Duán at Áth Iseal. Beyond the line of trees on the other side of the road is Lough Lár, and the High Road runs alongside it. This is the eastern border of Doire Coill, and here I leave you."

"Thank you, Seancoim of the Bunús Muintir," Mac Ard said. "I promise you that I'll tell Rí Gabair of your help. Is there some way I can have him reward you for bringing us here safely?"

"Tell Rí Gabair to leave Doire Coill alone," Seancoim answered. "That will be reward enough for the few Bunús Muintir who are left."

Mac Ard nodded. Jenna went to Seancoim and hugged him, then stroked Dúnmharú's back. "Thank you," she said.

"Take care of yourself," Seancoim whispered into her ear. "Be sparing with the andúilleaf; do not use it unless you must, or you'll find it difficult to stop. I also think you should be careful about showing the power of the cloch you hold. Do you understand?"

Jenna nodded. She hugged Seancoim again, inhaling his scent of herbs. "I'll miss you."

"I am always here," he told her. "Just come into Doire Coill and call my name, and I'll hear it." He let her go, and turned his blind eyes toward Maeve. "Take care of your daughter," he said. "She'll need your help with the burden she bears."

Maeve nodded. "I know. I thank you also, Seancoim. When I first met you, I didn't trust you, but you've kept your word to us and more."

"Remember that when you look on others," he answered. He gave a short bow to the three of them. "May the Mother-Creator watch your path. Dúnmharú, come— we have our own business to the south." He turned his back to them and walked off into the forest. Jenna watched until his form was swallowed in shadow, and the three of them made their way to the High Road.

10

The Taisteal

THE High Road, between the waist-high stone walls that bordered its path, was rough and muddy, with a scraggly growth of grass and weeds in the center between ruts carved by the wheels of carts and carriages. Mac Ard bent down to look closely at the road. "All the hoof marks are old. No riders have passed this way in a few days," he said. "That makes me feel a bit easier." He stood up, scanning the landscape. "I've come up on this side of Lough Lár a few times. Áth Iseal is no more than ten miles to the north, but there aren't many inns or villages along this side of the lake, so near to Doire Coill. It's too late for us to reach the town today, but we can camp along the lake's shore if we don't come across an inn. Tomorrow morning it should be an easy walk to the ford of the Duán, and once across to Áth Iseal I can hire a carriage to take us to Lár Bhaile." He smiled at Maeve, at Jenna. "We're almost home," he said.

Not our *home,* Jenna wanted to answer. *That's gone forever.* She clamped her lips together to stop the words and nodded encouragingly.

They walked through the afternoon. The High Road followed the line of Lough Lár, sometimes verging close enough that they could see the blue waters of the lake just to their right. At other times, the road turned aside for a bit to climb the low, wooded hills that held the lake in their cupped hands. As they approached the narrow end of the lake, the dark woods of Doire Coill turned westward and gave way to large squares of farmed and grazed land, defined with tidy stone fences. Occasionally, they would pass a gate in the fence that bordered the High Road, with a lane leading far back to a hidden farmhouse set a mile or more from the road. Jenna, used to the small homesteads and farms of Ballintubber, was amazed by the size of some of the fields. They saw workers in those fields, and once had to stand aside as a hay wagon drawn by a pair of tired, old horses squealed and creaked its way past them. The driver looked at them curiously, and said little to Mac Ard's hail. They passed no one at all on the road going in their direction.

Toward evening, they came to an empty field on the lough side of the road. The flickering lights of cook fires glistened there among several tents and four wagons. They could hear the nickering of horses and the occasional laughter of people. There was a sign hanging on one of the wagons, written in high black letters that were still visible in the dusk.

"What does the sign say?"

"You can't read?"

Jenna shook her head. "Neither of us know our letters," Maeve said, "but Niall could read. He said he'd teach me, but . . ." Remembered sorrow touched her face, and Jenna hugged her mam.

"No matter," Mac Ard said. "Once we're in Lár Bhaile, we can find teachers for you. Reading can be a useful art, though it's probably best that the common folk don't learn the skill. The sign says 'Clan Sheehan. Pots mended, goods sold.' " Mac Ard seemed to hesitate. "These are Taisteal camped for the night. They're coming down from the north, so perhaps they've heard something. If nothing else, we can probably buy shelter for the night here."

"Can you trust them?" Maeve asked nervously. "Some of the Taisteal who have come through Ballintubber were thieves and cheats, and often the goods you buy from them are damaged or poorly made. The last ones through fixed a leaking pot of Matron Kelly's and it began to leak again not two days after they were gone."

Mac Ard shrugged. "If I were buying something from

them, I'd inspect it well, but I doubt they're any more prone to be criminals than any other people. They roam, and so they're convenient to blame."

"Coelin came from the Taisteal," Jenna reminded her mam.

"I know," Maeve answered, but she did try to smile. "That's why I worry."

Mac Ard laughed at that. "We can't go farther today in any case," he said. "I'd rather spend the night among a group than alone, especially if the Connachtans are still out searching for us. Let's keep our eyes open and be cautious, but I don't think the Taisteal would risk assaulting a tiarna on the High Road so close to Áth Iseal."

They followed Mac Ard through a break in the High Road wall and into the field. Jenna could feel appraising glances on them as they approached, and the voices from the Taisteal camp went silent. Jenna knew little about the Taisteal: they were itinerants, moving in clannish groups throughout the lands and—if you could believe their tales—wandering everywhere through Talamh an Ghlas and beyond. They sold and bartered the goods they carried in their wagons, which sometimes included orphaned children they'd acquired along the way. Coelin had told her a little about his years with them. *"They treated me better than my own parents did,"* he said. *"But they also sold me without a single regret or tear when Songmaster Curragh indicated an interest and showed them his coins. In that way, I was just another pot or pan to them."*

As they came to the camp's perimeter, a man strode out to meet them. "Declan Sheehan, Clannhri of Clan Sheehan," he said, clapping his hand to his chest. Sheehan was an older man dressed in leather and wool, wrinkled and thin with a quick, almost nervous voice. He peered at them closely, and Jenna saw the other Taisteal also staring, with hands held conspicuously close to their waists. Jenna knew that they must be a sight, covered with the soil of three days' travel in the bogs and the forest. Their clothes were torn from the brambles, and the folds of Jenna's skirts were smeared with mud from waist to hem. "And how can the Taisteal help our fellow travelers this evening?"

"I am Tiarna Mac Ard from Lár Bhaile, of the Rí Gabair's court," Mac Ard said, and there was a snicker from one of the Taisteal behind Sheehan. "What I would like is a shelter for myself and my companions tonight."

"Ah, a tiarna . . ." Sheehan grinned, hands now on hips. "And two bantiarnas as well. We're honored to have the company of Riocha among us on such an evening. But . . ." He shook his head. "We Taisteal are poor, and have so very little to offer . . ." His voice, reedy and as thin as his body, trailed off as Mac Ard produced a bag from under his vest and poured out several coins. He plucked the single gold mórceint from among the coppers and held it up, turning it in front of Sheehan. Jenna marveled, too, wondering what it must feel like to be able to carry what was a fortune for her around in one's pocket. "We've become separated from our group," he said, "though we expect to meet them tomorrow, or perhaps even later tonight. We'd like two tents for tonight, some clean clothing if you have it, and would like to share whatever supper you have." Mac Ard flipped the mórceint to Sheehan; he snatched at it eagerly.

Jenna almost laughed at the transformation the gold piece had on the man. "Tiarna," he said. "I apologize. I couldn't . . . You seemed . . ." He turned to the others. "Hilde, where is that trunk we picked up in Áth Iseal? There was clothing in it. Bran, you and Edan can sleep in the wagon tonight. Tiarna, if you and the bantiarnas would come with me, I'll show you where you can put your things. Hilde . . . !"

The tent smelled of perspiration and badly tanned leather, but Jenna didn't care. A half hour later, rested and feeling refreshed with the clean, plain tunic and skirt that Hilde had produced, Jenna felt somewhat renewed. Her mam changed the dressing on her arm, and though her face showed concern, she did nod as she unwrapped it. "The old man knew his herb craft," she said. "This looks better than it did this morning." Maeve daubed on more of Seancoim's andúilleaf paste, rewrapped the arm, then handed Jenna a small mug of thick tea made from the leaves. "Here. You're sure you need this? He seemed concerned that you not drink too much of it."

"It still hurts, Mam," Jenna said. "And Seancoim told me to use it if I must." She drank the concoction, then grimaced. "The way this tastes, there's no danger of wanting more than I need." She made a face, and Maeve laughed, tousling her hair.

"Then I'm going to see how Padraic is faring in his tent." Jenna must have made a face, for her mam stopped at the entrance to the tent. "What?" she asked.

She couldn't form a sentence; the thoughts were too scrambled and confused. "Mam, are you . . . He's always near you . . . I see you smile, and . . ."

Jenna saw color rise on her mam's neck, but she only nodded. "I know," Maeve answered. "I won't lie to you, Jenna. 'Tis true, what you saying. I've never . . . well, it's been a long time since I felt that way about a man. Do *you* like him, Jenna? I'd like to know."

"I can see he's handsome, even with that scar. And he's helped us, Mam, saved our lives. But—"

"But?"

"He's Riocha. A tiarna. And we're not. I'm afraid what that would mean, Mam."

"I know," Meave told her. She tousled Jenna's hair as she used to when she was young. "I think about that, too. But I do like the man. May the Mother help me, I do. I don't know if you can understand, Jenna. Your da, Niall, there was a way I felt when I was around him, and in all the years since he's gone, I'd never felt that again, until now." Meave hugged Jenna. "But . . . how do *you* feel about Padraic?"

"I like him, Mam. When he smiles at you, I see that he means it." She kept the rest back: the worry she had that it might have been the same cloch she carried that he'd been searching for, that if he knew she had it his attitude might change.

"Thank you, Jenna," Maeve said. "That means a lot to me. None of this changes anything between us, darling. No matter what, you and I won't change."

Jenna remained silent. She could see in her mam's face that she knew that wasn't necessarily true, that neither one of them totally believed the words yet neither wanted to admit it. *If you go to him, it may change everything, Mam. It means that it's more likely you'll take his side against mine. It means that you'd be feeling things we can't share anymore. And it means that once we reach the city, I might lose you, and that scares me most of all.* But Jenna only nodded. "He makes you happy?"

Maeve smiled. "Aye, child. He does. That's something you'll understand soon enough for yourself, I'm sure."

"I hope so," Jenna said. "I hope so."

"You will. I know it," Maeve answered. "I can smell the stew. Clannhri Sheehan said that we should come and join them when we're ready. I'll be right back with Padraic. You're sure you're all right?"

"Go on, Mam. I'm fine. I think I'll go out and see the camp."

Maeve nodded and left. Jenna lay on the pile of sheepskins that served as a bed, fingering the smooth surface of the stone.

The Taisteal clan were all gathered around the largest fire, crackling in the center of the ring of tents and wagons. When Jenna came out of the tent, she could feel that everyone was watching her, even if they didn't look directly at her. She felt suddenly out of place and a little frightened. In Ballintubber, she would have had a name for every face. For the first time in her life, she was surrounded by total strangers. These were people to whom Ballintubber was just another village like a hundred others they'd seen, who had traveled from the cliffs bordering the Ice Sea to the southern tip of Talamh an Ghlas. Jenna suddenly felt provincial and lost.

She saw Clannhri Sheehan standing to one side, smoking a pipe and talking with one of the men. He saw her, said something to the man, and came over to her. "Ah, m'lady!" He glanced up and down at her as if inspecting a side of ham. "Now, doesn't that feel more comfortable? Here, let me get you some of the stew. Hilde . . ." Jenna started to protest, to say that she'd wait until her mam and Mac Ard came out, but Sheehan took her arm and ushered her forward.

She could feel the eyes of the clan on her as she came to the fire. She smiled, tentatively, and received a few smiles in return. They seemed to be several families: men and women as well as children, plainly dressed. She heard someone whisper in a voice that carried over the murmur of conversation: *"She's the one with the tiarna . . ."* No one spoke to her—that was also unlike Ballintubber, where strangers would have been immediately engaged in conversation and bombarded with a dozen questions about where they came from, where they were going, what their names might be and who they might be related to hereabouts. Instead, these people seemed content to stare and keep their speculations private. Most of the faces were friendly enough, and she supposed that she could have spoken to them and been answered kindly, but a few stared hard at her, with guarded faces and expressions. Hilde hurried to her with a bowl filled with fragrant stew, a small loaf of bread, and a wooden spoon. Sheehan took it from her and handed it to Jenna. "There, Bantiarna. Sit, sit and be comfortable." He sat next to her, speaking too loudly for her comfort. "It's not much, but the best we can offer. Don't often have Riocha staying with us, 'tis the truth, not with the Taisteal."

"Thank you, Clannhri," she said. "You're very kind." She started eating the stew, hoping he would leave her alone, but he didn't seem inclined to move or to be quiet.

"Aye," he said. "I knew him to be a tiarna as soon as I clapped eyes on him, I did, even through the mud and scratches. We Taisteal have the gift of that, you know, and Clan Sheehan best of all—we can see worth where someone else sees nothing. You've had a time of it, I could see, and I said to myself 'Sheehan, you need to treat these people well, who have had a bit of difficulty on the road.' What with all the trouble just to the north, and the lights in the sky, who knows what one might encounter? Some are already saying that this is the Filleadh, the time of magic come again, and creatures that have lain hidden for the last age will walk again. There are people out already hunting for the clochs na thintrí in the old places, as if a spell-stone like they talk about in the tales of the Before could be found strewn about for the taking."

Jenna tried to smile at that and almost succeeded. The stone hidden in her clothes seemed to burn with the mention, so that Jenna was surprised Sheehan couldn't see it. She placed her hand over the stone, as if to hide it. "I don't know about clochs," she said. "What about this trouble?"

Sheehan's face collapsed into a frown with a sad shaking of his head. He brushed what little hair he had left back with a thick-knuckled hand. "Ah, 'twas awful," he said. "Raiders came and burned one village, is what I hear, and killed several. Then they went riding all over the country, looking for someone from there. Word is they came as far east as the Duán before they turned back. Even came south on the High Road a bit, not more than a few miles from here."

Jenna shivered with remembered fear. The response must have been noticeable, for Sheehan lifted his hands as if to calm her. "Ah, there's no danger now, Bantiarna. But there's no doubt but that strange things are afoot. In fact, we've heard all manner of odd tales from people coming up the road recently: a party who says they saw a naked boy sunning himself on a rock at the north end of the Lough Dubh, and as soon as the boy saw them, he changed into a black seal and dove into the water. Just a hand of days ago, I was talking with a man who said he was attacked by a pack of huge dire wolves, which haven't been seen in this land since my grandfather's time, and another who was pursued by a troop of wee folk, no bigger than his knee and all armed with sharp little swords. Hilde herself saw a dog as large as a pony, with red, glowing eyes and mouth foaming, and the dog spoke, it did, spoke as plain as—"

"Did the dog talk as well as you, Clannhri, I wonder?" Mac Ard's voice interrupted the monologue, and Sheehan nearly fell, turning his head around to glance up at the tiarna. He stood and gave a quick bow to Mac Ard and Meave, who was on the tiarna's arm.

"Tiarna Mac Ard," Sheehan said. "I was just telling the

young Bantiarna about how strange the times have become, even for the poor Taisteal. Why, one might think—"

Mac Ard lifted his hand, and the man's voice cut off as if severed with a knife. "No doubt you have thought that we would like some of that fine stew, and something to drink if you have it," Mac Ard said, and Sheehan gave a nod of his head. He scurried off as Mac Ard helped Maeve to the ground and then sat alongside her himself. The gathering around the fire had gone entirely silent. Mac Ard glanced around, and faces looked quickly away. Conversations started up again, the noise level rising.

"Tiarna," Jenna said, keeping her voice low. "He said that Ballintubber was burned, and they've seen the mage-lights."

"Aye," Mac Ard said. "No doubt the rumors are everywhere now, maybe even in Dún Laoghaire itself by now. But I doubt that the Connachtans are still in the area, or that they burned Ballintubber to the ground. Rumors grow larger the farther they travel, and the Connachtans are likely to have scurried home by now." He glanced around the encampment. "But it wouldn't surprise me if they've left a spy or two behind, either some of their own or someone who is willing to send word to them for a few mórceints. There are faces here I don't like, and Sheehan talks more than is good for him. I don't think I'll sleep well tonight. I won't feel safe until we're back in Lár Bhaile."

Sheehan came back with stew for Mac Ard and Jenna, more bread, and cups of water. This time he said very little, glancing at Mac Ard with the expression of a scolded dog and hurrying off again. Mac Ard and Maeve talked, but Jenna only half-listened, leaning back on her arms and watching the fire. She wished someone would sing some of the Taisteal songs, and that thought made her think of Coelin, and she wondered how he was, if he'd been hurt by the Connachtans, or if Tara's even still stood and wasn't a burned-out hulk next to the road. She didn't want to go forward; she wanted to go back. She wanted to see Ballintubber again and Knobtop and all the familiar places. If it were within her power, she would erase the events of the past several days and happily go back to her old, predictable life.

She felt tears starting in her eyes, and she brushed at them almost angrily. "I'm tired," she told her mam. "I'm going up to the tent."

Maeve glanced at her with concern, but she kissed Jenna. "We'll do the same as soon as we eat," she said. "I'll check on you. Good night, darling."

"Good night, Mam, Tiarna." Jenna nodded to Mac Ard. She brushed at her skirts and walked away from the fire toward her tent.

She didn't notice that one of the men to her left excused himself from his companions and rose, following a few moments later.

11

Two Encounters

"BANTIARNA, a moment . . ."
    The voice came from behind Jenna, low and gravelly. Startled, Jenna turned. The man was brown-haired with a longish beard, and she found his age difficult to discern—he could have been as young as Coelin or nearer to thirty. His face was drawn and thin, his skin brown from the sun; his strangely light green eyes nested deep under his brows, glinting in the light of the fire. His clothing was plain, but more like that of a freelander than the Taisteal, and Jenna saw a bone-handled knife in its scabbard at his belt. His appearance was that of someone used to a life of labor, his body toughened and scarred by what it had experienced. He stopped a few feet away from her, as if he realized that she would shout for Mac Ard if he came closer. She moved a few steps toward the ring of light from the campfire.

"What do you want?" Jenna asked coldly.

"Nothing that will trouble you," he said. "A minute's conversation, that's all." When Jenna remained silent, he continued. "My name is Ennis O'Deoradháin. I'm not with the Taisteal; I have land nearby and happened to come here to see if the Taisteal had anything interesting to sell— my father was born here and also died here, several years ago. But in his youth, he wandered, and went to the west as a fisherman and came to the north. He married a woman there, and brought her back to Lough Lár."

"What has that to do with me?"

"My mam—may the Mother-Creator keep her soul safe—was an Inishlander. They say I'm more like her than my father. In some ways, I think that's true. They say one Inishlander knows another. Maybe that's true as well, or maybe the mage-lights have just sparked something in me that was dormant all this time." He stopped, staring at her.

"I'm from . . ." *Ballintubber,* she started to say, then realized that might not be something to admit either. ". . . Lár Bhaile," she said. "Not Inish Thuaidh."

O'Deoradháin nodded, though his eyes seemed unconvinced. "Mam always said that I had a weirding in me. She also told me that one of our ancestors was a cloudmage, and wielded a cloch na thintrí under Severii O'Coulghan in the Battle of Sliabh Míchinniúint. Of course, one never knows about family history that far back and to tell the truth it's a rare Inishlander family that *doesn't* claim a cloudmage or three among their ancestors, true or not. If all the stories are to be believed, the land must have been ankle-deep in clochs na thintrí."

With the mention of the mage-stones, Jenna's hand went to her waist, where her own stone was hidden. She immediately let her hand drop back to her side, but the man's eyes had followed her involuntary gesture. He almost seemed to smile.

"Your arm—you've hurt it." He nodded at the bandages wrapped around her arm; it seemed to throb in response.

"It's nothing," she said. "A cut, that's all."

"Ah." He nodded again. He glanced over his shoulder, as if making certain no one was close enough to overhear them. "One wonders," O'Deoradháin mused, "where Lámh Shábhála will be found if the Filleadh has really come, since the eldest cloch was taken from the Order of Inishfeirm and could be anywhere in Talamh an Ghlas by now. But then, you probably realize that already, since Clannhri Sheehan tells me that you're a Mac Ard. After all, your ancestors were once cloudmages themselves. I'm not surprised to see a Mac Ard on the road where the mage-lights have been seen. Not at all."

Jenna wanted to be away from the man, wanted to be alone, wanted to take the cloch out and hold it, wanted to

throw it away and never see it again. She'd understood little
of what he'd said—all that prattling about "Inishfeirm" and
some Order, but he spoke of "Lámh Shábhála," the same
name Riata had used . . . "You've had your minute, Ennis
O'Deoradháin, and I'm tired."

"True, I've had the minute, and more, and I've spoken
honestly about things that I probably shouldn't, out here
in the open." The man's left hand moved close to the hilt
of his knife, and Jenna wondered how quickly someone
would get to her if she screamed. Not soon enough, she
feared, if O'Deoradháin was skilled with his weapon. Her
bandaged hand went again to the stone; she could feel its
chill under the cloth, and her heart was pounding in her
chest. If she brought the cloch out, if she could use it as
she had with the men from Connachta . . .

But O'Deoradháin only smiled, gave a short bow, and
turned to walk back toward the fire. For a moment, Jenna
wondered whether she should follow and tell Mac Ard and
her mam what had just happened. But she couldn't make
herself go that way, not after what the man had said to her.

Instead, she went to her tent, half-running. Her arm
throbbed and burned, and she boiled water over the tiny
cook fire inside and made herself another cup of the andúilleaf tea.

The next morning, it was easy to forget the encounter.
Maeve was there in the tent, sleeping alongside Jenna—she
had wondered, after their conversation, if Maeve might stay
in the tiarna's tent that night. Jenna's arm still ached, and
she heated another cup of the brew to take away the hurt
before her mam rewrapped the arm with fresh bandages.
Outside, a warm, late autumn sun was shining, O'Deoradháin was nowhere to be seen, and they found that Mac Ard
had haggled with Clannhri Sheehan for the purchase of
three of the Taisteal's horses. They looked old and slow,
but a better prospect than walking the rest of the way to
Áth Iseal. By the time the sun was well up in the sky, the
Taisteal had packed away the tents into the wagons and
were jangling and plodding south along the road while

Jenna, Maeve, and Mac Ard rode north toward the ford of the Duán.

They moved through a landscape of green: farmland mostly, with occasional patches of wood. The High Road meandered, following the line of Lough Lár closely. Not long after they'd left, as they rounded a bend in the road, they heard hooves and the nickering of a horse coming up from an intersecting lane; a moment later, a rider came into view between a line of beech trees, a man wearing a plain clóca over pants and shirt. The hood of the clóca was up; the face in shadow. The man waved at them, then kicked his horse into a trot to meet them.

"Greetings, Tiarna Mac Ard, Bantiarnas. A beautiful morning. We seem to be going in the same direction, if Áth Iseal is your destination. May I join you? With brigands on the road, four is safer than one." He pushed back the hood, and Jenna saw that it was Ennis O'Deoradháin. His eyes glittered as he glanced toward her, but he kept his attention on Mac Ard, who frowned.

"It isn't brigands I particularly fear," he answered. "You have the advantage of me, since you seem to know me but your face isn't familiar."

"My name is Ennis O'Deoradháin." He gestured to the fields on either side of him. "This is my family's land. Not much, but enough to keep us fed. We're three generations freelanded, loyal to the Rí Gabair, and the name O'Deoradháin is well known around the west of the lough. And I know you because I was at the Taisteal's camp last night seeing if they had anything useful, and Clannhrí Sheehan has a mouth large enough to swallow all of Lough Lár itself." He smiled and laughed at his own jest, and the harsh lines of his face relaxed in his amusement. "And if it allays your fears, I'm hardly a threat to you, Tiarna. I doubt my knife is a match for your sword." O'Deoradháin swept his clóca aside, showing them that the only weapon he wore was the knife Jenna had seen the night before.

"In my experience, a knife kills as easily as any weapon," Mac Ard told the man, but his voice was easier. "But a freelanded man loyal to the Rí shouldn't be left alone to brigands, and the High Road's open to all, if you'd like to ride with us."

Jenna could have spoken. She saw O'Deoradháin's gaze flick toward her again, and she set her mouth in a firm, thin line of disapproval. Yet she held back. O'Deoradháin flicked the reins, and his horse moved out onto the road. For a time, he rode alongside Mac Ard, and Maeve, and they conversed in low voices. Then O'Deoradháin dropped back to where Jenna trailed behind. "And how are you today?" he asked. "Is the arm better?"

"It's fine," Jenna answered shortly. She didn't look at him, keeping her gaze forward to the road winding along the lakeshore. Lough Lár was narrowing, now no more than a few hundred strides across as they neared the falls of the Duán.

"So it seems you didn't mention our encounter last night to the tiarna."

"I didn't think it that important. I'd forgotten it myself until I saw you this morning." She answered him with the haughtiness she thought a Riocha would display. Now she did look over at him, and found him watching her with a strange smile on his lips. "Interesting that you'd happen to be going to Áth Iseal today, and at the same time."

"What would you think if I told you that wasn't entirely coincidence?"

"I'd wonder if I should make up for my error last night and tell Tiarna Mac Ard."

" 'Tiarna Mac Ard?' An awfully formal way to refer to your father," O'Deoradháin commented. Her face must have shown something at that, for he lifted his eyebrows. "Ah . . . I see I've been mistaken. Evidently Clannhri Sheehan didn't know as much as he pretended he did. You never can trust the Taisteal. I thought . . ."

"I don't care what you thought."

"This does shed a different light on things, though, I must say," O'Deoradháin persisted. "What is your name, then?"

She remembered that Mac Ard had commented on their name being Inish, and that O'Deoradháin had suggested that he thought her an Inishlander as well. She considered giving him a false name, but it didn't seem to matter now. Her mam would probably tell him, if he asked, or Mac Ard. "Aoire," she said. "Jenna Aoire."

The startled look on his face surprised her with its severity. For a moment, his eyes widened, and he seemed almost to rise up in his saddle. Then he caught himself, his features masked in deliberate neutrality. "Aoire. That's an Inish name, 'tis. So my guess wasn't so wrong after all."

"Aye," she admitted. "My father's parents were from the island, or so he claimed, though Mam says that they left the island when they were young."

O'Deoradháin's head nodded reflectively. "No doubt," he said. "No doubt." He shifted in the saddle, adjusted his clóca. "We should be in Áth Iseal by midafternoon," he said. "We'll be passing the falls in a bit; they're not as pretty this time of year without all the green, but they'll be impressive enough if you've never seen them before." It was obvious that he intended to change the subject, and Jenna was content to allow that to happen.

They heard the falls long before they saw them. Here, the High Road lifted in short, winding rises up a low series of hills, until they stood well above the level of Lough Lár. Away to the south stretched the dark waters of the lough; to the north, the road was hidden behind yet another set of low hills. Westward stretched checkered patches of farmland, meadow, and woods, and beyond that, like a green wall, was the forest of Doire Coill, lurking on the horizon.

A trail ran away from the High Road to a ledge overlooking the falls, and Mac Ard turned his horse in. "We've made good time this morning, and there's not a better day to see the falls," he said. "We'll eat here." As Mac Ard rummaged in the saddlebags for the food, Jenna and her mam walked to the end of the ledge, where the land fell off steeply toward the lough, so that they were looking down at the tops of the trees below. Ahead and to their left, the River Duán splashed and roared as it spilled down a deep cleft in the green hills, cascading white and foaming to the lake below while a white mist rose around the waters. The sunlight sparked rainbows in the mist that wavered, gleamed, and disappeared again. "Ah, Mam, 'tis beautiful," Jenna breathed. The wind sent a tendril of mist across her face, and she laughed in shock and surprise. "And wet."

"And dangerous, if you get too near the edge." O'Deoradháin spoke, coming up next to them. He pointed down toward the lake. "Not two months ago, they brought up a man from Áth Iseal who slipped over the edge and went tumbling down to his death. He was looking at the falls and not his feet, unfortunately."

Both Jenna and Maeve took a step back. "The mist has a way of enchanting, they say," O'Deoradháin continued. "The Duán weeps in sorrow here."

"Why in sorrow?" Jenna asked, interested despite herself.

" 'Twas here, they say, well back in the Before, that an army out of Inish Thuaidh met with the forces of the Rí of what was then the kingdom of Bhaile; Rí Aodhfin, I think his name was. The river ran red with blood that day, the stain washing pink on the shores of the lough itself, and the skies above were bright with the lightnings of the clochs na thintrí. Lámh Shábhála itself was here, held by an Inishlander cloudmage whose name is lost to the people around here."

The name of the cloch made Jenna narrow her eyes in suspicion, and she thought she felt the hidden stone pulse in response. *Aye* . . . The voice, a whisper, sounded in Jenna's head. *Eilís, I was* . . . "Eilís," Jenna said, speaking the name. "That was the Holder's name. Eilís."

O'Deoradháin raised an eyebrow. "Perhaps. It's as good a name as any, I suppose. You know this story, then?"

"No," Jenna answered, then shook her head. The voice was gone, and Jenna wondered whether she'd actually heard it, or if she imagined it in the sound of the falls. Maeve was looking at her curiously, as well. "Maybe I heard it at Tara's one night. One of Coelin's songs—he was always singing about battles and romances from other times."

O'Deoradháin shrugged. "Whatever the name, Aodhfin wrested Lámh Shábhála away from the Inishlander cloudmage during the midst of battle; then, for two hun-

dred and fifty years, Lámh Shábhála was held here in Talamh an Ghlas. They say that the mist of the falls is the
tears of the cloudmage who lost Lámh Shábhála, and that's
why it's dangerous. He, or she," he added with a glance at
Jenna, who was watching the water spilling down the ravine, "still seeks revenge for the loss."

"That's a pretty tale," Maeve said. "And an old one."

"This is an old place," O'Deoradháin answered. He gestured straight out from the ledge. "They say that back when
the first people came here to the lough, the falls were out
here. But the river's hungry, and it eats away a few feet of
the cliffs every year and so the lough keeps growing at this
end. One day, thousands and thousands of years from now,
the falls will be all the way back to Áth Iseal. We look at
the land, and from our perspective, it all seems eternal: the
mountains, the rivers, the lakes—they are there at our
birth, and there looking the same at our death. But the
stones themselves see that everything is always changing,
and barely see us or our battles and legends at all. We're
just ghosts and wisps of fog to them."

"Ah, you have a poet in you," Maeve said. " 'Tis well
said."

O'Deoradháin touched his forehead, smiling at Maeve.
"Thank you, Bantiarna. It's my mam's gift. She had a wonderful way with tales, especially those from the north. She
was from Inish Thuaidh, as I told your daughter."

Jenna refused to look back at him. "An Inishlander?"
Maeve said. "So was my late husband—or his parents were
from there, anyway. But he wasn't one for stories, I'm
afraid. He didn't speak much about his family or the island.
I don't think he'd ever been there himself."

"Perhaps not, but I've heard the name Aoire before, in
some of the tales my mam used to tell me." He seemed as
though he were about to say more and Jenna looked away
from the falls toward him, but Mac Ard came striding up,
and O'Deoradháin went silent at the tiarna's approach.

"I have our lunch unpacked," Mac Ard said. "We could
bring it out here, and eat while watching the scenery."

"That sounds lovely," Maeve said. "Excuse me. We'll go
help Padraic. Jenna?"

"Coming, Mam." She turned away from the falls, catching O'Deoradháin's gaze as she did so. "What is it you want?" she asked him, as her mam walked away.

O'Deoradháin shrugged. "Probably the same thing you want. Maybe the same thing you've already found." He nodded to her and smiled.

She grimaced sourly in return, and followed her mother.

12

The Lady of the Falls

THEY finished their lunch, and lay in the soft grass under a surprisingly warm sun. Jenna's arm was starting to throb again with pain, and she stood up. "I'll be right back," she said. "I'd like to take a walk."

"I'll go with you," O'Deoradháin offered, and Jenna shook her head.

"No," she said firmly. "I'd prefer to go alone. Mam, do you mind?"

"Go on," Maeve told her. "Don't be long."

"I won't be." Jenna walked away north, around the curve of the cliffs toward the falls. As she approached, the clamor of the cascading water grew steadily louder, until it drowned any other sound in white noise. Greenery hung over the edge of the ravine so that it was difficult to tell where the ground ended, and the mist dusted Jenna's hair and clothes with sparkling droplets. She moved as close to the edge as she dared. Foaming water rushed past below her, spilling down to the lough. With the touch of the mist, she thought she heard faint voices, as if hidden in the roar of the falls was a distant, whispering conversation.

At the same time, her right arm began to feel cold and heavy under the bandages, and the cloch na thintrí snuggled next to her skin flared into bitter ice. Jenna stopped, rubbing at her arm and flexing her suddenly stiff fingers, moaning slightly at the renewed pain. She started to turn back, thinking that she would fix herself more of the nasty-tasting andúilleaf, but stopped, blinking against the mist. There,

119

just ahead of her, was a break in the greenery, a narrow trail leading down toward the Duán right where it plunged over the cliff edge. She wondered how she could have missed seeing it before.

Follow . . . she thought she heard the water-voices say. *Follow* . . .

She took a tentative step forward, steadying herself against the bushes to either side. The path was steep and ill-defined, the grass underfoot slick and only slightly shorter than anywhere else, as if the trail were nearly forgotten. Once she slipped and fell several feet before she could stop herself. She almost turned back then, but just below, the path seemed to level out, curving enticingly behind a screen of scrub hawthorns. *Follow* . . . The voices were louder now, almost audible.

She followed.

Around the hawthorns, she found herself on a ledge below the lip of the falls. Water thundered in front of her, foaming and snarling as it thrashed its way over black, mossy rocks. The ledge continued around, cutting underneath the overhanging rocks at the top of the waterfall and disappearing into darkness behind the water.

Follow . . . Her arm ached, the stone burned her skin with cold. Her hair and clothes, soaked by the mists, clung to her face and body. She should go back, she knew. This was insanity—one slip, and her body would be broken on the rocks a hundred feet below.

Follow . . .

But there were handholds along the cliff wall, looking as if they'd been deliberately cut, and though the ledge was crumbling at the edges, the flags appeared to have once been laid by someone's hands. She took a step, then another, clinging to the dripping wall as the water pounded a few feet in front of her.

Then she was behind the falls, and the ledge opened up. Jenna gasped in wonder. She was looking through the shimmering veil of water, and the falls caught the sunlight and shattered it, sending light dancing all around her. The air was cool and refreshing; the sound of the falls was muffled here, a constant low grumbling that seemed to emanate

from the earth itself. The rock underfoot trembled with the
sound. As her eyes grew accustomed to the twilight behind
the falling water, Jenna saw that the ledge on which she
stood opened up behind her, sloping down and into the
cliff wall: a small, hidden cave. Something gleamed well
back in the recess, and Jenna moved toward it, squinting
into the dimness.

And she stopped, holding her breath. In a stony niche
carved from the living rock of the cliff, a skeleton lay, its
empty-socketed eyes staring at Jenna. The body had once
been richly dressed—a woman, adorned with the remnants
of brocaded green silk, with glistening threads of silver and
gold embroidered along the edging. The arms were laid
carefully along her sides, and under her head was a pillow,
the stuffing spilling out from rotting blue cloth, a few
strands of golden hair curling below the skull. Rings hung
loose on the bones of her fingers; jeweled earrings had
fallen to the stone alongside the skull.

*You look on the remains of Eilís MacGairbhith of Inish
Thuaidh, and I was once the Holder of Lámh Shábhála, as
you are now. . . .*

The voice was as liquid as the falls, and it sounded inside
her head. Jenna stepped back, her hands to her mouth,
until she felt the roar of the water at her back. "No," she
said aloud. "Be quiet. I don't hear you."

A laugh answered her. The skeleton stared. *Take one of
my rings,* the voice said. *Place it on your own finger . . .*

"No. I can't."

You must . . . The voice was a bare whisper, fading into
wind and the falls' louder voice. For a moment, Jenna
thought it had gone entirely, then it returned, a husk. . . .
please . . . one of the rings . . .

Her hand trembling, Jenna stepped toward the body
again and reached out to the hands crossed over the breast.
She touched the nearest ring, gasping, then pulled back as
the golden band wobbled on the bones. Taking a breath, she
reached out again, and this time pulled the ring from the
unresisting hand. She held it in her fingers, turning it: the
ring was heavy gold, inset with small emerald stones, fili-
greed and decorated with knotted rope patterns—an un-

common piece of jewelry, crafted by a master. The ring of someone who was once wealthy or well-rewarded.

She put the ring on her own finger.

At first nothing changed. Then Jenna realized that the hollow seemed brighter, that she could see as if it were full day. A bright fog filled the recess and the sound of the falls receded and died to nothing.

A woman, clad in the green silk that the skeleton had worn, stepped through the mist toward Jenna.

Her hair was long and golden-red like bright, burnished copper, and her skin was fair. Her eyes were summer blue, and she smiled as she came forward, her hands held out to Jenna. The sleeves left her arms bare, and Jenna saw that her right hand was scarred and marked to the elbow with swirling patterns, patterns that matched those on Jenna's own hand and arm.

On one of her fingers sat the same ring Jenna wore.

"Eilís," Jenna breathed, and the woman laughed.

"Aye," she said. "That was once my name. So you're the new Holder, and so young to be a First. That's a pity." Her hand touched Jenna's, and with the touch, Jenna felt a touch in her head as well, as if somehow Eilís were prowling in her thoughts. "Ah . . . Jenna, is it? And you've met Riata."

Jenna nodded. "How . . . ?" she began.

"You are the Holder," Eilís said again. "This is just one of the gifts and dangers that Lámh Shábhála bestows: the Holders before you—we who held Lámh Shábhála while it was awake and perhaps even some of those who held it while it slept—live within the stone also." Jenna remembered the red-haired man she'd glimpsed when she first picked up the stone. Had he been a Holder, once? "At least," Eilís continued, "some shade of us does. Come to where a Holder's body rests, or touch something that was once theirs, and they can speak with you if you will it. They will also know what is in your mind, if you allow it to be open. Tell me, when you met Riata, did he give you a token?"

Jenna shook her head. "No. He only spoke to me."

Eilís nodded at that, as if it were the answer she expected. "I met him, too. Riata prefers to be left alone in death. He knows that should you need him again, you can find him in the stone or go to where he rests. I went there once, myself. That's how I came to know him—a wise man, wiser than most of us Daoine believed possible of a Bunús Muintir. We're an arrogant people . . ." She seemed to sigh, then, and looked past Jenna as if into some hazy distance. "He told me I would die, if I followed my heart. I didn't believe him." Another sigh, and her attention came back to Jenna. "You will meet the shades of other Holders, inevitably, especially if you go to Lár Bhaile as you intend. And I'll warn you; some you will not like and they will not like you. Some will smile and seem fair, but their advice will be as rotten as their hearts. The dead, you see, are not always sane." She smiled as she said that, a strange expression on her face. "Be careful."

"Why didn't Riata tell me this?" Jenna asked. "There's so much I need to know."

"If he told you all, you would have despaired," Eilís answered. "You're new to Lámh Shábhála, and you are a First besides." She shuddered. "I wouldn't have wanted to be a First."

"Riata . . . he said that the stone was a curse, especially for the First."

"He was right."

Jenna shuddered. "That scares me, the way you say the words."

Her gaze was calm. "Then you're wise."

"Is the cloch evil, then?"

Eilís laughed, a sound like trickling water. "Lámh Shábhála—or any of the clochs na thintrí, for that matter— don't know good or evil, child. They simply *are*. They give power, and power can be put to whatever use a Holder wishes. Lámh Shábhála is First and Last, and so the power it can lend is also greatest. As to evil . . ." A smile. "You bring to the stone what you have inside you, that's all. In any case, evil depends on which side you stand—what one person calls evil, another calls justice. Let me see it," she said. "Let me see Lámh Shábhála again."

Jenna felt reluctant. She shook her head, the barest motion, and Eilís frowned, taking a step forward. "I mean you no harm, Jenna," she said. "Let me see the cloch I once wielded myself."

Jenna felt for the stone, closing her fingers around it through the cloth that hid it. "If Lámh Shábhála has the greatest power of all the clochs, how was it taken from you?"

Eilís' laugh was bitter now. "I said its power was greatest, but even the strongest can be overpowered by numbers or make a fatal mistake. Lámh Shábhála is chief among the Clochs Mór, the major clochs, but there are others that are nearly as powerful. Three of the Clochs Mór were arrayed against me, and I was isolated. Betrayed by . . ." She scowled, her face harsh. ". . . my own stupidity. By listening to my heart, as Riata said it would be. And so I died. *He* laid me here, the new Holder, the one who had betrayed me: Aodhfin Ó Liathain. My lover. He placed me here after he killed me and took Lámh Shábhála for himself. He kissed my cold lips with tears in his eyes. If you should happen to meet him through the cloch, tell him that I still curse his name and the night I first gave myself to him." Another step, and Eilís' hand reached out toward Jenna. "My cloch. Let me see it once more."

Shaking her head, Jenna backed up again. She wasn't certain why she felt this reluctance—perhaps the harsh eagerness in Eilís' features, or the way she had referred to the stone as hers. But Jenna felt a compulsion to keep the stone hidden—too many people had asked to see it already. Eilís took another step closer, and again Jenna retreated. There was a strange yet familiar roaring behind her. She glanced quickly over her shoulder, but there was nothing there, only the white-lit, ethereal fog. She could feel Eilís touching her memories again, and she tried to close her mind to the intrusion. The ghost laughed at her effort. "You're indeed young and unpracticed," she said. "So much to learn . . ." Her voice was honey and perfume. "I know your mind. You showed Riata the stone, didn't you? And Seancoim and that tiarna with you. Why not me?"

Jenna, reluctantly, reached beneath her clothing and pulled out the stone. "Here," she said to Eilís. "Here it is."

Eilís stared at the cloch, a hand at her breast as if she were having difficulty breathing. "Aye," she whispered. "That is Lámh Shábhála. And you don't know yet how to use it."

Jenna shook her head. "No. Can you tell me?"

"I can't," she answered, but then her eyes narrowed. "Or perhaps I can. Let me hold it. Give it to me . . ." She stretched her arm out.

"No." Jenna closed her fingers around the cloch, fisting it in her right hand.

"Give it to me . . ." Eilís said again. Her hand came closer, and Jenna took a final step backward.

Cold water hammered at Jenna's head and shoulders, driving her backward. The falls tore her away from the ledge and bore her under even as she screamed. She felt herself flung downward with the water, and she knew she was dead.

In that instant, the cloch burned in her hand, and she felt it open to her, as if she became part of the stone itself, her mind whirling with the patterns on her hand, with the identical patterns of the cloch, with the energy locked within it borrowed from the mage-lights. This was different than when she had unleashed lightning on Knobtop or when she had killed the soldiers. Then, there had been no conscious thought involved. This time, she felt herself will the cloch to release its energy, and it answered. The water of the Duán still pounded at her, unrelenting and merciless, but she was no longer falling . . .

Now you know . . . Eilís' voice whispered in her head.

Now you know . . .

Somehow, impossibly, Jenna was standing on the grass above the falls, in the sunlight. The cloch was no longer in her hand. There was no ring on her finger. She felt at the waist of her skirt: there it was, the familiar lump of cloch, and circular hardness alongside it: Eilís' ring.

Someone was crying, weeping in pain, and she realized it was her.

"Jenna! There you are! We've been calling . . . By the Mother-Creator, girl, you're soaked through! What's the matter?" Maeve came running up to her. Jenna sank into her embrace.

"My arm . . ." she cried. "It hurts so much, Mam." Sharp, red agony stabbed at her, radiating from her hand downward and into her chest. She shivered with cold, the wind biting at her drenched clothing. Her vision was colored with it, like a veil over her eyes. With Jenna leaning against her mother, they moved down away from the falls. As they turned, Jenna glanced down.

The falls flared white as the water cascaded over the edge of the ravine, and the mist touched her face like tears.

13

Smoke and Ruin

A STRIPE later, new wrappings with Seancoim's poultice slathered on the cloth and a mug of the andúilleaf brew had dulled the pain enough so that Jenna could ride. The wan fall sun had dried her clothes somewhat. She told the others that she'd slipped and fallen on the arm—the story appeared to satisfy them, and if she seemed wetter than the mist alone could have managed, no one mentioned the fact.

It was nearing midafternoon when they returned to the High Road. "A long lunch," Mac Ard said worriedly when they finally were riding north again. "It will be dark before we reach the ford at this rate. We still may not reach Áth Iseal tonight."

Jenna was silent on the ride. Again Mac Ard and Maeve rode together, and O'Deoradháin remained behind with Jenna, but his attempts to draw her into conversation failed. In truth, she barely heard him or saw the landscape as they approached the ford of the Duán. She held the reins of the horse loosely in her left hand, trusting the mare to keep to the road, and stared down at her bandaged arm, letting the fingers stretch and close, stretch and close. She traced the patterns of the scars with her gaze, feeling them even though they were hidden under folds of cotton.

Her thoughts were on Lámh Shábhála. The other times she had tapped the stone's power, she had felt no control of the process. But now . . . Even without holding the stone, she could touch it with her mind, as if she and the cloch were linked. She could place her thoughts there and imagine herself sinking into the unguessed depths of the cloch. She could see power flaring between the crystalline structures within the stone, and she could direct that force: she could send it flaring outward and control where it went, what it touched, what it did.

And she could see, at the center of the stone, a hidden well of another power, one that was as yet half-filled, and when she looked there with her mind, she could feel gossamer, invisible threads running away from Lámh Shábhála into the world. At the end of those threads, she knew, lay the other clochs na thintrí, the stones of lightning, waiting for Lámh Shábhála to restore their power.

She could not imagine how she would handle that huge reservoir, if the energy that already ran through Lámh Shábhála hurt her so much already. At the same time, she knew that she could not throw the stone away or give it to someone else. Lámh Shábhála wouldn't allow that. She would not allow it. Even contemplating that action made her arm throb through the veil of andúilleaf. She had opened the stone, but Lámh Shábhála had also opened her.

She could no more easily abandon the cloch now than she could discard her heart.

"I don't know how Tiarna Mac Ard feels," she heard O'Deoradháin saying though her musings, "but I don't like this. There's been no one on the road with us all day. The west isn't as well traveled as the east side of the lough, but still we should have seen a few others by now. Actually, I was surprised no other travelers stopped at the falls in all the time we were there."

Jenna nodded. She might have glanced at him, but Lámh Shábhála overlaid the sight. He may have continued to talk, but she was lost inside the stone, peering at its secrets.

By evening, with the sun sending long shadows eastward as it touched the treetops, they approached a crossroads where the lough road met with the High Road traveling up to Ballintubber and crossing over to the Duán. On either side of the road, oak trees overhung the stone fences; to the west, the outskirts of Doire Coill huddled close by across an overgrown field. Mac Ard suddenly pulled back on his reins to bring his horse to a halt, standing up in the stirrups and peering around them. "Can you smell that?" he asked.

The question brought Jenna out of her reverie. She sniffed, and the smell brought with it unpleasant memories. "Woodsmoke," she said, then frowned. "And something more."

"Too much woodsmoke," Mac Ard commented. "And an awful reek within it. I was past here a dozen days ago, on my way to Ballintubber. Where the roads meet there was a tiny village: a tavern and three or four houses." His face was touched with worry as he looked back over his shoulder. "And I share your concern about the quiet on the road, O'Deoradháin. I think we should ride carefully and slowly, and keep an eye about us. Jenna—"

Jenna started at the sound of her name. "Aye, Tiarna?"

"You should be most careful of all." His dark gaze held her, moving from her face to her arm. "I think you understand my meaning."

She closed her fingers around the hidden cloch. "I do, Tiarna."

A nod. "O'Deoradháin, you and I should ride ahead, I think."

They rode on, Mac Ard and O'Deoradháin several feet ahead of them. Jenna noticed that the tiarna swept his clóca back away from the hilt of his sword and that she could also see the leather-wrapped hilt of O'Deoradháin's knife. Alert now, they approached the crossing. The aroma of smoke hung in the air, and the odd scent underlying it grew stronger. The walls on either side of the road spread out suddenly, and in the clear space ahead of them, she could see a cluster of buildings. In the twilight, they seemed wrapped in a strange, dark fog, then she realized that the structures were roofless, the windows and doors gaping open like dead mouths, and that the fog was tendrils of smoke from still-smoldering timbers.

The scene was eerily deserted. No people moved in the midst of the rubble, no birds, no dogs. Nothing.

She also knew, then, what the other odor must be, and she swallowed hard. "The fires were set a day ago or more, by the look," Mac Ard said, almost whispering. His face

was grim. None of them wanted to speak loudly here; it
seemed disrespectful. "That worries me—I didn't think the
Connachtans would stay this long, or be so bold as to strike
this close to Áth Iseal with its garrison. Those who lived
here no doubt fled, the ones who weren't killed, but why
they haven't returned by now is what worries me more."

"Tuath Connachta, was it?" O'Deoradháin asked. "You
speak as if you've met them, Tiarna. Are the Tuatha at
war?"

Mac Ard glanced back at O'Deoradháin but didn't answer. "Let's see what we can learn here. Carefully . . ."

They moved closer to the ruins. Jenna could see now
that all that was left of the houses were the tumbled-down
stone walls, blacked with smoke. A few fire-blistered timbers leaned forlornly, with wisps of gray smoke lifting from
them. The ground was littered with broken crockery and
scraps of cloth, as if the village had been torn apart before
the fires were set. As if, Jenna realized, the attackers had
been looking for someone or something. There were no
signs of the residents of this place, though Jenna saw dark
shapes within walls of the houses that made her look away.

Mac Ard reined up his horse before the ruins of the
largest building—the inn, Jenna decided. He walked carefully over the stones and timbers, his boots crunching
through the wreckage and sending plumes of ash up with
each step. Once, he stopped and bent down, then came
back out.

"There are two dead in there," he said. "Maybe a few
more that I can't see. Some, perhaps most, I hope, ran
before the fire and are still alive." He looked around.
"There's nothing we can do here. I'll feel safer once we
reach Áth Iseal."

"If it hasn't been attacked as well," O'Deoradháin replied but Mac Ard shook his head.

"There weren't that many here, by the signs. A dozen,
perhaps a few more. This is the work of marauders, not
an army."

As Mac Ard spoke, Jenna closed her eyes for a moment.
The cloch burned in the darkness behind her eyes, and she
could see the webs of connection to the other clochs na

thintrí. One of those connections, she suddenly realized, snaked over to Mac Ard, and another . . .

She opened her eyes. Against the ruddy western sky, on a bare knife-edged ridge half a mile away, she could see a rider. "Tiarna," she said, pointing, and as Mac Ard turned to look, the rider turned his horse and vanished. A faint voice called in the distance, and others answered. Mac Ard muttered a curse and mounted.

"Ride!" he cried. "And let's hope that the crossing is still open."

They urged their horses into a gallop in the growing dark, moving quickly while they could still somewhat see the road ahead of them. At the juncture of the roads, they turned east toward the river, a few miles ahead. Jenna kept looking back over her shoulder at the road behind, expecting to see riders coming hard after them, but for the moment the lane remained empty. As they left the village, the walls closed in again to border the road, and they moved into a wooded area. There, night already lurked under the trees, and they had to slow the horses to a trot or risk being thrown by an unseen root or hole. By the time they'd emerged from the trees, the sun had failed entirely, the first stars emerging in the east. The waxing moon—now nearly at a quarter—lifted high above the west and painted the road as it swept down in a great curve over low, flat lands. Far ahead, a row of trees ran nearly north to south across their way, marking the line of the river, which sparkled just beyond. Across the Duán, the road lifted again; on the banks of the hills beyond, yellow light gleamed in the windows at Áth Iseal.

And between the four of them and the river stood three horsemen, moonlight glinting from ring mail leathers laced over their tunics. They didn't appear to see Jenna and the others yet, against the cover of the trees. Behind, from the direction of the village, Jenna could hear hooves pounding and men calling.

Mac Ard pulled his horse up "Trapped," he said, "and it's no good cutting across the field when the ford is ahead. Jenna?" Mac Ard looked back at her. "Can you . . . ?" He didn't finish the question, but Jenna understood. Wanly, she shook her head. Her arm already hung cold and heavy; she could not imagine what it would feel like to use the cloch again so soon. "These are the same people who killed the people in your village, who killed people you know, who burned your house and ran down your dog," Mac Ard reminded her, and Jenna lifted her head.

"If I must," she said wearily. She reached for the cloch, but Mac Ard stopped her hand.

"Not yet. If we can cut the odds down somewhat, we may not need to reveal what we have. O'Deoradháin, it's time to see how useful that knife of yours is. Maeve, Jenna, as soon as we have them engaged, ride on past. Go off the road around them if you need to. We'll follow as soon as we can. Now, let's see what we can do before they realize we're here."

He reached back and pulled the bow from the pack slung behind his saddle. Hooking a leg over one end of the weapon, he bent the bow and strung it, then nocked an arrow in the string. "I'm not much of a bowman but a rider's a large target."

He drew the bowstring back and let the arrow fly. Jenna tried to follow its flight but lost it in the darkness. But there was a cry from the riders, though no one fell. She could see them looking around, then one of them pointed toward the group and they came charging up the road toward them. Mac Ard nocked another arrow, letting them approach as he held the bow at full tension. Jenna could see muscles trembling in his arm. Then he let it fly, and one of the horses screamed and went down, the rider tumbling to the ground as the other two rushed past. "Now!" Mac Ard shouted, tossing the bow aside and drawing his sword. He kicked his horse into a gallop. "Ride for the ford!"

Maeve and Jenna both urged their horses to follow, but as Jenna kicked the mare's sides, O'Deoradháin's hand reached out and grabbed her reins. Mac Ard was already flying down the road with sword raised and a loud cry that they must have heard in Áth Iseal. Maeve's horse was close behind. "Let me go!" Jenna cried. Her horse reared, but O'Deoradháin held fast. Jenna tried to wrench the reins away from him, and reached for the stone, a fury rising in her.

"Wait!" he said. "It's important—"

"Let go!" she shouted again. Maeve had realized that Jenna hadn't followed and was stopped in the middle of the road between Jenna and Mac Ard. Jenna heard the clash of steel as Mac Ard and the riders met. O'Deoradháin continued to hold her. Jenna's fist closed around the cloch.

Her arm was ice and flame. Lámh Shábhála seemed to roar in her ears with anger as she brought it out. "Get away!" she screamed at O'Deoradháin, and at the same time, she opened the cloch in her mind, releasing just a trickle of its power. Light flared from between the closed fingers of her right hand, and a jagged beam shot from her hand to smash against O'Deoradháin, lifting him out of his saddle and throwing him against the fieldstone wall. He slumped down, but Jenna didn't stop to see what had happened to him. She was free, and Lámh Shábhála threw shimmering brilliance over her, as if she were enveloped in daylight. "Ride!" she called to her mam, and kicked her own horse forward.

Ahead, Mac Ard fought, but he was in desperate trouble without O'Deoradháin, the two horsemen flanking him. Jenna saw him take a blow to his sword arm, and his weapon went clattering to the ground. She clenched Lámh Shábhála tighter, lifting her hand. "No!" she screamed as swords were raised against Mac Ard, now weaponless and injured.

She imagined lightning striking the two riders. She visualized savage light darting from cloch to riders.

It happened.

Twin lightnings flared in searing lines from her fisted hand, slicing around Maeve and Mac Ard without touching them. The riders' swords shattered, molten shards exploding in bright arcs as hilts were torn from gloved hands and flung away. The lightning curled around the riders, lifting them in a snarling coil of blue-white and hurling them a hundred feet into the fields as their horses screamed and fled.

Behind them, there were shouts of alarm. Jenna turned.
Four more riders had come from under the trees. Jenna
waved her hand, and the earth exploded at their feet, a
line of bright fireworks erupting before them as horses
reared and bucked. The riders turned and fled back the
way they'd come. Jenna saw O'Deoradháin, back on his
horse, riding wildly south across the fields and away.

She let him go. The angry glare faded in her hand, and
Jenna screamed, this time with her own pain, as every muscle in her right arm seemed to lock and twist. She bent
over in her saddle, fighting to stay conscious. *You can do
it. Breathe. Keep breathing. You can't stop the pain, no, but
put it to one side* . . . The voice inside didn't seem be hers.
Riata? She fought the inner night that threatened to close
around her, pushed it away, and forced herself to sit up in
the saddle. She rode to her mother. "Mam, are you all
right?"

Maeve nodded, mute. Her eyes were wide and almost
timid as she stared at her daughter. "Jenna . . ." she
breathed, but Jenna shook her head. Cradling her right arm
in her lap, she flicked the reins with her left hand, going
to Mac Ard. He was standing, his sword now held in his
left hand, the point dragging on the ground, a spreading
pool of dark wetness soaking his clóca at the right arm.
Another cut spread a fan of blood across his forehead.

"You look awful," she said to him. "Padraic."

A fleeting smile touched his lips and vanished. "You
haven't seen yourself, Jenna. I can ride, though. And we
need to do that before those other riders decide to come
back. Where's that bastard O'Deoradháin?"

Jenna pointed away south, where a distant rider pounded
away across the moonlit fields. Mac Ard spat once in the
man's direction. Maeve came riding up, holding the reins
to the tiarna's horse. She dismounted and went to Mac
Ard. "We're binding this first," she said. "Riders or not,
you're losing too much blood, Padraic. Jenna can watch for
the attackers."

She looked up at Jenna, who nodded. "I'm . . . fine for
now, Mam," she said, hoping it was true. The edges of her
vision had gone dark, and her arm radiated agony as if the

very bones had been shattered. She took deep, slow breaths of the cold night air—*keep the pain to one side*—and forced herself to sit upright. If the riders returned, she wasn't sure she could use the cloch again. She thought of the andúilleaf in the pack: *As soon as we get to the town, you can have some, and that will keep the pain away* . . . "Go on. But you need to hurry, Mam . . ."

Maeve tore strips from her skirt hem, bandaging Mac Ard's arm and strapping the arm to his chest. "That will need to be stitched when we reach town, but it will do for now. Can you mount, Padraic?"

In answer, Mac Ard grasped the saddle with his left hand, put his foot in the stirrup and pulled himself up with a grimace. Astride, he looked around them: the empty-saddled horses now standing a hundred yards down the road, the bladeless hilts on the road, the broken bodies of the two men sprawled in the awkward poses of the dead in the field, the black furrow torn in the ground up the slope from them.

"So much for keeping this a secret," he said.

14

Áth Iseal

JENNA could not imagine a city larger than Áth Iseal. To her eyes, which had seen only Ballintubber, the town was vast, noisy, and impossibly crowded, though she knew that Lár Bhaile, to the south on the east side of Lough Lár, was the size of several Áth Iseals put together.

They ran into a squadron of men in green and brown, hurrying across the ford and up the road, having seen the lightnings and heard the fighting. On meeting Tiarna Mac Ard, three of the soldiers accompanied them across the ford, while the rest of the small force rode west in pursuit of the Connachtans. Tiarna Mac Ard, Maeve, and Jenna were taken to the Rí's House—lodgings reserved for the Rí Gabair should he come to Áth Iseal—and healers were sent for. Servants brought food and drink, and baths were prepared.

Jenna slept more soundly that night than she had since they'd left Ballintubber: only six days ago now, though it seemed far longer to her. When she awoke the next day, the sun was already high in the sky, masked by scudding gray rain clouds. She stood at the window, a blanket wrapped around her, shivering and yet delighting in the sharp cold and the fresh smell of the rain. The Rí's House had been built on top of the river bluff, and from her window, Jenna looked down on the clustered town. She'd never seen so many buildings in one place, all crowded together as if desperately seeking each other's company, the streets between them busy with people moving from place to place. A market square was just off to her left and down, packed with street vendors and buyers, bright with the awnings of the stalls. The sound of vendors' calls and high-pitched bartering came to her on the air.

For a moment, looking at the untroubled life below, she could almost forget the events of the past fortnight. But a twinge of pain from her arm brought back the memories, and she stepped away from the window again. She must have cried out, for someone knocked at the door to the room. "Young miss, are you awake? May I come in?"

"Aye," Jenna answered. "Come in."

The door opened, and a young woman no older than Jenna entered, bearing a tray with a steaming pot, a cup, and tea. A tentative smile was on her plain face, but there was also caution in her eyes as she set the tray down on the bedside table and bustled about the room, pulling clothing from a chest at the foot of the bed. She kept looking at Jenna as if Jenna were some sort of mythical beast, or as if she were afraid that Jenna might suddenly order her head lopped off.

"Here, Bantiarna. This will be good; see how the brown matches your eyes? The tiarna's already been to breakfast, and the other bantiarna, too—she's your mam, isn't she? I think she's very lovely, not at all like my own mam—but they asked that you come to them when you wake. The healer will be back here in just a bit to look at your arm again; I'll make sure someone runs to find him as soon as I leave you. That arm of yours must hurt, the way it's wrapped. Did it give you problems sleeping? You've evidently been through a terrible fight, from what I've heard. Goodness, the rumors that have been flying around here all morning . . ."

As the woman spoke, all seemingly in one gigantic breath, Jenna felt her arm cramp and tighten, her hand clenching involuntarily into a fist. She felt for the cloch—it was still there, hidden, and the feel of it caused her hand to relax, though the pain still radiated through her shoulder and into her chest. The servant was looking at her strangely, her mouth open though the words had stopped spilling out for the moment.

"Leave me," Jenna said abruptly before the young woman could take another breath and begin another monologue. "Those clothes are fine; I won't need your help."

The servant blanched, her face going white. "Young miss, if I've offended—"

Jenna waved her good hand to stop her. "You haven't. I just . . . I'd prefer to dress alone. Tell my mam and the tiarna that I'll be down shortly." She opened the door. "Please," she said, gesturing.

With a nod and bow, the servant left. Jenna closed the door behind her. She went to her pack, sitting at the side of the bed, and rummaged through it until she found the pouch of andúilleaf. She crumbled a bit of the herb and set it steeping in the teapot, then sank down on the bed. The bittersweet scent of andúilleaf wafted through the room, and that alone seemed to ease the pain a bit. For long minutes, she simply lay there, eyes closed, feeling the pain slowly lessen until she found she could move the fingers of her right hand again, then she went and poured herself a cup of the brew. As she drank, she pulled Eilís' ring from the pocket, looking at it and turning it in her hand. She needed to know more, but she didn't place the ring on her finger, uncertain. The specter of the ancient Holder had seemed so bitter, so fey. Not someone Jenna would voluntarily choose as an adviser. *Come to where a Holder's body rests, or touch something that was once theirs, and they can speak with you, if you will it.* With the memory of Eilís' words, Jenna sat up. She finished the andúilleaf tea, dressed quickly, and left her room.

She found her mam and Mac Ard in a parlor room leading out into an interior garden court, though when Jenna—directed by another servant—passed through it to get to the tiarna's room, she found most of the plants were now brown and dead. The doors were shut, and a fire was roaring in the hearth. Mac Ard was standing near the fire, one arm still bound to his body and another bandage over his forehead. Maeve was sitting near him. They had evidently been conversing, but both went silent as Jenna entered.

Food was laid out on a table near them, and Mac Ard

waved at it with his good hand as Jenna entered. "Have you eaten?"

"I'm not hungry," she answered. "What word is there on the Connachtans or O'Deoradháin?"

Mac Ard shrugged with one shoulder. "None. Three of the Connachtans are dead—I know their faces, and the Rí Connachta won't be pleased, as two of them are his cousins—and the others fled west, evidently leaving the High Road when it turned north. I sent men to the farm where we met O'Deoradháin—it wasn't his land at all, it seems. There's been no sign of him, and no freelander in the area knows him at all. I had someone find the Taisteal and speak with Clannhri Sheehan, who said that O'Deoradháin had come into the camp only a few hours before us. He was probably a Connachtan as well."

Three are dead, and two of them you killed. . . . Jenna swallowed hard, trying to keep her face from showing anything of her feelings. "There's talk all through Áth Iseal about mage-lights, clochs, and the Filleadh," Mac Ard continued. "The sooner we get to Lár Bhaile, the better. I'd like to set out tomorrow, if you're able."

The thought of more travel made Jenna grimace, but she nodded. "Whatever you think best. Whatever keeps us safe."

"You'll be safe now," Mac Ard told her. "From here, I can promise that. The Connachtans won't dare come this far east. I never offered you my gratitude, Jenna," Mac Ard said. "But I do now. That's the second time you've saved my life. It's a debt I'll do my best to repay."

"There's no debt," Jenna answered. "The first time, what happened was out of my control, an accident. This time . . ." She took a long breath. "I did it to save myself and my mam."

"And me?"

"Aye, and you. Because—" Jenna stopped, looking at her mam. Mac Ard's followed the gaze, his dark eyes glinting in the firelight. He nodded, as if he saw something in her face that he expected to see, and pushed himself away from the mantle.

"The cloch of yours," he said, his voice carefully neutral. "I thought it was a clochmion, one of the minor clochs, one of the least. I think we both know better now. I think I could name the cloch you're holding."

Jenna hurried to answer. "I didn't know, Tiarna Mac Ard. I just found it, that's all. I didn't know what it was."

"If you had, would you have given it to me? Would you give it to me now?"

Jenna didn't answer. She took a step back from him.

"You don't have to say anything," he said. "I can see the answer in your face." His eyes held hers for a few breaths longer before he looked away. "I have a dozen things to attend to if we're leaving tomorrow. Jenna, I'm glad you're feeling somewhat better. If you'll excuse me, Maeve . . ."

He left the room, passing close by Jenna. She could feel the breeze of his passage.

"Come here, darling," Maeve said as he left the room. She opened her arms, and Jenna sank into the embrace as if she were a small child again. As Maeve stroked her hair, tears came, surprising Jenna with their suddenness. She sobbed against her mother's breast as she hadn't done in years, and Maeve crooned soft words to her, kissing the top of her head. Finally, Jenna sniffed back the tears and pulled away, rubbing at her eyes with her sleeve. "How are you feeling this morning?" Maeve asked softly. Her eyes, concerned, glanced at the bandages around Jenna's arm. "You used andúilleaf again," Maeve said.

"I had to," Jenna answered. "It hurt too much."

Maeve nodded. "You should know, Jenna. Padraic and I—"

"You don't need to say anything," Jenna told her. "I understand, and if this is what you want, then I'm happy for you. Just don't let him hurt you, Mam."

"He won't," Maeve answered emphatically. Certainty tightened her face. "We talked for a long time. I know what he can do and what he can't do, and I'm comfortable with that. I understand his position; he understands mine. We're . . ." Maeve stopped and Jenna saw a broad smile spread across her face, twinned with a blush. "We're well suited for each other."

Jenna hugged her again, and Maeve stroked her hair. "Padraic is worried about you, Jenna," she said.

"Padraic doesn't need to worry." Jenna used his first name scornfully, as if she hated the taste of its familiarity. "This seems to be my problem, not his."

"He'd take the cloch and its burden from you, if he could."

Jenna's eyes flashed at that, and she stood abruptly, taking a step away from her mam. In the hearth behind her, a log crashed in a whirling cascade of sparks. "He can't have it. It's *mine*."

She pushed away from Meave, who let her go. "That's what he said you'd say, that you wouldn't, that you *couldn't,* willingly give it up now, even though it hurts you." Maeve smiled sadly. "I wish you could. I would do anything to stop you from being in pain, Jenna. I wish . . ." She looked away to the fire, then back to Jenna. "I wish you'd never found the stone. I wish Niall, your father . . ." She stopped.

"What about my da?" Jenna asked.

Maeve shook her head. "Nothing. He said nothing of this to me, but in looking back on how it was, I think he was always waiting for that cloch himself. I wonder now if he didn't bring it to Ballintubber himself, from Inish Thuaidh or wherever he came from before. If he'd lived, it would have been *him* who was up on Knobtop that night, not you."

"And then Tiarna Mac Ard would have come."

Her mam gave Jenna a knowing smile. "I loved your da, Jenna. But it's possible to be in love more than once in your life. It's even possible to be in love with two people at once, even if it's dangerous and even though you know that those feelings will inevitably cause everyone pain. One day you'll realize that. I'll always love your da, and always cherish my time with him. After all, he gave me you."

"And I'm all that's left. All the rest that we had is gone. I have nothing." Her voice was wistful and sad.

"Most of it is gone, aye, except for a few things of his I took before we left. Wait here a moment." Maeve rose from her chair and left the room for a few minutes, returning with a small wooden carving in her hand. "Remember this?" she asked, holding it out to Jenna: a block of pine fitting easily into her palm and poorly carved into a representation of a seal and painted a bright blue, though wood showed through at several places where it had been scratched.

"Aye," Jenna said. "The seal I used to play with when I was a baby." She looked at Maeve. "Why that?"

"Your father carved it, before he left for Bácathair. When you lost interest in it, I kept it because it was his last gift to you. I'd forgotten I still had it until I was trying to find a few things to take when we fled. Here . . . it isn't much, but you should have it back now."

Jenna held it in her left hand as memories surged back: sitting on her mam's lap at the table and laughing with her mam as the seal bobbed in a pan of water; tossing it angrily across the room one night because she was hungry and tired, chipping a crockery bowl in the process—she'd never told her mam that, letting her think the bowl had been chipped some other time. "Da made this? I never knew."

Maeve nodded.

. . . *touch something that was once theirs, and they can speak with you, if you will it . . .*

"Mam, may I keep this?"

Maeve smiled at her. "It's yours, Jenna. It was always yours."

She did nothing until after the evening meal, when she was alone again in her room.

The sun had sunk behind the hills. The night was dark, the moon and stars hidden behind a screen of clouds. The air seemed heavy and cold. Jenna had dismissed the servant for the night and sat in a chair near the fire, feeding it peat until the blue flames rose high and the light touched the far wall of the bedroom. She took the carving of the seal from the stand by her bed and set it in her lap, staring at the fire for a time. Then she took it in her right hand.

She stared at the carving, at the marks her da's knife had made shaping the wood, and seeing in her mind's eyes the shavings curling away under the blade. She could almost hear the sound of the dry scraping of sharp iron against soft wood. . . .

No. She *could* hear it.

She turned. Near the window, a man sat in a plain chair, holding a block of wood in one hand and a knife in the other. Shavings were piled in his lap. She could see the wall behind through the ghostly image. His face . . . Jenna gasped, realizing that the man who sat there, hair the color of fire, was the same she'd glimpsed when she'd found the stone. "Da?" she whispered.

He looked up. "Who . . . ?" he asked. He seemed confused, looking around. "Where am I? Everything looks so pale . . . Maeve, is that you? You're dressed so strangely, like a Riocha."

Jenna walked toward him, holding the battered, chipped seal out so he could see it. "I'm Jenna, Da. Your daughter. Seventeen years old now." He shook his head, wonder and fear and confusion all mingled in his gaze. His reaction was so different from that of Eilís, but then Eilís had held Lámh Shábhála when it was active and knew that the cloch contained its old Holders. When her da possessed Lámh Shábhála, it had been dead, just an ordinary stone wrapped in legend. Her da would have had no experience of the cloch's abilities.

"Wait," Jenna said. She imagined her memories opening to him, as if they were gifts that she could hand him, letting him see within her as Eilís had, only this time she directed the sharing, choosing what she allowed him to know. She could feel his gentle touch on her memories, and as he comprehended them he gasped, the knife and seal falling from his grasp. They made no sound, vanishing before they reached the floor.

"I'm dead. A ghost."

"Aye," she told him softly. "Or neither dead nor ghost, only a moment caught forever, like a painting. I don't really know, Da. But Eilís, the lady in the falls, told me that Lámh Shábhála carries its Holders. Which means you were one, too, even though the mage-lights weren't there for you. Here, do you remember?" She took the cloch out and held it so he could see the stone. He started to reach for it, then let his hand drop back.

"I remember, aye. I carried it with me, everywhere. Then, on Knobtop one day, I lost it. I was never sure how that happened. I go up there and look for it, all the time, still. Did I . . . ?"

"No, Da. You never found it, but I did, the night the mage-lights came."

The wraith of Niall nodded. "So the stone truly was Lámh Shábhála. I never knew for certain; for all I knew, it was just a colorful pebble, though I'd always been told it was a cloch, and supposedly *the* cloch, the Safekeeping. But it was dead—or waiting for the mage-lights—when I had it." He sighed. He looked at her for a long time, a slow smile touching his mouth. "You look like her. You have Maeve's eyes, and her hair."

"She always says I have your nose, and the shape of your face."

He laughed. "I remember her saying that, not long after you were born." He was silent for long moments after that, his face somber. "Why did you call me here, Jenna? If I'm dead, why did you rouse me? Why didn't you leave me to rest?"

"I wanted . . ." Jenna stopped. Now that she had called him, she wasn't sure what she wanted. There was so much. "I need to know what you know about the cloch. I need you to help me."

He stood and came toward her, reaching out his hand. She extended her own hand for his touch. She expected to feel his skin, or perhaps a waft of chill air. She felt nothing. Her fingers went through his as if they were mist. *Is that what would have happened with Eilís? She seemed so real, so whole, but she was trying to scare me. . . .* Jenna felt disappointment, and the figure of her da drew back, sighing. "You're a dream. Not real."

Jenna shook her head. "No. I'm real. It's you who aren't."

He may have believed her. He made no protest. "If this

is death, why is it so . . . ordinary? Why don't I remember dying? Why do I seem to be still in our house, and you standing before me like a ghost?"

"I don't know," Jenna answered. She looked at the carving in her hand. "Though this wasn't with you when you died, and it's all I have of yours. Maybe that's the reason. There's so much I don't know, Da. The stone was yours for a while—tell me why. Tell me how you came to have it. Tell me everything. Help me as you would have helped me if you were still alive."

He clasped his hands together, staring at them as if marveling at their solidity. "If I were still alive, *I* would have Lámh Shábhála," he answered. "Not you. I would have been on Knobtop that night."

"But I have it now, Da. Your daughter."

He looked at her. "My daughter," he said. "I never expected to have the gift of a daughter. For that matter, I never expected to fall in love at all . . ."

15

Niall's Tale

MY mam, your great-mam, was the one who took the cloch. No, that's not quite true. Actually, it was your great-da who stole it from where it rested . . .

"No, let me begin again. It's easier to start farther back. Let me tell you the story as my mam used to tell it to me. . . .

"She was born on Inishfeirm, an island just off Inish Thuaidh. Inishfeirm's best known for the Order of Inishfeirm, with their white stone buildings set high on the peak. From what my mam said, there weren't many residents of Inishfeirm outside the Order; of those few, most were fisherfolk, her family included. They knew the Bráthairs of the Order, though. Couldn't help it, since the Order dominated what social life there was on the island. They'd meet them in the streets or in the market, buying fish for their table or some of the greens that came over from the big island.

"My mam's name was Kerys Aoire. The Aoires weren't Riocha, just plain folk, but well enough off and one of the main families on the island, from what Mam told me. They were often invited by the Máister to dine at the Order Hall on the feast days. The Order was a contemplative one, devoted to the Mother-Creator. In the last decades of the Before, the Order was known for its cloudmages, but when the mage-lights failed, so did their prominence. By the time my mam was born, they were a curiosity from another age, a place to visit and hear the old tales, to see the spectacular scenery of Inishfeirm, with its buildings clinging like lichens

to the steep cliff walls of the mountain peak that formed
the isle, with the bright parapets of the Order, built five
centuries before, standing proud at the summit. Once, the
cells of the Bráthairs were crowded; now, half of them were
empty, though the Order still attracted occasional acolytes
from Inish Thuaidh, young men sent to serve by wealthy
families, mostly, and even a few from among the mainland
Riocha, primarily from Falcarragh in Tuath Infochla.

"One of the acolytes, a boy of eighteen summers named
Niall, caught my mam's eye. Aye, that's my name as well,
and I'm sure that tells you some of what happened next. I
don't know much about my da. Mam always claimed that
she wouldn't tell me his family name because she wanted
to protect him, but I'm not certain she ever knew it. I
suppose it doesn't matter. They fell in love, or at least lust.
My mam was probably your age, sixteen or seventeen, and
naive. It wasn't the first time a Bráthair of the Order and
a local girl had become lovers; I'm sure it wasn't the last,
either, though afterward I'll bet the Máister watched things
more closely than before.

"One of the treasures of the Order of Inishfeirm was its
collection of clochs na thintrí. Once, the Order's founders
had even held Lámh Shábhála, and three of the other
Clochs Mór had been theirs, as well as several of the minor
stones. But when the mage-lights failed, Lámh Shábhála
was given away or lost, though they retained the other
clochs. Over the centuries, they had accumulated more
stones reputed to be clochs na thintrí, though of course no
one could know for certain with the mage-lights long dead.
Some of the clochs had been handed down through families
for generations; others were purchased or found, and as to
their lineage and the truth of the claims made for them . . .
well, no one knew.

"Some two hundred years before my mam's birth, the
Order acquired a stone that was reputed to be the long-
lost Lámh Shábhála. I don't think anyone actually believed
that tale. Mam said that she'd seen the collection a few
times when the Máister would order it brought out for the
admiration of his guests, and some of the clochs were gor-
geous stones: gleaming, transparent jewels of bright ruby,

midnight blue, or deepest green, faceted and polished, some
of them as big as your fist. The one called Lámh Shábhála
looked puny and insignificant alongside them, at that time
wrapped in a cage of silver wire as a necklace. Even the
necklace was plain: simple black strands of cotton. The
Máister seemed somewhat skeptical about the claims. You
know how tales grow and change with each telling, and by
that time it had been four centuries and more since the
clochs were alive with power, so it's no wonder that no one
knew for certain what Lámh Shábhála had looked like.

"The Bráthairs were contracted by their families for life
to the Order. Marriage was forbidden to them. When Mam
twice missed her monthly bleeding, she told Niall. She was
afraid that he would go to the Máister, confess, and be
forbidden to see Mam again, and Mam would be left to
the shame of a bastard child. Certainly that had happened
before, and there were women on Inishfeirm who were
pointed out as local scandals. Now Mam thought she would
be one of them, a cautionary tale to Inishfeirm girls who
looked with love on one of the Bráthairs.

"But Niall was true to her. He promised Kerys that he
would go away with her, that he would take her to one of
the Tuatha where they might be married. And to prove
that his promise was in earnest, he gave her a token of his
love and also of his rejection of the Order. He stole what
he perceived as one of the least of the clochs, and gave it
to my mam.

"Aye, the very cloch you hold now.

"They managed to steal away at night, taking a small
currach that belonged to my mam's family. Though the
moon was out when they started, my mam said, they chose
the wrong night, for a quick storm came thundering out of
the west and south after they passed the last island and
were nearly across to Tuath Infochla. A currach is fine in
a calm sea; in the storm, in the huge wind-driven waves,
only a very lucky and very experienced sailor could have
kept the tiny craft afloat and neither Niall nor Kerys were
experienced or lucky. The currach foundered just off the
coast. Both Niall and Kerys went over—Mam, at least,
could swim well, and she knew to rid herself of her wet

clothes before they dragged her down. She said she never knew what happened to Niall. She heard him call once, but in the storm and night, she never saw him again. She called for him, called many times, but only the thunder and the hissing of rain answered her. She was certain she would die, too.

"But she did not. When Mam told the tale, she always said that a pair of large blue seals came to her, and kept her above water, her arms around their bodies as they swam toward shore. I don't know if that's true at all; in the midst of the storm and the terror, who knows if what you remember is true. What is true is that, gasping and choking on the cold salt water, she found herself on the rocky shore, naked and shivering.

"Around her neck, somehow, the necklace Niall had given her was still there.

"Mam saw a light high on the hill behind her, and she walked to a cabin. The shepherd family there took her in, set her by the fire, and gave her clothing and blankets. If the storm hadn't thrown Kerys ashore at that place, where there was a sparse shingle of beach and a house close by, she would have died anyway, of cold and exposure. She always wondered whether some faint power still lurked in the stone, that it brought the seals and found the beach and saved her so it would not be lost. Again, I don't know if that's true or not. Certainly the stone never did anything else for her . . . or for me. But I get ahead of my tale.

"The next day, the shepherd, his wife, their two children, and my mam went back down to the beach. They found shattered pieces of the currach, but nothing else. Niall's body wasn't ever found; he drowned, most likely, and his body was dragged to the bottom by the weight of what he wore, or tossed to the shore at the foot of one of the wild cliffs nearby and never seen.

"Kerys stayed with the shepherd family, whose name was Hagan, and I was born that winter. I don't know what tale she gave the Hagans regarding that night—for all I know, it may have been simply the truth. The Hagans kept to themselves, rarely going into the nearest village, and Mam said they told the villagers that she was a cousin who had come to stay with them. When the shepherd's wife died the next spring in childbirth, my mam remained, and eventually married Conn Hagan, my stepfather. They had two other children of their own. I can say little but good about Conn Hagan—he treated me as well as he treated his own children. If it was a hard life, it was no harder for me than for his own.

"There's not much more to tell. When I was sixteen, I felt the need to see more of Talamh an Ghlas than the few acres of our farm. When I left, Mam gave me the cloch and told me the tale about her and Niall. I set off north and came to Falcarragh, and sailed from there over to Inish Thuaidh, and lived on the island for a few years. I even visited Inishfeirm, though I didn't tell anyone who I was. I visited the Order, and they told me about the Before and the clochs na thintrí and Lámh Shábhála, the Stone of Safekeeping.

"I played the stranger with them, saying that I'd heard the Lámh Shábhála was also there at the cloisters, but they said 'no.' Many years ago, they told me, a cloch had been stolen from the cloisters, and though some had claimed that the stone was Lámh Shábhála, the Máister was unconcerned about the loss because the claims regarding the cloch were almost certainly false. If the stone was a cloch na thintrí at all (and the Máister doubted it) it had been no more than a clochmion, a minor stone. No one knew where Lámh Shábhála was, they told me. That cloch was lost.

"But I learned a lot about the clochs na thintrí from the Order of Inishfeirm and from other places, and I always wondered. Many of those I talked to spoke of the Return, the Filleadh, for they believed that the mage-lights would return soon, maybe within my lifetime. I thought that if this cloch was truly Lámh Shábhála, then I would be the First Holder. I would hold the renewed stone. I wandered more, leaving Inish Thuaidh and traveling the High Road south until I came to Ballintubber.

"And I found a new and more enduring type of enchantment in Maeve, and I stayed. . . ."

*   *   *

"What happened to the cloch, Da?" Jenna asked. "How did you lose it on Knobtop?" The phantom of her father glanced up from his chair, where he seemed to have fallen into a reverie after his tale. He shrugged.

"I lost it, or it lost me," he said. "I don't know which. I wore the necklace all the time. I walked often on Knobtop while in Ballintubber—I seemed to be drawn to the mountain, or perhaps it was the cloch that drew me there. After I married your mam, I'd take the flock up there nearly every day. One night, not a month after we married, I returned from grazing them there, and when I took off my shirt that night, I saw that the silver cage that had held the stone was empty. The wires holding the stone had moved apart enough for it to fall through. I looked for the stone for the next year, almost every day, combing the ground while the sheep grazed. I never found it. But I know if I'd seen the mage-lights over Knobtop, I'd have come running. But from what you've said, it seems I never had the chance." He seemed distraught and upset. "I wonder," he said finally. "I wonder if the cloch did it all: brought itself to Knobtop because it knew that the mage-lights would come there, pulled itself away from me so it could stay there. Or maybe that was just all coincidence. Maybe the mage-lights would have found the cloch wherever it was. I don't know."

As her da talked, Jenna became aware of light moving against the walls, colorful, swirling bands. She glanced at the balcony door; outside, the night sky was alive with the mage-lights, sheets of brilliance flowing as if in some unseen wind, dancing above her. "Da!" she cried. "There! Can you see them? Da?" She looked behind; he was gone. The wraith had vanished.

The cloch called to her, still in her hand from when she had shown it to her father's spirit. Jenna went out onto the balcony, into the chill night, into the blazing shower of hues and shades. She lifted the cloch to the sky, and the mage-lights coalesced like iron filings drawn by a lodestone. She could hear people in the streets below, shouting and calling

and pointing to the sky and to the tower on which she
stood, and behind her, her mam and Mac Ard hurried into
her room.

"Jenna!" Maeve called, but Jenna didn't turn.

The first whirling tendril of the mage-lights had closed
around her hand and the cloch, and the freezing touch
seeped into the patterns etched in the flesh of her arm: as
Maeve and Mac Ard rushed toward her and stopped at the
balcony doors; as the people below exclaimed and gestured
toward her; as the mage-lights enveloped her, encased her
in color as energy poured from the sky into Lámh Shábhála; as Jenna screamed with pain but also with a sense of
relief and satisfaction, as if the filling of the cloch's reservoirs of power also fulfilled a need in herself she hadn't
known existed. She clenched her fist tight around the stone
while billows of light fell from the sky and swept through
and into her, as she and Lámh Shábhála shouted affirma-
tion back to them.

Then, abruptly, it was over. The sky went dark; Jenna
fell to her knees, gasping, holding the stone against her
breast. Lámh Shábhála was open in her mind, a sparkling
matrix of lattices, the reservoir of power at its core stronger
now, though not yet nearly full. That would come, she
knew. Soon. Very soon.

"Jenna!" Her mam sank to the balcony floor in front of
her, hands clutching Jenna's shoulders. "Jenna, are you all
right?" Jenna looked up, seeing her through the matrix of
the stone. She shook her head, trying to clear her vision.
She blinked, and Lámh Shábhála receded in her sight. The
full agony of the mage-lights was beginning now, but she
would not lose consciousness this time.

She was stronger. She could bear this.

"Help me up," she said, and felt Maeve and Mac Ard
lift her to her feet. She stood, cradling her right arm to her.
She shrugged the hands away, and took a few wobbling
steps back into her room, with the tiarna and her mam
close beside her. She sat on the edge of her bed, as her
mam bustled about, shouting to the servant to bring boiling
water and the andúilleaf paste. Mac Ard knelt in front of

her, reaching out as if to touch her arm. Jenna drew back, scowling.

"It wanted me, not you," she told him. "It's mine now, and I won't let you have it. I won't ever let you have it."

She wasn't sure what she saw in his eyes then. "I'm sorry, Padraic," she said. "I didn't mean that. It's just the pain."

He stared at her for long seconds, then he nodded. "I'm not a danger to you, Jenna," he said, his voice low enough so that only Jenna could hear him. "But there are others who will be. You'll find that out soon enough." He stood then.

"I leave her to you, Maeve," he said, more loudly. "I'll send for the healer. But I doubt that he has anything that will help her now."

PART TWO

Filleadh

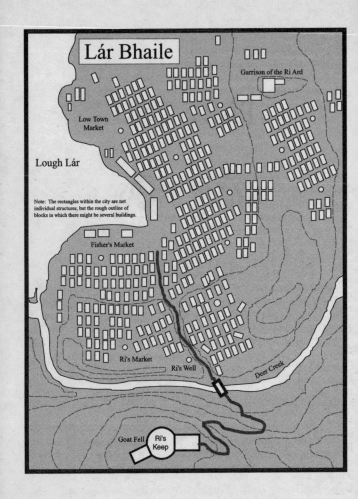

Lár Bhaile

Garrison of the Ri Ard

Low Town Market

Lough Lár

Note: The rectangles within the city are not individual structures, but the rough outline of blocks in which there might be several buildings.

Fisher's Market

Ri's Market

Ri's Well

Deer Creek

Goat Fell

Ri's Keep

16

Lár Bhaile

IF Áth Iseal felt large and crowded to Jenna, Lár Bhaile was immense beyond comprehension. The city spread along the southeastern arm of Lough Lár, filling the hollows of the hills and rising on the green flanks of Goat Fell, a large, steep-sloped mountain that marked the end of the lough. Along the summit of Goat Fell ran the stone ramparts of the Rí's Keep, twin walls a hundred yards apart, opening into a wide courtyard where the keep itself stood, towering high above the city. Behind those walls lived Rí Gabair, whose birth name was Torin Mallaghan, in his court with the Riocha of Tuath Gabair gathered around him.

Jenna could well imagine how Tiarna Mac Ard could have seen the mage-lights over Ballintubber from those heights, flickering off the night-clad waters of the lough.

She looked up those heights now from the market in what was called Low Town along the lake's shore, and they seemed impossibly high, a distant aerie of cut granite and limestone. Jenna judged that it had taken her at least a candle stripe and a half to ride down from the heights in Tiarna Mac Ard's carriage; it would take two or more to wend their way back up the narrow road that wound over the face of Goat Fell.

But that was for later. Now was the time for business.

Jenna glanced at the trio of burly soldiers who accompanied her. Neither the Rí nor Tiarna Mac Ard would allow her to leave the keep alone. At first, she hadn't minded,

not after the escape from Ballintubber. But in the intervening two months, the initial feeling of safety had been re-
placed by a sense of stifling confinement. She was never
alone, not even in the rooms the Rí had arranged for her
at the keep—there were always gardai stationed outside the
door and servants waiting just out of sight for a summons.
The cage in which she found herself was jeweled and
golden, plush and comfortable, but it was nonetheless a
cage.

"For your own safety," they told her. "For your protection."

But she knew it wasn't for her protection. It was for the
protection of the cloch.

Since she'd been in Lár Bhaile, the mage-lights had appeared here a dozen times. Each time, they had called her;
each time, she had answered the call, letting their power
fill the cloch she carried, now encased in a silver cage necklace around her neck, as it had been once for her da. Soon,
she knew, the well within Lámh Shábhála would be filled
to overflowing and the stone would open the way to the
mage-lights for the other clochs. Everyone else knew it,
also, for she saw that the Riocha were gathering here in
Lár Bhaile, and many of them wore stones that had been
in their families for generations, stones that were reputed
to be clochs na thintrí. They waited. They smiled at her the
way a wolf might smile at an injured doe.

The Alds had been consulted, old records pored over,
tales and legends recalled. They knew now that Jenna held
Lámh Shábhála, and they also knew the pain the First
Holder must endure when Lámh Shábhála opened the rest
of the clochs na thintrí to the mage-lights. They seemed
content to let Jenna be the First Holder.

She thought most of them also imagined themselves the
Second Holder, though at least Padraic Mac Ard didn't
seem to be among them. Wherever she went, there were
eyes watching, and she knew that the gardai whispered
back to the Riocha.

Jenna could sense that the gardai didn't like where she'd
brought them. They scowled, and kept their hands close to
the hilts of their swords. The four of them were at the end

of the market square; the stalls were small and dingy and
the crowds thin. Just beyond, a narrow lane moved south:
Cat's Alley, where the houses seemed to lean toward each
other in a drunken embrace, leaving the cobbled lane in
perpetual twilight. The central gutter was foul with black
pools of stagnant water edged with filthy ice, and a frozen
reek of decay and filth welled out into the square from the
open mouth of the lane. Jenna grimaced: this was where
Aoife, the servant she trusted most, had told her that she
would find a man named du Val, who kept potions.

"Back in Ballintubber," she'd told Aoife, *"we had a
woman who gathered herbs and knew the old ways. You
know, plants that can cure headaches, or can keep a young
woman from getting pregnant, things like that. Where would
I find someone like that here?"*

*Aoife had smiled knowingly at Jenna. "I do know, mis-
tress,"* she said. *"Down in Cat's Alley, no more than fifty
strides from where it meets Low Town Market. You'll see
the sign on your right."*

Jenna counted the steps, trying to avoid the worst of the
muck on the ground. Before she reached forty, she saw the
weathered board with faded letters: Du Val, Apothecary &
Herbalist. She couldn't read the words, but the tutors Tiarna Mac Ard had assigned to her had taught her the letters and she could compare then with the note Aoife had
given her. "Stay here," she told her escorts.

"Mistress, our orders . . ."

She'd learned quickly how to deal with the objections of
gardai. "Stay here, or I'll tell the Rí that you lost me in
the market. Would you rather deal with that? I'll be careful. You can stay at the door and watch me, if you'd like."
Her words emerged in puffs of white vapor; she wrapped
her clóca tightly around her. "The sooner I'm done here,
the sooner we can get back to the keep and some warmth."

They glanced at each other, then shrugged. Jenna pushed
open the door. A bell jingled above. In the wedge of pale
light that came in through the open door, she saw a small,
windowless room. The walls were lined with shelves, all of
them stuffed with vials of glass and crockery. Ahead of her
was a desk piled high with more jars, and beyond into dim

shadows were cabinets and cubbyholes. There was a fireplace to the right, but the ashes looked cold and dead.
"Hello?" Jenna called, shivering.

Shadows moved in the darkness, and Jenna heard the
sound of slow footsteps descending a staircase behind a
jumble of boxes and crates. A short dwarf of a man peered
out toward her, squinting, a hand over his eyebrows. "Shut
the door," he barked. "Are you trying to blind me?"

"Shut it," Jenna told the garda, then when he hesitated,
added more sharply, "do it!"

The door closed behind her, and as Jenna's eyes adjusted, she saw that some light filtered in through cracks in
the doors and shutters, and that candles were lit here and
there along the shelves. The little man shuffled forward to
the desk with an odd, rolling gait. He was dressed in a
dingy, shapeless woolen tunic and pants, held together with
a simple rope. His face reminded her a bit of Seancoim's—
the same bony ridge along the eyebrows, the flattened face.
She wondered if there wasn't Bunús Muintir heritage in
him somewhere. He glanced up and down at her appraisingly. "What can I do for you, Bantiarna?" he asked.

"Are you du Val?" He sniffed. Jenna took that for an
affirmative answer.

"I'm looking for a certain herb that none of the healers
in the keep seem to know," she told him. "I was told that
you might have it."

"The healers know shite," du Val spat. "They forget the
lore their ancestors knew. What are you looking for?"

"Andúilleaf."

Du Val said nothing. He came from behind the desk and
stood in front of her. He was no taller than her chest. He
stared up at her face, then let his gaze travel over her body.
He saw the cloth wrapped carefully around her right arm
and took her arm in his hands. Jenna didn't protest as he
unknotted the cloth strip and rolled it back. When her hand
was exposed past the wrist, he turned it over and back,
examining the skin with its mottled, scarred patterns. Then,
with stubby hands that were surprisingly graceful, he
wrapped the arm again.

"So you're the one? The one who calls the mage-lights?"

Jenna didn't answer. Du Val sniffed. "You don't have to tell me; I can look at your arm and see it. I've seen the mage-lights swirling around the keep and heard about the young figure that stands on the keep's summit at their bidding and swallows them. I've heard the name Lámh Sháb-nála bandied about. I've heard the rumors, little ones and big ones, and I know more about the truth of them than some of the Riocha up in the keep. I've seen the Riocha come to Lár Bhaile all of a sudden with bright stones around their necks, and I know that the eye of the Rí Ard in Dún Laoghaire looks this way as well, and he's also very interested in what's going on. And the goons outside—I suppose they're here to protect you and stop me from taking the cloch from you."

Jenna felt a shiver not born of cold run through her. "They're fast and strong, well-armed and mean, and they will kill you if you so much as scratch me," she told du Val. He seemed unimpressed. He scratched his side.

"Vermin," he said. "You can't get rid of them. Not here in their natural habitat: the city. How long have you been taking the leaf?"

"Almost two months now."

"Regularly?"

"Almost every day." In truth, it was every day. Sometimes twice. On the really bad days, the days after the mage-lights, even more. Du Val stroked his chin.

"You know that andúilleaf's addictive?"

Jenna shrugged. "It takes away the pain."

"So it does, so it does—though your healers would tell you that the leaf has no known pharmacological properties, if they recognize the herb at all. They wouldn't know where to find it, wouldn't notice it growing. That knowledge's lost to them. The Old Ones knew, the Bunús Muintir. The few of them who are still around know, too. They also know how careful you have to be with the leaf, if you don't want to end up needing it forever."

"If you're planning to talk me to death, I'll go elsewhere," Jenna told him, speaking to him in the tone she'd heard the bantiarnas use with their servants. "I have another source." She turned to go, hoping the bluff would work. She could feel tears welling up behind her eyes and knew that she couldn't hold them back once she closed the door behind her, no matter what the gardai might think. She was scared: lost in the need for the relief from pain the herb brought, lost in a level of society she didn't understand. There was no "other source"—she had no idea how she could find Seancoim again, or how she would find her way to Doire Coill without having to explain it to the Rí and Mac Ard.

"All right," du Val grunted behind her, and she wiped surreptitiously at her eyes before turning back to him. "I have the leaf. 'Tis expensive." He almost seemed to laugh. "But considering who you are, that's probably not a consideration, is it? Who else knows you're dependent on it?" When she didn't answer, he did laugh, a snorting amusement that twisted his swarthy, broad face. "If you're afraid that I'll use the information to blackmail you, forget it. You have worse worries than that."

He went to the back of the room, rummaging around in the shadowy recesses of a leaning, bowed case of shelving. He returned with a glass jar half-filled with brown leaves. "This is all I have," he said. " 'Tis old, but still potent." Jenna reached for the jar, and du Val pulled it back to his chest, scowling up at her. "First, it's two mórceints."

"Two mórceints?" Jenna couldn't keep the shock from her voice. Two mórceints was more than a good craftsman made in a year. Back in Ballintubber, that might have been more money than the entire village together saw in the same time.

"Two mórceints," he repeated. "And don't be complaining. There's few enough of us who would even know how and where to find this, and it grows in only one place anywhere near here."

"Doire Coill," Jenna said.

If du Val was surprised by her knowledge, he didn't show it. "Aye," he said. "The dark forest itself, and only in special places there. Two mórceints," he repeated, "or you can check your 'other source.' " He smiled at her, with black holes where several teeth should have been.

"All right," she said. She fumbled in the pouch she carried. At least Tiarna Mac Ard wasn't stingy with his money; she had the two mórceints and more. She counted out the coins into du Val's grimy, callused palm, then reached again for the jar. He wouldn't release it.

"Does someone know you're taking this?" he asked again.

"Aye," she answered. "My mam." It was a lie. The truth was that no one knew, unless Aoife suspected it.

He nodded. "Then tell your mam this: take the leaf no more than once a day, and for no longer than a month. Start with four leaves in the brew; cut the dosage by one leaf every week, or you'll be back here again in another month, and the price will be four mórceints. Do you understand that?"

"Aye," Jenna answered.

With the word, du Val released the jar and closed his fingers around the coins. He jingled them appreciatively. "A pleasure doing business with you, Holder."

"I'm certain it was."

He snorted laughter again. "I'll see you again in a month."

"I don't think so."

"The magic you're trying to hold is powerful, but also full of pain. There's no cure for it. You can look for ways, like the leaf, to dull it, or you learn to bear what it gives you. Either way, it will always be there. Better to accept the pain as it is, if you can."

"Do you charge for your platitudes, also?"

Du Val grinned. "For you, I can afford to give the advice for nothing."

"And that's exactly what it's worth," Jenna retorted. "I won't be back."

She immediately hated the way the words sounded, hated the intention to hurt that rode in them: she sounded too much like some of the Riocha at the keep, the ones she despised for their haughtiness. If du Val had shown that her words stung, she would have felt immediate remorse. She would have apologized. But the dwarf shrugged and moved away behind the desk. He puttered with the flasks and vials there, ignoring Jenna. Finally, she turned and

went to the door. When her hand touched the rope loop
that served as a handle, du Val's voice came from behind
her.

"I'm sorry for you, Holder. I truly am."

She took a breath. She opened the door, nodded to the
relieved glances of the gardai, and closed the door behind
her again.

She spent another candle stripe or so in Low Town Market, desultorily pretending to shop as an excuse for the trip.
The wind began to rise from off the lake, and she could
see storm clouds rising dark in the west beyond the roofs
of the houses, and finally told the gardai to fetch the carriage for the ride back. The carriage moved slowly through
the twisting maze of narrow lanes, heading always up
toward the stone shoulders of Goat Fell and the keep high
above. Jenna lay back on the seat, eyes closed, listening to
the sounds of vibrant, crowded life around her: the strident,
musical calls of the vendors; shouts and calls from the windows of the houses she passed; the laughter from the pubs,
seemingly on every corner; the sound of a fine baritone
voice lifted in song . . .

"Stop!" Jenna called to the driver.

The carriage jolted to a halt, and she got out, the gardai
hurriedly following her. She could still hear the voice, coming from the open door of a tavern just down the street.
She strode down the lane to the pub, squinting into a hazy
darkness fragrant with the smell of ale and pipe.

> *So over the sea they sped*
> *From Falcarragh where the mountains loom*
> *From home and bed*
> *To Inish and their doom . . .*

She knew the tune: the Song of Máel Armagh. She had
heard it once before she left Ballintubber. And she knew
the voice as well.

"Coelin!"

The song cut off in mid-verse, and a familiar head lifted.
"By the Mother-Creator . . . Jenna, is that you, girl?"

"Aye. 'Tis me, indeed."

Laughing, he set down his giotár and ran to her. He took her in his arms and spun her around, nearly knocking over a few pints. He set her down again, holding her at arm's length.

He kissed her.

"I thought you were dead, Jenna. That's what everyone was saying. The damned Connachtans killed the Ald, and Tom Mullin, too, when he tried to stop them. Then there were the killings down by your old house, and the fires . . ." Coelin was shaking his head; Jenna's finger still touched her lips. Now she placed the finger on Coelin's lips.

"Shh," she said. "Quietly. Please." That, at least, she'd learned from the Riocha: you never knew who might be listening to your words.

Coelin looked puzzled, but he lowered his voice so that only she could easily hear him against the murmuring conversations of the pub. "Anyway, the Connachtans went off in a fury, and we heard they were looking for you and your mam, and that tiarna—what was his name? Mac Ard?— but everyone figured you'd either been burned up in your cottage, or lost in the bogs." He stopped, looking at her closely, and glancing behind her at the trio of soldiers who watched carefully from the doorway. Coelin's eyes narrowed a bit, seeing them. "All the rumors were wrong, obviously, and by the looks of you, you're hobnobbing with the Riocha. And your arm—you have it all wrapped up. You owe me a tale, girl."

He was smiling, and she could still feel the touch of his lips on hers. "What about you, Coelin?" she asked. "How did you come to be here? And softly . . ."

He shrugged, grinning, but he kept his voice low. "If you remember, that tiarna of yours said I was good, that I should be singing to larger audiences than poor little Ballintubber could give me, so after things settled down, I thought I'd take his advice." He touched her cheek, though his gaze went quickly to the gardai. "After all, you were gone. Ballintubber just didn't seem to be where I wanted to be anymore."

"You still have the gift of words, Coelin Singer," Jenna

told him, but she was smiling back. "Pretty and beguiling and too charming."

"But not false," he answered. "Not false at all."

"Hah!"

His face fell in mock alarm. "You don't believe me, then? I *am* hurt." He laughed again, and gestured at the corner where his giotár rested, a few copper coins in the hat placed near it. "Can you stay and listen? Maybe we can talk more? I wasn't joking when I said that you owe me the tale of your adventures."

Jenna started to shake her head, then stopped. "I have a better idea," she said. "Come with me. I'm on my way back to the keep. You can sing for the Riocha there, and we can talk. Tiarna Mac Ard will remember you." She gestured at the hat with its coins. "And the pay's likely to be better."

"To the keep? Really?"

"Aye. Mam would love to see you again. We knew some of what happened in Ballintubber, but the Rí didn't want it known that we were here, not after what happened, and so it's been kept quiet. Mam will ask you a hundred questions, or more likely a thousand. Will you come?"

He smiled. "I could never refuse anything you asked, Jenna," he said.

17

The Rí's Supper

"COELIN!"

Maeve sounded nearly as glad to see him as Jenna had. She clasped the young man to her, then held him out at arm's length. "When did you leave Ballintubber?"

Coelin's gaze wouldn't stay with Maeve. It kept wandering past her to the rich embroidered tapestries on the walls of their apartment within the Rí's Keep; to the expensive, dark furniture; to the glittering trinkets set on the polished surfaces. "Two hands of days ago," he said. "By the Mother-Creator, I've never seen—"

"You have to tell me everything," Maeve said, pulling him toward a chair near the fire. Jenna laughed softly, watching Coelin marvel at the surroundings. "Start with the day the Connachtans attacked . . ."

Coelin told her, spinning the tale with his usual adroitness, and—Jenna suspected—a certain amount of dramatic license. ". . . so you can see," he finished, "I barely escaped with my life myself."

"That may still be the case," a voice said from the doorway. Tiarna Mac Ard stood there, frowning at the trio gathered near the fire. His dark beard and mustache were frosted with ice, and the furs over his clóca were flecked with rapidly melting snow.

"Tiarna," Coelin began. "I'm—"

"I know who you are," Mac Ard interrupted. "What I don't know is why you're here." He took off the furs, tossing them carelessly on a chair. As he did so, he grimaced—

the wound he'd taken on the road to Áth Iseal hadn't completely healed yet, and his right arm, Jenna knew, was still stiff and sore, its range of motion limited. He was dressed in riding leathers, and a short sword hung heavily from his belt. His left hand rested casually on the silver pommel of the hilt.

"I brought him here, Tiarna," Jenna said. "I happened to see him in the city, and we started talking, and I knew Mam would want to hear about Ballintubber, so . . ." She stopped, her eyes widening. "Did I do wrong?"

"Aye," Mac Ard answered, though his voice sounded more sad than angry. "I'm afraid that you did, Jenna."

"The boy isn't to blame, Padraic," Maeve said. "Or Jenna. She only did what I would have done, had I seen him."

"That may be," Mac Ard answered. "The deed's done, in any case. What we do now depends." He stopped.

"Depends on what?" Jenna asked.

"On whether Coelin Singer knows how to keep his mouth shut about certain things." Mac Ard strode up to the boy. He stood in front of Coelin, staring at the young man's face. "For various reasons, we've been careful to make certain that it's not common knowledge in the city that a certain two people from Ballintubber are here, or to know the circumstances under which they left the village. If I suddenly start hearing those rumors, I'd know where to place the blame and how to deal with the source. Am I understood?"

Coelin's lighter eyes held the man's burning gaze, though he had to clear his throat to get his voice to work. "I can keep secrets, Tiarna. I know that certain songs should never be sung, or only in the right circumstances."

Mac Ard took a long breath. He rubbed at his beard, melting ice falling away. "We'll see," he said. "It's a hellish evening out there," he added. "Cold, and full of sleet and snow. A fine end to the year. But a song or two performed well might be welcomed at the Rí's dinner tonight. Are you prepared to sing for a Rí, Coelin?"

Coelin's face broke into a helpless grin. "Aye," he nearly shouted. "For the Rí? Truly?"

Mac Ard seemed to smile back. "Truly," he answered. "Though you'll need to look better than you do now. Where's that girl? Aoife!" he called, and a young woman came out from one of the doors, curtsying to Mac Ard.

"Tiarna?"

"Take this lad and get him proper clothes for the supper tonight with the Rí. He'll be singing for us. Go on, then, Coelin, and practice until you're called for."

Coelin grinned again. "Thank you, Tiarna," he said. His gaze strayed to Jenna, and he winked once at her. She smiled back at him.

"You can repay me by keeping quiet," Mac Ard told him. "Because if you don't, I will make certain you never talk to anyone else again. I trust that's clear enough for you."

The grin had fallen from Coelin's face like a leaf in an autumn wind. "Aye, Tiarna," he said to Mac Ard, and his voice was now somber. "It's very clear."

"Good." Mac Ard glanced from Coelin, to Jenna, and back again. "I would not forget my place and my task, if I were you, Coelin Singer."

Coelin nodded. He left the room with Aoife, and did not look again at Jenna.

The Rí's suppers were in the great Common Hall of the keep, a loud and noisy chamber with stone walls and a high, dim ceiling. A trestle table was set down the length of the hall. Torin Mallaghan, the Rí Gabair, sat with his wife Cianna, the Banrion, at the head of the table, jeweled torcs of beaten gold around both of their necks.

Arrayed down either side of the table before the royal couple were the Riocha in residence at the keep.

Not surprisingly, there was a delicate etiquette involved in the seating. Immediately to the Rí's left was Nevan O Liathain, the first son of Kiernan O Liathain, the Rí Ard—the High King in Dún Laoghaire. Nevan's title was "Tanaise Ríg," Heir Apparent to the Rí Ard. He had come to Lár Bhaile at his father's request, as soon as the rumors of the mage-lights had reached the Rí Ard's ears.

Padraic Mac Ard sat at the Rí's right hand next to Ci-

anna, a sign of his current favor, and Maeve and Jenna
were seated after him. There were Riocha from most of the
tuatha present as well, and many of them wore prominent
necklaces with stones that were reputedly cloch na thintrí,
though none of them knew for certain. Jenna knew, however. She could open her mind to the cloch she held, and
see the web of connection from her cloch to theirs. A good
number of the stones were simply pretty stones, and those
who owned them would be disappointed when the Filleadh
came. But some . . . some possessed true clochs na thintrí.
One of them was Mac Ard, even though the cloch he held
was never visible.

Farther down, below the salt, were the *céili giallnai*—the
minor Riocha—then the Rí's clients and a few prominent
freepersons of Lár Bhaile.

Jenna hated these suppers, and usually pleaded illness to
avoid them. She hated the false smiling conversations;
hated the undercurrents and hidden messages that ran
through every word; hated the way Rí Mallaghan sat in his
chair like a fat, contented toad contemplating a plate of
flies before him; hated when his eyes, half-hidden in folds
of pale flesh, regarded her with an appraising stare, as if
she were a possession of his whose value was still in question. She wanted to dislike Cianna, the Rí's ailing wife,
whose eyes were always hollow and sunken, ringed with
dark flesh, but she couldn't, more out of pity than anything
else. Cianna was as thin as the Rí Gabair was corpulent
yet she wheezed constantly, as if the exertion of moving
her frail body about was nearly too much for her. Cianna,
unfortunately, seemed to have fastened on Jenna as a fellow sufferer and talked to her often, though she treated
Jenna like an addled child, always explaining things to her
in a breath scented with the mingled odors of cinnamon
and sickness. She leaned toward her now, bending in front
of Mac Ard and Maeve, the torc around her neck swinging
forward, glinting in the torchlight. Her dark, haunted eyes
fastened on Jenna's. "How are you feeling today, dear?
Did that healer I sent to you from Dubh Bhaile help you?"

"Aye, Highness," Jenna answered. "The arm feels a bit
better today." Actually, Jenna had endured the man's prod-

ding and poking, and had thrown away the potion he offered, taking instead some of the andúilleaf she'd bought
that morning. She could feel it easing the pain in her arm.

Cianna looked pleased. "Good," she said. "He's certainly
done much for me, though I still can feel the pain in my
back."

Jenna nodded. The Banrion had gone through three new
healers in the two months they'd been at the keep; each
time the Banrion seemed to get a little better, but then she
inevitably slumped back into illness and the current healer
was dismissed and another summoned. If her back was
hurting now, this healer would be leaving before another
fortnight. The Rí himself never seemed to notice—he'd perhaps seen too many healers already, and no longer inquired
after his wife's health. She'd borne him a son and a daughter early in their marriage; both were away in fosterage—
the son to Tuath Infochla, the daughter to Tuath Éoganacht. The Banrion Cianna had performed her duty and
could keep her title. As to the rest . . . well, the Rí had
other lovers, as Jenna already knew from keep gossip. For
that reason, she was careful when the Rí smiled at her—
two of the Rí's current lovers were as young as Jenna.

The Tanaise Ríg, Nevan O Liathain, had evidently been
listening to Cianna's conversation with Jenna. He looked
across to her as the servants set the meat trays on the table.
"Perhaps the pain will lessen when the other clochs are
opened, Holder," he said. "Or perhaps there is another
way to use the mage-lights that wouldn't cause a Holder so
much . . . agony." Jenna could hear the words underneath
what he said: *Perhaps you are too stupid and too common
to be the First. Perhaps someone of the right background
would be better able to use it . . .* O Liathain smiled; he was
handsome, with hair black as Seancoim's crow Dúnmharú,
and eyes of glacial blue. Thirty, with a body hardened by
training and an easy grace, his wife dead two years now
leaving him still childless, he turned the heads of most of
the available women in the keep, even without the added
attraction of his title. He knew it, also, and smiled back at
them indulgently.

But not at Jenna. Not at Maeve. Jenna had overheard

him talking to the Rí one night, a few days after his arrival. *"Why do you keep them?"* he asked the Rí, laughing. *"Listen to them. Their accents betray their commonness, and their manners are, well, nonexistent. I can't believe Mac Ard would be consorting with that stupid cow mother of the Holder—if I were going to take one of them to my bed, as disgusting a thought as that is, I would have chosen the girl, who's at least trainable. Better to have left them back scrabbling in the dirt, which is all they're suited for. One of us should take the cloch from this Jenna now, before she truly learns to control it, and be done with the charade . . ."*

She hadn't heard the Rí's answer. She'd slipped away, steeling herself to fight for the possession of the cloch that night if she had to, trying to stay awake lest the Rí's gardai enter her bedroom, but eventually exhaustion claimed her and she drifted off to sleep, awakening the next morning with a start. But the cloch was still with her, and the Rí Gabair, if anything, seemed almost conciliatory toward her when she saw him later that morning.

She smiled at O Liathain now across the table, but her smile was as artificial and false as his own. "Each cloch tells its Holder the way to best use it, as the Tanaise Ríg might learn one day should he actually have a cloch of his own." Her smile widened on its own; O Liathain wore what he thought was a cloch na thintrí around his neck; while it was certainly an expensive jewel worthy of a Rí, it pleased Jenna to know that it was simply that, not a cloch na thintrí.

O Liathain frowned and fingered the polished facets of his stone on its heavy gilded chain. He looked as if he were about to retort, but the Rí guffawed at the exchange. "You see, Nevan," he said to O Liathain. "The Holder is more than she appears to be. She has an edge on her tongue."

"Indeed, she does," O Liathain replied. He inclined his head to her. "My pardon." There was a distinct pause before the next word. "Holder," he finished.

Mac Ard speared a piece of mutton with his knife and set it on his plate. "The Tanaise Ríg is gracious with his apology," he said, but Jenna and everyone else who heard it knew the tone of his voice and the hard stare he gave O Liathain added another thing entirely: *and it was necessary if you didn't want me to take offense.* Maeve touched Mac Ard's arm and smiled at him. Mac Ard, at least, seemed protective of them, though Jenna noted that while he might spend the night with Maeve, he also hadn't offered to legitimize the relationship.

Mac Ard was playing his own game. They were *all* playing their own games. She had already learned that words and actions here were carefully considered, and often held more than one meaning. Jenna was already weary of ferreting out those meanings, especially since she seemed to be the prize at the end of the contest. She wanted straightforward talk again, the easy conversations she'd had back in Ballintubber with her mam or Aldwoman Pearce or the other villagers, words that were simply gentle and kind speech.

Mac Ard smiled at O Liathain; O Liathain smiled back. Neither one of them meant the gesture. Jenna would have made an excuse, as she often did, that her arm troubled her and she needed to retire. But Maeve leaned toward her. "Patience," she whispered. "Coelin will be singing in a few minutes."

Jenna brightened at that. She endured the barbed conversations around her until the doors at the end of the hall opened and Coelin walked through with his giotár. Mac Ard cleared his throat and leaned toward the Banrion and Rí. "I heard this young man in the village where the magelights first appeared, and he recently came to the city. He trained with the Songmaster Curragh, who came here now and again, if you remember. He really has an extraordinary voice, Highnesses. I thought you would enjoy hearing him."

"Well, then, let's hear him," the Rí said. He gestured to Coelin, and pointed. "Stand there, and give us this voice of yours."

Coelin bowed low, his eyes catching Jenna's as he did so. "Is there a song your Highnesses would like to hear?" he asked. "A story that Songmaster Curragh used to sing, perhaps?"

The Rí seemed amused by that. "Are you saying your voice is the equal of your Songmaster's, young man?"

Coelin shook his head but the charming grin remained

on his face. "Oh, no, my Rí. Songmaster Curragh always said my voice was the better."

There was a moment of silence before the Rí laughed, the rest of the table following his lead a moment later. "He seems to have a healthy ego, at least, Padraic. I suppose that's good. But we'll be the judge of his talent. Give me *The Lay of Rowan Beirne,* young man."

Mac Ard sniffed, as if the choice surprised him, and Jenna glanced at him curiously. Coelin strummed a chord on his giotár, his eyes regarding the ceiling of the hall as if the words to the song were written there. "A fine choice, Rí Mallaghan. Songmaster Curragh taught me that one, not long before he died. Let me think a moment, and bring back the verses . . . Aye . . ." Coelin's gaze came back down and he nodded his head to the Rí. "I have it now," he said. His gaze caught Jenna's again, and he winked. He began to sing.

On the cusp of summer Rowan came forth
Bright armor on his chest, around his neck the stone
He saw the army on Sliabh Bacaghorth,
The banners of the Inish waving as Rowan stood alone . . .

"Have you heard this song before?" Cianna whispered, leaning toward Jenna. Jenna shook her head.

"I don't believe so, Banrion," she answered. She wanted to add . . . *and I still won't have heard it, if you talk to me,* but held her tongue.

Cianna glanced at Mac Ard, next to her. "*He* knows it," she said. "Don't you, Padraic?"

"I do, Banrion," Mac Ard answered, his voice gruff and low.

"And do you enjoy it?"

"I think 'enjoy' is too strong a word, Banrion. I find it . . . illuminating. And an interesting choice for the Rí."

"Indeed." Cianna leaned back then. Jenna puzzled over the exchange for a moment, but then Coelin's rich voice drew her back, and she returned her attention to him, smiling as she watched him perform.

Jenna had indeed heard portions of the tale once or

twice, though greatly altered and changed in the retellings. She had heard folktales of the hero Rowan, who had a magic stone—though she hadn't realized until now that the stone was supposedly the one she held now, or that Rowan was anything other than a mythological figure. What Coelin sang now, though, gave the full background of the tales, and it was a history Jenna had never suspected. Rowan Beirne had been a Holder of Lámh Shábhála more than five centuries before, and the last Holder from Talamh an Ghlas. From the opening stanza on the eve of Rowan's last day of life, the lay moved backward in time to the hero's youth, to his first triumphs on the field of battle, to the unsurprising extolling of his skill with the sword and his prowess in battle, and to his consolidation of the smaller tuatha that were numerous around Tuath Infochla at the time.

But that wasn't what startled Jenna. Early in the lay, the verses gave the lineage of Rowan, and it was then that Jenna sat back in her chair, stunned, no longer even hearing Coelin's voice.

Rowan's mam was a woman named Bryth, and she held Lámh Shábhála before Rowan. Bryth's surname, before she married Tiarna Anrai Beirne of Tuath Infochla, was Mac Ard.

A Mac Ard once held Lámh Shábhála. . . . Jenna barely heard the rest of the song: how Rowan foolishly allowed himself to be drawn north out of Falcarragh to a supposed parley with the Inishlanders, where he was ambushed and murdered by assassins in the employ of the Inish cloudmage Garad Mhúllien; and how Lámh Shábhála was taken from Rowan's body and brought to Inish Thuaidh. She barely reacted when Coelin finished the song to the applause of the table, or when the Rí handed Coelin a small sack of coins and told him to return again four nights hence to entertain his guests at the Solstice Feast.

She sat clutching at the stone on its chain around her neck. She couldn't look at Mac Ard, and she fled the table as soon as she could make an excuse.

18

Secrets

"WHY didn't you tell us that your ancestors once held the cloch, Padraic? I don't understand . . ."

Maeve's voice trembled, and Jenna could tell that her mam was on the verge of tears. Mac Ard, standing near the fireplace of their chambers, made as if to move toward her, but she lifted her head and he stopped with a shrug.

"Maeve, would you have trusted me if I had?" he answered. "Or would you have thought that I'd come only to take it from Jenna?" He glanced at Jenna, seated next to her mam and still clutching the stone.

"I don't know what I would have thought," Maeve answered. "Because you never gave us the chance to know. Why would you have come at all, if you didn't want the stone?"

"I *did* want it," Mac Ard answered. "I won't deny that. Had I found the cloch on that damned hilltop, aye, I would have kept it for myself. I wanted to be the Holder of Lámh Shábhála. I thought . . ." He took a breath and let it out in a nasal snort. "When I saw the mage-lights—here, so close to me—I thought that it was a sign that it was my destiny to bring the cloch back to my family. But Jenna already had it, though I didn't know it. And when I did . . ." He raised his hands, let them fall. "If you remember, I *did* hold it once, after Jenna killed the riders, and I gave it back. Maeve, have I done anything, *anything,* to make you feel threatened, or to cause you to feel that I'm a threat to your daughter?"

Jenna watched her mam shake her head slowly.

"Have I made any attempt to take the stone from Jenna, even though I had the opportunity, even though I once actually held it in my hands, before she knew how to use it?"

"No," Maeve admitted. She touched Jenna's bandaged arm. "Though sometimes I wish you had."

"Then forgive me for not telling you all of the history I knew, but believe me when I say it was because I was afraid that you wouldn't trust me, and because I was afraid that you would think that I lied when I told you I loved you."

"Padraic," Maeve began, but the tiarna interrupted.

"No, let me tell you all now, so there aren't any more secrets. There isn't much to tell." He pulled a chair close to the two of them and took Maeve's hands. His attention was on her; he glanced quickly at Jenna and looked away again before returning his gaze to her mam. "All this took place five centuries ago, so I don't know what's true and what's been changed in all the telling and retellings over the years. That's too much time, and details change every time the story gets told. So I'm simply going to give you the bare, dry genealogy without any embellishment: Sinna Hannroia—a Riocha from a small fiefdom—once held Lámh Shábhála, and she fell in love with the Rí of another small fiefdom named Teádor Mac Ard, my several times great-da, and married him. The two of them had a daughter named Bryth and a son named Slevin. Sinna passed Lámh Shábhála to Bryth before her death, and as you know from Coelin's song tonight, Bryth later married Anrai Beirne— a purely political alliance, from what our family history tells us—and eventually became the mother of Rowan Beirne, who lost the cloch to the Inishlanders. In any case, I'm not of Bryth's direct line, which is dead now: Bryth had only Rowan, and Rowan left no children that anyone knows about. The Mac Ards of today, like myself, trace our lineage back to Bryth's younger brother Slevin. So, aye, once someone of my blood and my name was the Holder of Lámh Shábhála, but it was long, long centuries ago in the Before. I have hand upon hand of cousins with the Mac Ard name who can say the same. There are many tiarna, as well as people of more common blood, who can say the same because there have been *numerous* Holders over the years. If you're going to be afraid of all of those who share the same surnames, you're going to be fearful of half the Riocha. You can't blame me for history, nor hold me accountable for it." He kissed the back of her hands, lifting them to his lips. "That's the extent of it, Maeve. Don't be afraid of my name. Don't be afraid of me."

He smiled at her, and Jenna watched her mam smile in return. Then Mac Ard leaned forward and kissed Maeve. "I need to see the Rí," he said. "The Rí rarely does anything without a reason, and I wonder why he called for that song tonight. I think he and I should have a conversation. If you'll pardon me . . ."

"Go on, Padraic," Maeve told him. She continued to hold his hands as he stood. "And thank you. I do understand."

He kissed her hands again. "I'll see you later, then. Jenna, I hope you also understand," he added, and left the room. As he did so, Maeve placed her hands over her abdomen, pressing gently. Jenna's eyes narrowed, and she must have made a sound, for Maeve glanced back over her shoulder and Jenna saw that she noticed where her daughter's gaze lay. Maeve looked down at her hands herself, then back to Jenna, shifting in her chair so she faced her daughter.

"Aye," she told Jenna.

"You're certain?"

"I've not bled for two moons, and I've been ill the last several mornings. But it's far too early to feel the quickening and know for certain." Jenna saw a slow satisfaction move over her mam's face. "But it will come. I know it."

"Have you told the tiarna?"

"No. Not yet. I'll wait until I can feel the life. Then I'll tell him." She paused. "You're supposed to ask if I'm happy," she said.

She went to her mam and hugged her fiercely. "Are you happy?" she whispered, burying her head in her mam's scented hair.

"Aye," Meave answered. "I'm happy. I want you to be happy, too."

For a time, the two held each other, saying nothing. Finally, Jenna pulled away with a kiss to Maeve's forehead. "Will Padraic give the child his name, and you also, do you think?"

For a moment, Jenna saw uncertainty in her mam's eyes. "I don't know, Jenna. I don't know how the Riocha do things. I don't know all that Padraic can do and what he can't. It doesn't matter, though, as long he doesn't change the way he feels toward me."

"But it does, Mam," Jenna replied earnestly. "Everyone will know it's Padraic's child, and if he won't acknowledge it, they'll laugh at you, Mam. They'll give you their meaningless smiles and then snicker at you behind their hands. You know they will. It won't be Mac Ard who'll have to bear all that; it'll be you." Jenna knelt in front of Maeve, her hands in Maeve's lap.

She knew she shouldn't say it even as she spoke the words. "Mam, if this isn't what you want, well, Aoife knows an herbalist in Low Town. He'll have potions, like Aldwoman Pearce . . ."

"Jenna!" Maeve said loudly, and Jenna stopped. "I don't need your herbalist," her mam continued, more softly. "I don't *want* the herbalist."

"I know, Mam, but if after you tell him, what if he . . ."

"Jenna—"

. . . *what if he isn't as he seems? What if he's angry, or if he abandons you, or you find that the love he says he feels is just another Riocha word?* She couldn't finish it. She didn't want to finish it. She didn't want to believe it herself.

Instead she forced herself to smile, to lift up and give her mam another kiss and place her own hands on Maeve's stomach. *Inside, there is life. A brother, or a sister . . .*

"I trust him, Jenna," Maeve said. "I love him."

Her face was so peaceful and content that Jenna nodded. "I know," she said.

*   *   *

Jenna didn't see Coelin after his singing. She heard through Aoife that he'd left the keep late that evening, and that he had asked after her. She thought he might send word the next day; he didn't. The mage-lights came again that night, and after taking in their power, she was too exhausted to care about anything but fixing a brew of the andúilleaf to blunt the pain. At least, that was what she told herself.

More Riocha were arriving at the Keep each day as word spread that Lámh Shábhála had a Holder and that she was in Lár Bhaile. Most of them wore the green and brown of Tuath Gabair, though there were a few with the red and white of Tuath Airgialla, or the blue and black of Tuath Locha Lein. None wore Tuath Connachta's blue and gold. They were men, mostly, and a few women, with rich clothes and rich accents and bright jewels around their necks, and some of those jewels, aye, were clochs na thintrí. She was introduced to them and as quickly forgot their names and titles, though she could feel them watching her as she wandered about the keep, staring at her, whispering about her, and pointing at her bandaged arm.

Waiting. Waiting for Jenna to give them the power they wanted.

"Jenna . . ."

She heard Cianna's voice as she walked along one of the deserted upper hallways, trying to avoid the eyes. Jenna stopped and turned: the Banrion stood at the end of the hall, with two of her ladies. Jenna curtsied and dropped her gaze as she'd seen the Riocha do in the woman's presence. "Banrion," she said. "Good morning."

"Please, no courtesies here. Not between us. *Is* it a good morning for you, or are you simply being polite?" Cianna asked. She cleared her throat, a phlegm-rattled sound. "None of them seem good to me lately. I think the new healer's a fraud, like all the rest."

"I'm sorry to hear that, Banrion."

Cianna laughed, a sound that ended in a series of coughs. "It's what I expected, my dear. I'm not quite as stupid and self-involved as some would have you believe. I know that

I'm deluding myself—I don't think any healer can cure what's inside me. But I feel I have to try. Maybe, maybe one of them . . ." The Banrion's eyes glittered with sudden moisture, and she caught her lower lip between her teeth. She sniffed and shook her head, and the mood seemed to pass. She waved her hand at her attendants.

"Leave me," she told them. They scurried away, glancing at Jenna. "They're supposed to be here to help me, but they're really just the Rí's eyes," Cianna said to Jenna, her voice dropping to a husky whisper. "They tell him everything they see. Come with me for a few moments, before they rush back to tell me that the Rí insisted they return. We should speak somewhere where no eyes watch or ears listen."

Cianna took Jenna's arm. The Banrion seemed to weigh nothing; her hand looked that of a skeleton, poking from under the lace of her léine. She led Jenna along the hall and down a corridor, through a door and up a small flight of stairs. Taking a torch from one the sconces, she opened the door at the top of the stair, which led into a musty-smelling gallery. There were shelves along the gallery, and on them were items, most covered in gray layers of dust. Their feet left marks in the film of it covering the floor, and cloudlets rose wherever they stepped. Jenna sneezed. "Banrion, this can't be good for your lungs."

"Hush," Cianna answered, tempering the word with a smile. "Do you know where we are?" Jenna shook her head. "This is the Hall of Memories," Cianna continued. "These are artifacts from the long history of Lár Bhaile. Not many come here—my husband isn't one for sentiment and history. He dismissed the Warden of the Hall, whose task it was to preserve these things and clean them, and since then the hall hasn't been opened in years. Previous Rís, though, were rather proud of it and brought visitors here so they could view the artifacts."

"Remembering the past is important." She said it politely, wondering why Cianna had brought her here.

"Is that something you believe?" Cianna asked. "Is it true, Holder, that you can bring the dead Holders of that

cloch back to life and speak with them? That's what Tiarna
Mac Ard tells me. He said he thought you had done it
once, with an old Bunús Muintir Holder."

"Aye, that's true, Banrion," she told Cianna. She'd never
told Mac Ard or her mam about the others: the Lady of
the Falls and her own da. She still had Eilís' ring and Niall's
carved seal back in her room. She'd never tried to bring
Eilís back again, but she had talked to her da several times.
It had been disappointing, for he stared at her as if he'd
never seen her before, and she had to explain all over again
who she was. The dead, it seemed, did not retain the memory of being dragged back into this existence by Lámh
Shábhála. "If I'm near to where a Holder rests, or if I
touch something that was once theirs I can speak with their
shade. At least that's what I've been told."

"Then come here . . ." Cianna gestured at one of the
shelves. On it was a torc, the hammered gold incised with
swirling lines that made Jenna glance at her bandaged arm.
"Do you know why my husband chose to have that singer
give the *Lay of Rowan* two nights ago?" Jenna shook her
head. Cianna started to speak, then coughed a few times,
patting at her mouth with a lace handkerchief. Jenna could
see spots of blood on the ivory cloth. "This cough . . . it gets
worse. Damn that healer. This is the way it is for us, Jenna.
They let us suffer, me because I've already given the Rí
what he wanted and now he no longer cares; you because
they think you're weak and they can take what they want
from you later, when it's less dangerous." She coughed
again, nearly doubling over with the racking spasms.

"Maybe we should leave this room, Banrion," Jenna suggested, but Cianna drew herself up, her haunted, umber-
circled eyes widening.

"No. Listen to me, Jenna. There is talk. I hear it, though
they think I don't listen or care. But I do. They want you
for one thing, Jenna, and one thing only: to open the other
clochs to the mage-lights. They know that the First Holder
always suffers more than the Holders who follow—they're
content to let you take that pain for now, even though
some of them intend to take the cloch you hold, once
you've opened the others."

"Who?" Jenna asked. "Who wants it?"

"Some I know for certain," the Banrion answered. "Nevan O Liathain, the Rí Ard's son, covets Lámh Shábhála—he's made no secret of that. My husband does, as well; he's more ambitious than you might think. Galen Aheron, the tiarna from Infochla who arrived a few days ago, has said things that make me suspect he would try for it as well. And even Padraic Mac Ard . . ."

"You've heard *him* talking?" Jenna asked, her eyes narrowing. "Tiarna Mac Ard?"

Cianna shook her head. "No, in truth, though I think that's why the Rí called for the song, because he knew that Mac Ard had said nothing to you regarding his ancestors' history with Lámh Shábhála. The Rí is always careful with Mac Ard, because he knows that a Mac Ard was once Rí and that Padraic could contend for the throne of Tuath Gabair. My husband and Padraic aren't enemies, but they also aren't entirely allies. Mac Ard's said nothing against you that I've heard, but when he rode away from the keep weeks ago, when the mage-lights first came, I know he was eager to find the cloch. And if you were . . ." Cianna paused. Coughed. ". . . no longer the Holder, aye, I believe he would try for the cloch himself."

Jenna's right hand, the fingers stiff and painful to move, closed around Lámh Shábhála on its necklace. Cianna noticed the gesture, and her fingers touched Jenna's. "Your skin there is so cold and so hard, like the scales of a snake." She touched her cheek. "And so warm and smooth here." The Banrion smiled gently. "You're so young to carry such a burden, Jenna. But I was a cycle and more younger when I was sent to marry the Rí and was a mam by the time I was your age. Women often carry their burdens early." She smiled again. "And long."

Cianna picked up the torc from the shelf, brushing away the dust with a hand and pursing her lips to blow away the rest, though the effort cost her another fit of coughing. She held out the golden artifact to Jenna, though Jenna only looked at it, puzzled. "We have nothing of Rowan's or of Bryth's, but this torc was Sinna Mac Ard's, great-mam of Rowan Beirne. I don't know if she could give you answers to the questions you might have, but you may try. Take it, use it if you can."

"Banrion, I can't . . ."

"If anyone asks why you have it, tell them to come to me. That's all you need say. Keep it." She gestured around her, at the gray-covered shelves, at the dim recesses filled with hundreds of unseen items. "You can see how much the past is revered here." She reached out and touched the cloch where it rested between Jenna's breasts. "But they will grab for what they see as the future," she said. "And some of them are quite willing to kill anyone who would get in their way."

19

An Assassin's Fate

SHE could feel the strong tingling of a presence when she held the torc, and she knew that Cianna had spoken true—this had once been a Holder's beloved possession. But even though she found herself alone in the apartment when she returned, Jenna didn't let the cloch call the presence forth. The experience with Riata had been frightening at first yet ultimately rewarding, but the ghost of Eilís had scared and nearly killed her and as for her da . . . seeing him hurt too much and left her unsatisfied and feeling more alone than ever.

She doubted that Sinna's specter could help her at all.

She placed the torc among her clothes where Aoife was unlikely to find it, thinking that she might use it that evening. But the mage-lights came again and she went to them, and afterward Jenna was in too much pain for anything but andúilleaf and bed. After Maeve had fussed over her for a bit (with Mac Ard hanging in the background at the door of the room, staring at her, Jenna thought, strangely), she lay in her bed, holding the cloch in her hand and staring into the darkness of the ceiling, seeing not the room but Lámh Shábhála. She gazed into the crystalline matrix of the cloch, seeing the nodes gleaming and sparking with the stored power of the mage-lights, flickering tongues of blue-white lightning arcing between the facets. She let herself drop deeper into Lámh Shábhála's depths toward the seething well at its heart, and she seemed to stand on a precipice, looking down into a maelstrom, a thunderstorm so bright

that it nearly blinded her. The well was nearly full now—
no more than three or four more nights, and it would over-
flow, filling the cloch . . .

. . . then . . .

She knew what was supposed to happen, knew that Lámh
Shábhála was to "open the other clochs na thintrí." But
she didn't know how, didn't know what that would do to
her, how it might feel or how it might hurt her or what it
would be like afterward. She wondered if Tiarna Mac Ard
might know, but she couldn't—or wouldn't—ask him. She
was grateful to him for what he'd done to save her and her
mam, and she knew that Maeve loved the man and seemed
to be loved in return, yet she found herself holding back
when she might speak to him. There was no one she trusted
enough to ask that question who would know the answer.

There were the dead Holders, of course. Riata she might
ask, but she had nothing of his to bring him back; Eilís was
too fey. Her da she'd already asked, but he had never held
Lámh Shábhála while it was alive—he knew less than she
did.

She trembled, looking down into the depths, at the raging
energy trapped there. She ached to know, she *needed* to
know, if only to steel herself for the ordeal.

She let go of the cloch, and the image of it faded in her
mind, leaving only the darkness of her room. She threw
aside the bedclothes, shivering in the cold, and went quickly
to the chest holding her clothing, pulling out the torc Cianna had given her. Her hands tingled with the feeling of
the presence within it, and she thought she heard her name
called, a yearning summons. *They feel you just as you feel
them* . . .

She went back to her bed, wrapping the quilts around
her and snuggling her toes under the heated plate of
cotton-wrapped iron Aoife had placed beneath the covers
to warm the bed. She placed the torc around her own neck,
grimacing as the cold, burnished metal touched her skin.

Sinna . . . ?

Torchlight swam in the darkness.

Sinna, come to me. . . .

Jenna trembled, tugging the blankets tightly around her.

She was in her room, but the portion in front of her was overlaid with a hazy image of another time. There, the fireplace was roaring; torches were set in their sconces along the walls, and embroidered hangings covered stone walls no longer plastered and painted. In the shadows, someone moved, a woman with plaited, long gray hair, wearing a léine of yellow under a long clóca of green. Around her neck was the torc Jenna wore and from under the gold a fine chain held Lámh Shábhála. She stepped forward into the firelight, and Jenna saw that her movements were slow, her posture stooped, her face lined with the furrows of age. Her right arm was marked to the elbow with swirling curves of scars, in the pattern Jenna knew all too well.

"Ahh," the specter said, looking around. "I remember this room, though it's much changed. So it's happening to me, now—new Holders are calling me back." The smile was bittersweet. "I'm to be used as I once used others." Jenna felt the touch of the woman's mind on her own, and at the same time Jenna reached into her. "You're Jenna . . . and a First."

"Aye. And you're Sinna."

The woman nodded. "Aye. And long dead, it would seem. Nothing more than dust and a memory. Have you called me back before?"

Jenna shook her head, and the apparition sighed. "Good," she said. "At least I'm not replaying an old scene. I always hated that, myself, having to explain again who I was and what I knew. No wonder the dead are often so angry and dangerous. You've already learned to keep most of your mind closed off, so I assume at least one of us has given you a nasty fright before. And the cacophony of voices within the cloch . . ." She shivered and yawned. "It's summer here, and I'm still cold, and every joint in my body is aching. Being old is worse than being dead . . ." She shook herself out of her reverie and peered at Jenna again. "You're young, though—have they married you off yet, Jenna? Is that why you're here in Lár Bhaile's Keep?"

"No," Jenna answered. "And they won't marry me against my will. I won't allow it."

Sinna laughed at that, her voice husky. "Then you do live in a different age. In my time, you were fortunate if you married for love. I was lucky enough to have loved once: my dear, poor Ailen, who gave me this." She lifted the cloch, and at the same time, Jenna felt Lámh Shábhála pulse on her own chest, as if the cloch remembered the touch. "But the second time . . . Well, a Holder is a political prize, and Teádor Mac Ard was Rí."

It gave Jenna a strange satisfaction to learn that Sinna hadn't fallen in love with Teádor, as Padraic had told them, that it had only been a marriage of convenience. "You were the Holder of Lámh Shábhála. How could they make you marry him?"

Sinna shrugged. "I suppose they couldn't, not if I utterly refused. But a Holder who is a woman must also know how to play the game, if she wishes to stay the Holder. A Banrion is a powerful thing, too, and to be both Holder and Banrion . . ." Sinna smiled. "Teádor and I found love elsewhere, but we were well suited to be Rí and Banrion. What we had wasn't love, but we understood each other well enough, and for the most part we both wanted the same things. That was enough. And when my daughter was old enough, we used her to strengthen an alliance." She sighed and smiled inwardly, then her gaze focused on Jenna, who saw that one eye was cloudy and white with a cataract. "Why did you call me back, First Holder? What is it you wanted to ask me? Ask, and let this ghost go back to sleep."

Jenna flipped away the bed quilts. Suppressing a shiver as the cold air touched her, she swung her legs over the side of the bed and walked to where the old woman stood. "I'm First, as you said. And the other clochs na thintrí aren't yet opened. I want . . . I want to know what will happen when Lámh Shábhála is full and wakes the other stones."

"No one has told you?"

"They hint, but they don't say. Or perhaps they truly don't know," Jenna answered. "I've even talked to the Ald here. He says he doesn't know—it's been so long since the mage-lights came that the knowledge is lost."

Sinna sighed. Her hand lifted as if she were about to

touch Jenna, then dropped back. "So they do use you," she said. Her voice was soft. "Your time isn't so much different, then. I wasn't a First, Daughter. When I held Lámh Sháb-hála, the clochs had been active for generations and generations, nearly all the way back to when the first Daoine came to this land. I can't help you with that . . ." She stopped, turning slightly from Jenna and holding her hands out to the image of the fire, as if warming them. "Tell me, did I give the cloch to Bryth, or did someone else take it?"

"No," Jenna answered. "Bryth was the next Holder, and her son after that, your grandson."

Sinna nodded, firelight reflecting on her wrinkled skin and over the coarse gray hair. "That's good to know," she said. "It's a comfort, even though I'll forget as soon as you release me. I'm going to Tuath Infochla in a fortnight to meet her, and I intend to pass it to her then. So it seems I manage to do so."

"Another Mac Ard would like to hold Lámh Shábhála now," Jenna said, and with that Sinna turned back to her. "Ahh . . ." she breathed. "So the line continues."

"Not Bryth's," Jenna told her. "Your son's. Slevin."

Her face changed with that, as if she'd tasted sour fruit. "Slevin," she said, and the word sounded harsh and bitter. "Strange how distant we can become from our own children . . ." She stopped. "Jenna, do you feel that?"

"What?"

Sinna turned, her half-blind eyes peering toward the south window of the room. "Perhaps I can teach you something after all. See with the cloch, Jenna. Imagine . . . imagine that your skin is alive with its power, that it's like a shell around you, expanding, and you can feel everything that it touches, can see the shape of it as the power within you wraps around it. Can you do that?"

"Aye . . ." Jenna breathed. "I can." Perhaps it was because Lámh Shábhala remembered Sinna's touch, perhaps it was because Sinna's mind and hers were open to each other, but Jenna could feel her presence expand, filling the room so that in her mind she could see everything in it as clearly as if it were day. She let it expand farther, moving her awareness outward.

And stopped with a gasp.

"Aye," Sinna said. "Even the dead can feel that threat."

Outside, on the wall, a dark form crept upward in the night, hands already on the balcony and death lurking in his heart. The intruder pulled himself silently over the rail—with her eyes, Jenna saw nothing but the closed doors leading to the balcony, shut against the night and the cold air. But with the cloch, she saw the man crouch, then stand, and she saw the small crossbow in his hand and the quarrel smeared with brown poison.

"You see," Sinna said softly. "Lámh Shábhála can do more than throw lightnings. Watch; let me use the cloch . . ."

One of the balcony doors swung open, and a night-wrapped form slipped in with a breath of cold wind. At the same time, Jenna felt the stone around her neck respond as the ghost of Sinna moved forward, her body changing as Lámh Shábhála's energy surged through her, her shape suddenly that of Jenna herself, young and brown-haired, the torc gleaming around her neck. "You!" Sinna shouted, and the intruder turned, firing the crossbow in the same motion. The quarrel went through Sinna's chest, burying itself in the plaster behind her. Sinna laughed, and she was herself again, an old woman. Behind the dark wrapping of the assassin's head, his eyes were wide, and he looked from the ghost of Sinna to Jenna, standing near the bed. A knife flashed in his hand, but before he could move, Jenna felt Sinna's mind close over her own and—like a skilled teacher's hand guiding a student's—she let energy burst forward from the cloch, shaping the force as it flew, and the assassin was picked up as if in a giant's hand and slammed against the wall, grunting in pain and shock. A wisp of the cloch's power ripped the cloth from his head, so that Jenna could see his face.

"Do you recognize him?" Sinna asked.

Jenna shook her head—his features were those of a stranger.

"Then he was hired, and he has a name to tell you." The man was struggling, trying to push away from the wall and

move, but Jenna held him easily. "There, you have him,"
Sinna said, and Jenna felt Sinna's mind leave hers.

"I'll tell you nothing," the man grated out, writhing in
the grip of the cloch. His gaze kept slipping from Jenna to
the ghostly image of Sinna.

"No?" Sinna said. "Tighten the power around him,
Jenna. Go on. Squeeze him, Jenna. Make him feel you."

Jenna did as Sinna instructed, imagining the tendrils of
Lámh Shábhála's energy snaking around him, pulling tight
like a noose. The man grimaced, the lines around his eyes
and forehead deepening, and he spat defiantly.

"Good. I like defiance," Sinna said. "It increases the
pleasure when he finally gasps out the name we want. I
wonder if he's ever felt his ribs crack inside him, snapping
like a dry branch into a dozen knives of bone. I wonder if
he'll whimper like a kicked dog when the eyes pop from
his skull, or scream as his ballocks are crushed and ruined."

Sinna/Jenna yanked at the cords of energy, pulling them
tighter still. The man moaned, and Jenna glanced at
Sinna. "I can't—" she began, appalled, but with the shift
of attention, the assassin momentarily pulled away from
his invisible bonds. Before Jenna could respond, the
knife still in his hand moved. With a cry, he plunged it
into his own chest. Blood welled around the wound, and
flecks of red foamed at his lips. He wailed, his eyes
rolled upward.

He fell. The wind from the balcony brought the fetid
smell of piss and bowels.

Sinna sniffed. "Not a common assassin, then, but a loyal
and devoted retainer, to kill himself rather than talk," she
said. Her voice sounded eerily emotionless. "I would guess
that someone's becoming impatient."

Jenna gaped in horror at the foul corpse on the floor.
"Would you have done that, what you told him you
would do?"

Sinna laughed. "If he had come to me, in my time, rather
than to you? Aye, I would have done that and more to
stay alive. I *have* done it. And so will you, Daughter, if you
want to remain the Holder."

"No, I won't," Jenna said, the denial automatic. Sinna only smiled.

"Jenna!" Maeve's voice called from outside the room, and she heard footsteps pounding toward her. Jenna pulled the torc from her neck, and Sinna vanished as Maeve and Mac Ard rushed in, Mac Ard with his sword drawn. He stopped at the doorway, gazing at the crumpled body of the assassin. He hurried over to the man as Maeve went to Jenna. He prodded the assassin's body with the tip of his sword, then knelt and pressed his fingertips against the neck just under the jaw, grimacing at the smell. She saw him glance at the small crossbow on the floor near him. "Dead," he said, rising again. "And by his own hand, it would seem. Jenna, are you all right?"

"I'm fine," she answered, trying to keep her voice from trembling. Her arm ached, burning cold, and there was ice in the pit of her stomach, making her want to vomit, but she forced it down, forced herself to stand erect and pretend that she was calm. Later, she could allow herself to cry at the remembered fear and the death. Later, she could run to the andúilleaf and its relief. But not now . . .

"What happened here?"

Jenna pointed to the open door to the balcony, then to the quarrel embedded in the wall. "He climbed up from outside and shot that at me, but . . ." She paused, considering her words. She pulled away from her mam's embrace. "I knew he was coming," she said, more strongly, "and I swept the bolt aside with the cloch, then held him. He killed himself rather than be captured; if I'd suspected he would do that, I would have stopped him, but I was too late. No doubt he didn't want me to know who hired him." She watched Mac Ard's face carefully as she spoke— *certainly it wasn't Padraic, not after all he's done. He's had a hundred better opportunities if he wanted them . . .* Yet she watched. Mac Ard was frowning and serious, but she had seen him speaking with the Rí and knew that he could keep his thoughts hidden from his face. She couldn't stop the paranoia from creeping back into her mind. *He could easily tell an assassin where and when to find me.*

"You 'knew he was coming'?" he said, his head tilted, one eyebrow raised.

"Lámh Shábhála can do more than throw lightnings," she stated: *Sinna's words . . .* His eyes narrowed at that; his mouth tightened under the dark beard and he turned away from her. He went to the quarrel and pulled it from the wall, sniffing at the substance daubed over the point. "Aye, 'tis poisoned," Jenna told him.

There was anger and fury in Mac Ard's face, but Jenna didn't know if it was at the attempt, or at the failure of it. "The garrison will comb the grounds, and those on watch tonight will be punished for allowing this to happen," he said. "I'm sorry, Jenna. I will have gardai sent here immediately. This won't happen again."

How convenient that would be . . . to have his own people around me all the time. "Thank you, Tiarna, but I don't need gardai," Jenna said firmly.

"Jenna—" Maeve began, but Jenna shook her head.

"No, Mam, Tiarna," she insisted. "Get rid of . . . that." She pointed at the body. "Call the servants in to clean up the mess. But no gardai. I don't need them." She lifted Lámh Shábhála. "Not while I hold this."

20

Love and Weapons

"SO far," Jenna said, "they tell me that they think the assassin was sent from Connachta."

"Jenna . . ." Coelin's arm went around her shoulders at that. For a moment, Jenna tensed, then she relaxed into the embrace, moving closer to him as they walked slowly along the garden path. The planted array in the keep's outer courtyard rustled dry and dead in the winter cold, and a chill wind blew in off the lough, tossing gray clouds quickly across the sky and shaking occasional spatters of rain from them.

Coelin had arrived early for the feast celebrating the winter solstice, the Festival of Láfuacht, to be held that night. Aoife had come running into Jenna's apartment, bursting with the news that the "handsome harper" was in the keep and asking about her, and Jenna had sent Aoife to fetch him. Jenna could feel the warmth of Coelin's body along her side, and it felt comfortable and right. She knew there were eyes watching them, and that tongues would be clucking about the Holder and a lowly entertainer (and no doubt saying how "common blood will tell"), but she didn't care.

"You sound as if you don't believe them," Coelin said.

"I don't," Jenna said firmly. "What good would it do for Connachta to have me killed here, where someone else would simply become the Holder? That makes no sense unless the assassin himself was to be the new Holder, yet he wasn't from the Riocha families."

"But how else could someone from Tuath Connachta get

the stone? You said none of the Riocha from Tuath Connachta are here. If that assassin was so loyal that he'd kill
himself rather than be caught alive, he might be loyal
enough to take the cloch to his employer without keeping
it himself."

"Maybe. That's what Tiarna Mac Ard said, too." Jenna
shivered as the wind shook water from the bare branches
of the trees. "I don't think so. I think he was hired by
someone here."

"Who?" Coelin asked.

"I don't know. But I'll find out."

"Finding out could be dangerous."

"Not finding out is more dangerous, Coelin." She
stopped, moving so that they stood face to face, his arm
still encircling her shoulder. His face seemed bewildered
and innocent with all she had told him, and she knew that
she would have looked the same a few months ago, thrown
without warning into this situation where agendas were
veiled and hidden, and the stakes of the game so high.
Looking at him, she saw reflected back just how much she
had changed in the intervening months. *He is a harper, and
nothing more—right now singing is enough for him and all
that he thinks about. If he has ambition, 'tis to be a Songmaster like Curragh, who plucked him away from a life
of servitude.*

"Jenna, you should leave the investigation to Tiarna Mac
Ard and the others."

"One of the others may have sent the man in the first
place." She hesitated, not wanting to say the rest. "I can't
even rule out Tiarna Mac Ard."

His eyebrows lifted, widening his sea-foam eyes. "I
thought he and your mam—"

"They're lovers, aye," Jenna said. "But I'm not my mam,
I'm not his blood, and I hold what he was searching for
when he came to Ballintubber. Wouldn't it have been convenient, for him to be the first to find my body? He could
have plucked the cloch from around my neck before anyone could have stopped him."

"You don't know that, Jenna, and I don't believe it."

"You're right, I don't know that and honestly, I don't

believe it's true, either," she answered. "But I don't *know*. I don't know."

He was looking somewhere above and beyond her, as if he could find an answer written on the stones of the keep. He shook his head as if to some inner conversation. "Jenna . . ." he began. "This is so . . ."

Jenna reached up, twining the fingers of her left hand in the curls at the back of his head. She gently pulled him down to her. The kiss was first soft and tentative, then more urgent, her mouth opening to his as he pulled her against him. When at last it ended, she cradled her head on his chest. He stroked her hair. "Jenna," he said. "How can I help you?"

"I don't know yet," she answered. "But I will. And I'll ask when the time comes."

"And I'll be there for you," Coelin answered. He brought his head down to hers again, and she opened her mouth to his soft lips and his hot, sweet breath, and when his hands slid up to cup her breasts, she did not stop him.

"I can tell you this much about the assassin, Holder," the Rí Mallaghan told her, his trebled chins shaking as his mouth moved. Nevan O Liathain stood at the Rí's right shoulder, frowning appraisingly at her as the Rí spoke and stroking his thin beard. "He was not a Riocha that anyone here recognizes. I have people who would know such making inquiries in Low Town to see if he's a local, but I don't think so. We may never know who he was. I know that's of no comfort to you, but I assure you that the gardai here will be more . . ." He paused, and a smile prowled his face for just a moment. ". . . vigilant from now on," he finished.

Jenna knew that the gardai on watch that night had been imprisoned, and the sentry assigned to the north side of the keep nearest Jenna's room had been executed in front of the others as an example. The punishment had been exacted before she could protest and without her consent. She suspected that it never occurred to the Rí to inquire about her feelings—it was his domain, and he did as he wished.

It's also true that dead men don't talk, if they'd been told to look the other way and their knowledge of who gave them the order was now a danger. The Rí Gabair has the money and the knowledge and the desire, as much as anyone here.

She smiled blandly back at the Rí. "I appreciate your efforts, Rí Mallaghan. Your concern for my well-being is gratifying."

The Rí laughed at that, his body shaking under the fine clothing. "There, you see, Nevan—as fine a response as any Riocha could have fashioned. Tiarna Mac Ard has taught the girl well."

Jenna gave the Rí the expected smile, resisting the impulse to retort. *Tiarna Mac Ard may have helped, but I taught myself more by listening to the lies I hear around me every day,* she wanted to say. But she curtsied instead, as a Riocha would, and continued to smile.

"The Rí Ard is also concerned with your well-being," O Liathain said before Jenna could escape. "I have put the Rí Ard's garrison here in Lár Bhaile at Rí Mallaghan's disposal."

"That is kind of you, Tanaise Ríg," Jenna answered. "Some good has come of this incident, though. I've discovered that the stone I hold has greater and more varied powers than I'd thought. I may be able to discover who my enemies are on my own." She touched Lámh Shábhála with the scarred, patterned flesh of her right hand, looking from O Liathain to Rí Mallaghan. "And I'm certain the Rí and the Rí Ard would allow me to exact my own retribution. Wouldn't that be interesting?"

The smile on O Liathain's face wavered and for a moment Jenna wondered if she'd gone too far, but Rí Mallaghan also frowned. "The laws are the laws," Rí Mallaghan intoned. "An accusation would need proof—and proof that I as Rí can see."

Jenna inclined her head. "I've heard that the Rí Mallaghan has excellent methods for obtaining proof when it's needed," she responded.

The Rí snorted. "Taught well, indeed," he commented to O Liathain. Cianna drifted over to them before he could

say more, with Tiarna Galen Aheron of Tuath Infochla
accompanying her. Cianna touched Jenna's shoulder and
nodded to O Liathain's abbreviated bow.

"The servants tell me we should begin moving toward
the table soon, my husband," she said, her voice too fast
and colored with a slight wheeze. "Let me take the Holder
for a few minutes before we sit. Here, Tiarna Aheron
wishes to speak with you."

"Certainly," the Rí answered. "Holder, I will speak with
you later." Jenna curtsied to the Rí and O Liathain again,
and let Cianna guide her away. O Liathain's head moved
toward the Rí's ear before they were a step away, as Galen
Aheron bowed to the Rí.

"What did you say to the Tanaise Ríg?" Cianna asked
quietly as they moved through the crowd. "Poor Nevan
looked as if he'd swallowed a fish bone."

"I simply suggested to him that Lámh Shábhála might
have ways of uncovering treachery," Jenna said. Cianna
laughed at that, the laughter trailing away in a cough. She
stopped, drawing Jenna into a corner of the hall.

"I would be careful with what you claim, Jenna," she
said. "It's not good to put an enemy on alert with a bluff."

"I don't know who my enemies are, Banrion," Jenna
answered. "I thought that I might find out—and I wasn't
entirely bluffing."

"Ah," Cianna said thoughtfully, nodding. She gestured
at the room. "They're *all* your enemies, every one of them
here," she said. "Even me, Jenna. Any of us would take
the cloch and become the Holder, if we thought it would
gain us power."

"I think I can trust you, Banrion. Or you wouldn't have
said what you just said."

Cianna smiled. "Thank you, Jenna. But look at them.
There are more plots there than leaves in the forest, and
many of them concern you. In the last cycle, my husband
was nearly killed himself when one of the céili giallnai decided that he might increase his standing by allying with
one of the Connachtan families. He managed to actually
draw his blade at the table before he was cut down, not
five feet from the Rí. Trust is a rare commodity here,

Jenna. Don't take it lightly, and don't believe that it's eternal, either. Allegiances shift, friendships fade, love is ephemeral. Be careful."

Jenna glanced worriedly at the throng, at the faces overlaid with smiles and politeness. "How do you stand it, Banrion?" she asked. "Doesn't it drive you mad?" The crowd parted momentarily, and through the silken rift, Jenna saw Tiarna Mac Ard across the room, with her mam at his side and a quartet of the Riocha women also surrounding him. Maeve looked uneasy in the midst of the other women, her smile lopsided as her attention went from one to another of them, all of them obviously much more at ease and more skilled at the game of flirtation. Maeve's hand cradled her abdomen more than once. Jenna felt Cianna's gaze shift, following her eyes.

"There are rules even in this, Jenna. You've already learned some of them; if you want to keep the stone and also stay alive, you must continue to learn. You think Padraic Mac Ard doesn't understand how our society works? He does, all too well. That's why he doesn't marry your mam—because marriage to him is another weapon, one that often can be used only once, so he won't unsheathe it lightly."

"He uses my mam, then," Jenna said heatedly.

Cianna coughed, though it might have been a laugh. "I don't doubt that Padraic also loves her, or he wouldn't be so openly with her—he knows that his relationship with your mam dulls the blade of the marriage weapon, because it says that his true affection is elsewhere. He *does* love your mam, and that may have saved you as well, Jenna."

"You said to trust no one, and I wondered . . . I wondered if Tiarna Mac Ard sent the assassin."

Jenna felt more than saw Cianna shake her head. "Mac Ard would take Lámh Shábhála if he could, I agree. But I know him well, and his personality is more suited to the frontal attack. He can be subtle when he needs to be, but when action must be taken, he prefers to do it himself and openly. I wouldn't entirely trust him, if I were you, but I also doubt that the assassin was his man."

Jenna wasn't certain she was convinced, but she nodded

her head in the direction of the Rí, still in conversation with O Liathain. "The Tanaise Ríg, then," Jenna said, and watched Cianna purse her lips.

"Possibly," she said. "Hiring someone to do his killing for him is more his style, certainly—he wouldn't want to bloody his own hands. And through the Rí Ard, he has the money and connections; the assassin could have come from the east rather than the west. The Rí Ard used an assassin himself to kill his predecessor—or at least that's the rumor—and Nevan is more ambitious than even his father. Holding Lámh Shábhála *and* being Rí Ard: that would place him in a very powerful position indeed."

"You think it was him, then?"

Cianna shrugged. "Possibly," she repeated. "Maybe even probably. But there are other contenders here: my husband is certainly one; Tiarna Aheron, whose uncle is Rí of Infochla and who has been snatching any reputed clochs he can find, buy, or steal, is another. Jenna, *any* of the Riocha here could be the one."

Jenna's head whirled. She'd taken andúilleaf a few hours ago; the effects were already starting to fade, and her arm throbbed with a promise of pain to come. She looked out at the crowd and saw skeletons and ghouls underneath the fine clothing and polite speech.

A gong rang. "There, we're being called to table," Cianna said. "Come, walk with me. You will sit next to me tonight—we'll let Padraic move a seat farther down."

"Banrion?"

Cianna smiled. "Just a little object lesson, Jenna. Everyone will notice your elevation, though no one will say anything until afterward when they're alone. Even Mac Ard will gracefully make the shift, but he'll also see the message in it: that the Holder is now more important than the one who found her, and that what happens to you will be of intense concern to me." She coughed, and cleared phlegm from her voice. "That also means no one will question too much what you do, even if you should decide to consort with a simple harper."

Jenna felt her cheeks flush. "Banrion, I . . ."

"Oh, he's handsome enough, I'll grant you, and has talent for what he does. A little dalliance with him won't hurt you as long as you take the proper precautions—I'll make sure the healer sends a packet of the right herbs to you. But he can't help you, Jenna, not in this. Tell me, is it true you knew this Coelin in Ballintubber?"

"Aye, Banrion."

Cianna nodded. "Convenient that he should arrive here in Lár Bhaile just at this moment, don't you think?" she asked, but she gave Jenna no chance to ponder that question or to try to answer. "Come. All the tiarna are seated by now. Time to give them something to contemplate . . ."

"You were wonderful. The Rí and the Banrion were rapt—did you notice?"

Jenna could see the grin tugging at the corners of Coelin's mouth as she complimented his performance. "Aye," he said. "I did. I thought I might forget some of the words, but they came back to me in time. The captain said that I might be asked to sing again at an entertainment for the Tanaise Ríg in five days, and he gave me a gold mórceint for the evening. That's more than I saw for months in Ballintubber." The grin spread, and Jenna impulsively reached up and kissed him. She started to pull away, but his arms went around her and he brought her close, cupping his hand around the back of her head. The kiss was long and deep, and Jenna wanted more, but it was late and the carriages were already waiting at the gates of the keep to take the extra servers and entertainers back down into the town. "Jenna, when can I see you again?"

Stay, she wanted to say, but she remembered Banrion Cianna's admonitions, and there would be her mam's questions, and the pain in her arm was getting worse . . . "The day after tomorrow," she said. "You know the market in Low Town? I'll meet you there, when they ring the bells after morning services at the Mother-Creator's temple."

"I'll be there," he promised. He kissed her again, quickly this time, and held her hand—her left hand. He didn't touch the right. His fingers pressed against her. "The day after tomorrow will seem like forever before it comes," he said, and walked quickly away toward the gates across the courtyard. Jenna watched until he reached the gates and the gardai there pushed the inner door open. He went through, and she could hear that he was whistling. She smiled.

As she turned to go back into the keep, she saw movement at one of the windows: a shutter swinging closed. She glimpsed a face in the window just before the shutters pulled tight, shadowed in the dim light of the moon and the torches around the courtyard.

Tiarna Mac Ard's face.

21

A Familiar Face

"YOU will stay here with the carriage," she told the quartet of gardai Tiarna Mac Ard had sent with her. The protest was predictable, but when she invoked the Banrion's name, they went sullenly silent. *You see,* she wanted to tell Cianna. *You taught me well. I can play this game, too.*

Low Town Market was crowded today. Wagons had come in from the surrounding farms. There was little produce—the fields had long ago been harvested, but there were horses for sale, sheep brought in for slaughter, milk and eggs, pickled vegetables, dried herbs. A spice vendor in from the port at Dún Laoghaire had set up a display, and exotic aromas from the distant lands of Céile Mhór and Thall Mór-roinn wafted through the chill air. The sun beat down, driving away the worst of the chill. There was little breeze, and the respite from the cold had brought out most of the townsfolk. Jenna was surrounded by the movement and noise, the color and odors. Some of the tiarna from Upper Town were here as well, and they nodded to her as they passed, no doubt wondering why the Holder was walking unescorted through the city.

Jenna moved through the market, looking among the crowds for Coelin. The temple bells had rung as the carriage arrived at the market, but it would be easy to miss someone. She was beginning to wonder whether Coelin had forgotten her, and she closed her right hand around the cloch, remembering how Sinna had helped her. She let her

awareness drift outward with the stone's energy, seeing the
crowd with the power and looking for the spark that would
be Coelin. She could sense him, close by, and started to
turn even as she heard his voice.

"Jenna!"

She turned to see him hurrying toward her. With a grin,
he swept her up and spun her around once, kissing her as
she laughed. "I'll bet you thought I'd forgotten," he said,
wagging a finger in front of her face. She pretended to bite
at it.

"I did not," she answered. "I had perfect confidence in
you."

He snorted. "Hah! I saw your face when you turned."
He glanced around. "I'm surprised they let you come here
alone. I expected to see your mam, or servants at least.
Armed and surly gardai, most likely, after what happened
in your bedroom."

"Armed gardai I had," she answered. "But I sent them
away." *No, they're following* . . . The energy she'd released
before was fading slowly, but within the expanded shell of
awareness she could feel one of them. She turned her head,
and saw a garda ducking quickly behind the spice vendor's
stall. "Though they don't obey well. Don't look yet, but
near the spice vendor's stall . . ."

"Here, let's look at this cloth . . ." Coelin took her arm
and guided her over to the nearest stall, pretending to show
her the dyed wool there. "Ah, aye. I see. You have a
shadow, but not a very good one. Ring mail and leathers
makes one conspicuous. Do you really want to lose him?"

Jenna nodded, and Coelin took her left arm. "Come on,
then," he said.

With Coelin leading, they moved behind the stalls and
into one of the alleys. Jenna could sense the garda's sudden
consternation and feel him start to move through the crowd
toward the stall where they'd been, but Coelin was running
through a space between two houses, across a narrow courtyard, and on into another street. He paused, looking up
and down the street and behind them.

"You've lost him," she said to him.

"How do you know?"

"I know," she answered.

He didn't question that. He simply smiled at her and kissed her again. "We're alone, then." He glanced around at the people moving along the cobbled lane, most of whom were staring openly at Jenna, too well-dressed to be an occupant of one of these small, shabby dwellings. Away from the market square, the city had turned drab and dirty and crowded. The central gutter was choked with refuse, rotting garbage and excrement, and the fetid smell wrinkled Jenna's nose. The people were as shabby as their surroundings, dressed in rags and scraps of clothing. A child stared at her from a nearby door, her feet wrapped in muddy rags, her hair matted and wild, though her eyes were dark and clear. She smiled tentatively at Jenna, who had to force herself to return the gesture. "Well, at least we're not where anyone knows you," Coelin finished. He gave a mock, sweeping bow. "And now where would you have me take you?"

"Somewhere other than here."

Coelin glanced around, and she realized that he saw nothing unusual: these were the streets where he lived, too, and he didn't see the contrast, because he hadn't lived as she had for the last few months. Jenna could feel herself recoiling in instinctive disgust and revulsion. She could not imagine having to live here—she would rather call on the power of the cloch and destroy it, to cleanse the earth in fire and storm. And she wondered: *Is this the way Tiarna Mac Ard felt, when he first walked into our little cottage back in Ballintubber?* "There's an apothecary I need to see," she told him. "Du Val, in Cat's Alley."

He glanced at her curiously, then shrugged. "Let's go this way, then, to avoid the market."

They approached du Val's establishment from below the market. Jenna half expected to see one of the gardai standing outside the tiny shop, but none of these men had accompanied her on her first visit. A few dozen strides from the sign, she saw a man, dressed as a freelander, come out the doorway and turn away from her toward the market.

She stopped, her hand on Coelin's arm. "What?" he asked.

"That man . . ." She knew him. Without seeing his face, she recognized the walk, the posture, the *feel* of him: Ennis O'Deoradháin, whom she'd last seen fleeing through the fields just across the River Duán near Áth Iseal. Jenna held her breath, wanting to duck into shadows and suddenly wishing that she hadn't dismissed the gardai. Her hand went around Lámh Shábhála; if the man had turned, if he'd seen her and started toward her, she would have used the cloch and struck him down.

But he didn't turn, didn't seem to notice her at all.

"What about him?" Coelin asked. "Who is he?"

Jenna shook her head. O'Deoradháin was hurrying away, already at the end of the lane where it opened into the Low Town Market. "When . . . after we left Ballintubber, we met that man. I think he was part of the group of Connachtans who were pursuing us." *And if he's here in Lár Bhaile, if he's snooping around after me, then chances are he's the one who sent the assassin. . . .*

"Well, let's go after him, then," Coelin said, starting to pursue O'Deoradháin, but Jenna held him back.

"No," she told him. "He's already too far away, and he may have friends with him. Let's talk to du Val."

The shop was as pungent and dark as before, but du Val was in the front, bent over one of his tables with a mortar and pestle, grinding a small pinch of plant material into a powder. The dwarfish man glanced up as Jenna and Coelin entered, and grunted.

"It's not even been a month," he called out without preamble. "Well, this time the price is four mórceints, as I told you. And six the next time."

Jenna was glad for the dimness of the shop, so that Coelin could not see the flush that crept up her neck. "I hear you," she said. "Just get it."

Du Val sniffed. He set the pestle on the table with a loud *clunk*. His ugly, craggy face seemed to leer at her for a moment, then he turned and went back into the recesses of the shop. Jenna wondered what Coelin was thinking, seeing her spend four mórceints without a thought when he had been ecstatic to have received one the other night. She didn't dare look at him while they waited. Du Val returned in a few minutes with a pouch, which he extended to Jenna, palm up. When she reached to take it, he pulled his hand back. "Five mórceints," he said.

"You told me four."

One robed shoulder lifted and fell. "I changed my mind between then and now. Maybe the price will make you change yours about taking this, but if not, I might as well line my pockets with your foolishness."

Jenna felt the words like a slap, her cheeks reddening. "All I have to do is whisper to the Rí or Banrion, and they will have you in irons before the evening bells ring."

Du Val snorted and tossed the pouch of andúilleaf into the air and caught it again. "And if you do that, what happens when this is gone?" He gave her a lopsided leer. His glance went to Coelin. "I notice that you don't have your usual escort with you, only someone who makes his living singing for coppers and ale. Seems to me that you're being careful not to let anyone know you've come to see me, so I think I'm fairly safe from your threats, Holder."

"Jenna," Coelin said behind her. "Let's just leave. This man is a thief. I've seen the type of people who come in here."

"No," Jenna answered. She turned back to du Val. "Fine, I'll give you the five mórceints, but you'll also tell me something in return. There was a man who came from this shop just before we arrived. What did he want?"

Du Val sniffed. "I'm not in the habit of talking about my customers," he answered. "I'd also think that's something you'd be pleased to hear, Holder."

"His name is Ennis O'Deoradháin."

Du Val's lips pursed and he waggled his head. "So you do know him. Interesting."

"Why was he here?" When du Val didn't answer, Jenna's hand went to the cloch, with du Val's black gaze watching the movement. "The man's a danger to me, du Val. I'll do what I need to do to protect myself, even if means killing someone."

Du Val blinked, then cleared his throat and spat on the floor. "Brave words, Holder. I love the way you lift your chin and look down at me when you say that. It's so

haughty and practiced—you've obviously been watching the
Riocha around you. I also believe that's another bluff. I
don't think you're capable of striking a man down without
provocation. Not yet, anyway. Tell me, Holder, how did it
feel, when you killed the assassin?"

"I *didn't* kill him. He killed—" Jenna stopped. "How did
you know that?"

"I hear the things that run through the underbelly of this
city. That's one of the reasons people come to me."

"Like O'Deoradháin."

Du Val just stared at her.

"He sent the assassin, didn't he?"

The dwarf shook his head, like a parent disappointed in
a child. "Holder, you have no concept of who your real
enemies are. Or your real friends. That makes me wonder
if you will be holding Lámh Shábhála for much longer."
He held out his left hand palm up and waggled his fingers.
"Four mórceints," he said. "I'm giving you a discount for
not talking about O'Deoradháin."

Jenna untied a pouch from under her clóca and counted
out the coins into du Val's hand. He gave her the pouch
of andúilleaf, but held onto it for a moment as her fingers
closed around it. "Holder," he said, his voice gravelly and
low. "Please. You can't continue this. The leaf will consume
you. It will change you. It's already begun."

Jenna snatched the bag away. "I won't be back," she
told du Val. "If I need to, I'll find another source."

"You'll need to," du Val said somberly.

As they left the shop, Coelin stroked her hair and she
stopped, leaning against him. "Coelin . . ." she whispered.
She lifted her face to him, unable to stop the tears now
that she was outside. She wasn't sure why she was crying:
fear, or du Val's harsh words, or simply the confusion that
whirled in her mind. Coelin's thumb gently blotted the
tears, and he kissed her eyelids, then her mouth.

"What's the matter, Jenna?"

"Everything," she answered. "And nothing."

"Is it this O'Deoradháin? Are you scared of what he
might do?"

She nodded. It was as good an answer as any.

"Then I'll find him," Coelin said. "I have my sources, too. If he's down here in Low Town, I can uncover him. I'll find out where he lives, find out what he's asking. And you can send the Rí's gardai after him." He smiled down at her. "See?" he said. "You do have friends you can trust." He kissed her once more, his hand moving across the mound of her breast, and she felt herself yearn for more. "Come with me now, Jenna," he whispered. "Let me love you."

"I want to, Coelin. I want to so much."

"But . . . ?"

She opened her mind to the cloch, feeling the city around her with its power: her gardai were moving through the square, searching for her. One was close by, moving toward Cat's Alley. "I've been away too long already. I have to go back."

"Ah." The word held a bitterness in its tone. He looked away.

"Coelin, it's not that," she protested. "I do want you. I miss you every day."

"Then when, Jenna? When will we be together?"

"When you come to sing next. Afterward. I'll make arrangements."

He smiled at her and kissed her again. She pulled him close, not wanting to let go yet forcing herself to push him away. She nodded toward the far end of the lane. "They're coming for me now," she said. "Go that way."

"Jenna . . ."

"Hush," she said. "Don't say anymore. Go. Find O'Deoradháin for me. We'll be together soon. I promise."

He took a step backward, still looking at her, then turned. She watched him go, then turned herself and walked toward Low Town Market Square.

22

Proposals

THE mage-lights came that night and Jenna caught their power, crying out in mingled longing and agony. Afterward, the andúilleaf dulled only the worst of the pain, and, following a troubled sleep, she took it again early in the morning. The arm was still throbbing, a steady pulsing mirrored by a nauseous headache as she and Aoife moved toward her apartment from the common room, where she'd breakfasted with the Banrion.

"Holder, if you have a moment . . . ?"

Nevan O Liathain called to Jenna as she passed the door of his apartments. She stopped, closing her eyes before glancing inside as a wave of pain swept over her: the Rí Ard's son was standing near the fireplace. Rich, dark hangings adorned the walls, gleaming with bright colors; a woven carpet softened the varnished wood of the floor; the tables and chair were carved and expensive, unlike anything she'd seen in the keep. She suspected that most of the furnishings had traveled with O Liathain from Dún Laoghaire. O Liathain looked as rich and as handsome as his surroundings, his raven-black hair oiled, those strange, light blue eyes regarding her.

Jenna saw no way to politely decline. She nodded to Aoife and went to the doorway. "Good morning, Tanaise Rίg. Of what service can I be to you?"

O Liathain glanced significantly at Aoife, and Jenna waved to the servant. "Wait in the hall for me," she said. "I won't be but a few minutes." She hoped that was true;

she didn't know how much longer she could bear the headache, and she longed for another cup of the leaf. Aoife
curtsied and continued down the hall; Jenna took a step
inside the apartment.

"The door, please, Holder," O Liathain said. "Too many
ears and eyes . . ." Jenna pulled the door to, and O Liathain
took a few steps toward her, stopping an arm's reach away.
He moved with the ease of a dancer or a well-trained
fighter. "This is most improper, I know," he said. "Yet I
would speak with you privately, without curious ears listening." Another step. She could see his lips twist upward
in a momentary smile. "I would like to suggest something
to you that would be to our mutual advantage."

"And what would that be, Tanaise Ríg?"

Another vanishing smile, gone like frost under a spring's
sun. "I will forgo delicacy here, Holder," he answered. "Let
me be blunt. It's come to my attention that your mam is
carrying Tiarna Mac Ard's child. No, you needn't protest
or try to deny it—we both know it's true. I also know that
for the moment Padraic is unlikely to legitimize the child
or his relationship with your mam. Yet if he did so, if he
took your mam to wife, and acknowledged you as his own
daughter as well . . . well, then that would make you a
Riocha, wouldn't it?"

Jenna sniffed. "I am evidently not quite so awed by that
possibility as you, Tanaise Ríg. While I would like to see
the Tiarna Mac Ard acknowledge my mam and his child
by her, if that's the case, I have no interest in being named
his daughter."

A nod. An appraising, sidewise glance. "I believe you
miss the implications, Holder," he continued. "If you are
Riocha, then you are a peer to anyone here. And if, let us
say, the Holder of Lámh Shábhála were to marry, especially
someone with power himself, why, that would be an alliance to be reckoned with." O Liathain spread his hands
wide. "I hope I make my intentions clear enough for you."

He did. Jenna could feel a fist grasping her stomach and
twisting as he watched her, and for a moment the edges of
her vision went dark with the pounding in her temples and
her right arm. She struggled to show nothing on her face.

She lifted her hand to the cloch around her neck, and he stared at the patterns of scars on her flesh with a flat gaze. *He wants the power you hold. He will take it any way he can, through marriage if he can. He will try this, but if it doesn't work, he will try another way. He may have already tried another way.* Jenna knew what Cianna would tell her, that this was part of the game, and she must play the card as well and as long as she could. What she must not say was "no." It would not be good politics to have the heir to the Rí Ard's throne as an open enemy.

"Holder?" he asked, tilting his head. The gold-threaded patterns on his gray clóca shimmered as he took another step toward her. His hand reached out and took hers. He looked at Lámh Shábhála, cupped in her palm, the chain taut around her neck. "So small, this stone. And yet so many lust for it." His finger moved over the smooth surface, trapped in its silver cage, but his blue eyes held hers. "I understand that feeling."

He let the stone drop back to her chest. "Listen to me, Holder," he said. "I can apply enough pressure to Mac Ard to make him do as I say with your mam. I'm a reasonable person, Holder, and, I'm told, not unhandsome for a man of my age. I believe it is possible we could come to love each other in time, but if not . . ." He shrugged. "I would not expect fidelity of you any more than you would expect it of me, and as long as tongues aren't wagging throughout the tuatha, I would not care who you see."

Jenna could feel that her eyes were wide, that she must be showing the sick fright she felt inside. O Liathain nodded, as if what he saw on her face was what he expected. "I don't ask for an answer now, Holder. But soon I must. I would have you remember that there are . . . other ways. You may have thwarted the first attempts, but others might come, more difficult to prevent. Or perhaps a more efficient tactic would be not to attack you, but rather those you love."

"Tanaise Ríg, are you threatening me?"

O Liathain put his hand to his throat in theatrical horror. His eyes widened almost comically. "Me? Certainly not." Then his hand dropped, and his handsome face went seri-

ous. "I'm simply pointing out your vulnerabilities to you,
Holder. And offering you a solution to effectively negate
them. Think about my offer." The fleeting smile returned.
"I leave to return to Dún Laoghaire in three days. It would
be best to have an answer by then, so I might speak to my
da, the Rí Ard. I assume you know not to speak of this
to anyone."

He brushed past her then, going to the door. His hand
closed around the brass handle. "You'll be at the fete the
Rí and Banrion are giving for me in two nights?"

Jenna nodded, silent.

"I will look forward to seeing you then, and perhaps
speaking privately at that time." He swung the door open,
and gestured toward the corridor. "Have a good morning,
Holder."

She managed to hold her stomach in check until she and
Aoife had turned down the corridor toward her apartment.

Jenna spoke to no one, though the encounter with O
Liathain troubled her all day and most of the next. She
remained in her rooms, letting Aoife bring her meals with
the excuse that she was too tired and in too much pain to
dine with others. Cianna sent word that she would like to
see her at dinner that night, and Jenna told Aoife to let
the Banrion know that she would be there.

She could not hide forever, and perhaps Cianna would
be a confidante. Her mam had already gone down to the
common room with Mac Ard when the bells rang the sunset and Jenna left her room, Aoife accompanying her as
she had her own duties in the kitchen. They were nearing
the stairs when she heard her name called.

"Holder!"

"Tanaise Ríg." She gave him a perfunctory curtsy; Aoife
droppping nearly to the floor with hers, as was proper. O
Liathain was accompanied by a tiarna she'd seen at the
table, well down from her. His clóca was a somber gray,
the color of Dún Laoghaire, and he remained back as O
Liathain approached her.

"Are you on your way to supper? Good. We will walk
with you, then." O Liathain extended his arm to her; Jenna

hesitated, but there seemed no graceful way to refuse. She placed her left hand in the crook of his elbow, and he smiled at her. "Come then," he said.

They walked on, the other tiarna and Aoife a few paces behind.

"Have you thought of what we spoke about yesterday?" he asked.

"Truthfully, I've thought of little else."

"Has an answer come to you?"

"No, Tanaise Ríg. Not as yet."

His lips pursed, pushing out from the chiseled, perfect lines of his face. "Ah, I suppose that's what I would say in your place. But, as I said, I expect to hear from you before I leave Lár Bhaile to return home."

His face inclined toward her, he smiled, but the gesture never touched the rest of his face. The eyes were as cold as the waves of the Ice Sea as they approached the stairs leading down to the hall. "I . . . I shall have an answer—"

A cry—"Stop!"—and an answering wail cut off her words. O Liathain pushed Jenna to one side of the corridor and with the same motion, drew the sword girded at his side. Jenna moved back again, trying to see past the man and reaching instinctively for Lámh Shábhála. Her awareness went streaming out with the cloch's energy, and she felt someone die: a spark guttering out in the web.

"Aoife!" Jenna cried. She pushed past O Liathain's sheltering body and stopped. "No . . ."

Aoife lay sprawled on the flags of the corridor, bright blood streaming from a gash torn in her side. Her eyes were wide, her mouth open in her dying wail. O Liathain's tiarna was standing over her, his short blade held back at the end of the killing stroke, the honed edges dripping thick blood. "What have you done, Baird?" O Liathain roared at the man, his sword now pointing at his companion. Jenna could hear footsteps pounding up the stairs toward them, shouts of alarm, and the ringing of unsheathed metal.

Baird lowered his sword. "She intended to attack the Holder," he said. A booted foot prodded Aoife's limp arm. "Look—the dagger's still in her hand. She started to rush at your backs; I called, then I cut her down before she could reach you."

"No!" Jenna cried again. She went to Aoife, sinking down on her knees beside the body. She looked at Baird in fury, her right hand tight around the cloch, and the man backed away from her, his eyes widening in fear.

"Holder, no! I swear—"

"Jenna!" Mac Ard's voice snapped her head around. Padraic was standing, sword in hand, at the top of the stairs. Half a dozen other people crowded the landing behind him, Jenna's mam among them. Mac Ard pushed through them and came up to Jenna. "Do nothing with the cloch," he said to her. "Not here."

Jenna pointed at Baird. "He killed Aoife," she shouted. "How *dare* you tell me to do nothing!" Baird dropped his sword; the blade clanged discordantly on the stones.

"Tiarna Mac Ard," the man wailed, "Don't let her kill me."

O Liathain stepped forward. He had sheathed his own sword, and went to Mac Ard, placing a hand on the smaller man's shoulder. "Baird did as he had to," he said. "The girl tried to kill the Holder, and perhaps me as well."

"That's not *true!*" Jenna shouted. "Aoife wouldn't do that!"

"See for yourself, Tiarna," O Liathain told Mac Ard. "My man is blameless in this."

Mac Ard gave O Liathain a dark look, then stepped forward and went to one knee alongside Jenna. She was trembling, her hand quivering around the stone, and she could barely hold back the power, wanting to unleash it at someone, anyone. "Calm yourself, Jenna," Mac Ard whispered to her as he knelt. "We both need to be very careful here." He leaned over, taking the dagger from Aoife's hand and turning it before his face. The blade was long, the leather-wrapped hilt ending in a knob of yellowed whalebone carved as a twisted knot. "This was made in Connachta," he said, loudly enough so everyone could hear. "I know the hilt design—it's one they use in the ironworks of Valleylair."

"Then our cousins in Tuath Connachta have much to answer for," O Liathain said. "I'll give this news to my father, and tell him how they threatened my life and the Holder's."

"No doubt the Rí Ard will send a strong letter scolding the Rí Connachta in Thiar," Mac Ard responded, getting to his feet. He put Aoife's dagger in his belt; O Liathain watched, but didn't ask for the weapon. His face remained somber, but Jenna saw his eyebrows lower as he stared at Mac Ard.

"The Rí Ard will do what is within his power," O Liathain said. "This was a cowardly act; we can't condone it."

"Indeed," Mac Ard answered. He held his hand out to Jenna, still kneeling alongside Aoife's body. Jenna ignored the offer. Instead, she reached out and closed Aoife's eyes, then got to her feet by herself. She strode to O Liathain and stood before him, staring into his face. He returned the stare placidly, unblinking.

"I'm going back to my rooms," Jenna said: to O Liathain, to Mac Ard, to her mam and the others watching. "If anyone follows me, I *will* use the cloch. I, too, can do what I need to do." She spun on her toes and stalked down the corridor away from the carnage.

Baird shrank away to the wall as she passed. Behind her, there was only silence.

The Banrion first sent her handmaiden, who was visibly trembling when Jenna opened the door, holding a mug of andúilleaf brew. "The Banrion asks permission to visit the Holder in her chambers," the woman said. Her eyes flicked upward once to Jenna's face; otherwise, her gaze remained fixed on the floor, as if fascinated by the parquet pattern there. Jenna sighed.

"When?" she asked.

"My mistress waits just outside."

"Tell the Banrion that I'm only a guest here and these are after all *her* rooms, not mine. She may come in if she wishes."

Jenna drained the mug of its bitter contents; the handmaiden curtsied and fled. A few moments later, the door opened again and Cianna entered in a rustle of her ornate, silken clóca, her torc gleaming golden around her neck. As Jenna watched, she took a seat near the fire. She said nothing, only watched Jenna as she paced back and forth across the rug.

"He had her killed," Jenna said at last. "He didn't care that he was killing a person. She was just . . . an illustration to me of what he could do. A warning."

Cianna continued to sit quietly. Jenna plopped into the chair across from the Banrion, not caring about the lack of etiquette. Cianna raised an eyebrow, but otherwise didn't move. "I don't know what to do now," Jenna said.

"We *are* talking about the Tanaise Ríg?" Cianna asked, stirring finally. Jenna nodded. "I thought so. He departs in a few more days, and he grows impatient. Do you know *why* he leaves?"

Now it was Jenna who sat silent. She moved her head slowly from side to side, trying to keep back the headache that threatened to engulf her, starting to feel the brew send its welcome warmth through her body. "Tuath Connachta is gathering an army on its borders," she said. "They have demanded éraic—blood payment—for the death of Fiacra De Derga. Padraic tells me you may not remember that name, but he was the tiarna you killed in Ballintubber when the power of Lámh Shábhála first came to you. The éraic is the excuse for their aggression, and my husband has already sent back word that they may wait for their payment forever. Of course, what they *really* want is you . . ." Cianna stopped. She seemed to sigh. "Or more precisely, what you hold. We may be at war very soon, and the Rí Ard doesn't want his son and heir caught up in that collision. The Rí Ard knows he must stay above feuds between the tuatha if he wants to remain on his throne."

"The Tanaise Ríg wants me to marry him," Jenna said.

Cianna held her hands out to the low flames of the peat fire, rubbing them softly together. She didn't look at Jenna. "Does that surprise you? If *I* were Tanaise Ríg, I would have made that suggestion to you, too—just as soon as I had decided that it was too dangerous to take the stone from you myself."

"He threatened to do this. He hinted that to make me accept the offer he'd attack the people I loved. Aoife was to let me know that he meant it. That wasn't her dagger—I'm sure of that. That man probably handed it to her, then immediately killed her. I wasn't watching; she was behind me, both of them were." Jenna couldn't speak. The tears choked her throat and blurred her vision, the headache threatened to overwhelm her. If Cianna had opened her arms then, if the Banrion had called to her, Jenna would have sunk into her embrace like a child searching for the comfort of her mam. But the Banrion only watched, wheezing slightly as she breathed and hugging herself as if cold.

"You could do much worse than the Tanaise Ríg," Cianna said. "I told you before, marriage is a weapon. Now I'll tell you that once it's in your hands, you'll find the edge can cut for you as well as O Liathain."

That brought Jenna's head up and dried the tears. "You can't be serious."

"I am. Very much so."

"He killed Aoife."

"You killed Mac Ard's cousin De Derga and those with him. You killed two Connachtans more near Áth Iseal, I was told. And there was the assassin."

"All of that was different," Jenna protested. "With De Derga, I literally didn't know what I was doing. And the men near Áth Iseal—that was pure self-defense. They would have killed us had I not acted. The assassin was suicide; I was only trying to capture him."

"So he could be tortured and tell us what he knew, and *then* be killed." Cianna gave Jenna a wan smile. "I blame you for none of that, Jenna. You did what you felt was necessary, and you didn't worry that you were killing someone's son or brother or father or friend. That's as it should be, to protect yourself. But I would argue that's also what the Tanaise Ríg did, *if* he was responsible for Aoife's death."

"I didn't threaten the Tanaise Ríg. He wasn't in danger from me."

"The Tanaise Ríg, the Rí Ard, as well as Rí Gabair or

Rí Connachta or most of the Riocha for that matter, always feel threatened by a perceived stronger power. That's what you represent with Lámh Shábhála around your neck. If you aren't their ally, then you're their enemy. That's the way they see the world, in cold black and white. You are on their side or you are against them. There is no middle ground." Cianna lifted a finger against Jenna's burgeoning protest. "And your saying that it's not so doesn't change that perception. I know that's not your vision of the world. It's not mine, either. But it *is* theirs."

"I don't love him. I never could."

"What does love have to do with marriage? Do you think I love my husband?" Cianna gave a bitter, short laugh that ended in a barking cough. For a moment, she spasmed, leaning over as a series of coughs racked her body. Then she sat up again, wiping her mouth with a lace handkerchief, blotting away the blood on her lips. "Or that he loves me?" she finished. "It is enough that the two of you work together, with what he can do as Tanaise Ríg and eventually Rí Ard, and you with Lámh Shábhála."

"To do what?" Jenna asked.

"Whatever you can." Cianna closed her eyes, as if in pain. When they opened again, she smiled at Jenna. "You can't say 'no' to him. Not yet. But if it's not what you want, you can also delay, and see what tomorrow brings."

Jenna pounced on that, like a drowning person grabbing a stick extended from the bank. "How? How can I delay?"

"The Tanaise Ríg must leave, but you can tell him that you are in too much pain to travel—that much at least is close to the truth, and he knows it. You can tell him that once Lámh Shábhála has opened the way for the other clochs to feed on the mage-lights and you no longer have that burden on you, then you'll come to him in Dún Laoghaire and be his wife. Until then, you will stay here under Rí Gabair's protection. That's a reasonable compromise, and he won't be able to refuse it." Her shoulders lifted under her clóca. "And who knows what might happen in that time."

Relief flooded into Jenna, the tension slowly receding.

She went to the Banrion and knelt before her chair, taking the woman's hand in hers. "Thank you, Banrion. You are a friend where I did not expect to find one."

Cianna's face gentled, and with her free hand, she stroked Jenna's hair. "I'm pleased you feel that way," she said. "It's what I would want."

23

Answers

JENNA was escorted to the fete by Mac Ard and her
mam. As Maeve walked down the stairs, her clóca
moved against her body, and Jenna could see the slight
swell of her abdomen. She wondered if others saw it as
well; she wondered most if Mac Ard had noticed, and what
his thoughts might be.

The Banrion had sent Jenna one of her own clóca to
wear, trimmed in gold thread and in the colors of Tuath
Gabair. The clóca left her arms bare to the elbow, and
Jenna had not let her mam bandage the right arm. "Let
them see it," she'd told her. "Let them see what Lámh
Shábhála does to its Holder." The stone itself she also let
show, bright against the darker cloth. As a gem, it was
plainer than any of the gems at the throats of the tiarna
below, but its very plainness spoke of its power.

She'd taken a large draught of the andúilleaf before they
left. The herb roiled in her stomach as they descended the
staircase in the Great Hall toward the sound of pipes, bodh-
ran, and flute, all eyes on them. Most of the Riocha were
already there, the céili giallnai in their finest, the higher-
ranking Riocha already talking in polite circles, watching
the stairway for the Rí and Banrion who would enter with
O Liathain, their entrances as carefully choreographed as
the seating arrangements.

Halfway down the stair and looking at the faces upturned
to them, Jenna spotted Coelin, standing with his giotár near
the other musicians at the end of the hall. He had a broad

grin on his face, and she smiled back at him. Maeve noticed the exchange, for she saw her mam's focus shift for a moment and a brief frown cross her face. "Jenna," her mam whispered, leaning toward her. "Coelin has no importance here. Don't make a fool of yourself."

"You needn't worry. I'm not with child by him," Jenna answered. Her mam's hiss of hurt and irritation made Jenna immediately regret her words, but she made no apology. *It's the pain talking, Mam, not me* . . . They walked down the rest of the stairs in silence. They were immediately engulfed, several of the tiarna surrounding them, smiling and nodding. Jenna found herself torn away from her mam, who remained with Padraic as several of the unmarried women came up to him. Tiarna Galen Aheron of Tuath Infochla, resplendent in his clóca of green and gold, with a leine of fine white cloth underneath, was suddenly next to her. He was a burly man, muscular now in his prime, but Jenna suspected that the burliness would turn to fat soon enough, leaving the tiarna huge and slow. She also remembered that Cianna had named him as one of those who coveted Lámh Shábhála himself. She could easily imagine those thick fingers dropping a purse of gold mórceints into the palm of a paid assassin.

"Good evening, Holder," he said, his breath scented with mint. "A fine party for the Tanaise Ríg, don't you think? A shame he'll be leaving. Have you ever given any thought of going to Dún Laoghaire yourself?" He asked the question with a slight incline of his head, and with enough emphasis that Jenna wondered if he might not know, or at least suspect, what O Liathain had asked of her. If it hadn't surprised the Banrion, then others of the Riocha would certainly have suspected it as well.

"I would like to see Dún Laoghaire sometime," she answered, trying to return the smile. "Perhaps I shall, one day."

"Soon, possibly? After all, I would think—" Aheron paused as the musicians suddenly stopped playing and gave a loud, ornate flourish, his gaze going past Jenna's shoulder and up. "Ah, here comes the guest of honor now . . ."

The Riocha gathered in the Great Hall turned as one,

applauding politely. Jenna turned to see the Rí and Banrion at the top of the stair, with Cianna holding to both the Rí's and O Liathain's arms. O Liathain's eyes caught Jenna's for a moment; she looked down and away as Aheron glanced appraisingly at her. When the trio reached the foot of the stair, the Riocha closed around them, everyone talking at once. Jenna held back; she looked over her shoulder at the far end of the hall to where Coelin stood. He nodded to her. He seemed nervous and excited, his eyes wide, and she realized that he saw none of the underlying complexity— he was awed simply to be here. His naïveté almost made her smile.

"Good evening to you, Holder."

Jenna turned back quickly. O Liathain was standing before her, a cadre of tiarna behind him. He smiled at her, his gaze wandering past her for a moment to where she'd just been looking. She lowered her head, but he stopped her automatic curtsy by picking up her right hand. He held it, looking at the pattern of scars mottling her skin. "No bandages tonight," he said. "That's as it should be. A warrior should be proud of the scars of battle. There's no shame in them." He kissed her scarred hand. She tried to smile, feeling everyone watching, listening. "By the way, I was thinking of asking that young singer—the one from your village—to come to Dún Laoghaire and entertain us there. He has an excellent voice."

"Aye," Jenna answered, keeping her eyes downcast. "That he does."

"I wonder," O Liathain continued, "if you would have a moment to speak with me later this evening? More . . . privately." Jenna looked up; his blue eyes pierced her, demanding.

"As the Tanaise Ríg wishes, of course," she answered.

"Good." The corners of his mouth lifted. "I will look forward to that. In the meantime, I must speak to these good people I must leave behind tomorrow morning. Until later, then . . ." He kissed her hand once more, then released it, turning to the other Riocha. Jenna heard laughter, and O Liathain's rich voice starting another conversation. Someone spoke to her, and she smiled back politely, but she paid little attention to the words. She could feel the touch of O Liathain's lips on the back of her hand, and she was afraid to touch the stone around her neck.

The fete seemed interminable. Jenna wandered from conversation to conversation, occasionally finding her mam, Mac Ard, or Banrion Cianna, but without a chance to speak with any of them. The musicians began playing again, and she was asked to dance by the Rí—a request she could not decline—then afterward by Tiarna Aheron. Coelin seemed to have vanished; she could not find him in the crush of people. A stripe and a half later by the clock-candle near the stairs, the cold of the Great Hall was seeping into her bones despite the fires and the crowd and the dancing, and she could feel the old pain tingling in the fingertips and joints of her right hand. Jenna knew that she'd need to return to her room for more andúilleaf before the end, and she wondered how she could manage to leave without being noticed.

"Holder?"

Baird, O Liathain's man, was standing before her. Jenna could feel her face tightening as she glared at the man who had murdered Aoife. Her voice was frost and ice. "What do you want?"

"The Tanaise Ríg asks if you would come with me. He said to remind you that you promised him an answer and that he awaits you in a side chamber to hear it."

Jenna's stomach turned over and she could feel the acid burning in her throat. Baird had already turned to go. "This way, Holder . . ." She followed him down a side aisle of the hall. He knocked on a door near the south end.

"Enter," a muffled, familiar voice answered. Baird opened the door and gestured to Jenna to go through, closing it behind her and remaining outside.

O Liathain was seated on a chair, his legs propped up on the stone flags of the fireplace, his boots off. He gestured to a chair next to him. "Please," he said. His voice was oddly gentle, almost tired. "It's weary, standing and dancing all night, and I'm sure your feet are as sore as mine."

"Thank you, Tanaise Ríg." Jenna settled into the chair, feeling the welcome warmth of the fire wash over her. Neither of them spoke for several minutes. Jenna was content to have it that way, trying to think of what she might say to the man. When he finally did speak, his voice made her start.

"Have you reflected on our previous conversation?"

"I've thought of little else, Tanaise Ríg," Jenna answered truthfully. "After all, you . . . emphasized with Aoife just how important my answer was to you."

A look almost of pain played over his face in the firelight. "You are blunt, Holder. That can be an asset, if you use it in the right circumstances. But at the wrong time . . ." He let his voice trail off.

"And which is this—the right time or the wrong?"

He sat up in his chair, turning so that he faced her. "Here, we can speak openly, since there are just the two of us and my man holds the door."

"Aye. He seems to be a man who would kill someone if you ask him to do so, even if that person was entirely innocent of wrongdoing."

The right side of O Liathain's mouth twitched as if with some inner amusement. "Innocent? Let me speak frankly now, Holder. Did I order the girl killed? Aye, I did. Was the—well, shall we call it a lesson?—intended for you? Only partially. There was another who was even more distressed by the incident and it was mostly for that person's, ah, *benefit,* that I told Baird to do as he did. The girl was hardly innocent, Jenna. She may have been your servant, but she was doing the bidding of another. I happen to know that Aoife told that person's assassin where and when he could find you."

Jenna knew the shock of that statement showed on her face. "I don't believe that. Aoife wouldn't have betrayed me that way."

"It's true, nonetheless."

"Show me the proof. Tell me who this 'other person' is."

O Liathain took a long, slow breath. He put his feet back on the hearth, slouching again in his chair. "I will. In time. When I know you and I are . . . of one mind. Until then, you will have to trust me and trust my intentions. Did I order Aoife killed. Aye, I did. Did I do it only to demonstrate to you how far I would go to have you as my wife?" His lips pursed, his hands lifted palms up from his lap and fell again. "That was, I'll admit, a secondary consideration. But *only* secondary. I had Aoife killed to tell those who would harm you that you are under my protection, to show them that I knew more than they believed and that Dún Laoghaire has long arms." He looked over to her, the blue eyes reflecting fire. "What is your answer to me, Holder? Aye, or nay?"

"I . . ." Jenna's throat convulsed. She remembered Cianna's advice; it was all she had. She could not look at him and say no—he *would* kill her mam or Coelin. "You made another promise to me—that Mac Ard would also marry my mam and make her Riocha."

O Liathain nodded. "That he will do, when I put pressure on him. The Tanaise Ríg will not marry a commoner."

"Then your answer is aye," she said finally. "But Tanaise Ríg, I can't go with you yet."

His burgeoning smile transformed to a frown, darkly. "Why not?"

"You don't know how Lámh Shábhála hurts," she told him. The truth of that statement made it easier to say the lie she had been constructing for the last few days. "Lámh Shábhála will open the other clochs na thintrí soon—no more than four or five appearances of the mage-lights from now. I need to stay here until that happens—I *feel* that. Lámh Shábhála tells me this. The mage-lights would not follow me as far as Dún Laoghaire, and the cloch tells me to remain here, near the center of Talamh an Ghlas. I *must* stay here until Lámh Shábhála opens the other stones. When that happens, then I will come to you in Dún Laoghaire. I promise that it will be no more than a month from now, when you will be holding a cloch yourself."

He was fingering the stone around his own neck, the stone Jenna knew was only a jewel, no more. "How do I know you tell the truth?" he scowled. "Once I'm gone, you may decide that it's safe to change your mind."

"If we are to be 'of one mind' as you say, then you must learn to trust what I tell you also," Jenna answered. "And didn't you just tell me that the arm of Dún Laoghaire is long?"

"Indeed it is." He said nothing for a time. The fire crackled and hissed in the fireplace, sending a column of whirling sparks upward. Jenna moved her right arm so that the fire's radiance fell on the perpetually cold flesh, the welcome heat easing the growing discomfort somewhat. "Are you aware that Tuath Connachta is gathering an army and that they may attack Tuath Gabair?"

Jenna nodded. "The Banrion gave me the news."

"Did she also tell you that the Rí no doubt hopes for Lámh Shábhála to be part of that battle, if it comes to that, that he would love to see the lightnings of your cloch smash the enemy and send them fleeing for their lives back to the Westering Sea? No, you needn't answer; I can see by your face that she didn't. I can also see that the thought appalls you."

"I won't be used that way," she said. "As a weapon. To kill."

O Liathain vented a quick, unamused laugh. "Since we're being blunt, then let me say that you have no choice," he told her. "Lámh Shábhála is a weapon. It has *always* been a weapon. If you don't wield it in war against the enemies of those who protect you or if you're unwilling to protect yourself with its power, then someone will take it from you, someone who is willing to use it. I don't say that as a threat or to attempt to frighten you, Jenna. I say that simply because it's the bare truth, and if you don't accept it as such, your life will be a short one."

"I don't—" Jenna started to protest, then closed her mouth. *It is true. You know it. The blood is already on your hands, and there will be more* . . . She could feel twin tears course down her face. O Liathain made no move to comfort her. He watched, fingers prowling in his dark, gray-spattered beard.

"Here is what we will do," O Liathain said. "We will go back into the hall, together, with you on my arm. You will stay on my arm for a time and everyone will notice. Let

them talk. That's exactly what we want. We will also go to
the Rí and the Banrion, and we will tell them of our plans.
That way, my—let's deem it an 'investment'—in you is protected by their knowledge, and they will understand that
you must be kept safe or the Rí Ard and I will be most
upset."

Jenna sniffed, rubbing angrily at her eyes. "And Mac
Ard and my mam?"

"Mac Ard will notice the two of us together; he will see
us chatting with the Rí and Banrion. He will know what
that means; when I speak with him later, I guarantee he
won't be surprised." O Liathain reached down and picked
up his boots, pulling them over his stockings. He rose from
his chair and extended his hand to Jenna. "Let us make
our entrance," he said.

Jenna licked dry lips and rubbed again at her eyes. She
lifted her left hand to O Liathain and he shook his head.
"No, it should be the hand of power I hold," he said.
"That, I think, will send the message best."

His own hand felt cool and smooth under the stiff, unyielding flesh of her right hand. He placed her fingers on
his forearm, on the soft fabric of his léine.

With her hand on O Liathain's arm, they left the room
and went into the hall again.

He kept her with him for a candle's stripe.

O Liathain was correct: they were noticed. Jenna could
see the eyes on them, the heads that turned to nearby companions for quick, whispered comments. The Rí and Banrion accepted the news with nods and smiles and Cianna
nodded once to Jenna when the Rí and the Tanaise Ríg
were engaged in conversation. Her mam saw, too. Maeve
was shadowing Mac Ard, never on the tiarna's arm since
their arrival but always near him. She lifted her hand and
seemed to smile, but O Liathain moved then and Jenna
had no chance to speak with her.

Coelin sang, and O Liathain moved to stand directly in
front of the young man, his hand gently covering Jenna's.
Coelin faltered once, seeing them, and for the rest of his

performance his gaze always skittered past her, sliding over her face with an uncertain smile. When Coelin finished and left the hall to applause, O Liathain and Jenna moved from group to group for a time, until Jenna pressed O Liathain's arm.

"Tired, Holder?"

"Aye. Exhausted. And my arm . . . I need to retire for a bit."

"Certainly," O Liathain said. "These events are wearisome, aren't they? But I need to remain for a while longer. Baird will escort you back to your apartment."

"I don't need . . ." Jenna began. "That will be fine," she finished.

Baird left her at the door to her rooms, bowing to her as she left him. A girl no older than herself came scurrying out from the servants' quarters as she closed the door: Aoife's replacement, whose name Jenna didn't know yet. She was plain, her hair dull and close-cropped, and yet her eyes glittered with intelligence.

"Mistress, let me help you . . ."

Jenna waved her away. *She'll be someone's spy* . . . "I don't want help."

"But, Mistress, I'm—"

"Go now," Jenna answered sharply. "Leave me." The girl's eyes widened, then she made a hurried curtsy and fled the room. Jenna heard her voice whispering to the other servants as she closed the door behind her. Jenna went through the outer parlor to her bedroom. There, she removed the clóca the Banrion had lent her. She went to the chest at the foot of her bed and rummaged beneath the clothing there until she felt the packet of andúilleaf. She set a pot of water to boil over the fire and prepared some of the powdered leaf in a mug. She was sipping the pungent liquid when she heard the scrape of a footstep at the door. She whirled around, nearly spilling the potion, her right hand going instinctively to the cloch.

"Coelin . . ."

He smiled at her. "I thought you were about to strike me dead with that damned stone."

"How did you get in here?"

He grinned. "I have my ways. Do you want me to leave?"

"By the Mother, no," she answered. She set the mug down and went to him, her arms going around him and her face lifting for his kiss. The embrace was long and urgent, and she pulled him to the bed, enjoying the feel of his hands on her body and the heat of his response. He pulled away from her once, looking down at her with a question in his eyes, and she nodded to him. "Aye," she whispered.

Then they said nothing at all for a time.

Afterward, Jenna drew her leine over herself. There was blood between her thighs and on the bedsheets. She rolled away from him and took the cup of cold andúilleaf, sipping it as she sat on the side of the bed.

It was supposed to be different. While they were together in the few minutes of passion, she had lost herself and forgot everything to simply be with him, but when it was over . . . The insistent throbbing of her arm, the dead coldness of the scarred flesh called her back, and suddenly the andúilleaf was more important than being with Coelin. She sought solace in the sour milkiness of the brew, not with the man to whom she'd just given herself. She felt dead inside when she should have been feeling joy and release.

Did you do this because you wanted Coelin that much, or just so O Liathain couldn't be the first? She wanted to cry, but there were no tears inside her.

She felt Coelin move behind her, and his hand trailed from her head down her spine. She shivered and his arms went around her, cupping her breasts. She let herself lean back against him. "Are those the herbs you bought from du Val?" he asked. He kissed the side of her neck. "That potion smells awful."

"And tastes worse. But it helps."

"Mmm." He nuzzled the other side of her neck. His fingers started to drift lower, and she stopped them. "Jenna . . ."

"Hush," she told him. "It was wonderful. It was what I wanted."

She could feel his smile. "I thought, when I saw you with the Tanaise Ríg tonight . . ."

"I was doing what I had to do, Coelin. Nothing else. There's no love there. There never will be." That, at least, was only the truth. She turned her head, kissing him softly; Coelin grinned at her, then returned the kiss more passionately. When he tried to lay her down again, she shook her head. "No, not now, Coelin. My mam and Mac Ard will be returning soon, and I'm . . . sore. Later. There will be time. But for now, you'd better go." She stopped, looked into his green, soft eyes, and for a moment felt a surge of the old affection. "My love."

"My love," he answered, and kissed her again. With a sigh, he left the bed. "I nearly forgot," he said as he drew his tunic back over his head. "That man—Ennis O'Deoradháin. I found him. I know where he's living."

Jenna sat up, her eyes narrowing as remembered anger made her jaw clench. *If he sent the assassin, then he is also ultimately responsible for Aoife's death. . . .* "Where?" she asked.

"On Cooper Street. He has a room in a widow's house. Her name is Murrin. I've seen him a couple times now. Do you want me to do something with him? There are people I know in Low Town . . ."

"No," Jenna answered. "I will take care of O'Deoradháin myself."

Coelin's head went back at the ferocity of her words. "You're certain? He could be dangerous, and I—"

"I will take care of the man," Jenna said decisively. "Don't worry about him."

Coelin nodded reluctantly. "I should go, then," he said. He looked uncertain, an odd, strained smile on his lips, and he shifted his weight from one leg to the other, as if he wanted to say more. "I've been asked to play for the Rí again, next week. And the Tanaise Ríg said he would talk to his father about me."

The mention of O Liathain's title brought the coldness

back, and Jenna reached for the mug of brew, taking a long swallow and grimacing. "That's . . . good," she told Coelin. "When you come here again, we'll make plans."

He nodded. Turned.

"Coelin," she said. She could not keep the desperation from her voice. "Tell me that you love me."

He smiled, looking back over his shoulder. "I love you, Jenna. I always have."

And he left.

24

The Traitor

THE Banrion seemed concerned when Jenna came to her requesting half a dozen trusted gardai, but to her credit, Cianna did not ask Jenna why but only nodded in agreement. "Certainly, Holder. Let me call for Labras; he's a good man, and he can choose five others . . ."

Jenna lifted her hand. "No, Banrion. Not today. After the Tanaise Ríg leaves. Tomorrow morning. I need to go into Low Town then."

"Ah," Cianna had said. Just the one sound, then silence. "I'll make arrangements for them to be at Keep Gate at first bell tomorrow, then."

The Banrion started to move away, as if in dismissal, but Jenna cleared her throat. "Banrion, I would like to tell you why. It needs to be a secret between the two of us, though. You're the only person who has given me help, unasked for. Now I would ask it."

Cianna smiled softly. "Jenna, I will know anyway, whether you tell me now or not. The gardai will inform me where you take them, and why. The ones I would send with you aren't as blindly stupid as those you've borrowed before from my husband or Mac Ard. They won't let the Holder roam unaccompanied through Low Town, no matter what she says."

Jenna laughed with the Banrion. "I know. And that's why I came to you."

She told the Banrion about O'Deoradháin, how he had lied to them about himself on their way to Áth Iseal, how he had reacted during the attack by the Connachtans, that she'd glimpsed him in Low Town (though she said nothing about du Val), and how she now suspected the man had been responsible for the assassin.

Cianna's face was grim when Jenna finished. "Tell me where this man is, and I will have him fetched here for you," she said. "There's no need for you to expose yourself to danger, Jenna—and the Tanaise Ríg will be upset if you are injured while you remain with us."

Jenna shook her head. "Banrion, I will have Lámh Shábhála to protect me. Your gardai will be there only as a precaution. I want to do this myself. I want to see his face and hear his voice."

"Jenna—"

"Please, Banrion. I don't know any longer who I can trust. I can only trust myself."

Jenna saw Cianna gather herself for another argument, but the Banrion finally dropped her shoulders. She coughed softly a few times, rising from her chair. Servants appeared as if summoned by the rustling of fabric, and the Banrion waved them away. "Come, then," she said. "We should give our farewell to your future husband, and pretend that none of us is plotting anything."

"I need four to stay out here and make certain that no one leaves until I'm finished." Jenna gestured to Labras, a tall, burly man with hair so red it almost seemed to burn and eyes as gray as storm clouds. She wasn't sure she liked the man at all; he seemed to radiate violence, and the abundant scars on his face spoke to his familiarity with it. Yet if the Banrion trusted him . . . or maybe her reaction to him was only the haze of the andúilleaf. She'd taken two mugs of the brew before they'd left the Keep, knowing she might well be using the cloch, and the herb was like a fog over her mind that wouldn't quite clear. "Labras, bring someone with you and follow me."

She touched Lámh Shábhála once as the three of them strode toward the door of the small, two-story house. She could feel O'Deoradháin, could feel the pattern of his energy motionless on the second floor. She could sense no fear or apprehension in him.

She decided that would soon change.

An elderly woman came scurrying from the kitchen as they opened the door, stopping suddenly and gaping with an open, toothless mouth at Jenna and the armed men behind her. There were two elderly men in the front parlor, huddled over a ficheall board and staring with frightened eyes at the intruders: Labras with a drawn sword, his companion holding a nocked and ready crossbow. "You have nothing to fear if you stay where you are," Jenna told them. "Widow Murrin, you have a man here named Ennis O'Deoradháin."

"First door to the left at the top of the stairs," the woman said hurriedly, pointing, then hopping back as Jenna and the gardai pushed past her and up the stairs. Jenna heard the click of a door shutting as she reached the landing; in the expanded awareness of the cloch, she could feel O'Deoradháin's presence: still and quiet, even though she knew he must have heard the commotion below, the pounding of feet on the stairs and the jingling of the mail over the gardai's tunics. She could sense no danger in him, though, as she had with the assassin. He seemed to be waiting, calm. She started toward the door, but Labras shook his head. "He may have a bow or sword, ready to strike the first person through," he whispered. "Let me go in first." He seemed almost eager to do so.

"You needn't worry," Jenna said firmly. "He has a dagger, and it is in its sheath."

"How—?" Labras began, then saw her white-patterned hand touch the stone around her neck. An eyebrow interrupted by the pale line of a scar lifted and fell again. "So he has a dagger. You can see with that?"

"Aye," she told him. She pushed the door open. O'Deoradháin was leaning against a table on the far side of the room, arms folded across his chest.

"I was wondering how long it would take you to find me," he said. His gaze went past Jenna to the two gardai crowding the doorway. "You don't need them."

"No?" Jenna answered. "Strange. I expected you to be running like a frightened rabbit again, as you did the last time I saw you."

"If I were a 'frightened rabbit,' I wouldn't have come to Lár Bhaile at all," O'Deoradháin responded easily. "I wouldn't have made certain you saw me at du Val's. I wouldn't have made it so easy for that handsome, stupid boy with the golden throat to track me down."

His remark caused anger to flare in Jenna. She grasped Lámh Shábhála, opening it slightly with her mind so that the cold, blue-white power filled her hand. "You knew where I was," she spat. "If you wanted to speak to me, you didn't need this charade."

O'Deoradháin snorted. He took a step toward her, his hands down at his sides. She saw the well-worn leather of the scabbard there, and heard the gardai shift uneasily behind her. But the man stopped two strides from her. "Oh, aye. I could have walked right up to the gate—and Mac Ard would have had me killed immediately, or the Rí Gabair would have bound me in irons to be tortured until I gave them the answers they wanted, or the Tanaise Ríg might have had me dragged behind his carriage as he left for Dún Laoghaire, just for the pleasure it would give him. But I could never have gotten to *you*, Jenna Aoire. They might call me their enemy and be right, but I'm not *your* enemy."

Aye. That's why you sent the assassin, she wanted to tell him, mockingly. But she saw him through the eyes of Lámh Shábhála, not just her own, and though she could sense that he desired the power she held, there was no malice in him toward her, only jealousy and envy and sadness. The certainty in her failed. "Who's your master, then?" she asked. "Who sends you? The Rí Connachta?"

He laughed and glanced at the gardai. He gestured at Labras with his chin, his hands not moving. "I would rather not talk here. In front of them."

"You'll talk here, or you'll talk back at the keep. I'll ask you again, and I'll know the truth of what you say: are you with Tuath Connachta?"

Again, a laugh. "I gave you the truth when we met. I'm

of Inish blood. As to who sent me . . . I'm a Bráthair of the Order of Inishfeirm and the Máister there gave me this task."

Despite herself, Jenna found her interest suddenly piqued at the mention of Inishfeirm and the Order. She remembered her da Niall's tale, and her great-mam's and great-da's escape from that island. "And what task was that?"

"To bring you back to Inishfeirm so you could be taught the ways of the cloudmage."

Jenna bristled. The andúilleaf rang in her ears, Lámh Shábhála pulsed in her grasp. "What makes you think that I *need* your instruc—" In the fog of the andúilleaf, she nearly missed it: a sudden sense of danger, of attack—not from the man in front of her, but from behind . . .

"Jenna!" O'Deoradháin shouted at the same time. He flung himself forward as Jenna turned to look.

She caught a glimpse of Labras, no longer holding a sword but with a long dagger in his hand, his gray eyes not on O'Deoradháin but on Jenna and the dagger already beginning to make a sweeping cut that would have found her neck. O'Deoradháin hit Jenna in that same instant; as she fell she glimpsed O'Deoradháin parrying Labras' attack with his own weapon, the clash of blade against blade loud. Then she saw nothing as she struck the floor with a grunt and a cry, trying to roll away. As she tumbled, she heard a shout and a horrible, wet strangling sound: Jenna, on her knees, saw Labras fall, a new, second mouth on his neck gaping wide and frothing blood. The crossbow twanged, the bolt hissing, and O'Deoradháin staggered backward. The remaining gardai tossed the now useless crossbow aside and drew his sword. He moved—toward Jenna, not the wounded O'Deoradháin.

A shout of rage, the tendons standing out like ropes in her neck: Jenna let the power surge from the cloch. A torrent of agony rushed from the cloch, through her arm and into her body, and she threw that torment outward with a scream as light flared from her hand. The searing bolt lifted the garda from his feet and slammed him backward into the wall, lightning crackling madly about his

frame. The wood cracked and shattered beneath the force
of the blow, mingling with the cracking of bones; the body
dropped to the floor like a rag doll, neck and spine broken,
the wall blackened and smoldering behind him.

The echo of thunder rumbled in Jenna's ears and faded.
In the sudden quiet, she could hear O'Deoradháin groan
as he pushed himself to his feet. Jenna was breathing heavily, her body shaking. She stared at the garda's mangled
body. The eyes were still open; they gazed at her as if in
accusation. "I'm sorry . . ." she whispered to the corpse.

"*That* is what makes me think you still need to learn
how to use your cloch, Holder," O'Deoradháin said. That
near-contempt in his voice snapped her head around. His
left arm dangled uselessly, the quarrel from the crossbow
protruding from his shoulder and dark blood staining the
arm. His right hand still held his dagger, dripping red. He
went to the corpse of Labras and wiped the blade on the
garda's clothing. He turned to Jenna, sheathing the dagger.
"Your other men are coming," he continued, "and I don't
have time to talk." He was right; she could feel them rushing toward the house from their stations. "I'm not your
enemy. They may be."

Jenna shook her head; she could feel nothing in the others but concern and fear for their own well-being if she'd
been hurt. She wished she'd taken the same precaution with
Labras and his friend. "No," she told him. "They're loyal."

"To you, perhaps. Me, they'll kill."

"Stay, O'Deoradháin. You're right. We need to talk."

They could hear the first of the gardai rush into the
house. O'Deoradháin went to the window and glanced
down. He put a leg over the sill. "Then come with me."

There were footsteps pounding the stairs. "O'Deoradháin!" Jenna called. "Wait."

His shook his head. "Meet me below Rí's Market at
Deer Creek—third bell, two days from now." She could
have stopped him. She could have reached out with Lámh
Shábhála and held him with the cloch's energy—*or crushed
him like you did the garda* . . . Jenna lifted her hand but
rather than reaching out with the power, she pushed it
back, closing Lámh Shábhála. O'Deoradháin slid over the

windowsill, grimacing as he tried to maneuver with one hand. He lowered himself slowly down, until all Jenna could see was his right hand, holding the sill. Then he let go, and she heard him land on the soft ground outside, the sound followed by his running footsteps.

"Holder!" someone shouted, and Jenna turned from the window to see the gardai, swords out, staring horrified at the carnage in front of them. She could feel the fear in them as they glanced toward her, untouched in the midst of the butchery. And perhaps because she could sense that dread, perhaps because she needed to convince herself that she had only done what she'd needed to do, she lifted her chin and glared back at them.

"This is what happens to those who betray me," she said.

In her voice, she heard an imperious tone that had never been there before, and she wondered at it.

25

Preparations

JENNA had wondered whether Cianna would believe her. She shouldn't have worried. The Banrion uttered a gasp of horror when Jenna started to relate how Labras had attacked her, and she immediately sent away the servants, going to the door of her chamber and closing it firmly. "My child," she said, enfolding Jenna in her arms. Then she released her, a quivering hand going to the torc about her neck, gold braided with bright silver. "I can hardly breathe," she said.

"Let me call the healer," Jenna said, but Cianna shook her head.

"No." Cianna took a long, wheezing breath. "No. It will pass. I put you in terrible danger, however unintentional. I was certain Labras was one of those I could trust, but . . ." She bit at her lip. ". . . he was evidently in someone else's pay. How can you ever forgive me for making such a mistake? Had you been hurt, or the cloch taken from you . . . Jenna, I put you in such danger."

Jenna hurried to reassure the distraught woman. "You couldn't have known, Banrion."

A flush burned high on Cianna's cheeks. "No, Jenna. I absolutely *should* have known. For my own survival, as well as yours. Now I have to wonder who else around me is in the employ of another, who of those others I trust implicitly . . ." Cianna turned away, hunching over as a fit of coughing took her. "Damn this sickness in my lungs, and damn the healer for his own lies." Slowly, she straightened again, still turned away from Jenna. "What about the man you went to capture? Was he part of this, too?"

"He escaped, Banrion. When I used the cloch."

Cianna turned, touching a handkerchief to her mouth. There were clumps of clotted blood on the cloth. "My guess is that Labras was being paid in this O'Deoradháin's coin. To think that I was an unwitting accomplice—oh, this would have played so well for him—had you not been alert, Lámh Shábhála would have been his."

Jenna didn't bother to correct Cianna's perception. It would be a good lie for the time being, until she learned whose hand was actually behind the scenes. And she *would* find out.

The anger burned in her, alloyed with fear.

"I will have the rest of the gardai who went with you interrogated to see if there are others whose loyalty has been turned, but now I don't know if I can trust the results I would hear," Cianna continued. "I can't discount the possibility that my husband arranged for this, or the Tanaise Ríg, or even Padraic Mac Ard or one of the other tiarna here—maybe Aheron from Infochla; he seemed awfully fond of you the other night." She stopped, and touched Jenna's cheek. "You can trust *no* one, Jenna." A bitter smile creased her face. "Evidently not even me."

Jenna put her own hand, stiff and marked with the curling scars of the cloch, on top of Cianna's. She took the Banrion's hand and kissed it once. "It wasn't your fault, Banrion," she told the woman. "We both need to be more careful, that's all. And I've learned something from this: I can use Lámh Shábhála to look inside a person and see what's in their heart." Jenna frowned. "I won't be surprised this way again," she declared.

Cianna, pale and grim, nodded.

"The Holder Aoire," the page announced, and closed the door behind Jenna. The three men in the room were huddled together over a table, and they turned to look at her as one: Rí Mallaghan, Tiarna Mac Ard; and a man whom Jenna didn't recognize. She lowered her head and gave them a brief curtsy.

"Ah, Jenna," the Rí said. He was smiling, but there was
a grimness in his smile. "Thank you for coming so quickly.
Here, you should see this . . .." He beckoned to her, and
she came over to the table. She nodded to Mac Ard, then
glanced curiously at the other man. "Ah, you've yet to be
introduced to our Field Commander," the Rí said, noting
the direction of her gaze. "Holder, this is Tiarna Damhlaic
Gairbith, who has been away to the west watching the
Connachtans."

The man inclined his head to her. He wore his clóca
uncomfortably, as if he were unused to the long folds of
fabric. His face was hardened and assured from exposure
to wind and sun, his cheeks and forehead marred with the
white lines of scars, his gray-flecked beard thin over patches
of mottled flesh. His hands were on the table, holding down
a large piece of unrolled parchment; Jenna saw that the left
hand had but two fingers and a thumb.

Through Lámh Shábhála, Tiarna Gairbith radiated violence. This was a man at whose hands hundreds had died
and who would most likely be responsible for the death of
hundreds more if he lived. There was no visceral enjoyment
of death in him, though Jenna sensed a deep satisfaction
within him at the results of his campaigns, and he carried
no remorse or guilt at all in his soul. She knew that if the
Rí ordered it, he would slay her with the same pragmatic
lack of passion. But she could sense no direct threat in him
at all: to him, she was simply a piece in the game and he
would use her or not as the strategies of the game dictated.

The emotional matrix around Mac Ard and the Rí were
more complicated. There were strange colors and hues in
their shapes, nothing that was overtly threatening, but she
knew both of them wanted what she held and would take
it if the opportunity arose. With Mac Ard especially there
were tendrils of black secrets that snaked outward toward
Jenna, vestiges of hidden plots that involved her. She
wondered—more strongly this time—if Mac Ard were at
the heart of the attacks against her, if his involvement with
her mam weren't simply a subterfuge to allow him access
to her and Lámh Shábhála.

The Rí's emotions were simpler and yet more deeply

hidden. He was wrapped in plottings and deceptions. Under it all was the burning orange-red of ambition: the Rí Gabair would be Rí Ard, if he had the chance . . . and it took little imagination on Jenna's part to believe that the Rí might feel Lámh Shábhála would give him that chance.

The Rí moved aside to let Jenna stand next to the table. Lines were drawn on the parchment, and placed atop it were small triangular flags, some green and brown, others blue and gold. "This is Tuath Gabair," the Rí explained to Jenna. "There, see that blue area? That's Lough Lár. Here—" his stubby index ringer stabbed at the map. "That is Lár Bhaile, where we are now. Up here—" his finger moved up past Lough Lár to where a line of blue meandered, occasionally met by other, smaller branches. "That's the River Duán and the Mill Creek feeding into it, and Knobtop and Ballintubber." His finger touched the map again and again in concert with his words. Jenna nodded, but in truth the map meant little to her. How could marks on paper be Ballintubber or Knobtop?

"The flags," the Rí continued, "are where our troops and the troops of Tuath Connachta are currently located. Do you see here, southwest of Ballintubber, where the Connachta flags have bunched? That's where their main army is camped, right on the border. That's where they'll make the first push toward us."

As the Rí spoke, images came to Jenna. It was as if she were a bird, hovering far above Tuath Gabair and looking down. There was the lough, and just past it . . . "Doire Coill is in their way," Jenna said. "They can't go through that forest with troops."

Tiarna Gairbith snorted through his long nostrils: a laugh. "I thought you said the Holder knew nothing of war, my Rí," he said. The fingers remaining on his mutilated left hand traced one arc on the map, then another. "They will split their forces as soon as they reach the border of Doire Coill," he said. "One arm, the larger and slower, will go north to secure the ford of the Duán at Áth Iseal, then attack Lár Bhaile from the north. The other, smaller and swifter, will cross the Duán at the southern ford and come up to Lár Bhaile from the south. 'The Horns of the Bull,' they call it; the Connachtans have used the tactic more than once. They hope to split our forces to deal with the twin attacks; if one horn fails, the other might still impale us."

"But your troops won't let that happen," Jenna said, looking at the men. "If you know where they'll strike, you will have made plans against that. You have the advantage of knowing the land and deciding where to make your battle where you can use the ground to your benefit."

Again, the laugh. "I like this Holder," Gairbith said to the Rí. "No talk from her of negotiation, of somehow avoiding the conflict. Instead, she sees that the battle will come and prepares to meet it." He bowed to Jenna, approvingly, and she wondered whether the smile was genuine or if the man was simply mocking her. "Aye, we will do just as the Holder suggests," Gairbith answered, "but many will die doing that, and after we push them back to their own borders, we will be too weak to do more than watch them leave. Unless . . ." His voice trailed off. He looked at Mac Ard, who stood with arms crossed, lips in a tight frown, his eyes almost angry.

"Unless what?" Jenna asked, and Nevan O Liathain's words echoed in her memory: *". . . the Rí no doubt hopes for Lámh Shábhála to be part of that battle . . . he would love to see the lightnings of the cloch smash the enemy and send them fleeing for their lives . . ."*

Rí Mallaghan saw the realization on her face. "Lámh Shábhála has been in countless battles over the centuries, Jenna," he said, "many of them here in what is now Tuath Gabair. And while Lámh Shábhála is the only cloch na thintrí that is awake . . ." He spread his hands wide. "There is only one reason the Connachta are mounting their armies: they know Lámh Shábhála is here and they think to strike before you learn to wield the cloch as the cloudmages have in the past and my army comes to invade their land—because if *they* had the cloch, they would use it to strike us. They believe the only reason we haven't yet struck is because the cloch or the Holder is still weak. But you've learned so much already, Jenna. I ask you, how many lives will it cost if Lámh Shábhála does not enter the battlefield?

All we request of you is that you help us defend *you,* as the Holder."

The Rí's words were spoken in a voice like sweet butter, thick and freighted with an unconscious arrogance that spoke of his expectation that he would be heard and obeyed. His eyes, behind their enclosing folds of pale flesh, stared at her unblinking. When Jenna opened her mouth to begin a protest, she saw those eyes narrow. Through the cloch, she felt a sudden surge of malice directed toward her from the Rí, and she knew that if she refused, he would use that answer to justify other actions against her. As Cianna had told her with O Liathain, "no" was not an answer she could give him.

Is he the one, then? Has the Rí been stepping carefully only because the Tanaise Ríg was here also?

"Jenna *hasn't* fully learned to use Lámh Shábhála, my Rí," Mac Ard interjected before Jenna could decide what to say. "Not in the way of the legends of the Before. Not in the way the cloudmages of song used them. Your majesty knows the pain involved for Jenna when the mage-lights come. You also know that Lámh Shábhála's task right now is to unlock the other clochs na thintrí and that is what Lámh Shábhála has been teaching the First Holder—not the art of war. You ask too much of her too soon and place her in danger. You must remember, my Rí, that the Tanaise Ríg has expressed an interest in Jenna. He would not want her injured. Worse, what if the Connachtans should win the battle when Lámh Shábhála is involved? What if Rí Connachta were suddenly to possess the cloch? Do you think the Rí Ard or any of the other Tuatha would come to your aid, or would they sit and watch and wait and let the Connachtan vultures feed on the bodies of Lár Bhaile?"

Through Mac Ard's speech, the Rí's face had grown progressively more ruddy. "So it's Tiarna Mac Ard's counsel that I throw my armies against Connachta and ignore the weapon that could easily turn the battle? You would take the sword from my hand and have me do battle with a butter knife."

"I say better a duel with butter knives than risk giving your enemy your sword, that's all," Mac Ard answered.

"*I* have no plans to give the enemy this particular sword," Tiarna Gairbith interjected. "I will cleave the enemy's head from its shoulders with it and I will keep Lámh Shábhála safe—that's my pledge."

The Rí laughed at that. "There, you see, Padraic? My Commander has made his promise."

"*I* think," Jenna said loudly, and all three men turned their heads to her, "that everyone is talking as if I were incapable of making a decision for myself." Mac Ard glowered, Gairbith gave a quick, shocked laugh, and the Rí sucked his breath in with an audible hiss. For a moment, Jenna thought she'd gone too far, but then the Rí applauded her, three slow claps of his hands. His eyes were still narrowed and dangerous, but his voice was soft.

"The Holder seems to have no lack of courage in speaking her mind," he said. "That is good—a ruler should know the true feelings of those under him. I assume the Holder realizes that when the Rí asks for an opinion, she may give it. And when he issues a command, she will *obey* it. Without any question at all."

The malice she felt in him increased, a dark arm swirling around her in cloch-vision. She knew he wanted submission now. He wanted her to drop her head, perhaps even to fall to her knees to beg forgiveness for her audacity in questioning him. Instead, she touched Lámh Shábhála, letting a trace of its cold energy seep into her to fill her voice. "Is the Rí giving me a command, then?" she asked, and the words were edged like a blade, filled with a warning and menace. "Does he believe the Holder to be like a ficheall piece that he can move about the board? If so, I would remind him that the Holder is the most powerful of all his pieces and that it might even strike the hand that tries to move it to the wrong square."

Jenna could see the Rí scowl at the words, saw him blink and take a step backward while the fury brought color to his cheeks. Tiarna Gairbith put a hand to the hilt of his sword; she knew that if the Rí ordered it, that blade would flash out toward her. Mac Ard's hand was also on his weapon and in the cloch-vision his own emotions were chaotic and ambivalent: Jenna couldn't tell what he might do. Jenna clutched Lámh Shábhála, and all three men watched her fingers close around the brightening stone.

Mac Ard stepped out between Jenna and the Rí. "Jenna, the Rí is an excellent ficheall master, both in the game and in war. You need to trust his hand, for he wouldn't put a piece as important as you in needless jeopardy. Believe me in this. I have been with him all my life and my parents served him also. He won't ask more of you than you can give. All we are doing here is looking at the alternatives available to us for this threat. Nothing more. Rí Connachta has yet to make an irrevocable move. There is still some hope they will not."

Behind the Rí, Gairbith laughed again at that assessment.

In the cloch-vision, the Rí was a thunderhead ready to spew lightning and wind and hail. Jenna knew that she had just pushed the man as far as he could be pushed—the Rí was accustomed to obedience and deference, at least on the surface. He had known nothing else; he would tolerate nothing else. Whether she would do his bidding or not when the time came, she couldn't defy him now without using the cloch. And afterward . . . even if she walked out of this room still the Holder, what then? She would be a fugitive, a dangerous animal to be hunted down and killed.

Jenna's fingers loosened around the stone. They watched her hand drop back to her waist, watched her cradle the stiff, aching flesh to her abdomen. "I'm sorry, my Rí," she said, lowering her gaze so that she stared at the man's fat, sandal-clad feet below his clóca and hoping that her words sounded sufficiently apologetic. "I spoke too harshly. I . . . I'm still frightened by what happened yesterday, the attack by the Banrion's gardai."

"Ah, that. . ." The Rí nodded; his stance relaxed and his voice was now gentle. "An unfortunate occurrence, to be certain, but one that shows me that you are learning to use the cloch, eh?"

She nodded. "Aye, my Rí."

"Good," he said. She thought that he might pat her with a fatherly hand. The malice in her cloch-vision hadn't diminished, though; this was a man who would take her without a thought if he believed it to be to his advantage. There was no affection for her in his tone; only the satisfaction that came from watching her submit to his will. "Then we'll make our plans appropriately. Tiarna Gairbith will be in contact with you regarding the plans and I know Tiarna Mac Ard—" the Rí's gaze flicked over to Padraic and at the same time, Jenna saw the two of them in the clochvision, entangled in mutual webs of ambition and deceit "—will be helping us as well. I hope you understand, Holder Jenna, that we hold you in the highest esteem, and that everything we do here is for your benefit."

He said the words with compassion gleaming in his voice and deception in his heart.

Jenna smiled at him and nodded.

The mage-lights swirled in the night sky over the keep, and Jenna went to them. The bright communion was at once painful and joyous, and afterward Jenna staggered back into her room from the balcony, clutching her arm to herself, and half-fell into Maeve's arms. Her mam helped her back to her bed, where she sat, eyes closed, feeling only the power surging through her. "Andúilleaf," she managed to croak out. "Quickly."

The water was already boiling, the leaf already crushed in the bottom of the mug. Jenna heard her mam pour the water and smelled the aroma of the leaf wafting through the cold air. "Here," Maeve said, and Jenna felt a warmth pressed against her left hand. She took the mug and lifted it to her lips, sipping noisily against the heat of the brew.

"How many times more, Jenna?" There was a weary concern in her mam's voice.

"Is that what *he* wanted you to ask me?" Jenna answered. "Is he getting impatient to be a cloch Holder himself? You can tell him that it will be soon: two more appearances. Three, at most."

Maeve ignored Jenna's scornful tone. "And what then?"

"I don't *know*," Jenna answered heatedly. "If I did, I'd tell everyone so they'd stop asking these stupid questions of me."

She glanced up to see her mam bite her lower lip, looking away with hurt in her eyes. "I ask because I hate to see you in pain, Jenna," Maeve answered, her voice trembling with the sob she held back. "I've been hoping that once the other clochs were open, you wouldn't be . . . in so much . . ." Maeve couldn't finish. She covered her mouth with a hand, tears spilling over her eyes. Jenna wanted to go to her, to comfort her mam as she had comforted Jenna a thousand times over the years, but she couldn't make herself move. She hid herself behind the mug of leaf-brew, sipping and inhaling the steam as she watched her mam sniff and blot her tears with the sleeve of her léine.

Jenna could see the swelling curve of her mam's belly. She could feel the life inside, glowing like a banked fire in a hearth.

"Maybe," Maeve said, "Padraic should be *the* Holder." She wouldn't look at Jenna. "Maybe that's what should have happened."

"Is that what Da would have wanted?" Jenna retorted. "Or have you already forgotten him and the fact that Lámh Shábhála was once his?"

Maeve turned, her clóca flaring outward with the sharp motion. "I will *never* forget Niall. *Never.* And I can't believe that you'd be cruel enough to even suggest that."

Guilt made Jenna momentarily forget the throbbing coldness in her arm. "Mam, I'm sorry . . ."

There was a tentative knock at the door and one of the servants stuck her head in. "Pardon, m'ladies, but Coelin Singer is here asking to see the Holder."

Maeve was still glaring at Jenna. "Tell him he may come in," Jenna said.

"In *here,* Holder?" the servant asked.

"Do you not have ears?" Jenna snapped. "Aye, here. If the Tanaise Ríg doesn't like it, then he should have left his own people to stand guard."

The servant looked at Maeve, who shrugged. "The Holder obviously doesn't care to have anyone else suggest what she should do or question her commands."

The servant fled.

"Mam—" Jenna began, but then the door opened again

and Coelin entered. His face was full of concern and question, but he seemed startled when he saw Maeve.

"Oh, Widow Aoire," he said, nodding to Maeve and glancing once at Jenna questioningly. "I don't mean to disturb . . ." He gestured at the door. "I can wait in the outer room."

"Stay. Maybe you can talk some sense into the girl," Maeve said to Coelin. "I obviously can't tell my daughter anything. She would rather learn from her own mistakes, I suppose. Just see that you're not another one, Coelin Singer." Maeve didn't turn back to look at Jenna, but walked out of the room. The sound of the door closing was loud in the apartment.

"What was that about?" Coelin asked. "Jenna? I saw the lights, and thought that you might—"

Jenna shook her head. "Don't talk," she said. "Just . . . come here. Please. Hold me."

Coelin, with a glance back at the door, went to the bed in two long strides. He took Jenna up in his arms.

"Kiss me," she said. "Make me forget about all this for a little bit . . ."

And, for a time, she did.

26

A World Changed

DEER Creek ran at the bottom of a steep ravine. Above, to the north, was the city of Lár Bhaile; south rose the steep and stony flanks of Goat Fell with the Rí's Keep perched on top. Not far beyond the bridge that linked Low Town to Goat Fell and the ramparts of the keep, the creek widened and fanned out into a marsh-clogged mouth before flowing into Lough Lár. To Jenna's mind, Deer Creek was more river than creek, nearly twice as wide as the Mill Creek that ran past Ballintubber, deeper and faster.

And Deer Creek had seals; one, at least: on a flat slab thrusting out of the rushing water, a dark, shiny-furred head watched as Jenna made her way down the path from the Rí's Market Square. Getting away from the keep had been easier than Jenna had expected. After the incident with the gardai, no one voiced an objection when she left the keep unescorted except by two chambermaids. Jenna noticed that another carriage departed the keep immediately after they left, and that the square seemed particularly well-populated with gardai. Jenna had opened the cloch slightly, letting its energy spread out over the square—there were at least a half dozen tendrils of attention leading to her, none of them overtly dangerous but all watching.

And down in the hawthorn-choked ravine, another: O'Deoradháin.

The chambermaids were easy: she gave each of them a mórceint and told them to go buy whatever they liked. It

took time to lose the gardai, but she eventually managed
to lose all the watchers and sneak away, to the wooden
stairs leading down to Deer Creek and a small patch of
meadow there where a few people sat fishing despite the
cold. Jenna stayed under the trees, moving east along the
creek and away from the meadow, where someone glancing
down from the market above wouldn't easily spot her. She
saw movement out in the creek—the seal rose from the cold
water and clambered onto one of the flat rocks in the middle of the stream.

She could sense O'Deoradháin in the tangle of woods
huddled against the steep bank. Jenna shivered and
wrapped herself tighter in her clóca, one hand grasping the
stone on its chain, ready to open it fully and strike the man
down at need. "You could have at least picked a warm
place to meet," she called out to where he hid.

There was a rustle of dry brush and leaves, and O'Deoradháin stepped out. One arm was in a sling, but there was a
knife at his belt, and Jenna watched his free hand carefully,
knowing how quickly he could move with that weapon. She
stayed ready to strike if his fingers strayed near the hilt.
"If it were summer, the midges would be out. Would you
rather be cold or bitten to death?"

The seal out in the water gave a coughing roar, and
Jenna glanced again at the creature. It was a large bull, its
head up and alert and staring back at them. Its coat was
coal-black, yet deep blue highlights gleamed within it, like
sparks struck from a flint and steel. O'Deoradháin looked
toward the seal as well. "There aren't usually seals in
Lough Lár," he said. "Sometimes in Lough Dubh, aye, but
they don't usually come up the Duán this far."

"For an Inishlander, you know a lot about Tuath
Gabair."

"I've been here a long time now," O'Deoradháin answered, turning away from the seal and looking back at
Jenna. "Ever since the Order decided that Lámh Shábhála
might be in Gabair. Almost two years now."

Jenna cocked her head at that. "And how did you know
that Lámh Shábhála was here before the mage-lights
came?"

O'Deoradháin shrugged, grimacing as his bandaged shoulder moved. "Some in the Order know the magics of earth and water, the slow eternal spells. I know a bit of them myself. Ordinarily, that means little, but as the Filleadh approached and the mage-lights started to strengthen even though none of us could see them yet, those with the skill could feel the resonance through their own spells. They knew and they started to search, and they realized that Lámh Shábhála had once been on Inishfeirm and that they had lost the cloch. It wasn't hard, then, to know who had taken it—your great-da. What took time was discovering where he had gone and what had happened to him."

"So they sent you? Alone?" Jenna scoffed. "Why didn't they send everyone? Why isn't Gabair filled with people from the Order?"

O'Deoradháin gazed back placidly into her mocking stance. "If all of Inishfeirm suddenly came here, then everyone would suspect why and everyone would have been searching for the cloch. And there are only a few who are capable of being the Holder of Lámh Shábhála."

The way he said it lifted the hairs on Jenna's arms with a sudden chill that was not the cold air. "A few like you?" she asked.

O'Deoradháin nodded. "That's what I was trained to do." Jenna took a step back from him. "Jenna," he said. "Use the stone. Look at me. I'm not a threat to you. I'd take the stone from you if you gave it to me, aye. If you'd died the other day in my room, I'd have taken it then, too. But I won't harm you to become the Holder."

That might have been true; she could feel no danger to herself emanating from him. Yet . . . "I don't know that," she said. "Even with the cloch."

O'Deoradháin smiled, which softened his rugged face. "You're right. You *don't* know that, and I'll tell you that there *are* ways to hide yourself from a cloch na thintrí, even Lámh Shábhála."

"And you know them."

"I do."

"Then I can't trust you."

"Perhaps not," he answered. "But you can't survive alone. Not for long, and not with what you hold."

"I have those I can trust," Jenna replied with some heat, and—strangely—O'Deoradháin chuckled at that.

"Who? Mac Ard? The Rí and Banrion? That self-centered boy from your old village?"

"He's not—" Jenna began heatedly, then stopped, clenching her jaw as O'Deoradháin studied her, as the seal out in the river gave another moaning wail as if calling for a mate. "What did you want of me, O'Deoradháin?"

"Only what I told you: to bring you to Inishfeirm, so you can learn to use the power you hold."

"I *have* learned," she retorted. "I wouldn't be talking to you now if I hadn't. Three times someone has tried to kill me and three times I've killed them instead. I can see with the cloch, see what people are feeling toward me. I can tell whether a person holds a true cloch or a worthless stone. I can draw the mage-lights down to me and fill the stone with their energy."

"And did you *need* to kill them or even want to? Do you know that you see truth through the cloch? Do you know all Lámh Shábhála wants to do with that power or all it can do? Do you know how to deal with the *pain*, Jenna?" She must have shown something in her face, unwillingly, for he nodded. "Aye, that we can help you learn. But you must come with me back to Inishfeirm."

"I don't *trust* you," Jenna said again.

"I know you don't. But you're trusting the wrong people now."

"You don't know that."

"Unfortunately, I do," he answered calmly. "But I also know that you must learn things yourself to believe them. Let me start you on that path. I've done some investigation myself. Go to Night Mist Alley, just off Callaghan Street. Walk down to the third door on the left, the red one, and knock. And after you've been there and returned to the keep, *use* the cloch. Look at the ones you haven't bothered to examine yet because you trust them. And when you're done, if you think you might begin to believe me, then come to du Val again. He can tell you where to find me."

O'Deoradháin started to walk away; as if startled by his movement, the seal out in the river roared a last time and dove into the water with a soft splash. "O'Deoradháin, wait."

"No, Holder. There's nothing more to say. Go and see things for yourself and ask the questions you need to ask. When you need me again, I'll find you." He smiled at her. "I wanted to be the Holder, aye," he said. "But I think Lámh Shábhála has chosen wisely on its own." With a wave, he slid back into the undergrowth again, and she heard the sound of his retreat.

Out in the water, a dark shape slid away toward the lough.

Night Mist Alley was a dirt lane in the Low Town area. Even in the sunlight, it was dim, with the houses staring at each other across a muddy strip down which two people could barely walk abreast. Children were screeching and chasing each other through the puddles, filthy and snot-faced, and the adults Jenna saw stared at the sight of an obvious Riocha and her two chambermaids out where the royalty rarely walked.

The third door on the left was indeed red though the paint was scratched and peeling, and the door itself appeared to have been kicked, the lower panel cracked and bowed in. Jenna motioned to the maids to remain in the alley as she went to the door and knocked. There was no immediate answer. She knocked again. "Just a moment . . ." a woman's voice answered, and a few seconds later, the door opened. A woman blinked into the sunlight. "By the Mother—Jenna?"

Ellia, Tara's daughter, stood there. Jenna nearly didn't recognize her. She was heavy with child, one hand under the rounded bulk of her belly, her face and fingers swollen. After her initial surprise, she smiled at Jenna. "By the Mother-Creator, look at you," she said. "Don't you look wonderful! Oh, Jenna, it's so good to see you! Everyone thought you'd died when those horrible soldiers came. And to think you came here, like us."

"Us?" A feeling of dread was filling Jenna. She wanted

to rage, wanted to take Lámh Shábhála and bring a storm of lightning down on this house and this town and leave everything in flames.

"Aye." A possessive, triumphant smile lifted Ellia's lips. She turned slightly to call back into the darkness of the room. "Darling, come and see who's come to visit us. You're not going to believe this."

A sleepy grunt came from the interior. Jenna heard the sound of shuffling feet, then a man's form showed behind Ellia as she opened the door wider. The man took a step into the light. She knew who it was before she saw him, knew from the leaden stone that filled her stomach, knew because of the blackness that threatened to take her vision. Her world was suddenly shattered, crashing in crystalline shards around her.

Coelin.

Ellia's arm snaked possessively around Coelin's waist as he gaped at Jenna. "Look, love—it's Jenna! Back from the dead! Jenna, did you know that Coelin has sung for the Rí himself . . . ?"

Ellia must have continued to speak, but Jenna heard none of it. She stared at Coelin. He stared back, slack-jawed, rubbing at his eyes as if trying to rid them of a sudden nightmare. "Jenna, I . . ." he stammered, but Jenna shouted back at him in fury.

"You bastard! You damned lying *bastard!*" Jenna turned and ran from the alleyway, her maids hurrying after her with wide-eyed glances behind.

"Jenna!" she heard Coelin shouting behind her, and Ellia's now-shrill voice asking him what was happening. Jenna fled, helpless tears hot on her cheeks, unheeding of the people around her, staring. She only wanted to be away before the temptation to use the cloch grew too strong, before she gave in to the temptation to get revenge for this awful deception. *It's your own fault!* she railed inside. *You're so stupid. So naive and stupid . . .*

"Jenna!" A hand touched her shoulder and she whirled around with a cry, her right hand going to the stone around her neck, the radiance of Lámh Shábhála between her fingers already brighter than the sun. Coelin, panting, took a step backward from Jenna, his eyes wide. He was shoeless and half-dressed, his feet muddy, his legs bare under his tunic. His breath was a white cloud around him in the cold air. He spread his hands wide, as if to ward off a blow. "Jenna, listen to me . . ."

Her chambermaids flanking her, Jenna chopped at the air with her left hand. "You have *nothing* to say to me!" she shouted back at him. "*Nothing!* You disgust me, Coelin Singer. And I'm ashamed of myself for letting you . . ." She couldn't say the words. Fury obliterated them.

"Jenna, let me explain!"

"Explain what? Is that your child Ellia's carrying? Tell me now—is it?" Coelin started to shake his head, started to speak, and Jenna lifted the cloch. "Don't you dare lie to me again, Coelin, or I swear it's the last words you'll ever speak."

Coelin gulped and hung his head. "Aye," he said, his voice a whisper. " 'Tis mine." Then his head came up, and his green eyes gazed at her imploringly. "But, Jenna, I love *you* . . ."

"*Shut up!*" Jenna screamed at him. Light flared from her fisted hand, and shadows moved over the buildings around them. Someone shouted in alarm, and the curious crowd that had begun to gather around the encounter suddenly vanished. "No! Don't you *dare* say it. Who arranged this, Coelin? None of this was an accident, was it? Who made certain I'd find you, who told you to seduce me?" When Coelin said nothing, Jenna stamped her foot, the light flaring yet brighter. "Tell me!"

"Tiarna Mac Ard," Coelin sputtered. "He . . . he sent word that I should come here, said that you needed someone familiar, that I could help him help you . . ." He stopped. His hands lifted toward Jenna, then went to his sides. "Jenna, I didn't mean . . ."

She wanted to kill him. She wanted to hear Coelin scream in agony as the lightnings tore him apart. She wanted him to feel the pain and hurt that was coursing through her now. Her hand trembled around Lámh Shábhála but she held back the energy that wanted to surge outward. "Did you marry her?" she asked.

A nod. "Aye. When Tara realized that Ellia was with child, she came to me. What else was I to do, Jenna? At that time, I thought you were dead, and your mam and Tiarna Mac Ard, too."

"Do you tell Ellia you love her, too? Did you come to her after you'd been with me and snuggle down alongside her and give her the same words you give me?"

"Jenna—"

She spat at his feet. "I never want to see you again," she told him. "If I do, I swear to you that I'll use Lámh Shábhála to strike you down. Stand before me again, and I will leave Ellia a widow and your child fatherless. Go, Coelin. Go and find some way to tell Ellia about this. Maybe she'll keep you; maybe she'll even find the love in her to forgive you." She lifted her chin, her eyes narrowing. "But I won't," she told him. "I never will, and I am your enemy from this moment. Do you understand me, Coelin?"

He nodded, mute. He looked as if he were about to speak again, but Jenna tightened her fist around the cloch, and—wide-eyed—he turned and fled, walking then running back the way he'd come. Her breath fast and painful in her chest, Jenna relaxed her grip on Lámh Shábhála, and the stone's brilliance faded.

The street around them was empty and silent except for the ragged sound of her breath. "Come," she told the maids. "It's time we returned to the keep." They started down the lane toward where the carriage waited. As they walked, a man stepped out from between two houses and stood in the narrow street, barring their way. One of the chambermaids screamed at the sudden confrontation, but the man ignored her. One arm was in a sling, and he no longer seemed quite as dangerous. He looked at Jenna.

"Now you know," he said. "I'm sorry, Jenna."

"You could have told me, O'Deoradháin. Or did you get a perverse pleasure out of knowing I'd be humiliated?"

His head moved slowly in denial. "I took no pleasure in it, Holder. I would have preferred to tell you myself, but you wouldn't have believed me," he answered. "You know that, if you look inside."

She wasn't going to give him the satisfaction of a response. Her head was pounding, her arm ached, and there was a fury inside burning to be unleashed. "Fine. Now get out of my way. I'm going back to the keep."

"Holder . . ." He held out his hands, as if in supplication. "This isn't the way. You're angry, and you have reason to be. But you don't know the cloch well enough yet. There are too many people there, too many to confront."

Jenna coughed a single, bitter chuckle. "I thought you told me to go back and use the cloch."

"Not the way you're thinking of using it right now." He gestured to the tower of the keep, which could be seen rising above the rooftops. "I wanted you to know that the Riocha up there can't be trusted, that's all. I wanted you to use the cloch to see the truth in them."

"And you can teach me how to do that."

"Aye." He said it firmly. "I can. Come with me. Come with me now."

Her pulse pounded against the sides of her skull like a hammer; her arm seemed to be sculpted from ice. She couldn't think. She needed to get home. Needed to get andúilleaf. Needed to think. Needed to find a way to vent this rage before it consumed her entirely.

"Get out of my way, O'Deoradháin." Jenna started walking toward him.

She intended to push him out of the way, not caring about his size or the knife at his belt, ready to blast him dead with the cloch if she needed to do so. But as she reached him, he stood aside and let her pass, the two maids scrambling quickly after her.

"Holder, this is madness!" he called after her. "Please don't do this. Jenna, I can be your ally in this if you'll let me."

She didn't answer.

27

Bridges Burned

HER fury had gone cold and flintlike before the carriage reached the keep. Through the headache, through the agony in her hand and arm, the events of the last few months kept roiling in her mind and she could make no sense of it. They were *all* trying to use her; they were *all* lying to her: the Rí Gabair, the Tainise Ríg, Mac Ard, the Connachtans, Tiarna Aheron, even O'Deoradháin by his own admission.

They all had their agendas. She could understand that, yet it left unanswered the question of who was actively trying to kill her. Why would Mac Ard try to assassinate her and at the same time send Coelin to her? In any case, he could have taken the cloch easily before she knew what she possessed. What would the Tanaise Ríg gain by her death when he believed he could have Lámh Shábhála for his use by marrying her? Would Rí Gabair be willing to risk the enmity of the Rí Ard and those of the other tuatha by killing her?

I'd take the stone from you if you gave it to me, aye. If you'd died the other day in my room, I'd have taken it then, too. In that, certainly, O'Deoradháin was no different. Mac Ard might not strike against her, but Jenna had no doubt that her mam's lover would race to pluck Lámh Shábhála from her neck if she fell. Or the Rí or the Tanaise Ríg or Aheron or any of the tiarna.

Yet both assassination attempts required that someone know the keep, that they know the details of the society behind the massive walls, that they know Jenna's move-

ments. Who had known her and the keep that well? Who
would have had the connections and the money to hire an
assassin, to buy the loyalty of the gardai?

Jenna's next breath was a gasp as the carriage wheels
struck the cobbled surface of Deer Creek Bridge. A suspicion started to grow, one that left her feeling breathless
and sick. By the time Jenna stepped down at the High
Gates with an admonition to her chambermaids (that she
knew would be useless) to say nothing about what they had
witnessed, she had already made a decision. *And after
you've been there and returned to the keep,* use *the cloch,*
O'Deoradháin had told her.

She would do that, then. She would do exactly that.

She hurried to her rooms.

"Jenna, what's the mat—" her mam asked as she rushed
into the apartment, but Jenna hurried to her bedroom and
slammed the door shut. She locked it, then went to the
door leading to the servants' hall and locked that one as
well.

Her mam knocked and called, but Jenna ignored her.
She set water to boiling for the andúilleaf and dug under
the clothes in her chest until she found the torc of Sinna.
She placed it around her neck and let Lámh Shábhála
open . . .

. . . and there Sinna was again, the old woman with the
plait of gray hair, dressed in her léine and clóca, the fireplace blazing with a remembered fire, the walls of the room
overlaid with its older structure. Sinna turned as if surprised
and Jenna opened her mind to her, letting her see what
Jenna wished her to see. "Ah, Jenna," Sinna said, her voice
quavering with age, "so I've met you before." A sad smile.
"But of course I don't remember. I'm just a ghost."

"I need your help," Jenna told the old woman.

"Of course you do. Isn't that why we Holders always call
back our predecessors? The dead can't rest when the living
desire an answer." She sighed. "But your time will come,
when *your* spirit won't be allowed its peace, either. How
can I help you, Jenna First Holder?"

"I have been told that Lámh Shábhála can see the truth
in someone. Can that be done?"

Sinna's gray head nodded. "Aye. With Lámh Shábhála that's possible, though not with the other clochs na thintrí. If you know how to listen through the cloch, you can hear truth, though a person who holds another cloch can still hide truth from you. It's better if you learn to trust your own judgments. There are all sorts of truths, and not all of them are worth knowing."

"Show me."

Sinna smiled sadly. "Listen to me first. Sometimes it's not good to see the truth, Jenna. I can see anger and hurt and confusion in you already. Your thinking is clouded by that and by the potions you're taking. Jenna, sometimes you will find that you'd rather not know all the things that could be revealed to you." She gave a mocking, self-deprecating laugh. "I discovered that, too late."

"Show me," Jenna insisted.

"And what do you do when you discover the truth, Jenna?"

"If you want peace, if you want me to let you rest, you'll show me." Another nod, accompanied by a sigh. "All right, then," she said. "This is how I was taught to truth-see . . ."

"Banrion!"

Cianna turned as Jenna strode through the door to her chamber, two of the Banrion's attendants skittering nervously alongside her. Cianna waved the maids away. "Jenna," she said soothingly. "I'm glad to see you. There are rumors simply darting through the keep right now."

Jenna ignored that. The andúilleaf made her want to sleep and the walls around her seemed slightly hazy, as if she walked in a mist. Her hand closed around the cloch, the sleeve of her léine falling down to show the scars of her arm. She forced herself to focus. "I need to ask you this, Banrion—do you know who sent the first assassin?" she asked. "Do you know who told Labras that he was to kill me?"

Cianna coughed. Her eyes widened as if she were shocked by the questions, and her gaze was on Jenna's hand. "Of course not, Jenna. If I'd discovered that, I would have told you."

The words sounded sincere and almost sad. But even through the andúilleaf fog, Jenna could hear the broken, hidden tones, the umber notes that Sinna had shown her to be the signature of a lie. Jenna struggled to control her own face, to keep her voice calm even though she wanted to cry out her anger. She hadn't wanted her suspicions confirmed; she'd continued to hope that the certainty that had settled in the pit of her stomach since she'd spoken with O'Deoradháin was a sham—for if it was not, then she could no longer trust her own judgment. "Why would you ask, Jenna?" the Banrion continued. "You know that I would keep nothing like that from you. Who have you been talking with that filled your head with such notions?"

Jenna shrugged. *Focus* . . . "I overheard a most distressing conversation between two tiarna, and one of them was insisting that *you* were the one who hired the assassin."

Jenna watched the Banrion's face carefully as she gave her the fabrication. Cianna's face took on an expression of shocked disbelief. Her hand went to the torc around her neck and she coughed in quick spasms. "Surely you don't believe that, Jenna," she gasped. "I would never have . . . No, my dear, that's simply not true."

Yet it was. Jenna could hear it. She knew it.

It was Cianna who would kill her to hold Lámh Shábhála.

"Who are these tiarna? I will have them brought here this instant to answer to me," Cianna fumed. She rose from her chair, steadying herself as another coughing fit took her.

"No, you won't," Jenna told her.

For a moment, Cianna glared at Jenna. "You cannot take that tone with me—" she began, then seemed to catch herself. She smiled. "Jenna, I can see that you're upset. Let me call for some refreshments . . ." She lifted her hand, reaching for the bell rope near her chair.

"No," Jenna said again as she took Lámh Shábhála in her hand, allowing more of its energy to surge forth. Cianna started to cry out in alarm, but Jenna squeezed her right hand around the cloch, imagining the cloch's energy closing itself around Cianna's throat at the same time. The Banrion gave a choking gasp, her hands going to her neck as if to

tear away invisible fingers. Her face went dark red, her
mouth opened as she tried to draw in air. "There can be
no more lies between us, Banrion," Jenna told her. "Lámh
Shábhála can hear the truth, and I know who sent the first
assassin—when you knew that I would be in my room,
when you thought I might be weak or distracted by trying
to speak with the ghost of Sinna. After that attempt failed,
after you came so close to being discovered, you were too
frightened to try again until I stupidly played right into
your hands by asking for your gardai. I can imagine you
thought that incredibly convenient—kill me, kill O'Deoradháin, then blame my death on him while Labras brings you
back your prize before anyone else has the chance to claim
it. I can't believe that I was so naive as to believe you
afterward."

Cianna's face had gone purple. Through the anger and
the haze of andúilleaf, Jenna realized that the woman was
near unconsciousness and death. She relaxed her grip on
the stone, and Cianna took a deep, rattling gasp of a breath.
"Why did you want the cloch so badly, Banrion?" Jenna
asked. "What made it so valuable to you that it was worth
my life? Answer me, and I might let you live."

"Kill me," Cianna managed to grate out, her voice a
harsh croak. "Go ahead. You're no better than any of the
rest of them. I've heard them, all along. 'Poor Cianna. Such
a weak, pathetic creature. She's given the Rí all she could,
and now she's useless. It's a shame she doesn't die, so he
could marry again.' And you—do you think I couldn't see
the pity and disgust in your face? 'Poor Cianna . . .' Well,
with the cloch, no one would be saying that."

"I never—" Jenna began.

"You want more of this *truth*, Holder?" Cianna spat out,
interrupting. "Well, here's more: the Rí and Damhlaic
Gairbith have planned more than just the defense of Gabair. When the Connachtans attack, the Rí will take you
with him, let you use the cloch, then—when you're weak
and hurt and exhausted and the cloch is empty of power—
you will be unfortunately 'killed in the battle.' You'll receive all the plaudits and honors you desire, but you'll be
dead and the Rí will be wearing Lámh Shábhála. You see,

he's no different than me. And as to Nevan O Liathain, do you really think the Tanaise Ríg would have an interest in someone as common and plain as you if you weren't the Holder? Do you honestly believe he doesn't have his own plans to take Lámh Shábhála from you? You're a stupid, common child, and you don't deserve what you possess."

The rage was flooding Jenna's mind, a foaming, wild flood that swept away reason before it. She shouted back at Cianna, a wordless, guttural scream lost in the din of the fury. She lifted the cloch on its chain, her hand a trembling fist, and Cianna began a cry that suddenly choked into silence. Jenna's fist tightened. There was a sense of unreality to her action, as if it were someone else moving her hand, and it was not only Cianna's image that she choked—she imagined doing the same to Coelin, Mac Ard, the Rí Gabair, and the Tanaise Ríg and Tiarna Aheron and everyone who stared at her and whispered against her.

But they were not here. Cianna was.

Jenna felt something break inside the woman. A bloody froth bubbled on the Banrion's lips and she fell as Jenna turned away, stalking out of the room. The maids shrank back against the wall as the doors slammed against their stops with Jenna's thrust, and she strode across the anteroom and out into the corridors of the Keep.

Behind her there was a scream and a cry of alarm.

Jenna paid it no attention. She stalked through the wing toward her own rooms, pushing open the doors. "Jenna!" Maeve called as she entered. "What's happened?"

Silent, Jenna pushed past her into her bedroom. She grabbed the pouch of andúilleaf, placed the torc of Sinna Mac Ard around her neck. She pulled her traveling pack from its shelf, and stuffed some clothing in it. She put on her old coat, the one she'd worn in Ballintubber. She turned to leave.

Her mam was standing in the doorway, one hand at her swelling belly, the other on the thick, polished wood of the doorframe. There were tears in her eyes. "Jenna, talk to me," she said. "Darling, you look so . . ." She stopped.

"Get out of my way, Mam," Jenna said. "I'm leaving."

"You can't."

"I have to. I just murdered the Banrion."

Maeve gave a cry that was half-sob. She swayed, the hand on the doorframe going to her chest and Jenna pushed past her. As she started across the parlor, the door opened and Mac Ard entered, his dark face grim. He saw Jenna and his hand went to his sword. For a moment, Jenna blinked, seeing him.

"Don't do it," Jenna told him. It sounded like someone else's voice. "Show me a hint of steel, and I'll kill you where you stand, even if you are the father of my mam's child."

"Jenna," he said. "Listen to yourself. *Look* at yourself. If Lámh Shábhála or the andúilleaf has driven you mad—"

"Then *you'll* gladly take the cloch," Jenna finished for him. "So kind of you, Tiarna. Why don't you tell my mam *all* of your kindness, like the way you arranged for Coelin to come here to be my lover when you knew he was married to Ellia and she was with child. Tell her about that. Now move out of the way."

"I can't let you go, Jenna. I can't. I love you as my own daughter, but I also have my duty and my word."

"Move!" Jenna shouted at the man. The word tore at her vocal cords, a shriek.

"I can't," Mac Ard repeated.

Jenna screamed again. Her vision had gone dim, a red haze over everything, and she could see only what stood in front of her: Mac Ard. She lifted Lámh Shábhála, and it flared in her hand as her mam shouted behind her. Lightning crackled, wrapping around Mac Ard and lifting him. Jenna gestured and the man was flung across the room, his body slamming against the wall. He collapsed with a groan. Maeve ran to him, crouching down alongside him and cradling his head in her lap. He was moaning as blood poured from a cut along his forehead. Maeve wept, tears sliding down her face. "Jenna! Stop this . . . Please, darling, you must!"

Jenna spoke with a strange calmness in the midst of the red fury. "I can't stop it, Mam. I can't. It's too late for that. I'm sorry . . ." She tore her gaze away from Maeve, went to the door, and left the room.

* * *

She could hear footsteps pounding up the stairs. She sent lightning crackling down the long hall toward the sound and flames sprang up where the bright fingers touched. She ran the other way, to the back stairs the keep's help used. She ran down winding stone steps, scattering the few servants who were on them, and emerged into the courtyard. A tiarna was nearby, dismounting from his horse as two stable hands held the beast. "Holder—" he started to say in greeting. Jenna gave him no chance to go further—she let a pulse of energy flow from the cloch, smashing him in the chest. The horse reared and Jenna snatched the reins from the boy who was holding them, his face a frozen mask of terror.

She leaped onto the horse, not caring that her clóca rode up leaving her legs bare to the cold. "Holder, stop!" the boy shouted, but she kicked the horse into motion. Gardai were pouring out from the keep and an arrow hissed past her ear. Jenna crouched low on her steed's back, urging him into a gallop toward the gates.

There were men there, she saw, and the gates were closed. She reined up the horse, lifting Lámh Shábhála as the squad of men hesitated. She cried aloud, her hand alight with the power, the scars on her arm glowing. The squad scattered; brighter than the sun, a fist like that of a god arced out from the cloch and smashed into the gate. Metal screeched and wailed; stone cracked and fell. "Now!" Jenna shouted to the horse, kicking him again with her heels. She moved him carefully through the rubble and dust as more arrows shattered on the stones around her, then she was through onto the winding path leading down the steep slope of Goat Fell toward the town. Over the pounding of her mount's hooves, she could hear the commotion behind her. As she traversed the first of the switchback turns, she glanced back at the keep. Black smoke was pouring from the windows of the main tower, and a cloud of dust hung over the main gates, but a dozen mailed gardai on warhorses were already in pursuit.

Jenna kicked the horse again, and the stallion's nostrils snorted twin white clouds into the cold air as his hooves

tossed clods of half-frozen mud in the air. She would make
the bridge, she knew, but already her head threatened to
explode and her arm felt as if it was made of frozen granite.
Her vision had contracted so that she could see only what
was directly in front of her, and that poorly. She clutched
the horse's reins with her left hand, the right hanging limp,
her knees trying desperately to keep a grip on the saddle.
She heard more than saw the horse reach the bridge and
begin to gallop across, the hooves loud on the wooden
planking. She halted the stallion on the other side, pulling
him around so that she faced the bridge. Wearily, she
reached for Lámh Shábhála with a hand that felt as heavy
as the stones that formed the bridge's arches. She could
barely see. She squinted into her dimming sight, trying to
see her pursuers, ready to open Lámh Shábhála again and
take them and the bridge down. She swayed in the saddle,
and forced herself erect again.

"Holder!"

Jenna grimaced, her fingers fumbling around the cloch.
She could hear the riders approaching, but couldn't see
them in the dusk of her sight.

"Holder! Jenna!" the voice shouted again, behind her
and to the left. It sounded familiar, and she turned her
head slowly, her eyes narrowing.

"O'Deoradháin . . . You bastard . . ." She lifted Lámh
Shábhála, ready to strike the man down. He ran toward
her awkwardly, hampered by his sling-bound arm, as she
wobbled in the saddle, nearly falling.

"Can you ride?" He seemed to be shouting in her ear.
"Holder, listen to me! Can you ride?"

She nodded. It took all the effort she had.

"Then ride. Go to du Val's. The Apothecary. Go, and
I'll meet you there."

"The men . . ." Jenna muttered. "From the keep . . ."

"I will deal with them. Go!"

"It's too late," Jenna said. Her voice sounded noncha-
lant, almost amused. Strangely, she wanted to laugh. She
couldn't lift her hand to point, but nodded toward the bridge.
The riders from the keep were galloping around the final
bend in the mountain road. Sighting Jenna on the other side

of the bridge, they shouted and urged their horses forward. Jenna reached for the cloch again, wondering if she could open it in time, wondering if she had the strength to stay conscious if she did.

Something moved in front of her: O'Deoradháin, stepping to the end of the bridge as if he were about to hold back the onrushing gardai himself, one-handed. As Jenna watched, the man bent down and took a stone from the ground in his free hand. He held it in front of him, as if he were offering it to the riders. She heard his voice call aloud: *"Obair don deannach!"* He threw the stone to the ground, and it seemed to shatter and dissolve. The gardai's horses pounded onto the bridge, and at the same time, the bridge groaned like a live thing, a wail of wood and stone. The bridge decking writhed as if a giant had struck it from below as the tall stone arches to either side collapsed and fell away. Blocks of carved stone rained; support timbers bent and cracked like saplings in a storm.

The bridge fell, with the first of the riders on it. Horses and men screamed as they pinwheeled in air to the bottom of the ravine and crashed against the stones of Deer Creek.

There was a stunning silence. A gout of dust rose from the deep cleft. Jenna gaped. The gardai trapped on the far side stared down at the broken bodies of their companions.

O'Deoradháin alone was free of the stasis. Jenna saw him move, heard him groan with effort and pain as he pulled himself with his one good arm onto her horse, even as Jenna swayed and nearly fell. His arms went around her, taking the reins. He slapped them against the stallion's neck, kicked at its massive chest. "Go!" he shouted, wheeling the horse around.

Even as the first arrows arced toward them from across the ravine, they were galloping away toward the town, the onlookers staring in terror and fright.

They fled.

28

A Return

JENNA remembered little of the flight from Lár Bhaile, where O'Deoradháin took her or how they came to leave. There were flashes of images:

. . . du Val, his face peering down at her concernedly. His mouth moved, but she heard nothing of what he said. There was another face behind the ugly dwarf's—O'Deoradháin?— and Jenna tried to struggle up, but hands held her firmly . . .

. . . the pain as she was lifted. She could see nothing, but she could feel herself moving. There were voices: "We can't stay here. They'll be scouring the town in an hour. Not only the keep's gardai, but the Rí Ard's garrison as well." Another voice spoke. "A carriage, then? She can't ride, certainly." The first voice answered. "No, they'll be watching the High Road. If we could get across the lough . . ."

. . . a gentle rocking motion, the creaking of wood, the splashing of water and the smell of damp and fish. She looked up and saw stars above her, swaying softly . . .

There were still stars, and the smell of the lough and the sound of canvas rippling in a wind. Jenna sat up. She was in a small boat, a single small sail billowing in the cold night breeze. She was wrapped in blankets and she hugged them around her against the frigid air. O'Deoradháin was seated in the stern of the boat, the tiller in his hand, his left arm still bandaged tightly against his chest. Ahead, the shore was no more than a quarter mile distant. "Where?" was all she could manage to say. Her throat was raw and burning; the headache still pounded with every beat of her heart, and she wasn't certain she could move her right arm; it seemed dead. She touched her neck with her other hand: Lámh Shábhála was still there on its chain—that, at least, gave momentary relief. O'Deoradháin hadn't taken it from her.

"Nearly on the western shore of Lough Lár," O'Deoradháin answered. "And a bit north of Lár Bhaile as well. I've been looking for a good, low shingle where we can land."

"Andúilleaf . . . I need it. . ."

O'Deoradháin shook his head. "Don't have it. Du Val took it."

Jenna shivered at that. Anger burned, and she started to lift her hand to the cloch, but weariness overcame her. She sank back. "I'll die," she whispered. "I hurt so much."

"You might wish you died, but you won't. Not from the pain of Lámh Shábhála or withdrawal from the leaf. Perhaps from the Rí's soldiers, if they find us."

She remembered, suddenly, O'Deoradháin standing before the bridge, and it falling . . . "The bridge," she said. "You said you knew other magics, but you also said they were slow and weaker. That was neither slow nor weak."

If Jenna's praise pleased him, he didn't show it. His face was grim and sad. "Aye, much slower and weaker they are. But that spell was set earlier, before we met in the ravine and once the keystones were gone on the arches, the bridge itself did the rest. I thought that if we were to need to flee from the keep, that we would also need a way to slow up the pursuit. The spell took several at least a candle stripe or two of preparation, but then it was already done and set—all I had to do was speak the words."

He lifted his head to scan the shore, turning the tiller and adjusting the sail. "There, that's as good a spot as we're likely to find." A few minutes later, the keel grated on a tiny, pebbled beach along a small cove. Starlight dappled the tops of the trees on the shore while they held impenetrable darkness underneath, but across the lough and to the south, Jenna could see the yellow light of Lár Bhaile. O'Deoradháin leaped from the boat into the shallow water. Extending his good hand, he helped Jenna from the craft.

"I can't walk far," she told him.

"I know, but come dawn we'd be all too visible on the lough's shore."

"They'll see the boat anyway and know where we landed."

O'Deoradháin shook his head. "No," he said simply. He helped her up the bank to dew-wet grass. Then he went back down to the beach and shoved the prow of the boat away from shore. Jenna heard the bottom of the craft grinding against the bed of the lough, yet the boat continued to move outward. She saw two dark forms, blacker than the night, break the water's surface alongside the hull. Blue light shimmered from their bodies. Water splashed, the foam white, and the boat moved out into deeper water, floating free. The bow turned and faced south and east and it began to move away from them. O'Deoradháin came back to her and stood watching until they could no longer see the boat past the bend of the shore. He said nothing; Jenna decided she would not, either, though she wondered: *were those seals?* O'Deoradháin held out his hand to her. "We need to go as far as we can tonight," he said. "They'll find the boat tomorrow just south of Lár Bhaile, on the eastern side. If the Mother-Creator smiles on us, it will be a few days before they start looking on the western shore."

"And where are we going?"

O'Deoradháin shrugged. "North. To Inish Thuaidh."

"No," Jenna said.

"No?" In the darkness, it was difficult to see his face, but Jenna could hear his scowl and sigh of exasperation. "Holder, in the morning, all of Gabair will be out looking for you. When word reaches Dún Laoghaire, the Rí Ard will have his troops sent searching as well, and Tuath Connachta might very well consider this a wonderful opportunity to come look for you themselves. The other tuatha may do the same. Your only safety is to be gone from here as quickly as we can, and Inish Thuaidh is where you can best learn to use the power you have."

"No," Jenna repeated. She looked up, to where the wind tousled the heads of the trees. She could see nothing but the night sky and stars above them, but she could feel the first shy touch of mage-lights at the zenith. She knew that they would appear soon, no more than two stripes from now, and she was tired. So tired. *No!* she wanted to scream to them. *Not tonight. I can't . . .*

She struggled to her feet, staring into the darkness of the trees. She remembered other trees, the dark twisted oaks that stretched close to the shore of the lough, Seancoim's tenderness and aid . . . "I'm going to Doire Coill."

O'Deoradháin loosed a scoffing breath. "I didn't snatch you from the Rí's gardai to have you die under the haunted oaks."

Jenna shrugged. She took a halting step—it took more effort than she thought. "I've been through those oaks once before. I think I'm safer there than on the road. If you don't want to come with me, then I'll thank you for your rescue, Ennis O'Deoradháin, and may the path to your home be easy." Another step. She forced herself to stay upright. She turned toward the trees and forced her legs to keep moving. Suddenly she felt O'Deoradháin beside her, his hand under her arm, supporting her. When she glanced at him, he was shaking his head.

"Is it true, what they say of Doire Coill?" he asked.

Jenna nodded. "Aye. And yet no. The forest is old and alive in a way that other woods are not, and things live there that are dangerous. But Doire Coill is also beautiful, and none of the tales that I heard ever spoke of that. I have a friend there . . ." She closed her eyes, the weariness coming over her again. She looked back across the lake to the town, as if she could see the commotion and upset there. She had thought she had a friend there as well and she had left behind the one person whom she knew loved her unconditionally. *Mam, I'm so sorry. I hope I will see you again . . .* "At least I think he's a friend," she finished.

O'Deoradháin took a long breath. Let it out again. "Then I suppose it would be a shame for me to miss seeing the forest while I'm so close."

Two stripes and more passed while they walked to the west at as fast a pace as Jenna could manage. They crossed the High Road a half mile from the lough, moving across the stone fences into a field dotted with small trees that

must have once been farmland but was now long abandoned. A line of darkness loomed at the ridge of the hills
just beyond the field, and as they approached, they saw the
twisted, tall forms of oaks against the starlit sky. "Doire
Coill?" O'Deoradháin asked, and Jenna nodded.

"Seancoim said it came close to the lough at places.
We're lucky."

"Or not." O'Deoradháin scowled at the forest. "It feels
like the trees are watching us."

"They are," Jenna answered. She glanced at the sky and
thought she could see wisps of color curling above.
"Hurry," she said. "I won't be able to go much farther."
O'Deoradháin glanced at the sky also, though he said nothing. His arm went around her waist, and he helped her
forward over the rough ground.

The hill was steeper and taller than it had appeared from
the High Road. As they climbed, resting often, the two
could look back over the ground they'd covered and see
Lough Lár glimmering beyond the trees and, faintly on the
horizon, the hills where the city lay. There were trees now
as they neared the ridge, still widely spaced but undeniably
the offspring of the ancient oaks of Doire Coill. As they
started down into the valley beyond, the trees came suddenly closer together, and they had to walk carefully to
avoid tripping over roots or being smacked in the head by
low-hanging branches. At the bottom of the hill, they came
across a small stream meandering through the wood, and
Jenna sank to the ground. "No more," she said. "I'm too
tired."

"Jenna, we're two miles from the lough. Maybe less. We
should move on."

Jenna shook her head. "It doesn't matter. They'll know
where I am soon enough." She pointed to the sky overhead
through the winter-dry leaves and netted branches. Light
burned there, brightening even as they watched. As the
mage-lights grew, Jenna felt the desire in her to take their
energy grow as well, overwhelming the exhaustion. She
struggled to her feet again and took the cloch's chain from
around her neck. She placed the stone in her right hand,
forcing the fingers to close around it.

The mage-lights seemed to feel Lámh Shábhála's presence; they swelled, flashing like blue and green lightnings directly above her. She heard O'Deoradháin gasp. The power of the mage-lights crackled and hissed in her ears, and it seemed she could almost hear words in the din, speaking a language so old that it awakened ancestral memories in her blood. The scars on her arm seemed to glow, echoing the patterns in the sky above, and she lifted her hand, watching the colors converge and fuse over her. A funnel, a tongue slipped down from the display, bending and twisting until it touched her hand, engulfing it. Jenna cried out in mingled pain and relief as the power of the mage-lights poured into Lámh Shábhála. She didn't know how long the connection lasted: forever, or a stripe of the candle, or only a few breaths. She could see the force or the magic, brilliant as it surged into the niches within the cloch, as it filled the well inside the stone nearly to overflowing.

Once more . . . Jenna realized. *The next time the mage-lights come, Lámh Shábála will be able to hold no more.* . . .

But Jenna could hold no more herself. The primordial cold of the mage-lights burned her, and she could no longer bear it. She cried out, as the mage-lights danced above and waves of tints and hues fluttered in the sky. She pulled her hand away from the grasp of the lights, and there was a pulse of fury and thunder.

As Jenna fell away into darkness, she thought she heard the rustle of wings and the caw of a crow.

29

Awakening

SOMEONE'S head swam in her vision, and she could smell a scent of spices. Jenna blinked, squinting to make the features come into focus. She seemed to be in a cave. Torches guttered against the walls, and she lay on a bed of straw matting. The air was warm and fragrant with the smell of a peat fire. If O'Deoradháin was there, she couldn't see him. "Seancoim," she whispered. "Is that you?"

"Aye," a familiar voice answered. "I'm here."

"Lámh Shábhála," Jenna said, suddenly panicked. She remembered holding it, her fingers opening . . .

"It's around your neck," Seancoim answered. She felt his fingers take her left hand and guide it to her throat. She felt the familiar shape of the cloch in its silver cage. The relief lasted only a moment.

"Andúilleaf," she croaked. "I need . . . the leaf potion. You must have some. Give it to me."

"No," he answered, his voice gentle yet firm.

"Please . . ." She was crying now: from the pain, from the refusal. "Seancoim, it hurts . . . You don't know how it hurts . . ."

His blind eyes seemed to stare at her. Callused fingers brushed her cheek. On his shoulder, she could see Dúnmharú, the bird's black eyes giving back twin, tiny reflections of her face. "Jenna, what's hurting you most right now is the lack of the andúilleaf and not the sky-magic. I should never have given the herb to you in the first place. Some people can't stop once they take it, and eventually the crav-

276

ing becomes so intense that it drives you mad. You will
have to get through this without it."

"I can't," she wept. She huddled in a fetal position, cradling her right arm against herself, but nothing would warm
its cold flesh. Nothing would ever make it normal again.
The chill seemed to have crept all the way to her shoulder,
and she shivered. She couldn't see Seancoim anymore; her
vision was narrowing again, as it had in the keep, all her
peripheral vision gone until there was nothing there but
what was directly in front of her. The headache raged in
her skull, and she was afraid that if she moved, her head
would burst. "Seancoim . . ." she wailed.

"I'm here," his voice answered, and she heard his staff
clattering against stone as he moved. "I'll stay with you.
Here, drink this."

He pressed a bowl to her lips. She sipped the warm liquid, hoping irrationally that despite his words it was andúilleaf. It was not: sweet mint tea, with a hint of something
else. She swallowed, more eagerly than she expected, for
the taste made her realize how hungry and thirsty she was.
He gently laid her head back again. "Seancoim, just this
once. The mage-lights . . . it hurts . . ."

"I know it does," he told her. "But you can bear it."

"I *can't*," she answered, but the words were hard to
speak. She was sleepy; she could feel the weariness spreading through her, radiating out from her belly. "Where's
O'Deoradháin?" she asked. "He'll tell you what's
happened . . ."

"He's here. Just outside." Seancoim's face was receding,
as if she were falling away from him. "And he's told me
everything."

"It hurts," Jenna said again.

"I know," he answered, but his face was so tiny and his
voice so soft and it was easier to close her eyes and give
in to the urge to sleep.

"Seancoim?"

A hand brushed lank hair away from her face. "No, it's
Ennis," O'Deoradháin's voice answered. "Seancoim's gone
for a bit. Should I go look for him?"

Her head felt huge and heavy, and the headache still pounded. Her right arm was a log of ice cradled against her stomach. She tried to lift it and couldn't. She couldn't feel her fingers at all. Her body was trembling and despite the chill air, she could feel sweat breaking out on her forehead. A soft cloth brushed it away. Jenna licked dry, cracked lips. "Thank you," she husked.

"Feeling better?"

Her left hand felt for the cloch around her neck. When she felt the stone, she clasped it with a sigh. "Worse, I think. I'm not sure."

"Here, then. He left this; said to have you drink it when you woke up." The bowl touched her lips again and she drank the sweet brew. Afterward, she lay back. O'Deoradháin looked down at her worriedly. There was a cut across his forehead: a line of dried blood with black thread sewn through it to hold the gaping edges shut, and both his eyes were swollen nearly closed and blackened.

"What happened to you?" Jenna asked. "Did the Rí's gardai . . . ?"

O'Deoradháin shook his head. He touched the wound, his mouth twisting ruefully. "No. After you took in the mage-lights, you collapsed, and this crow came flying past me and an ancient Bunús Muintir appeared right behind me. I thought he was about to attack or cast a spell. I drew my dagger, and all of a sudden the old bastard cracked me on the head with his damned staff, a lot faster and harder than an old blind man had any right to move . . ."

Despite the pain, Jenna found herself chuckling at the image of Seancoim rapping O'Deoradháin over the head with his staff. O'Deoradháin frowned at first, then finally smiled back at her. "I'm glad you find that funny. I assure you I didn't at the time."

"If you wouldn't go pointing your weapon at people, it wouldn't have happened at all," Seancoim's voice answered from behind O'Deoradháin. A moment later, Dúnmharú fluttered past O'Deoradháin to land at Jenna's left side. She lifted her hand to stroke the glossy black feathers, and the crow cawed back at her. "He was rather insistent about protecting you," Seancoim told her. "Even when he'd been knocked on the skull. Doesn't listen well, either. I had to hit him twice more. I nearly left him there, but I decided that if he brought you this far, he deserved better." Seancoim shooed O'Deoradháin aside. He crouched down next to Jenna's pallet. His gray-bearded, flat face was solemn. The cataract-whitened eyes gleamed in a nest of wrinkled brown flesh. "It's time to get up," he told her.

Jenna shook her head. "No. Let me lie here. I couldn't . . ."

His gnarled, thick-knuckled hand reached down and took her arm. His grip surprised her with its strength as he pulled her up to a sitting position. Her head whirled with the movement, and for a moment she thought she would be sick. "Breathe," he told her. "Slow breaths, in through the nose, out through the mouth. That's it."

She could feel his hand on one side, O'Deoradháin's on the other, lifting, and she shook her head again. "It hurts. I don't want to . . ."

"You will," Seancoim answered. "You are stronger than you think. And there is something you must see." Suddenly she was standing on weak, wobbly legs. The room, she saw for the first time, was less a cave than a deep, sheltered hollow below an overhanging limestone cliff. Ahead of her down a grassy embankment was a creek, and beyond that the dark tangle of oaks and brush of the forest. They helped her walk down the embankment and out past the vine-fringed cliff wall into sunshine. Jenna squinted, but the heat on her shoulders felt good. The day was warm for the season; she could not even see her breath before her. "Sit here," Seancoim said, and Jenna was happy to do so, sinking down into the blanket of grass. "Look . . . Straight across the stream, near the tallest oak."

Jenna saw it then, in a shifting of shadows as it moved. At first she thought it was simply a stag deer, but then it came out from under the trees, and Jenna gasped as she realized that the animal was huge, taller than O'Deoradháin at the shoulders, with a rack of massive antlers that echoed the great branches of the oaks. Its coat was a brilliant russet with a white, powerful breast, and the black, gleaming hooves were larger than Jenna's hands. The crea-

ture was magnificent, almost regal, as it walked slowly
down to the stream's edge and lowered its crowned head
to drink for a moment. Then the head lifted again to gaze
across the river to the three people with eyes that seemed
calm and intelligent.

"That's a fia stoirm," Seancoim said quietly, answering
Jenna's unasked question. "The storm deer. In the Bunús
Muintir histories, they speak of herds of them, their hooves
so loud pounding against the earth that it sounded like
thunder. When the sky-magic died, so did they."

"Our stories are the same," O'Deoradháin said. "From
the Before, centuries ago. But if they all died . . ."

"Not all," Seancoim answered. "A few survived, hiding
in the oldest places. When I was young, I once glimpsed a
storm deer deep in Doire Coill. But in the past year, I have
seen dozens, and not in the depths of the forest but here
near the edge. I have seen other things, too, that were once
legend and are not as beautiful and gentle as these: dire
wolves, who have a language of their own; boars with long
tusks as sharp as knives, and whose bristles are gold; snakes
with white scales and red eyes, as long as any of us are
tall. From my brothers to the west, I have learned that a
dragon's scream was heard on one of the islands in the
Duán Mouth. And from another, that blue seals were gathering along the northern coast." Jenna remembered the
seals she'd seen in Lough Lár, the way their satin fur had
gleamed. She glanced at O'Deoradháin, but he would not
look at her. "The myths are awakening again," Seancoim
continued. "Things walk the land that have not been seen
in many generations. Even the trees of Doire Coill are
more awake now than I have ever felt them."

Almost as if in response to Seancoim's words, the wind
rose slightly and shook the branches of the oaks. The stag's
nostrils widened as it sniffed the breeze. The creature took
a last look at them before bounding away, its great hooves
thudding audibly on the ground as it departed.

"This is what you are caught in, Jenna," Seancoim said.
"Part great beauty, part great danger. As the mage-lights
are awakening the old creatures, so you are ready to

awaken the other clochs na thintrí. You will make a new world."

"I can't," Jenna said. The pain inside her, forgotten for a moment with the sighting of the storm deer, returned. "I don't know how. I'm scared, Seancoim. I'm so . . ." She couldn't finish the sentence. The tears came again in racking, terrified sobs, and she wanted more than anything else for her mam to be here, to comfort her as she had so many times. She had thought of herself as a woman now, an adult and self-sufficient, but she suddenly felt like a child again.

It was O'Deoradháin who came to her. "I can help you, Jenna," he told her, crouching down in front of her. "I can't do it for you because Lámh Shábhála has chosen you, but I can help you. If you'll let me."

His arms went around her, and for a breath she stiffened, ready to pull away. He started to release her, to back away, but she laid her head on his shoulder. She let herself fall into the embrace, allowing herself to believe that she was safe in her mam's arms again, imagining that she was home again and that none of this had ever happened.

But it wasn't an illusion that could last.

"There's another who will help you as well," she heard Seancoim say. "Or at least, I hope so. We'll go to him tomorrow."

30

Release

S HE remembered the valley.

The sight of the central dolmen, carved with the pattern of the scars on her arm and surrounded by the passage graves of the Bunús Muintir chieftains, still made her shiver. The day was gray and sullen with rain misting from lowering clouds, the water dripping heavily from the capstone of the dolmen as they stood under it. Only Dúnmharú seemed unbothered by the rain—the crow was perched above the entrance to Riata's grave, mouth open to the sky and occasionally shaking droplets from his feathers.

Jenna's mood matched the weather. Her stomach roiled and she'd thrown up nearly everything that Seancoim had put into her. The headache refused to leave, so that at times she could barely walk, and her right arm hung useless at her side. She'd leaned heavily on O'Deoradháin as they'd made the two-day journey to the valley. She remembered little of the time: it was a blur of pain and fatigue. She'd begged Seancoim for andúilleaf off and on, sometimes weeping, sometimes in a fury, once with a threat to use the cloch; he refused each time, though never with anger.

Jenna sank down with her back against one of the standing stones, not caring that the ground was soaked and muddy. "Now what?" she asked.

"We wait," Seancoim answered.

"Here?" Jenna spat.

"Here, or in Riata's cairn."

"Here," O'Deoradháin said. He cast a look at the blackness beyond the stones where Dúnmharú roosted, and shivered. "Graves aren't for the living."

"Riata isn't quite dead," Seancoim told him.

"Then that's even worse."

"Can we at least have a fire?" Jenna asked. "I'm cold through."

O'Deoradháin gathered together what kindling he could find and pulled his tinderbox from his pack, but the spark wouldn't catch despite repeated efforts. "It's too damp," he said finally. Jenna nodded miserably, and Seancoim hunkered down in front of the nest of kindling O'Deoradháin had built. He rubbed his hands together several times, chanting words that Jenna could not understand. He picked up O'Deoradháin's flint and struck it. A blue flame shot out, startling Jenna, and the kindling began to crackle. O'Deoradháin chuckled. "I'm beginning to think that I was lucky you only hit me on the head," he said to Seancoim.

Seancoim's grizzled, ancient face grinned back at him as he warmed his hands over the flames. "That you were, young man."

They stayed there under the dolmen as the sun lowered itself beyond the lip of the valley and the valley grew darker under the overcast sky. The rain stopped before sunset; as night fell they began to glimpse stars between the thinning clouds. Seancoim and O'Deoradháin talked as they waited, but Jenna said little, sitting on the ground with her knees drawn up and her right arm cradled against her. She stroked Lámh Shábhála from time to time. The cloch seemed almost restless, its image throbbing in her head, filling her vision with bright sparks. There was a tension in the air itself like the drone of some sepulchral pipe, so low that she couldn't quite hear it but only feel the sound, rumbling just below the threshold of perception.

A finger of light appeared above them, blue outlined in gold, wavering and brightening so that they saw the shadow of the dolmen sway on the ground in response. Jenna rose to her feet.

"So it is to be tonight . . ."

The voice spoke in her head, not in her ears: a resonant,

warm baritone. The others looked up as well, as if they'd also heard. "Riata?" Jenna glanced toward the entrance to his tomb. There was a wavering in the dimness, a mist that formed itself into a man's shape as she watched. "Do you remember me?"

She felt the now-familiar touch of another Holder's mind on her own, this one more powerful than most, strong enough so that she could not shut him out as he prowled her thoughts and her memories. The spectral figure of the ancient Bunús Holder drifted toward her. Jenna was vaguely aware of the others watching, Seancoim placidly silent, O'Deoradháin with shocked apprehension. "Ahh," Riata sighed. "Jenna. You are the First who came to me once before." More mage-lights had appeared in the sky, brighter and more brilliantly colored than Jenna had seen in previous displays. The largest manifestation was directly overhead, but the mage-lights flickered all the way to the horizon. The entire valley was illuminated, as if a thousand fires burned above. Riata's indistinct face glanced up to them. "Aye," he said. "Tonight."

Jenna clutched the cloch na thintrí. The fingers of her right hand, as if warmed by the glare of the mage-lights, moved easily now and closed around the stone. Lámh Sháb-hála was frigid in her palm, glowing in response to the swaying, dancing power above it. Jenna could sense the cloch yearning like a live thing, wanting her to open it, to fill it. The feeling was so urgent and compulsive that it frightened Jenna.

"Lámh Shábhála craves the power as you crave the andúi-illeaf," Riata murmured in her head. "You must control Lámh Shábhála as you must control yourself, or it will destroy you utterly when it consumes the mage-lights this night and sets free the other clochs na thintrí."

Riata's words filled Jenna with dread. Her breath came fast and shallow; she could feel her heart racing. "I can't do it," she gasped.

"You can. I will help you."

"As will I," O'Deoradháin said. He was beside her now. His hand touched Jenna's shoulder, and she shrugged it away.

"You *want* me to fail," she spat at him. "Then *you'll* take Lámh Shábhála."

"Aye, I would if that happened," he told her. His pale emerald eyes regarded her calmly. "But your failure isn't what I want. Not any longer. You can believe me or not, Jenna, but I will help you. I *can* help you. This is what I was trained to do."

"Listen to him," Riata husked. "Use the cloch. See the truth even if you want to deny it."

"You swear that?" Jenna asked O'Deoradháin, and she let the barest hint of the cloch's strength waft outward. Shaping it to her task was like holding one of the piglets back in their farm in Ballintubber: it wriggled, it squirmed to be away, and she could control it only with difficulty.

"I do swear it," O'Deoradháin answered, and the truth in the words reverberated like the sound of a bronze bell.

"Then what do I do?" Jenna asked.

"Start as you always have. Open the cloch to the lights."

Jenna let the image of Lámh Shábhála fill her mind: the crystalline interstices; the jeweled valleys and hills; the interior landscape of sparkling energy. Above, the sky responded, a surge of pure white light that was born directly above Jenna and rippled outward in bright spectral rings. The mage-lights flamed, the clouds were driven away as if by hurricane winds.

Lámh Shábhála pulled at the sky-magic, sucking in the power like a ravenous beast. *"No!"* O'Deoradháin and Riata shouted as one. "You must direct the cloch this time, Jenna," O'Deoradháin continued, his voice shouting in her ear but almost lost in the internal din of the mage-lights as they crackled and seethed around her. "You must go up to the mage-lights, not let Lámh Shábhála bring them down to you."

"How?" Jenna raged at him. "Do you think I can fly?" This was nothing she had experienced before with the cloch. She seemed to be in the middle of a coruscating storm, flailing and trying to hold her ground, nearly blind and deaf in its brilliance and roar. Riata's voice answered her, calm and soft as always, cutting through the bedlam.

"Think it," he said, "and it will be."

Her arm burned, the scars as bright as lightning. She lifted the cloch toward the sky and imagined rising into the maelstrom above. Her perception shifted: she was outside herself. She could see her body on the ground, arm lifted, and yet she was also above with the mage-lights running through and around and with her, the land spread like a tapestry below. She was Lámh Shábhála; she was the power within it. Voices and shapes surrounded her in the dazzling space and she knew them: all the ones who had held an active Lámh Shábhála before her: Severii O'Coulghan, who like Riata had been Last Holder; Tadhg O'Coulghan, his father who had held it before Severii; Rowan Beirne, Bryth and Sinna Mac Ard; Eilís MacGairbhith, the Lady of the Falls, and Aodhfin Ó Liathain, the lover who had betrayed and killed her to take the cloch; Caenneth Mac Noll, also a First, and the first Daoine to hold an active Lámh Shábhála. The Bunús Muintir Holders were there too—Riata, Dávali, Óengus. There were hundreds of them: Daoine, Bunús Muintir, and peoples unknown to her, stretching back thousands of years. And they spoke, a babble of voices that rivaled the sound of the mage-lights.

". . . So young, this one."

". . . She's too young. Too weak. Lámh Shábhála will consume her."

". . . I was a First and I died the night I opened the clochs, as will she . . ."

". . . let her undergo the Scrúdú, too. Now, before this happens, and if she lives . . ."

"Now is not the time for the Scrúdú. She must wait for that test until later, as I did. Lámh Shábhála chose her, and sent her to me." That was Riata, calm. "There· is a reason it was her . . ."

"What must I do?" Jenna asked them. Her voice was phosphorescence and glow. A hundred voices answered, a jumble of contradiction. Some were amused, some were hostile, some were sympathetic.

". . . die!"

". . . give up the cloch while you can . . ."

". . . hold onto yourself . . ."

She ignored them and listened for Riata's voice. *"Feel the presence of the other clochs . . ."*

"I do." She could sense them all, scattered over the land yet tied to Lámh Shábhála with streamers of green-white energy. The channels led to the well within the cloch.

"Fill the cloch now," Riata told her, though other voices wailed laughter or warning. *"Open it . . ."*

"You *are* the cloch," said another voice, fainter and paler: O'Deoradháin.

She imagined Lámh Shábhála transparent and without boundaries. Nothing happened. She drifted above the valley, snared in lambent splendor, but there was no change. She looked at her arm, saw light reflecting from it. A beam curled around her, and she willed it to enter her. Blue-green rays crawled the whorls of scars, and she gasped as the radiance entered in her and through her, surging into the cloch she held. Like a dam bursting under the pressure of a flood, the mage-lights suddenly whirled about her, following the path she had made, more and more of the energy filling her as she screamed in ecstasy and fear. Unrelenting, it poured inward. Lámh Shábhála was utterly full, too bright to gaze upon, shuddering and quivering in her hand as if it might break apart. And the pain came with the power: white, stabbing needles of it, driving deep into her flesh and her soul, a torment beyond anything she'd endured before.

The mage-lights were a thunderous cacophony into which she shouted uselessly. In a moment, she would be lost, swept away in currents that she could not control. She ached to release it, to simply let it pass through her, to end this.

"Hold onto the magic, Jenna!" The voice was Riata's or O'Deoradháin's or both. *"You must hold onto it!"* they shouted again, and she screamed back at them.

"I can't!"

"Jenna, Lámh Shábhála will open the way for the other clochs through you. It is too late now for anything else. The only choice to be made is whether you will use Lámh Shábhála or it you."

"*. . . too young . . . too weak . . . she will die . . .*"

"*. . . you see, even if she did this task, she would never have passed the Scrúdú later. Best she die now . . .*"

She couldn't hold the energy. No one could hold it. It clawed at her mind with talons of lightning, it roared and flailed and smashed against her. It bellowed and shrilled to be loosed.

"*. . . a moment longer . . .*"

Her hand wanted to open and she knew that if she let go of the stone the force would fly outward with the motion, uncontrolled and explosive. Lámh Shábhála burned in her palm; she could feel its cold fury flaying the skin from muscles, the muscles from bone. It would tear her hand from her arm. She closed her left hand around the right.

"*. . . Good! Turn it inward. Inward . . .*"

Jenna squeezed the cloch tighter, screaming against the resistance and the torture. She closed her eyes, crushing fingers together and shouting a wordless cry.

The sky went dark. The mage-lights vanished. For a moment, Jenna gaped upward, back in her body again. Light flooded around her cupped, raised hands as if she were grasping the sun itself.

"Now," O'Deoradháin said, his voice loud in the sudden silence. "Let it go—"

Jenna opened her hands.

A fountain of multicolored light erupted: from the cloch, from the scarred flesh of her arm, from her open mouth and eyes. It blossomed high above the valley, gathering like an impossible star for several breaths. Then it shattered, bursting apart into meteors that jetted outward along the energy lines of the other clochs na thintrí, the star fading as the meteors flared and faded themselves, arcing into the distance and away.

There was the sound of peal upon peal of thunder, then their echoes rebounded from the hills and died in silence.

The valley was dark under a starlit sky, and the sparks lifting from their fire under the dolmen stone seemed pallid and cold. Jenna lifted the cloch that had fallen back around her neck—it burned cold, but it was dark. She marveled at her hands, that they were somehow whole and unbloodied.

The pain hit her then. She fell to her knees, crying out, and O'Deoradháin and Seancoim laid her down gently. "Riata?" she called out.

"He's gone," O'Deoradháin told her. "At least I think so."

"It hurts," Jenna said simply.

"I know. I'm sorry. But it's done. It's done, Jenna. You've opened the way for the Filleadh."

She nodded. Her right arm was stiffening now, the fingers curling into a useless fist, sharp twinges like tiny knives cutting through her chest. She cried, lying there, and let O'Deoradháin place his arm around her for the little comfort it brought her. A familiar smell cut through the smell of woodsmoke: Seancoim crouched down by her, a bowl in his hand.

"Andúilleaf," he said. "This one time."

Jenna started to reach for it. Her fingers grazed the edge of the bowl and then stopped. She shook her head. "No," she told the old man. "I . . . I can bear this."

What might have been a smile touched his lips beneath the tangle of gray beard. His blind eyes were flecked with firelight; Dúnmharú flapped in from the night and landed on his shoulder. Seancoim dumped the contents of the bowl on the ground and scuffed at the dirt with his feet.

"You have indeed grown tonight, Jenna," he said.

PART THREE

THE MAD HOLDER

Inish
Thuaidh

Thall Coill

Gob an Tairbh
Baile
Nua

Cill Eanna

Farganlack

An
Ceann
Ramhar
An
Cnocan

⋯ Townland Boundaries
▲ Mountains
☙ Old Growth Forest

Carraig
na
Ghaill

Carrickagile

Coirebreckan

L. Áthas

Carravin

Ingean na nUan

Derginan

Loughnanskan

R. Béabhar

Dún Madadh

Glenn Aill

R. Teann

Be An Mhuillinn

Rubha na
Scarbh

R. Damh

Altandiven

R. Naofa
△ Sliabh Michinniúint
Dún Kiil
★ Dún Kiil

Ushet

Maoil na nDreas
Dún Kiil

Baile
na
Oiléanach

Port an Dúin

R. Salann

Na Clocha
Dubha

An
Ceann
Caol

Maddygalla

Shandragh

Inishfeirm

Inishdúin

0   5   10
Miles

31

Taking Leave

A DIRE wolf howled its worship to the moon goddess
from the next hill. A white owl with a wingspan as
wide as a person's outstretched arms swooped down from
a nearby branch and lifted again with a rabbit clutched in
its talons. The wind brought the enchanting song of the
trees at the heart of the forest. Mage-lights snarled the
stars.

"I have to go," Jenna said.

Seancoim nodded. Dúnmharú ruffled his wings on the
old man's shoulder as Seancoim's pale eyes plucked moonlight from the air. "I know," he said.

"Do you know why?"

He sniffed, almost a laugh. "Well, let me see if I can
fathom it . . . Because Lámh Shábhála aches to be used.
Because Jenna herself is tired of hiding and sitting. Because
you know that to the north are the people who are your
father's fathers, and there also lies the knowledge that you
lack as Holder. Because even though I tell you you're
wrong, you're afraid that if you hide here too long, your
enemies will come in too great a force for even Doire Coill
to resist and you don't want harm to come to me or the
forest. Because the winter's chill is gone and the land calls
you. Because you see the magic at work here and want to
see what it's done elsewhere. Because a blind old man is
poor company for a young woman. Are those your
reasons?"

Jenna laughed. "All but the last, aye. And more."

"And you'll be traveling with Ennis O'Deoradháin." It was more statement than question, and he was still smiling. "So that's the way it is, 'tis it? You've come to like the man."

"No!" The denial came quickly and automatically. "Not at all. But he's Inish, and knows some of the cloudmage ways and will help me get to the island. Do I trust him? I suppose I do to a point—he could have taken Lámh Sháb-hála from me easily when we were in Lár Bhaile and he didn't, but the man still has his own agenda and if I get in the way of that . . ." She shrugged. "And I *don't* like the man, Seancoim. Not that way." *And after Coelin's betrayal, I'm not sure I'll* ever *love anyone again that way,* she wanted to add, but pressed her lips shut.

Jenna and O'Deoradháin had wintered in Doire Coill. Seancoim had scoffed at Jenna's concerns that Rí Gabair and Tiarna Mac Ard—or the Rí Ard and Tanaise Ríg themselves—might try to invade the forest. "The forest will take care of itself, as I told Tiarna Mac Ard when you first came here," he answered. "Now the magic is unleashed again, and the forest is more awake than ever. They bring their own death if they wander here."

And yet they *had* come. The mage-lights of the Filleadh had told those in Lár Bhaile where Jenna had gone after she fled the city. In the days immediately following her escape, troops were dispatched to search for her on the west side of Lough Lár and some even ventured into Doire Coill. As Seancoim had predicted, few of those who entered the oak forest returned. But strangely, after the initial fortnight, no one came searching at all.

Jenna had wondered about that at first. Then she realized . . .

Nearly every night now, the mage-lights flickered in the sky, no longer only above the locus of Lámh Shábhála but from horizon to horizon, and the newly-released clochs na thintrí fed on them. The Riocha were scrambling for possession of the stones—and learning to control them—which created such turmoil and contention that finding Lámh Shábhála and Jenna was temporarily a secondary concern.

The night of the Filleadh, Jenna had opened three double hands of the major clochs (the Clochs Mór, O'Deoradháin had said they were called) and a hand of the minor stones—or clochmions—for each of the Clochs Mór: almost two hundred clochs na thintrí all told were now active.

Nearly every night, too, Jenna yearned for the andúilleaf and the solace it would bring against the continuing pain of holding Lámh Shábhála. But Seancoim would not offer it to her again, and she remembered too well the fog it had cast over her mind.

Little news reached Doire Coill from outside, but O'Deoradháin would sometimes go to search out a traveler alone on the High Road. He would bring back their tales to Jenna and Seancoim. Twice during their stay, other Bunús Muintir came to visit Seancoim—from Foraois Coill in Tuath Infochla, and the great island of Inishcoill off Tuath Airgialla—and they brought news of their own. Jenna knew from those contacts that word had been sent from Dún Laoghaire to all the tuatha that the Holder of Lámh Sháb- hála had been driven insane, that she had murdered a score of Riocha in Lár Bhaile including the Banrion Cianna her- self. A hefty blood price had been placed on her head, and it appeared that the Tanaise Ríg no longer had any interest in his marriage proposal.

Jenna was now the Mad Holder, to be killed upon sight.

Two months ago, near the time of the Festival of Fómhar, the three of them had watched from the western fringes of Doire Coill as an army approached from the west and another marched out from Lar Bhaille to meet it. They had seen in the distance the smoke and dust of battle, and Jenna felt the surge of power from several clochs na thintrí wielded as terrible weapons. From the travelers, they learned that other armies had been seen battling south and east, as well.

The tuatha were fighting among themselves, and the clochs na thintrí were among their implements of war.

Eventually, Jenna knew, someone would come searching for Lámh Shábhála, someone with an army or a few of the Clochs Mór or both at their backs, and they would stop at nothing to find her. Jenna had learned much about handling the cloch in the last months, but she didn't want to see Doire Coill at the center of a battle, even a victorious one.

And Seancoim was right. She was tired of hiding.

"When do you go?" Seancoim asked, his voice bringing her out of reverie. She shivered, then smiled at him.

"Tomorrow."

"Then I will enjoy tonight." Seancoim turned solemn, twirling a finger in his beard before he spoke. "You must realize that I'm not the only one who can guess which way Lámh Shábhála would travel."

"I know that. We'll be careful."

"Careful may not be enough."

She smiled at him and kissed his forehead. "Then come with us. I'd like that. Have you ever seen the Westering Sea, Seancoim? O'Deoradháin says that you look out, and see nothing but water and sky, all the way to the end of the world."

He shook his head sadly. "No. But this is where my destiny and my home are. I'm an old man, and I have my apprentice to train."

"Apprentice? Since when do you have an apprentice?"

"You've not met her. She stays on her own most of the time inside the forest. She's learned most of what I have to teach her but not all. No, Jenna, thanks for your offer, but I'll stay here and make certain that you have a place to which you can return one day."

They were standing at the northern edge of Doire Coill, near where Mac Ard, her mam, and she had first entered the forest—less than a year ago, though it seemed that everything had changed in that time. The High Road was less than a quarter mile away, turning here in a great sweeping curve to the north, where a day's walk away waited Knobtop and Ballintubber. Jenna wondered about her home, wondered what they said about her and her mam when they gathered in Tara's Tavern of an evening. Perhaps there were already tales of the Mad Holder, and One Hand Bailey or Chamis Redface regaled anyone who would listen with fanciful tales of Jenna as a child.

"Even back then it was obvious that she was fey and

dangerous. Why, once Matron Kelly scolded her, and Jenna made a motion like this, and Matron Kelly's cows gave no milk for an entire week. Tom Mullin once caught her stealing apples from his orchard and chased her off his land, and the very next day as he rode to Aldwoman Pearce's house, may the Mother-Creator rest her soul, his horse threw him for no reason at all and he broke his leg. He's walked with a limp since that day. I tell you, we were all careful what we said and did around the Aoires . . ."

"You don't get to choose how you're remembered," Seancoim said, as if he sensed what she were thinking. "That's up to those who are left behind." He touched her right arm. "Come with me," he said.

He turned and walked back into the forest, Dúnmharú flapping heavily ahead of them. He turned away from the faint path they'd followed, slipping into the darkness under the trees. "I can't see," Jenna said, hesitating.

"Then take my arm . . ."

Holding onto the elbow of a blind man, she moved into the night landscape of the forest. They walked for nearly a stripe, it seemed, Jenna stumbling and occasionally pushing away a stray branch, while Seancoim was sure-footed and easy with Dúnmharú's guidance.

They skirted a fen, and Jenna realized that the sound of the forest had changed at some point. She could no longer hear the animals: the grunt of the deer, the occasional howl of a wolf, the rustlings and chirps of the night birds. Here, there were other sounds: leafy rustlings, the groan of shifting wood, the sibilant breath of leaves that sounded almost like words. The moon came out from behind a cloud, and she could see that she and Seancoim were surrounded by gigantic old oaks with gnarled, twisted branches and great trunks that it would take three men to encircle. They loomed over the two, and Dúnmharú stayed on Seancoim's shoulder rather than roosting in any of these branches.

The trees spoke to each other. Jenna could hear them, could *feel* them. They were aware; they knew she was there. Branches moved and swayed though there was no wind, one limb sweeping down to wrap about Jenna's right arm. She resisted the temptation to brush away the woody fingers, the leafy touch, and a few moments later it uncurled and swept away. "Can you talk to them, Seancoim?" she asked, her voice a hushed whisper. It seemed sacrilegious to speak loudly here.

"No," he answered, his voice as quiet as hers. "They're the Seanóir, the Eldest, and their language is older than even the Bunús Muintir, nor do they experience life as we do. But this place is one of the many hearts of Doire Coill. These trees were planted by the Seed-Daughter herself when she gave life to the land, and they have been here since the beginning, thousands and thousands of years. Here, feel . . ." Seancoim took Jenna's hand and placed it on the veined, craggy surface of the nearest trunk. She felt nothing for a moment, then there was a throb like the pulsing of blood; a few breaths later, another followed. "That's the heartbeat of the land itself," Seancoim said. "Slow and mighty and eternal, moving through their limbs."

Jenna kept her hand there, feeling the long, unhurried beats, her own breath slowing and calming with the touch. "Seancoim, I never . . ." She wanted to stay here forever, feeling this. There was a sorcery to the trees, an insistent lethargy, and she remembered. "When I was here before . . ."

"Aye, it was their call you heard," Seancoim told her. "And if the Old Ones here wished it, you would remain snared in their spell until your body died of thirst and hunger. Look around you, Jenna. Look around you with your eyes open."

"My eyes *are* open . . ." she started to say, then blinked. For the first time, she noticed that there were gleams of moonlit white in the grassy earth of the grove. She bent down to look and straightened with a stifled cry: a skull leered back at her, stalks of grass climbing through vacant eye sockets, the jaw detached and nearly lost alongside. There were dozens of skeletons in and around the tree trunks, she saw now: some human, some animal.

"The sun feeds their leaves, the rain slakes their thirst, and those who come here and are trapped by their songs nourish the earth in which their roots dig," Seancoim said. "This is where, when it's time, I'll come, too, on my own and by my own choice." Jenna continued to stare. She could smell the death now: the ripe pungency of rotting flesh. Some of the bodies were new, and the clothes they wore were dyed green and brown.

She should have been horrified. But she felt the throbbing of the trees and the earth and realized that this was as it should be, that the Seanóir fed on life in the same way Jenna fed on life. She ate the meat of animals that had once been alive, and soaked up their juices with bread from the wheat that had waved in fields under the sun a month before. This was simply another part of the greater cycle in which they were all caught. There was no horror here. No malevolence, no evil. The trees simply did as their nature demanded. If they killed, it was not out of hatred, but because their view of the world was far longer and broader than that of the races whose lives were impossibly fleeting.

A branch came down; it lifted the cloch at Jenna's neck and let it drop again. "They know Lámh Shábhála," Seancoim said. "It is nearly as old as they are. They know it lives again." He went up to the largest of the trees and lifted his hand. A branch above wriggled, and a large acorn dropped into his palm. "Here," he told Jenna. He folded the nut in her left hand, closing her fingers around the acorn and putting his own leathery hands over hers. "For the Seanóir, the mage-lights signal a time of growing. Even the seasons themselves are too fast for them. The lights are the manifestation of a burgeoning centuries-long spring and summer for them, and this is their seed. Take this with you when you go, and plant this where you find your new home. Then you will always have part of Doire Coill with you. Make a new place for them."

Moonlight shimmered through moving branches, and the leaves spoke their words. Jenna nodded to the Seanóir, the ancient oaks of Doire Coill.

"I will," she said. "And I'll always remember."

They left that morning before the sun rose, their faces toward the constellation of the Badger, whose snout always points north. They said little besides idle talk of the

weather, and if O'Deoradháin noticed that Jenna paralleled
the High Road and that Knobtop crept slowly closer to
them as the sun rose behind a wall of gray clouds, he said
nothing. By evening, they were close to Ballintubber, with
Knobtop rising high on their right hand, its bare stony summit still in sunlight even though the marshes on either side
of the road were wrapped in shadow. As they approached
the Bog Bridge, O'Deoradháin placed his hand on Jenna's
arm. "Are you sure?" he asked.

"I need to see this."

He looked as if he were about to argue, but he swallowed
the words and shrugged. "Then let's hurry, before we're
walking in the dark."

A few hundred strides beyond the bridge, they came to the
lane which led to Jenna's home. The lane was overgrown, the
grass high where once the sheep had kept it cropped close
and the hay wagon had worn ruts in the earth. Jenna turned
into the lane, hurrying now down the familiar path, around
the bend she recalled so well. She wasn't certain what she
expected to see: perhaps the house as it had once been, with
her mam at the door and Kesh barking as he ran out toward
her, and smoke curling from the chimney.

Instead, there was ruin. The house had mostly returned
to earth. Only a roofless corner remained, overgrown with
vines and brush. Where the barn had been there was only
a mound. She walked forward with a stumbling gait: there
was the door stone, worn down in the center from boots
and rain, but it sat in the midst of weeds, the door itself
only a few blackened boards half-buried in sod and grass.
The chimney had collapsed, but the hearth was still there,
blackened from the fire that had destroyed the house, and
her mam's cooking pot, rusted and broken, lay on its side
nearby.

Here was where she had slept and laughed and lived, but
it was only a ghost now. The bones of a dead existence.
The silence here was the silence of a grave.

"I'm sorry," O'Deoradháin said. Jenna started at the
sound of his voice; lost in reverie, she hadn't heard his
approach. "I can imagine it looked beautiful, once."

She nodded. "Mam always had flowers on the windowsill,

red and blue and yellow, and I knew every stone and crack in the walls . . ." A sob shook her shoulders, and she felt O'Deoradháin's arms go around her. His touch dried the tears, searing them with anger. She shrugged his embrace away, her hands flailing. "Get off me!" she shouted at him, and he backed away, hands wide and open.

"I'm sorry, Holder," he said.

Jenna's right hand went automatically to Lámh Shábhála, touching the stone. A faint glimmer of light shone between her fingers, turning them blood-red. "You don't ever touch me. Do you understand?"

He nodded. His face was solemn, but there was something in his pale green eyes she could not read, a wounding caused by her words. He turned away and dropped his pack from his shoulders as Jenna slowly relaxed.

She let go of the cloch and its light faded. Her arm ached, as if in memory of how Lámh Shábhála had awakened here, and she wished again—fleetingly—that Seancoim had put andúilleaf in her pack. "We might as well camp here tonight," she said, trying to sound as if the confrontation had never happened and knowing she fooled neither of them. "It's obvious no one's come here since . . ." She stopped, and genuine wonder filled her voice. "Shh! What's that?"

"What?" O'Deoradháin glanced in the direction Jenna was pointing. Well off in the field where Old Stubborn and his herd used to graze, there was movement: pairs of pale green lights gleaming in the twilight, like glowing eyes. There seemed to be hundreds of them, just above the level of the tall grass, shifting and moving about, blinking occasionally. And they spoke like a crowd of people gathered together: a low, murmuring conversation that raised goose bumps on Jenna's arms. There were words in their discussion, she was certain, then—distinctly—a horn blew a shrill glissando. The lights went out as one, and a wind rose from the field and swept past them and up the lane. In the twilight, Jenna could glimpse half-seen shapes and feel ghostly hands brushing against her. The horn sounded again: fainter and more distant, heading in the direction of Knobtop. The wind died as a few glowing eyes stared back at them from near the bend in the lane and disappeared again.

The horde had passed.

"Wind sprites," O'Deoradháin said. His voice was hushed and awed, as if he were standing in one of the Mother-Creator's chapels. Jenna looked at him in puzzlement. "My great-mam used to tell me tales at night, and she spoke of eyes in the dark, and horns, and the wind as they rushed by in their hunts. I thought the stories she told me were all legends and myths."

He shook his head. "Now I think the legends were only sleeping."

32

Ballintubber Changed

THE next morning, they walked up the High Road to
the village. The morning was a drizzle of mist and fog
that beaded on their clócas and hair, and the spring's
warmth seemed to have fled. As they approached, Jenna
began to sense that something was wrong. It was the silence
that bothered her. A Ballintubber morning should have
been alive with sound: the lowing of milch cows in their
barns; the steely clatter of a hammer on hot iron or bronze
from the smithy; the creak and rumble of produce carts
going out to the fields; the shouts and hollers of children;
laughter, conversations, greetings . . .

There was nothing. She could see the buildings up the
rise, but no sound wafted down from them to challenge the
birdcalls or their footsteps on the muddy road. O'Deoradháin noticed it as well; he swept back his clóca and placed
his hand on the hilt of his knife. "Perhaps they all decided
to sleep late this morning," he said, and gave a bitter laugh
at his own jest.

"Not likely," Jenna answered. Grimacing, she placed her
right hand around the cloch. She opened the stone and let
its energy flow outward, her own awareness drifting with
it. O'Deoradháin had offered to teach her some of the craft
of the cloudmage during their months in Doire Coill, and
she had—grudgingly—accepted his tutelage. She wasn't
sure how good a pupil she'd been, suspicious of her teacher's intentions and instruction, but she *had* learned a few
skills. She could sense life in the way the power flowed,

and that told her there were people nearby, though only
a few.

And there was something else, at the edge of what she
could detect: a pull and bending in her consciousness, as if
another cloch were out there as well. She brought up the
walls that O'Deoradháin had taught her to create around
the cloch, but at that moment, the hint of another presence
vanished. She put her attention there, to the south and east,
but it was gone. Perhaps it had never been there at all.

She opened her hand and her eyes. A shiver of discomfort traveled from wrist to shoulder, and she groaned.
"Jenna?"

"I'm fine," she told O'Deoradháin sharply. "Come on;
there's no one there we need to be concerned with." She
began walking rapidly toward the cluster of buildings.

Things *had* changed. The High Road was marked with
stone flags through the village, but grass grew high between
the flat rocks. Dogs would usually have come running to
greet newcomers, but the only dog Jenna glimpsed—black
and white and painfully reminiscent of Kesh—was bedraggled and thin, skulking away with lowered tail and ears as
soon as it caught a glimpse of them. The Mullin house,
near the outskirts of the village, hadn't been whitewashed
this spring as Tom and his sons usually did, and the thatch
roof sagged badly just over the doorway. The door hung
on one hinge, half-opened and leading into a dark interior.
"Hello," Jenna called as they passed, but no one came out.

"Not the place you remember, is it?" O'Deoradháin ventured. "You're certain there are people here?"

"Aye," Jenna answered grimly. "Near the tavern, I
think."

"*I'd* be drinking if I lived here."

Jenna gave him an irritated glance; he stared blandly
back at her. Turning her back on the man, she walked
quickly to Tara's Tavern. The village square was overgrown
and shabby, but peat smoke curled from the chimney of
the inn and she could smell bacon frying. The stone steps
leading up to the door were achingly familiar, and she
pushed open the door and entered.

"By the Mother—Jenna?" Tara's voice cut through the dimness inside, and the woman set down a tray of glasses with a clatter and a crash, and she came running from behind the bar. She stopped an arm's length away from Jenna and looked her up and down, her mouth open. "Would you look at you—all dressed up in a Riocha's clothes, and that silver chain around your neck." Tara's gaze snagged on Tara's scarred right arm, and the mouth closed. Behind her, O'Deoradháin entered, and Tara took a step back. "You've . . . you've not changed a bit," Tara finished, and Jenna smiled wanly at the obvious lie. "Sit down, sit down. You and your . . . companion take that table over there, or any you want. It's not like we're going to have a crowd, though once people hear that you've come back, I expect we'll see as good a one as I've had all year. I have bacon going in the pan, and good eggs, and biscuits I just made this morning. I'll get some tea for you . . . Sit . . ." Tara turned and scurried into the kitchen; Jenna shrugged at O'Deoradháin.

"It's a better breakfast than we're likely to have for a while," she told him.

"If it's not our last."

Jenna sniffed. "I *know* these people, O'Deoradháin. They're my friends."

"They were once, aye. But friendship can be as hard to hold onto as a salmon in a stream." He didn't say more, but slid behind the table nearest the door. She noticed that O'Deoradháin sat with his back to the wall where he could see both the door and the rest of the room, and his hand stayed on the hilt of his dagger. She took a chair across from him.

They weren't alone. There were two other tables occupied, one by Erin the Healer, who lived to the north of the village. He nodded to Jenna as if seeing her was no more unusual than seeing any of the rest of Ballintubber's residents. At the other table were two men she didn't recognize; travelers, evidently, since they had packs sitting next to their chairs. A head poked out from the kitchen: Tara's son Eliath. He was a few inches taller than Jenna remembered, and a new, puckered scar meandered from his fore-head to the base of his jaw. "Hey, Jenna! Mam said you were out here."

"Eliath! It's good to see you . . ."

He grinned and came over to the table. He glanced at O'Deoradháin, and the grin faded to a careful smile before he turned back to Jenna. "Good to see you, too. Everyone thought you and your mam were dead, when the Troubles started. Is your mam . . . ?"

"She's fine. She's in Lár Bhaile."

The grin returned. "Lár Bhaile? That's where Ellia went. She married Coelin Singer, did you know that?"

"I know," Jenna said, forcing a smile. "I saw her, big with child."

Tara had come up with a tray loaded with steaming mugs of tea and platters of food. She set them down on the table. "You saw my Ellia?" she asked. "Did she look well? Did she ask after us? We didn't . . ." Tara blushed. "I'm afraid we didn't part on the best of terms, and I haven't heard from her since."

"She looked lovely and wonderful and happy, and they're living in a fine house in the town," Jenna responded, giving them the lie she knew Tara wanted desperately to hear. "She'll be a mam soon, probably already is by now, since I saw her last a few months ago. Coelin's even sung for the Rí, and for the Tanaise Ríg when he visited there. She told me to give you her love when I came back to Ballintubber and to say that she missed you."

"Truly?" Tara sighed. "I should go there," she said. "The Mother-Creator knows there's not much here. Not since the Troubles and all the death. I should go and see her and the babe. And your mam, too. Maybe this summer, once the spring rains have stopped."

She wouldn't go, Jenna knew. Like the rest of them, she would never leave Ballintubber. "I'm certain they'd love that. Both of them."

Tara nodded. "You know, Jenna, I thought you were sweet on that Coelin yourself. The boy had half the young women of the village hanging on him, and my Ellia no different."

"I didn't have a chance with him," Jenna answered. The smile was difficult to maintain. "Not with Ellia."

Another sigh. Then Tara stirred. "But here I am prattling on about things and your food's getting cold. Eat, and drink that tea before it turns to ice—it's a cold day for the season, 'tis." Despite the words, Tara seemed content to stay there, standing before the table. "Are you back home? Will you be building a new place on your mam's land?" she asked, and her gaze drifted significantly to O'Deoradháin.

"No," Jenna said. "This is Ennis O'Deoradháin, Tara—he's a friend, a traveling companion. We're going north—"

O'Deoradháin cleared his throat. When she glanced at him, he smiled, though his eyes glittered warningly. "—and east," she finished. "Along the High Road up to Ballymote, then on to Glenkille and maybe even across the Finger to Céile Mhór."

Tara's eyebrows raised at the names. "So far? Child, I haven't been farther than a stone's throw from Ballintubber all my life, and you're going all the way to Céile Mhór? It's not safe traveling. Not any more. Not with the fighting and the lights in the sky, and the strange creatures that have been seen. Why, only the other night, Matron Kelly saw wolves with red eyes and as tall as horses on the hill near her house. A pair of them, howling and snarling and frightening her so that she was afraid to go out of her house for days. Killed four of her sheep—tore their throats out and picked them up in their mouths as if they weighed nothing at all. No, I wouldn't be traveling. Not me."

The two strangers had risen from their chairs. They passed by the table as they left without a word. Jenna saw O'Deoradháin's gaze following them as they opened the door and went out.

"I see you still have people stopping at the inn," Jenna said to Tara, nodding toward the door.

"Them? They're the first in a week. Came up from the south, they say, from Áth Iseal. The High Road's not as well traveled these days. And not much business of a night, either." She shook her head, wiping her hands nervously on her apron. "Not since . . . well, you know. That was a bad time, when those Connachtans came raiding. Killed

Aldwoman Pearce, and cut down Tom Mullins and all four of his sons not a dozen steps from here when they tried to help. And poor Eli; one of them opened up my boy's face just because he didn't move fast enough when they told him to curry their horses. It was awful. They burned half the houses, and some of the women they . . ." Her voice trailed off. Remembered horrors drained the color from her face.

"Aye. I understand," Jenna told her.

"We thought you and your mam and that tiarna were all dead, too. We saw your house burning like the rest, and those that went to look said there was no one there alive, though there were dead Connachtans and your poor dog. We thought you'd been burned with the house."

Jenna shook her head. She found she didn't want to talk about it. The days when the Connachtans had swept through in pursuit of the mage-lights and Lámh Shábhála had damaged Ballintubber but not truly changed the place. Ballintubber remained sleepy and forgotten; if it was lucky, it might stay so. For the first time, Jenna saw just how much she'd been altered by the events of the last several months. She was no longer the person who had lived here. This was no longer "home."

"We managed to sneak away, my mam and I and the tiarna," she told Tara. "It didn't seem safe to go back."

"So you went to Lár Bhaile," Tara finished for her. From the expression on her face, she seemed to find it alternately amusing and unbelievable that someone from Ballintubber would have made that choice. "And now you're . . . traveling." She said the word as if it were something mildly distasteful.

"And we'll be needing horses," O'Deoradháin broke in leaning forward. "Would you have two good steeds in your stable, or can someone in the village sell us the mounts? We'll pay in hard coin."

Tara shrugged, but Eli spoke up. "We have one, sir—a roan mare that's a good twelve hands high and strong," he said. "And One Hand Bailey has another he's been talking of selling, a big brown gelding, past its prime but still healthy. He was asking half a mórceint, and not getting it. He'd take less now, I'd wager."

"He can have his half a mórceint," O'Deoradháin told him. "And a mórceint to you and your mam for the roan and livery for the two. Here . . ." O'Deoradháin opened his purse and took out two of the coins, flipping them to Eli. "Go fetch the gelding and get them both ready for us, and you can have the other half mórceint yourself." Eli grinned; Tara's eyebrows went up again.

"Aye!" Eli almost shouted. "Give me a stripe; no, half a stripe," he said, and he was gone, running. Tara, after a few more minutes of conversation, excused herself to go back into the kitchen. Erin the Healer left with another silent nod to Jenna. O'Deoradháin sipped his tea and leaned back in his chair. He whistled tunelessly.

"Horses?" Jenna asked.

"I didn't like the way those two strangers stared at us, like they were memorizing our faces," O'Deoradháin answered. "I didn't like the fact that they came up the High Road from the south, either. If they've been traveling through Gabair, then who knows what they've heard and what they realize? I want to get as far away from here as fast as possible."

"So you're the little Rí here, eh?" She lowered her head in mocking subservience, then glared at him. "And I must follow your orders."

"I would point out that *you* made the decision to come here. I'm just making the decision as to how to leave. That seems fair enough." He gave her that strange, lopsided smile of his. "You know, I get the sense that you still don't like or trust me much."

"I don't," she told him. "Either one. I want to go to Inish Thuaidh; you do also. Our paths just happen to lie together at the moment."

"And when they don't?"

"When that happens, or if I decide I can't trust you, then we part."

O'Deoradháin nodded. He took a hunk of bread and gnawed it thoughtfully. "That seems fair enough, too," he said.

33

A Battle of Stones

THEY were three days out of Ballintubber, and it still
seemed strange to both of them that they'd encountered very few people. Though the land at the northern
borders of Tuath Gabair was sparsely populated and they
were traveling overland rather than on the road, the area
seemed oddly empty. Fields that should have been plowed
by now were fallow, with weeds and grass growing up
among the straggling clumps of wheat and barley. The day
before, they'd passed near one village, and though they
heard the sounds of children playing and saw several
women working the fields nearby, the only men they noticed were the old. O'Deoradháin turned grim at the sight.

"They've been sweeping the land, then, and pressing men
into service. The Rís are strengthening their armies," he'd
said, and Jenna hadn't wanted to believe him.

Now the proof lay before her.

They were walking through a wooded valley between two
tall ridge lines. The trees thinned, and they came out into
an open field where the hills swept wide apart in great
curving arms.

A mound of raw new earth cut across their path, and the
banner of Tuath Gabair flapped on a pole planted in the
dirt. Jenna glanced at O'Deoradháin; his face was grim, and
he pulled on the reins of his horse to pass to the left of
the mound.

He quickly brought his horse to a stop. "By the Mother,"
he breathed. Jenna came up alongside him. "Gods," she

said. Her stomach jumped, and she tasted bile in her mouth.

They were on a slight rise. The full expanse of the field lay spread out before them: trampled, torn, and bloodied. Black flocks of carrion crows fought and scrabbled over the bodies of soldiers; feral dogs lifted their heads from gory feasts to glare suspiciously at them. Flies buzzed and whined through the air. The bodies, Jenna noted, all wore the blue and gold of Tuath Connachta. There were two more mounds on the field, and on each Gabair's banner flew.

A few heads had been mounted on broken lances as a warning. O'Deoradháin rode his horse up to one of the trophies, the horse shying away from the smell of rotting meat and the crow-emptied eye sockets, and a cloud of flies rising from the face as O'Deoradháin leaned over from his saddle to peer at it. The jaw hung upon, the head gaping in eternal amazement. "A boy," he said. "No more than fifteen, I'll wager, and a pressman in his Rí's army. I'll bet he told his mam he'd be back a hero."

Jenna's stomach turned again, and she leaned over, vomiting quickly. She hung onto the horse. The wind shifted slightly, and the smell came to them: rotting, ripe flesh. The sweet sickly smell of death.

"Victory," O'Deoradháin said mockingly. " 'Tis a wonderful sight, don't you think?"

Jenna wiped her mouth and nudged her horse carefully forward. The horse nickered, its eyes wide and nervous. She looked down at a body to her right. The soldier sprawled awkwardly on his back, a broken sword still clutched in his hand. The rings of bronze and iron sewn on his boiled leather vest were ripped and broken over his abdomen, and a horrible wound had nearly split him in two. Scavengers had been at the body—the eyes and tongue were gone, his entrails pulled out and scattered, the flesh gnawed upon. White maggots crawled in and around his open mouth, in the sockets of his eyes. Jenna's stomach lurched again, and she forced the gorge back down.

O'Deoradháin was riding slowly around the field, occasionally looking down at the earth. Jenna stayed where she

was, not wanting to go out into the carnage. "What was
left of the Connachtan force retreated west," he said when
he returned. "They weren't pursued—from the looks of the
mounds, the Gabairan troops lost a good many men also,
and their commander decided to stay here and bury their
dead. They moved off to the east, through that pass there."
He glanced down at the body of the soldier by Jenna. "The
battle took place no more than two days ago, from the
signs." Jenna nodded; she was still staring at the body.

"Jenna?"

She wondered how young he'd been, how he'd looked in
life, whether he'd had a wife and family. She imagined the
body alive again, as if she could turn back time.

"Jenna?"

She lifted her head to find O'Deoradháin staring at her.
"There were clochs here, too," he said. "There are several
places where the earth is scorched as if by lightning strikes.
Boulders were flung about that had crushed men underneath, and trees ripped whole from the ground and tossed.
Since the Clochs Mór, unlike Lámh Shábhála, have only
one ability each, I would guess there were two or possibly
three of the stones here."

Jenna touched Lámh Shábhála. She could feel nothing
here now, but a sense of dread hung over her that she had
not felt since they'd left Doire Coill. For the first time, she
realized just how much the Filleadh had changed the world.
You caused this, she thought, her gaze on the field of destruction ahead of her. *This is all because of the cloch you
hold, and there will be more of it. Much more.*

"It's my fault," Jenna said.

O'Deoradháin nudged his horse alongside Jenna's,
though he didn't touch her. "No," he said firmly, though
quietly. "This isn't your fault. This is the fault of greed and
callousness and stupidity. You didn't force any of the Ríthe
into conflict; they were just waiting for the opportunity, and
Lámh Shábhála provided a convenient excuse."

The corpse leered up at her, a mockery in the bright
spring grass. "All these people dead . . ."

"Aye," O'Deoradháin said, "and yet more will die. That

I can guarantee. But their souls won't come wailing to you when they cry out for justice."

She still stared down, realizing that beyond this body another one lay, and another and another. . . . "I can hear them now," she told him. "They already call to me . . ." She was trembling, unable to stop the movement of her hands.

"Jenna, you've seen a dead body before." His mouth snapped shut, and she could imagine the rest of what he might have said: *You were responsible for their deaths, too.*

She looked at O'Deoradháin, her head shaking violently from side to side. "Not this many," she said. "Not like this, just . . ." She had to stop for a moment, her breath gone. Her heart was pounding in her chest. ". . . just scattered everywhere. Torn apart, half-eaten, discarded and un-mourned." She tasted vomit at the back of her throat again, and swallowed hard. *This is your legacy. This is your fate, too. Some day it will be you sprawled lifelessly there . . .* The land was starting to whirl around her, at the center the grotesque face of the dead soldier . . .

"Jenna." O'Deoradháin brought her back as she was about to fall. Harsh and unsympathetic, his voice struck like a slap. She took a breath, and the world settled again. "This isn't the last you'll see of this. You'll see more and worse, because you'll be part of it. You don't have a choice, not unless you want to give up Lámh Shábhála."

"Lámh Shábhála is mine," Jenna answered heatedly. Her hand went to the cloch, closing around it.

"Then look around you and get used to the sight, because you'll need to have a clear head and mind when a battle's raging around you, or someone will be taking Lámh Shábhála from your corpse." Then his voice softened; he started to reach for her, then let his hand drop back to his side. "The dead can't hurt you, Jenna. Only the living can do that. We can't stay here, and we can't go back. The war will follow us—my bet is that the Rí Ard is already stepping in to end these battles between the tuatha. They'll unite to find Lámh Shábhála; we can only hope to stay ahead of them, and maybe, *maybe* on Inish Thuaidh we can leave them behind. But we have to go now, before someone finds

us. And before night falls, because this place will be
haunted." He tilted his head toward her inquiringly.
"Holder? Are you listening to me?"

"I thought you said that the dead couldn't hurt you."

His grin was sheepish. "They can't. That doesn't mean
they won't try."

She said nothing to that. Instead, she flicked the reins of
her horse and touched her heels to the mare's sides, urging
the horse forward—not around the field of battle, but
through it. She would not look down, but she saw the bodies as they passed, and each of them seemed to call to
her accusingly.

O'Deoradháin slept under his blankets on the other side
of the fire. The flickering yellow light illuminated the
undersides of the leaves above them and plucked the white
trunks of the sycamores from the night in a circle about
them. She could hear him snoring softly, the loudest sound
in the stillness.

Jenna reached into her pack and laid the relics out in
front of her: the wooden seal her da had carved; the ring
of Eilís MacGairbhith, the Lady of the Falls; the golden
torc of Sinna Mac Ard. Of Riata she had nothing; the ghost
of the ancient Holder had made it clear to her that he did
not want to be awakened again unless she returned to
Doire Coill and the valley of cairns.

She stared at them, a fingertip brushing each and feeling
the spark within. *Da?* But he had never held the active
Lámh Shábhála, and the times she had called him up, he
had seemed more frightened and confused than she was,
and she had ended by comforting him. *Eilís?* Jenna had
called the Lady of the Falls only one other time after that
day in her burial chamber behind the Duán's waters, and
the ghost had been as angry and fey as during their first
encounter; though Jenna knew that the ghost couldn't
touch or harm her, she would call that Holder forth only
in great need.

Jenna picked up Sinna's torc. She started to place it
around her neck . . .

"You'll just have to explain to her again who you are because she won't remember you. She's not your friend. She doesn't care about you—to her, you're as much a ghost as she is to you."

Across the fire, O'Deoradháin was watching from his blankets, up on one elbow. "Her time wasn't like our time, and she isn't like you. At all. You need to find your own path, not tread along someone else's," he finished.

"Which is the path *you* want me to take, no doubt." She hated the disdain in her voice. She thought of offering an apology—*He's done nothing but help you, and yet you keep pushing him away*—but then it seemed that she'd waited too long. The muscles along his jaw clenched, and he blinked. She pretended to look away from him, to be absorbed in the torc.

"I'm not forcing you to go anywhere, Holder," he said. "Remember when I said earlier today that the dead can't hurt you? Well, they also can't help you."

" 'Only the living can do that.' Is that how that ends? Meaning I'm supposed to trust *you*?"

O'Deoradháin took a long breath. His eyes held hers, and she saw the hurt in them. "You do what you think you need to do, Holder, and believe what you must." He lay back down and snapped the blankets around him, turning his back to the fire and her.

Jenna held the torc in her hands for several minutes, watching the fire shimmering in its burnished surface. Finally, she placed it back in her pack. "I'm sorry," she whispered to the night, not sure to whom she was speaking.

The spring sun beat down on the bright carpet of silverweed, primrose, and heather in which Lough Crithlaigh rested; the sky was cloudless and deep. Yellow siskins, song thrushes, and warblers darted among the wildflowers. Mountains lifted gorse-feathered heads to the west beyond the hills, and they could see deer grazing near a foaming rill winding toward the lough. The day was pastoral; even their horses seemed affected, neighing and lowering their heads as if they wanted to linger here forever.

"Those are storm deer, not the normal red," O'Deoradháin commented, then glanced back at Jenna. "You're frowning."

Jenna turned in her saddle. She tried to give the man a smile and failed. "I'm sorry," she said. "It's just . . ." She stopped; he lifted an eyebrow. ". . . . a feeling."

O'Deoradháin pulled back the reins of his mount, his gaze searching the terrain.

They'd debated whether they should go through this expansive but open valley, or take the much longer and difficult path through the hills. She wondered now if they'd made a mistake. She touched the cloch, letting tendrils of energy spread outward. In that invisible cloud, there was a twin disturbance. She could sense it in the pattern of Lámh Shábhála's sphere, like a wave disturbed by the presence of unseen rocks just below the surface. "There are two other clochs na thintrí close by," Jenna said. She could feel a cold apprehension spreading out from her stomach. "Powerful ones: Clochs Mór. I can feel them."

O'Deoradháin rose up in his saddle again. "Where?" he asked. "In what direction?"

"I'm not certain," Jenna said. "To the south, I think. They're trying to keep themselves hidden, but one of the Holders isn't particularly good at keeping his wall up and so I can sense them both."

"By the Mother-Creator," O'Deoradháin cursed. His hands clenched into fists around the reins, the knuckles going white with pressure. "I was afraid this would happen. Well, we don't have a choice. All we can do is ride on, and see if they show themselves."

"O'Deoradháin, what should I do? What happens if they attack with the clochs, or if they're part of the army the Rí has raised . . . ?" Jenna remembered the battlefield and saw herself as one of the corpses. Her breath was coming fast, and panic roared in her ears.

"You'll do what you can," O'Deoradháin told her. "I will do what I can, also, but if the clochs enter the battle, you must deal with them." Then his voice gentled, and his eyes held hers. "You're the Holder of Lámh Shábhála, and it's stronger than the other clochs na thintrí. Remember that."

She did. She also remembered the words of the Lady of the Falls: *". . . even the strongest can be overpowered by numbers, or make a fatal mistake . . ."* "I don't know what to do."

"You will, if it comes to that," O'Deoradháin told her. "And if we're lucky, they won't see us. If we can reach the hills beyond the lough . . ."

They moved through the field toward the lough, the land sloping gently downhill to the water. There were beeches and sycamores lining the banks, and without speaking both of them urged their horses into a gallop to head for their cover. The storm deer glanced up; the dominant stag of the herd lifted an antlered head and gave a ululating cry, and the herd moved off at a canter to the east, their hooves trembling the ground with a low rumble. Jenna and O'Deoradháin reached the line of trees and moved just inside, then pulled up their mounts and turned. "Can you still feel them?" O'Deoradháin asked.

Jenna closed her eyes, touching the cloch with stiff and cold fingers. "Aye," she said. She looked at him, worried. "Closer now. There." She pointed up the slope they'd just traveled to the low ridge lined with trees.

A few breaths later, a half dozen riders appeared, emerging slowly from under the trees, perhaps half a mile away. All were dressed in green and brown, mail glinting under their colors. One of the group, even from that distance, seemed familiar to Jenna.

Jenna's heart jumped. "The man in front—with no helm. That's Mac Ard, I think."

O'Deoradháin cursed again. "Aye. You could be right." As they watched, a rider dismounted and walked carefully along the ridge. He stopped and pointed—it seemed to Jenna that his finger was aimed directly at her. "Damn, they've seen our trail," O'Deoradháin spat. "There's nothing for it, Jenna. They'll track us now, and once we leave the cover of the trees, they'll see us." Jenna only stared at him, as if by her gaze she could change his words. "There are six of them, Jenna. I can't deal with that many, even without the clochs na thintrí they have."

She knew what he was saying, though her head was shaking in denial. "I can't . . ."

"It was eventually going to come to this, Jenna, no matter what. We both knew it. You can either use the cloch now, while they're not certain how close they are to us, or later when they know who we are and where. Strike first, and you have the advantage."

"I don't know how to fight cloch against cloch."

"And probably neither do they, yet," O'Deoradháin persisted. "I suspect Lámh Shábhála will show you the way."

He was right; she knew it, could feel it in the very marrow of her bones and yet she resisted. The riders gathered again as the scout remounted, and they started down the slope toward where they were hidden, following the unmistakable path their horses had made through the tall grass. She watched the tall rider with the dark hair, certain that it was Mac Ard even though she couldn't see his face clearly. *He will have one of the clochs. It will be him you strike against, your mam's lover . . .*

She brought her right hand up, looking at the mottled skin. She opened her fingers with an effort, then closed them again around Lámh Shábhála.

She opened her mind fully to the cloch.

Lámh Shábhála was full with the power of the magelights, its crystalline interstices crackling and surging with the energy. The vision of it seemed to expand and spread out before her, rushing like a tidal wave over the land; when it struck the riders, the force broke and shattered on twin rocks, shimmering white. Jenna saw the world in doubled vision now: through her eyes and through Lámh Shábhála. With her eyes, she saw Mac Ard and one of the other riders suddenly pull up and stop while the other four continued on; through the cloch, two presences suddenly appeared, one as ruddy as heated coals, the other more the color of a cold sea, both throbbing and pulsing inside the horizon of Lámh Shábhála.

She knew what she had to do and yet she hesitated—in that hesitation, she could feel the other two clochs searching for her in the landscape of Lámh Shábhála. There was no doubt as to their intentions; she could feel the hostility, especially from the sea-colored stone. For the moment, though, she ignored them. She looked instead for the four riders and she released more of the stored energy within her cloch, gathering it in her mind and shaping it, then releasing it with a savage mental thrust.

With her eyes, she saw lightnings arc from her scarred right arm, flashing outward in jagged white-hot streaks toward the riders. Two of the riders were torn from their saddles and their mounts killed as bolts shot through them: shredding flesh, shattering bones, and boiling their blood. Thunder boomed and crackled. Jenna heard the screams of both men and horses, short and cut off as the force of the cloch ripped the life from them. She felt them die.

But in that same instant, the remaining two bolts were turned aside before they struck their targets: one meeting a similar bolt from the red cloch; the other shoved aside as if by an invisible hand from the other stone. The two colliding bolts exploded in a ball of blinding fireworks between the two groups; the one shoved aside gouged a crater from the earth just to the left of its intended target, whose horse reared and bucked. She saw O'Deoradháin break from cover with a cry, kicking his horse into a gallop and charging back up the slope toward the remaining riders. The one who had nearly been struck broke and fled; the other pulled his sword from its sheath and came for O'Deoradháin.

The two cloch Holders ignored O'Deoradháin and instead turned their attention to Jenna and Lámh Shábhála. Their clochs were now open; in her mental view, she could see them, twin expanding ripples in the white sea of Lámh Shábhála. The sea-foam color of one moved more rapidly, surging for the center that was Jenna. *"Don't let it reach you. Go toward it . . ."* The voice spoke in her head: *Riata,* she realized, come to her on his own. The other voices were there as well, the voices of all the Holders, a babble of contradictory advice: one telling her to flee, another to make the first strike now, yet another insisting that it was too late already . . . She ignored them and found Riata's voice again. *"Go toward it, not physically but with the cloch . . ."* She let her awareness slide forward . . .

The impact nearly stunned her. She was surrounded by howling winds and a hand that seemed to grasp at her,

squeezing the very breath from her lungs. Jenna gasped
and struggled. She could feel more and more energy pouring from the attacking cloch, then—in support—lightning
arced from its partner. Jenna screamed with the pain, the
electricity arcing through her, her body convulsing as all
her muscles contracted and the burning spear coursed
through her. The aqua light continued to pummel her like a
gigantic fist as she felt the other cloch gathering itself again.

Yet she could also sense that with each attack, the clochs,
including Lámh Shábhála, grew weaker, that there was less
force left for them to use. *"You are stronger . . . You can
hold more of the mage-light's power than they can . . ."* She
thrust back at the blue-green constriction that had wrapped
about her, unwrapping it like a sticky rope laced around
her body. She could feel energy draining from Lámh Shábhála as she fought back, but the crushing pressure was easing. She *pushed,* and the cloch fell back. She lifted an
ethereal arm and slammed it down; waves of pain and
alarm radiated from the center of the cloch's influence. The
red cloch released another bolt of lightning; shifting her
attention, she sent her own to intercept it and a momentary
sun flared between them. The aqua cloch was pushing back
now, the two of them grappling mentally like wrestlers
searching for a hold. The ruddy one held back, and Jenna
realized that Mac Ard was waiting, deliberately allowing
the other cloch to drain as much of Lámh Shábhála's power
as it could.

*He's planning to wait until I weaken myself dealing with
the other cloch, then strike . . . I wonder . . .* She sent her
awareness racing to the center of the other cloch: she could
see a face, strained and hurting as it fought her: Damhlaic
Gairbith, the Rí's commander. He tried to push her away;
she would not let him. She shouted at him, feeling her
throat go raw with the near-scream. *"Mac Ard's using you,
Gairbith! He intends to let you die fighting me!"*

Gairbith didn't reply—couldn't reply, she knew, for handling the cloch was taking all his concentration. But his
eyes went wide with fear and suspicion, and he looked away
toward where the other cloch pulsed blood red, watching
and waiting.

The truth was enough. Jenna felt Gairbith's focus shift
and with that the defenses he'd set around himself weakened. Jenna cried out, releasing a new flood of energy from
Lámh Shábhála. It raged forward, overwhelming Gairbith.
The mental connection between himself and his cloch
snapped. Through her true eyes, she saw one of the men
sway in his saddle and fall. In the middle of the field,
O'Deoradháin and another man were fighting, steel clashing as a sword rang against the Inishlander's long dagger.

Jenna nearly fell with Gairbith. The sudden release of
pressure made her gasp and Lámh Shábhála was nearly
drained. Weary, she turned her attention to Mac Ard.

"We don't have to do this, Jenna." She heard Mac Ard's
voice as if he whispered in her ear. "I don't want to hurt
you. Give up the cloch. Let me take it and I'll let you
go or take you back to your mam. Whatever you want. I
swear it."

The thought of losing the cloch was worse than contemplating death. "No," she answered. "Lámh Shábhála is
mine. It stays mine."

She heard no more words, but she felt his sadness.

Jenna could feel Mac Ard's cloch opening and knew he
was readying a strike. She didn't wait for it; she grasped at
the dregs of power within Lámh Shábhála and flung them
at him. The energy shattered against his cloch, absorbing
the lightning he hurled toward her. As it crackled around
him, she could feel Lámh Shábhála sucking the rest of the
life from his cloch until there was nothing left. She saw
Mac Ard's face go suddenly wide-eyed with fear.

Mac Ard's horse reared up as he yanked at the reins.
Faintly, she heard his cry of pain and frustration as he fled,
galloping into the trees and over the rise. Within Lámh
Shábhála, there was still power left, enough that she could
feel Mac Ard's cloch moving away until she could no longer
sense it at all.

She let go of the cloch. It was a mistake, she realized
immediately, for it was only the residual energy within
Lámh Shábhála that was keeping her upright. With the release of contact, a doubled wave of severe pain and exhaustion swept over her. She could still see O'Deoradháin

fighting close by, but the edges of her vision had gone black, the scene before her shrinking and condensing until it was only a pinpoint. Thunder roared in her ears, and the drumbeat of her blood. Her right arm felt as if it were on fire. She tried to lift it, tried to call out, but the darkness closed in around her and she felt herself falling.

She didn't feel the impact of the ground at all.

34

The Gifting

"*YOU see, she's weak and stupid. She doesn't deserve to be Holder . . .*"

"*You can't be seriously thinking she could survive the Scrúdú . . .*"

"*Next time they come after her, she'll die. The only thing that saved her was the inexperience of the others, and they'll learn . . .*"

"*She doesn't have the discipline . . .*"

"*Lámh Shábhála has chosen poorly this time . . .*"

"*Be quiet, all of you. She will learn, she may take the Scrúdú in time, and she is stronger than you think . . .*"

"Riata?" With the word, the voices faded. She could see nothing. Her eyes refused to focus though there was a whiteness all around her, and she was being jostled. She tried to move her hands or her legs and could not—something held her. She remembered the last thing she'd seen: O'Deoradháin and the other man fighting. If O'Deoradháin had lost . . . had she been captured? Had Lámh Shábhála been taken from her? She closed her eyes, gathering her strength.

This time, she could see. The whiteness was a cloth draped over a wooden framework above her face, the sun shining through it. She could lift her head, and saw that she was reclining on a crude carrier—canvas stretched and tied between two saplings. She could hear the slow clopping of two horses' hooves and smell their ripeness—the carrier she was in was being dragged along behind one of the animals, the saplings evidently tied to the saddle, and the jostling was the device bumping and lurching over the broken ground. Someone had tied her into the frame as well.

Her body felt as if it had been bruised and battered and she could easily have slipped back into unconsciousness. Her right arm throbbed as if someone were rhythmically pounding it with a hammer of ice. She wanted to scream for someone to bring her andúilleaf, the old yearning for the drug rising from the suffering. She gritted her teeth to stop from crying out, forcing herself to take long, slow breaths, sending her awareness deeper. She did cry out then, in relief rather than pain.

Lámh Shábhála was still around her neck. She could feel the cloch, as drained as she was, but alive and with her. *It will always be part of you now* . . . The last of the voices whispered to her. . . . *to lose your cloch is like losing your child. You can't imagine that pain* . . . "O'Deoradháin?" she called. Her throat felt as if someone had scrubbed it with a steel file.

The horse came to a sudden halt. She heard someone dismount, then footsteps. The cloth was pulled away from the frame, and Jenna was blinking up into a bright sky as a dark face eclipsed the sun.

"You're finally awake." The voice was familiar and deep.

"Finally?"

"It's been nearly two days," he told her.

"Two *days?*" She repeated the words wonderingly. "So long?"

"You learn to bear using the cloch against others as it happens more. At least that's what I was taught. We can hope that Tiarna Mac Ard suffered the same fate, though I suspect he's had more practice than you." He crouched down in front of her. "Can you stand? Here, let me loosen these ropes . . ." He unlashed her, and helped her out of the contraption. Her knees were wobbly but they supported her; O'Deoradháin, after helping her to rise, let her go as she took a few tentative steps. She recognized none of the landscape around her: tall, grassy peaks with steep rocky outcroppings, and limestone-boned ground underfoot.

There was an odor in the air that she couldn't identify, a fresh, briny scent. "Where are we?"

"In Tuath Connachta above Keelballi, near the northern border with Tuath Infochla. We're perhaps five or six miles from the sea. I'm hoping to reach a fishing village where we can find someone who'll take us to Inish."

"Mac Ard? The others?"

"I don't know what happened to Mac Ard or the other one who fled. The rest . . . are dead."

Jenna touched the cloch. O'Deoradháin's eyes followed the gesture. "The cloch Gairbith had . . . ?"

"Was that the man's name?" O'Deoradháin shrugged, then reached into a pocket under his clóca. "Here . . . It's yours now." He took her left hand, turning it palm up and placing in it a gold chain. At the end of the chain was a turquoise gem, faceted and gleaming and far larger than Lámh Shábhála. "There's his cloch na thintrí. I took it from the body after . . ." He stopped.

Memory of the battle was coming back now. Jenna remembered Gairbith's cloch going silent, and the man falling from his horse. "He wasn't dead," she said. "The cloch was drained, but Gairbith wasn't dead."

"He is now." O'Deoradháin's lips pressed together.

She stared at him; his eyes, nearly the color of the gem in her hand, returned the gaze, as if daring her to object. "You could have let him go," she said. "Taken the cloch from him, aye, and his horse—"

"Jenna . . ."

". . . but you didn't have to kill him. Without the cloch, he wasn't—"

"Jenna!" he said sharply, and Jenna blinked angrily, closing her mouth. "I don't expect the person who murdered the Banrion to lecture me about the choices I made. We aren't children playing a game, Holder. What do you think this Gairbith would have done with you, had the positions been reversed? Do you believe the Banrion's assassin was only going to threaten you? Do you think the Connachtans who came to Ballintubber would have left you alive after they plucked Lámh Shábhála from your neck? Frankly,

from what I've been taught, a cloudmage would prefer to be killed rather than have his or her cloch taken."

He snorted derisively, his hand slashing air in front of her. "You did the right thing with the Banrion, because if you'd left her alive she might have been the one to kill you later, or more likely, to have ordered your death. Now she can't. And as for Gairbith—he doesn't have to bear the pain of having his Cloch Mór ripped away from him, and he won't be able to seek revenge."

Jenna looked at the gold links pooled in her hand. She closed her fist around them. "I'm sorry for you, O'Deoradháin. I'm sorry that you live in such a harsh, self-centered world. There is a time for mercy."

"I've learned that mercy and forgiveness will usually get you killed, Holder. I notice that you 'murdered' the riders with Mac Ard without worrying overmuch about *that* action."

The lightning striking them down . . . "I did what I had to do. The difference is that I regret that action, even if it was necessary."

"I also do what's necessary to keep me—and you—alive, and I *don't* regret that. I don't intend to die because I was too busy worrying about whether I should defend myself."

Jenna lifted her head. "We *all* die, O'Deoradháin, when the gods say it's our time." Gairbith's cloch na thintrí was heavy in her hand. She looked down at the stone: beautiful and clear all the way down into its emerald depths, captured in a finely-wrought cage of silver and gold. Unlike Lámh Shábhála, this gem would be precious even if it couldn't draw the power of the mage-lights from the sky. She looked back at O'Deoradháin. "Why did you give me this?"

"It's yours. I didn't win that battle. You did."

Her fingers closed around it again. "Can I . . . can I use it?"

"No," he told her. "A Holder can use only one stone, and you have Lámh Shábhála—why would you take a lesser stone? But while you keep this one, no one else can use it against you. It's one of the Cloch Mór; better you have it than your enemies."

Her gaze went back to him, and she suddenly felt ashamed of her doubt and suspicion of the man. *He's done nothing but tell you the truth: about Coelin, about Mac Ard, about everything. He helped you even when it put him in danger, and he could have taken Lámh Shábhála from you several times now. He could have taken this clock na thintrí just as easily, and yet he hands it to you . . .* "O'Deoradháin, I'm sorry if it seems I don't trust you. I certainly—"

He wouldn't let her finish, shaking his head into her words. "You should be careful with your trust, Holder. You haven't exactly made good choices in the past."

"Give me your hand," she told him. His eyes narrowed and his lips tightened again. He held out his right hand, and she took it in her own. She placed Gairbith's cloch in his palm and closed his fingers around it. "Tonight when the mage-lights come," she told him, "take this and fill it as I fill Lámh Shábhála. Become its Holder."

Her hand stayed on his, and he didn't move it away. His gaze searched her face, and she felt herself blushing under the scrutiny. *You like this man more than you want to admit,* and the realization brought more heat to her cheeks. What she felt wasn't what she had once felt for Coelin; the heat inside her was different. With Coelin, the attraction had come from his flattery of her and his handsome face, and she knew now how false and shallow that had been. What she was feeling now came at her from all directions, and she found herself looking at O'Deoradháin with new eyes, and wondering if he were feeling what she was.

"This isn't the cloch I want to possess," he said gruffly. "You know that."

"Aye," she answered. "I know. I also know that if you take the one you want, it will be because I can no longer use it. And I also know that will be due to some other person's deed, not yours." She pressed his fingers more tightly around the stone, and smiled at him. "I think I'm making a good choice, this time."

Slowly, he nodded. His hand slid from her grasp and he put the cloch na thintrí's chain around his neck. The jewel gleamed on his chest for a moment before he placed it under his tunic.

"If you can ride," he said, "we should be moving. I'd like to make the coast by tomorrow evening. *He* won't let us rest." O'Deoradháin didn't need to tell Jenna who "he" was—she knew. "He'll follow us, as soon as he's able, and the next time he attacks he'll be more careful."

"I know he will," she agreed. "But we'll be stronger."

35

O'Deoradháin's Tale

THEY stopped to eat and rest near a narrow and long lough cradled between close green hills. The sun was high and peeked out occasionally between the clouds sweeping across the sky. Cloud shadows raced over the slopes, and the smell of the sea was in the wind from the west. Well out toward the western end of the lake, two fishing boats bobbed on the waves where the lough curved north and away toward the endless water of the ocean. Dark fingers of smoke smeared across the sky around the hills behind them, and underneath was a cluster of white dots.

"People," Jenna said. "I'm not sure I remember how to react around them anymore."

"If we're lucky, we won't meet too many of them," O'Deoradháin answered. "We'll make for that village. Maybe there's an inn where we can stay and clean up, and if we're lucky, find someone to take us up the coast. But they'll be asking questions of strangers." He nodded at Jenna's right arm and the swirl of scars. "You'll need to cover that arm of yours, and we'll need to devise a story to give them. And we can't show the clochs. Ever. Not here."

"I agree. But let's rest here for a bit. 'Tis beautiful, this."

"Aye. If you'd like to look about, go on. I'll take care of the horses and our food."

Jenna walked down to the shore of the lough as O'Deoradháin hobbled the horses. The lough's waters were fairly clear, not peat-stained like the waters of Lough Lár, and the water shifted from green to deep blue as the bottom fell away quickly. She sat on a rock that protruded out a bit into the water, taking off her boots and leggings and letting her feet splash in the cold water. She stroked the smooth surface of Lámh Shábhála: she had renewed its reservoirs with the mage-lights the night before, and O'Deoradháin had done the same with his cloch. She opened Lámh Shábhála slightly, letting its aura spread out over the lough, feeling for the presence of other clochs na thintrí. She could sense O'Deoradháin close by and feel the powerful emanations of his cloch even through the wall he had tried to erect around it; she could perceive the fisherfolk in their boats, their thoughts altering the pattern of faint energy she placed around them; and at the very edge of Lámh Shábhála's range, the clustering of many people in the village. But there was no one else. No one with intentions toward her.

Except . . .

There *was* something. Rising toward her, drawn to her, its attention steady on her.

Rising from below . . .

Fingers gripped Jenna's ankles, still dangling in the water. They pulled, hard and sudden.

Jenna had no time to cry out. Instinctively, she turned her body, trying to cling to the rock even as she was dragged down into the lough. Frigid water hammered at her lungs; she took a gulping breath as her head went under, her hands still scrabbling for purchase. Invisible, frigid hands pulled at her legs, her waist, her breasts, and finally closed around the chain of Lámh Shábhála. Her desperate fingers found a knob of rock, and she pulled herself up even as the hands tried to hold her down and rip away the cloch from around her neck. Gasping, Jenna's head broke the surface as she flailed for a higher handhold, pulling herself up. She screamed, letting go with her left hand and striking at her assailant.

She saw her attacker now, and shock nearly stole the breath from her. The creature's torso had risen from the water with her, its arms around her—the face nearly fea-

tureless, its body the blue-black of the depths as if it were
made of the water itself. A finned row of spines ran from
its smooth-featured crown down the back of its sinuous
body, and the hands that encircled Jenna and snagged the
cloch's chain were webbed, long-fingered, and wide. The
eyes were dead black and shining—emotionless, cold shark
eyes—and thin fanged teeth glistened in a gaping round
mouth. Jenna tried to scream once more but the creature
folded its arms around her and with a powerful wriggle of
its body and a splash, yanked her away from the rock and
back under the water. Lámh Shábhála's chain broke and
tore away; she grabbed for the cloch, but it vanished, drifting down.

Eyes open in terror, Jenna struggled, trying to strike at
the creature though the water softened and slowed her
blows. She pulled at the thing's hands, and felt it bite at
her shoulder and neck. It bore her down to the bottom,
turning her under its body. She felt rocks and mud on her
back and she knew that she had only seconds, that the first
breath she took would be her last. She saw another dark
form speed toward them, churning white foam on the dappled surface, and she despaired. Yet at the same moment
she was about to give up and take the breath that would
mean her death, the form above dove and struck her assailant hard. The creature shrilled in pain, releasing Jenna to
respond to this new attack. Jenna pushed herself up from
the rocky bottom, surging toward the rippling promise of
sunlight above. Her head broke the surface and she took a
desperate breath, her arms slapping at the waves. She could
feel herself going under again, the weight of her clothing
dragging her down. She gulped water . . .

A hand caught hers and pulled her up: O'Deoradháin.
She choked and gasped, bleeding and coughing up water,
as he helped her onto the shore. "Lámh Shábhála," she
managed to say. "They took it . . ." She started to plunge
back into the lough, but he held her back, grasping her
from behind. She struggled in his arms now, trying to get
loose, screaming and crying as she fought to dive back in
and find the cloch, but he was too strong.

"Jenna, you can't go back in there . . ." he was saying to her, his lips close to her ear as he hugged her to him. "You can't . . ."

She continued to try to break free, but exhaustion took hold and she hung limp in his arms, struggling to catch her breath. The surface of the lough showed nothing, then a silken head surged up through the small wind-driven waves several yards out: a seal. It roared at them once and dove again, surfacing closer to the shore. Bright blue highlights glinted in its ebon fur where the sunlight touched it. Metal glinted in the animal's mouth and Jenna cried out wordlessly. She pushed out of O'Deoradháin's grasp and floundered into the water toward the seal. It waited for her; wading in waist-deep, Jenna snatched at the broken chain with the silver-caged stone. Her hand closed around Lámh Shábhála; the seal opened its mouth and released the necklace at the same moment. Sobbing, Jenna clutched the stone in her hand. The seal stared at her with its bulbous chocolate eyes, its whiskered snout wriggling as if it were sniffing the air. "Thank you," Jenna told the seal, tightening her right hand around the cloch.

She would have sworn that the seal nodded. Its head lifted, the mouth opening, and a series of wails and coughs emerged: like words but in no language Jenna understood. Then, with a flash of shimmering lapis, the seal turned and dove back into the water.

"It said that the Holder should be more careful, and warned you that not only humans want to possess a cloch na thintrí, especially Lámh Shábhála."

Jenna turned. O'Deoradháin stood on the bank, his hand extended to her. "Come out of the water," he said. "I'll start a fire, and we can get you warm and dry."

She didn't move. Waves lapped at her waist. "You understood it?"

"Her, not it. And aye, I understood her." He stretched out his hand again. "Trust me, Holder. I will explain."

She ignored the hand. "I thought I knew you," she said.

His mouth twitched under the beard. "Not all. Come out of the water, Holder; I don't know if that creature will be back."

She took a breath, shivering. Then she reached for his hand. "Then tell me," she said as he helped her from the lough. "Tell me why the seals come to you."

He nodded.

I was perhaps four or five when I realized that my mam was . . . *strange*. I woke up one night in the bed I shared with my younger brother. I don't know what it was that woke me—maybe the sound of a footstep or the creaking of the door. I managed to get out of the bed without waking my brother. Our house was small: my sister—the youngest of us at the time—slept in her crib in the same room, beside my parents' bed. I could hear my da snoring. The moon was out and the sky was clear; in the silver light, I could see that where my ma should have been, the blankets were flung back. I called out for her softly so I wouldn't wake the others, but she didn't answer. I went out into the other room, but she wasn't there, either. The door to our cottage, though, was ajar.

My da was a fisherman, and we lived just above a rocky shingle of beach on the southern coast of Inish Thuaidh not far from the island of Inishfeirm where your family lived, in the townland of Maoil na nDreas. Sometimes, when the day was clear, we could even see Inishfeirm like a gray hump on the horizon to the south. But that has nothing to do with this story . . .

I walked out of the cottage. I could see my father's boat pulled up on the beach and hear the waves pounding against the shore. I thought I heard another sound as well, and I padded down toward the water. The wind was brisk, and the breakers were shattering on the walls of our little cove, splashing high on the cliff walls that rose out like arms on either side. In the bright moonlight, I could see seals out there on the rocks, several big ones, and they were calling loudly to each other, occasionally diving awkwardly into the surf and pulling themselves back up with their flippers. These seals, I noticed, were different than the small harbor seals that I usually saw. They shimmered in the moonlight, their fur sparkling with blue highlights. I watched them for a while, listening to what sounded like a

loud conversation. One of the bulls noticed me, for I saw
him turn his snout toward the beach and bellow. A few of
the other seals looked toward me too, then, and one
lurched from the rock into the sea and I lost sight of it. I
watched the others, though, especially that old bull, who
kept roaring and staring at me.

"Ennis . . . ?" I heard my mam call my name, and she
came from around da's boat to where I was sitting on the
beach. She was soaking wet and naked, and water dripped
from her hair as she crouched down by me, smiling. Her
eyes were as dark and bright as a seal's. "What are you
doing out here, young man?"

"I woke up and you weren't there, Mam," I told her.
"And I came out and saw the seals and I was watching
them." I pointed at the old bull and the seals gathered
around him on the rock. I laughed. "They sound like
they're talking to each other, Mam."

"They *are* talking," she said, laughing with me. She had
a voice like purest crystal, and she seemed entirely comfortable in her nudity, which made me comfortable with it also.
"You just have to know their language."

"Do *you* know the language?" I asked her wonderingly,
and she nodded, laughing again.

"I do. Would you like me to teach you sometime?"

"Aye, Mam, I would," I told her, wide-eyed.

"Then I will. Now, let's get you inside and back into bed.
It's cold out here." She lifted me up, but I struggled to stay.

"I'm not cold at all. Mam, what were you doing out
here?" I asked her, staring up at her face, her hair all
stringy and still dripping water from the ends, a bit of sea-
weed stuck near her ear. "Aren't *you* cold?"

"No, Ennis. I was . . . swimming."

"With the seals?"

She nodded. "With the seals. Maybe, someday, you can
swim with them, too, if . . ." She stopped then, and a smile
curled her lip. She rubbed my hair. "Come now. Back to
bed." She led me back to the cottage door and stopped
there. "Go on in," she said. "I'm going to swim a bit
more . . ."

She kept her promise. She taught me how to understand

the language of the blue seals. And, once or twice a year, she would leave our house late at night to "go swimming with the seals." I don't think my siblings ever noticed, but I did. I would see her slip out of bed and follow her. I think she probably knew that I was watching her, but she didn't seem to care and never paid any attention to me at all. She would stand at the water's edge and take off her night robe, standing naked under the moon with the seals all wailing and moaning and calling to her. She'd run toward the water, diving into the surf. Somehow, though I looked, I never saw my mam after that—she would vanish among the bodies of the seals and emerge hours later as light began to touch the sky, dripping wet but somehow not cold. If I were still there asleep on the beach, she would wake me and take me back to the cottage with her.

I asked her, the first time, why I never could see her after she went into the water and she told me I might understand one day. She also told me about the blue seals—that there was but one small group of them left in all the world here at Inish Thuaidh, but that soon a time would come when they would return in greater numbers, and that she hoped I would be part of those days . . .

Aye, my da knew. He seemed troubled by his wife's occasional forays into the ocean, but did nothing about them, or perhaps it was just that he'd learned over the years that this was simply part of her—he didn't speak to her about the seals, or her swimming at night, or mention any of it to us. "Your mam must do what she must," was all he would say the one time I dared to bring up the subject with him. "And if you're lucky, you won't share her curse and find yourself out there swimming in the moonlight." Then he turned his back to me as he mended his fishing net.

I didn't think of my mam as cursed, though. I saw the joy in her face as she came from the water. I saw the cavorting of the seals and the way they flew through the water and thought that it must be wonderful to be able to do that. I listened to their talk and sometimes tried to speak with them, though our throats aren't made to speak their words, and they would laugh at my poor attempts and answer.

And, one day after my body had started to grow hair and my voice had gone deeper, I *did* swim with them . . .

"You're . . . ?" Jenna breathed, and O'Deoradháin nodded solemnly. "I thought . . . I mean I've heard of changelings and such, but I'd always believed they were only tales."

"Not only tales. And not only me. Wasn't your grandmother mysteriously rescued by seals?—or maybe she unconsciously, under the stress of nearly drowning, tapped a part of herself she didn't know was there."

The fire O'Deoradháin had built while he told his tale crackled, and Jenna snuggled close to the flames, letting the welcome heat sink into her still-damp clothes. She glanced back at the waters of the lough, half-expecting to see the seal again, but it was gone. "Are *all* the blue seals . . . ?"

O'Deoradháin shrugged. "Some of them are changelings, aye, but not all and almost none can change at will. Most of those who can change are water-snared, nearly always a seal but changing for a few short hours a year into human shape. Somewhere, back in my family's past, a many times great-mam must have met a bull in his human form and loved him, and that blood manifested itself in my mam—she said that her sisters and brothers weren't that way, just as my siblings also weren't affected. But the blood occasionally shows to create the few Earth-snared ones like me or my mam, who feel the call of the water-part of us only rarely."

Jenna didn't know what to say. She looked up the sloping bank of the lough to where the horses stood, to the pack on her mare where her father's carved seal was hidden, and she remembered the blue paint he'd used to paint it and she wondered.

"They've followed me, as well as they can, since I left Inish," O'Deoradháin was saying. "They haven't told me why, just that 'the WaterMother's voice tells them that they must.' The WaterMother is their god, like our Mother-Creator. The 'voice,' I think, is a euphemism, a feeling they have or perhaps part of an old song-tale—all their history is passed down in songs since they don't write at all, and there are thousands of them. Their—I suppose I should say 'our'—memories are very good, and they pass the songs down generation to generation. I don't know them all yet, only a few hundred."

Jenna remembered the seal who watched them when they talked at Deer Creek, and the shapes in the water that had pushed their boat away after they'd crossed Lough Lár . . . "What was the thing that attacked me?"

O'Deoradháin shrugged again. He took a stick from the ground and pushed at the logs in the fire; sparks and smoke went whirling upward. "I don't know. Garrentha—that's the name of the seal who came to your rescue—didn't either. There are things that live in hidden places that we don't know, and more and more of them are waking as the mage-lights grow stronger. It's not only humans who want to hold the magic." He rose to his feet. "If you're dry and warm enough, we should go. I think we'd be safer in the village at night than out here."

Jenna glanced back at the lough. She nodded. "Are there other secrets you're keeping from me, O'Deoradháin? You ought to trot them out now, before we go farther."

He grinned at that, but the expression turned oddly serious when his dark eyes found hers. "I only have one," he answered. "I suspect you already know what it is."

She found herself blushing under his gaze, and she turned away rather than say more.

36

Ambush and Offer

THE folk of the village of Banshaigh had a name for the
creature: "Uisce Taibhse," it was: the water ghost. "No
one fishes at the eastern end of Lough Glas now," one
grizzled old man told Jenna and O'Deoradháin. "At least
not if you care about coming back. Too many boats have
been mysteriously sunk there—in broad daylight and calm
water—and many of those aboard lost. The Uisce Taibhse
is an evil creature—or creatures, since there is more than
one of them, and they don't like us. We've caught one
ourselves, snagged in our nets; it died out of the water like
a fish, but it fought like a mad, cornered dog to its last
breath. Why, if I had one of those clochs na thintrí the
Riocha are wearing now, I'd just kill them all . . ."

As would have happened in Tara's tavern back in Ballintubber, the newcomers to The Green Waters, Banshaigh's
only inn, were greeted with curious looks and many questions. Jenna and O'Deoradháin agreed on their cover story
before entering the village: they were cousins uprooted
from their homes in Tuath Gabair by the recent troubles
and hoping to return to the home of their uncle in Inish
Thuaidh. Banshaigh wasn't much larger than Ballintubber
and though the villagers were aware of the hostilities between Connachta and Gabair, they were far enough removed from the larger towns and the Riocha that they were
more sympathetic than hostile to the unfortunate travelers,
especially since O'Deoradháin seemed to know as much
about fishing as any of the locals.

Lough Glas, the green lake, was fed by springs, brooks, and rills running from the high hills around it, and fed from its western end into a mountain-flanked and marshy tidal basin and the sea. Aye, the village fisherfolk sometimes ventured out into the open ocean. Aye, there was one fisherman in the village who would doubtless be willing to sail them to Inish Thuaidh for a fair price—Flynn Meagher had a large enough boat and often sailed the coast, if never that far north.

They went to see Flynn Meagher the next morning near dawn, in a windy downpour.

Meagher was a burly, nontalkative man, who grunted as O'Deoradháin explained what they wanted. "Maybe six days out, six back, fewer if the wind is good," Meagher said finally. "Need to take another person to help me sail and I won't be able to do any fishing. A half-mórceint a day is what I'll need." His face showed that he expected the bedraggled strangers to turn and leave with that. When O'Deoradháin showed him three golden coins and placed one of them in Meagher's palm, he seemed astonished.

"A quarter-mórceint a day is twice as much as you should get, but we're in a hurry," O'Deoradháin countered. "I'll give you one mórceint now so you can hire your crew member and provision the boat. You'll get the other two when we get there."

Meagher stared at the money in his hand. Slowly, his fingers curled around the coin, then opened again. He seemed to be thinking. "Can't leave today. Tomorrow. Better weather, better tide."

"We'll be here tomorrow morning, then. Same time."

A nod. His hand closed around the money and disappeared under the oiled leather coat.

"He could take us a day's sail out, kill us while we're sleeping, steal the money and dump our bodies overboard for the fish," Jenna said as they walked back to the inn.

"Aye, he could," O'Deoradháin admitted. "We'll need to be careful. But we also have defenses he doesn't know we have, and I could sail that boat myself with your help if we needed to. Do you have a better plan?"

She didn't. But she didn't feel easy about the decision.

* * *

The next day they sold their horses to the proprietor of The Green Waters and went to meet Meagher at his boat near the end of the docks. The day promised to be a fine one, as Meagher had suggested, but despite the yellow glow on the horizon and the deep, nearly cloudless azure above, Jenna felt more and more uneasy as they approached their rendezvous. She opened Lámh Shábhála slightly, examining the space around them with the cloch's vision. There were several other people in the dock area, which was to be expected, but if there were other clochs nearby, they were well-shielded. They walked toward the small wooden shack on the shore where Meagher stored his nets and other equipment.

Jenna put her hand on O'Deoradháin's arm. "Wait," she said. She could feel several people in the immediate area, yet the only one she could see was Meagher, on his boat and waving at them. "There are too many—"

It was as far as she got. The door to Meagher's shack opened. Tiarna Mac Ard stood there, and she suddenly felt the concealing shields go down around the rubied jewel already grasped in his hand.

"*No!*" Mac Ard shouted as both Jenna and O'Deoradháin reached for their own clochs. "Don't move!" Several men now appeared around the dock area, at least a half dozen with arrows nocked in bows already pulled back at full draw. They wore no colors, but they were obviously gardai. "Those arrows are aimed at your friend, Jenna," Mac Ard continued. "I've seen what you can do, but I doubt that he's had enough practice yet to know how to use that cloch well. If they see him touch poor Gairbith's stone, though, they will fire."

Both of their hands went back to their sides and a grim smile came over Mac Ard's face. He took a few steps toward them, though he stopped several yards away. "Your mam sends you her love and concern, Jenna. When I saw her last, a month ago, she was big with your half brother— at least the midwife tells us she thinks it's a boy."

"Have you married her, or will this son be a bastard?" Jenna spat out, and Mac Ard's smile faltered.

"Marriage is . . . a tool," he answered slowly. "You know that, even if you don't like it. In my position, one should only use it at need."

"What about my mam's needs?"

"My heart is with Maeve, Jenna," he answered. "It will always be, whether I marry another woman or not. I don't know if you can believe that, but it's true and your mam knows it. And I know that my love is returned. She understands why I don't marry her; she also knows that I will always take care of her, as I'll take care of your brother when he's born. Despite what you might want to believe, I'm not a monster." He spread his hands wide as if he were about to embrace her, the cloch glinting in his right palm. "Give me Lámh Shábhála, freely, and I will also give you my promise that I *will* use the tool of marriage in a way that would please you. Your mam and my son, your half brother, would share my name. I would make her Banti-arna Mac Ard."

Jenna didn't answer but glanced at O'Deoradháin, and Mac Ard's gaze followed hers. "You're more resourceful than I'd thought, Inishlander," he said to O'Deoradháin. "I've underestimated you twice now. It won't happen again. I also see the way she looks at you. Poor Coelin would be jealous, I think, though I doubt his wife lets the young man out of her sight any more."

His regard came back to Jenna. "I'll let you and O'Deoradháin take this man's ship back to Inish Thuaidh," he told her, gesturing at Meagher's boat. "But Lámh Shábhála and Gairbith's cloch must be given to me. Now." He waited; Jenna only breathed, her mind whirling. "I need an answer, Jenna. You're not going to get a better offer. It's difficult, holding back bowstrings this long. I can see their fingers trembling. I'd hate to have one of them slip."

"You'll just kill us anyway," she said. "You would have killed me a few days ago."

Mac Ard shook his head. "Only if I'd had to. That time, I was defending myself from your attack and I seem to recall that it was you who struck first." He shrugged, and a faint smile appeared in the curl of his lips. "Aye, I'd kill you if it means saving myself. I don't apologize for that, either. If I wanted you *dead,* Jenna, I wouldn't be standing here talking with you. I'd have struck before you ever saw us."

"You can't leave us alive and go back to Tuath Gabair and the Rí, not with all these witnesses."

Mac Ard's empty hand gestured to the men surrounding them. "These are my personal gardai, loyal to me and not Rí Gabair," he responded. "They will see what I tell them to see. I don't have many options here, however. I can't take you back to Lár Bhaile with me—not after what you've done. For the Banrion's death alone your life is forfeit, and there are the gardai you killed afterward at the bridge and the death of Gairbith and his men. And there were those we sent into Doire Coill to look for you who never came back." He sighed, shaking his head. "All that would await you in Lár Bhaile is torture and an eventual execution; I couldn't stand the torment and sorrow that would bring to Maeve. But I *can* take Lámh Shábhála back and tell the Rí that I killed you and O'Deoradháin in battle, and no one will challenge that tale. Then you and the Inishlander can go to your island, once I have your vow that you'll stay there and never return here at all." His scarred head cocked toward her questioningly. "Well, Jenna? I offer you your life and your friend's as well as your mam's future, all in return for the clochs na thintrí you have. Is that not a fair enough trade?"

For a moment, Jenna considered the offer. She thought of how it would feel to take Lámh Shábhála from around her neck and give it to Mac Ard, to never hold it again, to never drink the addictive power of the magelights, to never see with its ferocious vision. To lose Lámh Shábhála forever. Jenna glanced again at O'Deoradháin and knew that he saw the answer in her eyes. She looked back at Mac Ard.

"No," she said.

And with the word, everything happened at once.

. . . Bowstrings sang as Jenna reached for Lámh Shábhála and opened it with a mental wrench. The arrows arcing toward O'Deoradháin burst into flame, the wooden shafts seared to quick ash, the barbed heads clattering on the stone flags. Lightnings crackled from Jenna's hands and she heard the screams from the gardai around her . . .

. . . O'Deoradháin opened his own cloch with a shout and sent a burst of hurricane wind toward Mac Ard even as the tiarna attacked with his own cloch. Their energy met in a thunderous maelstrom between them, but Mac Ard was stronger and O'Deoradháin was enveloped in snarling, flickering fury. He shouted once, a voice full of hurt and failure . . .

. . . Jenna saw O'Deoradháin fall to his knees and she struck with Lámh Shábhála as Mac Ard turned toward her. In the cloch-vision, she saw their two stones collide, like two giants formed of bright lightning wrestling with each other and grasping for holds. For several seconds, the tableau held, the power draining from their clochs with each moment. But slowly, slowly, Mac Ard's attack weakened under Lámh Shábhála's greater strength and endurance, giving way so suddenly that Jenna nearly stumbled herself. She could feel all the power spill from his cloch, and with her true eyes, she saw the tiarna fall. . . .

That quickly, it was over. Jenna released Lámh Shábhála, and the shock sent her to the ground, sitting abruptly on the stones. She fought to retain consciousness, not daring to fall into night as she had the last time. Darkness threatened to take her, her vision shrinking and the world seeming to recede as she fought to hold onto it, bringing consciousness back slowly: Meagher and his crewman cowering behind the single mast of his boat; the moans of Mac Ard's gardai; O'Deoradháin and Mac Ard both sprawled on the ground; the echo of thunder rumbling in the hills.

Jenna took a long, slow breath and pushed herself back up. She went to O'Deoradháin; he was breathing but unconscious. "O'Deoradháin?" she said, shaking him slightly, but he didn't wake. She took the long dagger from its scabbard at his waist, the keen edge ringing as it was unsheathed. "Come help me with him," she shouted to Meagher and the other man. When they didn't move, she lifted the cloch around her neck.

"Now!" she commanded, and they scrambled over the ship's side to her. "Put him aboard," she told the wide-

eyed and terrified fishermen. "You'll be taking us to Inish
Thuaidh, and be glad that I don't strike you down right
now for telling *them* we were here." A quick intake of
breath told her that she was right. "How much did Tiarna
Mac Ard pay you, Flynn Meagher? Tell me," she barked
into his frightened eyes.

"Four mórceints, mistress," he finally mumbled, his
head down.

"Then you've been paid in full and more. Take my companion to the ship." Meagher and the other man didn't
move, their heads still down as if they awaited an execu-
tioner's stroke. "Do it now!" she ordered, "And gently."

"Aye, mistress." Meagher and the other man lifted
O'Deoradháin carefully. As they placed him on the boat,
Jenna went to Mac Ard. She crouched beside him. He was
barely conscious; his eyes fluttered, and he seemed to almost smile. His hand still clutched at his cloch. "It seems
I've underestimated you as well, Jenna," he said. His eyes
moved to the dagger in her hand. He tried to lift his hand,
but it fell back to his chest. "At least make it quick."

She pressed the keen edge against the side of his neck
and blood drooled as Mac Ard inhaled and closed his eyes.
But she only held it there, and his eyes slowly opened
again. "Were you lying to me? Would you have let us go?"
she asked him. She showed him Lámh Shábhála. "You
know I can hear the truth, if I wish."

"It wasn't a lie," he answered. "I believe you're an
abomination and a great danger, but I would do nothing
that would hurt Maeve so much unless I had no other
choice."

She stared at his face, remembering the way he had
looked at her mam, remembering the softness when she'd
seen him sleeping with Maeve in his arms, back in Seancoim's caves. She pulled the dagger back and put it in her
belt. Then she reached down and wrapped the fingers of
her left hand around the chain of his cloch, pushing his
feeble hand away from the stone. "No," he moaned. His
lips were flecked with blood. "Ah, Jenna, don't do this.
Don't take the cloch. Think of how Lámh Shábhála is part

of you, how it would be like tearing away part of yourself
to lose it. Don't . . ."

She could see genuine fright in his eyes now, surprising
her. *Would I feel this way, if it were me laying on the ground
and Lámh Shábhála about to be taken from me?* With the
thought, a spear seemed to penetrate her heart, and she
gasped with imagined terror.

Aye, you would feel as he does, and worse . . .

"You knew I couldn't just give you Lámh Shábhála. You
knew I wouldn't be able to do that."

"I suspected it." His eyes went to her hand, still clutching
the chain of his cloch. "Now I know it." His gaze searched
her face. "I'm sorry, Jenna. I'm sorry you have to bear the
burden. I'm sorry I could not be your da for you."

"My *da?*" Jenna shouted in rage. "You could *never* be
my da!" Anger twisted her hand tight around the chain,
and with the rising fury she tore the cloch from around his
neck, the silver links parting as they ripped open his skin.

He screamed, a sound that held loss and terror, a wail
of grief and a shivering denial. His hands grasped for the
cloch, his eyes wide. *"No . . . !"* He was panting, and his
eyes were wild. "I'll kill you for this. I swear it!"

She stared down at him. "The next time we meet," she
told him, clutching his stone in her hand, "one of us *will*
die." The words came to her with a sense of truth, as if
she'd been given a glimpse of the future.

He moaned and shrieked, his eyes not on her but on the
cloch na thintrí she'd taken. Jenna turned and went to the
boat, trying not to listen to the mingled threats and pleas
he hurled at her back.

"Cast off," she told Meagher, and went to sit next to
O'Deoradháin, staring back at the village as the wind
snapped at the sail and bore them away.

37

The White Keep

S HE expected him to be angry. He wasn't. "You know it was a mistake to leave him alive," was all he said, his voice surprisingly gentle. "But you should know that in some ways, that was more cruel. He'll always feel the loss. Forever."

"They'll give him another Cloch Mór. Or he'll find one," Jenna answered.

O'Deoradháin nodded. "Aye, I agree. He will. And he will come after you with it, because you have wounded him—on the inside, where it will never heal."

She only nodded, her hand at her throat, and he smiled sadly at her. "You made the choice. You can't unmake it. And I'm not surprised that you couldn't find it in yourself to kill a helpless man." It was the last time he mentioned the incident.

The first night out, with the headland of the bay still to be rounded, the mage-lights began to glow. Meagher and his friend were watching, their gazes on the two and the mage-lights that were beginning to swirl above them. "You saw what the clochs can do at the village," Jenna told Meagher. She cradled her right arm, letting them see the patterns the lights had carved into her skin. "I'm telling you now that we can sense your intentions, also, while we're calling the mage-lights or even when we're sleeping. I *will* use the cloch if I feel threatened. Do you understand?"

They nodded silently, meek and terrified. Neither looked inclined to test the truth of Jenna's small lie. The mage-lights strengthened, their glow touching the waves with color.

"Jenna," O'Deoradháin said as Jenna steeled herself for the ordeal of filling Lámh Shábhála once again. "If you're willing, I'd like you to give me Mac Ard's cloch." She glanced at him, more quizzical than anything. "I'll give you Gairbith's in return," he added.

Jenna hesitated. "Why? They're both Clochs Mór."

"Because he'll come looking for *that* one," O'Deoradháin answered. "And I want him to come to me, not to someone who may not understand or may not be expecting him."

"Are you sure it's not just because he hurt you with it?"

O'Deoradháin shrugged. "And that, too."

Jenna handed the rubied stone to him. His mouth tightened as he bowed his head to take Gairbith's cloch from around his neck, and she heard him gasp as if stung when the chain was removed. "It's only Mac Ard's cloch in my other hand that lets me do this," he said as he handed the green stone to her. He was sweating, the lines of his face carved deep. "Even this hurts, though I held Gairbith's cloch for just a few days and have another cloch to immediately replace it. Take it from me, Jenna; I can't . . . I can't let it go."

Jenna reached over and pried his fingers from the stone until it dropped into her hand. O'Deoradháin took a long, shuddering breath, clutching Mac Ard's cloch to him. After a few minutes, he lifted his head again and shook it. Jenna could see tears in his eyes. "They told me during the training that no one could give up his cloch willingly. I always thought that was an exaggeration, but that was harder than I believed. I couldn't ever do that again," he said softly. "Never. If I'd kept the other cloch any longer, if I'd used it more . . ."

"Then fill Mac Ard's cloch now," Jenna told him. "Fill it and make it yours."

The mage-lights danced seductively, calling Jenna, and Lámh Shábhála's need tugged at her. She turned away from O'Deoradháin and looked up, lifting the cup of the cloch to the mage-lights to be filled.

*   *   *

The voyage took five days, hopping across the chain of small islands between Talamh an Glas and Inish Thuaidh. "There," O'Deoradháin said finally, pointing ahead across the choppy gray waves. "That's Inishfeirm. That's where we're going."

Jenna could see a gleam of brilliant white atop the blue-gray hump of the island, a white that shimmered in the pale sunlight filtered through thin gray clouds. As they approached the island, the patch resolved into stone towers perched precariously on the island's steep cliffs. A road wound back and forth from a village clustered around the sheltering arms of a bay up to the ornate and imposing structure on the heights. "The town of Inishfeirm, where your great-mam once lived," O'Deoradháin told her. The "town" looked small, larger than Ballintubber, certainly, but not as imposing as even Áth Iseal. "And the Order of Inishfeirm," O'Deoradháin continued, pointing to the high towers, "where I spent far too many years." He laughed at the memory. "Máister Cléurach will be surprised. It's been two years now I've been away, and I don't think he ever expected to see me again." He chuckled again, pointing. "There, see that dark speck making its way down the road? That's one of the Order's carriages—they've seen our ship and know it's not one of the island's, and have sent someone down to meet us."

A few stripes later, they pulled the ship up at the harbor, Meagher tossing a line to the crowd that had gathered to watch the strangers dock. Jenna thought their faces held suspicion and she saw O'Deoradháin glance up a few times at the buildings of the Order and frown, as if he spied something there that troubled him. But as they stepped onto the dock, the crowd suddenly parted and a blond-haired, dark-bearded man dressed in a clóca of pure white linen came striding toward them. He stopped, his face registering amazement and disbelief. "Ennis? Is that really you?"

"Mundy! By all the gods, you're as ugly as ever." The two men, laughing, met in the middle of the dock, hugging each other fiercely, kissing each other's cheeks. "So you're still here!"

"I am. I doubt you're going to believe this, but I'm now in charge of the acolytes—who'd have thought that someone as difficult as I was would end up having to herd the young ones and trying to keep them out of trouble."

"Who better? You know all the tricks, having done them yourself," O'Deoradháin laughed. "How's Máister Cléurach faring these days? And why aren't you holding one of the clochs by now?"

Mundy's expression turned somber at that. "Máister Cléurach's as well as can be expected, I suppose. These aren't good times for the Order."

"What do you mean? Is that why everyone is looking at us like we're tax collectors? With the mage-lights coming every night to the clochs now, I'd have thought—"

Mundy shook his head warningly, raising his hand. "This isn't anything to discuss here. I must ask you for some patience. In the meantime, you haven't introduced me." He glanced significantly at Jenna.

"This is Jenna Aoire," O'Deoradháin told him, and Jenna stepped forward. "Jenna, this is Mundy Kirwan, a Bráthair of the Order." O'Deoradham leaned toward Mundy, speaking softly so that only Jenna and Mundy could hear him. "She is the First, Mundy. She holds Lámh Shábhála; she brought the Filleadh."

Mundy's expression was simultaneously shocked and awed. "First Holder, I am honored. And Aoire . . ." He glanced again at O'Deoradháin with lifted eyebrows. "That's a name that's not unfamiliar here."

"I was told that my family was from here," Jenna told him. "A few generations ago."

Mundy nodded. "The Máister will undoubtedly want to meet with you immediately. Do you have belongings?"

O'Deoradháin lifted the pack he carried. "This is all."

"Then follow me. I'll take you up to the mountain, and we can get you rooms there . . ."

Mundy escorted them to the carriage, little more than a flat cart with wooden seats attached, open to the weather

without even the cover of an awning. A young boy in the
same white attire waited there with the two horses, though
the léine underneath his clóca was red, not white. Jenna
looked out curiously as they ascended the narrow, winding
switchback road up the steep hillside, more and more of
the panorama spreading out below them as they rose. The
sea was a rippling, shining carpet, dotted with a few nearby
tiny islands; well out to the north, stony cliffs blue with
distance rose on the horizon, the white line of distant
breakers underneath. "The shore of Inish Thuaidh,"
Mundy told her, noticing her gaze. "Those are the Bird
Cliffs. Thousands and thousands of seabirds nest there."

"I'd like to see that sometime."

"Perhaps you will." Mundy was sitting across from Jenna
and O'Deoradháin, his seat facing them. He turned back
from the scenery. "Aoire," he said, almost musingly, but
with an undertone that made Jenna's eyes narrow. "An
acolyte once stole a supposed cloch from the cloister and
ran away with a local girl. In at least one version I heard,
her family name was supposed to be Aoire."

Jenna glanced at O'Deoradháin. "We agreed that we
wouldn't try to hide anything from Máister Cléurach," he
told her. "And I trust Mundy."

The cart lurched in the ruts as they navigated one of the
tight hairpin turns of the road. Jenna felt a momentary
surge of irritation that O'Deoradháin would speak so
openly, but she forced it down, knowing that it was mostly
because she was uneasy about revealing the truth of how
she'd come to acquire the cloch. "Then maybe that version's the correct one," Jenna told Mundy. "Her name was
Kerys Aoire and she was my greatmam. And the cloch they
took was this." She pulled the stone out from under her
tunic. "This," she said, "is Lámh Shábhála."

"Lámh Shábhála . . ." Mundy breathed the word, leaning
forward to peer closely at the cloch. "So plain, compared
to the other ones. No wonder no one believed that it was
a true cloch na thintrí, or at best only a minor one. So we
did hold it for a time." An ironic smile touched his face.
"Máister Cléurach won't be pleased to hear that. Not after
what's happened here."

"What *has* happened?" O'Deoradháin asked. "There are marks on the walls of the central tower where it looks like fires have burned, and our reception was definitely cold."

"I'll let the Máister give you that news," Mundy responded. "It's nothing any of us like to talk about."

Máister Cléurach was a short, balding man with a fringe of snow-white hair that didn't seem to have been combed in days. He came bustling toward Jenna and O'Deoradháin between the desks of his two clerks. "Ennis!" There may have been pleasure in his shout, but Jenna couldn't see it in his face. The folds of his face settled comfortably in the lines of his frown. "By the Mother-Creator, I was certain we'd lost you. The last letter was a year ago . . ."

O'Deoradháin shrugged at the mild rebuke. "I wrote six months ago, and again three months ago as well, Máister. But the tuatha are unsettled, and who knows where those letters have gone."

"Aye, we know the tuatha are at war, and we know why." Máister Cléurach seemed to glare at O'Deoradháin as if he were the cause of it, and then the old man went to one of the arched, open windows of the cloister, staring back south and east over the waves.

"Máister Cléurach," O'Deoradháin said, "Mundy hinted that things aren't well here, and I saw marks on the walls. What's happened? Why aren't Mundy and you and some of the others holding clochs? The Order was founded to make cloudmages . . ."

The old man turned back into the room, blinking as if the pale light outside had blinded him. "Five months ago," he said slowly, "not long after the Solstice and just before the mage-lights heralded the Filleadh, ships carrying gardai came here out of Fallcarragh. When we realized that this was more than an unexpected visit, it was too late. The gardai wore the colors of both Tuath Infochla and Tuath Gabair. We closed the gates to the White Keep, thinking we could hold them in siege until help came from Rí Thuaidh, but we had acolytes who were from Infochla and Gabair and some of them betrayed us, opening one of the gates. The gardai came storming in, and though we de-

fended the cloister as well as we could, we're not trained
to fight. The betrayal of our acolytes went deeper—these
gardai also knew where the clochs na thintrí were kept."
The Máister sighed, his rheumy gray eyes flared. "They
took them all, Ennis. All."

"Máister . . ." O'Deoradháin breathed. "I didn't
know . . ."

Máister Cléurach grunted, interrupting him. "The clochs
na thintrí were all they were after. They fled as soon as
they had them, returned to their ships and sailed away.
When our Rí finally sent men and ships—too few of both,
and far too late—they were a fortnight gone. Then the
mage-lights began to appear everywhere in the sky, her-
alding the Filleadh, and we knew all hope to recover them
was lost. The Order may have the knowledge to teach
cloudmages, but now we have no clochs to give them." The
Máister's sour face regarded Jenna briefly, then returned
to rest on O'Deoradháin. "And what do you bring us,
Ennis, you who we sent out to find Lámh Shábhála? More
tales of failure, no doubt."

"I bring you Jenna Aoire," O'Deoradháin answered.
"The tale is hers."

"Aoire . . ." The word was a hissing intake of breath.
The clerks looked up from their work and Máister Cléurach's gaze returned to Jenna. He stared at her face. "Aye,
I see it now. The shape of your face, your eyes . . . You
could be an Aoire—a family whose fortunes, I must tell
you, have declined greatly in my time."

"My great-mam was Kerys Aoire," Jenna told the Máister, "and my great-da was an acolyte here named Niall,
though I don't know his surname."

Máister Cléurach visibly trembled as Jenna spoke, his
hands clenching together at his breast. "I know that tale
and those names, and I know Niall's surname," he answered. "I know because I was sent here as an acolyte the
following year, and the gossip about Niall Mac Ard was
fresh and new among the acolytes and Bráthairs, since
they'd known him."

"Mac Ard?" Jenna couldn't stop the words, which

stabbed her so that she could hardly breathe. "Niall was a Mac Ard?"

Máister Cléurach glared at her as if she were a dim-witted student. "Aye. That was his name. A well-known Riocha name in Tuath Infochla, and Gabair, too, where a Mac Ard was once Rí long ago. Most of our acolytes are Riocha. You would hear many famous names among them."

Jenna felt dizzy and nauseous. *My great-da was a Mac Ard . . . Did Padraic Mac Ard know that?* She glared at O'Deoradháin angrily. "You knew!" she said to him. "You knew and you didn't tell me."

He was shaking his head, and the confusion in his face seemed genuine. "No, Jenna. I swear I didn't. I knew the story, aye, but not the acolyte's surname . . . All that happened forty years before I came here as a boy. It was just an old cautionary tale given to the acolytes and Niall's last name was never mentioned. None of us were old enough to have known them, and the elder Bráthairs who might have been here then wouldn't talk about it."

"They were *told* not to talk about it," Máister Cléurach interrupted. "It was a foolish deed done by a naive young man that cost him his life, and what was important was that it not happen again, or we might lose one of the stones we knew were true clochs. What Niall stole was probably just a pebble and not a true cloch, and almost certainly not the cloch it was reputed to be."

"Máister," O'Deoradháin said, "Jenna is the First. The Holder of Lámh Shábhála."

The Máister's eyes widened in sudden realization and he frowned at her so harshly that Jenna took an involuntary step backward, her hand going to the cloch under her tunic. Her sleeve fell away, exposing the scars, and Máister Cléurach *huffed* once. He glanced back—the clerks were staring also, and he waved a hand at them. They scattered, leaving the room by the rear door as Máister Cléurach turned back to Jenna and O'Deoradháin. "Then . . ."

"Aye, Máister," O'Deoradháin told him. "The cloch Niall took was what it had been said to be."

"No . . ." Máister Cléurach protested, then his mouth snapped shut and his eyes narrowed. He seemed filled with a cold anger as he regarded Jenna again. "If you hold the cloch Niall Mac Ard stole from us, then Lámh Shábhála is not yours, but the Order of Inishfeirm's." He held out his hand, as if he expected her to place the stone there.

Jenna returned his glare. Her arm throbbed as she pulled the cloch out and forced the fingers of her right hand to close around it. She shut her eyes momentarily: no, there were no other clochs na thintrí here other than the ones she and O'Deoradháin carried. "Lámh Shábhála is its own," she told Máister Cléurach, "and it has chosen me."

His eyes stared greedily at the stone. "That is the cloch na thintrí I have had described to me. There is a record of it here: we have paintings and drawings of all the clochs na thintrí that were in our collection, and I recognize this— there was no other like it. So . . . *plain.*"

"And your Máister at the time thought the stories about the cloch being Lámh Shábhála were false, or that it was at best a minor stone," Jenna retorted. "That's what my great-mam believed; that was what Niall had told her."

"Indeed, that *was* Máister Dahlga's belief," Máister Cléurach responded. "He wasn't the most intelligent man and I heard him say that myself, but what else was he going to claim but that bit of wishful thinking? We thought the stone lost at sea—Niall's body was found a few days later on the coast of Tuath Infochla and brought back here; we believed your great-mam had suffered the same fate until two years ago, when we learned that she'd actually lived, and that her son—Niall's child—had left Tuath Infochla and traveled south. By then we also knew that mage-lights would return soon, and so we sent out some of the Brá- thairs to look for this offspring of Niall Mac Ard in case he still had the cloch that might be—" He stopped. His lips pressed together. "—that *was* Lámh Shábhála."

"You're mistaken if you believe you have any claim to Lámh Shábhála," Jenna told him. "Not after what my fami- ly's gone through. Not after what *I've* gone through." She looked at O'Deoradháin. "And I made a mistake coming here." She turned on the balls of her feet, ready to leave.

"Wait!" The note of panic in Máister Cléurach's voice halted Jenna in midstep. "Why did you bring Lámh Sháb-hála back here?"

O'Deoradháin answered. "She came to learn, Máister. She came because I told her that you would teach her to be a cloudmage, a Siúr of the Order. She came because this was her family's home and I told her that the Order would help her. If all that's wrong, and I've unintentionally lied to Jenna, then you can have my resignation. I'm leaving with her."

O'Deoradháin's rebuke put color in Máister Cléurach's cheeks. His chest expanded as if he were about to shout something in return, then he let the breath out with a sigh. "I'm sorry," he said simply. His hands opened in a gesture of apology, then fell to his sides. He sat on the edge of one of the desks, slumping. "I'm sorry," he said again. "It's just that it's all gone, everything Máister after Máister worked for over the centuries. *He* knows—" Máister Cléurach pointed to O'Deoradháin—"but do you? Do you know why the Order of Inishfeirm came to be?"

Jenna shook her head, silent, still half-turned away.

"Come with me, then," he said. He started to walk toward the door through which his clerks had gone, then stopped at the door when he realized that Jenna wasn't following. "It will be easier if you see," he told her. "I promise you that it's not a trap." He held the door open.

Reluctantly, with another glance at O'Deoradháin, she went through.

38

The Vision of Tadhg

THEY walked down a corridor of marble flags. Twin rutted hollows were worn in the hard stone, unpolished and stained: the marks of countless sandaled feet over countless years. Jenna realized then just how old the White Keep was. The halls of the Order were quiet; the conversations that drifted from the open doors they passed were whispered and hushed. Even the laughter she heard once had the sense of being muffled and held back. The occasional acolytes and Bráthairs—no females, Jenna noticed—they met in their walk gave a quick bow of obeisance to the Máister, but Jenna felt their eyes on her, curious and wondering.

They came finally to a set of ornate, twin doors of bronze, the metal cast with curling flourishes and spirals that Jenna knew all too well: the same lines that marked her arm. Máister Cléurach pushed the doors open and beckoned to her to enter.

The room was large, with columns of polished marble in two rows down either side. At the end of the hall was a huge statue, easily twenty feet high, larger than any carving Jenna had ever seen: the figure of a man, elderly yet still vital. He was a seeming giant, his clóca white and flowing as if in some unseen breeze, his skin tanned, the eyes a startling blue under grayish, thin hair. He seemed to look directly at them, his expression solemn yet pleasant. His right arm was raised, the fingers curled into a fist as if he held something, and on the dome above him were painted

the hues of the mage-lights, dancing in a black sky dotted
with stars. For a moment, Jenna couldn't breathe, staring
at the colossus. "Go on," Máister Cléurach told her.
"Look closer . . ."

Jenna walked down the wide corridor between the columns, her footsteps echoing loudly. The gaze of the statue
seemed to follow her, watching her as she approached. It
was only when she reached the railing set a few yards before the statue that its regard left her. "Go up to him,"
Máister Cléurach said. "Touch him." She could hear Máister Cléurach and O'Deoradháin following behind. She went
to the statue, her head reaching only halfway to his knee.
She spread her left hand on the leg, expecting to feel cold,
painted marble.

The leg was warm, and the flesh seemed to yield under
her touch. She drew her hand back with a gasp, half-
expecting the giant to be looking down at her with a sar-
donic grin. "That is the founder of our order and its first
Máister—Tadhg O'Coulghan, Holder of Lámh Shábhála
and the da of Severii O'Coulghan, who would be the Last
Holder." Jenna could hear amusement in Máister Cléurach's voice. "And no sculptor carved this image of him.
No, the chisel was Lámh Shábhála, the marble the stuff of
the mage-lights, and the artist Severii. He made this image
of his da with the dying power of the cloch in the last days
of the mage-lights." Máister Cléurach gave a soft laugh. "It
startles all the acolytes in the same way, the first time they
touch it. The statue has remained warm and soft and life-
like for over seven centuries now."

"I've never seen anything to equal it," Jenna said. She
touched the statue again, wonderingly. The detail was ex-
quisite: the pores of the skin, the fine hair of the legs. She
almost expected to feel the pulse of blood under her hand.

"Tadhg saw that the clochs na thintrí were being used
primarily as weapons, that the possession and holding of
them was the cause of dissent and war and death." Máister
Cléurach continued, his voice reverberating from the dome
above them. "He believed that they should be used not as
weapons, but as tools. He and a few followers built the
White Keep, using the powers of their clochs to create the

buildings, erecting in a few years the work it would have
taken hundred of laborers and artisans a dozen years or
more to create. Yet as the Holder of Lámh Shábhála, he
also could sense that the mage-lights were beginning to
weaken, that the time was approaching when they would
die completely and the power in the clochs would vanish
with them. He was right, for that would happen in his son
Severii's holding. Tadhg felt that there must be a reposi-
tory, a place where knowledge of the clochs and how to
use them could be kept alive over the long centuries of
their sleeping. That was the public task of the Order—to
keep safe the old knowledge, to be the place where the
Riocha and others would come to learn the ways of the
cloudmage."

"The Order's *public* task," Jenna said, emphasizing the
word, and Máister Cléurach nodded as if pleased.

"Aye, and as you suggest, there was also a private task.
Tadhg envisioned the Order gathering to it most of the
clochs na thintrí after their magic was gone and forgotten.
That, he knew, would be impossible at first, but as the years
and decades passed and the clochs were given to sons and
daughters, and then given to their sons and daughters, they
would become pretty jewels, their power forgotten or dismissed. Then, Tadhg believed, they could be bought or acquired in other ways—when a tiarna sent his son or
daughter here to be an acolyte of the Order, one condition
was that the child be given the family's Cloch Mór, should
they possess one. And if that acolyte took the vows of the
Order, then the cloch would be passed on not within the
family but into the Order. As Tadhg perceived it, long centuries later when the Filleadh came, it would be those of
the Order who held the majority of the Clochs Mór. It
would be the Order that created the cloudmages. It would
be the Order that ensured that the wars and strife and
fighting didn't happen again. It would be the Order that
put together a better world, one where the clochs na thintrí
were used not for death and fighting, but for life."

Jenna glanced up again at the statue, at the face of
Tadhg, imagining him saying those words. It was easy to
visualize that kindly face speaking. The words awakened

an echo inside her. Yet . . . "That's an admirable goal,"
she said. "But not an easy one. And 'better' for whom?
The Riocha? That's who holds the clochs, that's who send
their children to the Order, so even if the clochs hadn't
been stolen, you'd have been making cloud-mages of Riocha, and war is exactly what they've always used them for."

Máister Cléurach took a long breath yet didn't answer.
"This way," he said. "There's more to see."

They went out from Tadhg's Hall and back to the corridor. Máister Cléurach stopped before another door, this
one simple, thick wood. "Try to open it," he said.

Jenna glanced at him, but went to the bronze handle of
the door and pushed, then pulled. The door rattled in its
frame but wouldn't open. "It's locked," she said.

"Keep trying."

"Máister," O'Deoradháin interjected, but Máister Cléurach raised his hand, finger to lips.

"It's nothing *you* didn't try, Ennis. Let her."

Jenna looked at O'Deoradháin; he shrugged. Jenna
pushed and pulled again at the door, then again. The third
time, there was a *snap* and sudden pain like quick sharp
knives ran up her arm. "*Ow!*" she exclaimed, stepping back
and shaking her hand, which still tingled.

Máister Cléurach's expression was solemn, but she
thought she saw amusement in his eyes. "Most acolytes try
the door at one time or another," he said. "The truly persistent and curious are the ones who feel it, is that not so,
Ennis?"

"Aye, Máister," O'Deoradháin answered. " 'Tis."

Máister Cléurach placed his hand on the door. Jenna
heard him start to speak, then he stopped and removed his
hand. "You know the word, don't you, Ennis?"

O'Deoradháin took a step back, his eyes a bit wide. "No,
Máister. How would I . . . ?"

Máister Cléurach snorted derisively. "Don't treat me like
a fool, Ennis O'Deoradháin. I'm not as blind as some of
you Bráthairs might think."

With a glance at the old man, O'Deoradháin put his hand
against the wooden planks and spoke a soft word that
Jenna could not hear. A violet light glimmered around his

ringers. The door swung silently open. "The ward was placed on the door by Tadhg himself," Máister Cléurach said. "And 'tis no less strong now than when *I* was shocked by it, many years ago." He nodded toward O'Deoradháin. "The opening word is at best an open secret. Only the Máister, the Librarian, and the Keeper are supposed to know it, but acolytes and Bráthairs have sharp ears, and some elders aren't as careful as they might have been. Eh, Ennis?"

O'Deoradháin blushed and said nothing.

The room they entered was a library, Jenna realized, far bigger than the small chamber in the keep at Lár Bhaile, the interior airy with light from windows in the east and west walls, and filled with three rows of long tables. The smell of musty parchment filled the air, and scrolls sat in wooden notches along the south wall, while the north wall held leather-bound flat volumes. Also along the north wall was a large wooden cabinet. Its doors hung askew, torn from their hinges. An elderly Bráthair sat at a desk at the front of the room, a parchment spread out in front of him. As they entered, he bowed to the Máister and left the room, his right leg dragging the floor as if he could not bend the knee or move the limb easily.

"This room is where the knowledge of the Order is written down and kept," Máister Cléurach told Jenna. He walked over to the ruined cabinet. Shoving aside the broken doors, he pulled out one of several trays. She could see that the tray was lined with black velvet and separated into several compartments, all of them empty. Jenna heard O'Deoradháin suck in a breath as the Máister displayed the tray to them. "And here . . . Here was where our clochs na thintrí were stored: behind the locked and warded Library door, and the doors of this cabinet were warded with slow magics as well."

Máister Cléurach dropped the tray onto one of the tables. The sound was loud and startling. "Tadhg O'Coughan's vision was a long one and correct," he continued. "We *did* acquire many of the Clochs Mór over the centuries, and we kept the knowledge and we held to his dream." His fist slammed against the table. "And it was all taken

away. Stolen just before Tadhg's future came to fruition."
He glanced at them, his voice bitter, his mouth twisted.
"The same acolytes who betrayed us let the invaders into
this room, knowing the word as you did, Ennis. Librarian
Maher was badly injured resisting the gardai; you noticed
that he still hasn't fully recovered. Keeper Scanlan died of
his wounds that night. The acolytes and Bráthairs resisted
as well as they could with sword and slow magics, and
twelve of them died in the hall outside. The raiders took
the clochs, all of them. I suppose I should be grateful that
they left the books and scrolls or that they didn't set fire
to the library as they fled. But this . . . this was enough.
You've seen the consequences."

"I wondered," O'Deoradháin said. "I wondered why
there seemed to be so many Clochs Mór with the tuatha.
Now I know why. Tiarna Mac Ard and the Rí Gabair, or
perhaps the Tanaise Ríg—they must have planned this not
long after the mage-lights appeared in Tuath Gabair."

"Aye," the Máister nodded. "The clochs are again in the
hands of the Riocha, and again they are used for war."

Máister Cléurach shook himself from reverie, standing
again and rubbing fingers through the fringe of unruly
white hair. For the first time, the frown lifted from his face,
though he did not smile. "I will teach you, Jenna Aoire,"
he said. "I will teach you to be the cloudmage who holds
Lámh Shábhála."

"You'd teach a woman?" she asked, remembering the
acolytes she'd seen.

"In Tadhg's time and Severii's, when the clochs na thintrí
were still active, we had female acolytes here, and Siúrs of
the Order. Not many, true, but some of the Holders were
women—for Lámh Shábhála as well as other clochs, as you
must know. Aye, we would teach them. It was only after,
when the mage-lights had stopped, that we also stopped
accepting women into the Order. So few were sent us then
and so few came here on their own . . ." Máister Cléurach
shrugged. "Eventually habit or circumstance becomes the
rule, and rule tradition. But tradition broken is also soon
forgotten."

His hands seemed old and tired as he picked up the

empty tray and slid it back into its place in the cabinet. He pushed the broken doors together. "At least they didn't get Lámh Shábhála," he said. "Stay, and I will teach you what is in the books here. You will become a Siúr of the Order."

"And Lámh Shábhála?" Jenna asked. "The cloch my great-da stole?"

"You're its Holder and the cloch is yours," Máister Cléurach replied. "I would be pleased to have the First Holder also be a cloudmage of the Order." He gave her a rueful smile. "It seems you'll be the only one."

Jenna looked at O'Deoradháin, knowing what she wanted to do and wondering if he knew as well. He nodded to her. "Not the only one," Jenna told the Máister. "Ennis . . . ?"

O'Deoradháin pulled his cloch from under his clóca. The ruby facets gleamed in the light streaming into the library from the windows facing west and the lowering sun. "This isn't the cloch you sent me to find, Máister," he said. "But I hold the Cloch Mór that was once held by the Mac Ards of Tuath Gabair."

"And this . . ." Jenna reached into the pouch at her belt, bringing out the sea-foam green jewel that Tiarna Gairbith had once possessed. "This is another Cloch Mór, though I don't know its long history." She placed it on the table in front of Máister Cléurach. "I give it to the Order to do with as you will. Consider it payment for my tuition, and a small compensation for what my great-da took."

39

Training

IT was harder than Jenna imagined.

"Máister Cléurach is an excellent mentor," O'Deorad-háin told her the first day. "*If* you can stand him." That wasn't an exaggeration. The Máister had an encyclopedic knowledge of the lore of the clochs na thintrí and was seemingly able to cail up in his mind the pages of the entire library of the Order, but he was also sometimes impatient with Jenna, who became his only student. He was initially exasperated by the fact that Jenna could neither read nor write. At first he refused to go further until she learned her letters, then a few minutes later reversed himself after finding that Jenna's memory was quick, facile, and reliable.

"I suppose the Holder of Lámh Shábhála deserves differ-ent treatment than a common acolyte," he said grudgingly. "If you weren't halfway intelligent, you'd already be dead." It was as close to a compliment as she was to receive for the next several weeks.

The first day, looking at a scroll filled with the bright, painted images of clochs na thintrí, she let the scroll roll itself up once more and she held up her own cloch to his eyes. "Why didn't you know for certain that this was Lámh Shábhála, since the first two Máisters of the Order both had held this cloch themselves? For that matter, why didn't Lámh Shábhála get passed on to each of the Máisters in turn? I don't understand."

"You need patience," he replied. "The answers will come in time, when they will make the most sense to you."

"I want the answers now," she persisted.

"I'm the teacher, you're the student. I will determine when you're ready, what you'll learn, and when."

"Aye, I'm the student. And it's *my* duty to tell you when I don't understand something so that you can explain. Don't put me off with platitudes and pleas for patience. When I ask questions, tell me what you know or tell me that you *don't* know."

"You're an arrogant young lady."

"And you're a crotchety old man who is used to easily cowing the boys who are sent to you because you look sour and mean. Your appearance and reputation aren't going to frighten me, Máister Cléurach. A year ago, I might have been as terrified as any of them, but not now. Here's one thing I've learned in that time: when someone refuses to answer me, they either don't know the answer to my question or they're deliberately withholding it for reasons of their own. Which is it for you, Máister?"

They glared at each other for a few breaths, then Máister Cléurach snorted. "The Holders of Lámh Shábhála evidently have their obstinate streak in common," he said. "As well, evidently, as a tendency to view the world in dualities. One thing I hope you learn here is that things are more complicated than that. You're seeing conspiracies when the truth is more innocent and banal."

He shook his head, rapping his fingernails on the table a few times before continuing. "Here's your answer: Severii O'Coulghan was not Tadhg. Though he did serve as Máister here, which was his da's dying wish, the truth is that he didn't share Tadhg's sweeping vision for the Order. The clochs went dead late in his Holding, and Lámh Shábhála finally died a year or two afterward. Had Tadhg been the Holder then, he would certainly have given Lámh Shábhála to the Order as the ultimate prize of its collection. Then, when the mage-lights returned, we would have seen them shining *here* over Inishfeirm and known that the time of the Filleadh was approaching. We would have had Lámh Shábhála to protect us if raiders came to plunder the clochs. Severii had the cloch, though, not Tadhg. Rather than treasuring the cloch for the Order, he gave Lámh Shábhála as a gift to his lover." Máister Cléurach gave a sniff of derision. "Lámh Shábhála is not the most beautiful or most striking of jewels, as you know," he continued. "If anything, it's rather plain. And love, as you may also know, is an emotion that can fade and die like the mage-lights. Severii's lover one day abruptly left the island never to be seen again. With him went Lámh Shábhála."

Jenna's face must have shown confusion. *"Him?"*

Máister Cléurach shrugged. "Life is complicated," he replied simply and continued his tale. "No doubt Lámh Shábhála was eventually given away or lost or misplaced as something not particularly valuable. When Severii was asked by the librarian for a description of Lámh Shábhála, so that it could be painted and written down in our books . . ." Máister Cléurach went to one of the shelves and pulled down one of the bound volumes.

"The Book of Lámh Shábhála," he said, placing it before Jenna. He opened the stiff leather cover, the smell of dust and old paper wafting over Jenna. His bony forefinger pointed to an illustration on the first page: a cloch held in someone's hand: caged in silver wire; whorled with emerald-green and mottled gold; the size of a duck's egg and glinting as if transparent and full of hidden depths. Jenna could see hints of the actual stone in the representation, but this was Lámh Shábhála magnified and made far more jewellike than the reality.

"Obviously, that's *not* Lámh Shábhála," Máister Cléurach said. "Perhaps Severii deliberately lied to the artisan— wanting to make the loss of the cloch and his lover all the more poignant. Or it's possible that the artisan, knowing that this was Lámh Shábhála, the greatest of the clochs, could not see it as . . . well . . . plain, and Severii obviously never contradicted that image. So when a rather ordinary-looking stone reputed to be Lámh Shábhála *did* come back to the Order, you can understand why my predecessors doubted the identification when they looked here. That's also why, when your great-da stole it, Máister Dahlga could believe that it was a false cloch that had been lost, not Lámh Shábhála."

"I do understand," Jenna said. "And is what's written in this book also false?"

"In this book is written all that Tadhg and Severii told us of Lámh Shábhála, and all that we have learned since. Some of it is undoubtedly untrue or exaggerated or rumor; other portions are certainly true. You'll help us revise this at the same time you're learning from it."

"I have another question," Jenna said, and Máister Cléurach sighed audibly, though he said nothing, waiting. "Sometimes, when I've used Lámh Shábhála, I've heard the voices of all of its Holders. Some of them have spoken of a test, 'Scrúdú,' they call it. What is that?"

Máister Cléurach sighed. His fingers brushed the parchment where the false image of Lámh Shábhála was painted. "The Scrúdú . . ." he breathed. "Not all Holders need to know that."

"That's not an answer, Máister."

He glared at her, but continued. "Right now, Lámh Shábhála is like a Cloch Mór, more powerful and with more abilities than any of those, aye, but still a Cloch Mór. Many Holders have been content with that, and spent their years with the cloch that way. No one will think less of you if you do the same."

"Finish your answer, Máister. Please."

He snorted in irritation. "A few, a *few* Holders have found the full depths of Lámh Shábhála's power. To do so, they must first pass the trial they call the Scrúdú. I will tell you this, Holder Aoire: most who try fail."

"And if they fail?"

"If they're lucky, they die," Máister Cléurach replied. His stare was unblinking and cold. "If you believe that to be overdramatic, I assure you it's not."

"Is this Scrúdú in your book?"

"It's mentioned, but neither Tadhg or Severii ever risked the challenge. But the process, the way to begin and what happens then . . ." He shrugged. "*They*—the voices in the stone—will tell you later if you're foolish enough to make the attempt. I would advise you to first *learn* something about being a cloudmage."

Jenna started to speak, but Máister Cléurach closed the book sharply, surprising her so much that her mouth snapped shut again. Dust rose from the pages, so heavy that Jenna had to turn her head and sneeze. "You've used up your quota of questions for a month, Holder Aoire. If you have no interest in the lore we have to give you, you're welcome to leave. If not, then henceforth you'll learn *when* I'm ready to teach and not before. Is that quite clear?"

He glared at her, his head turned sideways, looking so stern that Jenna suddenly felt compelled to laugh. "Aye," she told him, as his face softened slightly in response to her laughter. "I suppose I can work on my patience."

Máister Cléurach might be old, but he was hardly decrepit. If anything, his stamina was greater than Jenna's. The schedule over the next weeks quickly fell into routine: every morning, O'Deoradháin would wake her by knocking on the door of her small cell, located near Máister Cléurach's own rooms. She broke her fast with O'Deoradháin in the same dining hall as the other acolytes and Bráthairs. O'Deoradháin then escorted her to the library, where she and Máister Cléurach worked until sundown.

Máister Cléurach had given over his other duties and students; Jenna's instruction was now his only task. She learned about the clochs na thintrí: their history, their behavior, their quirks, how previous Holders had dealt with handling their power. She was shown meditations that helped her deal with the pain of her interaction with the mage-lights, she was guided through the bright landscape she saw when she looked at the world through Lámh Shábhála's eyes. She and Máister Cléurach pored over the texts left by previous Holders of Lámh Shábhála, and Jenna realized that she had only touched on the surface of the cloch's abilities. As Máister Cléurach had said, some of what was stated in the book was false, but much more of it illuminated pathways within the cloch that Jenna had not even guessed at. The Máister pushed her and prodded her, never letting her rest, taking her past what she thought were her physical and mental limits, never accepting less than her best effort.

"Was he this way with you?" she asked O'Deoradháin after a particularly grueling day. "After all, he expected *you* to hold Lámh Shábhála had you found it. Did he drive

you like this?" They were standing on a balcony of one of
the White Keep's towers, overlooking the crags and cliffs
atop which the cloister perched. The houses and buildings
of the village were a collection of dots far below already
in deepening shadow. Only the upper rim of the sun was
still visible, the clouds above burning molten gold and rose,
the waves of the sea tipped with shimmering orange. A
sparkling column of wind sprites lifted from the cliffs halfway down the mountain, and several seals had hauled out
of the sea, roaring and honking where the waves crashed
foaming onto black rocks.

"Consider it a good sign," O'Deoradháin grinned. "He's
hardest on the ones he feels have the most potential. The
time to worry is when he's easy on you."

"You still haven't answered my question. Was he this
hard on you?"

O'Deoradháin smiled again. "That would be telling,
wouldn't it?" Jenna laughed and his smile grew broader.
"I knew you could do that," he said.

"Do what?"

"Laugh. Enjoy yourself."

Jenna felt herself blushing, and she glanced down toward
the village so that she wouldn't have to look at him. Her
flight from Lár Bhaile now seemed ages ago, and over the
intervening months her feelings toward O'Deoradháin had
been slowly changing: from suspicion and caution to grudg-
ing admiration, to friendship, to . . . she didn't know how
to term what she felt now. *Or perhaps you're simply afraid
to give it a name, for all manner of reasons* . . . Below, the
seals were leaping into the waves, one after another, dozens
of them. "Are those blue seals?" Jenna asked to shift the
subject, but O'Deoradháin moved closer to her to peer over
the balcony's stone railing. She could feel the heat of his
body against her side.

"I don't think so," he said. "Just the normal harbor seals.
There's a family of blues here, but they're usually on the
other side of the island."

"Are they . . . ?"

"The ones I first swam with?" he finished for her softly.
"No. That was on Inish Thuaidh itself. But I've been with

this group, when I felt the need. They know me, and Garrentha, who saved you at Lough Glas, is one of the Inishfeirm family." His hand touched hers on the railing—her right hand. She didn't move away this time. His fingers interlaced with hers, pressing gently. Though the fingers of that hand, as always, moved only stiffly and with some pain, she pressed back. "Jenna . . ." he began, but his voice trailed off. The throng of wind sprites rose in the darkening air, chattering in their high voices as they swarmed past Jenna and O'Deoradháin before darting around the bulge of the tower.

"What were you going to say, Ennis?" Jenna asked, and O'Deoradháin chuckled. "What?" she said into his laughter.

"I think that may be the first time you've called me by my given name."

She smiled back at him. "Is that wrong? Is that too familiar for you?"

"No," he answered, still smiling. "I like the way you make it sound."

They were still holding hands. "Ennis . . ." she began, and this time the tone was different.

"I know. You don't have to say it."

Her eyes searched his. "What do you know?"

"I'm a bit too old for you. A bit too strange. A bit . . ." He shrugged. He let her hand fall away from his grasp. "I understand all that. Truly. But I hope you know that I will always be your ally. When you need my cloch to stand with you against the other Clochs Mór—and I don't think that can be avoided—I will be there."

He started to turn away. She reached out with her left hand and touched his arm. "Wait, Ennis."

His head tilted, his gaze questioned. Jenna reached up for him, slowly, wondering at the gesture even as she made it. She brought his head down to hers. The kiss, when it came, was softer and sweeter than she expected, and longer. There wasn't the bruising urgency there'd been with Coelin; there also wasn't the awkwardness. This was deeper and stronger.

It was more frightening.

The fright overwhelmed her. She turned her head, breaking off the kiss. His breath was warm at her ear. She heard him swallow.

"I'm sorry, Jenna," he said. "I shouldn't have . . ."

"Tell me that you have no more secrets, Ennis."

A quiet, tentative laugh. "None that I know of."

"Then tell me that you won't hurt me the way Coelin did."

His arms closed tight around her, pressing her close. "Not the way he did, no. I can't promise that I'll never hurt you, Jenna. But I'll promise that I'll love you, for as long as you want me."

"Ennis . . ." She didn't know how to say it, to tell him how scared she was of this, how confused. How she didn't—couldn't—trust her own feelings, not after Coelin's betrayal. That the things he had told her about himself *did* matter, even if she said they didn't. Her heart pounded against her ribs as if shaking the cage of its confinement; her pulse throbbed in her temples, and the pain of her arm came again, making her close her eyes. She shook her head. "I'm not ready . . . I don't know . . ."

He nodded. She could see the hurt in his eyes. His hands left her. "Ah," he said. He tried to smile. "I understand," he said. "I do."

She wanted to explain it all to him, but she had no words.

The seals called plaintively below them, and the sun's disk slipped below the line of the sea.

40

The Rí's Request

"JENNA?"

The knock on the door was tentative, and the husky whisper was that of Ennis. Jenna blinked sleepily. It was dark in the room, though dawn was just beginning to paint the sky. Jenna reluctantly put the covers aside and drew her night robe closer around her in the cold air as she sat up.

After their conversation a few days before, she'd hoped he might come to her, that he might begin the conversation again, that he might kiss her and she would let herself open to him. She'd also feared the same thing, not knowing what she wanted. There was an awkwardness now when they were together, when their arms accidentally brushed. She wanted to be next to him; she was frightened to get too near. *Not now. Not this way* . . . she thought as she moved to the door. *No! Let him in. You want the feel of his body on yours, his mouth* . . . another part of her shouted. She opened the grille in the center of the door and peered through, and all the voices inside died as she saw his face.

"Ennis? What's the matter?"

Ennis' face, candlelit, filled the opening on the other side of the grille, serious and unsmiling. "Máister Cléurach would like to see us in his rooms immediately."

"What's wrong?"

His lips twitched under the beard. "Nothing's *wrong*. We have . . . a visitor. A Riocha from Inish Thuaidh, from the

Rí's court in Dún Kiil. He's on his way up from the village;
a runner was sent ahead to alert us."

Jenna felt her stomach lurch. *You can't escape the politics, even here* . . . "I'll be there as soon as I'm dressed."

Her stomach settled, and the voices returned. She could
do it; she could unlatch the door, let him slip inside . . .
But Ennis gave her no chance to act on the impulse.

"Good. I'll tell Máister Cléurach that you're on your
way. Quickly!" With that, Ennis turned, and she saw the
yellow glow of his candle moving off down the corridor.

Máister Cléurach glanced up from his desk as they entered. One of the acolytes was already there with a tray of
tea and scones, placing it on a table to one side of the
room. He bowed out as Máister Cléurach waved toward
the tray, taking a sip from his own cup. If Máister Cléurach
knew about the attraction between Ennis and Jenna, he
gave no indication, though he looked at them strangely,
standing close but not too close to each other. "Have some
tea. Get yourselves warm and awake."

"Who'd they send, Máister?" Ennis asked.

A single shoulder lifted. "The runner didn't know. All
he said was that it was a tiarna who claimed to be here at
the Rí's request. And who was anxious enough to get here
that he crossed the water at night. He'll be here soon; I've
been told the carriage is already at the main gate."

Jenna cupped her right hand around the welcome
warmth of the steaming mug. "What does he want?"

"There are still other allegiances among the Bráthairs
and acolytes," Máister Cléurach answered. "We haven't
been able to eradicate all the spies among us. I'm certain
that rumors have left the White Keep and gone to Inish
Thuaidh as well as the mainland, saying that the Holder of
Lámh Shábhála was here. At least our visitor's from Thuaidh and not another troopship from one of the tuatha. I'd
hoped to have another few weeks to prepare before this
started, but it would seem—"

There was a knock at the door. Máister Cléurach sighed.
"Would you let him in, Ennis?"

There were a quartet of people in the corridor: three

gardai in blue and white, and one other who stepped in through the open door, leaving the gardai behind.

It wasn't a him. It was a woman.

She was tall, with long white-blonde tresses trailing from underneath a hood the color of spring grass, and Jenna decided that the woman was older than Maeve by several years. Her large eyes were the same deep green as her overcloak, dominating a round face networked with fine wrinkles. She shrugged out of the overcloak and tossed it uncaringly over the nearest chair. Her clóca was a lighter shade of green and finely embroidered; the léine underneath snowy white. An ornate, thick torc of beaten gold hung around her neck, and rings adorned her fingers. Máister Cléurach came hurrying from behind his desk to greet her, and to Jenna's surprise, bowed low as he approached. "Banrion," he said. "I would not have thought that Rí MacBrádaigh would send *you* on this errand."

"I insisted, Máister Cléurach," the woman said. "Or do you think that the return of the Holder of Lámh Shábhála to Inish Thuaidh isn't important enough for me?" Her voice was pleasant and low with a hint of amusement just below the surface. But there was a careful posturing to her tone and stance, as if she kept her emotions well concealed and intended them to remain so. She glanced at Jenna and Ennis, and Máister Cléurach coughed.

"My pardon, Banrion. This is Holder Jenna Aoire and Ennis O'Deoradháin, both cloudmages of the Order." Jenna, startled at the title given her, looked quickly at Máister Cléurach, but his eyes told her to say nothing. He nodded at the woman. "And this is Banrion Aithne MacBrádaigh, wife of the Rí Thuaidh, lonhar MacBrádaigh."

The woman's verdant gaze rested on Ennis for a breath, then went to Jenna, cool and appraising. Jenna, unlike Ennis, didn't politely lower her head, meeting the woman's eyes. "Ah," the Banrion said with a slight twist of her lips. "So very young. I expected someone older and more . . ." she paused, as if considering the next word, ". . . sinister in appearance," she finished. "For being the Mad Holder who gleefully murders Banrions, you look innocent enough."

Jenna flushed, taken aback. For a moment, she could not

speak at all though her mouth opened in protest as Banrion
MacBrádaigh continued to stare at her. "That wasn't my
intention. Truly. Banrion Cianna was ill and weaker than I
thought. I wish it hadn't happened."

The Banrion gave a slight nod at Jenna's protest. "Then
the rumors of the destruction of the bridge to Rí Gabair's
Keep and the death of twenty or so gardai are, no doubt,
exaggerated as well. Or were also not intended."

"There is some exaggeration there, aye, Banrion." Jenna
blinked. "But I won't deny there was also intention—it was
my life or theirs. I chose mine."

Again the lips curled in a slight smile. "A choice most
of us would make, I think. So you *are* more complicated
than you appear." The heat on Jenna's face increased as
the Banrion's gaze dropped to Jenna's right arm. "The
marks of the Holder . . . May I see Lámh Shábhála?"

Her tone held the expectation of obedience. Reluctantly,
Jenna pulled the cloch out from under her léine. The Banrion took a step toward her and leaned closer to examine
it, but made no move to touch the stone. After a few moments, she stepped back again. "It's plainer than I would
have thought."

"That's an oversight others have made," Jenna answered,
"mistaking an ordinary appearance for weakness."

The Banrion laughed aloud, clapping her hands twice,
the sound loud in the cold morning. "And you have a bite
to your words as well. Excellent. I can understand how that
fool Torin Mallaghan managed to underestimate and lose
you. He may be Rí Gabair, but he holds his title mostly
for his name, not his ability. And that woman he married.
My niece's blood was more her mam's than that of my
brother." The Banrion laughed again at the expression on
Jenna's face. "Aye, Cianna was my niece. Rí Mallaghan
thought that perhaps it might be a good alliance; as usual,
he was mistaken. You needn't worry, Holder. I had no love
for her conniving, scheming soul. But you might be advised
to avoid my brother; a da's love for his daughter is less
objective, I'm afraid."

She turned from Jenna back to Máister Cléurach. "The
Rí requests that you and your cloudmages appear at the

court. There are . . . implications that must be discussed. The Comhairle of Tiarna will be meeting in Dún Kiil in a fortnight, and they are anxious to meet the First Holder. As you might expect, there are complications to Holder Aoire being here in Inish Thuaidh, and we've already received open threats from Tuatha Gabair, Infochla, and Connachta, insisting that she be returned to them for various crimes committed in their territories." Aithne smiled thinly. "I don't think any of us are fooled as to the actual reason they'd like to have the Holder. It's the prize she wears, not her that they want."

This time Máister Cléurach lifted his head. "The Order is not subject to the Rí's commands," he told the Banrion. "That's clear in Severii's Charter, as I'm certain the Banrion is aware."

"I'm aware of the charter, Máister," Aithne answered calmly, "even if a charter seven centuries and more old is hardly relevant to today's situation, and I suspect the signatures at that time were made more under duress than by actual agreement with Severii's desires. I said it was a request, not a command, yet the importance of this can't be denied. After all, I was sent, not some anonymous messenger, and the Comhairle has been summoned. The Order may have its independence, but Inishfeirm is the Rí's land and the Order but a small part of the island. Nor do I see an army here to protect you should the Tuatha decide to attack."

"The Rí should have thought of that a few months ago."

Jenna saw the folds around the Banrion's eyes tighten at the remark, but Aithne still smiled grimly. "That was an unforeseen and a terrible mistake on *all* of our parts—I'd remind you that your request for help was rather after the fact. Perhaps my husband would have stationed a garrison here if there had been a suggestion from the Máister that the Order's clochs na thintrí were so vulnerable." Her hand waved, dismissing their words. "None of that can be undone now. It would be more terrible to make a second mistake, now that we realize the import of the clochs."

"I agree, Banrion. But I must still consider this. Will you stay with us? I could have one of the acolytes take you to the guest cells, and you're welcome to break your fast at our table . . . ?"

Aithne's lips tightened slightly. She glanced at the tray with its tea and few scones. "No," she said. "I'll return to my lodgings at the Black Gull. I think that may be slightly more comfortable. But only slightly." She picked up her overcloak and wrapped it around herself. She strode toward the door, and Ennis barely managed to open it before she reached it. Jenna wondered if she would have bothered to open it herself. Jenna heard a conversation suddenly go silent as the gardai outside straightened and fell in to flank the Banrion. Aithne turned back and nodded to Máister Cléurach, Jenna, and Ennis. "Holder Aoire, it was good to meet you. Máister, I'll expect to hear your answer this afternoon before my ship departs. I trust it will be one that the Rí and the Comhairle hope to hear, and we'll take ship together."

The footsteps of the Banrion and her entourage echoed loudly in the marbled halls.

"We only have one answer, you realize," Máister Cléurach told them as they stood on the balcony watching the Banrion's carriage wind away down the long road to the village. "Making her wait for it is just so much pettiness. But it feels good, nonetheless."

Jenna almost laughed. "She's frightening. Those eyes, the way she stands, the tone in her voice."

"You haven't met Rí MacBrádaigh, Jenna," Ennis told her. "Behind his back, they call him the Shadow Rí. It's Banrion Aithne who is the true power in Inish Thuaidh. *She's* the one the Comhairle of Tiarna listen to. The Banrion didn't come here because the Rí requested it; she came because that's what she wanted to do."

"And she knows we'd realize that," Máister Cléurach finished. He took in a long breath as the Banrion's carriage vanished behind the trees at the first switchback, and let it out again loudly. The cloud that emerged from his mouth echoed the mist that cloaked the base of Inishfeirm and hid the sea. They seemed to be standing on an island floating in fog. "The Banrion has her faults, but she's fair and what she does, she does with all of Inish Thuaidh in mind, not just herself. I might not entirely like her, but I do respect her. Most dangerous of all would be to underestimate her."

"I don't think that will happen, Máister," Jenna answered. *I did that once before, with Cianna. . . .* Jenna felt the hair at the base of her neck rise with the memory, and a twinge of pain sliced up her right arm.

"Go prepare yourselves to leave," Máister Cléurach told them. "I'll send a messenger to her after the noon meal and tell her that if she will wait until tomorrow morning, we'll accompany her." The elderly man snorted. "She'll likely bite the head off the poor acolyte I send, but it will do the Banrion good to spend a night here in the Black Gull's beds, don't you think?"

"I doubt the innkeeper will ever forgive you, Máister," Ennis commented.

A fleeting smile was the only answer.

41

Cloch Storm

THERE were seals at the harbor quay. Jenna was disappointed to see that they were the common brown harbor seals and a few grays.

Jenna wandered down to see them as she and Ennis waited for the Banrion's entourage and Máister Cléurach to arrive. The Banrion's ship, the name *Uaigneas*—Loneliness—emblazoned across its prow, cast a long shadow over the harbor front, and Jenna glanced at the ship as she walked along the beach with Ennis. *Uaigneas* dwarfed any craft Jenna had seen before, with a sparred central mast that seemed to prick the lowering clouds and six oars per side for use when the wind died. She could see several sailors on the deck and more swarming near it where it was docked alongside a long wharf extending out into the bay. The sides of the ship were painted in the blue-and-white colors of Inish Thuaidh in sweeping curves that were reminiscent of the long swells of the ocean.

"She's magnificent, isn't she?" Ennis said. Jenna nodded, silent. His hands touched her shoulder; before he could move away again, she leaned back against him, luxuriating in the feel of his closeness. But though he remained where he was, he wouldn't put his arm around her and his voice was carefully neutral. "We Inishlanders know how to build ships. Infochla may claim to have rule of the Westering and Ice Seas, but though they have more ships, ours are the better. The Banrion's ship is one of the best, which is why her captain was unafraid to sail at night. Inishlanders understand and respect the sea because it surrounds us. Even in the middle of Inish Thuaidh, the ocean's but a day's ride away and its whims and its moods touch the entire land."

A hoarse roar punctuated the end of Ennis' sentence, and they both turned to look. A quartet of blue seals was hauling out on the rocky beach. Jenna glanced at Ennis; he nodded to her. "Go on," he said and for the first time that morning, a smile touched his lips. "They've come to see you, not me."

She approached the group: a bull, two cows, and a pup. They watched as she and Ennis walked closer, their utterly black eyes glistening, their glossy fur rippling with sapphire highlights. The bull hung back, but the pup waddled awkwardly forward; when Jenna crouched down in front of the animal, it nuzzled the hand she held out. The pup's breath was warm, its fur damp velvet. The larger of the two females came forward also. Up close, the seal smelled of brine, an odor Jenna found strangely pleasant. As the female came closer, Jenna took in a breath of wonder: the cow's fur was mottled in color: dark gray swirls and curlicues interrupted the blue-black and the fur there was stiff and wiry, as if the animal had been injured.

The pattern in the cow's fur was the same as the scars on Jenna's right hand.

The cow spoke, uttering a long string of moans and gargles and Jenna glanced back at Ennis. "She offers welcome to their land-cousin, the Holder," he said.

"Land-cousin?"

Ennis lifted a shoulder. "The blood of the Saimhóir—that's their name for themselves—is mixed with many Inish families. They say the Saimhóir can sense when a human has but a touch of their blood in their ancestry. She's saying that you're one of them." The seal spoke again, a bark and a braying cough. "She also says that I'm a poor translator and you should use the cloch."

"The cloch . . . ?" Jenna touched it. Curiously, she opened it slightly until she saw the seals in both her own vision and that of the cloch's energy. She closed her eyes, then opened them again, startled, when she heard the seal's voice.

"Land-cousin, can't you taste the salt in your blood? Thraisha is my name and Garrentha, who fought the dark-beast that attacked you, was of my milk." The words came overlaid with the sound of the seal's own language and came not from her ears but through Lámh Shábhála. Around Thraisha, there was a strange radiance in the cloch's vision, something Jenna had never experienced before.

Jenna laughed in wonder, glancing back at Ennis with wide eyes. "Thraisha, you can understand me now when I speak?" Jenna asked, and she knew the answer immediately: her voice came back to her altered into the moans and calls of a seal.

"The language of Saimhóir is part of your blood, and Lámh Shábhála allows you to tap that part of yourself," Thraisha responded. "And I have chased and swallowed Bradán an Chumhacht, the first bright salmon of the mage-lights, which has come back to us. I am like you and I bear the marks. Aye, I understand you through Bradán an Chumhacht as you understand me through Lámh Shábhála."

Jenna blinked. "You've eaten a *fish* that gave you the ability to tap the mage-lights?"

Thraisha gave a series of pants that translated as laughter to Jenna's ear. "And you have a stone that gives you power?" she said, mimicking Jenna's tone of astonishment. "Why, the land is *full* of stones." She laughed again. "The sea has changed as the land has changed, and things swim under the waves that have not been glimpsed since the last change of currents. Did you think that you humans were the only ones who could tap the power above or who could use the slow magics? The gods made us all; why should they gift only you?" The seal lifted her gray, bristled muzzle. "I am First for the Saimhóir as you are First for your kind. I understand your pain; I have endured it also."

With the words, a foaming, cresting wave of force rose from within Thraisha and enveloped Jenna. For a moment, as the false surf swept over her, Jenna felt the memory of the Filleadh, the agony she'd felt as she'd opened all the clochs na thintrí to the mage-lights . . . and at the same time she saw herself as Thraisha, undergoing the same brutal trial underneath the sea and nearly dying as the energies tore at her. It had been worse for Thraisha, Jenna realized—she had nearly succumbed, saved only by her bull mate who had lifted her to the surface and held her above the water for long hours as Thraisha lay senseless. Jenna cried out, a wail of her own remembered torment all mingled with Thraisha's suffering as she sank to her knees in front of the seal, not caring that the rocks were wet or that the spray from the slow breakers washed over her legs and clóca. Her arm ached and throbbed, the fingers of her right hand knotting as muscles cramped and protested. Thraisha lurched forward and Jenna cradled the seal's head against her breast as she might a child, her breath choked with a sob. She heard Ennis start forward behind her, then stop as the bull roared once at him in warning.

"We are closer than sisters of the milk," Thraisha said softly. "We know, you and I. We know . . ." Thraisha's head pulled away and Jenna reluctantly let her go. "Bradán an Chumhacht isn't Lámh Shábhála; what it gives me is not what the stone gives you," the seal said to her. "One gift it brings to me is a small foretelling, a glimpse of possibilities. I am seer and this is what I've seen: our fates our linked together, my sister-kin. That's why I wanted to meet you."

"What do you mean? How are we linked?"

Thraisha moved her head from side to side with a gurgling wail. "That I don't know. I can't see it. But I know we will be together again, and in one vision of those possible futures, we die together. I've seen Bradán an Chumhacht swim from my dying mouth and Lámh Shábhála fall to the ground from your hand."

The bull roared loudly behind them and Thraisha gave a snort. "Your people are coming and I must go now. We'll talk again." With a lurch and a roll, the seal turned to leave. The bull waited, but the other female and the pup had already slipped back into the water, calling to Thraisha.

"Wait!" Jenna cried. She stumbled to her feet, Ennis running forward to help her up. "I want to know more."

"You will," Thraisha called. "We both will, when it's time." Thraisha was at the water's edge; she half-fell, half-dove into the water. The bull lumbered after her. A mo-

ment later, her sleek head reappeared. "Beware the
storm," Thraisha called to her. "It doesn't follow you; it
travels with you."

"Thraisha . . . !"

The blue seals dove as one. She could see their muscular
bodies just below the surface, seeming to fly in the water, as
graceful in their element as they were clumsy on the land.

"Mages!"

The voice came from the wharf. Jenna and Ennis turned
as one, Jenna releasing her hold on the cloch at the same
time. As the cloch-vision left her, the brilliance seemed to
wash out of the world, leaving the colors muted and gray.
The Banrion was standing there looking down toward
them. Máister Cléurach stood next to her; behind, their
luggage was being loaded into *Uaigneas*. "Consorting with
seals isn't something I expected of the First Holder,"
Aithne commented. "I especially didn't expect to hear you
growling and wailing like one of them. Will we find you
chirping at gulls, as well?" She didn't wait for an answer.
"The captain says we should sail now, while the tide is
running out. We're boarding."

The Banrion gestured to them and strode purposefully
toward the ship, the gardai falling into place alongside her.
Máister Cléurach stared a moment longer, then followed
her.

"Jenna . . . ?" She glanced back to the water, its rolling
surface now unbroken. Thraisha and her companions had
vanished. Ennis' hand stroked her right arm, trailing down
the stiff flesh and falling away again. "We need to go."

She nodded.

Inishfeirm lay only five miles off the coast of Inish Thuaidh, but they were making for the harbor of Maddygalla,
twenty miles eastward around a cliff-walled headland—a
full day's journey. Jenna had to admit that the *Uaigneas*
was far more comfortable than the small fishing boat in
which she and Ennis had made the crossing from Talamh
an Ghlas. The ship rode the waves easily with a gentle
rocking motion, the sail billowing on the mast above them,
spray curling from the bow as it cut the gray-green water.

Jenna stood with Ennis at the starboard rail; the Banrion and Máister Cléurach were talking near the stern. Jenna watched the water, wondering if she might see the shapes of the seals pacing the boat, but there was nothing but the occasional gull or cormorant diving for a fish. Behind, Inishfeirm slowly receded, the White Keep glinted atop the summit as the sun moved in and out of clouds.

"What are you thinking?" Ennis asked. He was standing next to her, a careful arm's length away. She leaned toward him, enjoying his closeness and attention, imagining that she could feel the warmth of his body against the chill sea breeze.

"I'm thinking that we're walking into another snake's nest like the Rí's Keep in Lár Bhaile. I'm thinking that there are still too many things I don't know. I'm wondering if I have a baby brother by now or if I'll ever see my mam again. I'm wishing that I had the courage to say . . ." She stopped herself. . . . *to say to you all the things I want to say.* She sighed, and gave him a wan smile. "I'm wondering about Thraisha's words. Did you know about her, Ennis?"

"Aye, a bit. I knew the tales the Saimhóir told about the mage-lights and Bradán an Chumhacht, and I knew from Garrentha that her milk-mother had eaten the salmon." His hand was near hers on the railing. If she moved, she could touch him. "I figured that she'd come looking for you."

The sun cloaked itself again though its light still danced on the waves well out from them. Jenna shivered. "Are there more? Other things like the cloch na thintrí held by other creatures?"

"Probably. The books in the library talk of eagles and wolves having their own magic and they hint of dragons with the same. There may be others."

She glanced up at his shadowed face. "When did you last see a dragon?"

He smiled back at her for a moment, the expression lightening his face, and she started to laugh with him. Jenna lifted her hand, put it on top of his. He looked down at their intertwined fingers as he spoke. "Never. Máister Cléurach says he doubts they exist at all. But I hope he's wrong.

Now *that* would be a sight . . ." He suddenly dropped his hand away from the railing, his gaze moving past her shoulder. "Banrion," he said. "Máister. Good morning."

That earned Ennis a grunt from Máister Cléurach and a flick of the Banrion's eyes before her gaze went to Jenna. "We hardly need to make polite small talk here. Let me be blunt. You don't seem to like me, First Holder," Aithne said.

"Banrion—" Jenna began, but the woman raised her hand.

"You don't need to either acknowledge that or try to smooth it over. I simply state the fact. The truth is, Holder Aoire, I don't much *care* if you like me or not. All that matters to me is that I understand where your loyalties lie, so that I know how we can work together. Your mam, I understand from Máister Cléurach, is the consort of Tiarna Mac Ard of Gabair and is carrying his child."

Her tone made it clear that she felt the word "consort" was closely related to "whore," and the quick shift of her gaze to Ennis indicated that she might feel that Jenna was little more than that herself. Jenna's eyes narrowed as if she'd been slapped, and it was difficult to keep her voice civil. "Aye, Banrion, that's true, if she hasn't already delivered the baby." The wind freshened slightly, and Jenna felt a drop of rain touch her cheek. "But as to my loyalty . . ." Deliberately, she put her arm through Ennis', who nearly jumped before his mouth spread into a grin. "This man helped me where no other would. And the Order and Máister Cléurach have taken me in and I owe them for their kindness. Past that, I am loyal only to Lámh Shábhála. My enemies are those who would try to take it from me." Jenna started to remove her arm from Ennis's, but he brought his arm in to his body to hold her.

"That's well said," the Banrion answered. The wind tossed her light hair, lifting the glossy strands from her shoulders as it turned around to blow from the northwest. A splatter of rain drummed over the wooden deck and Jenna glanced up to see the clouds gray and lowering over the boat, though well out in the channel she could still see sunshine, and the White Keep shone far behind. "You'll find that most of the Riocha here share your attitude. Inish

Thuaidh isn't Tuath Gabair, where the Rí's word is law.
Ask Máister Cléurach how difficult it is to get the Comhairle to agree on an action, even if the Rí wishes it."

Above them, canvas snapped angrily, and *Uaigneas*
heeled over abruptly, causing all of them to reach for ropes
and railing to keep their balance as a wave crashed white
and gray over the side of the ship, drenching them. Thunder grumbled somewhere close by, and the day had gone
as dark as twilight, though sunlight played on the horizon
all around. Sailors scurried across the deck as the captain
came over to them. "You told me this would be a fair day
for sailing," the Banrion shouted at him over the rising
wind.

The captain had a hand in the pocket of his oiled overcoat, as if the shifting deck were solid ground and he were
out for a stroll. "That is what all my experience said, Banrion," he answered. "But blows like this can come suddenly
and without warning. You and your guests should go
below—it's becoming dangerous up here."

Another wave pounded the ship, the prow lifting high
then falling, sending Máister Cléurach sprawling. Ennis reluctantly let go of Jenna and helped him back to his feet
as the rain began to fall in earnest, cold and stinging. The
captain alone seemed unperturbed by the ship's motion,
one hand still casually in his pocket. Jenna could see nothing past the rippling gray curtains: Inishfeirm had vanished,
as had the chalk cliffs of Inish Thuaidh. The captain
shouted to his men to reef the sail which was threatening to
tear apart in the gale, and to man the ship's oars. "Banrion,
please," he said. "I can't be responsible if you stay on
deck."

The ship lurched, turning as the captain shouted directions to the man at the tiller. Jenna followed Aithne to the
small deckhouse and down the short flight of stairs into a
cabin barely large enough to hold the four of them and the
trio of gardai. The wind howled and cold seawater poured
in through the hatch before Ennis and one of the gardai
managed to push it shut. *Uaigneas* rolled again, more
sharply this time, and they heard an ominous cracking and
splintering above, accompanied by a scream. Then the ship

seemed to shake off the waves and finally right itself, lifting
first bow, then stern. "The captain's turned her to run before the wind," Ennis said. "We're going where the storm
wants to take us."

A garda abruptly and noisily threw up. Jenna fought not
to be sick herself from the smell and the seawater and the
ship's wild careening. For an interminable time, like the
others, she huddled in a corner of the cabin, leaning against
Ennis with eyes closed as she tried to sleep, her hands out
to brace herself. She must have managed to actually doze
for bit, but a sharp roll of the ship brought her awake again.

"Beware the storm . . ." Thraisha had said that before
she left, and Jenna wondered if she'd glimpsed this. She'd
said more, as well. Jenna took a breath, trying to remember
as the ship seemed to rise, hesitate a moment, then plum-
met back into the sea. *"It doesn't follow you; it travels
with you."*

Jenna remembered the sunlight, playing on the horizon
and the peak of Inishfeirm. The storm hadn't come streaking from across the sea toward them; it had developed rapidly above them.

". . . it travels with you . . ."

She fumbled under her soaked clothing for the chain that
held Lámh Shábhála. She let her mind touch the cloch as
she forced stiff fingers to wrap around the stone; her awareness drifted outward with the cloch's energy.

Aye. There . . .

Another cloch na thintrí was aboard, its bright energy
spraying outward and upward, and she could sense the
mind wielding it: one that knew the waters of the channel,
knew the ship and how much wind and heavy seas it could
handle. *Driving us east and south with the storm, toward
Talamh an Ghlas . . .*

Jenna pushed herself to her feet, trying to maintain her
balance on the rolling, wet planking and still hold onto
Lámh Shábhála. "Open the door!" she shouted above the
shrieking wind and the drumming of the rain. "Ennis! I
need you!"

Ennis noticed Jenna's hand on her cloch, and he immediately clenched his own. The Banrion noticed as well. "Open it!" she ordered the nearest garda. "Go with the Holder."

The garda pushed open the door; water and sheets of sleeting rain poured in as the garda, then Jenna and Ennis, forced their way up the stairs to the deck. "Can you feel it, Ennis?" Jenna shouted to him, blinking against the assault of rain and wind. The crew was at the oar seats, drenched and grim-faced with the task of keeping the ship from being swamped in the heavy seas.

"Aye!" Ennis pointed to the bow of the ship, near the tiller. The captain was there, his gaze turned up toward the sky. One hand remained in the pocket of his overcoat.

"I'll hold him," Jenna shouted to him. "You and the gardai take him." Ennis nodded. Jenna let herself fall into Lámh Shábhála's worldview. There, the captain's Cloch Mór was a maelstrom of gray and black, swirling and rotating and as yet unaware of her. Psychic winds howled and screeched around it, and Jenna knew those could be directed at her as easily as they now pushed at the ship. She opened Lámh Shábhála fully, letting its radiance swell outward until it touched the cloudy black; as it did, she felt the captain's awareness shift, sensing the attack even as she brought her cloch's energy down on and around the interior storm. It battered her, the winds tearing at Lámh Shábhála's hold like a furious animal. The cloch's strength surprised Jenna, and for a moment the maelstrom nearly slipped through as doubt entered her mind. A gust of wind slammed into Jenna, sending her staggering backward. She went to her knees, gasping and taking in water from the rain and the waves, but she held onto the stone, pushing back again at the other cloch's dark energy.

She had no choice. She could feel the power draining from Lámh Shábhála with every passing second, but she knew that the same was happening to the captain's stone. Lámh Shábhála burned in her hand, searing her flesh with ice, and she forced herself to hold tightly to it, knowing she would pay afterward.

A bolt of lightning cleaved the inner vision, and from the deck there was a cry of pain and alarm. The maelstrom faltered; Jenna pressed in against it and it collapsed completely. Jenna could see Ennis and the gardai rush the captain, taking him down.

Ennis' hand reached down, pulling the cloch from the captain. There was a scream, a wail of wild distress and loss. The wind slowly died; the rain fell to a drizzle. The waves fell.

"Well done, Holder." The Banrion was standing at the entrance to the cabin, and Máister Cléurach emerged behind her. The crew, appearing dazed, were gazing about them in bewilderment as Ennis and the gardai dragged the captain forward. The man was weeping, and he stared at Ennis, struggling to be released. "Give it back!" he cried. "I have to have it. You must give it back!" In Ennis' hand was a large crystalline stone, which he gave to Máister Cléurach. The older man held up the gem: a mottled smoky-gray like an approaching thunderhead.

"It's named Stormbringer," Máister Cléurach said, his face grim. "I know it—it's one of the clochs na thintrí stolen from the Order." He walked up to the captain, now moaning in the hands of the gardai, and abruptly slapped him across the face. "Thief!" he spat. "And worse—you're a traitor." Máister Cléurach pointed eastward.

Under the clearing sky, they could all see four ships well away to the east. Three of them flew green-and-gold banners from their masts, and one green and earth-brown: Tuath Infochla's colors, and Tuath Gabair's. Jenna was still holding Lámh Shábhála, not daring to let it go because she was still borrowing the cloch's strength to hold off the pain that would come. She could feel faintly, at the outer edge of the cloch's vision, the presence of two more Clochs Mór out where the ships lurked. "You were sending us to them. You were to hand over the Banrion and the First Holder."

The man's head hung down. He didn't dare to look up at them. "My cloch," he whispered. "Please . . ."

"You, First Mate!" Banrion Aithne called out to one of the crewmen, who hurried forward. "You are now Captain. Bring us around and take us back to Inish Thuaidh." The man bowed, and began shouting to the crew. They hurried up the mast and started to unfurl the sail. Aithne turned

back to the former captain as the *Uaigneas* started a slow
turn back north and west, putting its stern to the waiting
ships. "Your life is forfeit," she told the weeping man. "Kill
him and toss the body overboard," she told the garda holding the man. "His friends may want to recover the body
before the sharks find it, but I doubt it. *That* will end his
pain." The garda's hand closed around the long knife at
his belt and the captain blanched, closing his eyes. The
Banrion held out her hand to Máister Cléurach. "And the
Cloch Mór I claim for the Rí."

"No!" Jenna shouted. The garda stopped his thrust in
mid-motion; Aithne's head swiveled to regard Jenna with
eyes of green ice.

"No?" she asked, her eyebrows raised. "I remind you,
First Holder, that you are on a ship I command."

"And you and your ship would have been in *their* hands
and your husband paying your ransom if I hadn't been
here," Jenna answered. "The cloch was stolen from the
Order of Inishfeirm and cloudmages of the Order have won
it back again."

Aithne sniffed. Jenna could see her considering her next
words. "I suppose that's a fair statement," she said finally,
though Jenna knew that did not reflect her true feelings.
"And what would *you* do with the traitor, First Holder?"

Jenna didn't answer the Banrion directly. Instead, she
turned to the former captain. "Look at me," she said, and
he lifted his head slowly. "I hold Lámh Shábhála, and it
can hear truth," she told the ashen-faced man, though it
pleased her to see a flicker of uncertainty also cross the
Banrion's face. "Tell me a lie and I'll let the Banrion's
order stand. Tell me the truth and you might manage to
live. How did you come to hold Stormbringer?"

"I'm sorry, Holder, Banrion," he said. "I didn't want
this . . ." He stopped, his face stricken. "My son . . . he
was in fosterage to my cousin, a tiarna in Infochla. Two
weeks ago, a man came to me with the cloch. He offered
me . . ." The man gulped. "He seemed to know that this
would happen. He told me what the cloch could do and
said he would show me how to use it. He promised that if
I brought you and the Banrion to them, I would be made

Riocha myself and could remain as the Holder of Stormbringer. And if I failed. . . . He made no direct threats, but
I understood that my son was a blood-hostage, and he
would pay for my failure. Holder, my son is all I have. My
wife is dead, there are no other children . . ."

He sagged in Ennis' arms, his face to the deck. "I'm
sorry. I'm sorry I betrayed you and the Banrion. I'm sorry
that my weakness will almost certainly mean my son's
death." His head came up again. "Kill me," he said to
Jenna. "I've lost my son; I've lost the cloch. It hurts too
much. Kill me and let me rest. At least my son and I can
be together in the womb of the Mother-Creator."

He closed his eyes, as if awaiting the dagger's thrust. The
garda looked at Jenna, then at the Banrion, who shrugged.
"Leave this judgment to the Holder," she said.

They were all staring at her. Jenna took a long breath,
not certain what to do. There were no good decisions here,
she realized. She felt sorry for the man; he'd been well-
trapped by Infochla. Now, his livelihood was lost and he'd
be forever branded a traitor, his son likely dead. Jenna
closed her eyes, her fingers still around Lámh Shábhála,
her arm beginning to throb with the pain of using it. In the
cloch's vision, she could feel each of the people on the ship,
and in the water, nearby . . .

"Throw him over the side," she said to the garda. "Toss
him in the water."

Ennis started to protest, and the Banrion chuckled. "You
surprise me, Holder. A slow drowning rather than a
quick death . . ."

"Do it!" she told the garda, with a look of warning to
Ennis. Ennis let go of the man and the garda pushed him
toward the railing. He glanced back at Jenna as the captain
stared down at the cold water rushing by. "Go on," Jenna
told him.

The garda pushed hard at the captain's back. He tumbled
over the side. The Banrion took a step to the rail and
glanced down. Already the man was behind the boat,
thrashing at the waves, gasping as the frigid water leeched
the strength from his body. "Well, that's done," she said.

"Holder, Máister . . ." She moved away, gesturing to the new captain.

Jenna stood with eyes half-closed, watching and listening through the cloch. A trio of Saimhóir were close by: Thraisha was not with them, but Garrentha was. *Go to him,* she whispered in the voice of the stone, knowing the seal would hear her. *Keep him alive and take him to the other ships.*

In her head, there was a warble of acknowledgment from Garrentha.

She released Lámh Shábhála, gasping as the pain came to her fully, forcing herself to take slow, deep breaths. Máister Cléurach looked at her, hefting Stormbringer in his hand. Ennis gave her a concerned frown, and nodded.

"This will be the last Cloch Mór we take alone," she told them. "They'll know now that one Cloch Mór isn't enough against Lámh Shábhála, and they won't make that mistake again." For a moment, she felt she could glimpse the future, and it was dark and bloody. She watched the sails behind them and felt the touch of dread. Jenna rubbed at her dead, cold arm as if she could scrub away the marks there. The pain ripped from hand to shoulder and into her chest. Her body trembled with it; she closed her eyes and clenched her jaw to keep from crying out. Ennis rushed over and took her in his arms and she let herself relax into his grasp, allowing him hold her up. When the worst of the spasms passed, she pulled away from his embrace and looked at the ships of the tuatha again, growing smaller in the distance.

"I don't know that we can survive when they all come," she said.

42

Dún Kiil

Lár Bhaile and the Rí's Keep were more magnificent. Áth Iseal was larger. Ballintubber seemed more inviting.

At first glance, Dún Kiil was a gray town on a gray mountainside beyond gray water. Jenna knew the impression was unfair—the weather had gone to drizzle by the time they reached the seat of Inish Thuaidh and the clouds were a landscape of unbroken, featureless slate overhead. The bright colors of the doors and the flowery window boxes were muted, and most of the people in the streets were intent on getting to their destinations and out of the weather.

The keep dripped. Jenna could hear the rhythmic, echoing *splat* of water striking the stone flags, as if the gods were keeping time to the Rí's welcoming speech.

Rí Ionhar MacBrádaigh of Inish Thuaidh was not an impressive speaker or an impressive man. His complexion was pallid, his voice mild, his physique potbellied and flabby. Jenna could understand why they called him the Shadow Rí behind his back; already it had been made clear to her that the true negotiations would take place with the Banrion and the Comhairle of Tiarna. It was also clear to her that the alliance of the Inishlander Riocha was a fragile thing that might—and often did—break apart at any moment. Already, half a dozen of the tiarna and bantiarna to whom she'd been introduced had leaned forward and whispered conspiratorially to her that they wished to speak

with her in private, intimating that they were the true
power behind the throne. There was Kyle MacEagan of Be
an Mhuilinn, short of stature and wide of girth, but whose
eyes blazed with a sharp intelligence and piercing awareness; Bantiarna Kianna Cíomhsóg of An Cnocan, a dark-
haired woman whose beauty and grace was still untouched
in her third decade, and who, Ennis whispered in Jenna's
ear, was the match of any of the men with a sword.

There was also Árón Ó Dochartaigh of Rubha na Scarbh,
whose cheeks were as flaming red as his hair and who towered a full head above Ennis. He was also Banrion Aithne's
brother, and the da of Banrion Cianna. He glared at Jenna
with undisguised animosity, and she knew that she already
had at least one open enemy in the court.

There were other rulers of other townlands among the
thirteen chieftains of the Comhairle whose names had already slipped Jenna's memory. They stood before the
throne, watching her as the Rí spoke and the rain dripped
through the roof of Dún Kiil Keep. Behind the Comhairle
stood the minor Riocha and the céili giallnai—a hundred
or more people gathered under the cold, seeping stone
vaults of the keep.

After the first day, Jenna was already weary of the politics and beginning to despair of the chances of the Inishlanders' ability to hold off a concerted attack. Máister
Cléurach must have sensed her thoughts, for he inclined
his head toward her through the Rí's droning speech. "We
Inishlanders come together quick enough against a common
foe, First Holder," he said. "And when there's no outside
foe, we make do with ourselves."

". . . and so we bid welcome to the First Holder, who
has brought Lámh Shábhála back to Inish Thuaidh, where
it belongs." The Rí finished with a nodding bow to Jenna,
and there was polite applause from the gathered Riocha.
Árón Ó Dochartaigh made no pretense at all: he simply
glowered.

The Rí stepped down from the steps of the throne as
servants began to circulate through the room with trays of
drinks and appetizers. The sound of conversation obliterated
the softer *tink* of falling droplets. The Rí approached Jenna,

Ennis, and Máister Cléurach, and Jenna curtsied. "No, no,"
Ionhar clucked, lifting her back up. He smiled, and Jenna had
a sense that this was a gentle man, someone who would be
more comfortable with a book or a goblet of wine in his hand
than a sword. His hands were soft and uncallused; the hands
of a scholar, nor a warrior. Under the rich cloth of his clóca
and léine, the muscles of his arm sagged.

"I should be bowing to you, Holder, since it's through
you that the Banrion was returned to me. Such awful
treachery, and from someone I trusted." He shook his oiled
and well-coifed head. "This is an ill omen, I'm afraid. I
would like to speak with you at length, Holder. Your tale,
what I've heard of it, is a strange one, and I thought—"

"You thought that you would keep the Holder from her
well-deserved rest, my dear?" Banrion Aithne came up behind Ionhar in a rustle of silk. "This has been a long and
difficult day for her. The tale should wait for another time,
I think. Besides, I wanted to steal Lady Aoire away for a
bit and thank her myself. I have a gift for her."

Aithne, smiling, detached Jenna from the Rí's attention,
leaving Ennis and Máister Cléurach still talking with the
man. Ennis' gaze followed her as she moved away, her arm
through the Banrion's as the older woman escorted her
through the throng in the Hall. It wasn't only Ennis who
watched; Jenna could feel the gathered nobility's appraising
eyes on them. The Banrion maneuvered them to a small
door hidden in an alcove. A garda stood there; silent, he
opened the door for them, closing it again behind them.
Jenna found herself in a smaller, comfortable chamber, the
air warm with a blazing fire in the hearth and bright tapestries covering the walls with golds, reds, and browns.

In the room, also, were Kyle MacEagan and Kianna
Cíomhsóg. The two flanked the fireplace. MacEagan nodded his head to Jenna; Bantiarna Kianna simply lifted her
glass goblet. "Would you like some wine, Bantiarna Aoire?"
the woman asked.

"That title doesn't fit a common sheepherder from Ballintubber," Jenna said. "I'm not Riocha, Lady. Please call
me Jenna, or Holder, if you prefer."

The woman simply smiled. "That's simple enough to

remedy. I don't think we'd allow the First Holder to remain common. Do you, Banrion?"

Aithne smiled at Jenna. "Hardly." She gestured to one of the chairs before the fire. "Please sit, Holder."

She brushed her fingers against Lámh Shábhála, hoping none of them would notice the quick grimace of pain as she let the cloch's energy drift quickly out. She immediately felt two holes in the field where Banrion Aithne and Kyle MacEagan stood: attempts at shields. The hole around Banrion Aithne was strong; the one about MacEagan much smaller. *Tiarna MacEagan has a clochmion and the Banrion has a Cloch Mór that she didn't have on the ship. Where did she get it?* Jenna wished now that she'd used Lámh Shábhála in the main hall to see how many more of the clochs na thintrí were gathered here. *Does Árón Ó Dochartaigh also possess a cloch, like his sister?*

Jenna smiled, letting her hand drop away, and took the offered chair; the Banrion took her seat opposite her, though the other two remained standing where they were. "I said I had a gift for you. I do. Here . . ." She reached under her chair and brought up a small packet wrapped in paper and secured with a ribbon. Jenna untied the ribbon and unwrapped the paper. A familiar smell wafted out as she did so, and she stared down at the pile of dried, brown leaves there. "On the ship, I saw the cost of using Lámh Shábhála, so I asked my healer what the ancient Holders used to ease their pain. He said some of them used this, an herb that the Bunús Muintir knew. You grind the leaves and make a tea . . ."

"I know," Jenna said, perhaps a bit too harshly. "Andúilleaf. Thank you. I've . . . used it in the past." *It would be pleasant to use it, just once again, to feel all the pain and cold leave your body for a time . . .* She set the packet on a table next to her chair. *You'll leave it there. You won't pick it up. You won't use it again . . .* At the thought, pain shot up her arm again, and she grimaced. They watched her, reminding her of crows standing on a tree limb watching a dying rabbit. *They'd take Lámh Shábhála from you in an instant, if they thought they could . . .* "I assume there's another reason I'm here, Banrion."

Aithne smiled; the other two chuckled as if sharing a secret joke. "Evidently Máister Cléurach has already told you that while my husband may have the title, the Comhairle actually reigns. And we three . . . we hold the Comhairle. Four more tiarna and bantiarna on the Comhairle have pledged their votes to us when needed. The Rí will sign what I place before him. So what we decide here—" her hands spread wide—"becomes law." Aithne glanced at MacEagan, and Jenna saw a look pass between them, an affection that made Jenna wonder whether there was more between the two than simple concern for their land or friendship.

But Kianna stirred and drew Jenna's attention away from them. "You realize that the Rí Ard won't leave you alone here. The Ríthe of the Tuatha are afraid of Lámh Shábhála, if not of you. They'll come here, and they'll bring an army of thousands, supported by all the Clochs Mór they can muster."

Jenna thought of Mac Ard and the Rí Mallaghan of Gabair. She thought of Nevan O Liathain and what he would advise his father, the Rí Ard. "I know," she answered.

"We remember the last time a Tuathian army came here. It's been engraved in the tales we tell our children, in the history the sages keep, in the very bones of the land. We remember the battles and the destruction," Kianna continued. Her finely-chiseled face frowned, placing lines around her mouth and eyes. "We remember the deaths of our ancestors: men, women, and children alike. We remember the smell of corruption and smoke when Dún Kiil was sacked and burned. We remember the flare of the clochs na thintrí as they tore at the very land and changed it forever." Her eyes held Jenna's. "We remember, and we wonder how we can prevent that from happening now. To us. To our children. To our towns and lands."

Jenna couldn't speak, held in Kianna's stern, unblinking gaze. She had no answer, didn't know what the woman wanted her to say. She opened her mouth, then closed it again.

"You frighten the Holder, Kianna," the Banrion said, her voice holding a soft amusement, and the spell was broken. "She's such a young thing . . ." Kianna took a step back, though the frown didn't leave her face.

"Young or no," she said, "she has to understand the cost of her being here—the cost to *all* of us."

"I'm sure she does," the Banrion purred. "Don't you, Jenna?"

"I do." Jenna put her spine against the chair's back, rubbing at her arm. She could smell the andúilleaf, seductive and enticing. "I know they'll come. I don't want that, but I can't stop them. As long as Lámh Shábhála is here, they'll come."

"'As long as Lámh Shábhála is here . . .'" MacEagan commented. The brogue of Inish Thuaidh sat firmly in his tenor voice. "Aye, that's the crux, is it not?"

"Would you have me leave, Tiarna?" Jenna asked him. She sighed. "Then give me a boat and I will sail for Céile Mhór, perhaps, or—" She stopped as the man laughed.

"You misunderstand, Holder," he said. "If you leave, then the likelihood is that Lámh Shábhála will fall into the hands of the tuatha. If that happens, then Inish Thuaidh will inevitably fall to the Rí Ard. We'd fight and resist, we'd run to the hills and hide, coming out to kill them when they least expect it. We would die to the last rather than submit but eventually we *would* be conquered, because we couldn't stand against the massed power of the clochs and the army the Rí Ard can raise. But while Lámh Shábhála is here, we might yet prevail." He moved across the room to the window, pushing the stained glass panels open. "Holder, I'd like you to see this."

Jenna rose, going to where the tiarna stood. Looking out, she could see the ramparts of the keep, built into a mountainside overlooking the harbor. Everything was cloaked in mist from the rain, but Jenna imagined that on a clear day the view would be breathtaking: the blue deep water, the curving strips of white sand, the houses set in the lush green foliage that cloaked the mountainside, the sheer black rock of the cliff on which the keep perched.

"They call this Croc a Scroilm, the Hill of Screaming. When Máel Armagh of Infochla brought his ships of war to Inish Thuaidh, when his cloudmages brought him safely through the storms our mages called up to stop him, it was here his fleet landed, and here that the first battle was fought. Then, there was no keep, only the flat top of the mountain. The pregnant women, the young mothers and their children, the elderly and infirm of Dún Kiil fled here when the Infochla fleet sailed into the harbor and they watched the battle from above. We had no army waiting for them since it was thought he would come first to attack Inishfeirm, where Severii O'Coulghan, the Holder of Lámh Shábhála, waited. Here there were only a few hundred gardai and maybe a thousand pressmen, and only a single cloudmage with her Cloch Mór. It was a slaughter, and quickly over. Those Inishlanders Rí Armagh captured—men and women both, for many of the women fought alongside their men—he brought bound and hobbled to the base of the mountain below these cliffs where those gathered above could see. With a wave of his hand, he had his archers fire into the helpless captives, while those above wailed in sorrow and terror and helpless disbelief. Then, Armagh ordered his soldiers to climb the mountain; when they reached the mourning crowds, his soldiers raped the women and their daughters and killed the sons and old men, throwing their violated bodies over the side of the mountain to join the bleeding corpses of their slaughtered loved ones. Some, according to the tale, jumped over the cliff on their own rather than submit. They fell, all of them, screaming . . ."

Jenna's hand had gone to her throat as MacEagan spoke, imagining the horror of that scene. "We remember," MacEagan finished. "We will *always* remember. It was Severii who began the construction of this keep after the Battle of Sliabh Míchinniúint, where Rí Armagh met his fate. They say it's the tears of those who died here that drip inside the keep when it rains. I don't know if that's true. I do know that the roof's been repaired and rebuilt and redesigned a dozen or more times over the centuries, and still the tears fall. I think *they* remember, too."

Jenna turned away from the window, MacEagan closing it behind her. She saw that the stained glass depicted the scene he'd just described: a woman, her mouth open in a silent cry, tumbled over black, jagged rocks. "What is it you're asking of me?" she asked the trio.

Banrion Aithne answered. "Some of the tiarna advise us to wait, to prepare our armies for the inevitable. That's the advice my husband listens to, because it means he can sit in comfort and do nothing. But while we sit, the tuatha make their own preparations. We've learned that the Rí Ard has ended the conflict between Tuath Connachta and Tuath Gabair, and that he is actively working to have the tuatha join together. If they *all* come, fully prepared and allied, we can't stand."

"What does your brother say?" Jenna asked.

Aithne almost laughed. "So you've felt the knives in his glare? Árón will be against anything that involves you, I'm afraid. I'll deal with that when the time comes. But . . ." She paused. "We here in this room believe that time must be soon."

The bright shattering of glass tore Jenna's gaze away from Aithne—Kianna tossed her wineglass into the fireplace.

"The Banrion is right," she said. "We must strike first. Before the Tuatha are ready."

The mage-lights came, and Jenna wearily pulled herself from the bed to answer their call. As she lifted Lámh Shábhála to their glowing strands of energy, she could feel Ennis doing the same somewhere nearby, and also Máister Cléurach opening Stormbringer, which he had taken for himself after having given Gairbith's cloch to Bráthair Mundy Kirwan. The mage-lights seethed and roiled above her, and Lámh Shábhála sucked greedily at them, filling itself. Afterward, her arm throbbed and ached, and it trembled as she released the cloch, the pain shooting deep into her joints.

She went to the small chest of drawers beside the bed. She pulled out the packet of fine, soft paper.

"I must consider this," she'd told them. "I need to speak to Máister Cléurach and Ennis, for what you're asking also concerns them. I need to think . . ."

The Banrion had nodded and given her that small, cold smile. "Then we'll talk tomorrow evening," she said. "But

*there is only one answer, Holder. I think you already
know that."*

Jenna had said nothing. She'd walked quickly from the
room, but on the way, without conscious thought, she'd
taken the packet Banrion Aithne had given her . . .

She put water over the hearth fire to boil, holding the
packet on her lap and watching the steam start to curl from
the small iron pot. When she heard the first chatter of the
boil, she took two of the leaves, crushed them in her left
hand, and sprinkled them into the pot. The bitter smell of
andúilleaf filled the room and she sniffed it gratefully, already feeling the pain easing in her arm and shoulder. She
poured some of the thickening tea into a mug.

For a long time, she sat there, just holding it and inhaling
the aroma. She could almost taste it. She felt her body
yearning for the brew, her hands trembling around the
mug, and yet she waited. She could hear the voices in her
mind, the voices of all the old Holders.

*. . . go ahead. I was a First Holder and it's what I
needed, too . . .*

*. . . aye, and you were mad with it a mere five years later,
Caenneth: homicidal, fey, and insane, and hated by those
around you . . .*

. . . I could take it or not. I was never in thrall to it . . .

*. . . that's what you wanted to believe . . . that's not what
they said after you were dead . . .*

*. . . it was all that kept me from going crazy with the
pain . . .*

The arguments echoed in her head, contradictory. Her
arm throbbed and sent stabbing flashes through her shoulder and chest. Finally, she started to lifted the mug to her
lips.

There was a harsh knock on her door. "Jenna! Please
open the door. I need to talk with you."

"Go away, Ennis."

"Jenna, open the door. I'm not going away." Again, the
knocking came. With a sigh, Jenna set the mug down and
opened the door. Ennis walked in. His right arm was bare
to the elbow, and she could see the markings of the mage-
lights beginning to scar his flesh as it had hers—not as deep,

not as defined, but they were there. Seeing her gaze, he
rubbed at the arm.

"It aches and throbs when I use the cloch or call the
mage-lights to me," he said. "But it's bearable. I don't hold
Lámh Shábhála. I didn't have to open the clochs na thintrí
to the lights. I don't have to bear the power you wield."
He glanced at the mug steaming on the table. "Is that what
you need?" he asked softly.

"I don't know." She bit her lower lip. Her right hand
was shaking, and she pressed it against her stomach. "I'm
afraid, Ennis," she said. "It hurts so much, and the leaf . . .
the leaf keeps the pain away, at least for a little while, but
I wonder . . . I wonder if I hadn't been taking it . . . the
Banrion . . . I was so confused, so angry . . ." She stopped.
Her breath was coming in short gasps, her chest tight. The
room swam in unshed tears.

He was close to her, but he wouldn't touch her. "You
can't change what happened, Jenna. You didn't have a
choice then."

"But I *did*." Her voice was nearly a whisper. "And I
have a choice now."

"About the andúilleaf?"

She shook her head. "No."

"The Comhairle, then?"

A nod. "I told Máister Cléurach . . ."

"I know. And he told me. What do you think?"

Jenna lifted her head. "I think they're right. There will
be war, no matter what we do, and if we strike first, we
have the best chance of prevailing. I also I think it would
be horrible and I don't want to be part of it. The clochs
na thintrí shouldn't be weapons of war, Ennis, but that
seems to be all they're ever used for—to gain power."

"Then tell the Banrion and the Comhairle that your answer's 'no.' "

"And there's even more death as a result. Right here.
For good or ill, this is my home. This is where my ancestors
came from, and Ballintubber's lost to me now. The Rí Ard
and Tanaise Ríg both stand against me. There's nowhere I
can go in Talamh an Ghlas. This is my home, the only one
I have. Shouldn't I defend it?"

"You're arguing against yourself, Jenna, and that's an argument you can't win." A gentle, sympathetic smile touched the corners of his mouth, creasing his cheeks. His hand lifted, brushed her cheek, and fell away. "Listen to your heart. What does it say?"

Jenna gave a bitter laugh. "I don't *know*. I can't hear it through all the confusion." She picked up the mug of andúilleaf.

"Will that help you hear it, or just cloud your mind more?"

A shrug. "Right now, I need something to lean on. To help. This is what I have."

"You have me."

Jenna started to speak. Blood pounded at her temples. She took a breath. "Ennis . . ."

His hand closed around hers on the mug, so tightly that she gasped. "If you need this, then fine. I trust your decision and won't stop you. But I'll be here, too. I'll give you what I can, whatever you want to take from me. I'll stand with you in whatever decision you make. I'll . . ." He stopped. He was very close, his green eyes not letting her look away.

"Let go of the mug, Ennis," she told him. For a moment, he continued to stare. Then he took a step back, letting go of her hand.

She looked down at the milky brew inside the cup, at the promise it held. Very softly, she set the mug down again. She walked over to Ennis, put her left hand around his neck and pulled his head down.

She pressed her mouth to his. He tasted sweet, and she opened her mouth to him, an urgency and need rising in her. His arms went around her, drawing her close, his hands tangling in her hair. Her lips clung to his, moist and soft, as he lifted his head.

"Jenna . . . ?" he husked.

"Aye," she whispered back to his question. "This is what my heart says. And for right now, anyway, this is what I want."

43

The Dream of Thall Coill

*S*HE *was there, in the upheaval and the blood* . . .
   Sliabh Míchinniúint, the Mountain of Ill Fate, burned
as if it were an ancient, slumbering volcano come to vile
life, spewing rivers of molten lava down on its blackened
and broken slopes, the earth steaming with gray-white mists
under the assault. Only this was no natural fury; this was
the terror of a battle of cloudmages. Beneath black clouds
the armies clashed, and she was one of them: an Inish clans-
woman roaring her defiance at the armored troops of Rí
Máel Armagh, shouting her hatred of the banners of green
and gold gathered in a writhing island of steel and flesh in
the valley below. She rushed down on them from the slopes
among the hundreds of her fellow clansmen, her throat raw
with the battle cry they called *"caointeoireacht na cogadh,"*
the massed sound of it like the thousand-throated scream
of an angry god. Overhead, the cloudmages called down
lightning and fire as great explosions clawed at the mountainside with shrieking hurricane winds and twisting black
funnels. She and her fellow clansfolk slammed into the Infochla troops with an audible clash of iron on iron, bronze
on bronze, the impact stunning. Her first slash hewed off
the sword arm of a young Infochla soldier. The soldier—
no doubt a pressman boy of no more than fourteen, his
face still pimpled—screamed a thin shriek of terror and
shock, the arm pinwheeling to the ground still clutching the
sword, blood spraying wildly over both of them. A blow
struck her from the side, the bronze shoulder plates of her

403

leathers dimpling under the impact. She went down on her
knees, crying out as she swung her own weapon, blinking
away the blood and seeing the edge of her sword slice
through the thin mail of her attacker and cut deep into
his abdomen. She struggled to her feet, knowing she was
screaming, feeling the sound ripping her throat but hearing
none of it in the ferocious din of the battle. There was
blood everywhere and no way to know if it was hers or her
enemy's. She saw a flash of green and gold; she slashed at
it blindly. All around her, Infochla soldiers fell, and still
the Inishlanders pushed forward, trampling the dead into
the mud underfoot. Above and around them, the clochs
raged, illuminating the battlefield with their bright, awful
lightnings. Something struck the ground near her with a
deafening *ka-RUMPH*: she saw searing, yellow light and a
dozen and more soldiers, Infochla and Inishlander alike,
screamed as the fire consumed them in an awful moment,
leaving behind nothing but blackened skeletons that stood
in an eerie imitation of their last poses for a few seconds
before dropping to the ground like broken dolls.

This was chaos. This was slaughter.

*"This was how it was, Holder. This is how it would
be . . ."* The voice seemed familiar, one of those who spoke
to her when she used the cloch.

"Severii?" she asked, knowing that he'd been there at
the battle, but she was now somewhere else, standing at
the edge of a high cliff in a small open space surrounded
by the dark, brooding presence of ancient oak trees.
Nearby there seemed to be a presence, but she could not
see it. It was as if there was a blank spot in her vision
where the presence lurked, so that it vanished whenever
she tried to look directly at it. *Is this Doire Coill?* she wondered, and someone answered as if she'd spoken aloud, a
woman's voice this time.

"No, this is Thall Coill. This is the source and the place
of Scrúdú . . ."

Jenna turned around—there was nobody with her. And
yet . . . there was. She saw them: a couple—a woman and
a man, perhaps in their early twenties, both of them leaning

against the trees at the edge of the clearing as if impossibly
weary. They panted, their breath steaming about them in
clouds although Jenna herself felt warm. Around the woman's neck, outside the soiled, ragged clóca, was Lámh Shábhála. Jenna's hand went to her own breast: no, Lámh
Shábhála was still there, on its chain, and yet . . . "Hello?"
she called to the two, but though the woman's eyes were
searching the cliff top, she didn't seem to see Jenna standing there or to hear her voice. She took a step forward,
staggering to where Jenna sensed the presence, and fell to
her knees. The man started to come forward and she raised
a hand to hold him back.

"No, Tadhg, I have to do this myself. Stay back.
Please . . ."

Tadhg . . . The name hit Jenna with a shock—could this
be Tadhg O'Coulghan, the Founder of the Order? Jenna
could see the conflict in the man's face, the love and concern for the woman.

"Peria, come back. You don't need to try the Scrúdú.
You hold enough power with Lámh Shábhála the way it is
now. We can go back, be content with ourselves. Think of
Severii if you won't think of me; the boy will never know
his mam . . ."

Jenna had the sense that this was an old argument, one
that both of them had been going over and over for many
days now, the protest and responses so automatic that they
weren't even heard. The woman was shaking her head into
Tadhg's argument, pushing herself up from the muddy
ground. "I may be the Last Holder, Tadhg," she told him.
"I've told you what the voices say—it's the first few Holders or the last few who have Lámh Shábhála when it's the
strongest. By undergoing the Scrúdú, the Firsts can create
the path for the others to follow; the Lasts can forge a
legacy to last until the mage-lights come again. I have to
try."

"Almost all who try, fail. You told me that's what all the
old Holders said, Peria."

"I won't fail."

"You don't know that. You can't."

Tadhg started forward again, and again she lifted her hand. He stayed, but Jenna could see him trembling with fear.

Taking a long breath, Peria moved to stand near the edge of the cliff and then turned her back to the sea, standing within an arm's reach of Jenna yet not reacting to her at all. Again, she looked all around her, her gaze passing through Jenna as if she weren't there. She stared at the place that was dark and blank in Jenna's sight.

The woman took Lámh Shábhála in her right hand, the loose sleeve of her léine falling back, and Jenna saw the familiar scarred flesh mirroring her own damaged arm. Grimacing with pain, Peria closed her stiff fingers around the cloch, her eyes closing as she opened it to her mind. Above the meadow there was a sudden burst of brilliance, a showering of stars that sent black shadows racing away into the forest. Peria's face lifted, the radiance forcing her to squint as she looked up. The mage-lights, brighter and more colorful than Jenna had ever seen them, twisted and writhed above her, their forms bending toward her, dancing downward . . .

. . . touching . . .

Peria screamed, a long, drawn-out ululating cry, a wail of despair and desperation. Peria's eyes were wide open now, staring fixedly into the glare of the mage-lights. Jenna didn't know what Peria saw in her mind through the cloch-vision, but it obviously terrified her. Her mouth was working, pleading silently with something or someone that only she could see or hear, and Jenna saw her hand clench tighter around the cloch, as if she were forcing herself to hold onto it when every instinct was telling her to let go, to release the power and save herself. Tadhg evidently saw the internal struggle also, for he surged forward with a cry. With his first step toward her, the mage-lights flared, an arc of blue fury lashing out to strike the man, hurling him backward. He got to his feet and tried once more; again, the mage-lights threw him back. This time, he didn't rise.

Peria didn't notice Tadhg's defeat. She'd sunk to her knees, as if beaten down by the power above her, though her face still stared at the mage-lights in stricken, helpless horror. "No!" Jenna saw her mouth the word, her free hand raised as if in supplication. The mage-lights flayed the sky, so powerful that Jenna could hear them, shrieking like a raging hurricane. "No!" Peria said again, this time an audible shriek nearly lost in the raging storm of the lights. "I *can't!*"

As if in answer, the mage-lights pulsed in one gigantic flash. They slammed down to earth, engulfing Peria. She screamed as if she were caught in the midst of an inferno, her body contorted in agony. As Jenna shouted with her, Peria was smashed into the ground. The crack of bones and spine was horrible to hear, a dry, awful snapping like a handful of dry twigs. Her flesh tore; vertebrae ripping from her back, a femur erupting bloody and white.

The mage-lights vanished.

Jenna stood, stunned, in the sudden silence and dark.

"*Peria!*" The cry shattered the stasis. "Oh, Gods, *no!*" Tadhg had risen to his feet; now he ran to the broken body at the cliff's jagged extremity. He sank down beside her, pulling her to him. Horrified, Jenna saw Peria's head lolling, attached only by flesh and muscle, blood pouring from her mouth, nose, and eyes. Tadhg cradled her body, rocking back and forth, sobbing and wailing as Peria's lifeblood stained his clothes, calling her name over and over again.

This was worse than the battle, this was worse than anything Jenna had ever seen. Jenna could feel tears flooding her eyes in sympathy.

"*That is how my mam died,*" the voice came again as Jenna watched Tadhg lay Peria's shattered body on the ground, as she saw him take the cloch's chain from around her neck and put it over his own. "*That is how my da came to hold the cloch . . .*"

"But what *was* that?" Jenna asked the voice. "What was she doing?"

"*Something only fools or the very strong should attempt,*" came the answer, but it was another voice, a familiar one.

"Riata?"

There was no answer or rather there were many, a babble in which she could distinguish no one person. The cliff-side meadow and forest vanished, and Jenna was standing in a white, cold fog, and the voices came to her from the air around her.

". . . do this . . ."

". . . no, you must not! It will be your death as it was mine . . ."

". . . you have the chance where those who come after you may not . . ."

". . . Lámh Shábhála will always be primarily an instrument of war . . ."

". . . it needn't be that way . . ."

". . . she can't change it. She hasn't the will for the Scrúdú . . ."

". . . she's weak . . ."

". . . let her die . . ."

Then Riata's voice came again. "She will make her own choice, in her own time, as I did."

"Riata! Please, I need to know more . . ."

The fog dissolved in an unseen wind. She was in a room, her room, the room where she had lived in Lár Bhaile, and in the bed Maeve groaned, her hair damp with perspiration, knees up and legs open and the sheet wet and bloodied under her. A midwife bent over Maeve, her hands between Maeve's thighs as another woman stood ready with a blanket and knife. "Push now, love; the babe's nearly out. I have the head—curls as red as the sunset. All we need are the shoulders. Bear down, and push!"

As Jenna walked to the bedside to stand near her mam's head, Maeve groaned again, her face tightening, her hand fisted in the blankets and body trembling. Then she gasped in sudden relief, and the midwife laughed. "There!" A thin cry sounded. The midwife's assistant hurried forward with knife and thread. Jenna glimpsed the squalling infant as the midwife toweled him clean and swaddled him. "Tell the tiarna he has a son," the midwife said to her assistant. "He's waiting in the other room." Then she turned back to Maeve, tucking the baby carefully in the crook of her arm. Maeve touched the newborn's pudgy, purple-red cheeks. "He's a beauty. Do you have a name for him?"

"Aye," Maeve answered. "His name is Doyle . . ."

"He's beautiful, Mam," Jenna whispered, standing alongside the bed. Maeve's head lifted almost as if she heard Jenna, and Jenna leaned over, reaching out to stroke her mam's sweat-damp hair . . .

"Jenna?" A new voice intruded, and she ignored it, but then her mam and her old room were gone and she was reaching out to nothingness. *"Jenna?"* the voice called again.

"Jenna?"

She came awake with a start, realizing that her fingers were clutching Lámh Shábhála, and that Ennis' arm was around her. The moon threw silver shadows over their bed. The sky was dark, the mage-lights having long ago died away. "You were turning and calling out," Ennis said sleepily. "I thought you were having a nightmare."

Jenna released the cloch, cuddling into Ennis' embrace. "I'm . . . fine," she said. "If you'd just hold me for awhile."

His lips touched the back of her neck. His breath was warm down her spine. "I'll do that," he said.

They were in Máister Cléurach's chambers in the keep. He'd stared at the two of them when they'd first arrived, their hands clasped together defiantly and openly. "I knew this could be a problem," he said. "I expected better of you," he snapped at Ennis, then glared at Jenna. "I'd tell you that you're too young, but youths never understand that until it's too late and the mistake can't be undone."

That had started the conversation. It had gone downhill since then, with Jenna relating her dreams of the night before as servants brought in their breakfast.

"Thall Coill?" Jenna saw Máister Cléurach's frail form shudder at the name. "What insanity have you been listening to, girl? You mustn't go there."

His words were like a slap in the face. *He's treating you like you're his misbehaving daughter . . .* "So the dream was real? There is such a place? There is a test called Scrúdú?"

"There is, and that's all you need to know."

"It's not your decision," she told him angrily.

"It certainly is," he retorted. "I'm Máister of the Order, and if I'm to teach you, then you'll damned well listen to me."

"You're a frightened old man," she retorted. "Why should I listen to you?"

Ennis put his hand on Jenna's shoulder. "Jenna—" he began, but she shrugged him away.

"Don't, Ennis," she told him. "I know how you feel about him and the Order, but *I don't*. I don't." She pushed away the plate of sausages and bread in front of her. "I don't know enough about anything," she finished more softly.

"That you don't know enough is something that we can *all* agree on," Máister Cléurach answered. The argument didn't seem to have affected his appetite. He gestured at Jenna with a fork full of sausage. "Lámh Shábhála holds a shadow of all its old Holders, as it will hold a wisp of you after you die—an image of your personality, though not your true soul. Well, not all of the Holders were good people or entirely sane at the end of the Holding, and a lot of those Holder-shadows would laugh to see you fail because it would mean that you're no better than they were, and any advice they give is poisoned with that attitude. As for Thall Coill . . . none of the Daoine Holders—*none* of them, girl, not a single one—ever lived through Scrúdú, if it *is* truly a test and not just some old Bunús Muintir fable. If you could *read*—" Máister Cléurach paused for emphasis, "then you might have seen what Tadhg wrote after Peria's death. He thought that this 'Scrúdú' was nothing but a rumor circulated by the Bunús Muintir to gain some small revenge on the Daoines. There's no test and no reward; opening Lámh Shábhála at Thall Coill, the center of the mage-lights, kills the Holder. That's what he believed." He shoved the sausage into his mouth, talking as he chewed. "You can't trust the Bunús. Those who do so are fools."

Ennis' eyes widened, and he started to protest, "Um, Máister . . ." But Jenna had already pushed her chair back from the table, the legs screeching angrily. She stalked toward the door.

It opened before she reached it.

"Good morning, Holder. I trust you broke your fast satisfactorily." Banrion Aithne stood in the corridor. Next to her was a red-haired giant: her brother. The sight of Árón

Ó Dochartaigh's surly glower made Jenna's throat close. She took a step back as the Banrion nodded to her attendants to remain outside, then swept past Jenna into the room. The tiarna entered behind her, and Jenna stood well aside. As casually as she could, she mentally opened the cloch at her throat. The wash of emerald energy spread out like a rushing tide and immediately broke on another cloch's presence, sparkling and foaming.

Árón held a Cloch Mór. He'd also made no attempt to shield the stone from her cloch-vision. It gleamed in Lámh Shábhála's vision under his léine.

"Máister Cléurach, Ennis, would you leave us for a moment, please?" the Banrion asked. Máister Cléurach bowed to the Banrion and left quickly; Ennis hesitated until Jenna shook her head slightly to him, then walked over to Jenna and embraced her.

"I'll be just outside," he told her and kissed her, the Banrion watching with an amused expression as Ennis and Árón exchanged stares. After the door closed behind them, she sat in Máister Cléurach's chair at the table.

"I don't believe you actually had a chance to meet Árón, Holder Jenna," she said. "I know he was very interested in seeing you."

Jenna let her hand drop from Lámh Shábhála, and the doubled vision of the cloch vanished, leaving the world momentarily washed-out and colorless. She could see hints of Cianna's features in her da's face: he was hearty and full where Banrion Cianna had been sickly and thin, but the sharp, straight nose, the high cheekbones, the set of his mouth echoed that of his daughter, and now that she knew to look for it, she could see it in Aithne as well.

Árón glared, towering over Jenna. His hands were clenched in fists, cords of muscle standing out under the sleeves of his tunic. He didn't extend his hand; she would have been afraid to take it. She saw his gaze travel from her face to her right arm. "Did it make the First Holder feel powerful," he asked, "to have Lámh Shábhála crush the life from someone as frail and ill as my daughter?"

The words brought a searing flush to Jenna's face, and for a moment, tears blurred her vision. She blinked angrily.

"No," she answered. "It did not. But let me ask, Tiarna,
does it make you feel proud to know that Cianna pretended
to be my friend while she twice sent others to kill me?"

Now it was Árón whose face burned red. The hatred
radiated from him, palpable, and Jenna realized that she'd
made a mistake: this was a man who loved his daughter,
as blindly and unconditionally as any parent. He would
not—he *could* not—see any evil in her. He would have
protected Cianna in life without thought; he would do the
same in death. Jenna would forever and always be the cruel
murderer who had stolen that love from him.

And he faced her now.

The Banrion's *tsk* was a torrent of cold water into the
heat. Jenna and Árón both turned to her to find her shaking her head. "This won't do," she said. "The Rí Ard would
be laughing himself silly, seeing the Inishlanders at each
other's throats as usual. This is exactly what he wants. It's
time to set aside your grief, Brother. Are you planning to
demand éraic of the First Holder? Well, she has no blood
payment to give you and we need her as an ally."

"*I* don't need her at all, Sister," the man retorted, swinging around to her angrily. "It's you and the fools on the
Comhairle who think that. *We* don't need her. The Rí Ard
also knows his history and will recall that every army the
Tuatha have sent here has been broken by the Inish. If—
and, unlike you, I think it's no certainty, Aithne—the Rí
Ard manages to get the tuatha to work as one and come
against us, we will break them again—*without* Lámh Shábhála." His gaze flicked toward Jenna. "And I don't trust
the Order, which has already failed Inish Thuaidh by losing
their clochs to the Tuatha. In fact, Sister, I find it interesting
to note that it was within a few weeks after the clochs na
thintrí were stolen from the Order that the First Holder
chose to open them."

"I knew nothing about that, Tiarna," Jenna told him.
"And I didn't choose the timing of the Filleadh."

A sniff. The huge man pulled himself up to his full, towering height. "So you say, Holder. Yet if I were the Rí
Ard . . . how convenient for me that the First Holder would
show herself to be a threat to the Riocha; that she would

dare to kill a Banrion and destroy a keep; that she would then flee to Inish Thuaidh. Curious, too, that along the way the person sent to pursue her would be the very tiarna who shares a bed with her mam—and she just happens to defeat him publicly in her flight. Wouldn't it be tragic if during the battle Lámh Shábhála suddenly turned against us, as it was intended to do all along."

"This is insane," Jenna protested. "You're concocting a conspiracy where none exists."

Árón ignored Jenna, his voice riding over hers. "Why, if I wanted to create an outside threat to pull the Tuatha together just when they were starting to war among themselves, I could ask for nothing better. What does it cost, after all? Only the death of a sickly woman who would probably die soon anyway of the consumption in her lungs, and whose husband already has the children which were all he ever wanted from her."

"Árón!" The rebuke was sharp. Aithne pushed herself up, the chair scraping back as she confronted him. "This is *not* why we came here. We were in agreement, we were going to put together a plan . . ."

Árón towered over his sister: a mountain standing before a wisp of cloud. "I listened to you once before, Sister, when you told me that it would be good for Inish Thuaidh and for Cianna to have her marry Rí Mallaghan. But I do agree with you that there's a threat to Inish Thuaidh looming." He pointed at Jenna. "The threat stands *there*. I know that now. I came with you because I wanted to see her. I wanted to listen to her voice. I wanted to look into the eyes of the person who killed my child before I made my final judgment. Well, I've looked, and I'm not impressed. I see no remorse or sorrow in her gaze, and I tell you, Aithne, that if you go into battle expecting her aid, you will find yourself crushed between the cloudmages of the Tuatha in the front and Lámh Shábhála at your unprotected back—because that's exactly what they plan for you to do."

"Tiarna," Jenna said, her hands wide, "I'm sorry for what I did. Truly. I wish I could undo it, but—"

Árón spat, deliberately and loudly. The globule pooled on the wooden floor a scant fingertip from her feet. "I have no more to say to you, First Holder," he told Jenna. "I'll give you the warning you were too cowardly to give poor Cianna. From this day forward, *I am your enemy*. Remember that."

The door shivered and trembled on its hinges as it slammed shut behind the man. The sound rang in Jenna's ears for long seconds.

44

Juggling Possibilities

THAT evening, Rí MacBrádaigh declared that the Feast of First Fruits would take place in three days.

"What," Jenna asked Ennis, "is the Feast of the First Fruits?"

He kissed her throat before replying, and Jenna lifted her chin with a trembling gasp at the touch. His mouth traveled from throat to chin to mouth, and then he pulled slightly away from her, smiling down as he rested on one elbow on the bed, his other hand at the loose collar of her night robe, undoing the satin ribbon tied there. "The Feast of First Fruits . . . Have you seen the blackberry vines on the columns of the Temple of the Mother-Creator?" When Jenna shrugged, he continued, his fingers slipping under the cloth of her gown. "Traditionally, the Feast takes place close to the Great Festival of Méitha, when the Draíodóiri who keep the temple first see that the vines show ripened berries. In truth, though, the Draíodóiri are sometimes told by the Comhairle that now would be a good time to proclaim the feast, regardless of the state of the vines—a few green berries can easily be dyed to provide justification."

The memory of Áron's declaration in Máister Cléurach's chambers was a distraction to the pleasure of Ennis' roving hand. "And because of what happened today with the Banrion, her brother, and me, this is one of those times."

Ennis nodded. "I would think so, given the timing. I'd wager that this was the Banrion's doing to try to dissolve some of the tension." His thumb grazed her nipple; his hands cupped her breast. She closed her eyes, taking a breath, and he laughed softly. His mouth came down again, brushing her lips. "Do you want to talk about this now?"

"No," she answered. "Not now."

"Then what do you want?" His lips touched hers once more, moist and warm, more insistent this time. She opened her eyes as he drew away, loving the way he watched her. "I just want to be with you."

"That's all I want, too," he told her. His hand had moved lower. "I would like that forever."

"Is that a proposal of marriage, Ennis O'Deoradháin?"

"It's quite possible," he answered, almost teasingly. "But I also know it's not what the Banrion or Máister Cléurach or probably even your mam would advise. They would tell you that the Holder of Lámh Shábhála should use marriage as a tool and use it when it's most advantageous."

His voice had gone serious. His hand was still. "Do you think I care what the Banrion or Máister Cléurach would advise?" Jenna asked him. "Do you think I need their approval? And my mam . . . She would tell me that I should do what my heart says. And my heart says that I love you, Ennis."

She sat up abruptly, on her knees on the bed as she pulled the night robe over her head. Underneath, she was naked except for the chain holding Lámh Shábhála. "All I want is what is best for the two of us," she told him. "Is that what you want?"

He gazed at her. "Aye," he husked.

"Then you are overclothed," she said.

The Feast of First Fruits.

Street vendors appeared as if by summoned by magic. Booths were hastily erected around the main square of Dún Kiil, selling everything from hand crafts to potions. Street musicians, jugglers, and sleight-of-hand magicians stood on every corner. Bright banners were hung around the square and from the tessellated walls of the Keep high above. Carts groaning under the weight of apples, early corn, freshly slaughtered pigs, and new-brewed ale rumbled into town from the outlying farmlands. A sense of desperate gaiety infected the population; there was talk of little else. The Comhairle suspended their meetings (though Jenna suspected that the Banrion, Tiarna MacEagan and Banti-arna Cíomhsóg still gathered to talk), and the lesser Riocha and céili giallnai came in from the nearby townships, filling the inns and the taverns and swelling the population of Dún Kiil.

Jenna and Ennis moved through the laughing, shouting throngs in the street. As they walked from between the pair of standing stones that marked the entrance to the square, Ennis stopped Jenna and pointed. To their right, a juggler with a hatchet, flaming torch, and dagger wove bright, dangerous patterns in the air. As they moved closer to watch, despite her determination to keep this a day strictly for merrymaking, the sight of the juggler made Jenna think of the choices she was juggling herself: to side with the Banrion and attack the Tuatha now; to go back to the Order and learn more from Máister Cléurach, know-ing that the Tuatha would almost certainly invade the is-land; to seek the path of Thall Coill and the Scrúdú, wherever that might lead. Perilous choices all, with their own keen edges ready to cut, and she wondered how long she could keep them all in the air before she had to choose one.

"He's good, isn't he?" Ennis said. Jenna started, then smiled at him.

"Aye," she answered. "He is." She dropped a mórceint in the juggler's hat; the boy grinned at her and tossed the torch high, letting it spin several times as he struck the ax head deep into a small log standing end up to his right, jabbed the dagger point first into the wood alongside the quivering ax, then caught the torch before it hit the ground and blew it out. He bowed extravagantly. Jenna and Ennis applauded, as did the small crowd that had gathered around to watch.

"You make that look easy. What's the hardest thing about juggling?" Ennis asked the juggler as he laid the smoking torch atop the log.

The boy chuckled and reached down into a large cloth bag behind him. He brought out three leather balls, juggling them high and slowly so that they could easily see the pattern. "There's just one ball in the air and two in your hands," he said as he juggled. "It's that simple." He stopped and handed the balls to Ennis. "Try it," he said with a grin. "Start with two in your right hand and toss one of them high over to your left hand."

Ennis shook his head and started to hand the balls back, but Jenna laughed. "No, no, no," she told him. "You asked the question. Now you have to try."

Ennis grimaced. Standing spread-legged, he tossed the balls up in the air—right, left, right—and they all plopped immediately to the ground. Jenna and several of the people watching applauded laughingly. The juggler grinned. "You just have to remember that the ground always wins, Tiarna, Bantiarna." He reached down, flipped the torch up and caught it. "The Mother-Creator designed our world so that when you toss something up, it comes back down. That makes juggling possible, but it also means that no matter how good you are, eventually you'll make a mistake." He pulled ax, dagger, and unlit torch from the log and started the cascade again: ax, dagger, torch, ax, dagger, torch, ax— but this time they saw the dagger spin a little faster, so that it turned over one and half times, starting to come down into the juggler's hand blade first. With a comic expression of horror, he snatched his hand back at the last instant. The dagger clattered on the cobblestones of the street. "You just have to know when something's about to cut you and remember to let it go," he said.

The boy adroitly slipped his toes under the blade near the hilt and kicked the dagger back into the air—and suddenly he was juggling again. Jenna and Ennis applauded once more, watching for a bit before tossing another coin in the boy's hat and walking on. "I think you missed a career as a street performer," Jenna told Ennis.

"I think you just enjoy seeing me make a fool of myself."

Jenna laughed and pulled him close, hugging him. "I love being with you," she said. "I enjoy not having to think about anything for a few hours." She felt Ennis' muscles tense under her hand. "What?" she asked.

They stopped. Ennis pretended to look at the cloth hung

at a weaver's stall. "I can tell you want to say something,"
Jenna said. "What?"

"I spoke to Máister Cléurach this morning, before we
left."

"And?"

"He feels very strongly that you should come back to
Inishfeirm. He believes that the more of the cloudmage
discipline you can learn before the invasion comes—and
we all know it's coming—the better chance we'll all have."

"And what does he think of the Banrion's plan?"

A shoulder lifted his clóca. "He understands her position
but doesn't agree. No army's ever come to Inish Thuaidh
and conquered it. And no Inish army has ever left here to
invade the Tuatha."

"No army's ever had this many Cloch Mór with them,"
Jenna answered. "And no Rí Árd has ever put together an
alliance of *all* the Tuatha, and if this one has . . ."

Another shrug. They moved away from the weaver's stall
to the next, a potter's booth, bright with glazed mugs and
bowls. Ennis picked up a bowl: golden brown swirled with
blue. "So you agree with the Banrion: strike first before
they strike us."

Jenna sighed. "I don't know who I agree with," she said.

"Attack first, or wait. You don't have any other options.
At least none that I can see."

There's Thall Coill . . . she thought, but didn't voice it,
forcing the thought away. The day was bright and warm,
and the festival atmosphere filled Dún Kiil, and she wanted
nothing more than to forget for a few stripes the decision
ahead of her and just enjoy herself. Her hand brushed
Ennis', and she tangled her fingers in his. "Shut up," she
said.

He looked at her, startled, and saw her smile gentle the
words. "We don't have to talk about this now," she said.
"Tomorrow is soon enough."

"But—" he began, then stopped himself. He took her
hand and put it behind his back, pulling her close and kissing her. Jenna leaned into him, reveling in his presence, in
the affection that radiated from him. He had, all unexpected, become her sanity in this. When she was with him,

she felt complete, as if he been designed to sustain a part
of her, as Lámh Shábhála had fulfilled another part.

*It was never like this with Coelin. Never. This is what my
mam must have felt for my da . . .* With that thought came
its corollary: *And what she feels now for Mac Ard, also.*
She recalled her last sight of Mac Ard, screaming with the
pain of his loss as they left Banshaigh and Lough Glas.
Jenna's fingers convulsed around Ennis'. He returned the
press of fingers, his other hand trailing down Jenna's spine
as he held her, and she let the memory go.

"Let's not talk about anything but ourselves today," she
whispered to him. "Let's just enjoy this."

He grinned at her. "That sounds wonderful to me," he
answered. He took a long, appreciative sniff of the air.
"Smell that?" he said. "Someone's making milarán."

"Milarán?"

Ennis grinned. "You don't know what a milarán is? Well,
it's time you found out."

Jenna would find that a milarán was a griddle cake made
with honeyed batter and drizzled with molasses and spices.
It was both sticky and delicious, and part of the fun of
eating one was to lick the clinging syrup from each other's
fingers and mouth. They watched a street magician make
scarves appear from empty boxes and coins vanish and reappear seemingly at will. They laughed and shouted en-
couragement to a pair of dwarves fighting a mock battle
with wooden swords and groaned with feigned disappointment as their chosen champion fell. They listened to the
start of a storyteller's tale and helped fill his bowl with
coins so he'd finish the story. They ate a midday meal at
an inn near the waterfront, and in the afternoon went walking along the harbor way.

"Look!" Jenna said. "Aren't those Saimhóir?" She
pointed to a trio of dark shapes in the water, moving steadily toward the shore. The glint of blue highlights shimmered
in their black fur. Jenna brushed Lámh Shábhála with her
right hand and laughed. "Thraisha!" she called happily,
then tugged at Ennis' hand. "Come on!"

They ran down the wharf to where the harbor ended in
a jumble of dark rocks. The seals were just hauling out of

the water as they arrived, and Thraisha gave a warble and
huff of greeting. Jenna held Lámh Shábhála in her hand,
opening the cloch so that the cloch-vision overlaid her own
and Thraisha's words came to her. Thraisha glowed brightly
in the flow of the mage-lights' energy.

"May the currents bring you fish, sister-kin," Thraisha
called. "A foretelling came to me that you would be walking here today. I came to tell you first that the stone-walker
you gave to Garrentha was saved. The stone-walkers in
their islands-of-dead-wood-that-move . . . what is the word
you use for them?" Jenna felt the touch of Thraisha's mind
on her own, and she allowed the intrusion, let the seal
rummage through her thoughts. "Ah. 'Ship'—that's it. Garrentha kept the stone-walker afloat until the ships came.
The stone-walkers in those ships pulled the stone-walker
from the water, then the ships moved away from Nesting
Land to Winter Home."

Jenna nodded. "Good," Jenna told her. "Tell them that
I thank Garrentha for doing that." She glanced at Ennis.
"And perhaps the captain was reunited with his son. I
would like to believe that."

Ennis shrugged, and she saw that he held no such hope.

Thraisha turned to the other seals, moaning and panting
in their own tongue for a few moments. Then she turned
her head back toward Jenna, the blue-white pulse of Bradán an Chumhacht rising within the seal. "I came also to
tell you another foretelling. I dreamed last night, and in
that dream I saw several ships coming from Winter Home
to Nesting Land." Thraisha lowered her head, her black
eyes looking mournful and sad. "These ships were full of
stone-walkers in hard shells that gleamed in the sunlight,
and they had sticks of bright stone in their hands. They
came to Nesting Land at this very place and hauled out
onto the rocks and the stone-walkers who lived here
swarmed from the dry hills to meet them. I saw smoke and
fire. I smelled the scent of stone-walker blood. I heard cries
of pain and screams of rage. And I saw you, sister-kin."

Thraisha paused before she continued, as if she didn't
want to say more. "I could feel something incomplete inside you, as if you'd failed to do something you were ex-

pected to do. I could feel it like a hollowness in the fire of your soul. You stood there alone and called lightning down from the skies with Lámh Shábhála, but other sky-stones were there also, held by the hard-shelled ones, and they gathered against you. I was here, too, but I was too far away and others clochs were set again me and I couldn't reach you. You looked for help but even though those with you held sky-stones of their own, they were beset themselves and none came to your aid. I saw you fall."

She stopped, and Ennis shook his head. "Your dream is wrong, water-cousin," he told her. "My cloch will stand with Jenna as will any others held by the Order."

Thraisha gave a coughing pant. "I did not see *you* in my dream, land-cousin," she said. "I'll admit that surprised me. I know you would be there, if you could."

"Then the dream is wrong," Ennis insisted. "It was a dream and nothing else."

The seal wriggled in what Jenna decided was the equivalent of a shrug. "That may be," she said. "I only tell you what came to me. But it had the feeling of a foretelling."

"Do you see what *will* be, or only what might be?" Jenna asked.

"I see what I see," Thraisha answered. "I don't know more than that." Another cough: "I'm sorry, Holder. When I came, I could see joy in your face and I have destroyed that with my words. I wish I could give it back to you."

Jenna glanced back at the town. They could hear the sound of laughter and see the tops of the banners fluttering from the roofs of Market Square, just past the warehouses and fisheries that flanked the harbor front. The gaiety struck a false note now, like a song sung just off-key. Jenna could look at the harbor and imagine it filled with the warships of the tuatha, could practically see the smoke of burning houses while below the streets of Dún Kiil were chaotic with battle. As she stared, her right arm throbbed, her fist convulsing with the pain as if she were already there, the power of Lámh Shábhála arcing through her and breaking against the massed might of the Cloch Mór.

"It's only a possible future you see," Jenna said. "It must be. The Water-Mother sent you a vision in warning. After

all, Thraisha, if what you see *must* happen, then what use
is there in telling me? If it's destiny, then there's nothing I
could do to change it. Any action I take would still inevitably lead to the same point."

Thraisha wriggled again. "I don't know the way of gods,
yours or mine. I see what I see," she repeated. "If it's
destiny, then I know I'll soon be here with you again. I
saw more, sister-kin. When you fell, the clochs turned to
me and I could not swim against that current. Their magic
drowned me and Bradán an Chumhacht swam from my
mouth. So if it's destiny, then it's not only your death. It's
also mine."

"It's a glimpse of maybe," Jenna insisted. "That's all.
A warning."

"I hope you're right, Holder," Thraisha answered. Her
companions were chattering loudly behind, and she turned
her head toward them, her fur glistening with the movement as she listened and then looked back to Jenna. "The
sweetfish have started their evening run, and it's time for
us to feed," she told Jenna. "I will see you again, sister-
kin, and I will help you any way I can." Her gaze went to
Ennis. "And you, land-cousin, I bid you farewell."

Thraisha waddled toward the water, moving awkwardly
over the rocks and dropping into the water. One by one,
her companions slipped into the water with her. Their
heads regarded Jenna and Ennis for a moment, then they
ducked under the next swell and were gone.

45

Torn Apart

THEY walked back to the square. Though Jenna tried
to pretend that nothing had changed, the joy had been
drained from the day. The gaiety and laughter around
them only served as a contrast, making darker the shadows that wrapped around Jenna with Thraisha's words.
She realized now that there would be no escape from the
burden of Lámh Shábhála, not until it was taken from her
(and with the thought, a bolt of agony shot up her right
arm as if it had been torn loose from its socket) or she
was dead.

She could not escape the world: not with love, not with
festivals, not by turning her back on it and secluding herself. She must *be* the First Holder.

"Come on," she told Ennis, taking his hand. She pulled
him toward the square and for the next few stripes, she
went from one vendor's booth to another, watched all the
performers, examined all the wares with a fierceness and
energy that surprised Ennis. She plunged into the fair as if
she could obliterate herself in its bright celebration. By the
time torches were lit along the square and the bonfires
roared on the three hilltops around the city, Jenna was
exhausted and certain that she knew what she must do.

They took supper in one of the inns just off the square,
and afterward strolled out toward the crowd gathering
around a temporary stage at the north end for a performance by a group of mummers. They were stopped by a
page from the keep, who came running up to them.

"Mages! There you are! I've been looking for you for over a stripe now . . ."

Ennis laughed at the boy, panting, his hands on knees as he tried to catch his breath. "What is it, Aidan? Is Máister Cléurach wondering where we got to?"

"Not Máister Cléurach," Aidan answered, gulping air. "It's the Rí. The procession to the square is ready to start and he wishes the two of you to be at his side when he enters." He nodded toward one of the side streets leading away from the square. "Follow me," he told them. "I was told to take you this way."

They followed after him down the narrow lane. Jenna could nearly touch the houses on either side and little light made its way here from the square, only the milky light of the moon providing illumination. There were few people here, all of whom pressed back to let the three well-dressed Riocha pass. Aidan was well ahead of Jenna and Ennis, stopping near an intersection and waving. "This way! Hurry!"

They heard the horns announcing the Rí from the square behind them. Ennis stopped, a hand on Jenna's arm. The page was looking back toward the square with a puzzled expression. "I thought—" Ennis began.

The page collapsed to his knees, his eyes widening as if startled. His mouth opened but no words came. He fell face-down into the mud of the lane. Three arrows protruded from his back.

"Jenna!" Ennis yelled. He pushed her into a doorway across the street as more arrows suddenly hissed past them. Ennis grunted, and Jenna saw a wooden shaft blossom in red at his shoulder. He staggered backward against the wall across the lane from her. His eyes on her, he shook his head as she started to run across to him. His hand closed around his cloch.

A moment later, she did the same, ripping open Lámh Shábhála so that its power roared out like a rogue wave.

She could sense Ennis and his cloch, along with a trio of Cloch Mór lurking just down the lane. Several dozen people were moving toward them from the front as well as behind. She had no chance to identify any of the ambushers or judge their intentions: the three Cloch Mórs arrayed against her struck.

They concentrated on Jenna. As she crouched in the doorway, a rush of heavy wings beat the air above her. She looked up to see a demonic horror above: twice as tall as herself, skin burnished like bronze over massive muscles, clawed fingers and feet, and a brick-red face scowling with anger under folds and horns. Leathery wings sprang from the creature's back. Looking at the thing dredged an elemental feeling of revulsion and horror from her, as if this were a creature formed of ancient racial fears or memory. Jenna wondered at first if it was simply an illusion, but the apparition slammed into the structure above her, its claws ripping deep into mortar and plaster. The mage-demon was real and physical enough. The house shuddered at the impact, and Jenna had to use part of Lámh Shábhála's power to shield herself from falling stone and beams. The creature howled, roaring words in no tongue that she had ever heard before as it started to fall toward her, but she pushed it away. It snarled and spat, slamming again into the second story of the house as its great wings flailed the air. In frustration, it ripped away at the house, pulling it apart as if it were made of paper and throwing pieces of the ruin down toward her.

Dust made her blink her eyes, but she kept the shield in place above her, pushing the splintered, hard rain away from her.

She could do little more than fend off the mage-demon. In her cloch-vision, she saw a stream of pure energy—a blue so brilliant it was nearly white—come snarling toward her. She threw up a wall of her own power barely in time, and the color broke against it, sizzling and burning.

Fire erupted in the street in front of her, molten gobs splattering against Lámh Shábhála's wall. In the dust, Jenna saw a figure standing nearby, seemingly formed of lava and flame, glowing orange-red and covered with scabs of black, visible both to her eyes and the cloch-vision. The lava-creature lifted its hands and a glowing boulder erupted from them, arcing toward her. Jenna pushed back at the new assault, sending a blast of furious wind from Lámh

Shábhála. The boulder went black and fell, shattering ten feet away in a gout of fury. Jenna could feel the heat, searing and intense. The building was aflame above her.

The cloch-beast continued to tear at the structure, and she could sense the house starting to collapse around her. The roiling clouds of dust and smoke were so thick that she could see nothing as she flung herself back into the lane. Bowstrings sang from somewhere above and arrows arced toward her; with a flick of energy, she sent them to streaks of fire and ash. But some of them got through, hissing past or ricocheting from the doorway in which she now crouched.

I can't keep this up . . . I can't . . .

A strobe of lightning illuminated the dust clouds as it streaked away: Ennis attacking. Down the lane, there was a cry of distress and the massive lava-creature grunted and shifted its attack to Ennis, though the blue-white beam still pounded at the defensive wall Jenna had erected. "Jenna! Back to the square!" she heard Ennis shout in the confusion. She thought she saw a glimpse of his figure, then the dust closed in again as the second story of the house fell in with a splintering, long crash. Someone screamed in the rubble. The mage-demon attacked directly once more, hovering above her with an audible whoomp-whoomp of wings before it plummeted down; Jenna formed the energy of Lámh Shábhála into hands and reached for it. The beast reared back as the hands caught and held it, fiery arcs of drool flying from its mouth and its wings flapping desperately, clawing at the unseen fingers that held it. Jenna could *feel* the claws, as if they were ripping into her own skin, and she screamed.

Jenna forced herself to focus, to fend off the beast and still hold back the others. She knew now how Lámh Shábhála had been beaten in the past—she could not put her attention anywhere long enough to counterattack; inevitably someone would get through. She could sense that the other Cloch Mór Holders in the city were now aware of the battle: Máister Cléurach, the Banrion . . . She could only hope that they would enter the fray soon. She gave way, the mage-demon following, backing down the lane and

hoping Ennis was doing the same. She could feel him struggling against the fire cloch.

She heard his voice, calling out, "Jen—" and then cut
off. She screamed her own pain and fear as the lava-
creature stomped back toward her. *Hold them. They have
to be weakening . . .* Already the cloch-beast's struggles
were failing, though the other two clochs continued their
assault. For an instant, she let down the wall, shouting
against the pain as the energy stream burned her, as the
clinging fire of the lava-creature struck her clothing. She
channeled the flow of Lámh Shábhála toward the hands
holding the mage-demon, imagining them crushing the life
from the thing: the beast gibbered in panic, limbs flailing
now in desperation. She heard bones cracking, and the soft,
ugly sound of the body rupturing.

The cloch-beast vanished in a wail as down the lane she
heard an echoing cry from its Holder. Jenna threw the wall
back up again, pushing away the other two clochs' assault.
She'd fallen without knowing it, nearly losing hold of Lámh
Shábhála. Her clóca was scorched, her skin burned underneath. She forced herself to stand again, readied herself to
release the wall now and counterattack.

Raging chaos shifted abruptly into silence and dark. In
her cloch-vision, the other two clochs vanished. She could
sense them still, but they were dim and inactive. The Holders were moving away, quickly, as if on horseback. She
flung furious lightning bolts toward them, but it was already
too late. They were gone.

"Ennis!" She called his name, coughing in the dust, trying desperately to see either with her eyes or through Lámh
Shábhála. "Ennis!"

He wasn't there. The dust was settling; she could see the
street and the rubble strewn across it, but there was no
sign of Ennis, and she could not feel him or his cloch with
Lámh Shábhála.

He was gone. Taken.

"Ennis!" she called again, knowing in her heart it was
useless. Footsteps were running toward her from the direction of the square. Jenna whirled, her hand on Lámh Shábhála, ready to strike.

"Holder!" One of the Rí's gardai—a sergeant by the insignia on his shoulder—came to an abrupt halt, staring in disbelief at the destruction around him and Jenna's battered appearance as half a dozen soldiers came hurrying behind. "Are you hurt?"

"I'm fine," she said. "Mage O'Deoradháin has been captured." Jenna waved her arm. "Quickly! We have to find him!"

The sergeant barked orders and his men scattered, but Jenna knew it was too late.

Too late.

PART FOUR

THE SHADOW RÍ

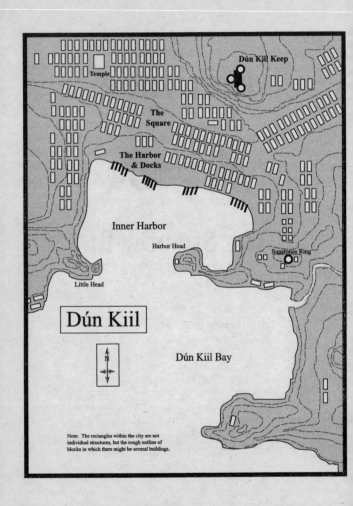

Temple

Dún Kiil Keep

The
Square

The Harbor
& Docks

Inner Harbor

Harbor Head

Little Head

Sunstones Ring

Dún Kiil

N

Dún Kiil Bay

Note: The rectangles within the city are not
individual structures, but the rough outline of
blocks in which there might be several buildings.

46

Decisions

"IT was my brother," the Banrion said. "Or at least I have to make that assumption. He's gone, along with all his retainers."

Jenna had been carried to her chambers in the keep and the healer sent for. Máister Cléurach had come rushing in as well, refusing to leave in case he might need to defend her with his cloch. Guards were set outside the doors and in the hallways, and trackers were sent in pursuit of Árón Ó Dochartaigh.

Now, several hours later, Jenna lay bandaged in her bed, the cuts, scrapes, and burns on her body salved and wrapped, her right arm and chest throbbing with fiery needles each time she breathed or moved. She kept finding her gaze snagged on the set of drawers across the room where the bag of andúilleaf sat. The only thing that kept her from telling them to bring her the leaf was knowing how disappointed Ennis would be if she started using it again.

She wasn't sure how long that would mean anything. She was afraid that Ennis might never have the chance to know.

The Banrion Aithne sat alongside the bed, at her left hand, and for the first time Jenna seemed to see genuine anguish on her face. Her haughtiness and stiff certainty were gone. "I've sent word that the Comhairle will meet tomorrow, and we'll send an edict to the Rí that Árón and those with him are to be proclaimed traitors, with the price of death on their heads if Holder O'Deoradháin is harmed." A trace of her old confidence returned to her. "The Rí *will* sign the warrant, of course."

"Where has your brother gone?" Jenna asked. Her throat was raw; it hurt to talk. It hurt to move. It hurt simply to lie there.

"If I know him, he's riding hard for the mountains of Rubha na Scarbh. That's where we both grew up, and he knows the paths and hidden places as well as anyone. There are caverns and lost valleys there where he can hide for years, and an army would not be able to dig him out. The people there are like him: grim and solitary folks, fiercely loyal to their clan-kin; they won't care about the proclamation. They'll hide him and protect him."

"So you're telling me that the warrant means nothing."

Aithne shrugged. "If we can find him before he reaches Rubha na Scarbh, it means everything. It's a long ride over hard country, and there are several townlands to cross with people who will wonder why a tiarna and his people are passing through so quickly. But once he's there, in his own land . . ." She shook her head. "I won't lie to you, Holder. In his land, *he* is the only genuine Rí, even though he doesn't claim that title. Inish Thuaidh isn't like the Tuatha of Talamh an Ghlas. We may fight, clan against clan, but we'd resist together if the Rí MacBrádaigh tried to use the power given him by the Comhairle to take out one of us— because we would fear we'd be the next. The warrant may cause someone to betray Árón; we can hope for that. There will be people there who consider themselves more loyal to me than to him. And we can send a few troops in to look for him, though not an army."

Máister Cléurach stirred from the chair in which he'd been sitting all evening. "The Banrion tells you the truth, Jenna. We Inishlanders covet our little independences. We take oath first to clan, then to townland, and last to Dún Kiil."

"If they . . ." *Kill,* Jenna started to say, but she wouldn't utter the word. *"Speak ill and you make it true"* was an old saying, one she'd heard her Aldwoman Pearce or her own mam utter many times. ". . . hurt Ennis at all, I swear by the Mother-Creator Herself that I will kill him. I don't care if he's your brother, Banrion. I don't care about anything. I *will* kill him."

The Banrion smiled thinly. "You're an Inishlander, Holder. I would expect nothing else."

"There were two other Cloch Mór Mages with him. Who were they?"

"We don't know."

"You hold a Cloch Mór yourself, even if you hide it from everyone. Show it to me."

Aithne started, sitting back in the chair and glancing at Máister Cléurach. But she didn't deny the accusation. Her hands went to her neck, and she slowly lifted a fine, silver chain there. From under her léine, a blue stone emerged, a finger's length long and cut with intricate facets. "Do you recognize it?" Jenna asked Máister Cléurach, who leaned forward to look closely at the gem, then shook his head.

"No. It's not a stone that the Order held."

"I wasn't a party to the Inishfeirm raid and I wasn't with my brother tonight, if that was your suspicion, Holder," Aithne said. "I can understand why you'd be cautious. But I was with the Rí. You can ask any of the Riocha or half the townspeople. I had nothing to do with this. Or you can use Lámh Shábhála and judge the truth of what I say."

Jenna held Aithne's gaze for a long breath, then closed her eyes. "Put the cloch away," she told her. "You're probably wise not to let others see it."

The Banrion tucked the gem back under her léine and leaned over to hold Jenna's hand. "I promise you that all that can be done is being done. Get yourself well again—that's the best you can do for him right now." With that, the Banrion left the room in a rustle of linen and a whiff of musk oil.

"She'll do as she promises," Máister Cléurach said. "I know that much."

"I hope you're right." Jenna pulled herself up on the bed, grimacing as freshly-closed wounds pulled. "I should have been able to stop it. I should have been stronger."

Máister Cléurach sniffed. "There were three Clochs Mór set against you. I think you did as well as anyone could have. I could read you the histories, or you could listen to

the Holders' voices inside Lámh Shábhála. There have been
Holders who have fallen against two clochs, or even one
that surprised and overwhelmed them before they could
react. You fought three, and you might have beaten them
had they stayed to play it out. But I don't think they truly
expected to defeat Lámh Shábhála. They would have taken
that gift if it had happened, but I wonder if all along the
real target wasn't you, but Ennis."

"Why? Why would Árón want Ennis?"

"Do you love Ennis?"

The question made Jenna blink. "Aye," she answered,
feeling the truth in the gaping wound inside her, one that
no Healer could cure. "I do."

Máister Cléurach's mouth tightened; his eyes narrowed.
"And Árón Ó Dochartaigh loved his daughter," he said.

She knew he was right, knew it even as she shook her
head in reflexive disagreement. The tiarna wanted to hurt
Jenna as she had hurt him, and that realization was a sword
blade in her gut, ripping and tearing at her soul. "No . . ."
she whispered, and the word was not so much a denial as
a plea.

The light shifted in the room, a wavering brightness that
dimmed for a moment the yellow glow of the candles. Outside, the mage-lights touched the sky, wrapping around the
moon and calling to her. Jenna flung aside the covers.

"You can't," Máister Cléurach said. He rose, as if to
guide her back down. "You're too weak and it will hurt
too much. The lights will come again tomorrow or the
next day."

Jenna pushed his hands away. "So might the next attack
or the chance to help Ennis. I need Lámh Shábhála full.
Lámh Shábhála *wants* to be full." Biting her lips to keep
from crying out, she swung her legs over the edge of the
bed. Máister Cléurach, without saying anything, brought a
woolen shawl and draped it over her shoulders. He helped
her up, held her as she walked across the room and pushed
open the doors to the balcony. The cold night air bit into
her and she shivered. The mage-lights crawled and sparked
from horizon to horizon between the shreds of clouds. Everywhere, she knew, the cloudmages were lifting their

clochs to sky. That's what Árón would be doing, she was
certain, and the other two who had been with him.

She took Lámh Shábhála in her right hand. The mage-
lights curled and swayed above her in response. She lifted
it to the tendrils of light snaking down from above, closing
her eyes as the icy touch burned along her hand and wrist
and arm and Lámh Shábhála greedily sucked in the power.

She had drained the cloch nearly dry. When it was full
again, when the mage-lights reluctantly drew away from
her, she would have fallen if Máister Cléurach had not been
there to catch her. "Get the Holder a solution of kala bark
for the pain," he snapped at the healer as they came back
into the chamber. He helped her onto the bed and patted
her forehead with a warm, wet towel. He took her cold
right hand between his gnarled fingers and rubbed life back
into it. "Come back with me to Inishfeirm, Jenna. There
are still things I need to teach you. There's nothing you
can do about Ennis now—it's out of your hands. You can
help him most by being as strong as you can."

She shook her head.

"Why not? You can't be seriously thinking of doing what
the Banrion has suggested. Jenna, you—" He stopped, and
she saw suspicion widen his gray, sad eyes. "You intend
to go to Thall Coill." He invoked the name as if it were
a curse.

She grimaced as pain rippled through her arm, her hand
tightening into a fist. "You said it best, Máister," she told
him. "I can help Ennis most by being as strong as I can
possibly be."

The Comhdáil Comhairle, the Conference of the Comhairle, was as boisterous and loud as Jenna had been led
to believe it would be. Rí MacBrádaigh sat in his chair at
the head, his pallid face propped on a hand as he listened,
his eyes so close-lidded that Jenna wondered if he wasn't
dozing. The Comhairle was arrayed down either side of the
massive oaken table, much scarred and discolored from
years of use. There were six chairs down the right side,
seven down the left. One chair on the left side—Árón Ó
Dochartaigh's chair—sat vacant. Jenna and Máister Cléu-

rach were seated at the far end of the table, facing the Rí
and the tiarna. This afternoon, the hall was also crowded
with the minor tiarna and the céili giallnai, standing behind Jenna.

Even though the sun shone beyond the great, tall stained
glass windows behind the Rí, the keep still dripped, a sullen
plop-plop-plop that could be heard whenever the Comhdail
Comhairle lapsed into silence.

That was not often. It seemed that everyone wanted their
chance to speak. Jenna decided that the falling water was
less the tears of those slaughtered on Croc a Scroilm and
more the gods weeping for the waste of words. Most of
the tiarna railed against Árón Ó Dochartaigh's audacity in
ruining the Feast of First Fruits, the destruction and loss of
life—over a dozen bodies had been pulled from the burning, charred rubble of the lane—and the temerity in taking
Cloudmage Ennis as a hostage. But as the Banrion had
predicted, once the indictment had been made, they all
stopped short of calling for concerted action against him.
Despite the loud and brave talk, they were content with
the verbal condemnation of Árón, and no one wanted to
pursue him once he was in his own land.

". . . we know that a tiarna's land is his own, and if
Tiarna Ó Dochartaigh is back in Rubha na Scarbh, there
will be no pulling him out." That was Kyle MacEagan,
looking sour and irritated as he glanced up and down the
table. "The Rí should issue a warrant, but then we must
wait. Tiarna Ó Dochartaigh will send word, and soon, as
to his intentions. Do you not agree, Banrion? You know
Árón better than any of us."

Banrion Aithne rose, nodding to MacEagan and her husband, the Rí. "I do know Árón," she said, "and even
though we share the same blood, I agree with those who
say that we must condemn this action with the strongest
terms possible. And I also agree with Tiarna MacEagan:
though I speak in the Comhairle for my husband's townland of Dún Kiil, Rubha na Scarbh was my home, and I
know it and its clans well. Árón won't be found if he
doesn't wish to be found. I believe—"

There was a crash as the doors to the hall were thrown

open. Everyone turned, and even the Rí looked up sleepily. A bedraggled garda entered, looking travel-stained and tired. He held up a leather pouch toward the Comhairle. "For the First Holder," he said. The Banrion gestured for the man to come forward; a moment later, the Rí did the same. He moved through the press of tiarna, who stepped aside, and placed the package in front of Jenna. "We followed Tiarna Ó Dochartaigh's path from Dún Kiil," he said. "He had a dozen riders with him, at least. They stopped at Néalmhar Ford to water their horses. We found this hanging on a tree branch at the crossing, with a note that it was to go to you, Holder." He gestured at the bag. "I rode here as quickly as I could. None of us opened it." He said that last sentence quickly, as if he feared that Jenna would strike him down with Lámh Shábhála.

"Thank you," she told him, as gently as she could. The Comhairle was staring at the pouch, knotted shut with a leather cord. Jenna untied the cord and opened the flap. She turned the pouch and a necklace slid out along with a sheet of parchment on which she could see the black scrawl of words. The necklace was silver and a cage of fine silver wire hung from one end. The cage was empty, but Jenna knew what had once sat there: Ennis' cloch, the one she had taken from Mac Ard.

"Oh, Ennis . . ." she breathed, hand over her mouth to stop the cry that wanted to wail and shriek its way forth. *"Don't,"* Mac Ard had pleaded when she took the cloch from him. *"It would be like tearing away part of yourself to lose it. Don't . . ."* Now it was Ennis who had had his cloch na thintrí ripped from him, it was Ennis who must have cried out in pain and loss, suffering more than if Árón had cut him open with his sword and left him to bleed to death. "Ennis . . ." Tears dripped onto the paper, the sepia ink running where the water touched, and Jenna blinked furiously, grasping the necklace in her hand, wishing she could read the words and also glad that she could not. She handed the note to Máister Cléurach. "Máister, what does the note say?"

He read it slowly, aloud:
"To the First Holder Aoire—

"I send you this token as proof that I hold Holder O'Deoradháin as hostage against the blood payment you owe for my daughter's murder. The éraic I demand is this: you will give me Lámh Shábhála, for you have shown that you are not fit to hold it. You will send the cloch to me via my sister, the Banrion, who will bring it to Rubha na Scarbh. Once I have the cloch in my possession, I will release my hostage. If I do not have Lámh Shábhála by the Festival of Méitha, I will send back your lover's body for you to mourn as I mourned my daughter."

Máister Cléurach laid the paper down on the table as if with great weariness. "It is signed," he said, "by Tiarna Árón Ó Dochartaigh."

They were all staring at Jenna. She could feel their gazes, hot against the aching cold dread that had seeped deep into her with each word. "The Festival of Méitha is in ten days," the Rí said, the first words he had spoken all morning, and it brought everyone's attention to him. The Rí shrugged as if surprised. "We have a lot to do before then," he said. "All the preparation for the festival . . ." He lapsed into silence, his mouth shutting abruptly. He waved a hand indulgently. "But go on. Go on."

Banrion Aithne audibly sighed.

Tiarna Kianna Cíomhsóg rose and pointed to the parchment in front of Jenna. "This changes everything," she said. "Árón has made the affair not treason but éraic, a personal matter of honor between himself and the First Holder in which the Comhairle needn't involve itself." Several of the other tiarna around the table muttered in agreement. Jenna saw annoyance flit over the Banrion's face; Aithne nodded to MacEagan, who immediately interjected.

"He may have tried to do so. But it remains that Tiarna Ó Dochartaigh disrupted the holiday, destroyed the Rí's property, and killed several of his subjects. *That* isn't éraic; that is lawlessness and a breaking of the oaths of fealty and peace we've all sworn to the Comhairle and the Rí. The Comhairle should still recommend that the Rí issue the warrant against him."

Banrion Aithne rose then, nodding to MacEagan. "And I, sadly, must agree with Tiarna MacEagan." Her voice was tinged with soft regret. "Even though Árón is my brother, he has violated the peace of the Rí and deserves to pay for that . . ."

Jenna wondered why Aithne would argue against Árón, but Máister Cléurach leaned toward her and whispered. "Oh, she'll make him pay—by bleeding his personal estate dry to come up with the honor-price against the warrant and replacing him in the Comhairle with another tiarna whose gratitude will give her his vote. Leave it to the Banrion to turn her brother's rash judgment to her own advantage."

The Banrion continued to speak. ". . . but Tiarna Cíomhsóg is also correct in that the hostage taking is now éraic, and neither the Comhairle or the Rí can interfere in that." Aithne looked directly at Jenna, and though the sorrow still throbbed in her voice, her gaze was as hard as flint. "I wish it were different, First Holder. I wish the decision weren't so painful and difficult for you, or that I had wise counsel to give you. I don't. You must make your own decision as to how to respond to the éraic's demands. I can only offer myself as your servant to carry Lámh Shábhála to my brother, if that is what you decide."

47

Voices

SHE wished she could speak with Seancoim. She wished she could sink into her mam's arms and simply sob. She wished Ennis were there, warming the other side of her bed.

But the night was cold and empty, and there was no one but Jenna herself and the voices inside Lámh Shábhála. She stroked the stone, listening . . .

". . . *give it up! Aye, it will hurt and may even kill you, but holding the cloch will end up being more pain for you than this, and death is a final release. Save the man you love . . .*"

". . . *give up Lámh Shábhála, and you'll die unhappy and young. You'll hate him for having made you lose the cloch, that wonderful love of yours will turn sour and bitter and you'll end up with nothing. Nothing at all . . .*"

". . . *go there yourself and attack the man. If you lose, at least you've fought . . .*"

". . . *only a stupid fool would give up Lámh Shábhála for a lover . . .*"

". . . *only an utterly selfish one would keep it at the cost of a lover's death . . .*"

"Riata, talk to me," Jenna said, but if his voice was there in the babble, she couldn't distinguish it from the dozens of others. Jenna rolled from the bed, grimacing as the healing wounds and burns pulled and complained, and went over to a chest at the foot. Under the clothing were nestled the torc of Sinna Mac Ard and the carved blue seal her father had made. She picked up the seal, caressing it and holding it against Lámh Shábhála. A moment later, the moonlight streaming in from the windows shimmered, and she was looking at the interior of her cottage in Ballintubber, and her da glanced up in surprise. "Who are you?" he asked, as he had every time.

And as she had every time, she told him, and watched his disbelief slowly turn to acceptance. She told him about Mac Ard and Maeve, about Ennis. "I don't know what to do, Da," she said finally, unable to stop the tears. "I don't know . . ."

Niall put down the block of wood he was carving. He walked toward her and a hand went out to touch her in comfort, but it moved through her as if Jenna were no more substantial than air. He looked at his hand as if it had somehow betrayed him. "What if it were you, Da?" Jenna continued as Niall stared at the offending fingers. "What if holding the cloch meant that you lost Mam?"

"I never held a cloch na thintrí when it was alive," he answered. "It's not hard to give up something that had little value to you. I would give away a thousand stones like that to keep Maeve." He put his knife to the wood and a brown shaving curled away. "I'm sorry, Jenna. Truly I am. But I can't help you; I can't imagine needing to make the choice or the choice being that important." His sad, lost eyes gazed at her, and she was struck by the softness of his face and his hands. *He wouldn't have been strong enough to hold Lámh Shábhála. It would have destroyed him.* The thought was so like the cold, judgmental voices she'd heard in her head that she gasped, knowing it was her own voice she heard. She opened her hand and the carving fell to the floor. "Da, I'm sorry . . ." she whispered as Niall and the cottage vanished, leaving her alone in the room.

She left the carving where it fell, picking up a shawl and leaving her chambers. The guards posted outside started to follow her, but she gestured to them to stay. She hurried down the stairs and corridors of the keep and outside to the courtyard. "I need to go down to the town," she told one of the pages on duty there, and he scurried off to wake the stable master and bring a carriage. Half a stripe later, she left the carriage at one end of the wharf. "Stay here," she said to the driver. "I'll be back soon."

In the darkness, the harbor area was quiet, though she could hear laughter and singing from the tavern facing the docks, and the waves lapped the piers as mooring ropes groaned and hulls knocked gently against pilings. Jenna strode quickly to the end of the wharf where she and Ennis had gone the night of the Feast of First Fruits. She walked from the planks onto the wet, dark boulders there and sat, staring out over the water. She touched Lámh Shábhála, her attention drifting with its energy over the sea, calling.

There was an answer. Several minutes later, as she sat shivering in the cold night breeze, a head appeared in the waves, the waves splashing white and phosphorescent around it. A grunting warble: "Sister-kin." The Saimhóir hauled itself awkwardly out of the water and onto the pebbled beach.

"You knew," Jenna said. It was not so much an accusation as a statement, nor did Thraisha deny it. "When we left, you told him 'Farewell.' You knew."

The black eyes glinted in moonlight. Blue light shimmered in the satin fur, mottled with the pattern of the mage-lights. She smelled of brine and fish. "I knew that my land-cousin wasn't with you in my foretelling, and I had the sense that I wouldn't see him again."

Tears filled Jenna's eyes with that, and Thraisha waddled over until she could put her head in Jenna's lap. Jenna stroked the silken fur, crying. A drop fell near Thraisha, and she lapped at the water, tasting it. "Why do you give the salt water?" Thraisha asked. "Is it an offering to your gods?"

"No," Jenna answered, sniffing. "I'm crying because I know that I could change your vision. All I have to do is give up Lámh Shábhála."

"You can't do that." It was not a warning or a caution, only a statement of fact.

"Why not?" Jenna railed. "Why shouldn't I? What's Lámh Shábhála brought me that's so wonderful I can't bear to let it go? I've lost my mam, lost my home. I've had to endure more pain than I thought possible; I've killed peo-

ple and had them try to kill me." She yanked the stone
from around her neck, holding it in her hand, the chain
dangling. "Why *not* give it up?" she shouted. She took her
arm back, bringing it forward with a sharp, throwing
motion.

But there was no answering splash out in the water. Her
hand remained closed and when she opened it, the stone
was still there, glinting in her palm.

"Jenna, stroke my back." Jenna placed Lámh Shábhála
around her neck again, and reached down to Thraisha, her
fingertips grazing wet fur: "No—harder, so you can feel
beneath," Thraisha told her. Jenna rubbed the patterned
fur, and underneath the skin of her back and sides, she
could feel the lines of hard ridges. "Those are scars and
wounds that are still healing," Thraisha said. "Not from
harpoons or the teeth of the seal-biter. These are from my
own kind, because they wanted what I have and tried to
take it from me. Because they think that I'm wrong in what
I do."

Her front flippers slapped rock as she moved, and Jenna
saw that the left one was torn, as was her tail. "So it's no
different for you."

"No, sister-kin." In the cloch-hearing, Thraisha gave a
bitter laugh, as Jenna's own ears heard a soft warbling.
"Stone-walkers and Saimhóir both came from the loins of
the Miondia, and those lesser gods are all brothers and
sisters from the womb of the same deity, even if we give
Her different names. We *are* cousins and share more traits
than we like to admit. There are a few who believe as I
do, but only a few."

"What is it that you believe?"

Thraisha looked up at Jenna. "That we're to do more
with the gifts we've been given than use them as weapons.
That we who come First can mark this time and shape it
so that it will be different and better than all the times the
mage-lights have come in the past. That your fate and your
choices—*yours*, sister-kin—are important to the Saimhóir
because you hold Lámh Shábhála, who opened the way for
all and who might still guide us." She huffed, her nostrils
flaring at the end of the dark muzzle. "But there aren't

many who agree with me. Most believe that Saimhóir and stone-walkers should stay apart, that our changeling land-cousins are abominations, and that the Bradán an Chum-hacht should be used only for the needs of the Saimhóir. 'The stone-walkers live on the dry stones and their concerns aren't ours. We only meet them at the water's edge, and that's not enough. Use your gift for your own kind.' That's what they tell me."

"I hear the voices of all the old Holders," Jenna said. "I've never heard any of them speak much of the Saimhóir."

Again the laugh. "Then perhaps it's time one did."

"I didn't want this," she said. "I didn't ask for it."

"I know," Thraisha answered. "I didn't either. But it's ours, and the question is what will we do with it."

"You've already seen it in your foretelling. You've seen my death and yours. You've seen it all fail."

A cough, a moan. "Perhaps. Or, as you said, maybe that was only a vision of what could be, not what must be." Her head lay back on Jenna's lap, as if she were tired. "What do you think Ennis would tell you?"

"He would tell me not to worry about him and to do what I felt was right." She stroked Thraisha's head. "It should have been Ennis with Lámh Shábhála. Not me. It would have been better that way."

"It wasn't what Lámh Shábhála wanted," Thraisha answered. "It chose you, and there was a reason for that."

"Then it should tell me what it is."

"I think it has," Thraisha answered. "You just haven't listened. You need to listen now—to your head, not your heart."

"But Ennis . . ."

"Ennis is lost," Thraisha said. "I think you know that."

"No!" Jenna shouted the denial, screamed the word as if she could burn away the void inside her with the fury as she scrambled to her feet, pushing Thraisha away. In the tavern, the singing stopped, and someone opened the door, spilling yellow light over the dock and silhouetting a man's figure. "I won't *let* him be lost!"

"Hello out there!" the figure called. A few other heads appeared behind it. "Is everything all right?"

"I'm . . . fine," Jenna said, turning to wave at the people in the tavern door. "Sorry. I just . . . slipped."

The door closed. After a moment, the singing started up again.

When Jenna turned back, Thraisha was gone. The waves lapped the stones silently.

48

Glenn Aill

THE party that left Dún Kiil on horseback was tiny:
Jenna, Máister Cléurach, the Banrion Aithne and a
quartet of gardai along with six attendants. They were escorted for the first day by the Rí and several tiarna and
bantiarna of the Comhairle and their followers, but the others turned back when they came within sight of Sliabh
Míchinniúint, where long ago Máel Armagh had been defeated by Severii O'Coulghan. The group traveled on alone:
beyond the townland of Dún Kiil into Maoil na nDreas
and Ingean na nUan, and finally past the leaning, gray
stone marker of the Ó Dochartaigh clan.

Jenna could well believe that Rubha na Scarbh could
effectively hide Árón Ó Dochartaigh or a thousand others.
The landscape was violent and wild, with sudden cliffs,
great mountains of greenery-hung granite; boulder-clogged
lowlands and hummock-strewn bogs. Mist and clouds
draped the slopes and thunder rumbled in the valleys. They
followed wandering sheep and goat trails or no path at
all, coming upon "villages" of three or four houses where
suspicious, grimy faces peered at them from shuttered windows. For every mile they traveled northwest, it seemed
they traveled four up and down, or had to detour for half a
day around an escarpment that flung itself across their path.

They saw a herd of storm deer, their hooves striking
sparks from the rocks, the noise of their passage obliterat-
ing the storm. The next night, wind sprites lit the air around
them in the mist and fog. From the pine forests bristling

on the mountains came the howls of wolves that sounded
like sibilant, long chants. Red, glowing eyes watched them
from the darkness, and once there was a call that none of
them could identify at all: a chilling long moan that raised
the hair on the back of their necks, then was answered
from across the valley.

"The land is changing," Máister Cléurach said. "The Old
Ones are slowly waking from their long sleep. You woke
them, Jenna."

A rider had come up to their party that morning, as they
moved deeper into Ó Dochartaigh's land. A white banner
fluttered from his spear, and his scabbard was empty of its
sword. He'd glanced at Jenna, Máister Cléurach and their
escorts, then handed the Banrion a note. "I wasn't told the
Holder would be coming, or the Inishfeirm Máister," the
man said. "The tiarna . . ."

"Is my brother so defenseless that a dozen riders are a
threat to him?" the Banrion asked, and the man flushed.

"The Holder—"

"—wishes to see that the hostage is delivered into her
hands as was promised," the Banrion snapped. "Nothing
more. Tell Árón that she is here to give him the éraic he
demanded. Or if he prefers, we can ride back to Dún Kiil
and he can be content with nothing."

Jenna had remained silent, staring back as the rider's
eyes narrowed and his mouth tightened. Then, with an arrogant sniff, he wheeled around and galloped away. The Banrion had unrolled the parchment. "He'll meet us at Glenn
Aill," she said. Her eyebrows raised as she glanced at
Jenna. "This is what you want, isn't it, First Holder?"

Jenna felt a flush rise in her cheeks. "I don't know of
any other way to get Ennis back." Máister Cléurach came
up to them, listening. Jenna couldn't look at him, afraid of
what Aithne might see if she did.

The Banrion seemed mostly amused by Jenna's statement. "Love is a phantom, Holder. It lives but a few years,
then withers away and leaves you wondering how you could
have ever thought you liked this sad person sharing your
bed." She paused, her head tilting slightly as she regarded
Jenna. "I think we're more alike than you want to believe,

Jenna, and *I* certainly wouldn't give up what you have for
that."

"I suppose I don't have your cynicism, Banrion."

Máister Cléurach, grunted but said nothing. Aithne
smiled at Jenna. "I would call it realism, Holder. Besides,
your sacrifice leaves my brother as the Holder of Lámh
Shábhála."

"I would have thought that was something you might
prefer."

"Love is a phantom," Aithne repeated, "whether 'tis between lovers or between siblings. I hold no illusions as to
whether Árón would allow any lingering affection for me
to stand in the way of what he wants."

"And that is . . . ?"

"He would like to see a true Rí sitting on the throne at
Dún Kiil, one who wouldn't need or want the Comhairle.
With Lámh Shábhála, he could well have that." Her gaze
lingered on Jenna, and Aithne seemed to sigh. "I wish you
trusted me more, Holder. I think we both actually want the
same thing." She kicked heels into her horse's side.

"Does she know?" Máister Cléurach asked softly as the
Banrion moved up the trail. Jenna shook her head.

"I don't think so."

"We may have made a mistake in not telling her."

"If so, it's already made," Jenna answered. "We've gone
too far to take the chance now."

The Banrion stopped, looking back at the two of them.
She waved her arm. "We go this way," she said.

They were in their second day of storm.

" 'Tis no worse than others I've seen," Máister Cléurach
said. "The sea is a fey mistress and we're no more than a
speck in her hand—there's no escaping her whims, not in
Inish Thuaidh."

Jenna huddled sullen and miserable on her horse. The
reedcoat she wore flapped in the gale force winds that
shredded the gray-black clouds above and pushed them
firmly across the sky. The persistent and steady rain, blown
nearly horizontal, had penetrated every fold and gap in the
reedcoat and plastered her hair to her skull under the hood

she held over her face. Her mount plodded through the deluge, great clumps of mud clinging to her hoofs and fetlocks, her mane dripping and the leather saddle and reins sodden. The clouds ran aground on the tops of the steep mountains to either side of them, a thousand dancing and splashing rills and streams plummeting down their sides toward the river whose banks they followed.

It helped, a little, that the others in their small party were suffering with her. Máister Cléurach sniffled and coughed, the gardai and retainers grumbled and muttered. Only the Banrion Aithne seemed unaffected by the weather, sitting uncomplaining on her black mare as she peered around her.

"Another few hours," she said. "We're nearly there."

Glenn Aill emerged from the storm and haze like an apparition: a curving half-moon rampart of native stone thirty or forty feet high, its horns facing outward toward them. Huddled high on a steep mountainside and adorned with draperies of vine and moss, the fortification could have been part of the landscape. Dour, small windows peered out from two towers at either end of the structure; a single massive oaken door at the center led out into a cramped, winding path through fifty yards of *chevaux de frise*: pointed, tall rocks set like thousands of teeth bristling in the gums of the earth, through which an army would have trouble advancing at any speed. The rocks gave way to a long, sloping meadow separated by stone fences into dozens of small fields planted with various crops or grazed by sheep, all running down to a narrow black lough that filled the valley in front of them. A stone-walled bridge with wooden planks arched over the water. No more than two riders could have ridden across it abreast. "Glenn Aill was built over two hundred years ago and has never been taken by force of arms, though there have been attempts," the Banrion said. "Beyond the walls is the keep, also built of stone. Even if the outer wall and keep were overrun, there are corridors leading back into caverns in the mountain where you could hide forever, or come out far from here."

"You lived here?" Jenna asked. Aithne nodded, her gaze on the fortifications looming above.

"Now and again, when there was need," she answered. "Normally, there are only a few families of attendants here to keep the place ready. Our parents retreated here once, when the chieftain of Carraig an Ghaill attacked us over a dispute about grazing lands. I remember watching the battle—they never got farther than the bridge before they turned and retreated again. And my family would come here every so often, just to visit."

Jenna glanced at the forbidding scene, and Máister Cléurach shifted in his saddle. "Such a lovely holiday spot," he muttered, droplets falling from his white beard as he spoke. The Banrion only smiled.

"I think that right now Árón feels it's quite lovely," she said.

They rode over the bridge. The workers in the field stopped to look at them, and up on the mountainside, the great door in the wall opened. Several riders emerged, making their way through the *chevaux de frise*. "We should wait here," the Banrion said. "Out of any archer's range."

They pulled up their horses. The rain pummeled them as the riders made their way down the long slope. "This is your last chance, Holder," Aithne said to Jenna. "We could still turn and leave." Jenna only shook her head.

The riders stopped a few hundred yards from them. Árón was at their head. He reined in his horse and lifted a hand. "I expected no one but my sister," he said, his voice sounding distant and muffled in the storm.

"I need to see Ennis," Jenna called back to him. "I need to know that he's still alive."

Árón made a gesture, and two horsemen from the rear came forward. On one steed was Ennis, his hands bound together in front of him. The other was one of Árón's men, with one hand on Ennis' arm and a long dagger placed firmly against his throat.

"Ennis . . ." Jenna nearly sobbed the word. He sagged in his saddle as if desperately weary, and his green eyes were clouded with pain. His hair was disheveled and plastered to his skull with the rain; his skin was pallid and drawn. He stared at Jenna, pleadingly, and shook his head, water splattering on his face so that he blinked. He looked beaten. Defeated. Jenna nearly despaired, seeing him.

"Jenna," he husked. "Don't—" He stopped with a gasping intake of breath as the man holding him jabbed the blade against his throat.

"Be quiet," Árón warned him. "You are to say nothing."

She wanted desperately to go to Ennis, to rip the bonds from his hands and kiss him, to hold him in her arms again. And yet . . . he gazed at her like a lost thing, with no hope or joy in his eyes at all. *Is this the way Mac Ard was after I took the cloch from him? Is this what I would look like once Lámh Shábhála is gone—or worse, since it's woven itself so deeply into me . . . ?* She started to urge her horse forward, but Árón lifted his hand and the man holding Ennis pressed the dagger tight. "Move this way, Holder, and he dies. You know what I want. Give it to my sister. Now!"

Jenna let her hood fall back, uncaring of the rain. She brought her hands up and touched the chain around her neck. Muscles jumped in her face; she tightened her mouth, closing her eyes.

She lifted the chain from around her neck, the stone swinging in its silver cage, and handed it into Aithne's waiting hands. She bowed her head, clutching herself around the waist and cradling her right arm to herself as she gave a sobbing cry. Aithne glanced at the stone in her hand. Her lips lifted slightly, and Jenna quickly dropped her gaze away from the Banrion's face.

Árón's laughter came from up the hill. "Well, you are stronger than I thought possible, Holder. You should have heard your lover scream when I plucked the cloch from his hands," he called down to them. "Aithne, you may come forward now."

Máister Cléurach, alongside Jenna, leaned toward her. "She knows," he whispered.

"Maybe. It doesn't matter. Árón takes the stone, sends Ennis to us, and we go," Jenna replied.

"And after that?"

"We ride hard and fight if we must."

Jenna heard the Banrion slap her horse's neck with the reins, heard the animal take a few steps forward through the mud. Then she stopped, halfway between the two groups. "It's not much of a jewel, Árón," she said. "But I wonder . . . how it would look on me?"

"Aithne!" He shouted the name, a call of fury. Máister Cléurach hissed in irritation. Jenna glanced up to see Árón's horse rear in alarm, and nocked crossbows appeared from under the cloaks of his companions. "Don't be a fool, Sister. You'll wear that cloch for no longer than a breath. The moment you take it in your hand and try to claim it will be your last."

Aithne laughed. "Such glorious threats. What will you do with it, Brother? Use it to promote yourself? Such a banal and selfish purpose."

"Aithne, I warn you. The blood we share won't stop me from giving the order."

"Oh, I know it won't." Jenna watched Aithne heft the stone in her palm, as if in thought. "In truth, I gave this almost no thought until just now, when I took it into my hand . . ." She lifted her head up. "The truth is, Árón, that I trust the Holder Jenna more than I trust you. But . . ." She clucked at the horse, urging it forward again. As she came alongside Árón, she nodded her head to Ennis.

"Let him go now," Jenna heard her say. "That was the agreement."

"Give me Lámh Shábhála." He held his hand out, palm up.

"Let O'Deoradháin go," Aithne repeated.

"When I have Lámh Shábhála in my hand. Not before."

Aithne glanced over her shoulder toward Jenna, then placed the necklace in his hand. He stared at it, then his eyes lifted to find Jenna's gaze and he raised his voice to her. "I'm sorry," he said. "This is still not sufficient payment for my poor Cianna." He nodded to the man holding Ennis.

The knife moved, slashing deep, and blood fountained even as Jenna's hand belatedly closed around the true cloch, hidden in a small pocket in her clóca. "Ennis!" she screamed. "Ennis!"

He was already falling, his eyes open and unseeing, a froth of red foam on his lips.

Jenna was sobbing as she ripped open Lámh Shábhála with her mind. Unthinking, she threw its power, wild and raw, toward Árón. He was still holding the necklace in his hand, not yet realizing that it was a false stone. He was defenseless, his own cloch still resting untouched at his breast. She wanted to see him crushed and smashed, wanted the lightnings of the cloch to snap and burn around his screaming, broken body. She saw the lightning flash and crackle, arcing toward him, then . . .

Just before the fury struck Árón, Jenna saw another lightning strike her own, and the two exploded in a white fireball and thunder. Another bolt followed, and Jenna was forced to shove it aside.

That is Ennis' cloch, she realized. *They've given it to someone.*

Chaos erupted. Her senses lost in the cloch's, Jenna was vaguely aware of shouts and curses. She tried to follow the cloch's energy back, to see who possessed it, to kill him because he had what should have been Ennis'.

". . . Lámh Shábhála! Use it!"

". . . *she* still has it!"

Jenna was vaguely aware of what was happening around her. Máister Cléurach's hand convulsed around the stone about his neck; immediately the storm howled a thousandfold with Stormbringer's energy. A hurricane wind tossed men from their saddles and pounded against the walls of Glenn Aill. She saw Árón's fist close around the false Lámh Shábhála, then his face convulsed with a curse as he tossed it aside. Aithne had turned her horse, galloping back toward them as Árón lifted his own cloch.

Jenna, though, kept her attention on the person using Ennis' cloch. *You bastard . . . I'm almost there . . . I can feel you . . .*

A stream of energy—sapphire and white streams hissed and snarled, reminding Jenna all too well of the ambush in Dún Kill—flared from the Keep and struck Aithne, hurling the woman backward from her horse.

. . . there! I can almost see your face . . . The winged

demon appeared in the air above them, shouting rage; the
lava-creature spewed orange flame as the other two Clochs
Mór that had attacked Jenna and Ennis in Dún Kiil now
opened.

    . . . *by the Mother-Creator!*

Jenna saw the figure holding Ennis' cloch, standing at
one of the windows of the towers on the wall. She saw his
face and she nearly released Lámh Shábhála with the
shock.

She knew now why the cloch was handled so well and
easily. She knew now who had helped Ó Dochartaigh plan
the ambush. She knew now that there was another reason
Ennis had been taken.

The new Holder was also its old one: Padraic Mac Ard.

In the cloch-vision, it was as if they faced one another
in the same room though a quarter mile or more separated
them. His mouth moved, his eyes almost sad. "Jenna . . ."
The word was loud in her hearing, even through the
clamor. She recoiled backward, the vision of Mac Ard receding as if she were falling away from him impossibly fast.
She found herself back in her body, the roar of the battle
around her.

"Jenna!" Máister Cléurach shouted. His face was grim
and strained, his flesh pale as he lashed out with Stormbringer against the other clochs. He pointed at Aithne, but
even the gesture allowed an opening, and the lava-beast
threw globules of fire that the winds of Stormbringer hurled
aside only barely in time. The field workers were running
away in panic; the rows of wheat nearest Jenna and the
others were now ablaze. The Dún Kiil gardai had gone to
Aithne, swords drawn uselessly. One went down with a
crossbow quarrel in his breast.

The mage-demon flapped its dragon wings above Aithne,
claws out as it stooped like a hawk and plummeted. At the
same moment, blue lightning erupted again from Árón's
hand. Jenna imagined a wall above the Banrion and she felt
Lámh Shábhála shudder in her hand as the demon struck it,
as the searing energy from Árón's cloch battered at the
shielding force. The demon, growling in frustration, tore at

the shield; Jenna could feel it as if the claws were gouging at her own flesh. Aithne rose groggily, and she touched her own cloch.

A new demon appeared, the twin of the first. It hurled itself at the other and they came together with a roar.

Mac Ard sent lightning that tore at the earth directly in front of Jenna. Her horse reared, sending her falling to the ground. Her right elbow struck a rock in the mud, and her arm went numb. She was no longer holding Lámh Shábhála. The world snapped back into drab confusion, the power of the Clochs Mór now just half-glimpsed whirlings in the air, the shrill howling of wind, and the flickering of pale light. One of the stone fences exploded, shards of rock flying everywhere. A fragment sliced across Jenna's left arm, leaving a long cut that gaped white for an instant before blood welled up. Jenna cried in pain and frustration. Her right arm throbbed with the pain of wielding the cloch as she scrabbled in the mud. *There*—she saw the cloch, an arm's length away, and flung herself at it. Her hand closed about it . . .

. . . and the fury rose again: around her. Inside her.

"Mac Ard!" She screamed his name. She reached deep into the well of energy within her cloch, grasping it all, holding the power with her mind and shaping it. She could see him, could feel the lightning that writhed like snakes in his hands. She hurled the whole force of Lámh Shábhála's energy at him. He sensed the attack and pushed back at it. Árón, too, felt it, and his Cloch Mór turned to aid Mac Ard. For a moment they both held, then, with a cry, she broke through. Árón swayed in his saddle, senseless. Mac Ard, in his tower room, crumpled.

Jenna herself sagged, suddenly weary. She took a breath, ready now to finish it, to kill them . . .

There were cries and shouts around her—she saw one of Ó Dochartaigh's riders pluck the tiarna's unconscious body from his horse and turn to gallop back up the hill. The others followed, retreating as the other two Clochs Mór pushed back Máister Cléurach and the Banrion's renewed attacks. Jenna flung the cloch's rage at them, and one of

the Mages gave a cry and fell as the lava-beast wailed and
vanished. The door to Glenn Aill opened to let the remaining riders in, then shut.

She could feel the remaining Clochs Mór close also, their
Holders releasing the stones, though Máister Cléurach continued to hurl Stormbringer's energy toward the walls and
towers.

"Máister, it's over," Jenna heard Aithne say wearily.
"They've gone. They'll be in the caverns and gone before
we can get to them."

The old man lifted his hand. With a curse, he released
the cloch. The storm was simply a cold, soaking rain once
more. All but one of their gardai were dead; the Banrion's
attendants seemed to have fled. Three of the Ó Dochartaigh retinue lay on the ground, and . . .

"Ennis!" Jenna ran to him, ignoring the pain and fatigue
of her body. "By the Mother . . ." She sank into the mud
beside him, pulling him into her lap. His eyes were open,
and the long gaping wound across the side of his neck no
longer pulsed, but seeped thick and red. The ground below
him and his léine were soaked with it, and the blood covered Jenna's rain-slick hands as she cradled him.

"Ennis . . . Oh, Mother-Creator, no . . ." His name was
a wail, a keening of grief. The rain splattered on his still
face, on his unseeing eyes, and she rocked back and forth
in the muck and grass, willing him to stir, to take a gasping
breath, to speak, to live. She cried, praying to the Mother-
Creator, to the Seed-Daughter from whom the Miondia,
the lesser gods, had sprung, to Darkness in His own realm,
to any god that might bring him back. She touched Ennis'
face, still warm in the cold rain, and stroked his hair.

"He's gone, Jenna." Máister Cléurach's voice, at her
shoulder. "Jenna, I'm so sorry . . ."

He's not gone!, she wanted to rail at him. *I won't let him
be gone. There has to be something, some way to change
this* . . . But no words came out. She looked up at Máister
Cléurach, stricken dumb, her mouth open as she shook
her head.

She took Lámh Shábhála in her hand. She held the cloch,
opening the small store of energy still left within it. She

held the energy, not knowing how to shape it or change it so that she could bring his soul back from where it had fled. The brilliance of the mage-lights shimmered around her, and it meant nothing. She let go of the cloch and fell over Ennis' body, weeping.

She lay there for long minutes until gentle hands pulled her away.

49

Leave-taking

THE attendants, returning now that the battle was over, argued that with the rain it was impossible to cremate the body, but Jenna insisted that a pyre be built in the nearest field. Jenna watched as they sullenly constucted the pyre in the downpour, sitting by Ennis' body and refusing to move whenever Máister Cléurach or Aithne came to join her, though she didn't resist when they tended to her injuries. The tears came and went on some internal tidal rhythm; the grief filled her like a cold moonless sea, heavy and deep. The sun sank below the mountains beyond Glenn Aill; the rain subsided to drizzle as mist and a few stars emerged between ragged clouds.

"The pyre's ready," Aithne said. Jenna felt the Banrion's hand on her shoulder. The woman had said little since the battle. She crouched down alongside Jenna and took her hands, still clutching Ennis' stiffening body. "They need to take him now," she whispered, nodding to her attendants. They came forward silently and took the body as Aithne helped Jenna to her feet. She stood unsteadily, her legs weak with exhaustion and hours of sitting.

They placed the body atop the framework of logs and branches, and placed the bodies of the gardai who had died to either side of him. One of the retainers came forward with a burning torch and touched it to the base of the pyre. A pale blue flame flickered then went out. "The wood is soaked, Banrion," he called. "We used what little oil we

had, but . . ." There was a hint of pleasure in his words,
the ghost of an unspoken reprimand.

"I'll do it," Jenna said. She shrugged away the Banrion's
hands, drawing a breath as she found Lámh Shábhála's
chain, recovered from where it had fallen and around her
neck once more. She lifted the cloch, closing her eyes and
coaxing the remaining essence from deep within the well
of the stone.

She imagined fire: a flame of elemental force, burning
purer and hotter than a smelter's furnace. She placed the
image under the pyre and released it. With an audible
whump, the pyre burst into flame. White smoke billowed
as the moisture in the wood went immediately to steam and
evaporated. The pyre hissed and grumbled, but it burned so
aggressively that the attendants all moved well back. Shadows lurched and swayed behind them as the flames leaped
up to envelop the bodies, the light from it touching even
the walls of Glenn Aill. Jenna poured the last dregs from
Lámh Shábhála into the pyre; the flames roared in response, sending a whirling column of furious sparks pinwheeling into the night sky.

She watched as the flames devoured the corpses. She
imagined Ennis' soul soaring free, dancing in the glowing
ash toward the sky and the Seed-Daughter's welcome to
the afterlife. She watched until the pyre collapsed in a tornado of sparks; until it was no more than glowing embers;
until she saw above them the mage-lights snarling the sky
and felt the yearning, seductive pull of Lámh Shábhála
toward them.

"I know you're exhausted and hurting, Holder, but you
need to renew your cloch," Aithne said softly, startling
Jenna. "Árón and the others will be doing the same, and
it's a long and possibly dangerous ride home."

Máister Cléurach, off to one side, had already opened
his cloch to the lights. Aithne stood near Jenna, her face
gentle and sympathetic. The Banrion looked battered and
sore: a bruise discolored her cheek and puffed one side of
her mouth. Her clóca and léine were scorched, torn, and
filthy, and blood had soaked through along one arm where
a long cut trailed down nearly to her wrist. She'd been

burned on the other arm—Jenna could see the blisters that glistened on the woman's left hand, running up beyond the sleeve of her léine.

Jenna nodded. "Banrion, I'm sorry . . ." she began, then faltered. So much had happened that demanded an apology: that she hadn't told the Banrion about the false Lámh Shábhála she and Máister Cléurach had prepared; that she hadn't trusted Aithne; that Aithne had been injured protecting her . . . "I wish I'd told you before what the Máister and I had done."

"I wish you had also," Aithne said and the agreement cut deeper than any of the wounds. "But I knew, or at least suspected. And I understand why you kept your own counsel and didn't tell me."

"Árón was your brother, and I didn't know how you'd react. I thought it might work, and it was the only way I could think of to get Ennis back, and . . ." A deep sob racked her from the center of her being, a grief so huge and terrible that for a moment she thought she couldn't bear it. Aithne put her arms around Jenna, pulling her close. Jenna wept on the Banrion's shoulder, letting the lamentation rise within her and give voice to her bereavement as Aithne stroked her hair and kissed the top of her head as her mam might have done.

Her mam . . .

Jenna gently pulled away from Aithne, pushing the grief back down within herself. "Banrion, during the battle, Lámh Shábhála showed me the face of one of your brother's allies. It was Tiarna Padraic Mac Ard, of Tuath Gabair, holding the cloch they'd taken from Ennis. And the other clochs . . . Máister Cléurach is certain that at least one of the other Clochs Mór was among those stolen from Inishfeirm."

Aithne's face went grim. "That's a strong accusation," she responded. "Árón is stubborn and foolish. He thinks mostly of himself. But you call him a traitor to Inish Thuaidh now. And *that* is something I find hard to believe."

"I know what I saw," Jenna answered. She gestured at the sullen orange embers of the pyre. "I'm also realizing, now, how the loss of someone you love can mark and change you. And your brother's right: I was responsible for that. I bear the blame."

Aithne said nothing. Her gaze went from Jenna to the pyre. Finally, she placed her hand over her Cloch Mór. "I've been told the name of this cloch is Scáil," she said. "'Reflection,' because it steals the power from another Cloch Mór and uses that force to defeat the attack. Árón gave the cloch to me, after I returned from meeting you at Inishfeirm. He said that it had been in our clan for centuries, but though he was eldest and it belonged rightfully to him, he had another. I used the cloch with Árón so that I could learn to understand how it worked. In those few minutes when our clochs were linked and struggling against each other, I also saw Árón's mind mirrored in my own." She paused, taking a slow breath and looking away from Jenna. "I saw the rot in his soul," she continued. "I don't think you made him that way, Jenna. I think Cianna's death only exposed that vein within him and gave him an excuse to turn to it more and more. If the Rí Ard promised Árón that he would be made Rí in Dún Kiil, then my brother might well listen and betray kin, clan, and oath. But I still hope not. I still hope that there's some other reason why he would tolerate Mac Ard's presence here."

Aithne sighed. She glanced up at the sky, then down at her cloch. "We don't have much time, Holder," she said. "And whatever my brother is or whatever he plans, you will need Lámh Shábhála. Let's use the mage-lights while we can, and worry afterward."

The day dawned surprisingly clear and warm. The field workers came out from Glenn Aill, staying well away from the encampment over which flew the banner of Dún Kiil and Rí MacBrádaigh. Of Árón Ó Dochartaigh and his people, there was no sign. Jenna let Lámh Shábhála open slightly; in the wave of cloch-vision she felt no other Clochs Mór aside from those with the Banrion and Máister Cléurach. If Árón and Mac Ard were still lurking in the area, they weren't where they could immediately attack.

Ennis' pyre still smoldered in the field, wispy tendrils of smoke rising from the ash. "Holder?"

Jenna turned to see Aithne and Máister Cléurach already mounted on their horses. The attendants were packing the last of the supplies onto the pack animals and the Banrion held the reins of Jenna's horse. "It's time to go back to Dún Kiil," Aithne said. "We need to make plans. I'll make certain that the Comhairle puts a watch on our coast immediately, but I don't have much hope that we'll catch Mac Ard before he returns to Talamh an Ghlas and tells the Rí Ard what's happened here. If you're right and my brother has allied himself with the Rí Ard and the Tuatha, then we can expect them to attack soon. Possibly before the Festival of Gheimhri and winter. I've been talking with Máister Cléurach; he wants you to go back to Inishfeirm at least through the month of Softwood to continue your study with Lámh Shábhála."

Jenna walked over to them and took the reins. She swung herself up on the horse, tucking the long clóca between her legs. She stared at the pyre, then lifted her gaze away from Glenn Aill to the north and east where mountains lifted stony heads in the sunshine.

"*. . . You can determine the shape of this age . . .*"

"*. . . It doesn't have to be this way . . .*"

"I don't think my path leads to Inishfeirm or Dún Kiil," she said.

Máister Cléurach followed the direction of her gaze, and his mouth tightened under his beard. "You can't be thinking of Thall Coill. Jenna, don't be stupid—"

He stopped as Jenna's head snapped around and she glared at him. "If you think that I'm at all concerned about the possibility of dying, you're mistaken, Máister."

He sniffed and frowned. "I didn't think that at all, First Holder. In fact, it doesn't surprise me at all that you'd choose a suicidal course. So far, your recent choices haven't proved to be particularly wise."

The words stung, her face reddening as if he'd slapped her across the cheek. "The difference between us is that I don't judge wisdom by how little the action might cost me."

Aithne gave a short laugh, but Máister Cléurach's eyebrows lowered like white thunderheads over the sea.

"Jenna," he said, his placating tone at odds with his face, "at Inishfeirm, I can show you what the other Holders of Lámh Shábhála have said about Thall Coill and the Scrúdú. Why, neither Tadhg or Severii O'Coulghan would attempt that, not after Tadhg witnessed Peria's death, and Tadhg was one of the most accomplished cloudmages."

"So you believe that because Tadhg was afraid of the Scrúdú, I should be also. No doubt that's more of what you call wisdom."

"Tadhg watched the woman he loved die there," Máister Cléurach answered, all the softness gone from his voice. It was steel and bone. "You of all people should appreciate that. Don't push away those who are only trying to help you, Holder. You need us more than you can imagine."

"Don't try to impose your will where it doesn't belong. I am the First Holder, not you."

The two glared at each other. The Banrion rode up between them, so that their horses shifted and the eye contact was broken. "I think the Holder is fully aware of your feelings, Máister Cléurach," she said. "Jenna, I won't presume to tell you what course to follow. I only ask you to consider this: if you go to Thall Coill and fail, then you leave Inish Thuaidh open to the Rí Ard."

"If I don't, then probably Inish Thuaidh falls anyway. And right now, Banrion, I have to say that I find I don't really care. Inish Thuaidh was my great-mam's home and I love this land, too, but ultimately the land will remain, no matter who is called Rí in Dún Kiil. Will the lives of these people change?" She gestured at the field workers. "They'll just switch one master for another, that's all. No matter who rules, the crops will have to be planted, tended, and harvested, and the stock will have to be fed and watered. I know. I was once one of them and I cared nothing for the Riocha in their keeps and estates. When you say Inish Thuaidh will fall, you mean yourself."

If Aithne felt the lash of Jenna's words, she showed none of it. "Then perhaps you made a mistake not handing over Lámh Shábhála to my brother yesterday," she answered with a gentle reproof. "The Rí Ard's interest in Inish Thuaidh is mostly because you're here, after all. If you'd given him Lámh Shábhála, it might be that no army would come here at all."

Jenna's hand had gone protectively to her breast, where the cloch was hidden under her léine. "Jenna," the Banrion continued, "there are times we're drawn into something all unwillingly. No matter what you do, the Rí Ard considers you now to be part of Inish Thuaidh. You're their enemy; nothing you say or do will change that, not until you no longer hold Lámh Shábhála." Aithne stopped then, her gaze sliding to Jenna's right hand and past to the white ashes of the pyre. "You had something I've never had, however short the time," she said. "I envy you that, Jenna. What do you think *he* would tell you? Can you hear Ennis' voice?"

"Aye," Jenna answered immediately. "I listened all night for it, asking him the same question. I heard the answer."

"This is nonsense," Máister Cléurach said. "Banrion, we have no time to waste here."

"Should I tie the First Holder to her horse and drag her back to Dún Kiil?" Aithne answered. "Is that something you want to try, Máister?"

Máister Cléurach glowered but said nothing.

The Banrion gave Jenna a soft smile. The torc about her neck glinted with the movement. "Your Ennis spoke to you, truly?"

Jenna nodded. "I hear him here," she said, touching her breast.

"Surely you're not thinking of telling her to go," Máister Cléurach said. "That would be a tragedy for all of us, including Jenna."

Aithne sighed. "It's not a decision any of us need to make yet. Jenna, the High Road to the townland of Ingean na nUan is still two days' ride from here, and that's the road you'd need to travel to An Ceann Ramhar and eventually Thall Coill. We'll ride together at least that far, then we'll see." She looked at Máister Cléurach warningly. "And we'll speak of this no more today. A few days of thinking might do us all some good."

50

Roads Taken

THERE were barrows where their path met the High
Road, which was little more than an unmarked trail
heading vaguely northeast down from the hills. In the storm
and rain, Jenna had noticed neither the High Road nor
the barrows when they'd passed before. The mounds were
overgrown, appearing as stony, weed-infested hillocks in
the field alongside the path, the low sun draping long shadows behind them.

"They're old Bunús Muintir graves," Banrion Aithne
said, noticing Jenna's attention. "There are a few barrows
here in Rubha na Scarbh, and more in the northern townlands. As children, we were told they were haunted. We
were warned to stay away from them or the wights would
rise from their slumber and come for us. No more than
tales, I'm sure. I know that I was shooed away from them
more than once, and Árón as well. They say there are still
Bunús living in the hills and people still saw them occasionally, though I never did." She inclined her head to Jenna.
"There's only another hour or two of light. There's an inn
we could reach in that time and stay in dry and warm
rooms."

"On the road to Dún Kiil?"

A nod.

"I'm staying here tonight," Jenna said. Máister Cléurach
groaned audibly.

"I don't care to sleep another night with rocks digging

into my back," he said. "I'm an old man and I've been too many days away."

"Then go on," Jenna told him. "Leave me here. I'm going no farther today."

Máister Cléurach looked at the Banrion. "Rocks," he said. "In her head, too."

"If we stay out here, anyone can see our fire from the hills around us," the Banrion said to Jenna. "I know those with my brother will have eyes out there, reporting to him where we are. I doubt he would dare attack after the last time, but I don't know that for certain. He'd be less likely to do so if we're in a village, where others might be more inclined to side with the Rí in Dún Kiil."

Jenna said nothing, sitting on her horse and staring down to where the High Road led off through the heather. She felt more than heard the Banrion's sigh.

"We'll stay here," Aithne told the attendants. "Make the camp ready."

The mage-lights that night were faint and weak, soft filaments that glowed fitfully and vanished. Jenna watched them while sitting between the barrows, away from the encampment and the fire, a blanket around her shoulders. Both the Banrion and Máister Cléurach had come to her earlier—Máister Cléurach demanding and gruff, Aithne soothing and understanding, but both attempting to convince her to return to Dún Kiil. To both of them she gave the same reply: "I'll decide by morning."

She didn't know what she expected to happen during the night to ease the conflict within herself. The thoughts chased themselves, ephemeral and changing, impossible to hold or examine. She felt the conflict deep in her soul; when she tried to muddle through the choices in front of her, Ennis' face rose before her and the grief welled up again, overcoming her.

Once, she opened Lámh Shábhála, but there was only more confusion and contradiction in the voices of the old Holders and she closed it again quickly, returning to the near-silence of the night.

In the darkness there was the rustling of dark wings. A

form appeared on the barrow to her left, a particle of night
with black eyes that stared at her. A yellow beak opened.
The creature cawed once.

"Dúnmharú?" At the name, the crow cawed again and
spread wide wings, gliding down to land in the grass in front
of her. Its head cocked inquiringly at her. "Dúnmharú, is
that really you?"

The crow cawed once more as she reached out toward
it. It didn't move, but let her touch the soft, black feathers
of its head and back. She glanced about her. "Seancoim, is
he here, too?"

Dúnmharú hopped backward, then flapped away again
to the barrow, alighting there and cawing again. When
Jenna got to her feet, the crow flew up again and landed
just past the end of the grave, moving away from the fire
and the encampment. Another caw. Jenna glanced back to
where the Banrion and Máister Cléurach were' sleeping,
then followed after the bird. Fly several feet and wait; fly
several feet and wait . . . The pattern went on for some
time, until Jenna was well away from the camp, moving
steadily down and east into a wooded valley. Dúnmharú
led her along the bed of a stream tinkling merrily as it
descended the slopes, until it finally merged with a river
wending southward through a stand of sycamores. Dúnmharú cawed again, loudly this time, and flew off with a great
flapping of wings, circling high and disappearing into the
leaves of the trees.

"Jenna!"

The call was soft in the darkness, the voice familiar. She
saw a flickering gleam of white beard in the shadows, and
Seancoim stepped out toward her, leaning on his staff of
oak.

"Seancoim!" She rushed to him, enveloping him in her
arms and taking in the familiar smell of spices and herbs
that exuded from his body and clothing. "I can't believe
you're here. How did you know, how did you get
here . . . ?"

The old Bunús Muintir seemed to gaze past her with his
cataract-white eyes, his hand holding hers. Dúnmharú came
flapping down from the branches above to land on his

shoulder in a flurry. "You still overlook the slow magics,"
he told her. "It was always the fault with most of you
Daoine. You'll likely ignore them entirely now, with the
power you wield with the clochs na thintrí." He took a
long, slow breath and let it out again. "I saw, I heard," he
said. "Once this was Bunús Muintir land, and some of us
still live here, hidden." His blind eyes looked aside, but
Dúnmharú regarded her with steady, bright eyes. "I came
as quickly as I could. But it seems I've come late. I saw
the pyre two nights ago, and I felt your anguish. I'm sorry,
Jenna. I knew that there was to be love between the two
of you. Even when you denied it back in Doire Coill, I
knew. I'm sorry."

The tears came again then, sudden and hot, pushing from
deep within her. She'd thought that she cried away all the
pain, but it returned now, redoubled, and she realized how
much she'd been holding away, hiding it from Aithne and
Máister Cléurach and herself.

"You'll always feel this pain," Seancoim murmured in
her ear as he held her. "It will always be with you. You'll
hear a sound or smell something, and it will remind you of
him and you'll feel the loss all over again. But it will stop
hurting you so much. You'll get used to carrying the grief,
as you're starting to carry the pain of Lámh Shábhála without thinking about it."

"I was there. I saw them kill him and I couldn't *do* anything to stop it."

"I know. And that's not your fault. You need to mourn,
but you also need to move past the grief. You're still here,
Jenna, and while you are, you can't forget this world. If
you're going to Thall Coill, I knew I should be with you."

"Thall Coill . . ." She repeated the name, sniffing and
wiping at her eyes. "That's what some of the Holders told
me. Riata . . ."

"I know. I saw his spirit, wandering restless from his
grave and looking north. Come with me; we have a long
way to travel and night is the best time." He hugged her
again, then started to move away into the trees. Jenna
began to follow, then glanced back up into the hills, where

the campfire glimmered like a yellow-orange star. "You can choose only one path, Jenna," Seancoim said.

"How do I know which is the right one?" Jenna asked him.

"You don't," he answered. "And you never *will* know. Not until the Seed-Daughter calls your soul back to Her and whispers the tale of your life in your ear. But you need to choose now. Go with them, or with me."

"I'll go with you," Jenna answered, and with the words she could feel the doubt dissolve within her. She gave a final glance back at the campfire, wondering whether the Banrion or Máister Cléurach realized yet that she was gone. Soon they would, but Jenna felt certain that she knew what the Banrion's decision would be: *We can't waste time searching for the Holder. She's made me a promise, and she'll keep it if she can. We return to Dún Kiil . . .*

Jenna turned to Seancoim, and followed his shuffling steps into the deep shadows of the sycamores, Dúnmharú flitting ahead above them.

As Seancoim had indicated, they moved by night and rested by day, slipping through the landscape while the people in the villages and farms slept. They met other Bunús Muintir: they crossed the River Teann in a currach oared by a Bunús they met on the shore, apparently waiting for them. Seancoim and the other man spoke in their own language briefly, the Bunús occasionally glancing at Jenna, but he either didn't speak the Daoine language or had nothing he wanted to say to her. When she thanked him for his help, he merely grunted and pushed his boat away from the shore, paddling back the way they'd come.

Jenna remembered the maps she'd seen in Inishfeirm and Dún Kiil. Though she couldn't read the markings on them, both Ennis and Máister Cléurach had pointed out to her the townlands and geography of Inish Thuaidh. Ingean na nUan, through which they walked now, was a lush land of rolling hills, punctuated here and there by the wide, checkered expanse of farmed lands, with small villages that re-

minded Jenna achingly of Ballintubber, tied together with
the narrow ribbons of rutted dirt roads. They avoided the
settled areas, keeping to the forest that wound in and
around the farmland. As the nights passed, they moved
steadily eastward and the land started to rise again. With
each dawn, as they settled in to rest, Jenna could see the
mountains ahead of them less blue with distance, looming
higher until their path started to lift toward them and they
were walking ·in green, narrow valleys where rills and
brooks rushed frantically down steep slopes toward them,
half-hidden in bracken and thickets. They turned northward
now, and when they were forced to climb up to one of the
ridgelines, Jenna could glimpse off to the east the shore of
Lough Áthas; then, a few days later, to the north, the endless expanse of the Westering Sea, its waves touched with
the milk of moonlight. Jenna wondered if, somewhere out
there, Thraisha or her kind swam. But they never came
close enough to the shore for Jenna to call for the Saimhóir
with the cloch. Seancoim now turned north and east,
roughly following the coastline but staying with the spine
of mountains, steep hills, and drumlins bulwarking the island from the winds and storms that the sea often flung at
it, and passing into the townland of An Ceann Ramhar.

This townland was sparsely settled, and the villages grew
even smaller and farther apart as they continued north.
They began seeing large herds of storm deer, their hooves
striking thunder from the land. Wind sprites wafted in
clouds through the branches of trees, and the red, glaring
eyes of dire wolves could be glimpsed watching them as
they passed, though none attacked. There were other
sounds and calls in the dark, and glimpses of creatures
Jenna couldn't identify. Even the more normal creatures
seemed strange. She saw eagles flying high overhead with
wingspans wider than she was tall, and they called to each
other with voices that sounded almost human; there were
enigmatic ripples in the dark lakes, odd footprints in the
earth.

"The land has almost fully awakened here," Seancoim
said one morning as they settled into an overhanging hollow in a hillside to sleep. He lit a small fire with dead

branches, striking the tinder into reluctant flame with flint
and steel. Dúnmharú flapped over to roost on a nearby
branch, his head down on his breast. "It spreads slowly,
but soon all places will be like this. When the mage-lights
last faded, hundreds of years ago, these creatures faded,
too, remembered only in the tales of the old people. In a
few generations, they were nothing more than myths and
legends, and those who claimed to see them were ridiculed
and laughed at. Now the mage-lights bring them back from
the hidden, lost places where they rested."

"All the fables are real?" Jenna remembered the tales
she'd heard back in Tara's Tavern: from Aldwoman Pearce
or Tom Mullin or in the songs Coelin sang.

"Not all. But most are based on some truth, no matter
how twisted and distorted they've become over time. In
another twenty or thirty turns of the seasons, everyone will
have seen the real meaning of the Filleadh." Seancoim
groaned as he settled back against the rocks. He rummaged
in his pack for an earthenware pot, filled it with water from
one of the skins, and set it at the edge of the fire. He
unrolled a packet of dried fruit and meat and passed it over
to Jenna. "In Thall Coill, the awakening is nearly
complete."

"Tell me about Thall Coill," Jenna said, breaking off a
bite of the smoked meat. "Tell me about the Scrúdú. I
asked En—" She started to say the name, and her throat
closed. She forced back the sudden tears, swallowing.
". . . Ennis," she continued, "but he didn't know much
about it, and Máister Cléurach simply wouldn't talk about
it at all."

Seancoim shook his head, his white, featureless eyes
seeming to stare at the fire. "I won't, either," he said. "Not
until it's time."

"Máister Cléurach believes that it's not real, that it's a
Bunús Muintir trick to kill the Daoine Holders."

"Is that what you think?"

"I don't believe you would do that to me."

Seancoim didn't answer, only nodded sleepily. The eastern sky was lightening, though the sun was still behind the
hills. The clouds were painted with rose and gold. "If I fail

at Thall Coill," Jenna said, "I want you to take Lámh Shábhála."

Seancoim laughed at that. "Me? An old, blind man? A Bunús Muintir?" He laughed again, setting his pack behind his head as a pillow. "No," he answered. "It's not a burden I want. Not now. If you fall, I'm certain that Lámh Shábhála will find itself another Holder, all on its own—one that it wants." He turned on his side, facing the fire. "And if you don't let me rest these old bones, we'll never get there and you won't have to worry about it at all."

The mountains curved away east to their end at the long bay that jutted deep into Inish Thuaidh. Here, they were taller and stonier than their green-cloaked brothers and sisters to the south, thrusting jagged peaks into a steel-gray sky, piercing the clouds so that they bled rain and oozed a mist that cloaked the summits and sometimes fell heavily into the valleys below. This was wild land, and if there were Daoine here at all, Jenna saw no sign of them. "The only towns of your people are well off to the south, in the farmlands away from the coast," Seancoim told her, Dúnmharú sitting on his shoulder. He pointed away with his walking stick to the hazy triple lines of ridges, one atop another, receding into the mist, and gestured to the ramparts yet to the north of them, a wall of stone. "Past there is the peninsula of Thall Coill."

"Do you know the way through? Have you been here before?"

"No," Seancoim answered. "But we'll be shown the way, I'm sure."

"What do you mean?"

"Be patient," he told her.

They rested there that day, and Seancoim roused Jenna before sunset. They broke camp and trudged northward, toiling steadily upward between walls of gray rock spotted with lichens and garlanded with slick green mosses. To Jenna, it seemed that Seancoim wandered, moving left or right at random, their progress erratic. He said nothing, but seemed to be waiting. As they trudged on, walking in deepening twilight while the peaks above them were still

touched with the last rays of the sun, Jenna had the sense
of being watched, though she saw nothing and no one. The
feeling persisted; it was so strong that she touched Lámh
Shábhála and opened it slightly, letting the cloch's energy
be her vision. She could sense life around them, but she
recognized none of the patterns it made in the cloch-vision.
Somewhere, near the edge of the cloch's sight, though,
there were pinpricks of radiance less bright than a Cloch
Mór: some of the clochmion, the minor stones. She started
to mention it to Seancoim, but he simply grunted and shook
his head at her, and she subsided into silence.

They walked on, and the feeling of being watched persisted and strengthened as the sun vanished and the sky
above darkened to ultramarine, then black. The crescent
moon had yet to rise, but the constellation of the Oxcart
wheeled ahead of them. The birds had settled into their
roosts and Dúnmharú was nearly unseen as he moved from
rock to rock ahead of them.

Suddenly Dúnmharú gave a *caw* of alarm and hopped
quickly into the air. The mound of rocks on which he
perched seemed to shiver and lift and change, until . . .

. . . the mound shifted like molten glass and solidified
again, taking on the shape of a bulky, humanlike form
standing shorter than Jenna or Seancoim, nearly as wide as
it was tall. It raised its arms, then cracked them together
again with a sound like two boulders smashing. A few seconds later, there was an echoing clamor to their right, and
two other rock piles began to move, flowing slowly into
similar forms. In the darkness, their exact shape was difficult to see, but there was a scraping sound as they walked
forward with a rolling, side to side gait. They wore no clothing, their bodies a light brown-gray color like slate yet with
a glossy sheen like fired pottery, their limbs thick and muscular. They stopped a few yards from Jenna and Seancoim
as Jenna reached for Lámh Shábhála, ready to use the cloch
at need. Thick eye ridges curled downward on the lead
creature's face; its rough-hewn features frowned. Again, it
clashed hands together, and this time Jenna saw sparks
jump as the hands came together.

Seancoim answered with a like gesture, the sound of his

handclap almost comically soft in contrast. The creature
uttered a low, warbling tone and seemed to nod, its head
inclining slowly first to Seancoim then Jenna. It stretched
a thick-fingered hand out to Jenna, beckoning once.

"Seancoim?"

"They are Créneach," he answered. "Have you never
heard of them?" Jenna shook her head. "If you'd been
brought up here, you would have," he continued. "They
belong to yet another one of the old tales: the Clay People
who live in their mountain fastnesses. The Hewers of Rock,
the Eaters of Stone, the Dwellers In Darkness, the Boulder-
folk. There were a dozen names for them in my childhood."

Jenna touched the cloch as the Créneach gestured again
to her, its voice a liquid sibilance almost like a bird's call.
As she did so, she felt that same presence of a clochmion,
focused in all of the Créneach before her—not hung about
them like jewelry, the way she carried Lámh Shábhála, but
inside. A part of their being.

Glancing back once at Seancoim, she went forward
slowly, stopping an arm's length from the creature. Now
that she was close, she could see umber eyes that reflected
light back at her as it stared up toward her, as a cat's eyes
might. The skin was unnaturally smooth, flecked with color
like polished granite, and muscles bulged in arms, the torso,
and legs. The unclothed being in front of her seemed to
possess no gender at all; like its two companions, there was
only a smoothness where she would have expected to see
genitalia. The Créneach had no nose; instead, twin fissures
ran between the eyes, each curling outward and under the
deep eye sockets. The nasal openings flexed as the creature
inhaled deeply in Jenna's direction, still venting its warbling
noises. It leaned closer to Jenna, its head level with the
cloch hanging on its chain. It snuffled and a trill of musical
notes came from its mouth. A long tongue flicked out, a
flash of purple. Before Jenna could react, the creature
licked at Lámh Shábhála, the long, thin tip snaking between
the silver wire of its cage before retracting. The creature
smacked its lips, its eyes half closed as if considering the
taste as Jenna's hand went belatedly to the cloch. She
closed her hand around it, stepping back. The Créneach

gave a final smack and turned to its companions; they conversed loudly in their own language for a moment.

Jenna opened Lámh Shábhála, and in the cloch-hearing, words mingled with the warbling voice as the Créneach swiveled to face her again. "Soft-flesh bears the All-Heart. She returns to us. Soft-flesh will follow." It beckoned as the trio turned and started to waddle away between the rocks.

"Wait!" Jenna called to it, wondering if it could understand her through the clochmion inside it as Thraisha had understood her. "Who are you? What do you want?"

It looked at her. "You may call me Treoraí, for I've come to escort you," it said, then continued to walk away.

Jenna glanced at Seancoim. He was already shuffling to follow them, his staff clattering against the rocks. She released the cloch, not wanting the Créneach to overhear her. "You're going to follow them?" she asked. "Seancoim, we don't know them or what they might intend to do."

"They seem to know where they're going," he answered. "And I don't. Have you a better idea?"

He smiled at her. Dúnmharú cackled on his shoulder.

Jenna grimaced, but she followed.

51

The Tale of All-Heart

TREORAÍ and its companions led them on a winding, upward path between two peaks. After a long climb, Treoraí turned abruptly, descending by a set of steep and narrow stone steps into a barely-visible cleft. They followed the stairs down, then walked another mile or so before again turning through a jagged fissure into a short passage and out into a small valley. The moon had risen by then, and Jenna could see a few other Créneach there as well as the black openings of caverns set in the overhanging, furrowed cliffs that lined the hidden spot. There were no more than fifteen of the creatures; in the cloch-vision, Jenna could sense that each of them held within it a clochmion . . . and that there was one spot of greater brightness: a Cloch Mór.

She had stopped at the entrance, though Seancoim continued on. Treoraí gestured for her to come forward. "Soft-flesh, bring the All-Heart," it said, the words sounding in her head while her ears heard the musical trill of its voice. Jenna hesitated, but Seancoim was standing there also, with the Créneach around him and seemingly unconcerned. Dúnmharú flew over to Jenna, circled her once with a harsh caw, then flew back to Seancoim. She took a hesitant step forward as the Créneach gathered around her like a crowd of strangely-sculpted children. They sniffed and their tongues flicked out to touch her right hand, curled protectively around Lámh Shábhála. The touch of them was strange: cool and smooth, yet strangely hard—like fired and glazed pottery that was impossibly pliable. She could hear the whispers as they huddled close, their voices crowding inside her head.

". . . the All-Heart . . ."

". . . ahh, the taste . . ."

". . . it comes back to us . . ."

". . . bring the Littlest to see . . ."

Jenna saw one of the Créneach push forward as the others made way. It carried a small form in its arms: an infant Créneach, the tiny body smooth and marbled with color, its arms waving as each Créneach they passed touched it with its tongue. There was a brilliance in the cloch-vision: the Cloch Mór was within the child.

"This is our Littlest," Treoraí said. "Given to us in the return of the First-Lights. It carries a Great-Heart within it, so we know that the All-Heart is pleased with us and our long wait." Treoraí took the infant from the other Créneach, cradling it close. "It will have life while the First-Lights stay, and when the lights return to their search, it will go with them."

"I don't understand," Jenna said, shaking her head. "The All-Heart, the lights . . . I don't know what you mean."

"Then listen," Treoraí answered. Its tongue ran along the child's face, like a caress, and the infant mewled in soft contentment. "You bear the All-Heart, so you should know . . ."

Back when there was only stone in the world and the First-Lights gleamed, before the coming of the soft-flesh things, there was Anchéad, the First Thought. Anchéad wanted a companion, and so took a pebble from Itself and let the First-Lights wrap around it. The First-Lights gave the pebble of Anchéad life and awareness, and from this piece grew the god we call Céile. Within Céile, Anchéad's pebble grew, always pulling the First-Lights toward it. For a long time, Anchéad and Céile dwelled together, but Ceíle found that Anchéad still sometimes yearned for Its solitude and would often go wandering by itself, leaving Céile alone for years at a time. So Céile also became lonely, and like Anchéad, broke away a pebble from Itself and held it out to the First-Lights, and they came and gave it life and shape also, though the fire of its life did not burn as deeply as Céile's. Each time that Anchéad went wandering, Céile would break off another part of Itself, until there were a dozen or more children of Céile. Sometimes her children even broke off fragments of themselves and made their own children, but their hearts were even weaker than their own and shone only dimly.

The children and grandchildren of Céile were the first of the Créneach.

One day, though, Anchéad went wandering and never returned, and Céile sorrowed though the Créneach tried to give It comfort. The First-Lights felt the grief and loss of Céile, and in sympathy they left and went to search for Anchéad. As they faded, so did Céile's life and those of the Créneach. When the First-Lights had gone completely, Céile and Its children and grandchildren fell down lifeless, and the wind and rain wore away the form of their bodies until all that was left were their gleaming hearts.

The soft-flesh things came, and they took away many of the hearts they found for themselves, for they loved the way the hearts looked—Céile's heart was one of those that was taken.

And so it was until finally the First-Lights returned again from their unsuccessful search for the lost Anchéad. The First-Lights found Céile's heart and they went to it, filling it once more. But the soft-flesh things held the heart now and the First-Lights could not bring Céile back, nor any of Its children or grandchildren who had also been taken. But the All-Heart that had been within Céile was able to stir and waken the hearts of all Its children and grandchildren: those hearts the soft-flesh things possessed could hold the power of the First-Lights, but only the few who had not been touched by the soft-flesh things could revive and have form and shape again as Créneach.

Without Céile, though, none of the Créneach could take of themselves and make children. The First-Lights saw that and sorrowed, and so they gave a gift to the Créneach: they found a pebble that was like the heart of the Créneach and gave it life and form, and that one was the Littlest, and its light shone as bright as the first children of Céile.

That is the way it has been ever since: the First-Lights go to search now and again for Anchéad and we Créneach die. Our bodies crack and crumble to pebbles and dust, and the hearts within us fall away. Those hearts the soft-flesh things find and take will never live again as Créneach. When the First-Lights return from their search, they go first to the All-Heart and awaken it once more, and the All-Heart in turn awakens all of Its children and grandchildren. Then the First-Lights find the hearts that have not yet been touched and bring us back.

And they also wake a new Littlest or two . . .

Jenna found herself staring at Lámh Shábhála as Treoraí finished the tale, still cradling the infant in its arms. She tried to imagine her cloch burning with the mage-lights energy inside the god Céile, only to be found after the long, slow erosion of her body. She thought of *all* the clochs na thintrí—Cloch Mór or clochmion—having first been born in the Créneach . . .

Truth or fable . . . There was no way to know. All she knew was that the Créneach believed it, as Jenna believed in the Mother-Creator and Seed-Daughter, as Seancoim believed in the god he called Greatness, as Thraisha believed in her WaterMother. Perhaps they were all mingled, all shades of the same truth. Jenna looked around her at the Créneach, and inside each of them burned an undeniable cloch na thintrí: that, at least, was truth.

"I hold the All-Heart that was inside Céile," she said, and Treoraí nodded with slow precision.

"I am Eldest here," it said. "This is my twelfth Awakening. I've seen the quick growth of soft-flesh things like you, who can change the very land. I have felt the All-Heart close by twice before: when I was Littlest, and also at the end of my last life." Jenna could hear the awe enter its voice, then, and its eyes were on the stone in her hand. "But this is the first time any of us here have actually seen it. It is a great gift for all of us, and for the Littlest."

". . . *my twelfth Awakening* . . ." The import of that staggered Jenna—if true, the Créneach before her was unimaginably old. From Riata's time to her own was thirteen centuries or more, and that would have encompassed only a portion of two of Treoraí's "awakenings." Most of the voices within Lámh Shábhála were the more recent Holders; of the Bunús Muintir Holders, only Riata's voice was easily heard, and he had been the last active Bunús Holder. There must be older, fainter voices buried deep within the cloch, going back and back to the dim mist of legend and myth.

And here, one of the legends walked.

Jenna glanced at Seancoim, who was leaning placidly on his staff, and then she bent down, looking at the smooth, shiny face of the Littlest in Treoraí's arms. She could feel the Cloch Mór shining in the chest of the infant, a jewel with a radiance stronger than the moon. She dangled Lámh Shábhála over it, as she might have with a child. It didn't reach for the cloch, but its tongue darted from its mouth, sliding over the stone in its silver cage and withdrawing. The Littlest chirped then, birdlike, as if in satisfaction.

"It will remember," Treoraí said. "We will all remember the taste of the All-Heart. Soon enough, when the Littlest has grown, we will leave here, each on our own, to search for Anchéad while the First-Lights still glow in this land, but we will remember."

Treoraí handed the Littlest to one of the other Créneach, and clapped his hands together again. "But I forget that the soft-flesh things are always in a hurry, for your lives are short. We could stay here for several darknesses, remembering all the old tales of the All-Heart and our long search, but you would grow old in that time, so—" Treoraí stopped, abruptly. He turned away from her, as if he'd forgotten she was there, and lifted his gaze toward the sky.

The first wisps of the mage-lights glimmered into existence, a feathery curtain dancing in the sky, and the Créneach responded, clapping their hands together once in unison. The resulting boom was deafening, and both Jenna and Seancoim put hands to ears as the Créneach clapped again, the explosion of sound repeating from the nearby peaks, each time fainter and more distant. The Créneach lifted their hands toward the sky and the brightening mage-lights, as Jenna felt the insistent pull of Lámh Shábhála and mirrored the gesture with her own right hand. The mage-lights curled and fused above the valley, lowering until their slow lightning flowed around them in multicolored stream-ers. One stream wrapped itself around Lámh Shábhála, fill-ing it eagerly; around her, Jenna saw the Créneach standing surrounded by the glow, their mouths open and the mage-lights swirling in as if they were swallowing them. The Créneach crooned, a twittering, musical sound almost like chimes stirring in a wind.

Lámh Shábhála filled quickly, and Jenna released it with a gasp of mingled pleasure and pain. The Créneach paid no attention to them at all, their attention all on the bath of light in which they were immersed. Seancoim came up to her, his arm supporting Jenna as she slowly let the cloch-vision recede.

"We'll stay here tonight," he said. "Go on and rest, and I'll watch . . ."

52

The Protector

SHE was more exhausted than she'd thought. She fell asleep quickly and when she woke, it was dim morning, the sun lurking behind a thin smear of charcoal-gray cloud. The valley, in the daylight little more than a narrow canyon, was empty. Seancoim was poking at a tin pot boiling on a small campfire while Dúnmharú pecked halfheartedly at the ground. Jenna's right arm ached and throbbed. She grimaced as she sat up, rubbing at the scarred flesh.

"Where are the Créneach?" Jenna asked.

Seancoim pulled the pot from the fire with a stick. He sprinkled herbs from a pouch into the boiling water and Jenna caught the scent of mint. He set the tea aside to steep. "Still here," he answered. He pointed with the stick in the direction of a rock pile against the cavern wall. "That is Treoraí, I think."

Jenna went over to the pile: undistinguished broken granite, glinting here and there with flecks of quartz—she would have walked past it unknowingly a hundred times. The rocks were loose and in no semblance of any shape: ordinary, plain and common, as if they had tumbled from the cliff walls years ago and been sitting there since. The only hint that this might be something out of the ordinary was a lack of weeds or grass growing up in the cracks between the boulders. She started to reach toward it with her right arm, but a flash of pain ran through her with the movement, and she cradled the arm to herself, stifling a moan.

When the spasm had passed, she touched one of the larger boulders with her left hand: it was rough and broken, not at all like the skin of the Créneach had been. "You're certain?"

"Aye," Seancoim answered. "When the sun rose, they all sat. As the light came, they seemed to just melt into what you see now. Before they went to sleep, though, Treoraí told me that we would find the path to Thall Coill through the other end of the valley. It also said to tell you that the Créneach will always honor the All-Heart, and even the Littlest will always remember." Seancoim poured the tea out into two chipped-rim bowls and handed one to Jenna. "Here. You'll need this: it's kala bark."

"Not andúilleaf?"

He didn't answer that, simply gave her a grimace of his weathered face. "We have a long walk today."

Jenna nodded, sipping her tea and staring at the rock pile as if it might reassemble itself again into Treoraí. "We *did* see them, didn't we, Seancoim?"

The old man smiled briefly, the beard lifting on his flat, leathery face. "Aye," he told her. "We did."

"And is it true, what they told me—that each of the clochs na thintrí is the heart of a dead Créneach?"

Seancoim shrugged. "It's what they said." He took a long draught of his tea, and tossed the dregs aside. He wiped the bowl and placed it back in his pack. "We should go. These mountains are best passed through in daylight."

They packed quickly, then set off again. The path led upward toward a saddle between two peaks. Eagles soared above them, huge and regal, and Dúnmharú stayed on Seancoim's shoulder, not daring to challenge them. Their pace was slow as they made their way through broken, trackless ground, sometimes needing to detour around cliffs and slopes too steep to climb. They reached the ridge by midday, and finally looked down over a long, curving arm of forested land spread out into the distance before them. Fogs and vapors curled from the treetops, indicating hidden streams and rivers and bogs below the leafy crowns. The sea pounded white against the rocky coastline, until it all merged into indistinct haze. It was cold in the heights, as if summer had never reached here, and Jenna shivered in her clóca.

"Thall Coill," Seancoim said, though he appeared to be looking well out into the distance. "And there—on the coast—can you see the open rise where the cliffs lift from the sea? I can see it with Dúnmharú's eyes, but . . ."

Jenna squinted into the distance, where there was a speck of brown and gray against the green. "I think so. Is that where . . . where I must go?"

"Aye." He exhaled, his breath white. "That place is called Bethiochnead, and it's our destination. But we won't get there standing here. Come on, at least it will be warmer farther down."

They took the rest of the day to toil downward over the intervening ridges, through fields of bracken and hawthorn into glades dotted with firs, and finally into the shadow of Thall Coill's oak-dominated fastness. There was no sharp demarcation, no boundary they that they crossed, but they could sense the ancient years lying in the shadows, the long centuries that these trees had witnessed, unmoving and untouched. By evening, clouds of wind sprites were flowing between the trunks of the oaks like sparkling, floating rivulets, and a herd of storm deer swept over the last stretch of open field, their hooves drumming the earth.

Jenna felt as she had in Doire Coill. This was a land alive in a way that she could not understand. There were places here older even than the ancient forest near the lough. As if guessing at her thoughts, Seancoim halted next to her. "We'll have no fire here tonight," he said. "I don't think the forest would like it, and I don't know what it can do. And beware the songs you might hear. Thall Coill is said to have a stronger, more compelling voice than the Doire. These trees were here when we Bunús came to Inish Thuaidh; they will still be here after you Daoine are as scarce as we are now. Thall Coill doesn't care about us—only about itself."

Jenna shuddered, feeling the truth of the statement. "We can't get to that place you saw tonight," she said. "I think we should stay here and not go any deeper into the forest tonight."

"I think there may be a better place to stay." Seancoim plunged the end of his staff into the loamy earth. He took a long breath, and called out into the gathering dark as Jenna watched him curiously. There was movement in the shadows, and from under the trees, two Bunús Muintir emerged.

They were both male, one nearly as old as Seancoim; the other much younger. Like Seancoim, they were dressed in skins, their feet wrapped in leather. They had the wide, flattened faces of the Bunús, their skin the color of dried earth. The young one, with a matted and tangled beard, was armed with a bow and a bronze-bladed sword; the older, his chin stubbled with patchy gray, had only a knife and an oaken staff. The expressions on their faces were suspicious and decidedly unfriendly. The old one held out his staff and spoke a few words in their guttural language. Jenna understood none of the words but the intent was clear: they were not welcome here.

Seancoim replied in the same language, and Jenna belatedly reached for Lámh Shábhála, so she could understand what was being said. The gesture drew the attention of the younger man; he pointed to Jenna's arm as he spoke to his companion, evidently noticing the scars there. He nocked an arrow and started to pull back the string of his bow. Jenna's fingers closed around the cloch, ready to defend herself and Seancoim, but the older one grunted and gestured to his companion. The younger Bunús slowly released the tension on the bow, though he kept the arrow fitted to the string.

The old one spoke in the Daoine language, his voice even more heavily accented than Seancoim's, his words slow and full of effort as he tried to find the words. "Go back," he said. "You should never have been brought here." He glared at Seancoim.

"She holds Lámh Shábhála, Protector Lomán," Seancoim told him.

"I know what she holds, and I know who you are, too—Seancoim Crow-Eye. A Protector should stay with the forest he has been given to guard."

"My pledge-daughter Keira watches in my place," Seancoim answered. "I'm old, and Dúnmharú is ancient for his kind. Soon I'll be blind again. The Greatness has given me another task. Doire Coill is Keira's, now."

Lomán scoffed. "So Seancoim has abandoned his charge . . ." He nodded to his companion. "You see, Toryn, this is what comes of being too close to the Daoine. You fail in your duty and give it over to someone who's not yet ready, who is still learning the slow magics. Doire Coill will fail, like so many of the other old places." He lifted his grizzled chin. "But not Thall Coill."

"You underestimate Keira," Seancoim answered quietly. "You always did. She's been away from me and doing the work of the Protector for over two hands of years now. I see you still don't trust Toryn and keep him close so you can correct his mistakes."

Toryn visibly flushed at that, and the bow came up once more. Seancoim lifted his staff even as Jenna started to open Lámh Shábhála. "Do you really want to match our skills, Toryn?" Seancoim asked. "It would be a shame. Lomán's getting too old to begin with a new pledge-child."

Toryn glared; Lomán spat on the ground. "Put your bow away, boy," Lomán said. "Don't let him goad you into foolishness. It's not Crow-Eye you have to worry about; it's the Holder. Slow magic can't stand against Lámh Shábhála, even when it's wielded by a girl-child."

"I'm not a child," Jenna snapped back angrily.

Lomán didn't answer directly, but his eyes showed his contempt. "You misunderstand if you think I'm being anything but kind to you, Holder. I'd love nothing better than to see you fail here—with none of your own people around you. It's been a thousand years and more since a Bunús Muintir held Lámh Shábhála. I wonder . . . what would a Bunús Holder be able to accomplish? Perhaps the Daoine could be made to regret what your ancestors did to us, eh?"

"What would happen to Lámh Shábhála after I'm gone isn't my concern," Jenna answered. "If I fail, I fail."

"Then you have a death wish."

"I'm not afraid of death," Jenna answered. "I've seen too much of it."

Lomán's eyes narrowed at that. "Maybe not such a child, now . . ." he muttered. "But you've chosen a poor adviser if you're listening to Seancoim." His gaze went back to Seancoim. "You think she can survive Scrúdú, Crow-Eye? You can look at this stripling and believe that?"

"Riata believes it," Seancoim answered.

Lomán made a sound like a kettle too long on the fire. "Riata's long dead."

"His body, aye, but his spirit is still restless and he has spoken to Jenna. He seems . . . impressed by her."

Lomán snorted again. "The Daoine are a weak race. They conquered us only because they were so many and we were so few. They conquered us because their swords were iron and ours were bronze. But even with steel and numbers, they still wouldn't have won had our clochs na thintrí not been decades asleep when they came." One shoulder rose and fell. "We would have pushed the Daoine back to Céile Mhór and beyond if the clochs had been awake. But go ahead, Crow-Eye. Let her try. I think Toryn would be a good Holder, afterward."

The youth grinned at that, cocking his head appraisingly toward Jenna. "It's about time that Lámh Shábhála came home to Thall Coill," he said. His voice was thick and low, blurred with the Bunús Muintir accent, a voice of confidence and certainty. "I'll be happy to escort the two of you to Bethiochnead, and afterward . . ." He grinned again, showing his teeth. "Lámh Shábhála will come back to us, and perhaps we can obtain a few of the Cloch Mór, then who knows? It may be that the Bunús Muintir will emerge from our forests and hills and take back what was once ours, an age ago." Dreams flashed in his eyes, widening his smile.

"Come with me, Holder," he said. "Let me show you Thall Coill."

It was Toryn who led Jenna and Seancoim through the trackless forest, Lomán refusing to accompany them. "I've

no interest in watching your Daoine die," he told Seancoim. "That's your task, since you brought her here. And
I'm too old to want Lámh Shábhála."

The forest . . .

A spine-backed form slunk away through the snarl of
seedlings to their right. A patch of moonlight struck blue
highlights from a whorled shell taller than Jenna, glimpsed
in a meadow bordering the shoulder of a black stream. The
smell of sulfur and rotting meat wafted from a fissure
bound in vines. Air colder than winter or the heights of
the mountains spread from a pond whose glowing water
was the color of buttermilk fresh from a churn. Calls and
hoots and shrill cries erupted from the darkness around
them.

And the tree-song . . . Jenna heard the call of the ancient
oaks, the green life in the most ancient and lost hollows of
Thall Coill, a compelling whisper that rustled the leaves
above them, that caused the oaks to bend down with many-
limbed branches, that hushed the call of the mage-lights
nearly invisible under the canopy of the forest. Thall Coill
had a stronger, more insistent voice than Doire Coill, a call
that echoed down in the very fibers of Jenna's being. The
voice of the forest awoke primitive echoes, as if pulling at
impossibly ancient ties between the trees and her most distant ancestors. More than once, Jenna found herself stray-
ing from the path, wandering away as Seancoim and Toryn
continued on. The first time it happened, Seancoim called
to her, breaking the spell, and Toryn laughed. "She's
weak," he told Seancoim. "The Old Ones would snare her,
and we'd find her bones years later, sitting against their
trunks."

Jenna flushed, embarrassed that she could succumb to
the trees' singing, but she noticed as Toryn turned away
that there were tufts of moss in his ears, and that Toryn
pushed them in deeper as he strode away.

You're not the only one . . . Seancoim nodded to her,
with a quick smile; he had noticed as well. "Everything
beautiful is also dangerous," he said to her before turning
to stump along after Toryn.

As Jenna followed along behind them, she tried to see

the forest with Seancoim's eyes. It was beautiful in its way, she had to admit. The oaks, their massive trunks wound with vines of mistletoe, with girths so wide that two people could not have encircled them with their hands, were survivors from when Thall Coill, Doire Coill, and the few other old growth forests had dominated all of Talamh An Ghlas, penetrating far into Céile Mhór and even to the great continent of Thall Mór-roinn. The Daoine were still in their homelands then; the Bunús Muintir were nothing but a series of family-based clans scratching out a subsistence existence under the trees, their culture just starting to coalesce.

Walking here, Jenna felt as the first peoples must have felt: insignificant and small in the midst of this ancient life. The forest was a single creature, a vast and intricate organism in whose bowels she walked, and within its body was mystery, danger, and, aye, great beauty. If the forest desired, it could crush her with its sheer weight. It tolerated her because she was too small to do it any real harm.

She understood for the first time why the Bunús Muintir could worship a goddess whose earthly form was an oak tree.

They walked for hours, Toryn (deliberately, Jenna was certain) keeping a quick pace that made it difficult for Seancoim to stay with him. Jenna remained at Seancoim's side; Toryn would at times be so far ahead of them that he was barely visible in the moonlight filtering down through the trees. Each time, Seancoim sent Dúnmharú angrily flying to the young man, screeching at him from a nearby branch until he stopped to wait, hands on hips, while they caught up with him again. And each time, as they approached, he would start off once more without a word.

Jenna had decided she despised the man by the time false dawn tinted the horizon with rose and ocher.

The call of the Old Ones had faded; Jenna could hear the rhythmic pulse of the sea crashing against rock. The land was rising steeply under them, the trees thinning quickly until they gave way entirely to a grassy swath. Here, the bones of the land showed through the dirt: furrowed lines of bare gray limestone, the cracks sprouting a few weeds clinging to the thin film of earth at the bottom. At the top of the rise, the land simply stopped at a sheer cliff while—nearly a hundred feet below—waves gnawed at the feet of the island. The wind blew in steadily, cold and misty. And there . . . where in her dream of Peria and Tadhg had been only the sense of a presence that would not allow itself to be seen . . .

It might have been a huge cat or, perhaps, a dragon. The statue stood a few strides from the cliff edge, gazing out to sea as if it were protecting the forest or the island from unseen invaders. The statue was carved of jet-black stone, glassy and volcanic in appearance and unlike any rock Jenna had seen in the area. The head was perched thirty feet above them on a massive four-legged body, sitting down on its haunches with its tail wrapping around its left side and curling away to end abruptly at the cliff edge. Along the sloping back, there were two ridges where wings might once have been, though there was no evidence of them having tumbled to the ground around them. The monument's features were blurred by the weight of centuries, polished by wind and sand, eroded by rain until all that remained was the obscured outline of what the creature had once been.

"Bethiochnead," Seancoim said as Jenna gazed up at the creature. "It was here when we Bunús Muintir came. No one knows who erected this or exactly what it is."

"The Greatness Herself put Bethiochnead here for the Bunús Muintir to find," Toryn said from the side of the statue. "It still holds Her power."

Seancoim shrugged. "That's what some believe, aye," he told Jenna. He glanced at Toryn. "But not all. There may have been other races here before the Bunús and Daoine, and they may have made this. Some think it was the Créneach who sculpted it, that this is a representation of one of their gods. Others think it may *be* a Créneach, solidified by some magic, or else a mythical creature snared by a spell, or . . ." He stopped, tapping his staff on the rocks as if testing their stability. "Its origin doesn't matter. It only matters that it's here. This is the center. This is where the mage-lights are strongest."

"What do I do?" Jenna asked. She clutched her right

arm to herself. It felt colder and more lifeless than ever, though there was no pain. She could only move the fingers with great effort. The scars on her flesh were pure white, as if etched with new snow.

"You rest," Seancoim told her. "And sleep if you can. When you're ready, I'll tell you all I know."

53

Bethiochnead

SHE hadn't thought she could sleep, but she did. In her dream, she was with Ennis in Ballintubber, entering Tara's Tavern. Coelin was there inside, and Ellia with several small children around her, all of whom looked like miniature Coelins. Everyone was singing and dancing, and Ennis and Jenna joined in with them. In the midst of the dancing, without warning, the door opened with a sudden crash like thunder. A form stood there in darkness, cloaked in black with its face hidden and sending a surge of unreasoning fear through Jenna. She grabbed Ennis by the hand and they ran—that agonizing, skin-crawling slow run of dreams where the legs refuse to cooperate no matter how hard you try. Somehow, she and Ennis retreated into the fireplace and through another door at the back of the chimney, which led them outside again. It was raining, and Kesh was barking and running circles around her. Mac Ard was shouting something from inside the cottage (for when Jenna looked about, they were back at the old house), only when she glanced up it was her father Niall whose face she saw at the window. Her mam was outside with Jenna, and Jenna felt a stab of jealousy because Ennis was so close to Maeve, his arm around her waist . . .

Jenna woke up, feeling a sense of incredible loss sitting heavy on her chest as the remnants of the dream faded quickly in the light of reality.

It was late afternoon, and the clouds had cleared. The statue cast a long shadow that reached the cliff edge and disappeared. She seemed to be alone, though Seancoim's pack was next to hers. She sat up, the blanket around her shoulders, and saw Dúnmharú come flapping out of the woods. The crow circled the statue once but didn't land on it, coming instead to rest on a nearby boulder. The bird cocked its head at her; a moment later, she saw Seancoim and Toryn walking up the slope from under the emerald cave of the oaks. She stood, shivering a bit despite the warm sun, as they approached. Toryn was staring at her; she ignored him. Seancoim handed her an apple. "Here, you should eat something. Did you sleep?"

Jenna took a bite of the apple, letting its tart sweetness awaken her, and shrugged. "A bit." She glanced at the statue. "What do we do now?" she asked.

"That depends on you. You're still resolved to try? You realize that only a few times has anyone gone through the Scrúdú and survived?"

"And none of those were Daoine," Toryn added. When she glanced at him, he smiled.

"I don't care about me," she told them. "If I die, I can be with Ennis. If I don't, then maybe his death will mean . . . will . . ." She stopped. The heaviness returned to her chest, not allowing the words out. Seancoim nodded as Dúnmharú hopped up into the air and, with a flap of black wings, landed on the old man's shoulder.

"All right," he said. He came over to her and hugged her. She let herself fall into his herb-scented embrace, her arms going around him. "You can do this," he whispered to her. "You can."

He released her, his blind gaze looking past her out to the sea. "Stand in front of Bethiochnead, Jenna," he said. "Take Lámh Shábhála in your hand, and open the cloch. That's all you need to do. The rest . . ." He patted her cheek, smiling gap-toothed at her. "You'll have to tell *us,* afterward."

He walked with Jenna around to the front of the statue. She could hear the waves roaring against the rocks; she could feel the wind tousling her hair and the sun warming her face; she could smell the salt breeze mixed with mint and loam. The colors of the landscape seemed impossibly saturated, the green of the grass like glowing emerald, the limestone ribs of the land speckled with white and red and soft pink. She wondered if she would ever see them again. She wondered how much it would hurt.

Her hand closed around Lámh Shábhála. She willed the cloch na thintrí to open, and felt the power go surging forth.

She was still standing near the cliffside, but the land now ended several feet farther out. And the statue . . .

It was no longer ruined and half missing. The legs and chest rippled with carved tendons; the feet were cat-clawed, seeming to tear into the rock on which the creature sat. The body was scaled, feathered, and brightly painted: the red of new-shed blood and the blue of a child's eyes, the simmering yellow of the yolk of a hen's egg. The expanse of wings spread majestically from its back, ribbed and fingered like some gigantic bat's, with black, leathery skin pouched like sails between the ribs. The tail was complete, with a barbed, bulging tip at its end.

The head had a long muzzle, the mouth partially open to reveal twin rows of daggered white teeth. The ears were like a cat's also, though between them were scales like staggered rows of painted shields; its eyebrows were two fans of spines, meeting above the muzzle and running back over the middle of the skull. The eyes were frighteningly human; the large, expressive eyes of a child, and as Jenna gazed at the statue, the eyes blinked and opened. Though the mouth didn't move, a low, stentorian voice purred.

"So. Another one comes after all these years."

Jenna could feel the power flooding from the statue; above, the mage-lights curled, visible even in the bright sunlight. The trees of the forest beyond writhed and swayed as if they, too, were alive and capable of pulling roots from ground and capering about. "Who are you?" Jenna asked. Her voice sounded thin and weak in this charged atmosphere.

The eyes blinked once more. A shimmering change rippled through the body from spiny crest to curled-claw feet and when it passed, the thing was no longer painted stone but living flesh. It stretched like a cat waking from a nap, the wings snapping and sending a rush of wind past Jenna. "I am An Phionós," it said. "I am the First, and you are now in my world."

Its voice was Ennis'.

"Stop that!" Jenna shouted at the creature, and it reared its great head, the mouth curling in a near-laugh, the eyes flashing.

"Ah, my dear Jenna. Do you think you're so strong that you can command my obedience?" it asked with seeming mirth, still with Ennis' inflection and tone. Then the mocking amusement left, along with the memory of Ennis' voice. An Phionós hissed, steam venting from its nostrils. Magelights flickered around it in a bright storm. "Are you stronger than me, Jenna? Do you remember Peria's fate? Do you remember how she screamed as I crushed the life from her? I give you this boon: release Lámh Shábhála now, before it's too late."

Jenna's fisted hand trembled around the cloch. She could feel An Phionós bending its will to her, insinuating itself into her muscles and prying at her fingers, loosening them. Yet with the intrusion she also caught a glimmer of the entity's mind, and she realized that, despite its fury and insolence, An Phionós didn't actively seek her death. It had no choice as to how it must act. "Why do you do this?" she asked, gasping as she fought to keep hold of the cloch.

An Phionós laughed, a bitter and wild sound. "One should never offend a god," it answered. "Their revenge is swift and eternal, and that's why I sit here forever waiting. You, at least, have a choice—let go of the cloch and live, Jenna, or continue to hold it and die."

"And if I hold it and don't die?"

"That won't happen. But if you do . . . there are depths within Lámh Shábhála that you have only glimpsed, and the shaping of this entire age could be yours." Again the laugh. "I hope you don't think that's a gift. It would be the greatest burden of all." An Phionós bent down close to her. The scent of rotting meat drifted from its mouth. "Re-

lease the cloch, Jenna. I have nothing for you but pain."
An Phionós' hold on her hand vanished; it sat back on its
haunches again. "Make your choice now."

Jenna glanced wildly about her and An Phionós snorted.
"Your friend can't help you. Look . . ." The air shimmered,
and for a moment Jenna caught a glimpse of Seancoim, his
mouth open in a shout, trying to push forward toward her
as the mage-lights threw him back. Then he was gone again.
"He doesn't see what you see. He sees only your struggle,
not me." An Phionós' front paws kneaded the earth, tearing at the limestone. His voice was Ennis' again, and now
Ennis' eyes gazed down at her from An Phionós' face, a
single tear rising and sliding down a scaled cheek to splash
on the rocks. "I don't want you to die, my love. Don't
do this."

"Stop!" Jenna screamed again. She raised the cloch, pulling the chain from around her neck and lifting it high. Her
fist tightened around it. "Here! Here's your answer."

An Phionós bared its teeth. The wings spread wide; the
claws gouged new furrows in the stone. Mage-lights
snapped and shattered around it. "Then we begin," it said.
It drew in a great breath, pulling in the mage-lights as if
they were smoke. Its neck arced, the head reared back and
it exhaled in a roar, blinding light rushing from its mouth.
Jenna reflexively interposed a wall with Lámh Shábhála;
the mage-lights crashed upon it like a furious tidal wave.
Jenna stumbled back against the assault, the pressure of it
driving her to her knees as An Phionós vomited forth an
unending stream of raw power. Jenna's hand tightened
around Lámh Shábhála, wrenching the cloch fully open.
She imagined the wall growing, expanding, pushing back:
slowly, she stood. She thought of the wall as a mirror-
smooth lake, reflecting back what came to it as the Banrion's cloch had done. The wall shifted with the thought and
she found herself wielding a weapon as the shield gathered
in the energy thrown at her and hurled it back at An Phionós. The beast staggered back at the first impact, roaring
in wordless pain.

Then it nodded to her, as if in satisfaction. "So it won't
be simple. Good. You would have disappointed me if it

had, Holder. After so many years, to be awakened only for a moment . . ."

It was pacing now, the scale-armored body striding back and forth before the hoary, vine-laden oaks: fifty feet long without the enormous barbed tail, half again as high to the crown of the head, the wings folded against its back. Then the wings opened, and a hurricane wind lashed Jenna as it took to the air, rising high above. The mage-lights encircled it like arms, burning like a second sun so that An Phionós was silhouetted against the glare.

Jenna waited for the inevitable attack: fireballs; thunderbolts of bright power; burning thickets of spears and swords; blasts of winds; demons or giants or a flight of angry dragons. None of it came.

The silver bands holding Lámh Shábhála dug into her palm. The landscape shifted around her again: she floated in a featureless void with An Phionós. The forest, the cliff, the sound of the seas, even the mage-lights—all of them were gone, though she could feel their energy supporting her. An Phionós swept its wings leisurely, circling slowly around her, and she waved her arms to follow its movement as if swimming in the emptiness.

"It's just the two of us, Jenna," it said, still circling. "That's all it's ever been. The shape of the energy doesn't matter. Each cloch na thintrí bonds to its Holder in a different manner, in the form that a long sequence of Holders has worn into it like grooves in a road. Most Holders follow that same path because it's easiest to see and hold to, and that's why the clochs na thintrí tend to be used in the same way each time a new cloudmage uses them. Very few have the strength to shape the power of their cloch na thintrí in a new way, to give it a new form that might suit them better. It's no different with Lámh Shábhála."

"Are you intending to talk me to death?" Jenna asked.

An Phionós laughed. It stopped, hovering in front of her with slow beats of its leathery wings. "Perhaps. Do you die that easily?"

"No," Jenna answered. "I don't plan on dying at all."

The teeth bared again. "No? Even to be with him?"

Now Ennis stood before her. He smiled, almost shyly,

holding out his hand. "Jenna," he said. "I wish . . . There was so much I wanted to tell you, just to say one last time that I loved you . . ."

She wanted to take that hand, wanted desperately to take him in her arms, to bruise her lips with his kisses. She started to lift her left hand, then forced it back to her side. She looked at An Phionós, not Ennis. "You can't seduce me with false images," she told it.

The huge, scaled head lifted. "Not false," it said. "That *is* Ennis, or the spirit that was once him. I brought him here. He awaits you, Jenna, on the other side of death."

"It didn't hurt," Ennis said to her, his familiar voice awakening a deep longing in her. "You should know that. I felt the knife move and the heat of my blood pouring out, then . . . I don't know. It was as if I were outside myself. There was no pain, just a slow fading and a feeling of regret, and I was gone. I watched you cry over the body, Jenna, and I tried to touch you and comfort you. I tried to tell you that I was still with you, but I couldn't. I *am* with you, Jenna, each day. And we'll be together again."

She listened to him, shaking her head in denial and disbelief, and Ennis glanced over at An Phionós. "Death doesn't hurt, Jenna. All you have to do is accept it."

"I will make it easy and quick," An Phionós told her. A forepaw lifted, the scythes of its claws scissoring in the air. "One stroke. One quick flash . . ."

"Ennis . . ." The word was a sigh, a plea. Jenna closed her eyes, letting Lámh Shábhála's force flow out to him. Where it touched the body, she felt strings leading back to An Phionós. She could feel An Phionós trying to push her away with its own power, but she concentrated, letting more power flow from the cloch. She formed the energy into hands and ripped away the strands of connection even as An Phionós tried to stop her. Ennis wailed, his body went pinwheeling away like a rag in a storm, finally vanishing in a point of white light that made Jenna squint and throw her hand in front of her face. A wave of intense cold flew past her.

"It's just us," Jenna told An Phionós. "No ghosts. No lies. No tricks."

"There's no trick in what I said," it told her. "I *can* make this painless and fast for you. You simply have to allow it."

"No."

She could hear the shrug in its voice. "Then it will be the other way." Muscles bunched and wings flexed. An Phionós stooped like a hawk about to swoop down on a helpless field mouse. The wings folded in and the apparition fell in a rush, plummeting toward her. Jenna raised her cloch, concentrating its force on the onrushing creature, pushing back at it. Jenna grunted with the impact as An Phionós seemed to dissolve, slipping through the web of force like water through a sieve. Jenna searched for it with the eyes of the cloch: *there!* She hurled lightning at the mage-glow that was An Phionós, but it swept the bolts aside.

Frantically, she created a creature like An Phionós, molding it from mage-stuff and launching it at the creature. They collided in a snarl of talons and wings and teeth, and Jenna felt the concussion as if it were her own body that smashed into her opponent. She was flung backward—screaming, her eyes rolling back in her head, a red-shot blackness threatening to drown her—and she fought to hold onto consciousness. Her own fingers curled and slashed as she gouged at An Phionós, and for a moment, the creature retreated. Jenna breathed, gulping and tasting blood.

"This is good," it said. "Usually the Daoine are so weak." An Phionós looked at her, and it seemed to Jenna that its eyes saw past the surface of her skin and deep into her being. "But you're not just Daoine, are you? Part of you is also Saimhóir, and much farther back, there is also Bunús Muintir. Ah, that surprises you, does it? You're a mongrel, and mongrels are often the strongest."

Then An Phionós came again with a roar; Jenna fought back in the form of the mage-creature, but An Phionós was immensely strong, far more powerful than any of the clochs she had encountered. In the space of a few breaths, her mage-creature was shredded and fading like smoke.

Lámh Shábhála was nearly empty; there was nothing left but the dregs of power. Jenna was no longer floating in nothingness. The hard gray rocks of Bethiochnead pressed into her back, and she lay looking up at a storm-lashed sky.

An Phionós hovered over her. "Now," it whispered, "even the mongrel falls."

Jenna threw a final bolt at the creature. The attack was weak and slow; An Phionós pushed the flickering brilliance aside contemptuously. "You're an empty vessel, Jenna," it told her. "Do you remember Peria? Do you remember how I crushed her? Do you remember the sound of bones cracking and splitting and ripping through flesh? That's what will happen to you now."

An Phionós descended. It picked up Jenna in its talons as she beat futilely at the beast with her fists, the scales scraping the flesh from her knuckles. She felt the knife-edge points digging into her flesh. Its head came down; its too-human eyes regarded her almost sadly. "You came so close," it said. "Closer than you know. Perhaps . . ."

Its claws closed around her, She felt them begin to tighten, felt her ribs crack. An Phionós was inside her head now, its awareness flooding her. She was still holding Lámh Shábhála. Mage-energy crackled inside her with An Phionós' intrusion. "Now," it said gently. "You'll be with him again. I promise you that much . . ."

The pressure against her body increased. Jenna screamed in terror and pain. The mage-energy burned her. She tried to push back with Lámh Shábhála, but there was nothing there. She took her awareness deep into the cloch, deeper, to the utter bottom of the well, and there . . .

A glimpse . . . A hope . . .

"No!"

The pressure was suddenly released. An Phionós dropped her, and Jenna gasped in pain and surprise as she fell back to the ground, struggling up to a sitting position with her legs folded underneath her. The beast coiled above her, the wings and body blocking the sky. *"Why did you come here?"* it raged at her. "I can take *your* life if you give it to me, but I can't take a life that doesn't come here willingly—She whose servant I am won't allow that. Why would you do this?"

It glared at her, mouth gaping dangerously, then the eyes and its voice softened. "You don't know, do you?" it asked.

Jenna shook her head. "I don't understand. No."

"Look," An Phionós answered. "Look within yourself."

An Phionós gestured, and Jenna saw herself as the creature saw her: a form of energy and light, her heart beating like a candle fluttering in the wind, and in her belly, a tiny flame burned.

"Mother-Creator . . ." Jenna breathed. She cupped her abdomen, as if she could warm her hands in that small radiance.

"Aye," An Phionós answered. "You're with child. You didn't know?"

Jenna could only shake her head mutely. An Phionós snorted. It came to earth, resting again as she had first seen it: sitting on its haunches, the wings down against its body, the tail wrapped around one side, staring down at her as she lay in front of it. "There can be no finish to this Scrúdú," it said. There was a note almost of triumph in its voice. "I let you live."

"But I found the path," Jenna told the creature, still cradling herself and staring in wonder at the sparkle of life in her womb. She raised her head as the cloch-vision faded. "I saw the way to defeat you."

An Phionós shook its head. "Perhaps," it said. "And perhaps not. You'll never know now."

"Why not?" Jenna asked. "I could come back, after the child is born . . ." She stopped, realizing that what An Phionós had said was the truth.

"Aye," it said. "You nearly died this time, with no certainty that what you found would have helped you. Could you undergo this again, knowing that you might leave your child motherless and abandoned? The child will bind you here, Jenna. This time, you fought without caring that you might die; the next time, your focus will be divided." Its voice was sad. "There's but one time in your life to test yourself this way, Jenna. Now you must leave the Scrúdú to some other. Perhaps to the child inside."

Its voice became less heard than sensed, the years and decades and centuries seeming to pass as she watched An Phionós became simply a statue once more, its features eroding and fading. "You saw inside Lámh Shábhála. You glimpsed the possibilities. But you'll always wonder if you'd

really found the way, Jenna," its dying voice husked. "And
so will I . . ."

The fog around them cleared. She was back in Thall
Coill, kneeling on the cold ground with Seancoim hurrying
toward her, and she let herself fall.

54

Fire and Water

"**J**ENNA!"

Through half-opened eyes, she could see Seancoim hurrying to her, and Dúnmharú cawing in alarm at her side as she rolled and pushed herself up on one side with her left arm. Scrapes and cuts oozed blood along her body; the smell of ozone hung in the air like the aftermath of a thunderstorm. She was still clutching Lámh Shábhála, but the cloch was empty and drained. Her world swayed around her and she steadied herself, trying to keep from falling back into unconsciousness. Her head pulsed with a ferocious headache; her right arm, now that she released Lámh Shábhála, fell dead and useless at her side.

She felt as if her body had been placed on the anvil of the gods and pounded.

The spice of Seancoim's presence was at her side. His hands cradled her. "Jenna . . . You're alive! I thought . . ."

"So did I," Jenna answered. The rocks dug into her side, her legs, her elbow. "Help me up, Seancoim."

"Can you stand?"

"I think so. Probably." Toryn had come over to her as well, and she felt both of them lifting her.

"You passed the Scrúdú," Toryn said, his voice awed. "You met the beast and defeated it. We saw the mage-lights, we heard your cries, saw you fighting with something unseen . . ."

Jenna shook her head. The movement sent the world dancing again and she would have fallen if not for the

505

hands holding her. "No," she said when the land settled once more. She glanced at the ruined visage of An Phionós. "No," she repeated. "I didn't win."

"But you're alive," Seancoim protested. "The Scrúdú kills those who fail."

"Aye," Jenna answered. "But not me." She touched her abdomen. "Not us."

"Us?" Seancoim asked, but Toryn interrupted before Jenna could explain.

"But you've found the full power of Lámh Shábhála," he said. "You wrestled with the beast and were given that gift."

Again, Jenna shook her head. "No. I used every bit of energy within Lámh Shábhála. And I thought, for a moment . . ." She tried to lift her right hand to the cloch and couldn't. "Mother-Creator, it hurts. It hurts so much . . ."

"Jenna, here. Sit." Seancoim lowered her to one of the rocks. "I'll start a fire, mix some andúilleaf . . ."

He hurried away. Toryn stayed with her, his gaze appraising and cold. "Lámh Shábhála is drained? The struggle must have been awful."

Jenna shuddered at the memory. "Aye," she answered. Toryn nodded. Seancoim had gone downhill a bit to the edge of the forest. They could see him gathering deadwood, Dúnmharú fluttering around him.

"Let me help you," Toryn called. He walked down toward the old man, stooping to gather up branches. "Go on," Jenna heard Toryn say finally. "There's a few more branches here. I'll be right behind you."

Seancoim started up the hill, one arm around a bundle of dry sticks, the other around his staff. Toryn turned as if to follow. Jenna saw the intention in the younger man too late. *"Sean—!"* she began as Toryn swung the heavy oaken limb he held. Jenna saw Seancoim fall an instant before the dull, sickening sound of the impact came to her. Dúnmharú screeched, diving at Toryn as Jenna tried to stand. She forced her right hand to move as Dúnmharú raked its talons over Toryn's cheek; Toryn swung the crude club at the bird and missed. Jenna's hand closed around Lámh Sháb-

hála and she tried to open the cloch (the crow rising again
in a fury of black wings, coming back to attack once more),
but there was nothing there, no glittering store of mage-
energy. Nothing.

The club swung again, striking Dúnmharú down to earth
in a heap of ebon feathers. Toryn lifted it again and
pounded it back down on the small mound. As Jenna cried
out, Toryn flung the club aside. He spread his hands: fire
erupted between them.

He gestured toward the unmoving Seancoim.

"No!"

Small, tiny blue flames erupted over Seancoim's figure;
thin tendrils of white smoke rose and began wafting away
toward the forest. Jenna screamed again and started running toward Seancoim, even as the flames thickened and
went to orange and yellow, as the smoke began to billow
in earnest. Seancoim didn't move. Jenna could hear the
flames crackling, burning as if Seancoim were made of
paper and tinder. In the space of her first two limping
strides, he was engulfed in an inferno. The impossible heat
washed over her, and she knew no one could survive that.
Toryn, already running up the hill, caught her before she
could move again.

Jenna battered at Toryn with her fists, first trying to push
past him to get to Seancoim, then tearing herself from his
grasp and backing away from him. "Sometimes slow magic
is quite effective," he said, grinning as she struggled.
"Crow-Eye was a useless old man anyway, but he did make
you quite a nice fire, don't you think?" She was still holding
Lámh Shábhála in her hand, and she saw his gaze on it.

"No," she said in a voice that trembled. "It's mine."

His smile was lopsided. "I won't ask you to give it to
me. I know that's something Holders can't do. But I *will*
take it from you. It took me a full day to create the spells
to hold the slow magic so I could use it at will, but I made
two of them. Seancoim could have deflected the spell if
he'd been awake—even old and decrepit, he was strong in
the slow magic. But you don't *have* the slow magic, do you?
All you have is a cloch na thintrí that's been exhausted. I
don't think a bit of fire will hurt Lámh Shábhála."

Jenna continued to back away. She was alongside the statue as Toryn glanced back at Seancoim. The fire was already dying. Jenna could glimpse a blackened, withered skeleton through the smoke. "At least he was unconscious when it happened," Toryn remarked. "Can you imagine what it would feel like to be consumed while alive and awake? Your flesh crackling and turning black like bacon too long in the fire; the fat of your body hissing and sputtering as it boils, the flames feeding on your face. Flesh gone, muscle and tissue seared and crisped as you scream and shriek in agony . . ." Jenna continued to back away; Toryn stalking her, step for step. She could sense the air at her back, could hear the crumbling edge of the cliff under her feet. Toryn stopped. "Are you sure you don't want to give me the cloch?" he asked, his hand held out to her.

"No," Jenna answered. She touched her stomach. "I'm sorry," she said.

Toryn seemed to shrug. He lifted his hands again, speaking a phrase in his own language. She saw the flames appear before him.

Jenna turned away. The cliff edge was two steps away. She ran toward it, and leaped.

She expected death.

The wind rushed past her, roaring. And she felt her body changing, altering as she plummeted toward the water. Her clóca and léine slipped away, torn from her new, sleek shape by the rushing of air, and she fell naked to the waves.

She had almost no time to contemplate the alteration of her body.

Jenna hit the water with a stunning impact that ripped the breath from her lungs. She expected to feel the shock of the frigid ocean, but somehow the water felt impossibly warm and pleasant. Still, the shock of striking the surface nearly made her lose consciousness; she was disoriented, her sense of direction lost underwater. Her body, already sore and battered, screamed with abuse; her vision seemed sharper yet somehow distorted. She could see the wavering

light of the waves well above her and her lungs yearned
for air. She reached out with her arms and kicked with her
legs to stroke for the surface. They responded though the
feel was strange, and she could not see hands or arms even
though the light came quickly closer. She broke the surface
with a gasp, swallowing spray along with the wonderful cold
air. She almost immediately went under again.

Something, someone was under her, lifting her . . .

She emerged into the air once more, coughing and spitting water, and she was held up as she retched and splut-
tered and finally took another shuddering breath. A head
emerged from the waves.

Jenna started to speak in surprise and relief—
"Thraisha!"—but what emerged was a croak and moan.
She looked back along the length of her own body.

The chain of Lámh Shábhála gleamed against black fur
touched with blue highlights, the caged stone still with her.
Jenna barked in surprise; Thraisha's eyes gleamed; she almost seemed to laugh. High above them, at the cliff edge,
Jenna saw Toryn staring down, his face pale. Thraisha followed the direction of Jenna's gaze, her body rolling easily
in the white surf. She spoke, but with the emptiness within
Lámh Shábhála Jenna understood none of it. Thraisha
started swimming, pushing Jenna's body in front of her,
moving away from the rocks and outward. Toryn shouted
something, his voice faint against the roar of wind and
waves. Jenna tentatively tried to help Thraisha and swim
on her own—the body ached and complained, but she managed a few strokes. They swam out beyond where the
waves broke, and Jenna realized that Thraisha was making
for the blue-gray hint of coastline to the south, where a
tongue of land curved outward.

She could not swim long and had to stop, exhausted.
Thraisha stayed with her, patiently keeping Jenna afloat on
the waves. Swim and rest; swim and rest.

The journey took hours. The sun was nearly setting when
they came to a table of low, wet rocks and could crawl out
of the water.

*   *   *

"You threw yourself from the cliff a stone-walker and landed a Saimhóir." Thraisha seemed amused by what she'd seen. "Welcome to the sea, land-cousin."

The mage-lights had come; Jenna had been able to renew Lámh Shábhála, and with the cloch she'd regained her ability to speak with Thraisha. She was still in seal form—far more comfortable than any human one in this environment. She marveled at the new feel of the world around her and her heightened senses. She had never known that the taste of the ocean was so complex, that she could sense where the mouth of a river shed fresh water, or whether the bottom below was sandy or rocky, or where the kelp beds lay. Swimming unbounded by gravity was a luxuriant pleasure, the feel of the water against her fur like the stroke of a lover's hand. Underneath the water, she could hear the sounds of the ocean: the distant, mournful calls of whales, the splash of brown seals feeding nearby, the flutter of a school of fish turning as one, the grunts and chirps and clicks of a thousand unidentified animals.

Yet her new body retained marks of the old: her right flipper was scarred and balky, the fur marked all the way to her spine with the shapes of the mage-lights. She still ached, every movement sending a reminder of the punishment she'd endured.

"How long can I stay this way?" she asked Thraisha after she'd recounted to the Saimhóir what had happened since they'd last talked. "Ennis, he said that most changelings were either Water-snared or Earth-snared, able to change for only a few hours."

Thraisha grunted agreement. "He was right. But your blood runs strong with the Saimhóir strain and with the power of the mage-lights. You can stay this way until you will yourself to return to your birth form. But there's danger in that, as well. The longer you remain Saimhóir, the more difficult it will be to make the change back. And I would believe that the longer you stay Saimhóir, the more likely it is you will lose the ability to use the cloch na thintrí. Lámh Shábhála is a servant of the stone-walkers, not of the Saimhóir."

In the radiance of the cloch, Jenna could sense the faint

stirring of the life inside her. She wondered what would happen to the child if she remained Saimhóir. "I need to go back. To Inishfeirm, perhaps." She looked at the cliffs of the headland, a hundred yards away from the rocks on which they lay. They were lower here than at Thall Coill— looming like a blue-green line of thunderclouds on the horizon at the end of the curving shore of the island—but still high. And beyond them, she knew all too well, were trackless miles of steep hills and drumlins.

She would be naked. With no resources but Lámh Shábhála. Without Seancoim . . . The thought stirred the deep sorrow in her. *You've lost the two people who cared most for you. You're alone. Alone . . .*

Jenna found that while a Saimhóir could feel anguish and grief, they could not cry.

Thraisha stirred. "We could swim there, faster than you could walk. I would stay with you."

"I can't ask that of you. You told me: the interests of the Saimhóir aren't those of my people."

"You are both," Thraisha answered. "And we're linked, you and I." She coughed, and the heads of two more blue seals broke the water near them. They hauled out of the water alongside Thraisha.

"It's a long swim around the Nesting Land," Thraisha said. "Rest today, and feed yourself while the sweetfish are running. Then we'll begin."

55

A Return

OWAINE often went down to the shoreline in the mornings. He'd help his da and his older brothers push the boat off the half-moon shingle where it was beached and tied every night, even though he knew that it was the burly arms and legs of his brothers and not his tiny form that was sliding the tarred and weathered wood along the wet sand. When the waves finally lapped at the prow, his da would ruffle his hair. "That's good enough, little one. We'll take it from here. Watch your mam for us until we get back." Then they would push the boat out into the swells, his da leaping into the boat last as his brothers rowed out a bit. He'd see his da readying the nets as the boat cleared the surf and headed out to the deeper water past the headland.

Owaine would watch until he could no longer see the boat—that would not be long, since his eyes were short-sighted and everything quickly became a blur—then he'd go exploring before his mam called him back to the cottage up the hill. Usually, he scrambled around the clear tidal pools that collected between the black rocks, trying to catch the small bait fish that were sometimes trapped as the tide went out, or poking at the mussels and clams. Sometimes he'd come across odd presents the sea had tossed up on the shore for him to find: a boot lost by some fisherman; a battered wooden float from a fishing net; strange, whorled shells with enameled, sunset-pink interiors; driftwood polished by the waves and twisted into wondrous shapes.

Today Owaine walked to the north side of their small beach, to where the waves broke against the rocky feet of the Inishfeirm. The wind was cold; the salt spray wet his hair and made him blink. Mam wouldn't let him stay out long today; he knew she'd be calling him back to help her and his two sisters: there was butter to be churned and the chickens to be fed. He half-slid, half-crawled along the rocky shoreline, wet to his thighs. He thought he heard the call of seals just beyond a screen of boulders, and he clambered over to them to see. Once his brothers had said they'd seen a family of blue seals on the shore, but Owain hadn't been there that day. Blue seals occasionally visited the island, he knew, and it would be exciting to glimpse them, since they were so rare. Bragging about it afterward to his brothers would be best, though . . . Maybe he could make it sound even more exciting than it was.

Owaine pulled himself up the surf-slick face of the last boulder. Beyond was another tiny rocky beach. He caught a blurred glimpse of black fur sparkled with blue fire, but then movement at his end of the beach caught his eye. He gasped and nearly fell from his perch.

A young woman was standing there, walking out of the water. She was naked, her black hair hanging in wet, dripping strings, her body sheened with water. She seemed exhausted and her right arm appeared to be injured, scarred and hanging limp at her side. She wore a silver chain around her neck, with a pendant swinging between small breasts. To Owaine, she seemed to be perhaps a little older than his sisters.

A naked lady on the beach was going to be a far better tale than blue seals, but he wondered if anyone was going to believe him.

He must have made a noise, for her head turned and she looked at him. "Don't be frightened," she said, the words accompanied by a soft smile. Her voice sounded hoarse, as if she hadn't used it for a long time. She made no attempt to cover herself; she didn't seem to notice her nudity at all. She cleared her throat. "This is Inishfeirm, isn't it?"

He nodded, wide-eyed.

"Good. I wasn't certain, since I couldn't see the White

Keep from this side, but that's what they said it was. Do you have a cottage near here?"

They? Owaine wondered who she might mean but decided not to ask. Instead, he nodded solemnly.

"What's your name?"

"Owaine." He blinked as the apparition took a few steps toward him. He crouched, ready to jump down from the boulder and run. The woman walked gingerly, the way Owaine did when he sat too long with his legs under him and they were all tingly and heavy. He decided he could stay where he was. "Owaine Geraghty. Who are you?"

"My name's Jenna. I need to go to the White Keep. Do you know if Máister Cléurach has returned there yet?"

Owaine shook his head. He'd heard that name, of course—everyone on Inishfeirm knew it—but his family had little to do with the White Keep and the cloudmages. He'd seen a few of the acolytes, even talked to them a bit when they bought the fish his da brought to the market, but he'd never seen the old Máister, who—his brothers and sisters all told him—was a cross and nasty man who sometimes liked to beat the acolytes with willow branches, just for fun. They told him other more imaginative and awful things about the keep and the Bráthairs and their Máister and what happened to the acolytes there, but Owaine wasn't sure how much to believe since, after all, none of his siblings had ever actually been to the White Keep. Still, some of it might be true and Owaine couldn't imagine why anyone would want to meet Máister Cléurach, who seemed to be part monster.

Of course, this woman could be a monster herself, which might explain her appearance . . . But the woman smiled again, and she didn't seem dangerous at all. "Don't worry, it's all right," she said. "How about you—do you have a home near here? Is your mam there?"

"She's back there in the cottage." Owaine pointed to the whitewashed walls just visible high up in the green hills.

"Will you take me to her?" She seemed to have realized her state for the first time, one hand covering her breasts, her scarred and stiff-looking right hand over the dark fleece at the joining of her legs. "I suppose I need some clothes . . ."

Being in the White Keep reminded Jenna achingly of Ennis. She almost sobbed, seeing her own tiny room again. But Máister Cléurach arrived not a minute after the wide-eyed acolyte closed the door behind himself.

"I didn't think I would see you again, frankly," he said without preamble.

"I'm pleased to see you again, too, Máister."

He sniffed at that. He stared at her, his eyes dark under the white-haired line of his brows. "The rumors are flying through the keep that you've returned from Thall Coill, that you appeared naked on the shore in a blaze of sorcerous light, that you passed the Scrúdú and now understand the deepest places within Lámh Shábhála."

One corner of her mouth lifted. "I've returned from Thall Coill. The rest . . ." She shrugged. ". . . are just rumors."

"What happened?"

She wasn't certain that she wanted to tell him. But once she started, she found that there was a catharsis in telling him all that had happened since they'd parted ways after Glenn Aill. Máister Cléurach let her talk, occasionally interjecting a question to clarify some point. An acolyte came in with a lunch of bread, fruit, and water, then left. She told him everything except the fact that she was pregnant.

She didn't know why she kept that back, only that it felt right to do so.

Máister Cléurach listened, then grunted. "I still don't understand," he said. "Why did this An Phionós not kill you as it did Peria?"

She'd prepared a lie for that, knowing the question would come. "We fought to a draw," she said. "I wasn't able to defeat An Phionós, but neither did it have the power left to kill me."

"Hmm . . ." Máister Cléurach ran fingers along his bearded jaw. "And you have the changeling blood, too. Like Ennis."

The mention of the name made her blink. "Aye," Jenna answered. "Or I wouldn't be here and Lámh Shábhála would be lost in the ocean."

"I doubt it." He plucked a slice of apple from the tray and chewed it thoughtfully. "Lámh Shábhála has a way of finding its own path to a Holder. By now, someone else would have found it washed up on a shore, or in the gullet of someone's fish dinner." He swallowed. "I've already sent word to Dún Kiil that you've returned."

Jenna nodded. "I thought you would. So the Banrion's back there? Is she well? Is there word about the Rí Ard and the Tuatha? Mac Ard?"

"Nothing about Mac Ard," he answered, "but we hear that the Rí Ard and his son have gone to Tuatha Gabair, Airgialla, Connachta, and Infochla, and sent messages to Locha Léin and Éoganacht as well. Mundy Kirwan—you remember him; Ennis' friend—is strong with the slow magics, and he has felt Clochs Mór gathering near Falcarragh. I think the war comes soon; the Comhairle agrees with me. And that makes me wonder. Why did you come back here, Jenna?"

"I don't know," she answered honestly. "I thought . . . I thought it was the only place I belonged right now."

"Then you'll fight with Inish Thuaidh."

The memory of Thraisha's foretelling came to Jenna again, as it had all too often over the last days. . . . *You stood there alone, and you called lightning down from the skies with Lámh Shábhála, but other sky-stones were there also, held by the hard-shelled ones, and they gathered against you. I was there, too, but I was too far away and others' clochs were set against me and I couldn't reach you. You looked for help, but even though those with you held sky-stones of their own, they were beset themselves, and none came to your aid. I saw you fall . . .*

"This is my home. This was Ennis' home. And I know that my presence is the reason for the war if it comes." Jenna shrugged. "I didn't choose this path, Máister. But it seems to be the one I have to walk."

Máister Cléurach grunted again. "Then I'll do my best to make you ready for it," he told her. "We can start today."

                              *   *   *

She hadn't been certain what she wanted, but Máister
Cléurach certainly had no such doubts. He immediately resumed his role as Jenna's mentor in her studies of the
cloudmage art. Most of that time was spent in the library,
as Máister Cléurach set Bráthair Maher to pulling out dusty
and half-crumbling rolls of ancient parchment. There were
exercises and meditations; reading and history lessons; the
beginning of her study in the slow magics of earth and
water.

Jenna fell into the routine almost gratefully. It allowed
her no time to think, the work kept her mind occupied and
held the grief and worry at arm's length, at least during the
days. The nights were a different matter. She didn't sleep
well, despite the exhaustion of the days and the mage-
lights' nightly call. Then the ghosts threatened to overwhelm her as she cried with her head buried in her pillow,
seeing Ennis' face or Seancoim's. She clutched her stomach where the first flutterings of life quickened. She listened to the calls of the seals far down the jagged cliffs
of Inishfeirm, and wondered whether Thraisha was out
there somewhere, even though she couldn't feel her with
Lámh Shábhála.

But the days . . . The days she could tolerate.

". . . and as you see, Severii claims that even when Lámh
Shábhála seems to be devoid of energy, there is still a reservoir of power within it, one that he was unable to tap.
Which is what he thought was the place that would be
opened through the Scrúdú—"

Máister Cléurach stopped, causing Jenna—seated next to
him looking at the mostly undecipherable marks on the
yellowed roll of parchment—to glance up. An acolyte
cleared his throat from the doorway of the library; behind
him, another figure lurked. "Máister," the acolyte began,
but Máister Cléurach was already on his feet.

"Banrion," he said. "This is a surprise."

Aithne gave a cough of laughter. "Then you don't know
me well at all, Máister. Holder Jenna, it's good to see you
again. I wanted to give you my condolences on the death
of your friend Seancoim. It must have been terrible, losing

two people so close to you in such a short space of time."
The sadness in her voice seemed genuine, as did the sympathy on her face. "And I also wanted to welcome you back."
She held her hand out to Jenna, who took it. Aithne's fingers pressed against hers. "I was afraid I would never see
you again," Aithne said. "I knew when we woke that morning and found you gone that you'd taken the path to Thall
Coill. Come, walk with me a bit and tell me about it. Máister Cléurach's dry reports are fine, but I'd like to hear your
own words. Máister, if you don't mind . . ."

Jenna didn't particularly want to relive any of it again,
but she could think of no way to politely refuse. Leaving
Máister Cléurach and the library, the Banrion walked with
Jenna along the stone corridors of the White Keep, her two
gardai accompanying them just out of earshot.

They walked for a few minutes, hand in hand, Aithne
telling Jenna about their own trek back from Glenn Aill
and the response of the Comhairle to the news of Árón's
treachery. ". . . My own best guess is that my brother,
Tiarna Mac Ard, and the others with them have left Inish
Thuaidh and slipped the net of ships we placed around
the island. They're probably in Falcarragh with the Rí Ard
by now."

They'd come to the bronze doors cast in the shapes of
the mage-lights: the Temple of the Founder. Aithne pushed
the doors open and they entered. Six acolytes were there
with a Bráthair of the Order, who bowed to the Banrion
and Jenna and quickly escorted his charges out of the room.
The Banrion and Jenna walked down between the twin
rows of marble columns as they exited, approaching the
immense statue of Tadhg O'Coulghan. He seemed to watch
them advance, his right hand raised as if he were about to
cast the power of Lámh Shábhála down at them from the
mage-lights swirling in the painted dome above him. They
stopped just under the dome, with Tadhg looming above
them.

"How long has it been?" Aithne asked.

Jenna's brows wrinkled, puzzled. "Banrion?"

Aithne pressed her fingertips against Jenna's abdomen,
gently. Jenna flushed, and the Banrion smiled. "Sometime

dry reports have buried nuggets. You came here with nothing, and among the documents Máister Cléurach sent was a list of everything you'd been given, a quite detailed list. What was interesting to me was what wasn't there: no sponges, no cloths. A surprising omission for a young woman who should be expecting her monthly bleeding. I wasn't certain, though, until I saw you." The Banrion chuckled softly. The sound reverberated from the dome. "How long?"

"Two months, Banrion. Nearly three." Jenna sighed—with the admission, a surprising sense of relief washed through her; she hadn't realized how much it had pained her to have no one in whom to confide.

"Is Ennis the da?"

Jenna nodded. "So Máister Cléurach knows as well?"

"Actually, I doubt it. He didn't mention anything in the reports, I didn't speak to him about my suspicions, and he's not . . . as observant about these things. I didn't know until I saw you, and even then I wasn't certain. Your condition isn't really visible yet, but I see a slight curve to your stomach where there was none before, and I doubt that the Order is feeding you *that* well." She smiled. "Combined with the rest . . . The question now is what to do about it. My healer has potions that can start your bleeding again even at this point, if that is what you want."

Jenna was shaking her head before the Banrion finished. "No," she answered. "This is all I have left of Ennis. I . . . can't."

Aithne nodded. "I thought that would be your answer. Do you remember Tiarna Kyle MacEagan of the Comhairle?" Jenna nodded, recalling the short, stocky man who with the Banrion and Kianna Cíomhsóg controlled the Comhairle. "He and I have been good friends for many years," Aithne continued. "I like the man—he's a good person, wise and quick-witted. He knows when to speak and when to hold back what he knows. He's also . . . unmarried."

Jenna started to protest, realizing what Aithne intended to suggest, but the Banrion held up a hand. "Let me finish," she said. "Tiarna MacEagan . . . well, let us simply say that

he doesn't have any interest in our gender beyond friendship. A marriage between the two of you would legitimize
both you and your son or daughter. He would be a good
father as well as a guide and companion for you. You
would have as much leverage over him as he would have
with you: he wouldn't care if, in time, you have other lovers
as long as you gave him the same freedom. And he would
acknowledge as his own any children that came as a result."

Twin knots of tension burned in the corners of Jenna's
jaws, clamped tight as Aithne spoke. The gardai stood near
the door of the room, talking softly among themselves and
carefully looking away. *No!* she wanted to shout. *No! This
is not what I want.* But she pressed her lips shut, taking a
breath and glaring at the face of Tadhg high above. "And
you, Banrion," Jenna asked. "What do you get out of
this?"

Aithne nodded as if in satisfaction. "You learn well,
Holder. Aye, I'll benefit from this arrangement, also. It
keeps the Holder of Lámh Shábhála bound to Dún Kiil and
Inish Thuaidh. It means that Tiarna MacEagan, Bantiarna
Cíomhsóg and I will have an even stronger hold on the
Comhairle. It means that you will fight with us against the
Rí Ard, because that time's coming very soon. I wanted to
strike first, as you recall. I still believe that would have
been the best strategy, but that time's past. The invasion
will come well before the Festival of Gheimhri. There isn't
much time." She looked meaningfully at Jenna's clóca.
"There isn't much time for you to make *your* decision,
either, Holder. Soon enough your secret will be . . . obvious
and then Tiarna MacEagan would no longer be able to
make the offer."

"You've already broached this with Tiarna MacEagan?"

"No. But I'm confident his thinking will be the same as
mine." The Banrion reached out and touched Jenna's hair,
stroking it gently. "He's truly a good person, Jenna," she
said. "If you allow it, he could be a loyal friend even
though you never share a bed. I made certain that Máister
Cléurach gave him the Cloch Mór of the fire-creature you
destroyed at Glenn Aill, and he is learning to use it. He
could be an excellent ally if you have political desires. I

know that you say you don't, but that may change in time. You could do far, far worse for a husband. Do this now in the next few weeks, and no one will question that the child is his—it will simply come early, as some children do. But if you wait . . ." Aithne shrugged.

Ennis . . . Jenna's thoughts whirled, confused. *I miss you so much . . . What do I do?* Jenna started to speak, then stopped. She backed away from the Banrion, pacing around the base of the statue. "I can't give you an answer," she said. "Not here. Not right now."

"You already have," Aithne answered. "You haven't said 'no.' Think about this conversation, Jenna. I will be here for another day, perhaps two. I've come to tell Máister Cléurach that he must bring the Bráthairs of the Order to Dún Kiil along with the few clochs na thintrí they hold so that we can prepare for the Rí Ard's invasion. We could go back together, meet with Tiarna MacEagan, and make the announcement to the Comhairle." Aithne sighed, her face soft with sympathy. "This is a lot to put on your shoulders, which have already borne more than their share of pain. I know that, Jenna. I don't mean this to sound as cold as it will, but Ennis is gone forever. We can't bring him back. I think he would understand this and approve, because it's best for you." She gestured at Lámh Shábhála. "I know that you can hear the old Holders. Listen to them. How many of them have done the same thing I'm asking you to consider?"

Jenna remembered Banrion Cianna's words to her back in Lár Bhaile—that seemed so long ago now, though it had been less than year—regarding Tiarna Mac Ard's reluctance to marry Maeve: *". . . marriage to him is another weapon . . ."* Even Ennis had said it once: *". . . They would tell you that the Holder of Lámh Shábhála should use marriage as a tool, to be utilized when it's most advantageous."* She suspected that Ennis would have understood, all too well.

Jenna stared at the Banrion, her face stricken, her head shaking from side to side not so much in denial as in confusion. Aithne gathered Jenna to her, hugging her close. "Go, and think about this," she whispered in Jenna's ear. "I'll keep Máister Cléurach away from you until tomorrow. Then come and give me your answer." Her lips brushed Jenna's hair. "In the end it must be your decision, Jenna," she said. "Not mine."

56

Covenant

A N attendant, a younger man, opened the door for Jenna and Aithne and motioned them in.

The room was the same one in which she'd first met Tiarna MacEagan. The sun streamed through the stained glass window depicting the horror of Croc a Scroilm, sending bright hues shimmering on the walls. MacEagan sat in one of the chairs near the fire, sipping an amber liquid in a cut-crystal goblet. Bantiarna Kianna Cíomhsóg sat across from him. Jenna brushed her cloch with her finger and let it open slightly: MacEagan wore the Cloch Mór she remembered all too well from Glenn Aill and the attack during the Feast of First Fruits. Kianna, who had no cloch at all the last time they'd met, now had a clochmion, perhaps the one that had been MacEagan's.

MacEagan set down his glass and rose as Jenna and Aithne entered, going immediately to Jenna after a quick glance at the Banrion. She found herself searching his face, looking at his body. The crown of his head was but a few finger's width higher than her own, and streaks of pale scalp showed through the dark strands at his temple. Still, the lines around his eyes crinkled deep when he gave her a wry smile, and his eyes were kind and lingered easily on her face.

"Holder," he said. "This is awkward for both of us."

"Aye," Jenna answered, not allowing herself to respond to the smile. " 'Tis that."

"Banrion Aithne has told me about her, umm, *proposal.*

I want you to know—it would be acceptable to me. It would, in fact, be good for me. And I hope for you as well."

Jenna lifted up a shoulder under her clóca. She remained silent and MacEagan looked again at Aithne. "I'll leave the two of you to discuss this," the Banrion said. "Banti-arna Kianna, why don't we walk and plan the defense of Dún Kiil?" Kianna pushed herself from her chair; she and the Banrion linked arms and left. The attendant remained, gazing with a strange intensity at MacEagan, who nodded to him.

"You may go, too, Alby," he said. "I'll call for you later."

"Tiarna—"

"Go on. Please." Alby bowed stiffly and left. The door closed loudly behind him. Jenna cocked her head toward MacEagan, raising an eyebrow. "Aye," the man said. "Alby is more to me than simply my squire. I tell you that so there won't be any secrets between us. There can't be, not if this is to work." He gestured toward one of the chairs and Jenna sat, watching as MacEagan seated himself across from her. The odd smile was still on his face, and he folded his hands quietly on his knee.

"I'll never love you," Jenna said flatly.

He seemed to take no offense, his face unchanging. "Perhaps not. And certainly not love in the way you loved Ennis O'Deoradháin. I wouldn't expect or want that of you. But I hope that you could come to like and respect me, at least. I think we can be friends, Holder Aoire, and I would say that I have love for my friends."

Another shrug. More silence. Finally, MacEagan rose and went to the window. He pushed open the stained glass panels, sending colors shifting across the room. He stood there limned in sunlight before turning back. "I know the Banrion has outlined what I can offer you, Holder, and I won't go over that again, only tell you that I would endeavor to be as a father to your child. I would offer your child everything I would offer a child of my own."

"And what is it *you* intend to gain from our . . . arrangement?" Jenna asked him. "In your words, not the Banrion's."

He brought steepled hands up to his mouth, bowing his head for a moment in thought. "I get to use your reflected power," he answered finally. "Bluntly, that's what I receive. We know—Aithne, Bantiarna Cíomhsóg, and I—that Rí MacBrádaigh won't live much longer. When he dies, a tiarna of the Comhairle will be elected Rí in his place. A tiarna married to the Holder of Lámh Shábhála would be a powerful figure, don't you think? Maybe even enough to be more than a Shadow Rí—and we control enough votes in the Comhairle to guarantee the outcome. And you . . . you would be Banrion and would take my place on the Comhairle."

"What of Banrion Aithne?"

"She would have her ancestral lands in Rubha na Scarbh to rule, especially now that her brother has proved to be a traitor. She would still be among the Comhairle, representing her townland, and the Comhairle is the real power in Inish Thuaidh, not the Rí. *And* she would also know our secrets, which would ensure that her voice was adequately heard. She loses nothing but a husband she doesn't love, like, or respect and a title she won't mourn."

"Because hers was a political marriage," Jenna spat. "Like the one we're discussing."

"Aithne went into her marriage knowing it would be no more than it is," MacEagan responded. "I have higher expectations."

"You shouldn't."

"But I do," he persisted. "Oh, not for physical love—neither one of us want that of the other. But I do admire you, Holder Aoire. Your youth, your background—there aren't many like you who could have gone through what you have and survived, much less flourished. You're stronger than most believe, including, I think, yourself."

"I don't need false flattery, Tiarna MacEagan."

He went back to the chair, sat, and took the glass in his hand again, swirling the liquid before taking a small, appreciative sip. "I've said nothing false, Holder. And my given name is Kyle. I would be pleased to have you use it."

"I still haven't made a decision," Jenna answered. She paused, took a breath. "Tiarna," she finished.

MacEagan gave a sniff that might have been a chuckle. "How can I help you make that decision, then? Tell me what you need."

"There's nothing you can give me. It's something I have to feel. Back in Ballintubber . . . My marriage would never have been arranged; I wasn't important enough for that. It's the poor who can most easily marry for love, and I always expected that, if I married, it would be that way. I expected that we would have little more than the land we worked, that it would be hard, but it would be all right because we would care for each other. This—" Jenna swept a hand through the air.

"You can still have love," MacEagan said. "I don't intend to keep you from that."

"But it would always have to be a secret love. You might know, and perhaps Aithne, but it would have to be hidden from everyone else."

"Aye," MacEagan responded. He blinked. "As mine is. Now." He took another sip of the whiskey and set the glass down once more. "I've already given you my trust, Holder. I've already made myself vulnerable to you so that you would feel safe. I can't force you into this marriage, and wouldn't even if I could. But I do think it could be advantageous to us both. I will give you one other promise—if one day you find a love that you can't bear to keep hidden from the rest of the world, then I will go with you to the Draíodóir and sign the dissolution. All you have to do is ask."

"You say that now."

"I'll put it in writing, if you wish."

Jenna could feel her hands trembling. She placed her right hand over her left, trying to conceal the nervousness. In the three days since the Banrion had made the suggestion back in Inishfeirm, she had agonized over this. The night the Banrion had come, she'd gone to the harbor and called Thraisha, but no matter how wide she cast the vision of Lámh Shábhála, she couldn't find her. The Holder within the cloch na thintrí had been useless, yammering contradictory advice. She had found Riata in the babble and spoken with him, but he had only sighed. *"The Daoine*

way isn't ours," he said, more than once, and didn't seem
to be able to comprehend the implications, so foreign to
his culture. She'd called her da from the carving of the blue
seal, and he had listened sympathetically, but in the end all
he could tell her was to do what she thought best. She
wished more than once that she could talk with her mam
again—she wondered what Maeve's advice might be,
caught up as she was in the same snare—but her mam was
with Mac Ard. She closed her eyes every night and called
to Ennis' spirit, trying to bring him to her to tell her what
to do . . . but the only answer had been the wind and the
steady, relentless sound of the surf against the rocks.

"You are the only one who can make the decision," Riata
had said finally. *"You are the one who has to live it."*

"Write it, then," Jenna said. "And we will marry, Kyle
MacEagan."

"Please leave us, Keira," MacEagan said to Jenna's attendant. The young woman—no older than Jenna herself—
lowered her gaze, curtsied quickly, and vanished, closing
the door to the bedchamber behind her. MacEagan smiled
at Jenna, sitting on the edge of the bed and pulling her
night robe tightly around her neck. He held a bottle of
wine and two goblets.

"I thought I would come and say good night, Jenna," he
said. He remained standing at the door. He nodded toward
the polished wood behind him. "You can trust her. Keira's
been with me since she was twelve; she knows how to keep
her mouth shut and eyes averted when they need to be. Or
if you have someone else you feel you can trust more . . . ?"

Jenna shook her head, mute. MacEagan—*my husband,*
she thought. *I wonder if I will ever stop shivering when I
hear that*—continued to smile. " 'Bantiarna Jenna MacEagan of Be an Mhuilinn, Holder of Lámh Shábhála.' I imagine that will sound strange to you for a while."

"I think it may always sound strange," Jenna answered.

"If asked, Keira will swear that I spent our wedding night
here in this chamber," MacEagan said. "But Alby has put
together a room for me just across the hall. I thought . . ."
He lifted the wine and gold-rimmed goblets. "We should

at least share a drink together first. I would like that, if
you're willing. It's been a long and tiring day for both of
us."

That was certainly true enough. Banrion Aithne had
given Jenna a clóca of finest white silk that had come all
the way from Thall Mór-roinn. Jenna had let Keira and
the other attendants dress her, feeling numb and somehow
detached, as if she were watching this happen to someone
else. The wedding had been in the Great Hall of Dún Kill
Keep; she entered the hall to find the Rí and Banrion,
the entire Comhairle, Máister Cléurach and several of the
Bráthairs of the Order, and many of the minor Riocha of
the city in attendance. The dripping of the stones punctuated the droning voice of the Draíodóir brought from the
Mother-Creator's temple to conduct the ceremony. Jenna
stood next to MacEagan, not truly hearing the words, and
when the Draíodóir handed her the traditional oaken
branch to break, symbolizing her departure from her previous family, the dry *crack* of the stick had sounded impossibly loud and she had dropped the half she was to give to
MacEagan, startled. The party afterward had been interminable. A singer had begun the *Song of Máel Armagh,* his
baritone voice so much like Coelin's that Jenna felt her
breath go shallow for a moment. The food in front of her
seemed to taste of ashes and paper. A seemingly eternal
line of well-wishers passed their table. Jenna had wondered
what they were thinking behind their carefully smiling
faces, their choreographed movements, their polite and
empty words. . . .

MacEagan poured the wine and handed one of the goblets to Jenna. She took it, but stared down into the well of
purple liquid without drinking. She felt as if she wanted to
cry, but her eyes were almost painfully dry. "I don't feel
much like celebrating," she said.

"I'm sorry you feel that way, Jenna. Truthfully." She
glanced up; there was genuine empathy in his face, a distress that carved deeper the lines around his eyes. "I realize
I can't ever fill the void Ennis left in you; perhaps one day
someone will. But I do promise that in the meantime I
won't make the emptiness larger."

"What does that mean?"

He sat on the bed near her, leaving a hand's width between them. When she moved away, he remained where he was. "It means that I'll stand with you even if others won't. The truth is, when the time comes to finally choose sides—and it's coming sooner than anyone except perhaps Aithne, Kianna, and I believe—neither you nor I know where the final lines will be drawn and who will stand where. People do strange things when they think it's to their advantage, or when it seems to be the only course they can take."

"Like marrying someone they barely know."

The corner of his lips twitched; it might have been a smile. "That's one example, aye. You began a new age when you woke the clochs na thintrí, Jenna. We still don't know the rules of it yet, or how it will change us. We only know that it *will* change us." He lifted his goblet. "So would you drink with me? To the future beyond the Filleadh."

Jenna felt the infant stir within her, a fluttering deep in her stomach. She wondered what kind of world the child would be coming into. *Not one I thought a child of mine would have a year ago, nor one I would have chosen . . .*

"To the future," she said.

The clink of the goblets touching gilded rims seemed as loud as the crash of a closing door.

57

The Battle of Dún Kiil

"*I'M so scared,*" she'd admitted to MacEagan that morning. "*I don't know if we can stop them.*" She didn't mention Thraisha's dream, which had haunted her more and more in the last few weeks: the images of death and loss. She hadn't mentioned that to anyone, but she felt the certainty of it, more firmly each day. She felt as if she were walking a path that was already set for her, unable to turn aside or change it. Part of her, at least, was already reconciled to the inevitability of failure.

The first signs of the coming battle were the white sails on the horizon beyond the arms of the Inner Harbor, well out in Dún Kiil Bay.

They knew the armada was coming from Falcarragh—their own fast scout ships had come scurrying back as soon as the fleet had been sighted. The first battle of the war had already been fought and lost: the much smaller fleet of Inish Thuaidh had engaged the enemy as soon as it rounded Falcarragh Head and turned west toward the island. The tattered remnants of the Inish fleet—five ships of twelve oars, one of twenty: their rams broken, their single sails torn, the hulls dark with smoke and blood—had landed at the end of An Ceann Caol a week ago; an exhausted courier had staggered into the keep with the news two nights afterward.

And now the sails could be seen in the morning light.

Jenna stood in the golden dawn with MacEagan, Aithne, Kianna Cíomhsóg, and Rí MacBrádaigh. They gathered on the south tower, gazing out over the town, the bay, and the sea. The wind was laden with the scent of salt and fish. Soon, Jenna suspected, the primary smell would be the coppery odor of death.

The sails . . . Jenna could count at least twenty of them; more seemed to appear every few minutes. "Forty oars, at least two hundred troops on each," MacEagan said, answering the unasked question. "Perhaps a few less than they started out with, if our ships were at all successful in ramming and sinking theirs. But I imagine that we're looking at a force of up to ten thousand men."

Ten thousand . . . It seemed an inconceivable number. It seemed even more inconceivable to imagine such a horde in battle.

Everyone glanced down from the ramparts to Dún Kiil itself. The town bristled with troops and weapons. Officers shouted orders to trained gardai as well as conscripts from the surrounding lands. The town steamed with the smokes of the forges, the smithies hammering out weapons even as the invaders approached. Catapults sat on the harbor front and out on the headlands, ready to hurl fiery boulders at the Rí Ard's ships as they approached.

But there were not ten thousand here. There was less than half that.

"How many Clochs Mór do they have?" Kianna Cíomhsóg asked. The bantiarna's sword was already unsheathed, clenched in a muscular hand. Her bright red hair hung braided and long, shimmering against the dull leather armor around her torso. Aithne shrugged.

"The runner said that the captains claimed there were at least three single hands of them used during the sea battle. But that could be an exaggeration."

Or an undercount . . . None of them would say it. Jenna remembered the night of the Filleadh and the power she had unleashed. *Three double hands of Cloch Mórs were opened then* . . . MacEagan had one, as did Aithne, Máister Cléurach, Ennis' friend Mundy and one other Bráthair of the Order. One single hand. The Rí Ard could have two double hands and more.

One of them, she was certain, would be Árón Ó Dochar-

taigh. He would be out there, as would Mac Ard and the
TanaiseRíg, Nevan O Liathain . . . *Ironic, isn't it, how
firmly you turned the little bastard down when he offered
you marriage. Won't he be amused to find you married here,
when you could have been the Tanaise Banrion, to one day
be Banrion Ard . . .*

So much would have been different, if she'd accepted.
She might never have met Ennis again, but he would be
alive. She would never have gone to Thall Coill, and Seancoim would still be walking in Doire Coill with Dúnmharú
on his shoulder. Maybe that would be better.

*You can't go back and change any of it. That's not within
even Lámh Shábhála's power.*

"We should retreat now," Rí MacBrádaigh muttered,
staring down at his troops. The Rí's eyes were wide as he
turned to look back at the others gathered with him, and
his dry white hair was wild in the wind. "We could leave
a small force here to hold them back and give us time to
rejoin the families we've already sent back to the mountains." He looked from one to another of them, as if
searching their faces for some agreement. Jenna turned
away so she didn't have to see him. "Doesn't that make
sense?" he asked. "We could harry them from the mountains, cut them down bit by bit when it was safe, maybe
find a better place to make a stand, maybe even Sliabh
Míchinniúint again . . ."

"Which we'll do if it becomes necessary," Aithne told
him, speaking to him like a stern parent to a misbehaving
child. "Not all of them will land here. And none of their
Holders are trained cloudmages, nor do they have Lámh
Shábhála." Jenna felt everyone look to her with that pro-
nouncement. She could think of nothing to say. *I'm not
your salvation,* she wanted to say. *Don't look at me as if I
were.* She felt ill, nauseous. She placed her hand on her
stomach, pressing it tightly.

"We'll meet them as they land," Kianna said. "I need to
go speak with those who will be fighting with steel. Banrion, I leave the strategies for the cloudmages to you. Rí
MacBrádaigh, will you go with me? Our people would like
to see their leader."

"I . . . I don't know what to tell them," the Rí stammered, looking frightened, and Kianna exchanged glances with Aithne.

"I'll tell you what to say," she told the man. "All you'll need to do is keep a brave face on." She gestured toward the keep; the Rí, with a final look back at the sails on the horizon, shuffled slowly toward the archway to the balcony, with Kianna following.

Banrion Aithne sighed. "We shouldn't stay here, that's for certain," she said. "The keep will be an obvious target for the clochs. Better that they not know where we are. Jenna, where do you want to make a stand?"

"Down at the harbor," Jenna answered. "We'll need to be close as they come in so they're within range of our clochs; if we must, we can retreat back up toward the keep and the mountains with the rest of the troops."

Aithne, Jenna knew, could have blamed her for this. *Maybe she was right, all along. Perhaps if I'd listened to her, if we'd made the attack on Falcarragh first before the Rí Ard was ready as she and the Comhairle wanted . . . She could say that it's my fault, that the Rí Ard wouldn't come here at all except for me . . .* But there was no accusation in Aithne's voice or face, only a solemn acceptance of their task. "Then that's where I'll stand as well. I'll tell Máister Cléurach to meet us there." With that, she swept away toward the keep, leaving Jenna and MacEagan alone.

"We'll get through this," MacEagan told her. "The tuatha have never been able to conquer Inish Thuaidh. The Rí Ard will suffer the same fate as the rest, and fifty years from now, the bards will be singing the *Song of Kiernan O Liathain* the way they sing of Máel Armagh now, and laughing at the man's foolishness."

"I hope you're right."

"I am. We might lose this battle, but we'll prevail. Inish Thuaidh is a hard land, and the Tuathians are soft. They will break here, as they always have." He stopped. His hand lifted as if he were about to touch her shoulder, then dropped back to his side. "*You'll* live, Jenna," he said. "And so will your child."

Jenna nodded. On a pole on the keep's tower, the blue-

and-white flag of Inish Thuaidh snapped in the wind. Far
out to sea, she could see the banners fluttering above the
sails: the colors of the Tuatha: green and brown, blue and
gold, green and gold. She could see the oars churning the
water as the sun glinted on mail and steel.

"They'll be here soon," she said. "Then we'll know."

The battle for Dún Kiil began with a single sound: the
k-thunk as the arm of a catapult was released out on Harbor Head and a flaming ball went hurtling across the late
afternoon sky. It splashed into the water in an eruption of
water and steam a dozen yards short of the lead boat just
entering between the inner bay's arms. Four more fireballs
followed; two of them struck the ship and burning oil and
grease splattered over the deck. Faint screams could be
heard from the crew, and the oars splintered and fell as
those on the ship leaped into the water, some of them
aflame. Jenna, standing next to MacEagan near the end of
the dock, heard a ragged cheer go up from the troops as-
sembled close by.

The cheer nearly immediately went silent. The catapult
nearest the fleet erupted in a gout of black smoke, pieces
of shattered timber flying through the air. There were more
screams, but this time it came from the Inishlanders man-
ning the catapult.

The Clochs Mór had entered the battle.

The sky near the entrance to the inner bay darkened and
swirled with storm clouds as a gale force wind blew out to
sea, howling and shrieking and laden with blinding curtains
of rain: Stormbringer awakened. Jenna could see the ships
gathered near the harbor entrance and already trying to
avoid the flaming hulk of the lead craft, suddenly heel over.
Sails went down—cut or torn, she didn't know—and oars
lashed the water, pushing the boats forward against the
tempest. Two more catapults fired, and another ship was
bathed in a gushing inferno; a moment later, fireballs hissed
away from the incoming ship, and both catapults exploded.
The ships pushed on.

The Inner Harbor had been closed off with chains and
nets hung just under the water between Little Head and

Harbor Head. The first few ships hit the barriers and were stopped, but only for minutes before they were cleared. The first ships moved into the Inner Harbor.

Smoke was beginning to drift over Dún Kiil, laden with the scent of charred wood and the burning oil; curtains of ·driving rain obscured the bay. A constant roar dinned in her ears, the wordless cry of the massed thousands. Kianna Cíomhsóg raised her sword a hundred yards away, her mouth opened as she shouted something to the troops; Rí MacBrádaigh was with her, a sword clutched in his hand also, though its point dragged the ground at his side.

"Jenna, it's time." MacEagan's hand closed around his Cloch Mór. He nodded to her. "I'll be with you."

Jenna took Lámh Shábhála in her right hand.

She sent her mind into the cloch.

The world faded about her for a moment, then the doubled vision of the cloch-world came to her, brilliant and saturated. Jenna gasped in wonder and terror—so many clochs, so many points of brilliance set like burning suns about her: at least twenty of the Clochs Mór, and dozen upon dozens of the clochmion as well, faint pinpricks against the glory of their powerful cousins.

Some of them she knew, their colors and shapes familiar: Ennis' cloch wielded by Mac Ard; Árón Ó Dochartaigh, the nameless tiarna with the Cloch of the mage-demon. Nevan O Liathain was out there, and other tiarna she had met at Lár Bhaile. They were out there, and they were aware of her as well—she could feel their minds turn as the greater sun of Lámh Shábhála rose.

They saw her. The first attack came before she could draw breath.

A wave seemed to tower in front of her, a surging surf of green whose crest glowed white. It loomed high, ready to fall like an immense tower down on her. She could feel the inexperience of the Holder behind the cloch's attack—there were holes in the wall of energy before her. With near contempt, Jenna shaped Lámh Shábhála's power, gathered up the wave, and threw it back to its source. The emerald wave crashed over one of the ships just entering the Inner Harbor; a thin, single scream cut through the

noise of the rising battle. The Mage had squandered all the
energy in the cloch in one flurry, and Lámh Shábhála
greedily sucked it out, emptying the cloch utterly and spitting it back over the ship. More screams came, this time
from the people around the Holder; the luminescence that
had marked the cloch's position vanished like a snuffed
candle.

One . . .

The Clochs Mór of Inish Thuaidh were alive now, attacking on their own, and Jenna realized that no matter
how much she might have disliked Máister Cléurach's tutelage, the quality of the Order's teaching showed. The Inishlander cloudmages were superior to any of the Tuathian
Mages—she saw Mundy Kirwan's cloch open and tendrils
of blue-green death streak outward across the water, thrusting aside the defenses of two Clochs Mór and smashing
into one of the ships, its touch setting the hull afire as the
boat capsized. Most of the Tuathian Mages were inexperi-
enced, their handling of the mage-light's power awkward
and tentative. For the first time, Jenna began to have
some hope.

Sudden flights of arrows arced from the bay, a thousand
barbs streaking down through the smoke, surprising Jenna
with their suddenness, and Jenna barely managed to throw
a shadow of Lámh Shábhála's power toward them. The
arrows closest to her burst into flame and went to drifting
ash, but those to either side did not and soldiers fell,
screaming in pain or silent in death. The assault brought
back to Jenna the realization that it would not be the clochs
only that won this battle. Even Lámh Shábhála couldn't
stand alone against an army.

And not all the clochs had entered the fray.

A shout went up from the western end of the harbor—the
first of the Tuathian ships had landed, the soldiers on it
swarming out to be met by Kianna Cíomhsóg and her van-
guard. The *caointeoireacht na cogadh*—the war-keening—
burst from their throats as they charged. Jenna heard the first
clash of steel on steel as men rushed past her, moving toward
the battle. Another ship landed; a second mass of arrows
was launched hissing through the air; again, Jenna spent a

tithe of Lámh Shábhála's energy to destroy those raining down toward her.

"Jenna!" she heard MacEagan call. "Fall back! Keep yourself behind our troops." She felt MacEagan's arm on hers, and she allowed him to pull her back through the press of soldiers until they stood in the shadow of the tavern. His face was drawn, his hand white around the cloch. His eyes closed and he groaned, staggering, and in her cloch-vision, Jenna saw the fire-creature recoil as a thicket of glowing spears thrust into its torso.

Through the smoke at the edge of the harbor front, Jenna saw a banner of green and brown appear, waving above a troop of mailed knights not thirty yards away. Then the smoke obscured them as a squadron of Inishlander troops rushed past Jenna toward them.

The mage-demon appeared in the air over the harbor front, tendrils of smoke writhing about it like a mad cloak. It shrieked, its head seeming to search the city, then it folded its wings and fell toward Jenna.

From there, what little vestige of order remained disintegrated into chaos, and Jenna was too busy to see what happened anywhere but in front of her.

The demon fell upon them, claws and horrible mouth open in fury. Jenna sent a pulse of energy toward it, nearly too late: a taloned hand slashed air so close to her face that she felt the wind of its passage. The creature slammed into the wall of the tavern, timbers cracking and stone walls tumbling in. Splintered wood and sharp fragments of shattered stone splattered over Jenna; she ducked instinctively, raising her left hand to protect her face.

The mage-creature howled in rage and pain, leather wings lashing as part of the roof collapsed and dust rose in a gray pall. It stalked out of the ruin, thrusting aside shattered roof beams, as Jenna stood again. She sent her mind into the well of the cloch, sending arcing bolts of energy toward the beast. It howled and screamed as they struck and went down to its knees. Jenna prepared a second strike, knowing that alone the creature couldn't survive against Lámh Shábhála. But it was not alone, suddenly.

Behind you . . . ! She could hear the scream of a chorus of ancient Holders in her head.

Light flared in her cloch-vision, slashing toward her from two directions within the Inner Harbor: firebolts accompanied by streaks of azure lighting, both of them all too familiar to Jenna: Mac Ard and Árón Ó Dochartaigh. Cursing, Jenna brought the energy she'd gathered to bear on the new attack: mage-power exploded so near her that she was thrown back, landing on the paving stones with a grunt, her clóca torn and skin scraped away on her left arm and side. Almost, she lost her grip on Lámh Shábhála; the cloch-vision shuddered, blinked, then returned. The demon pulled itself erect again . . .

. . . but a form of molten rock hurtled past in front of Jenna, colliding with the demon with a screech of rage; MacEagan, somewhere close by, shouted in unison with the creature. A fury surged through her, overlaid with the memory of Árón's murder of Ennis. She reached out with Lámh Shábhála, rushing back along the lines radiating from Árón's cloch with the full force of her own cloch. But two additional clochs had joined in the attack; Jenna felt an unseen force drape around her; where it touched, it clung like a stinging spider's web. The net constricted, pulling tighter, and she had to divert some of the force of Lámh Shábhála to push it back and allow herself to breathe. At the same moment, she felt the touch of a cloch on her mind. There was disconcerting sense of invasion, then it went away . . .

. . . and Ennis was standing before her, smiling, his hands out. "Ennis . . ." Jenna breathed. Ennis, still smiling, raised a sword that appeared impossibly in his hands and slashed at her. She fell back, raising her left hand, and the blade cut deep in her forearm, opening a long wound through which bone shone white for a moment before blood poured from the gaping cut. The blade finished its diagonal slice at her hip, opening a shallower wound along her right side. The strike intended for Árón Ó Dochartaigh went wild, vanishing as she lost control of the power. Ennis was still smiling as he raised the sword—dripping red along its keen edge—once more.

"Ennis!" She screamed his name. A line of fire hurtled toward her—Mac Ard—and she barely managed to turn the fireball aside; she could feel its terrible heat as it exploded in one of the buildings behind her. She heard screams from behind but couldn't turn to look. The net tightened around her; in her cloch-vision, she could feel the snarling power of Ó Dochartaigh's and Mac Ard's clochs gathering for another stirke.

Ennis—smiling fixedly like a mad creature—brought the sword down.

Jenna brought up a shield of Lámh Shábhála's energy. Where the power met Ennis' sword, the blade hissed, smoked, and sheared away. Screaming wordlessly, Jenna sent the red-tinted fury past the useless weapon, hurtling into Ennis' body, burning and tearing at it as if it were her own hands even as she cried. Ennis screamed in pain, calling her name like a curse, and she wept even as she pulled at the ribbon of energy that linked his image to the cloch that had created it. She could feel the Mage at the other end shrieking with agony as she raked the phantom with Lámh Shábhála's power, and that fueled the anger even more. She ripped every last erg of energy from the other's cloch and sent its remnants hurtling toward the netting laced around her. The impact loosed the constriction, and she rolled aside as azure lightning and red-orange fireballs both gouged craters in the earth at the spot where she'd been standing an instant before.

For a moment, she was free, but the cloch-vision roiled with bright points of power even as she threw shields around Lámh Shábhála to keep it hidden. Some of them were matched with the clochs of the Inishlanders: Máister Cléurach, MacEagan, Aithne, Galen . . . Most of the Tuathian clochs were set against the Inish troops, but she could feel several searching for her. She wished she could make sense of the uproar and confusion around her. Men were shouting and yelling and moaning all around her; there was movement and the bright sound of clashing steel; the scent of blood and death, but she was standing alone in a small circle of calm. She spun around, looking for MacEagan, but though she could sense his cloch close by, she couldn't see him. "MacEagan!" she shouted. "Kyle!" There was no answer.

She thought for a moment she glimpsed Kianna through a gap in the clouds of smoke, sword lifted and bloody, hacking at two Tuathian solders, then the smoke covered her again. Where Aithne, or Máister Cléurach or Rí Mac-Brádaigh might be, she had no idea. She tried to walk and nearly went down; pain shot through her right hip, and she looked down to see her clóca ripped and covered with gore, her left arm slathered with blood and the wound gaping and raw. The sight of it made her nauseous and weak and she nearly fell. Her fingers loosened on Lámh Shábhála, and the cloch-vision faded, the world going gray and dim. She forced herself to stand erect, to pull strength from the cloch.

"This is what war is like . . ." The voices came from within Lámh Shábhála.

". . . we warned you . . ."

". . . it's pain and blood and loss and death . . ."

". . . it's only in the songs and myths that war is glorious and brave and only the enemy is hurt . . ."

Jenna felt despair and hopelessness wash over her. *We're going to lose. We need to call the retreat now, before it's too late.*

But there were sea-green points of magic-imbued light, moving out in the water. One of them was very familiar. "Thraisha!" The blue seals moved among the ships of the Tuatha. Through the confusion of the battle, Jenna heard the sudden shouts of alarm aboard the boats and the splintering of wood. In the cloch-vision, Thraisha's brilliance flared, and Jenna saw, out in the Inner Harbor, a ship suddenly heel over as if a giant hand had pushed it; at the same time, one of the cloch-lights winked out, extinguished.

The Tuathian Mages now seemed to realize that they were being attacked from the sea and Jenna felt many of them turn away to deal with this new threat. Limping and slow, Jenna made her way toward the water. She felt the ground underneath move from stone flags to hard-packed earth to wooden planks as she reached the quays. She passed bodies, both Inishlander and Tuathian; she passed

wounded who looked up at her beseechingly, moaning or
calling out to her—she ignored them, lost in the cloch-
vision.

Mac Ard was still there, searching for her, and Árón Ó
Dochartaigh also. She was near enough now that she could
see the ships on which they stood, Mac Ard out near Little
Head, and Ó Dochartaigh a few hundred yards out and to
the south of her, his ship rowing in. *"Strike before they find
you . . ."* She heard the whispered advice, and plunged her
being into Lámh Shábhála, gathering up as much of the
cloch's power as she could hold, keeping the shields around
her as she prepared, then dropping them as she threw the
wild energy toward Ó Dochartaigh. Too late, he saw the
attack and sent pulses of blue toward it, but the white-hot
force was hardly blunted. Jenna followed the lines back,
imagining that she handled lightning with her bare hands
and shoved it, pushing it back at Ó Dochartaigh. She saw
his face in her cloch-vision, glimpsed his hatred as he realized that Jenna was there. "This is for Ennis!" she shouted
at him, not knowing if he could see or hear her, not sure
if it was truly his face or simply a shadow of it glimpsed in
the cloch-vision. His lips shaped words, but she held the
lightings and thrust them directly into that mouth. Lámh
Shábhála tore at him, shredding flesh from bone, his hair
aflame, his eyes bulging . . .

And he was gone. The cloch-light went dark, and she felt
him, finally, die.

She had no time to savor her revenge, no time to feel
any emotions at all. Lámh Shábhála was revealed again,
and Mac Ard and the other cloch wielders saw her. Red
violence streaked toward her; she thrust it aside and the
piers to either side of her erupted in splinters and flame,
the heat of Mac Ard's attack rushing over her. The net-
thrower was at her again, tossing its webbing about her.
She could feel the attention of other clochs turning to her
now. A giant wolf howled, leaping from nowhere toward
her, mouth open and slavering. She speared it with Lámh
Shábhála, tossing it into the water as somewhere a Mage
howled in concert. Another wolf followed, and another . . .
She dropped the pier from underneath one, then hurled

the other into the fire of the docks Mac Ard had destroyed.
The netting pulled tight around her as her attention wandered, tendrils closing around her throat, the ends writhing
and pushing at her mouth. Her arms were trapped, and she
felt herself being pulled toward the water, her feet lifting
from the ground.

Jenna was deep into the reservoirs of Lámh Shábhála
now. She forced herself to concentrate, to find the power
to pull away the cloch-bonds around her . . .

. . . she felt them loosen, and at the same time, aqua light
blossomed near her. *"I'm here, sister-kin, as I promised,"* a
familiar voice boomed in her head, and she saw Thraisha
lash out at the person holding Jenna while—through her
eyes—she saw Thraisha clambering out of the water onto
the broken pilings of the quay. In the cloch-vision, Thraisha
was a darting, sleek blue presence, liquid and graceful, severing the threads surrounding Jenna and sending them recoiling backward. *"There . . ."*

Freed, Jenna staggered backward. A sinister, double
boom reverberated in her head and red flares came streaking toward her: Mac Ard. She reached into Lámh Shábhála,
imagining a wall, but Thraisha's presence interposed itself
before she could use the energy. Blue inundated red, each
pushing against the other. Mental sparks flew, like a grinding wheel sharpening a blade, energy flowing from both of
them toward the point of impact. Thraisha moaned, and
Jenna heard pain and weariness in the call. The net-weaver
had returned, and strands were coiling around Thraisha.

Jenna sent her mind into Lámh Shábhála, and in her
anger, she knew that this was the moment. She would
smash Mac Ard now, overwhelm him and end this. End it
forever. Thraisha's vision had been false . . .

. . . a noise . . . not heard with the senses of Lámh
Shábhála, but with her own ears . . .

. . . a hammer blow between her shoulder blades, sending
her crumpling to the pavement . . .

. . . the shock of the blow loosening her grip on the cloch,
so that it rolled free of senseless, stiff fingers . . .

. . . scuffed boots in front of her face, and laughter. Jenna
looked up to see the face of a Tuathian soldier . . .

. . . the pain coursing through her as she groped for Lámh Shábhála, a loss as intense as the moment she saw Ennis fall. She cried aloud, moaning and trying to reach the cloch, knowing that Thraisha was now alone against Mac Ard and the others, that Thraisha couldn't stand against them all . . .

. . . The soldier's hand, grimy and broken-nailed, reaching for Lámh Shábhála as well . . .

". . . When you fell, the clochs turned to me, and I could not swim against that current . . ."

Jenna saw Thraisha's glimmering blue-and-black body skewered by scarlet lightning. The bolts ripped through the seal, nearly tearing her body in half. Her dying eyes seemed to stare at Jenna as the force of the strike from Mac Ard's cloch toppled her back into the water. Blood spewed from the riven corpse and stained the waves, and a silvery form wriggled away from Thraisha's open, silent mouth.

". . . Their magic drowned me, and Bradán an Chumhacht swam from my mouth. So if it's destiny, then it's not only your death . . ."

Jenna wondered if death could hurt more than the pain of losing Lámh Shábhála.

58

Retreat

"SO you're the Mad Holder . . . and this must be Lámh Shábhála." Jenna looked up from the ground to see the soldier holding the cloch, and the sight of it caused her mouth to open and release a wailing cry that sounded more animal than human. She shuddered, reaching uselessly for the cloch, and the man kicked her scarred arm aside. He grinned down at her: a red-bearded face stained with black gore, a long cut down his left cheek and through one side of his mouth dripping blood. The deep gash through his lips widened sickeningly as he grinned at her. He was missing teeth, and his voice was slurred with his injuries. " 'Tis mine now, 'tis."

Jenna blinked, peering up through the acrid smoke that wrapped the harbor. The man didn't see the movement behind him. There was a flash of steel and the Tuathian's head was suddenly separated from its shoulders, rolling away. The body stood for a moment, fountaining blood from the stump of the neck before it collapsed, nearly falling on top of Jenna.

"Sometimes," she heard someone say, "it's just more satisfying to use a sword."

A hand was reaching for her—"Let's go, Jenna . . ."—but she slapped it away, scrambling over to the body, tearing at the fist holding Lámh Shábhála's chain and ripping the cloch away from lifeless fingers. "Mine!" she proclaimed, closing her right fist around it.

"Jenna!"

She whirled around at the shout, snarling. Lights flared wildly, confusingly, in the sudden cloch-vision. She started to tear Lámh Shábhála open, to send its power hurtling blindly at the person in front of her, but she could not hold the power; it burned her so that she screamed, her right arm in agony. Hands caught her as she fell.

"Mother-Creator, you've been wounded! Didn't you hear the call for retreat? Come on . . ."

Jenna blinked away blood, trying to see the face. "Ennis?"

"No, it's MacEagan," came the soothing voice. "Lean on me, Jenna. That's it; let me support your weight. We have to leave now . . ."

. . . there was the flickering of candles and the smell of wet stone, and a form moving in the twilight . . .

"Here, Holder. Please sip this . . ."

She could smell the andúilleaf in the crude clay mug the old man was holding out to her. For a moment, disoriented, she thought it was Seancoim and her heart leaped inside her, but then her vision cleared and she recognized him as the Banrion's healer. He held out the mug toward her; she pushed it away. "No, I won't drink that."

"It will take away the pain."

"No!" She pushed at it again even though she could feel herself yearning to drink it, to lose herself and the suffering in the leaf's milky embrace. The healer grimaced and pouted, but he put the andúilleaf aside. Jenna was relieved; she didn't know if she could have resisted if he'd insisted a third time. She tried to raise herself up, and the movement pulled at the stitched and healing wounds, making her cry out and bringing back all the anguish: in the wounded left arm, in the scarred right, her head, her stomach . . .

. . . her stomach. She touched her abdomen, relieved to feel an answering stir. The healer grunted. "The babe is fine," he said, and responded to Jenna's shocked look with a faint, conspiratorial smile. "Aye. The Banrion told me since I was looking after you and she felt I needed to know. But no one else will know unless you tell them. At least not until it's obvious. That's another reason you need to rest, Holder."

"I need to understand—"

"Understand what?" a new voice intruded. Someone had thrust aside a woolen curtain Jenna hadn't noticed before, letting in a stream of sunlight that made her eyes water and blink, revealing the stone walls of a small cavern. The curtain dropped down behind the silhouetted form and the room went dark again.

"Ah, Tiarna MacEagan," the healer said. "Holder, I'll leave you with your husband, then. Maybe he can get you to drink the infusion."

Husband . . . Jenna found herself turning the strange word over in her head as the healer left the room. MacEagan walked over and sat at the edge of the blankets on which she lay. A long cut crossed his forehead, scabbed brown with the skin an irritated red along the edges, and one hand was wrapped in bandages. "Infusion?"

She shook her head. "You're hurt."

"Have you seen yourself?" he answered. "At least I'm walking. It's a rare person out there who *isn't* wounded, and there are far too many familiar faces missing." A sadness came over his own face.

"Alby?"

MacEagan smiled momentarily. "No, he's alive, though he took injuries like the rest. He wouldn't leave me, even though he's more a liability with the sword than an asset."

"I'm glad to hear that. I know how you would have felt if you'd lost him."

Again the smile came and vanished. "That's kind of you to say. Still, it was a terrible battle, and a terrible cost we paid."

The sounds and memories flooded back to Jenna in disjointed, unconnected fragments: the initial assault, the confusion, the bitter victory of killing Árón, the struggle with Mac Ard, Thraisha's sacrifice, the stunning moment when she lost Lámh Shábhála . . . She reached for the stone with a gasp. Aye, it was still there, but drained entirely of power. "I remember . . . You came, I think, and helped me up . . ."

She shook her head. "I don't remember anything past that. It's all gone. And it was only yesterday."

"It was two days ago," he told her. "You were badly hurt. I wasn't sure you were even going to live." He told her then: how the two of them together fended off another attack from Mac Ard and the Tuathian Holders with Lámh Shábhála and his own cloch, falling back past the square and finally finding what was left of the Inishlander defenders near the base of the Croc a Scroilm; fighting their way through another wave of Tuathians; Kianna falling near the harbor and the Rí MacBrádaigh severely wounded, but fighting his way to them; finally reaching the winding road to the keep, then making their way into the deep clefts beyond.

It was like a tale to Jenna, unreal. There was no memory of it in her at all. He might as well have been speaking of a battle fought a century ago with other people.

"Where are we now?" she asked after he'd finished.

"In the mountains north of the city." His lips twisted. "In the same caverns that Severii O'Coulghan used when he retreated after Máel Armagh's attack. We can only hope that this will turn out the same. The Tuathians hold Dún Kiil for now. Scouts have told us that more ships are coming from Falcarragh, and that the banner of the Rí Ard flies above the keep."

Jenna sat up, grimacing as her body protested the movement. For a moment, the cavern whirled around her and she thought she might lose consciousness, but she closed her eyes until the spinning passed. She started to raise her left hand to MacEagan, then realized it was bound to her side. Instead, she reached out with the stiff lump of her right. She could see the scars of the mage-lights beyond the stained sleeve of her léine. "Help me up again," she told him.

"You should rest," he told her.

"There's not time for that, and I'm not the only one hurt. I need to talk to the Banrion and I want to see those who fought with us." She reached out again. "Help me." She paused. "My husband."

He responded with a quiet smile. Then he stood, crouched down again, and took her hand and arm. "Let's walk together, then, wife."

Jenna found that they were encamped in a narrow valley nestled between tall, steep slopes covered with purple heather and thickets. Bright rills capered down the sides to a small river curling through the valley bottom before vanishing into the misty distance, where the indistinct backs of more mountains loomed. The hillsides were studded with hollows and shallow caves eroded from the soft limestone that protruded from under the thin skin of earth, and crude tents and lean-tos littered the ground. Campfires lifted columns of white smoke into the fog. The remnants of the Inishlander army had rejoined their families, but Jenna saw many tents where solemn-faced women hugged silent children to them. They would nod silently toward her as she passed. Jenna expected to see anger and blame in their faces, but there was none; there was only the aching loss. She wished she had words of comfort for the widows, for the fatherless children. She could only gaze back at them, echoing their pain. One of them clutched at Jenna's clóca as they passed, and Jenna stopped. The woman could have been no more than a year or two older than Jenna, with a child nuzzling at her breast under the red-dyed léine of mourning, and a boy that might have been three years old at her side. "Holder," she said, "My son . . . he wanted to see you . . ."

Jenna knelt down in front of the woman. The boy peered out at her from under his mam's arms; she pushed him forward. He held back for a moment and seemed to gather his courage, lifting his face and frowning sternly. He took a step toward Jenna.

"What is your name?" she asked.

"Mahon." The boy's voice was serious and quiet. "My da died."

"I know," Jenna answered softly, with a glance at his mam. "He was a brave man."

"Did you know him? His name was Deelan. Deelan MacBreen."

"No," Jenna told him. "I'm afraid I didn't. But I wish I had."

"When I'm older, I'm going to be a soldier like my da. Mam said she would give me his sword, and I'll come fight with you."

"I hope, Mahon, that won't be necessary." Jenna looked again at Mahon's mam. She was smiling, sadly, all her attention on the boy. She felt the pressure of Jenna's gaze and looked at her with eyes the color of the sea at night. "I'm so sorry for your loss," Jenna told her. "There aren't any words I can say that can give you comfort, I know."

The woman settled her baby at her breast, stroking the infant's head. "It was the choice he made, Holder, the choice of any Inishlander." The woman's face went grim and almost angry. "Drive them back out, Holder," she said. "Make sure his death wasn't wasted. That would give me comfort."

Jenna didn't know what to say. She nodded without knowing why, she brushed the boy's disheveled hair, and stood up again, grimacing with the effort that movement required. "We should go," MacEagan said. Numb and hurting, she let him lead her away.

And where they passed the soldiers who had been there at Dún Kiil—with arms bound or heads bandaged, limping or curled on their pallets, huddled with their families—she heard them whisper her name; saw them nudge one another as she approached. They looked at Jenna and they straightened, bowing. They lifted their sheathed weapons in quick salute. They smiled. They held out their hands to her as she passed. "Holder . . ." they said. "So good to see you . . . A good morn, 'tis it not? . . . Pleased to see that you're up and about . . . We were praying to the Mother-Creator for you . . ." She nodded back, and tried to smile in return. She touched their outstretched hands and watched the tentative smiles widen.

"They saw the Holder of Lámh Shábhála fighting for them," MacEagan whispered to her, sensing her bewilderment. "They saw the power of the cloch, and they know that some of their own lives were spared because the Clochs Mór of the Tuathians had to contend with you and

couldn't be used against them. They saw you wounded and
yet continuing to battle and that gave them strength to do
the same. They watched you cover their retreat with Lámh
Shábhála until both it and you were exhausted." He lifted
his chin toward the valley littered with tents. "You're quite
the hero, Jenna, whether you believe it or not. Some of the
rumors . . . well, you'd be amused."

"I'm not a hero," Jenna said. "I'm not . . . anything."

"But you are. You're the First Holder, and you brought
Lámh Shábhála back to Inish Thuaidh, defying the Rí Ard
and defeating the mages he sent to stop you. You restored
the Order of Inishfeirm to its glory. You routed the traitor
of Glenn Aill, who conspired against the Comhairle and
the Rí MacBrádaigh. You went to Thall Coill to undergo
the Scrúdú and returned again triumphant. You're the
Changeling who can be seal or eagle or dragon at will. You
woke the Rí MacBrádaigh from the slumber of his rule and
gave his sword the strength of twenty men. You stood
against the massed Clochs Mór of the Rí Ard and very
nearly defeated them all."

Jenna had begun shaking her head long before Mac-
Eagan finished the litany. "But that's all wrong. I didn't do
those things. They're exaggerations, half-truths, or out-
right lies."

"It doesn't matter whether it's the truth or not. Not anymore. The point is that *they* believe it, and more. You give
them hope and strength and courage." MacEagan frowned
then, his face grim. "And right now, that's what we need
most."

"I don't want this," Jenna insisted. "I never did."

"Want it or not, it's been given to you. Come, the Banrion's anxious to see you."

The Rí's tent was set near the river, its bright panoply
of banners seeming to mock the weariness, loss, and pain
around it. The gardai stood back as Jenna and MacEagan
approached, and she heard a moan emerge from the flap
held aside for them.

Inside, in the warm light of candles, was a bed holding
the Rí, the Banrion sitting in a chair alongside. Jenna could

smell the strong aroma of andúilleaf. She cradled her cold right arm to her waist.

"Any change with him?" MacEagan asked as they entered, and Aithne shook her head in answer.

"None. The healer says that it's a matter of time, that's all." Aithne chuckled, mirthless and short. "It's strange. I had no respect for the man until now. From what I was told, he fought like a man possessed, screaming the *caointeoireacht na cogadh* and rallying everyone after Kianna fell. 'There was a pile of bodies at his feet,' one of his gardai told me, 'so high that the Rí could not even step over them. He wouldn't leave until we had Bantiarna Cíomhsóg's body, and even then he stayed at the rear protecting the wounded as we fled.' He was a poor husband and a weak ruler. But he found his strength in the end. I wish I'd seen it." She sighed, reaching over to brush away a strand of white hair curling over the Rí's forehead. Her eyes found Jenna's. "I'm glad to see you walking and somewhat recovered, Holder. We'll need you now, more than ever."

Jenna must have shown confusion at that, as Aithne stood and came over to her in a rustle of her clóca. "We lost this battle," she said to Jenna, "but it cost them far more than they anticipated. They thought they would crush us completely with one, swift blow and never have to wage a campaign. They thought they had enough Clochs Mór to guarantee the fall of Lámh Shábhála, and enough troops to smash all resistance. They were wrong and they know that now. I suspect the Rí Ard isn't altogether pleased with his son's generalship."

"Nevan O Liathain planned this?" She could well believe it—the glory of leading the combined forces of the Tuatha would have attracted the man as a guttering candle calls to a moth.

"Aye," Aithne replied, "that's what we've been told, but his victory's cold. None of our cloch Holders are dead and we've recovered another of the Clochs Mór. Eight of their Mages died—before you fell unconscious, you told us that—so seven of their clochs either have new, inexperi-

enced Mages or were lost entirely in the harbor. They lost
nine ships to the catapults and Stormbringer, and during
the hand-to-hand fighting we destroyed at least a third of
their forces. Winning the battle cost them so much that
they couldn't follow us, but were forced to wait for
reinforcements."

Jenna heard little of the end of it. Talking of the battle
brought back snatches of memory: *Árón's face, screaming
in agony and frustration and anger as she killed him* . . .

"Banrion, your brother . . . He was with them."

Her lips tightened and lines folded around her eyes. "I
know," she said. "You told me that also."

"I'm sorry."

"No, you're not," she answered. "You had no reason to
feel anything but hatred for my brother."

"I'm still sorry for your loss. He was your brother; I
know you cared for him. And if I'd not come here—"
Jenna stopped. "If I'd not come here, none of this would
have happened. None of it."

The lines deepened in Aithne's face. Her gaze flicked
once toward MacEagan, and she stepped forward, cupping
Jenna's face in a hand and lifting her chin. "You came,"
she answered. "That can't be changed. And my brother
made his own choices—you didn't force them on him, nor
did you tell the Rí Ard and Tanaise Ríg to bring their
armies here. You're not responsible for their actions, Jenna,
only your own. Do I mourn Árón? Aye, I do. I *will* miss
him, and I'll always remember his strength and his love for
our family. But I didn't agree with his last decisions. He
knew when he chose to stand with the Rí Ard that his
choice might mean *my* death as Banrion, and still he did
so."

She released Jenna's face, going back to the chair by the
bed and sitting. "Let me tell you one other thing, Jenna, a
choice I made. I saw you during the battle. I could feel the
clochs set against you, and there was a moment when I
could have come to your aid. But I didn't—because Árón
was among those fighting you. Instead, I set my eyes elsewhere." Her hands were folded on her lap, her head tilted
to one side as she stared at Jenna, her gaze unblinking. "I

stone in her palm. She half-closed her eyes, willing the fingers to open. They obeyed only reluctantly, lifting until she could see folded lines crossing her palm then refusing to move farther. She moved the hand to her breast, leaning forward slightly so that Lámh Shábhála slipped between the fingers into the hand. She looked at it: the plain, ordinary stone trapped in its web of fine silver.

"Aye," she told them. "I agree with you. We can't wait."

59

Death on the Field

THE mage-lights rippled and flowed, and Lámh Sháb-hála suckled at them like a ravenous infant, drawing down the power. Jenna sagged, her knees buckling with the sense of relief, the energy of the lights easing the aching of her muscles and the bitter chill along her right side. The world around her seemed saturated with color again, no longer so gray and dim. Her awareness seemed to swell out, encompassing the entire valley where the Clochs Mór of MacEagan, Aithne, Máister Cléurach, Galen, and the others were also renewing themselves; and at the outer edges of her senses she could feel the pinprick presence of the Tuathians' clochs also feeding on the same energy—all of them linked to the sky, all of them tied together.

She could pluck them if she wanted, like the strings of Coelin's giotár. She reached out with the cloch, found the blood-red strand of an all-too familiar cloch, and followed it back. Faintly, she could feel the mind behind the energy—and that person sensed her at the same time.

"*Jenna . . .*" The voice was a dark husk, the tones familiar. "*So you are still alive. I told them you were, but they still hoped . . .*"

"*Aye, Tiarna, I'm alive. How is my mam? My brother?*"

She could feel the surprise in Mac Ard's mind. "*You know?*"

"*Lámh Shábhála told me.*" He didn't respond. She felt him try to close his mind to her, and she pushed aside the curtains he drew over himself, enjoying the frustration and

556

fear she felt in response. *"You can't hide from me, Mac Ard. I am your bane. You hold the Cloch Mór I gave to my lover, and I intend to take it back."*

"It was mine first, as you know since it was you who stole it from me."

"Stole? Won it, perhaps, and only after you attacked me twice. If I'd been able to glimpse the future, I'd have killed you then. I left you alive only because of my mam. Tell me about her, Mac Ard."

Again, he threw up a shield; she broke it down as quickly. He tried to mask the flare of anger he felt, and that pleased her. Grudgingly, he answered. *"Maeve's well enough, and waiting in Falcarragh with my son."*

The mention of the child, her half brother, made her think of the baby in her own womb, the child she would never see. *"Your bastard, you mean."*

"I love Maeve, Jenna, as I've told you before, and I treat her as well or better than any wife. I have acknowledged publicly that the child is mine; there's no secret there. No matter what you want to believe, Jenna, I'm no monster. I never was your enemy. Never. You forced that upon yourself, like all the rest."

"Aye, none of this could possibly be your fault," Jenna taunted. *"You're so faultless and noble."*

"Your mam misses you," Mac Ard said, ignoring the comment, *"and she is afraid for you. I think she may even be afraid of you after what you did in Lár Bhaile. And she hates this war."*

"As do I."

"Then end it, Jenna. Surrender yourself and Lámh Sháb-hála and we can negotiate a peace. You can't win this, Jenna. Inish Thuaidh can't stand alone against all the Tuatha."

Jenna sent scorn hurtling through the mage-lights, not allowing him to see the doubts that his statement caused to stir within her. *"Believe what you will. Tell Nevan that I remember his words at Lár Bhaile, how he said that everyone must know that the arm of Dún Laoghaire is long. Well, I know that now, but he will find that the arm of Inish Thuaidh may not reach as far, but it is stronger. Tell him that."* Lámh Shábhála was full. She closed her eyes, reveling in the sense of completeness and power that the lights gave her. She released the cloch.

Mac Ard and the rest of the clochs na thintrí vanished. The mage-lights began to dim in the sky.

The Rí MacBrádaigh died that night.

The Comhairle met briefly in the Banrion's tent, deciding that the issue of a successor must wait, though they gave control of the Inish forces to Tiarna MacEagan. After a long conference, it was decided to strike Dún Kiil in three groups: the largest force taking the heights on which the keep sat, and two pincer arms coming in from the west and east along the lower valley where the main roads ran. The west and east attacks would occur simultaneously, hopefully diverting the attention of the Rí Ard's forces and drawing them down toward the harbor so that the assault on the keep would have the advantage of surprise. They already knew that the Rí Ard, the Tanaise Ríg, and most of the Tuathian Mages were in the keep, and it was there that the battle would be won or lost. There were secret passages into the keep that the Riocha had used for centuries to flee or enter in secret: the Banrion sent Tiarna Ó Beolláin of Baile Nua along with several squads of soldiers along those hidden paths with the task of opening the gates and doors of the keep from the inside as the main force approached.

As for the cloudmages, two would go with each of the initial waves both to protect them and so that they appeared to be legitimate attacks: Mundy and another Bráthair were assigned to the eastern forces and Máister Cléurach and the new cloudmage with the west. MacEagan, Aithne, and Jenna would remain with the main force.

The encampment woke before the dawn and began to move, assembling in the narrow valley, then moving up toward the low pass to the south. Their faces grim and set, they left behind the tents of the camp followers and their families as well as those too seriously wounded to walk. Many of those who went with the army were limping or still bearing blood-stained bandages from the battle a few days before, Jenna no less than any of them. She walked with the cloudmages in the midst of the column: Banrion

Aithne, MacEagan, Galen, Máister Cléurach, Mundy, and two other Bráthairs of the Order, one of them new to his Cloch Mór.

Jenna felt as if she were walking into the face of her own doom.

Not long after noon, they were within a few miles of the city. There, the forces divided, and the main group waited for a few candle stripes to allow the others to begin the encirclement. Finally, with the sun already lowering in the west, they rose and started to climb up the long slope to the plateau where Dún Kiil Keep stood brooding and weeping over its town.

Jenna plodded along with the others. There was very little talk, all of them lost in their own reveries, their own hopes and fears, wondering perhaps if they would still be alive after this day.

Jenna felt only a dull fatalism. The miles she'd trudged that day had been exhausting on their own, a challenge for the slowly healing cuts and scrapes of her body, for muscles torn and taken to their limits only a few days before. She shivered under her thick woolen clóca, and her right arm was a block of flesh-colored ice against her side.

If Jenna herself was quiet, the voices inside Lámh Shábhála were not.

"*. . . this is too soon. The last time nearly killed you . . .*"

"*. . . you'll be with us, one of the ghosts within Lámh Shábhála, yammering at the next Holder . . .*"

"*Be still!*" The voice was a near-roar in the mental din: Riata's voice. "*Leave her alone if you have nothing to say that will help her.*"

"*Riata!*" Jenna thought to him, closing her mind's ears to the rest of them. "*I'm so scared.*"

"*Those who are the bravest are those who know what they face and still go to meet it,*" Riata answered.

"*I'm not brave,*" Jenna answered. "*I just want this to be done and over, even though . . .*" She couldn't say the words. But Riata knew or guessed her thoughts.

"*If you want to live, then you must use what you've learned. Go deeper into the stone, Jenna. Remember where you went at Bethiochnead. Find that place again.*"

"I don't know if I can. I only glimpsed it once, in pain and desperation. Riata, I don't care if I live. Not anymore. It doesn't matter."

"Find it!" Riata insisted, then his voice was gone again, drowned in the babble of the other Holders. Jenna forced them away from her, shoving them back down into the recesses of Lámh Shábhála.

"Are you all right?" She heard MacEagan's voice only faintly. Opening her eyes, Jenna realized that her hands were clasped over her ears as if the voices of the Holders had been physical and real. She lowered them, shivering as the cold reality of the mountains returned to her.

"I'm fine," she told him. Alby was standing just behind the tiarna, his soft hands around the hilt of a sword. "Is it time?"

"Nearly." MacEagan's gaze moved off to the ridge beyond which the Keep stood. "No matter how this ends, it will be remembered. The bards will be singing of it for the rest of time."

"I hope you have the chance to hear that song."

He didn't notice the stress on the "you." "So do I," MacEagan answered. "Win or lose, I've sent too many people to their graves today." He smiled wanly at her. "Of course, if we lose, I won't have to worry about the guilt, will I now? And if we win, why, I can console myself with the necessity of it all. I wonder if every leader feels that way."

"I doubt most of them think of it at all," Jenna answered.

He chuckled quietly; at the same time, the bass growl of thunder rolled loud from the south and west of them. A thunderhead appeared there, dark against the bright sky. "Máister Cléurach and Stormbringer," he said. "It's begun." Already the soldiers were rushing all around them, and the banner of Inish Thuaidh waved at the head of the column. They began to move quickly, a bright swarm over the rocks and mosses of the hills.

Jenna heard the faint clamor of battle as they crested the rise. The tri-towered ramparts of the keep were black outlines drawn on the sky, the town unseen past the cliffs of the Croc a Scroilm, but the wind off the bay sent to them the ringing of iron and bronze and the cries of the combat. Jenna opened Lámh Shábhála as they reached the summit: aye, the Clochs Mór were awake now and fighting. So far at least, MacEagan's tactics had been successful—the clochs were all intent on the two arms already attacking the town, perhaps waiting for Lámh Shábhála to appear in one place or the other. There were Clochs Mór awake in the keep and not yet engaged—Mac Ard's among them—but she could feel their attention focused outward.

That could not last long, she knew. She wondered how close they would get before someone on the walls looked behind and saw them.

It wasn't long. There was no outcry that Jenna heard, but she felt the shift in attention within Mac Ard. "Now!" she cried aloud to MacEagan and Aithne. "They know we're here."

Gouts of too-red fire spat from the window of the north-ernmost tower, rushing toward the front ranks of the troops. Jenna stretched Lámh Shábhála's fingers toward them, touching each with the cloch's power: they exploded in brilliant flame a hundred yards short of the target. A cheer went up from the Inishlanders and they began to run toward the keep. Jenna heard the first ululations of the *caointeoireacht na cogadh,* shrieking from their throats as they charged toward the castle . . .

. . . *she ran with them, half blind with the overlay of the cloch-vision. The rush carried her along, and she glimpsed MacEagan and Aithne near her. The air was loud with the keening and the rattling of mail and the thudding of feet on the earth . . .*

. . . even as the last glare of the fireballs faded, Jenna ripped at the tower with the cloch as if tearing the stones apart with her own hand—great blocks tumbled away from the window where Mac Ard had been. He was a raging, throbbing scarlet in the cloch-vision, like a volcano spewing lava. Jenna could feel the heat of him, and she countered with the cold of the void, wrapping him in blue-white ice, placing more and more of it around him as he melted away each layer desperately. The glow was beginning to dim as he poured more energy from his Cloch Mór to keep her

away, and for a moment, she dared to believe that she
could end it here . . .

    . . . *they were close to the keep now, and arrows filled the
air in a deadly rain. She saw the man beside her suddenly
drop, a feathered shaft sprouting from his neck as blood
spurted, but then he was gone under the rush. The main
gates to the keep loomed ahead, but they were still shut* . . .

    . . . something snarled, and a whip of arcing yellow
slapped down across her shoulders. Jenna whirled and saw
a dragon's face, jaws open with needled teeth as it clamped
down on her shoulder and coiled the rest of its body around
her. Jenna howled, the teeth digging deep into her, the
writhing scales flaying the skin from her body everywhere
it touched. "MacEagan!" Jenna shouted, but even as she
called, she realized that both MacEagan and Aithne were
each struggling with a rival Cloch Mór and couldn't come
to her aid. Mac Ard was nearly free of his confinement.
Jenna imagined herself growing larger, her skin hard as
stone, and energy flowed from Lámh Shábhála into her.
The yellow coils of the dragon's body snapped and broke,
and she followed fading energy back to its source—a young
man, his face pale and frightened as he realized who he
faced—but she saw him only for an instant as Lámh Shábhála tore at his Cloch Mór, draining it. She thought she
could hear the young man whimper, and Jenna wondered
if she had killed him . . .

    . . . *The charge faltered with the sight of the closed gates,
the front ranks spreading out along the walls as the arrows
continued to arc down on them. "The doors were supposed
to be opened!" someone shouted. "We can't go forward* . . ."

    . . . furious now, Jenna swept the cloch-vision about,
searching for Mac Ard, but she was given no chance to find
him. The mage-demon landed just outside the keep, towering above the onrushing Inishlanders, and it roared as it
plunged into their ranks, tearing and ripping with its clawed
hands and feet. She saw it storm forward and pick up a
man bodily, legs and arms flailing, and rip the body apart
as if it were a rag doll, blood and entrails splattering as it
tossed the broken corpse aside. The war-keening faltered;
the advance slowed like a tide striking a rising seabed. The

beast laughed, its wings spreading and blotting out the setting sun, and it bent to its terrible task once more. Jenna
shouted and unleashed Lámh Shábhála again, reaching out
with arms of energy to pluck the thing up and smash it
down on the ground again before it could react to the attack. She sent thunderbolts raining down on it, striking it
again and again and yet again. The creature bellowed as
she tore at it, and she heard the mirroring cries from its
Holder within the keep. In the cloch-vision, a coiling line
of gold led from the mage-creature back to the Cloch Mór
which spawned it, and Jenna sent of blade of energy down
on it, severing the link. The mage-demon howled once
more and vanished, and Jenna would have finished it
then . . .

. . . the arrows no longer fell, but something else did:
several hands of round balls arced over the walls, rolling
into the midst of the Inishlanders. Where they fell, great cries
of anguish went up. One fell near Jenna and she saw that it
was not a stone but a severed head, the eyes still wide open,
long black hair matted with mud and caked blood. She recognized the gory features even through the distortion of the
death rictus: it was Tiarna Ó Beolláin, and she knew then
that those who had been sent to open the keep from the
inside had failed. The last glow of sunlight was fading; darkness was falling, and when she looked up at the walls of the
keep, she saw the first stars glitter in the dome of the sky . . .

. . . light blazed all around her, suddenly. A half-dozen
flares of power, multihued and dangerous, Mac Ard among
them. Jenna reflexively threw up shields as they attacked
as one, and she was suddenly contending with attacks from
all sides, the snarl and blinding light of mage-energy pounding at her. Mac Ard sent his fire; she caught it with Lámh
Shábhála and threw the flame toward the great glowing
wolf that was leaping toward her. Spears of golden sunlight
cascaded from the shield, but she couldn't respond fast
enough to the others. A stream of rich azure slithered
through, burning her while a funnel of utter black whirled
above, its mouth twisting ravenously. She could feel the
power of Lámh Shábhála being leached away by the
tornado . . .

. . . *the war-keening had died. Around her, the soldiers milled, confused and stymied. Rams were brought forward to break down the gates, but archers on the walls cut down half the men wielding them. The gates shuddered with the impact but held. MacEagan's lava-creature—bright in the growing darkness—came lumbering forward to smash open the iron-barred wood, but the mage-demon, returning to the battlefield, met him, the two struggling before the gates so that none could get past. The moving shadows of their contest played over the faces of the soldiers, and Jenna could see the despair and resignation there. Jenna knew that the gates must go down now or they must retreat. To stay would mean being decimated by the archers on the walls and the Clochs Mór* . . .

. . . This was the end, Jenna realized, even as she fought the Clochs Mór arrayed against her, even as she tossed wild power around her and threw them all momentarily back. She was stronger, aye, but they would bear her down under sheer numbers. The Inish hope had been that the army could gain the keep, that sword and spear would cut down a few of the Mages or cause them to look elsewhere. Mac Ard's cloch attacked her again, and this time she could not push it aside. The force struck her, enveloping her in fire, and she screamed as the blow sent her reeling backward and her freshly healed wounds ripped open again. Unseen hands caught her and held her upright, but they, too, shouted in pain as they touched Mac Ard's blaze. Jenna held Lámh Shábhála aloft in futile defiance, gathering power in the fist of her mind and sending it smashing down to where she sensed Mac Ard standing—but the other clochs interposed themselves, shunting the energy aside or absorbing it themselves. She could feel their realization that victory was to be theirs, that they were enough to overwhelm Lámh Shábhála. Their colors circled her, like hungry wolves harrying an injured but still dangerous storm deer stag. They would come in for the final kill now, and Jenna found that the anger inside her, even toward Mac Ard, had dissolved into resignation. She hadn't wanted this fight in the first place, and people all around her were dying, all because of the cloch she held . . .

. . . *the men around the mage-demon hacked at it, but it kicked them aside as if they were bothersome flies. It leaped upon the lava-creature, and Jenna saw its clawed hands grasp the glowing head and twist it. A sound came like stones splitting, and MacEagan's cloch-created creature was gone. She saw MacEagan, several yards away, collapse as Alby wailed, dropped his sword, and sank down alongside him, cradling the unconscious tiarna in his lap. The mage-demon began rampaging through the Inishlanders closest to the gate, and Jenna saw men starting to retreat in panic into the gathering night, pushing back against the ranks behind them* . . .

. . . her cloch-vision was filled with the lights of the Tuathian Holders. She gathered a shield around her; they broke it down. Lámh Shábhála was weakening now; she was using its stores quickly. She could prepare a final stroke, perhaps aiming it at Mac Ard, or she could simply allow it to happen—quickly and hopefully without too much pain. The mage-demon had fastened its eyes on her, and was plowing through the soldiers between it and her . . .

. . . *now. It's better that we die now,* she told herself and her unborn child. *If we die, this ends. The Tuathians will have what they want, and Inish Thuaidh will have to retreat and then negotiate for peace, but the battle will end. In the final tally, we will have saved hundreds of lives. Won't that be better* . . . ?

. . . but there was something else in Lámh Shábhála's vision now, moving swiftly toward them from the tumbled rocks at the feet of the mountain close to the keep, and there was the sound of rocks clashing together in furious handclaps, a storm of sound, and mingled with it a musical warbling that Jenna remembered well. She blinked, wonderingly. *The Créneach . . . !*

In their valley near Thall Coill, she had never seen them move this quickly. They were surprisingly graceful despite their size and appearance, their craggy bodies sliding among the amazed Inishlanders. The mage-demon howled, fluttered its leathery wings and flung itself at them; one of the Créneach slapped at it with a bouldered hand and the

mage-demon shattered like glass. Several more of them
went to the gates of the keep. The archers sent a hail of
arrows down at them, but the shafts clattered and broke
on their smooth, dark skin. The Créneach placed their
hands on the great doors and their fingers seemed to sink
into the wood as if the oak were no more substantial than
newly-churned butter: they ripped the gates open, splinters
and shards of reinforcing metal flying, the portcullis torn
out and flung aside as if it were made of sticks. The Inish
troops cheered; they began to surge forward again. A ferocious battle was quickly underway at the ruins of the gate
as the defending soldiers within came forward to meet
the Inishlanders.

"Holder of the All-Heart!" Jenna heard Treoraí's voice,
mingled with the warbling sound of its true language. "We
tasted the need of the All-Heart, and so we came." Jenna
wanted to answer, but the clochs had not forgotten her with
the appearance of the Créneach; as she heard the call and
felt Treoraí's presence approaching from behind her, they
attacked again as one. Forms and shapes and colors swept
over her like a tide, too quickly for her to do more than
glimpse them. A dire wolf flew at her; she split it asunder
with a blade of energy; lines of bright color wrapped
around her like a snake; she tore them away. The yellow
dragon coiled above her; the black funnel began to draw
power from her; Mac Ard's fire spitting at her like great
glowing meteors.

In the cloch-vision, an ebon wall interposed itself between Jenna and the others. They shattered against it, energy flaring in a mad explosion. For a moment, the wall
held, but the massed clochs continued to strike, battering
it. With her own eyes, she saw Treoraí shamble forward to
stand facing her, and she heard the shrill trill of Treoraí's
voice. "The Soft-flesh must give in to the heart that you
hold in your hand," it said. "Find Céile inside. You
must—"

"I can't," she told Treoraí, not knowing if the Créneach
could hear or understand her. "It's too late."

"If not for you, then for the life you carry," Treoraí
answered. "You can, if—" Its hand plunged into its own

chest, ripping a fissure in its body, and emerged again holding a tiny blue crystal. "Give this to her . . ." Treoraí's voice went silent as the clochs broke down the wall. Jenna heard the sound of falling stone; before her, the bodily form of Treoraí collapsed into a heap of rocks and boulders. The crystal fell to the ground.

The Clochs Mór surged toward her.

60

The Gift of Death

THEY hammered her down. They took her cowering to her knees.

Jenna shrilled her pain to the world, nearly losing her grip on Lámh Shábhála as she fell. Her own sight was gone now; there was only the terrible light and agony of the cloch-world, and she sank down inside Lámh Shábhála as she had with An Phionós at Bethiochnead, desperately seeking a place to hide from the assault. The voices of the Holders shrieked at her or laughed or shouted contradictory advice.

She burrowed deeper, seeking escape. The Clochs Mór followed her. She tumbled into a crystalline, twisting well. The faces of the ancient cloudmage Holders flashed past her: the Daoines, then the Bunús Muintir, then tribes and peoples for whom she had no names at all, falling deeper into the past. And there, at the bottom . . .

Lámh Shábhála throbbed like a live thing, waves of colors pulsating around her. This was the place she had glimpsed during the Scrúdú, the place she'd not been able to reach. She went toward it as the Clochs Mór continued to pummel her, and again she was held back. "No . . ." a voice whispered. *"You're not allowed here. You have not passed the test."*

"Then I'll die!" she shouted back.

The voice sounded amused. *"We thought that no longer mattered to you."* The energy of the Clochs Mór crackled around Jenna, and she pushed back at them. She could feel the baby in her womb, frightened and in pain because Jenna was in pain, suffering because she suffered. The voice at the heart of Lámh Shábhála seemed amused. *"So that's why you fight, even though you still don't understand. What have you brought me?"*

Jenna could only shake her head in confusion and terror. *"I don't know what you mean? The cloch?"*

"No. There, in your hand." Jenna could see blue light radiating from between the fingers of her left hand—the crystal that Treoraí had pulled from itself. She held it out, felt the presence take it from her. The light danced away in darkness. *"Ah, such a gift . . ."* The voice seemed to sigh. *"So my children ask me to help you. How can one refuse one's own . . ."* The voice faded, and Jenna thought it had gone. Then the feeling of nearness crawled over Jenna's skin again. *"All the hearts of my children connect to the mage-lights through you. You fight yourself when you fight them."*

"What do you mean?"

"I will give you a gift for the sake of my children, though I don't know if you are capable of using it. This once, in this moment, you must accept what they give you," the voice answered. It was sounding fainter now, and Jenna felt herself being pushed away, rising through the levels of the cloch once more back to reality. *"Accept it . . ."* the voice said again, a whisper.

Jenna lay like a broken doll on the cold ground before the keep. The power of the Clochs Mór played around her, keeping away the Inish soldiers who were trying to reach her and pull her free. The pile of stones that had been Treoraí were at her right hand, and the mage-lights had appeared in the sky above. She could feel the threads connecting all the clochs na thintrí: running through Lámh Shábhála and into the sky, creating loops of energy, endless circles and spirals . . .

"This once, in this moment, you must accept what they give you . . ." That's what the voice of Lámh Shábhála had said.

Jenna let the shields fall. The energy poured into her and through her. She marveled at the feel of it. She seemed to have been thrown entirely away from her body into some new reality where she was with all the clochs, and their energy filled her, but it no longer hurt, not with the mage-lights in the sky. Instead, she had become a vessel, and they filled her to overflowing. She held the power in her hand.

She rose. She found five of the Clochs Mór and took hold of them.

She thought.

The wind blew cold and salty. The mage-lights flared and vanished, but their radiance seemed to remain, illuminating the cliffside and the weathered, ruined statue of Bethioch-nead.

Six people stood there, each with a cloch na thintrí in his or her hand, all of them battered and bruised and bloody, all but one of them with confusion on their faces.

"Where are we?" Banrion Aithne asked. She stood next to MacEagan and Máister Cléurach, both of whom stared up at the statue. "Holder, did you do this?"

"Aye, I did," Jenna answered. "I think I did. I'm not entirely certain." Power filled Lámh Shábhála as it never had before, so potent that her body seemed to vibrate with it. She felt like a piece of parchment trying to hold back a frothing torrent. *Is this what it would have been like if I'd passed the Scrúdú?* she wondered. *How can anyone handle this?* The energy buzzed in her head, making her giddy and delirious. Her face burned with it so that she was surprised that she wasn't literally glowing. Her voice seemed too loud and too fast. She wanted to laugh. "Banrion, Tiarna Mac-Eagan, Máister Cléurach, this is Nevan O Liathain, the Tanaise Ríg, and Tiarna Padraic Mac Ard. And *this*," she swept a hand about to indicate the cliffside on which they stood, "is the place they call Bethiochnead, in Thall Coill."

Before she'd finished talking, she felt O Liathain's Cloch Mór open; before he could use it, she clamped an ethereal hand around it, letting the power flow not to his stone but to her, the Tanaise Ríg gaping in astonishment as nothing happened. The feel and color of the energy was all too familiar to Jenna, and she did laugh now, high and maniacal. "Why, Tanaise Ríg," Jenna said. The power of his cloch wriggled in the grasp of her mind, and she saw him grimace in pain and cry aloud, falling to his knees. "So it was *you* who wielded the mage-demon. I should have known. I'm sorry, I really can't allow him to walk here."

Mac Ard and O Liathain were truly frightened; she could see it in their faces. MacEagan, Aithne, and Máister Cléurach seemed bewildered, uncertain of whether they should attack the Tuathians or wait. Jenna could feel all the clochs; she held the strings to them in her mind like puppets, but they were puppets who had wills of their own and who fought the control. She could not hold them long, not when the energy ached to be used, rattling the bars of her mind. She heard her voice again. "Tanaise Ríg, you were right to name me the Mad Holder. You were right to call me dangerous. But you want to know why you're here now, don't you?" Jenna realized she was babbling, but she *had* to talk, had to find some way to dissipate at least some of the energy or it would consume her utterly. "That's simple enough. I will have an end to this war. Now."

Mac Ard and O Liathain looked at each other; O Liathain had risen shakily to his feet again. His voice, even through the fear, was still oily and smooth and dangerous. "That's what we all want, isn't it, Holder? But it wasn't us that started this, after all. After Lár Bhaile . . ." A shrug; a glance at Aithne. "Even the Banrion understands that, I'm sure. After all, Cianna was your niece." His gaze went back to Jenna, but he kept glancing at the others. "Killing us also won't end the war, Holder. It will only convince everyone of how dangerous you are. *Everyone.*"

Jenna was trembling now. *"I give you a gift for the sake of my children, though I don't know if you are capable of using it . . ."* Jenna closed her eyes, trying to stop the buzzing in her head. Her scarred arm felt as if it were aflame, the pain crawling along the lines the mage-light had carved into her flesh; she had to bite her lip to keep from screaming. She could tell that the clochs wanted to return to where they had been; it was only Lámh Shábhála holding them here. It was as if she had lifted all five of them into the air: if she let go, they would return, falling back instantly to Dún Kiil; but the effort of holding them was draining her.

"You are Tanaise Ríg," she said to O Liathain, and her voice was a shout, tearing at her throat. "You will be Rí Ard one day. You *can* end this. You will end it, or—" Jenna stopped.

"Or you will kill him?" Mac Ard finished for her. He stepped forward, putting himself between Jenna and the Tanaise Ríg. One side of his mouth lifted. "I'm sure you could, Jenna. That seems to be your answer for any disagreement. Kill me, kill the Tanaise Ríg. Then what happens when the Banrion or your new husband or the Máister do something you don't like. Do you kill them also?"

"Be quiet!" Jenna shouted at Mac Ard, wondering if he could even hear her over the shrilling, singing energy that filled her. The cloch pulled at her, struggling to be free of her grasp. The strain of holding them here was too much, too much.

"Don't you see?" Mac Ard continued, and he was no longer talking to her but the others. "We are dealing with a rogue Holder. That isn't something I want to admit since Jenna's the daughter of the woman I love, but none of us can deny it. She's a danger to everyone around her. She can—she *will*—kill those she perceives as standing against her. She is mad. How long before it's one or all of you that she turns on?"

"Shut up!" Jenna roared at him. She ached to strike at him.

Mac Ard glanced at her, almost pityingly. "I love her mam," he said to all of them. "I would have loved Jenna as a daughter, if she would have let me. I tried to be a guide for her, tried to be like a da. But she rejected all of that. Even her mam is frightened of her now—she would tell you that if she were here. Holding Lámh Shábhála has been too much for Jenna. It's turned her fey."

"No!" Jenna lashed at Mac Ard with the denial, the power arcing around him, and throwing him backward so that he slammed into the base of the statue. He fell on his side on the ground. He spat blood.

"End this?" Mac Ard said, speaking not to her but to the others. He wiped at his mouth, trailing red over the sleeve of his léine. "Aye, we *can* end this, if all of us work together. Lámh Shábhála is strong, but not as strong as all five of us."

Mac Ard struggled back up, one hand on the centuries-blurred stone of the statue, the other still holding his cloch. His hair was matted and bloody, and his dark eyes were intent on Jenna. She could feel him reaching for the energy within his cloch. She started to reach for it as well, knowing she could stop him, knowing that it didn't matter that O Liathain was preparing to attack as well. But the others . . . Aithne was staring at her, and Máister Cléurach, and Mac-Eagan. In the charged atmosphere of Lámh Shábhála, she could *hear* them, could feel their doubt and hesitation.

"Aye," O Liathain said. "If we are together, one of us will be the new Holder, and I promise this as well: however it ends, whichever one of us takes Lámh Shábhála, I will take the armies of the Tuatha home. Remove the Mad Holder, and we will have peace."

There was the same hunger in all of them. Despite the strong ties to their own clochs, the lust to hold Lámh Shábhála was still greater. Mac Ard knew the desire better than any and had tapped it. Jenna felt the change. No one spoke, but in that moment, four clochs attacked as one. The strands running from them through Lámh Shábhála to the mage-lights brightened and came together in Jenna's mind as if like a sinuous, multicolored dragon. The mage-demon snarled near the statue, fire burned near her, storm clouds gathered and lightnings flickered overhead, even a pale copy of Lámh Shábhála appeared.

They came at her at once. Jenna tried to hold them, tried to turn the energy but still it came, the mage-creature raking claws over her, fireballs slamming into her, the storm thundering . . .

A creature of fire arose, standing in front of Jenna, and it leaped at the mage-creature, taking it down. "I promised I would stand with you no matter what," MacEagan's voice said. "My wife."

With MacEagan's sudden defense, Jenna felt momentary

doubt grip the others. Their attack, for a moment, faltered. It was enough.

Jenna imagined her hand, seizing each of the Cloch Mórs and strangling the link to the power of the mage-lights, spilling the energy within them. Savage, unfocused energy exploded, striking the earth around them, scoring the black rock of the statue, charring the trees at the edge of the clearing, hissing over the cliff into the cold ocean. Jenna held them all, and they could not escape.

"You've all betrayed me," she said into their fear and despair. "You've all shown your true faces. Now . . . now is *my* time."

They were huddled together: O Liathain, Mac Ard, Máister Cléurach, Aithne. Jenna reached out with Lámh Shábhála; behind them, the statue of An Phionós shuddered, tilting as she ripped it from the ground that had held it for so long. She brought it high overhead, dirt and rocks falling from the encrusted base. Its shadow was dark and massive. In Jenna's head, the dead Holders shouted: *"Let it fall . . . kill them . . . you must smash them to end the threat . . ."* And Riata's voice: *". . . you must live with what you do . . ."*

"All I need do is release the monument," she told Mac Ard and the others, "and this is over. Do you think, Tanaise Ríg, that your armies will stay when I return your broken and crushed body to them? Will they continue to fight when they see the full might of Lámh Shábhála before them, or will they flee back to their Tuatha like scolded dogs? Tiarna Mac Ard, I won't have to worry about you ever again. Banrion, Máister Cléurach, I won't have to wonder whether your advice and actions are intended to help me or yourselves. I'll demonstrate to everyone— *everyone*—that the Holder of Lámh Shábhála is not to be trifled with."

The energy within her could no longer be held. Jenna shuddered with the effort of holding it. With a cry half of fury and half of pain, she smashed the statue down with all her pent-up anger. The cliffside shuddered and rocks and boulders fell away into the sea. The crash was deafening, the impact so hard that the massive stone of the statue itself cracked, a fissure opening along the creature's back.

Jenna sobbed.

The others stared at the statue, now plunged at an odd angle into the ground back where it had been. None of them spoke. None of them dared.

Finally, Jenna took a breath. "There is always a choice, and we cloud-mages have chosen the path of vengeance and death too many times already. I choose another. I was told that the First Holder can sometimes change the course of her time, and perhaps that can be done without the Scrúdú. Tanaise Ríg . . ."

His voice was small. "Holder?"

"You said that no matter how this ended, you would take your armies back. It's ended, and I charge you to keep that pledge and to add to it: swear that you will never lead another army here to Inish Thuaidh. Will you do that?"

"Do I have a choice?" His face was grim and twisted, as if he were tasting sour milk. He glared at her. "Aye, Holder," he answered. "You have my word."

"Then go and keep your oath." Jenna closed her eyes for a moment. In the cloch-vision, she found the thread of his Cloch Mór and released it from her hand, letting it free. She heard a gasp and a cry, and there was a sense of something torn away from her, leaving her weak. When she opened her eyes again, O Liathain was no longer there.

"Máister Cléurach?" The old man would not look at her. "Stormbringer fits you. Take your gloomy presence back to Inishfeirm, with your pledge that you will remain there for the rest of your time."

Máister Cléurach nodded; Jenna released him and with a crackle of distant lightning, he was gone, and with him, more of the power of the clochs.

"And what of me?" Aithne asked. A wry smile touched her lips. "Holder, I'd tell you that I was sorry, but that would be false. I made my choice, too."

Jenna's eyes were still closed from the effort of releasing Máister Cléurach. Wearily, she forced them open. "Would you make it again?"

The smile wavered, then steadied. "I tell you 'no' as I stand here and I mean it. But I don't expect you to believe that. And if the moment came again, in a different time and place, who knows?"

"That, at least, is honest," Jenna answered. She took a long breath, considering. "The Comhairle must elect a new Rí," she said finally. "Once I would have said that you should take your husband's place and simply be Banrion. But not anymore. I ask for your pledge that the Comhairle elect someone more suited to the task."

Aithne glanced at MacEagan before answering. "I give you my word," she said.

Jenna turned to MacEagan, holding out her left hand to him. She hugged him once, fiercely. "Husband," she said, smiling. "I would send you back with the Banrion, with my thanks for your help."

MacEagan grinned. "It was my duty," he answered. "And my desire." He nodded to Mac Ard, going somber. "But I don't want to leave you with him."

"I hold him," Jenna answered, "and you're needed more in Dún Kiil. Alby will be worried."

"Then send me there, and I'll do what should be done."

Again, Jenna submerged herself in the cloch-vision, finding Aithne and Kyle and loosing them from Lámh Shábhála's grasp. Their departure burned her with its swiftness. Now the mage-energy no longer filled her, and she could feel the pain of her body: the wounds, the ravagements of wielding Lámh Shábhála, the weariness from lack of sleep and worry, the loss and grief.

She opened her eyes. Mac Ard stared at her. "So it's just the two of us," he said. "What do you ask of me, Holder? What is *my* punishment?"

"Be my mam's husband," Jenna answered. Exhaustion throbbed in her voice. The gift given to her was almost gone, and Jenna felt only relief. "Marry her."

"That's all?"

Jenna nodded. It was too much effort to speak. She couldn't hold Mac Ard's cloch much longer; it shivered in her mind, struggling.

"Then I will do that. I give you my word." Mac Ard

sniffed, wiping his bloodied lips with his sleeve. He shook his head. "You should not be the Holder, Jenna," he said. "Everything you do tells me that. You're weak."

Jenna's cheeks colored. Her lips tightened. "Leave me, then," she said. She started to release him, to send him back as she had the others. But where the rest had departed willingly, Mac Ard did not. His cloch remained, burning red before her, the glow growing rather than diminishing. "You're too weak," she heard his voice repeat, almost sadly. "Especially right now. But I will keep my word to you, Jenna. Take that with you to the Mother-Creator as some comfort. I will marry your mam, afterward."

She felt his cloch open and turn its power toward her. "No!" she screamed at him, but an inferno had already erupted. The mage-energy licked hungrily at her, the heat taking her breath. Mac Ard was sending everything toward her, emptying his cloch. She tried to throw up shields but they were weak and late, the fire burning through them in an instant. There was little left in Lámh Shábhála, and Jenna knew that if she miscalculated here, if she did not use enough of what remained to her, then Mac Ard would win. He would take Lámh Shábhála from her—he would kill her.

He would kill the life inside her. He would kill all that was left of Ennis.

"No!" Jenna screamed into the assault. She sent herself spiraling deep into the cloch, gathering all that she could of the mage-energy. There was no subtlety or finesse to her response; it was a blunt weapon, wielded with all the remaining strength she had. Even as the fires surrounded her, she sent it out, hurtling multicolored lightnings into the red center of Mac Ard.

They struck, blinding her. She heard him scream as the fire of his cloch vanished.

For several seconds, there was no sound but the wind and the faint crash of the waves far below, though her ears still rang with the furious sound of the clochs. Jenna blinked into the starlight above Bethiochnead. Mac Ard was lying on the ground a few feet away. She went to him, looking down into the open, staring, sightless eyes. His mouth was open, his chest still. Kneeling beside the body, she closed his eyes and took the Cloch Mór from his fisted hand.

"This," she said, "was never yours."

Jenna straightened. The movement made her momentarily dizzy, and she had to close her eyes to stop the world from spinning around her. She wanted nothing more than to collapse. But she couldn't. Not yet. Not here.

Only the dregs of the mage-energy were left. Lámh Shábhála couldn't take her back to Dún Kiil or return Mac Ard's corpse. She lifted her head, looking toward the moonlit oaks ringing the cliffside. "Protector Lomán!" she called. "I know you're there watching. Step out!" There was no answer for several breaths and she started to call again. Then two figures emerged from the shadows and began walking slowly toward her, one of them leaning on an oaken staff. The Bunús Muintir stopped several feet from her.

"Holder," Lomán said, but Jenna's eyes were on the boy with him, who would not look at her directly though she saw him glance with fright at the broken statue before sending his gaze back to the ground. She had expected Toryn to be with the old Protector, but this boy was blond and no more than fourteen, far younger than Toryn.

"Where's your apprentice?" Jenna asked Lomán.

"Toryn is . . . gone," Lomán answered. His scraggly beard sagged as he frowned, and the boy with him shuddered. "When I learned what he had done to Seancoim Crow-Eye and you, I sent him to the oaks, the Old Ones. He feeds their roots now. I'm sorry, Holder. Seancoim was right; I chose poorly and taught badly for Toryn to do such a thing. Aye, I would gladly have allowed him take Lámh Shábhála if you'd failed in the Scrúdú, but to kill Seancoim and to try to take the cloch by force . . ." He shook his head, grimacing. "I'm sorry if I've cheated you out of the revenge you might have wanted for that."

Jenna gave a laugh that sounded more like a cough. She gestured at the body between them. "I think, Protector, that I've had my fill of revenge."

The apprentice visibly brightened at that statement, venturing a small smile. Lomán *hmmed,* clearing his throat; his breath wheezed asthmatically. "Holder," he said. "How can I help you?"

"You know the way to the nearest Daoine village?"

A nod.

Jenna pointed again to Mac Ard. "Good. I know that you also know herb lore: I want you to treat this body so that it can make a long journey, then take it to that village. Tell them there that the Comhairle wishes the tiarna's body returned safely to Dún Kiil. That's all. Consider it a partial payment for your poor choice of apprentice."

His eyes glared, a flash of irritation that he hid almost immediately. "It will take several days to do as you ask," Lomán answered.

"I don't care," Jenna told him. "Do it." Neither of the Bunús Muintir moved. Neither of them seemed to want to be near her. Jenna lifted the cloch. "Now," she said.

For an instant, she wondered if Lomán, like Toryn, might try to use the slow magic against her. But the ancient Bunús snarled something to his apprentice in their own language and the younger man moved quickly over to Mac Ard's corpse. He picked it up, draping the tiarna's body over his shoulder. His back bowed under the burden, he walked away toward the trees. "This will be good for the young one here. He has much to learn, and I . . . well, I don't have a great deal of time left to teach him." Lomán bowed to Jenna, bending stiffly from the waist. "There is a cavern nearby where you can stay, Holder, until the body's prepared."

"I have my own way home," she told him. "Just do as I've asked." Lomán nodded silently at that and turned to follow his new apprentice into the forest. Jenna watched until they had gone.

She wanted to sleep, to give in to the exhaustion and pain. But she forced herself to walk down the slope, away from Bethiochnead to where the cliffs lowered and she could find a way down to the water. She clambered down over the slippery rocks until the salt spray of the waves touched her face, refreshing her. The moon dappled the ocean as she stood on the rocks at the water's edge.

Not far out from the shore, a dark body lifted its head above the waves. Jenna heard the grunting cough of a seal. She brushed her fingers against Lámh Shábhála. There was barely enough power remaining. "Thraisha . . . ?" Jenna whispered hopefully into the wind, feeling the presence of Bradán an Chumhacht there.

"Not Thraisha," a voice said, the words sounding in her head as her ears heard more throaty gruntings. "Garrentha."

"Garrentha. I thought for a moment . . ."

Garrentha gave a bark, and in Jenna's head a sad laugh echoed. "I know," Garrentha said. "I was there at the battle, too, and we both saw my milk-mother die. When her body went back into the water, I saw Bradán an Chumhacht swim from her mouth, and I chased it and swallowed the power myself. I struggled with it for a day, then felt you gathering the power of the stones, and Bradán an Chumhacht allowed me to follow you here. A small foretelling . . ." Garrentha barked, and Jenna heard the laugh again. "I thought you would need me."

"I do," Jenna said. "More than you know."

"Then I'm here for you," Garrentha answered. "In that first foretelling, I saw more, as well, and I'll tell you now: those who came here to wage war are preparing to leave. And tomorrow, the stone-walkers who live here will meet in their stone house."

"The Comhairle, aye. Kyle will be the next Rí," Jenna said, anticipating, but Garrentha's head moved quickly side to side.

"They will not choose a Rí. They will instead elect a . . ." Jenna felt the touch of Garrentha's mind on hers, searching for the word. ". . . a Banrion to lead them."

"Aithne," Jenna breathed.

Again, a bark/laugh, making Jenna tilt her head in puzzlement. "No. Not Aithne herself, though the choice of person will be hers," Garrentha said. "But there's time enough for you to worry about stone-walker things later. Now you should listen to the Saimhóir within you . . ."

Jenna nodded. She stripped away her filthy, tattered clóca and léine and pulled the boots and stockings from her feet, standing shivering and naked on the shore. She slipped the chain of Ennis' cloch around her neck next to Lámh Shábhála and stepped into the water. The waves that lapped her feet were icy, and she drew in a hissing breath, but the cold vanished a moment later as she continued to walk forward, and suddenly she was no longer walking at all but diving into the waves.

Two sleek bodies swam away, black fur shimmering blue in the moonlight.

PART FIVE

REUNION

61

The Banrion

INISHDUÁN was a barren flyspeck of an island pushing out of the waves halfway between Inish Thuaidh and Talamh An Ghlas. Over the course of history, it had been controlled by both Tuath Infochla and Inish Thuaidh, but in fact no one much cared who owned the small tumble of rocks. No one lived there, no one visited except a few fisherfolk; the earth there was thin and unarable; the wind scoured entirely clean much of the single peak that formed the island. Someone had once tried to establish a herd of wild goats there; even the goats had been unhappy. Seals clambered over the rock at the shoreline while gulls, terns, and other seabirds nested in the steep cliffs rising out of the sea, spotting the gray rocks with white—the seals and birds seemed to be the only animals that much cared for the island.

Undesirable, empty, the isle was well-situated for this meeting. Standing in front of a white tent billowing in the harsh, steady wind, Jenna watched the tiny rowboat approaching her from one of the two ships anchored just offshore, one flying blue and white, the other green and brown. A pair of gardai in green-and-brown clóca stepped out as Jenna's own gardai helped pull the boat onto the wet, narrow shingle. A woman was seated in the boat, stepping out once the craft was ashore. The passenger approached the tent slowly, and Jenna could see that she was holding a baby in her arms. She seemed to glance from Jenna to the blue-and-white banner fluttering on the tent poles, then strode purposefully forward off the wet shingle, leaving the gardai behind as she came to a stop a few strides from Jenna.

"Mam . . ." Jenna breathed. She started to move to her, to take her in her arms and embrace her.

Maeve had changed much in the intervening months. Her face was heavier and paler, the dark hair now liberally streaked with gray. Semicircles of brown flesh hung under her eyes, and she stared at Jenna with such scorn that Jenna stopped where she was, her hand still raised. Maeve's gaze went from Jenna's face to the golden torc around her neck, below to where Lámh Shábhála hung on its chain, and further down to her rounding belly. "Married, and with child. A Riocha," she said. The last word was uttered as if it were a curse. "And more. They tell me you are now Banrion MacEagan. They also say that you rule alone, that your husband is not the Rí."

"That's true," Jenna said. "It was the decision of the Comhairle."

Maeve sniffed. Her eyes shimmered with tears and she looked away. Jenna heard a sob, and she put her hand on Maeve's shoulder. The baby stared at her from within its swaddling, the chubby face solemn. With the touch, Maeve sniffed and brushed at her eyes with a sleeve, the gesture almost angry. She took a step back from Jenna. "It's too late for that," she said. "Maybe once . . . Not now."

"Mam—"

Maeve shook her head. "I've always heard that the Inishlanders are strange, and you . . . you fit them well. I can barely believe the stories I've heard about you." She stroked the baby's head; Jenna could remember Maeve doing that with her, long ago. "I can barely believe even what I've seen. You're the Mad Holder, the changeling, the warrior, the great cloudmage, the Banrion." She paused. Her breath hung for a moment like a white cloud between them before the wind tore it away. "The murderer of your brother's da and my lover."

The cold air pulled tears from Jenna's eyes. She wanted to answer angrily: *What about me? I'm your daughter, your own flesh and blood and all you have left of Niall, and he would have killed me. You're talking to me like an unwelcome stranger. Have I hurt you that much? Do I mean so little to you now?* She forced the anger down, taking a breath. "Mam . . . If I could have changed that, I would have. He gave me no choice."

"Is that what you told yourself about Banrion Cianna also, Daughter?" Maeve retorted. "Would you say that to the widows of all the gardai dead because of you? 'Poor me! I had no choice!' I tell you this, Jenna, because it's what I thought every night since you fled Lár Bhaile: you should have stayed in Ballintubber. You should have given that stone-embodied curse you found on Knobtop to someone else. Everything since you took Lámh Shábhála has turned to dust and ashes." Maeve barked a short, bitter laugh, looking at the tent. "Often quite literally." The baby stirred and gave a cry; Maeve rocked him in her arms and he settled down once more. Jenna saw the face again briefly as Maeve brushed aside the swaddling—a mass of red curls, bright blue eyes, a small mouth with pouting lips: a handsome face. A tiny hand closed around one of Maeve's fingers. Jenna wanted to ask to hold the infant, to be able to look closely at him.

"That's my brother?"

Looking down at him, Maeve's face had softened for the first time. "Aye. His name's Doyle Mac Ard." She looked back to Jenna and the hardness returned to the lines around her eyes and mouth. "Padraic's final will gives the boy his surname and an estate—Padraic showed the document to me before he left Falcarragh and the Rí Ard has confirmed it. At least Doyle will have that, even though they will always whisper that he is 'the bastard Mac Ard child.' " Her gaze drifted past Jenna to the tent. "Padraic's body's in there?"

"Aye. I brought it with me from Dún Kiil." Jenna's acknowledgment was less than a whisper. Maeve walked past Jenna. As she passed, Jenna started to lift her hand to touch her mam, but Maeve cast her a cold stare. Jenna watched her go to the tent, lift the flap, and walk inside. After a moment, Jenna followed her.

Mac Ard's body was wrapped in cloth saturated with

unguents and oils: Lomán's work. The gardai had laid it on
a low pyre built of logs brought with them from Inish Thuaidh. The smell of oil was thick in the tent, cloying. Maeve
didn't seem to notice, though Doyle started crying again.
Maeve rocked him as she stood staring at the body, standing at the edge of the pyre. "It took weeks to bring him
back from Thall Coill," Jenna said to Maeve's back. "I
didn't know what you would want, whether you would want
to send him to the Mother here or take the body home to
whatever end he desired. Tell me what you want, and I'll
have my gardai take care of it."

"What I *want* is for Padraic to be alive," Maeve answered, still facing the pyre. "Can you give me that, Jenna?
Can the First Holder, the new Banrion, do that for me? Is
that within your vast power?"

The questions tore holes in Jenna's soul. She felt the
child inside her stir, and she placed her hands protectively
over her stomach. "No." The wind snapped the canvas of
the tent, punctuating the word. "Mam, I'm so sorry."

Maeve swiveled. "What of the Cloch Mór that Padraic
held? Give me that, so I can give it to Doyle as his legacy
as a Mac Ard."

Jenna shook her head. "I can't—I won't—do that. It
belongs . . ." Jenna paused, taking a breath. *It belongs to
the child I carry. It's Ennis' legacy.* ". . . to Inishfeirm and
Inish Thuaidh."

Maeve nodded, her mouth tightening. "Then can you at
least manage to give me a torch?"

Jenna went to one of the tent posts, where two circles of
copper held a smoldering brand. She pulled it from the
rings and gave it to her mam. "You may leave now,"
Maeve told her.

"Mam—"

Maeve shook her head vigorously, the flame flickering in
her hand. "I'm not your mam. I'm the woman who loved
your enemy. My allegiance is to the Rí Ard, not the woman
who calls herself Banrion in the pigsty of Dún Kiil. Leave
me to say farewell in private. Go back to your ship and
your island and forget me. Give me that much."

Jenna's mouth hung open; a dozen unsaid replies filling

her head. A gulf wider than the Westering Sea separated them, and Jenna could think of no way to bridge it. The infant Mac Ard was crying again, but Maeve's face reflected only a stoic suffering. Jenna started to take a step toward her but Maeve's eyes narrowed warningly and she stopped. Finally, Jenna ducked her heard and left the tent, going out into the wind again. Her gardai were waiting for her. They looked at her questioningly.

"We're leaving," she told them.

Jenna sat in the boat as they rowed back to their ship, gazing backward at Inishduán. She saw Maeve come out of the tent, Doyle cradled in one arm. Smoke gushed white around the central pole as Maeve walked down to the beach without looking back. A few seconds later, the first flames appeared, leaping high into the air. Smoke rolled gray with the oils, the wind smearing it west and south toward Talamh an Ghlas.

They arrived at the ship. Hands reached down to help Jenna up onto the deck. Standing at the rail, she looked back to the island: to the boat that was carrying Maeve and Jenna's half brother back to their own vessel; to the conflagration rising high into the sky.

"Are you ready, Banrion?" the captain asked.

Jenna nodded. "Aye," she said. "Take me home."

APPENDICES

Ellia	Tara's daughter, enamored of Coelin
Matron Kelly	Ballintubber resident, keeps cows
Niall Aoire	Jenna's da (father)
Chamis Redface	A Ballintubber resident who teased Jenna as a child
Rafea	Ballintubber resident, weaves cloth
Sean	Matron Kelly's son, brain-damaged by fever
Eliath	Tara's youngest son
Padraic Mac Ard	A tiarna (lord) who comes to Ballintubber
Conhal	Mac Ard's horse
Máel Armagh	An ancient king of Tuath Infochla who tried to conquer Inish Thuaidh and failed
Severii O'Coulghan	The Inish chieftain who defeated Máel Armagh
Buckles	A resident of Ballintubber, an old man
Fiacra De Derga	A tiarna from Tuath Connachta, a cousin of Mac Ard
Rí Gabair	The king of Tuath Gabair
Rí Connachta	The king of Tuath Connachta
Daragh O'Rheallagh	A resident of Ballintubber, killed by a falling tree in Doire Coill
Widow O'Rheallagh	The wife of Daragh
Dúnmharú	Seancoim's companion crow, and his eyes
Seancoim	The old guardian of Doire Coill
Seed-Daughter	Goddess: the daughter of the Mother-Creator, who planted the first seeds

Ruaidhri	Bunús Muintir chieftain, died in the Battle of Lough Dubh
Crenél Dahgnon	Daoine king who fought Ruaidhri at the Battle of Lough Dubh
Riata	Bunús Muintir chieftain, the last of the Bunús cloud-mages
Dávali	Bunús Muintir cloudmage who possessed Lámh Shábhála before Riata
Óengus	Bunús Muintir cloudmage who possessed Lámh Shábhála before Dávali
Declan Sheehan	Head of Clan Sheehan, one of the roving Taisteal bands
Edan	One of the Taisteal
Hilde	One of the Taisteal
Bran	One of the Taisteal
Ennis O'Deoradháin	Inishlander who meets Jenna in the Taisteal encampment
Aodhfin Ó Liathain	Rí of the small kingdom of Bhaile, Holder of the cloch after Eilís MacGairbhith
Eilís MacGairbhith	A Holder of the Lámh Shábhála, killed in the Battle of Lough Lár by Aodhfin Ó Liathain
Kerys Aoire	Jenna's great-mam, who fled from Inishfeirm when she became pregnant
Niall	An acolyte of the Order of Inishfeirm who fell in love with Kerys Aoire. Jenna's great-da. His last name is unknown
Conn Hagan	Head of the family that took in Kerys Aoire after her flight from Inishfeirm, and eventually married her

Torin Mallaghan	The Rí Gabair
Aoife	A servant girl in Jenna's employ at Lár Bhaile
Du Val	An apothecary in Lár Bhaile who supplies Jenna with leaf
Kiernan O Liathain	The Rí Ard, or High King
Nevan O Liathain	The Rí Ard's first son and Tanaise Ríg (Heir Apparent)
Cianna Mallaghan	The Rí Gabair's wife
Rowan Beirne	Holder of Lámh Shábhála from 648–651
Bryth Beirne (née Mac Ard)	Mam of Rowan, Holder of Lámh Shábhála from 622–648
Garad Mhúllien	The Inish cloudmage who took the cloch from Rowan Beirne in the year 651
Anrai Beirne	The tiarna who married Bryth Mac Ard—da of Rowan Beirne
Ailen O'Curragh	Holder of Lámh Shábhála from 597–612
Sinna Mac Ard	Original surname Hannroia, married to Ailen O'Curragh and then Téador Mac Ard, mother of Bryth Mac Ard, Holder of Lámh Shábhála from 612–622
Slevin Mac Ard	Bryth's brother, and the ancestor of Padraic Mac Ard
Galen Aheron	Tiarna from Tuath Infochla, at the Rí Gabair's Keep
Baird	One of Nevan O Liathain's men, a tiarna
Murrin	The widow woman from whom O'Deoradháin rents a room in Lár Bhaile

Labras	One of Cianna's gardai
Damhlaic Gairbith	Commander of the Rí Gabair's forces
WaterMother	The chief god of the blue seals
Garrentha	The blue seal who rescues Jenna from an attack by an underwater creature
Flynn Meagher	A sailor from the village of Banshaigh
Máister Cléurach	Head of the Order of Inishfeirm
Mundy Kirwan	A friend of Ennis O'Deoradháin and a Bráthair of the Order of Inishfeirm
Tadhg O'Coulghan	Founder of the Order of Inishfeirm, and da to Severii, the Last cloudmage of the Before
Maher	Librarian of the Order of Inishfeirm
Scanlan	Keeper of the Order of Inishfeirm, killed when the White Keep was invaded
Aithne MacBrádaigh	Banrion of Inish Thuaidh
Ionhar MacBrádaigh	Rí of Inish Thuaidh
Thraisha	A blue seal on Inishfeirm, the First of the Saimhóir
Árón Ó Dochartaigh	A tiarna of Inish Thuaidh from the townland of Rubha na Scarbh, Headland of the Cormorants
Kyle MacEagan	A tiarna of Inish Thuaidh from the townland of Be an Mhuilinn, Bay of the Mill
Kianna Cíomhsóg	A bantiarna of Inish Thuaidh from the townland of An Cnocan, the Hillock
Peria Ó Riain	A Holder of Lámh Shábhála, from whom the cloch passed to Tadhg O'Coulghan

Aidan	A page from the Keep at Dún Kiil
Treoraí	"The Guide," one of the Créneach
Littlest	An infant of the Créneach
Anchéad	The Créneach name for the Mother-Creator
Céile	Literally, "Spouse," the companion Anchéad made for Itself, and from whose body came the All-Heart, perhaps analogous to the Daoine "Seed-Daughter"
Lomán	The Bunús Muintir who is the Protector of Thall Coill
Keira	Seancoim's pledge-daughter in Doire Coill
Greatness	The Bunús Muintir term for the Mother-Creator
Toryn	Lomán's pledge-son in Thall Coill
An Phionós	"The Punishment," the statue-creature in Thall Coill
Owaine	A young child on the island of Inishfeirm
Alby	Tiarna MacEagan's attendant
Keira	Jenna's attendant in Tiarna MacEagan's household
Mahon MacBreen	A child whose father Deelan was killed at the Battle of Dún Kiil
Deelan MacBreen	Killed in the Battle of Dún Kiil
Tiarna Ó Beolláin	A tiarna of Baile Nua, killed in the assault on Dún Kiil Keep

PLACES:

| An Cnocan | A townland in Inish Thuaidh |

An Deann Ramhar	A townland in Inish Thuaidh
Áth Iseal	A village on River Duán, where the High Road crosses the river
Bácathair	Capital city of Tuath Locha Léin, on the west coast of the peninsula
Ballintubber	The village where Jenna was born
Banshaigh	A village on Lough Glas in Tuath Connachta
Be An Mhuillian	A townland in Inish Thuaidh
Bethiochnead	The "Beast-Nest," the location in Thall Coill where the Scrúdú takes place
Cat's Alley	A back street in Lár Bhaile
Céile Mhór	The far larger peninsula to which Talamh an Ghlas is connected by the Finger, a strip of mountainous land
Croc a Scroilm	The "Hill of Screaming," the mountain that faces Dún Kiil Bay
Doire Coill	The "Forest of Oaks"
Duán Mouth	The mountain-girdled and long end of the River Duán, which ends in an island-dotted bay
Dubh Bhaile	A city in Tuath Gabair, south of Lár Gabair on the Lough Dubh
Dún Kiil	Seat of Inish Thuaidh
Dún Laoghaire	Main city of the peninsula, seat of the High King
Falcarragh	Capital city of Tuath Infochla
Foraois Coill	Another old growth forest, in Tuath Infochla
Glen Aill	A fortress mansion in Rubha na Scarbh (Inish Thuaidh)

Ice Sea	The sea to the north of the peninsula
Ingean na nUan	A townland in Inish Thuaidh
Inishcoill	A large island off the coast of Tuath Airgialla, entirely covered in old growth forest
Inishfeirm	A small island off Inish Thuaidh, home of the Order of Inishfeirm and of Jenna's great-mam and great-da
Knobtop	A small mountain outside Ballintubber, on whose flanks sheep are often grazed
Lár Bhaile	A city on Lough Lár, the seat of Tuath Gabair
Lough Crithlaigh	A lake on the northwest border of Tuath Gabair
Lough Dhub	A lake on River Duán, scene of one of the final battles between the Bunús Muintir and Daoine
Lough Glas	A lake on the coastline of Tuath Connachta
Lough Lár	"Center Lake," a large lake nearly in the center of the peninsula, very near Ballintubber
Maoil na nDreas	A townland in Inish Thuaidh
Néalmhar Ford	The crossing of the River Néalmhar, the Gloomy River, in Inish Thuaidh
Rubha na Scarbh	A townland in Inish Thuaidh, home of Árón Ó Dochartaigh and Banrion Aithne MacBrádaigh
Sliabh Bacaghorth	A mountain in Tuath Infochla near Falcarragh, where Rowan Beirne lost Lámh Shábhála
Sliabh Colláin	A mountain in a southern county of the peninsula, also the title of a song

Sliabh Míchinniúint	The battle at the end of the previous incarnation of the mage-lights where the forces of Infochla were defeated by the Inishlanders
Talamh an Ghlas	"The Green Land," the peninsula on which the events of the novel take place
Thall Coill	The "Far Forest"
The Black Gull	The only inn on Inishfeirm
Thall Mór-roinn	The "Far Continent," the distant mainland, of which Talamh an Ghlas is a peninsula of yet another larger peninsula, Céile Mhór
Thiar	A city on the west coast, the seat of Tuath Connachta
Tuath Airgialla	The Tuath in the northeast corner of the peninsula
Tuath Connachta	The Tuath to the immediate west of Tuath Gabair
Tuath Éoganacht	The Tuath in the south of the peninsula
Tuath Gabair	The Tuath in which Jenna was born
Tuath Infochla	The Tuath in the northwestern corner of the peninsula
Tuath Locha Léin	The Tuath in the southwestern corner of the peninsula
Valleylair	A location in Tuath Connachta, famous for its ironworks
Westering Sea	The ocean to the west of the peninsula

TERMS:

Ald	The "Eldest," a title of respect for the local repository of history

Andúilleaf	A plant from which an addictive narcotic can be obtained
Banrion	The feminine form of Rí: "Queen"
Bantiarna	The feminine form of tiarna: "Lady"
Before, the	The time of myths, when magic ruled
Black haunts	The spirits of the dead who come and take the soul of the living when it's their time to die
Blue seals	Intelligent seals, black, but with a sheen of electric blue in their fur
Bradán an Chumhacht	"Salmon of Power," the blue seals' analogue to the clochs na thintrí, it is through eating one of the Bradán an Chumhacht that a blue seal can tap the energy of the mage-lights
Bráthair	The title for those who have dedicated themselves to the Order of Inishfeirm
Bunús Muintir	The "Original People," the tribes who first came to Talamh an Ghlas, and whose remnants still can be found in the hidden places
By the Mother-Creator . . .	A familiar mild curse, as we would say "By God . . ."
Caointeoireacht na cogadh	The war-keening; the ululating and terrifying war cry of the Inishlanders as they charge their foes; the cry in conjunction with their ferocious aspect has sometimes sent foes retreating in panic
Céili giallnai	The lower grade vassals of the Rí
Cinniúint	Máel Armagh's ship
Clóca	A long cloak worn by the Riocha over their clothing, usually in the colors of their Tuath

Cloch Mór	The major clochs na thintrí, the ones with large abilities
Cloch na thintrí	Literally, "stone of lightning," the stones that gather the power of the mage-lights
Clochmion	The minor clochs na thintrí with small powers
Clock-candle	Device used to keep time: a candle of standard diameter with colored wax at fixed intervals; one "stripe" equals roughly one hour
Cloudmages	Sorcerers of old who took power from the heavens to create their spells
Colors	The various Tuatha have colors that show allegiance: Tuath Gabair = green and brown Tuath Connachta = blue and gold Tuath Infochla = green and gold Inish Thuaidh = blue and white Tuath Airgialla = red and white Tuath Locha Léin = blue and black Tuath Éoganacht = green and white
Comhairle of Tiarna	The Council of Lords, the actual governing body of Inish Thuaidh
Comhdáil Comhairle	The "Conference of the Comhairle," the meeting of all chieftains in Inish Thuaidh
Corn Festival	Autumn feast in Ballintubber
Créneach	Literally, "Clay Beings," a race of sentient beings who inhabit the mountains near Thall Coill
Currach	A small, dug-out boat used by the fisherfolk of Inish Thuaidh
Da	Father

Daoine	Literally, "The People," the society to which Jenna belongs
Dire wolves	Large, intelligent wolves that speak a language
Draíodóir	Those consecrated to serve the Mother-Creator, in essence, the priesthood, though it is not restricted by gender; the plural is Draíodóiri
Eneclann	Honor-price, the amount a person can owe by his/her status
Éraic	Payment of blood-money from a slayer
Feast of Planting	One of the great quarterly festivals, taking place in late March
Fia stoirm	Storm Deer, a giant deer, previously thought extinct
Ficheall	A board game similar to chess
Filí	Poet
Filleadh	The "Coming Back," the prophesied return of magic
Fingal	To slay your own kin; one of the worst crimes
Freelanded	A term meaning that the land is owned by the person living there; to be freelanded is to be one step down from being Riocha, or nobility
Garda	The police of the large cities, or the personal protectors of a tiarna, also a term for "guard;" the plural is gardai
Giotár	Stringed instrument, guitar
Great-da	Grandfather
Great-mam	Grandmother
Is ferr fer a chiniud	"A man is better than his birth"

Kala bark	An analgesic used for headaches and minor pain, non-addictive, but not anywhere near as strong as andúilleaf
Knifefang	An extinct or mythical carnivore of the land
Lámh Shábhála	The cloch na thintrí that Jenna holds
Léine	A tunic worn under the clóca
Maidin maith	"Good morning!"
Mam	Mother
Milarán	A breakfast griddle cake from Inish Thuaidh, sprinkled with molasses and spices
Miondia	The Lesser Gods
Mórceint	A fairly large denomination coin
Óenach	An assembly held on regular occasions to transact the private and public business of the Tuath
Pledge-son/daughter	Bunús Muintir term, a younger person adopted by an Elder as his or her successor
Quern	A stone mill using for grinding grain and corn
Rí	King
Riocha	The nobility
Saimhóir	The name the blue seals call themselves
Scrúdú	The test which allows a Holder to fully open all of Lámh Shábhála's capabilities, often fatal
Seanóir	The Eldest, the oak trees of Doire Coill and the other Old Growth forests

Siúr	"Sister"
Stirabout	A meat stew
Taisteal	The "Traveling," an itinerant group of peddlers of anything, from orphaned children to hard goods
Tanaise Ríg	The Heir-Apparent
The Badger	A constellation used for navigation, as the snout of the badger always points north
Tiarna	The title "Lord"
Tuath	Kingdom
Turves	Turf cuttings, peat
Uaigneas	The Banrion Thuaidh's ship: *"Lonliness"*
Uisce Taibhse	Literally "Water Ghost," a race of intelligent creatures living in fresh-water loughs, sometimes antagonistic to humans
Wind sprites	Nearly transparent, small and sentient herd creatures, once thought to be entirely mythical, nocturnal

SAIMHÓIR TERMS:

Bradán an Chumhact	The "Salmon of the Mage-Lights," the analogue of a cloch na thintri
Bull	Adult male seal, bulls are less common, and are "shared" by several adult females
Cow	Adult female seal
Haul out	The term for leaving the water for the shore
Land-cousin	Those humans with Saimhóir blood in their ancestry

May the currents bring you fish	A common polite greeting
Milk-mother	The cow who suckles a youngling, not necessarily the same cow who gave birth to the infant. In Saimhóir society, the young are often suckled by another cow. There is generally a stronger attachment to the milk-mother than the birth-mother (unless, of course, they happen to be the same).
Milk-sister/brother	A seal who has shared the milk of the same mother
Nesting Land	Inish Thuaidh, only on this island the Saimhóir breed, on the northwest shores
Saimhóir	The name the blue seals call themselves
Seal-biter	The shark, which feeds on seals
Sister-kin	A term of endearment
Sky-stones	The cloch na thintrí
Stone-walker	A human
Sweetfish	Any of the small fish that make up the bulk of the Saimhóir's diet
WaterMother	The chief god of the Saimhóir. It is possible, though not proved, that the WaterMother is simply another manifestation of the human's Mother-Creator
Winter Home	The peninsula of Talamh an Ghlas, where the currents are warmer and the fish more plentiful during the coldest months

THE DAOINE CALENDAR:

The Daoine calendar, like that of the Bunús Muintir, is primarily lunar-based. Their "day" is considered to start at sunset and conclude at sunrise. Each month consists of 28 days; there is no further separation into weeks. Rather, the days are counted as being the "thirteenth day of Wideleaf" or the "twenty-first day of Capnut."

The months are named after various trees of the region, and are (in translation) Longroot, Silverbark, Wideleaf, Straightwood, Fallinglimb, Deereye, Brightflower, Redfruit, Conefir, Capnut, Stranglevine, Softwood, and Sweetsap.

The solar year being slightly more than 365 days, to keep the months from recessing slowly through the seasons over the years, an annual two-fold adjustment is made. The first decision is whether there will be additional days added to Sweetsap; the second proclaims which phase of the moon will correspond to the first day of the month that year (the first day of the months during any given year may be considered to start at the new moon, quarter moon waxing, half moon waxing, three-quarter moon waxing, full moon, three-quarter moon waning, half-moon waning, or quarter moon waning). The proclamation is announced at the Festival of Ghéimri (see below) each year—any extra days are added immediately after Ghéimri and before the first day of Longroot. All this keeps the solar-based festivals and the lunar calendar roughly in line.

This adjustment is traditionally made by the Draíodóiri of the Mother-Creator at the Sunstones Ring at Dún Laoghaire, but the Inish Thuaidh Draíodóiri generally use the Sunstones Ring near Dún Kiil to make their own adjustments, which do not always agree with that of Dún Laoghaire. Thus, the reckoning of days in Talamh an Ghlas and Inish Thuaidh is often slightly different.

The year is considered to start on the first day of Longroot, immediately after the Festival of Ghéimri and any additional days that have been added to Sweetsap.

There are four Great Festivals at the solstices and equinoxes.

Láfuacht: (in the first week of Straightwood)	Marks that true winter has been reached and that the slow ascent toward the warmth of spring has begun. Generally a celebration touched with a somber note because the rest of winter must still be endured.
Fómhar (in the second week of Brightflower)	Marks the time to prepare for the spring planting to come and the birthing of newborn stock animals. This festival was an appeal to the Mother-Creator and the Miondia (the lesser gods) to make the crops grow and the livestock fertile. A time of sacrifices and prayer.
Méitha (in the third week of Capnut)	Marks the height of the growing season. In good years, this was the most manic and happy festival, celebrating the plenty all around.
Gheimhri (in the fourth week of Sweetsap)	Marks the onset of autumn. This is a date fraught with uncertainty and worry as the crops are harvested and the colder weather begins. Though this holiday often spreads over more than one day, it is also laden with solemn rites and ceremonies to placate the gods who awaken with the autumn chill.

The following is a sample year with corresponding Gregorian dates. However, bear in mind that this is only an approximation and will differ slightly each year.

1st day of Longroot (New Year's Day) = September 23
1st day of Silverbark = October 21
1st day of Wideleaf = November 18
1st day of Straightwood = December 16
    Festival of Láfuacht: 7th day of Straightwood (December 22)
1st day of Fallinglimb = January 13

1st day of Deereye = February 10
1st day of Brightflower = March 10
 Festival of Fómhar: 11th day of Brightflower (March 20)
1st day of Redfruit = April 7
1st day of Conefir = May 5
1st day of Capnut = June 2
 Festival of Méitha: 19th day of Capnut (June 20)
1st day of Stranglevine = June 30
1st day of Softwood = July 28
1st day of Sweetsap = August 25
 Festival of Gheimhri: 28th day of Sweetsap (September 21)

HISTORY:

Time of Myth

Though details and sometimes names vary, similar tales are shared by both the Bunús Muintir and Daoine people, which indicate a common mythological base and possibly a shared tribal ancestry. The following tale is just one of many, and is the primary Daoine Creation Myth.

The Mother-Creator had intercourse with the Sky-Father, and gave birth to a son. But their son was sickly and died, and she laid him down in the firmament, and his skeleton became the bones of the land. In time, the Mother-Creator overcame her grief and lay again with the Sky-Father, and gave birth to Seed-Daughter.

Seed-Daughter flourished and in time became as beautiful as her mother, and she attracted the attention of a son of the Sky-Father, Cloud. From that triple union came the plants living in the soil that covered her brother, the Earth. Seed-Daughter was also coveted by Darkness, and Darkness stole her away and took her in violence. When Seed-Daughter escaped from Darkness and came back to Cloud and Rain, sor-

rowing, she was heavy in her womb, and
from her time of confinement would
come all the Miondia, the Lesser Gods.
The Miondia spread out over the lands,
and from their couplings emerged the
animals in all their varieties.

After the rape by Darkness, Seed-
Daughter could conceive no more. She
wept often, sometimes fiercely, which we
see even now in the rain that falls.

Year–2500 (approx.)	The first of the Bunús Muintir tribes reach Talamh an Ghlas, after traversing from Thall Mór-roinn, the mainland, into Céile Mhór, the larger peninsula to which Talamh an Ghlas is attached. These Bronze Age people created their society in Talamhan Ghlas, which lasted until the arrival of the Daoine tribes in Year 0.
Year –75 (approx.)	The disappearance of the mage-lights for the Bunús Muintir people. The mage-lights would not reappear again until after the arrival of the Daoine and the collapse of Bunús Muintir society.
Year –70 (approx.)	Death of Bunús Muintir chieftain and cloudmage Riata.
Year 0	The first of the Daoine tribes enter Talamh an Ghlas, crossing over the "Finger," the spine of mountainous land connecting Talamh an Ghlas to the peninsula of Céile Mhór, and also arriving by ship at Inish Thuaidh, on the western coast at Bácathair and in the south at Taghmon. They would encounter and eventually displace (and interbreed with) the Bunús Muintir people.

Year 105   The Battle of Lough Dubh, where Rí Crenél Dahgnon defeated the last Bunús Muintir chieftain Ruaidhri.

Year 232   The first recorded mage-lights appear over Inish Thuaidh. The Inishlanders would eventually learn to harness the power of the mage-lights through the cloch na thintrí, the "lightning stones" of Bunús Muintir legend. This is the beginning of what will be popularly called the "Before" by the people of Jenna Aoire's time.

Year 711   Máel Armagh, Rí of Tuath Infochla, sets out to conquer Inish Thuaidh, and is defeated and killed in the Battle of Sliabh Míchinniúint by Severii O'Coulghan, the Inishlander chieftain.

Year 726   Last reported sighting of mage-lights over Inish Thuaidh. End of the "Before." Over four centuries will pass before the mage-lights return.

Year 1075   A reputed cloch na thintrí is stolen from Inishfeirm by an acolyte named Niall (last name unknown) and is given as a pledge of love to Kerys Aoire.

Year 1111   Niall Aoire, son of Kerys Aoire, arrives in Ballintubber and meets Maeve Oldspring, whom he will marry.

Year 1113   Jenna Aoire born in Ballintubber.

Year 1129   On the 18th day of Longroot, mage-lights reappear over the village of Ballintubber in Tuath Gabair. This heralds the beginning of Filleadh—the "Coming Back."

THE HOLDERS OF LÁMH SHÁBHÁLA

(Dates given in Daoine years and in chronological order. Entries in **boldface** indicate the cloch was active during the time of Holding.)

THE BUNÚS MUINTIR HOLDERS (from Year–160)

–144 to–160	**Lasairíona (F)**
–129 to–144	**Óengus (M)**
–113 to–129 Dávali (M)	

–113 to –70   **Riata (M) The last Bunús Muintir holder of an active cloch. The magelights failed in the last years of his Holding, and Lámh Shábhála would rest again for three centuries.**

–70 to -63   None. During these years, the cloch remained in Riata's tomb.

–63 to –63   Breck the Tomb-robber (F) For two days, until she was caught and executed.

–62 to –53   None. Again, the cloch rests in Riata's tomb.

–53 to –42   Nollaig the One-Handed (M). Nollaig, like Breck, stole the cloch from Riata's tomb but held it for years, until he was caught pilfering other items from the chieftain Lobharan's clannog. The cloch and other items once belonging to Riata as well as from the other tombs there were found among Nollaig's belongings. Some of the treasure was returned to the tombs, but Lobharan kept the stone. Nollaig lost his hand.

–42 to –27   Lobharan (M)

–27 to –15	Ailbhe (F) Lobharan's daughter.
–15 to 11	Struan (M) Ailbhe's son, father of Cealaigh.
11 to 37	Cealaigh (M) First war chief of the Bunús, who were now actively fighting the Daoine in the north of Talamn an Ghlas. He would wear the cloch in battle under his armor, and was never defeated on the field—he died of an illness.
37 to 42	Mhaolain (M) Mhaolain was Cealaigh's successor as war chief, who (like Cealaigh) wore the cloch as a talisman for victory. When he was finally defeated by Dyved of the North Holdings' army, the cloch passed from Bunús Muintir hands to those of the Daoine.

THE DAOINE HOLDERS

42 to 57	Dyved of the North Holdings (M)
57 to 59	Salmhor Ó-Dyved (M) Dyved's son, killed in battle against the Bunús Muintir. The cloch was among his effects, but none of Salmhor's heirs seems to have inherited the cloch. From here, it passes out of history for nearly two centuries until the mage-lights come again in 232.
59 to 232	The Lost Years. Sometime during this period, the cloch was moved from the North Holdings (a small kingdom in what would later be part of Tuath Infochla) to Inish Thuaidh. No one knows for certain who held the stone during this time, though several people in later years would claim that their ancestors had been among them. Since

none of the Daoine had seen the mage-
lights, it's doubtful that they understood the significance of the stone beyond its recent history as a talisman of
the Bunús war chiefs.

There is a legend that the Bunús Muintir recovered the cloch after Salmh-
or's death on the battlefield, and that
the Bunús themselves took the cloch to
Inish Thuaidh to hide it. Another legend claims that the cloch was thrown
into the sea, and that a blue seal
brought the cloch to Inish Thuaidh.
The truth of any of these claims can't
be verified.

232 to 241	Caenneth Mac Noll (M) The first Daoine cloudmage, and the return of the mage-lights in the skies. Caenneth was not of royal lineage, but a simple fisherman of Inish Thuaidh, yet he would come to understand the sky-magic, and would reactivate the other cloch na thintrí. Caenneth would die in Thall Coill, attempting the Scrúdú.
241 to 263	Gael O Laighin (M)
263 to 279	Fearghus O Laighin (M)
279 to 280	Heremon O Laighin (M)—died testing himself against the Scrúdú.
280 to 301	Maitlas O Ciardha (M)
301 to 317	Aithne Lochlain (F)
317 to 329	Nuala Mag Aodha (F)
329 to 333	Ioseph MacCana (M) Died testing himself against the Scrúdú.
333 to 379	Lucan O Loingsigh (M)
379 to 382	Naomhan McKenna (M)

382 to 392	Kieran MacGairbhith (M)
392 to 401	Eilís MacGairbhith (F) Killed in the Battle of Lough Lár by Aodhfin '' Liathain, and the control of the cloch moves south from Inish Thuaidh to the mainland of Talamn an Ghlas.
401 to 403	Aodhfin Ó Liathain (M) Rí of the small kingdom of Bhaile.
403 to 416	Dougal Woulfe (M)
416 to 432	Fagan McCabe (M)
432 to 459	Eóin Ó hAonghusa (M)
459 to 4O6	Eimile Ó hAonghusa (F)
463 to 480	Dónal Ó hAonghusa (M)
480 to 487	Maclean Ó hAonghusa (M)
487 to 499	Brianna Ó hAonghusa (F)
499 to 515	Lochlainn O'Doelan (M)
515 to 517	Maitiú O'Doelan (M) Perhaps the only Daoine from Talamh An Ghlas to attempt the Scrúdú. He came to Thall Coill stealthily via ship in company with his good friend Keefe Mas Sithig. He did not survive the attempt.
517 to 529	Keefe Mas Sithig (M)
529 to 541	Conn DeBarra (M)
541 to 577	Barra Ó Beoilláin (M)
577 to 591	Uscias Aheron (M)
591 to 597	Afrika MacMuthuna (F)
597 to 612	Ailen O'Curragh (M)
612 to 622	Sinna Mac Ard (F) The young lover of Ailen O'Curragh, who after O'Curragh's early death married Teádor Mac

Ard, then the Rí of a fiefdom within what is now Tuath Gabair.

622 to 648   Bryth Beirne (nee Mac Ard) (F) Daughter of Sinna and Teádor Mac Ard. It is during Bryth's holding that the Inish cloudmages began to secretly plot to bring the cloch back to the island. Negotiations were begun with Bryth, including possible arrangements of marriage to the Rí of Inish Thuaidh, but she refused despite Rí Mac Ard's interest in that political union, and eventually married Anrai Beirne, a tiarna of Tuath Infochla.

648 to 651   Rowan Beirne (M) Bryth's son Rowan foolishly allowed himself to be drawn north out of Falcarragh to a supposed parley with the Inishlanders, where he was ambushed and murdered by assassins in the employ of the Inish cloudmage Garad Mhúllien. Lámh Shábhála was taken from Rowan's body and brought to the island.

651 to 662   Garad Mhúllien (M) The cloch returns to Inish Thuaidh. Garad would die testing himself against the Scrúdú.

663 to 669   Rolan Cíleachair (M)

669 to 671   Peria Ó Riain (F) Mother of Severii, lover to Tadhg O'Coulghan. She died in Thall Coill testing herself against the limits of the cloch with the Scrúdú. Tadhg would take the cloch from her body and become Holder himself.

671 to 701   Tadhg O'Coulghan (M) Founder of the Order of Inishfeirm based on the tiny island of the same name just off the coast of Inish Thuaidh. Tadhg was the

da of Severii, the Last Holder. It was Tadhg who began the process of codifying and bringing together all the lore of the clochs na thintrí, as well as Lámh Shábhála.

701 to 730   Severii O'Coulghan (M) The last person to hold an active Lámh Shábhála until the mage-lights returned in 1129. The mage-lights had ebbed to nothing by 726.

730 to 731   Lomán Blake (M) Lover of Severii, and a wastrel who sold Lámh Shábhála to pay off gambling debts.

731 to 741   Donnan McEvoy (M) Kept Lámh Shábhála, hoping that the mage-lights would return. They didn't. Donnan, a gambler, was killed in a tavern brawl in Dún Kiil, after which the stone passed into the possession of Kinnat Móráin, who owned the tavern and confiscated the dead McEvoy's belongings.

741 to 753   Kinnat Móráin (F)

753 to 779   Edana Ó Bróin (F) The daughter of Kinnat Móráin, who found the stone in her mam's jewelry chest after her death due to the Bloody Flux. Edana and her husband took over the tavern. She had no idea that the stone was Lámh Shábhála; she kept it only because it had been her mam's. She happened to be wearing it on the day Doyle Báróid came to Dún Kiil on business and stopped in the tavern for a drink and a meal.

779 to 831   Doyle Báróid (M) A Bráthair of the Order of Inishfeirm, who recognized

that the unprepossessing stone around
Edana's neck was similar to the description of Lámh Shábhála in the Order's library. He purchased it from
Edana, and brought it back to Inishfeirm. He would eventually become
Máister of the Order. On his death, the
cloch was put in the collection of the
Order.

831 to 1075   During these two and a half centuries,
there was no single Holder of the
stone. The stone resided in the Order
of Inishfeirm's collection of clochs na
thintrí.

1075 to 1093   Kerys Aoire (F) Kerys fell in love with
a man named Niall, one of the Brá-
thairs of the Inishfeirm Order. Niall, as
a pledge of his love, stole the cloch and
gave it to Kerys. Because the Bráthairs
were contracted by their families to the
Order and were forbidden to marry,
Kerys and Niall fled Inishfeirm. Their
small currach foundered in a storm;
Niall drowned, but Kerys, pregnant,
survived. She would give the cloch to
her son, also named Niall.

1093 to 1113   Niall Aoire (M) In traveling, he came
to Tuath Gabair and the village of Ballintubber, where he fell in love with
and married a woman named Maeve
Oldspring. Niall would lose the stone
(or perhaps the stone lost him) while
walking on Knobtop, a hill near
Ballintubber.

1113 to 1129   None. During these years, the cloch lay
on Knobtop.

1129   Jenna Aoire (F)

The Known Clochs Mór,
Their Current Manifestations & Holders:

Stormbringer (color: smoky-gray)	Inish	•Captain of *Uaigneas* •Máister Cléurach	Ability to control weather within a small defined area. Able to call rains, gale-force winds, and lightning. Though the direction of the winds can be controlled, the lightning cannot—it will strike randomly and unpredictably.
Blaze (color: bright red)	Inish	•Padraic Mac Ard •Ennis O'Deoradháin •Padraic Mac Ard	A fireball/lightning thrower
Snarl (color: blue-green)	Inish	•Damhlaic Gairbith •Ennis O'Deoradháin •Mundy Kirwan of the Order	Capable of putting out ethereal, constricting tentacles with strength well beyond anything an unaided human could resist.
Firerock (color: ruddy)	Inish	•Tiarna, ally of Árón Ó Dochartaigh, •Kyle MacEagan	Creates a creature of glowing lava
Scáil (color: opaque silver)	Inish	•Aithne MacBrádaigh	Can mirror the effect of any other Cloch Mór, mimicking its power.
Demon-Caller	Tuatha	•Nevan O Liathain	Creates a winged demon-creature
Waterfire (color: sapphire)	Tuatha	•Árón Ó Dochartaigh	Produces blue streams of fiery, arcing energy.
Snapdragon (color: yellow laced with red)	Tuatha	•A tiarna of the Tuatha	Creates a whiplike dragon whose tail wraps about its opponent, causing incredible pain as it chews at the flesh
Rogue	Tuatha	•A tiarna of the Tuatha	Creates a tsunamilike burst that crashes over its target, inundating it.
Sharpcut	Tuatha	•A tiarna of the Tuatha	Calls into being dozens of glowing, yellow spears that slice through flesh as if wielded by an unseen infantry.

Weaver	Tuatha	•A tiarna of the Tuatha	Creates a stinging web of force that constricts around its victim.
Nightmare	Tuatha	•A tiarna of the Tuatha	Give the Holder the ability to read the mind of an enemy and create images of that person's worst fears or greatest loves.
Wolfen (color: amber crackled with black)	Tuatha	•A tiarna of the Tuatha	Calls into being gigantic, ethereal wolves which attack at the Holder's command.
Tornado (color: black)	Tuatha	•A tiarna of the Tuatha	An energy-sucker. Does no damage, but pulls power from another Cloch Mór, eventually draining it
GodFist	Tuatha	•A tiarna of the Tuatha	Creates an ethereal fist that can crush a person like an insect—the more spread out the effect is (such as over several people) the less power it can generate.

Curt Benjamin

Seven Brothers

"Rousing fantasy adventure."
—*Publishers Weekly*

Llesho, the youngest prince of Thebin, was only seven when the Harn invaded, deposing and murdering his family and selling the boy into slavery. On Pearl Island, he was trained as a diver—until a vision changed his life completely. The spirit of his long-dead teacher revealed the truth about Llesho's family—his brothers were alive, but enslaved, living in distant lands. Now, to free his brothers, and himself, Llesho must become a gladiator. And he must go face to face with sorcerers...and gods.

Book One:
THE PRINCE OF SHADOWS   0-7564-0054-6
Book Two:
THE PRINCE OF DREAMS   0-7564-0114-3
Book Three:
THE GATES OF HEAVEN   0-7564-0156-9
(hardcover)

To Order Call: 1-800-788-6262

Kristen Britain

GREEN RIDER

As Karigan G'ladheon, on the run from school, makes her way through the deep forest, a galloping horse plunges out of the brush, its rider impaled by two black arrows. With his dying breath, he tells her he is a Green Rider, one of the king's special messengers. Giving her his green coat with its symbolic brooch of office, he makes Karigan swear to deliver the message he was carrying. Pursued by unknown assassins, following a path only the horse seems to know, Karigan finds herself thrust into in a world of danger and complex magic....   0-88677-858-1

FIRST RIDER'S CALL

With evil forces once again at large in the kingdom and with the messenger service depleted and weakened, can Karigan reach through the walls of time to get help from the First Rider, a woman dead for a millennium?   0-7564-0209-3

To Order Call: 1-800-788-6262

Emily Drake

The Magickers

A long time ago, two great sorcerers fought a duel to determine the fate of the world. Magick was ripped from our world, its power kept secret by a handful of enchanters. The world of Magick, however, still exists—and whoever controls the Gates controls both worlds.

Book One:
THE MAGICKERS   0-7564-0035-X

Book Two:
THE CURSE OF ARKADY   0-7564-0103-8

Book Three:
THE DRAGON GUARD   0-7564-0141-0
(hardcover)

To Order Call: 1-800-788-6262

DAW 15

Irene Radford
Merlin's Descendants

"Entertaining blend of fantasy and history, which invites comparisons with Mary Stewart and Marion Zimmer Bradley"   *—Publishers Weekly*

GUARDIAN OF THE PROMISE
This fourth novel in the series follows the children of Donovan and Griffin, in a magic-fueled struggle to protect Elizabethan England from enemies—both mortal and demonic.   0-7564-0078-3

*And don't miss the first three books
in this exciting series:*
GUARDIAN OF THE BALANCE
0-88677-875-1
GUARDIAN OF THE TRUST
0-88677-995-2
GUARDIAN OF THE VISION
0-7564-0071-6

To Order Call: 1-800-788-6262

Melanie Rawn

"Rawn's talent for lush descriptions and complex
characterizations provides a broad range of drama,
intrigue, romance and adventure."
—*Library Journal*

EXILES

THE RUINS OF AMBRAI	0-88677-668-6
THE MAGEBORN TRAITOR	0-88677-731-3

DRAGON PRINCE

DRAGON PRINCE	0-88677-450-0
THE STAR SCROLL	0-88677-349-0
SUNRUNNER'S FIRE	0-88677-403-9

DRAGON STAR

STRONGHOLD	0-88677-482-9
THE DRAGON TOKEN	0-88677-542-6
SKYBOWL	0-88677-595-7

To Order Call: 1-800-788-6262

Tad Williams

THE WAR OF THE FLOWERS

0-7564-0135-6

To Order Call: 1-800-788-6262